NEVER SCREW UP

Also by Jens Lapidus

Easy Money

NEVER SCREW UP

JENS LAPIDUS

Translated from the Swedish by Astri von Arbin Ahlander

MACMILLAN

First published in Sweden in 2008 as *Aldrig Fucka Upp*
by Wahlström & Widstrand, Stockholm.

First published in English in 2013 by Pantheon Books
a division of Random House, Inc. New York

First published in Great Britain in 2013 by Macmillan
an imprint of Pan Macmillan, a division of Macmillan Publishers Limited
Pan Macmillan, 20 New Wharf Road, London N1 9RR
Basingstoke and Oxford
Associated companies throughout the world
www.panmacmillan.com

ISBN 978-0-230-76734-8

Copyright © Jens Lapidus 2008
Translation copyright © 2013 by Pantheon Books, a division of Random House, Inc.
Translated from the Swedish by Astri von Arbin Ahlander

The right of Jens Lapidus to be identified as the
author of this work has been asserted by him in accordance
with the Copyright, Designs and Patents Act 1988.

1 3 5 7 9 8 6 4 2

A CIP catalogue record for this book is available from the British Library.

Printed and bound by CPI Group (UK) Ltd, Croydon, CR0 4YY

Visit **www.panmacmillan.com** to read more about all our books
and to buy them. You will also find features, author interviews and
news of any author events, and you can sign up for e-newsletters
so that you're always first to hear about our new releases.

For Jack

"I'm a copper," he said. "Just a plain ordinary copper. Reasonably honest. As honest as you could expect a man to be in a world where it's out of style."

—RAYMOND CHANDLER

NEVER SCREW UP

PART 1

1

The taste of metal in his mouth didn't tally. Like when you drink juice after brushing your teeth. Total confusion. But now—actually—it did tally. Mixed with fear. Panic. Mortal terror.

A grove. Mahmud on his knees in the grass with his hands over his head, like some fucking Vietcong in a war flick. The ground was wet; damp seeped through his jeans. Might be nine o'clock. The sky was still bright.

Around him stood five *blattes*. Each one = model lethal. True soldiers. Guys who'd sworn to always have each other's backs. Who chowed on small-timers like Mahmud for breakfast. Every day.

Khara.

A chill in the air, even though it was nearly summer. Still, he could smell the sweat on his skin. How the fuck had all this gone down? He was supposed to be living Life. Had finally caged out—free as a bird. Ready to grab Sweden by the balls and twist good. Then this. Could be game over now. For real. Every fucking thing.

The gun was grinding against his teeth. Echoing in his head. Light was flashing before his eyes. Scenes from his life. Memories of whiny social-service hags, pretend-to-give-a-shit counselors, half-baked racist teachers. Per-Olov, his teacher in middle school: "Mahmud, we don't do things like that in Sweden. Do you understand?" And Mahmud's response—in a different situation, the memory would've made him smile—"Fuck yourself, this is how we do in Alby." More movie clips: cops in the concrete who never understood what Sven Sweden's shitty urban rearing did to guys like him. Dad's tears at Mom's funeral. All the buzz with the guys at the gym. The first time he got to put it in. Hitting bull's-eyes with water balloons from the balcony on dog walkers down below. Shoplifting in the city. The chow hall in the pen. Him: a true Millionaire, a housing project kid from the Social Democratic Million Program high-rises, on his way up, like a deluxe gangster. Now: free fall. Wipeout.

He tried to whisper the Shahadah despite the gat in his mouth. *"Ash-Hadu anla-ilaha illa-Allah."*

The dude holding the piece in his grill looked down at him.

"You say something?"

Mahmud didn't dare move his head. Glanced up. He couldn't say shit with the gun filling his mouth. Was this dude slow or something? Their eyes met. The guy still didn't seem to get it. Mahmud knew him. Daniel: on his way up, becoming a name, but still not one of the big *blattes*. Thick eighteen-karat gold cross around his neck—true Syriac style. Right now he might be the one bossing. But if his brain'd been made of blow, the sales price would hardly cover a candy bar.

Finally: Daniel understood the situation. Pulled the gun out. Repeated. "Did you want something, or what?"

"No. Just let me go. I'll pay what I owe. Promise. Come on."

"Shut it. You think you can play me? You gotta wait till Gürhan wanna talk."

The piece, back in his mouth. Mahmud remained silent. Didn't even dare think of the Shahadah. Even though he wasn't religious, he knew he should.

Pounding thought: Was this it?

It felt like the woods around him were spinning.

He tried not to hyperventilate.

Fuck.

Fuck, fuck, fuck.

Fifteen minutes later. Daniel was getting bored. Fidgeted, looked unfocused. The gat was squeaking worse than a rusty old subway car against Mahmud's molars. Felt like he had a baseball bat in his mouth.

"You think you can do whatever you want, huh?"

Mahmud couldn't respond.

"You really think you could boost from us, huh?"

Mahmud tried to say no. The sound came from far back in his throat. Unclear if Daniel understood.

The dude said, "Bottom line: nobody boosts from us."

The guys farther off seemed to sense that things were buzzing. Came closer. Four of them. Gürhan: fabled, fatal, fat cat. Inked all the way up his neck: *ACAB* and a marijuana leaf. Along one forearm: the Assyrian eagle with wings spread. Along the other forearm, in black Gothic lettering: *Born to Be Hated*. Vice president in the gang with the same name. Southern Stockholm's fastest growing gang. One of the most dangerous people Mahmud knew of. Mythic, explosive, insane. In Mahmud's world: the more insane, the more power.

Mahmud'd never seen the other three dudes before, but they all had the same tattoo as Gürhan: *Born to Be Hated.*

Gürhan gesticulated to Daniel: Pull out the gat. The VP took it himself, aimed at Mahmud. Half a yard away. "Listen. It's pretty simple. Get the cash and stop dicking around. If you hadn't made a fuckin' mess to begin with we wouldn't have to play this game. *Capice?*"

Mahmud's mouth was dry. He tried to respond. Stared at Gürhan. "I'm gonna pay. Sorry I tripped up. It's on me." Heard the tremble in his own voice.

Gürhan's response: a hard slap with the back of the hand. Exploded in Mahmud's head like a shot going off. But it wasn't a shot—a thousand times better than a shot. Still: if Gürhan flipped out, he was really screwed.

The dude's neck muscles were stretching out the layered texture of the marijuana leaf on his skin. Their eyes met. Locked. Gürhan: huge, bigger than Mahmud. And Mahmud was far from a twig. Gürhan: infamous psycho-bandit, blood-loving violence addict, gangster Olympian. Gürhan: eyebrows more scarred than Mike Tyson's. Mahmud thought: If it's possible to see someone's soul by looking in their eyes, then Gürhan doesn't have one.

It was a mistake to say anything. He should've lowered his eyes. Groveled for the VP.

Gürhan yelled, "You cunt. First you fuck up and get collared. Then the five-oh confiscate the goods. We checked the court sentence. You didn't think we were gonna do that, huh? We know there were over ten thousand ampoules missing from what they got. That means you boosted from us. And now, six months later, you start trippin' when we want back the dough you owe. What, you gonna play hardball now 'cause you done time? It was three thousand fucking packs of Winstrol you lifted. No one steals from us. You a slow learner, *habibi?*"

Mahmud, panicked. Didn't know what to say.

In a low voice, "I'm sorry. Please. Sorry. I'm gonna pay."

Gürhan impersonated him in a shrill voice: "I'm sorry, I'm sorry— stop speaking gaylish, you fucking fairy. You think that's gonna help? Why'd you start messing?"

Gürhan grabbed hold of the revolver with both hands. Cocked the top break. The bullets fell out, one by one, into his left palm. Mahmud felt his body relax. They could smack him around. Beat him bloody. But without a gat—they probably didn't plan on ending him.

One of the other guys turned to Gürhan. Said something curt in Turkish. Mahmud didn't get it: Was the guy giving orders or showing appreciation?

Gürhan nodded. Pointed the gun at Mahmud again. "Okay, this is the deal. There's one bullet left in this cylinder. I'm gonna be nice to you. Normally, I'd just pop you. Right? We can't be tolerating a buncha clowns like you who bitch as soon as things sour. You owe us. A lot. But I'm in a good mood tonight. I'll spin, and if you're lucky, it's meant to be. You walk."

Gürhan held the cylinder up against the pale sky. Clearly visible: five empty chambers and one with a bullet in it. He spun the cylinder. The sound was reminiscent of the wheel spinning on a roulette table. He grinned widely. Aimed at Mahmud's temple. A clicking sound when the hammer was pulled back. Mahmud closed his eyes. Began to whisper the creed again. Panic took over. The flashes of light in front of his eyes returned. His heart was pounding so hard his ears almost popped.

"Okay, let's see if you're a blessed *blatte*."

A click.

Nothing happened.

NOTHING HAPPENED.

He opened his eyes again. Gürhan grinned. Daniel laughed. The other guys howled. Mahmud followed their eyes. Looked down.

His knees were wet from the damp ground. And something else: along his left jeans leg. A long stain.

Loud laughs. Jeers. Cruel grins.

Gürhan handed the piece back to Daniel.

"Next time maybe I'll fuck you instead. You little girl."

Frenzied feelings. Hope versus fatigue. Joy versus hate. Relief—but also shame. The worst was over now. He would get to live.

With this.

Curtain.

* * *

VIOLENCE AGAINST WOMEN

Over the last ten years, the number of reported cases of violence against women has increased by 30 percent, to around

24,100 reported cases, according to the numbers provided by the Swedish National Council for Crime Prevention. This is probably due, in part, to the fact that more cases of abuse are reported, but also due to an actual increase in violence. Meanwhile, the number of cases that go unreported is high. In previous studies, the Swedish National Council for Crime Prevention has estimated that only one in five cases are reported to the police.

In about 72 percent of reports, the woman is familiar with the perpetrator. Most often, the man and the woman have had a close ongoing or ended relationship.

In 21 percent of the total number of cases, the perpetrator was brought to justice. This means that the prosecutor, after an investigation, has found that there is reasonable suspicion that the person has committed the offense and will proceed with the prosecution, or that the prosecutor has decided to dismiss the case (if, for example, the person in question is a minor or if the crime is of a negligible nature), or that the person in question is issued a fine and/or a suspended sentence.

Violence against women and children is a societal problem that has been given quite a bit of attention over the last few years. This is due both to the creation of new laws (regarding, among other things, restraining orders, and gross violation of a woman's integrity) and through other measures, such as the formation of a National Center for Battered and Raped Women, as well as a focus on new educational initiatives. The attention of individual organizations has also played a significant role, for example through the creation of hotlines for women and young girls in around half of the counties in the country. Despite the significant measures that have been taken, the problem remains—thousands of women are abused and humiliated each year.

The Swedish National Council for Crime Prevention

2

Niklas was back.

He was living with his mother, Marie. Tried to sleep now and then, between the nightmares. In the dream world he was hunted, tracked, punished. But, just as often, he was the one holding the weapon or kicking defenseless people. Just like it'd been when he'd been down there. In reality.

The couch was too short to sleep on, so he'd put the leather cushions on the floor instead. His feet stuck out in the cold, but it was okay—better than being folded up like a Leatherman in a three-seater—even if he was used to that kind of thing.

Niklas saw a sliver of light through the crack in the door. Mom was probably reading ladies' magazines in there—just like she'd always done. Biographies, memoirs, and gossip. An unvarying interest in other people's failures. She lived vicariously through news of B-list celebrities and their divorces, alcoholism, and affairs. Maybe their tragic lives made her feel better. But it was all a lie. Just like her own life.

In the mornings he remained where he was, on the cushions. Heard her get ready for work. Wondered what his life in Sweden would be like, life as a civilian. What was he supposed to do here, really? He knew what kind of jobs would be suitable: security personnel, bodyguard, soldier. The last was out, though. The Swedish armed forces wouldn't hire someone with his background. On the other hand, it was what he knew.

He stayed at home. Watched TV and made omelets with potatoes and sausage. Real food—not dried stuff, tins, and canned ravioli. The grub down in the sandbox'd almost ruined his taste for quality meat, but now it was coming back. He left the apartment a few times. To jog, grocery shop, run errands. Not a lot of people out in the middle of the day—he ran senselessly hard. Drove the thoughts away.

He was living on borrowed time. His mom couldn't handle his staying with her. He couldn't handle his staying with her. Neither could handle knowing they couldn't handle it. He had to release some pressure. Find a place to live. Make a move. Something just had to work out.

After all, he was back in easy, safe Swedeland. Where everything could be arranged with a little willpower, gung-ho, money, or Commie connections. Niklas didn't have connections. But he did have willpower—harder than the armor on an M1A2 Abrams tank. Mom called him cocky. Maybe there was something to it. He'd been cocky enough to hold his own down there with guys who'd fuck with you for much less than a stupid English mispronunciation. And money? He wasn't sitting on a lifelong fortune—but it was enough for now.

He was standing in the kitchen, thinking. The secret to a good omelet was cooking it under a lid. Get the eggs to coagulate faster on the surface to avoid slime on top and burning it on the bottom. He piled on diced potatoes, onions, and pieces of sausage. Topped off with cheese. Waited for it to melt. The smell was fantastic. So much better than all the grub he'd had down there, even on Thanksgiving.

His thoughts were dreary. He was back—felt good. But back to what, exactly? His mom was present absent. He didn't know who he knew in Sweden anymore. And how was he doing, really? If he truly let himself feel, for once? Confusion/recognition/fear. Nothing'd changed. Except for him. And that was terrifying.

During the first years he'd been gone, he'd come back once a year or so. Often got R & R around Christmas or Easter. But now it'd been over three years since the last time. Iraq was too intense. You couldn't just up and leave. He'd hardly even spoken to Mom during that time. Hadn't been in touch with anyone else, either. He was who he was. Without anyone knowing. But on the other hand—had anyone ever known?

The day crept by in slow motion. He was sitting in front of the TV when she came home. Still full from the omelet. Watching a documentary about two guys skiing across Antarctica—the most meaningless shit he'd ever seen. Two clowns playing at fake survival—there was a camera crew there too, obviously. How did they survive if it really was as cold and awful as they made it out to be? Pathetic people who knew less than nothing about survival. And even less about life.

Mom looked much older than when he'd been home last. Worn out. Tired. Grayed, somehow. He wondered how much she drank. How much she'd worried about him during all those nights after watching the news. How often she'd seen Him with a capital H—the man who'd destroyed their lives. The last time Niklas'd been home she'd claimed they didn't see each other anymore. Niklas believed that about as much as Muqtada al-Sadr believed the United States wanted the best for his people. But all that was over now.

She was strong, somehow. Had raised a punk kid on her own. Refused welfare. Refused to give in and retire early like all her girlfriends had. Toiled through life. On the other hand, she'd let Him come into her life. Let Him take control over her. Humiliate her. Wreck her. How could they be so different?

She set a grocery bag down on the floor. "Hello, hi. So, what've you been up to today?"

He could tell how much pain she was in just by looking at her. He'd understood already on his first day back in Sweden: her back'd given up. Still, she kept working—part time, sure, but still: what was the point, really? Her face'd never exactly radiated joy. The wrinkles between her eyes were deep now, but she'd always had them. They formed an expression of constant worry. She'd lower her eyebrows, scrunching them up, making her most noticeable wrinkles deepen by almost half an inch.

He kept studying her. Pink cardigan—her favorite color. Tight jeans. A necklace with a gold heart around her neck. Her hair had blond highlights. Niklas wondered if she still had it done at Sonja Östergren's salon. Some things never change, as Collin used to say.

She was actually the nicest person in the world. Too nice. It wasn't fair.

Marie. His mother.

Whom he loved.

And still despised.

Because of that—the niceness.

She was too weak.

It wasn't right.

But they would never be able to talk about everything that'd happened.

Niklas put the groceries away in the kitchen. Went back into the living room.

"I'm moving out soon, Mom. I'm going to buy a firsthand rental contract for an apartment."

There they were again: the wrinkles. Like cracks in a desert road.

"But Niklas, isn't that illegal?"

"No it's not, actually. It's illegal to sell rental contracts, but not to buy them. It'll be fine. And there's no other way to get a rental in this city, you know that. Stupid socialist housing system. But I have some money and no one's going to rip me off. Promise."

Marie mumbled something in response. Went into the kitchen. Started making dinner.

Insomnia was having its way with him. Not even during the worst nights down there, when the grenades'd made more noise than a New Year's Eve fireworks display in the middle of the living room, had his sleep been this shitty. Earplugs used to be a blessing; his CD player, salvation. But nothing helped now.

He lay watching the gap under his mother's door. Lights off at twelve-thirty. For some reason, he already knew he wouldn't be able to sleep. He turned over and over again. With every turn the sheets slipped more and more to one side of the cushions. Got twisted. Annihilated the chance of sleep.

He was thinking about what he'd bought the other day. Unarmed, he was unsafe. Now he felt better. He'd arranged what he needed. His thoughts drifted on. He considered his work options. How much of his résumé should he include, really? He almost chuckled to himself in the dark: maybe in-depth knowledge of more than forty types of weapons wasn't the kind of thing that was valued too highly in Sweden.

He thought about Him. He had to get out of this apartment, away from this building. It was giving him bad vibes. Difficult memories. Dangerous intimacy.

Niklas was planning to live according to his own philosophy now. A temple of thought he'd been building meticulously over the past few years. Ethical rules only mattered to yourself. If you were able to rid yourself of them, you'd be free. All that stuff died down in the sandbox. Morality dried up like a scab that disappeared on its own after a few weeks. He was free—free to live his life in the way that suited him best.

He thought about the men. Collin, Alex, the others. They knew what he was talking about. War made humans become self-aware. There is only you. Rules are made for other people.

The next day, he tried an off-the-books apartment broker. The guy sounded shady over the phone. Probably a nasty type. Niklas'd gotten his number from an old school bud, Benjamin.

First he had to leave a message on the illegal broker's voice mail. Four hours later: a call from a hidden number.

"Hi, I'm a broker. I heard your message. You're interested in looking at some properties. Is that correct?"

Niklas thought, Some people lived well off other people's crises. The guy was a snake. Consistently avoided words like *apartment, contract*, or *off the books*—knew not to mention anything that could be used against him.

The broker gave him instructions: I call you, you never call me.

They arranged to meet the following day.

He stepped into McDonald's. Totally beat, but ready to meet the broker. The place looked just as he remembered it. Uncomfortable metal chairs, cherrywood-colored paneling, linoleum flooring. Classic McDonald's smell: a mix of hamburger meat and something rank. Ronald McDonald House donation jars by the registers; ads for Happy Meals on the tray covers; young, downy-lipped dudes and swarthy chicks behind the registers.

The difference since he'd been here last: health fascism. Mini carrots instead of french fries, whole-wheat buns on the burgers instead of the traditional white bread, Caesar salad instead of extra cheeseburgers. What was people's problem? If they didn't exercise enough to burn normal food they should think twice before they even went into this place. Niklas ordered a mineral water.

A man walked up to his table. Dressed in a long coat that almost dragged on the ground, under which he was wearing a gray suit and a white shirt. No tie. Slicked-back hair and empty eyes. A smile so wide it looked like his head was going to split in half.

It must be the broker.

The man extended his hand. "Hi, I'm the fixer."

Niklas ignored his hand. Nodded at him. Point: You may be the fixer I need—but that doesn't mean I'm going to kiss your ass.

The broker looked surprised. Hesitated for a moment. Then sat down.

Niklas didn't skip a beat. "What do you have for me and how does it work?"

The broker leaned forward. "You seem to be a straight shooter. Aren't you going to eat anything?"

"No, not now. Just tell me what you have and how it works."

"All right. I've got listings anywhere you want. I can get you something south of the city, north of the city, Östermalm, Kungsholmen. I can get you something in the royal Drottningholm Park if you're interested. But you don't look like the type." The broker laughed at his own joke.

Niklas remained silent.

"But remember, if you ever come claiming we've met here to discuss what we're discussing, it didn't happen. I'm in a meeting with some colleagues right now, just so you know."

Niklas neither heard nor understood what the broker was talking about.

"Yeah, so, I've got myself covered in case of rotten eggs. Just so you know. If anything unpleasant happens, I have witnesses who'll say I was busy with other stuff somewhere else right now."

"Okay. Good for you. But you didn't answer my question."

The broker smiled again. Got going. Spoke rapidly. He was difficult to understand. Niklas had to ask him to repeat himself several times. The guy's confident style didn't match his jumbled manner of speaking.

He described the listings in detail: in all the inner-city neighborhoods. Collaborations with landlords of luxury apartments, single-family homes, state-owned rental co-ops. Magnificent apartments in the inner city, one-bedrooms with eat-in kitchens on Södermalm or studios in the boroughs. According to him: safe, good-value deals.

Niklas already knew what he wanted. A one-bedroom in an area just outside the inner city. Preferably near Mom.

The broker explained the routine. The preparations. The timing. The process. The guy looked like he thought this was all a game.

"First we'll register you at a rental out in the boondocks for a few months—a place with a short tenant wait list attached to it. Everything'll look good on paper. That's where you'll be registered and since there was a short wait list, no one will wonder how you got your hands on it. I'll deal with the landlord. After a few months, we'll exchange the apartment for the one you're actually going to buy. That way, the trade will look completely clean. After that, the seller will have to be registered at the same apartment you traded from—that is, your fake apartment—for at least two months. Credibility is everything in my field, as I'm sure you understand."

Problem. This wouldn't cut it—Niklas had to get a place this week already. He had to get out of Mom's apartment. Fast.

The broker grinned. "Okay, I think I know your problem. Did your chick kick you out, or what? Shredded clothes? Trashed stereo? Things tend to go a little *High Chaparral* when they're mad."

Niklas held his gaze. Stared for two seconds longer than normal social codes would allow if he were laughing it off as a joke.

The broker finally got the message—this was not the time to try to be funny. "Whatever," he said. "I can still help you. We'll get you a sublet for those three months when you'll need to wait. Does that work? I can put you in a sweet one-bedroom, five hundred and forty square feet, in Aspudden. If you want it, you can have it next week. But it'll cost a little extra, of course. What do you think?"

He needed something even sooner. "If I pay more, can you get it faster?"

"Faster than that? You're really cutting it close, I have to say. But sure, you can get it the day after tomorrow."

Niklas smiled inside. That sounded good. He had to get away.

Better than expected, actually.

To disappear so quickly.

3

The Southern District might not have the most incident reports per capita, but it always had the most major crime. The City District, downtown, definitely topped the numbers, everyone knew that, but that's because the scum from south of Södermalm came into the city and did a lot of petty shit there. Shoplifted, pocketed cell phones, harassed, started bar brawls.

Thomas thought, The south—real ghettos that the politicians don't give a damn about. Fittja, Alby, Tumba, Norsborg, Skärholmen. Everyone knew the names of the northern shit holes: Rinkeby and Tensta. Diversity aid and cultural organizations abounded. Support efforts were focused. Project money rained down. Integration institutes invaded. But in the south, the gangs ruled for real. Iraqis, Kurds, Chileans, Albanians. The Bandidos, Fucked for Life, Born to Be Hated. You could spend ages burping up calamities. Topped the Swedish lists in number of firearms, number of guys who refused to talk to cops, number of reported blackmail attempts. The criminals organized, copied the MC clubs' hierarchies, pulled together their own steel-fisted gangs. The teen punks followed the examples set by older bank robbers/drug dealers/thugs. A well-trodden road. To a shit life. The list was endless—all the facts were there. In Thomas's eyes, didn't matter what you labeled those niggers and losers—they were all scum, the lot of them.

He'd heard all the theories that the social-service ladies and the youth psychologists droned on about. But what were they really supposed to do with all those behavioral, cognitive, dynamic, psychiatric, blah-blah-istic hypotheses? No methods worked anyway. No one could clean it up. They spread. Reproduced. Multiplied. Took over. Once upon a time he too might have thought there was a way to stop it. But that was a long time ago now.

Things used to be better. A cliché. But as Lloyd Cole sings, the reason it's a cliché is that it's true.

Yet another night on the beat. Thomas was driving calmly. Let his hands rest on the wheel. Knew he'd get his ear chewed off at home for signing up for the night shift all week. He didn't really need the extra money—even though that's what he told Åsa. A police inspector's base salary wasn't even worth a tenth of the drugs he confiscated on a regular night. It was an insult. Ridicule. A loogie in the eye of all the honest men who really knew what needed to be done. So if they took back a little, it was only right.

There were five or six of them who took turns driving these routes together. Circled the areas around Skärholmen, Sätra, Bredäng. Damned the development to hell. Skipped the PC bullshit and the Commie fake-empathy crap. They all knew the deal—break the swine or roll over and die.

Thomas's partner tonight, Jörgen Ljunggren, was sitting in the passenger seat. They usually switched sometime around 2:00 a.m.

Thomas tried to count. How many times'd he and Ljunggren slid through the slowly darkening summer nights like this? Without unnecessary chitchat. Ljunggren with his paper cup of coffee, always for too long—until the coffee got cold and he hurried off to get a refill at the closest all-night place. Thomas often with his thoughts elsewhere. Mostly focused on his car at home: zinc treatment for the new original detailing, parts to the differential in the back axle, the new tachometer. A project of his own to long for. Or else he yearned for the shooting range. He'd just bought a new pistol—a Strayer Voigt Infinity, made to his specifications. Thomas was lucky in that way, he had more than one home. First the cruiser with the guys. Then his own car at home. Then the shooting club. And then, maybe, home-home—his house in Tallkrogen.

Jörgen Ljunggren suited Thomas well—he preferred people who didn't babble too much. What came out was mostly nonsense anyway. So they were quiet. Shared meaningful looks sometimes, nodded, or exchanged short remarks. That was enough for them. They liked it that way. Mutual understanding. A worldview. It wasn't complicated: they were here to clean up the crap flooding the Stockholm streets.

Ljunggren was one of the best on the squad. A good guy to have on your side when things heated up.

Thomas felt relaxed.

The police radio was spewing out commands. The Stockholm County Police Department used two frequencies instead of one: the 80 system for City, the Southern District, and the Western District, and the 70 system for the rest. In accordance with the rest of the organization. The fact that there were two systems instead of one: inefficiency was the middle name of this operation. No one ever woke up to realize a new age'd dawned. You couldn't keep trudging along in the same old tracks anymore. His thoughts ran on a loop: The rabble organized completely differently these days. It wasn't just some Yugos and washed-up Finns running amok. The bottom-feeders stayed fresh. Professional, international, multidisciplinary criminals. New methods were needed to get at them. Faster. Smarter. Tougher. And as soon as someone wanted to do something about it, the media started whining about the new laws as if they were intended to hurt people.

The radio crackled. Someone needed assistance with a shoplifter at a twenty-four-hour bodega in Sätra.

They exchanged glances. Grinned. Forget it, they weren't taking a crap job like that—let some greenhorn cadet take it. They ignored the call. Drove on.

Approached Skärholmen.

Thomas downshifted, slowed. "We're thinking of going away for Christmas again."

Ljunggren nodded. "That's nice. Where were you thinking?"

"Don't know. My wife wants to go somewhere warm. Last year we did Sicily. Taormina. Real nice."

"I know. You didn't talk about anything else for three months after."

Laughs.

Thomas turned off toward the Storholms school, outside of Skärholmen's center. Always worth taking a look at the schoolyard. The punks usually got it into their heads to go there at night—sit on the back of park benches, roll a fatty, as they say, smoke up, and enjoy their short lives.

Dig the irony: the same kids that usually played hooky all day flocked to the schoolyard at night—to smoke themselves stupid. If they were still sitting on those benches five years from now, jobless, they could only blame themselves. But they complained that it was society's fault. Moved on to heavier stuff: moonshine, hash, aimies. If unlucky: brown sugar. Talk about free fall. Welfare and social services. Worked a couple corners. Flipped a few grams and pulled some suburban break-ins. Their parents could only blame themselves—they should've taken their responsibility ages ago. The police could only blame themselves—should've clamped down right off the bat. Society could only blame itself—if you gather that much riffraff in one place, you're asking for trouble.

The lights in the schoolyard could be seen from far away. The gray concrete school building lay like a giant Lego block in the darkness behind the yard.

They stopped the car. Got out.

Ljunggren grabbed the white baton. Completely unnecessary—but correct. The other feeble expandable baton didn't always cut it.

"Maria always needs to be so damn cultural. Wants to go to Florence, Copenhagen, Paris, and God knows where else. There isn't even anything nice to look at over there," Ljunggren said.

"Can't you look at the *Mona Lisa*?"

Chuckles, again.

"Yeah sure, she's about as hot as a fucking bag of wieners."

Thomas thought: Ljunggren should swear less and show his wife who's in charge more.

He said, "I think she's kinda hot."

"Who, the *Mona Lisa* or my old lady?"

More laughter.

For once, the schoolyard was empty. Except for under one of the basketball hoops, where a red Opel was parked.

Thomas lit his Maglite. Held it at head height. Illuminated the license plate: OYU 623.

"That's Kent Magnusson's car," he said. "I don't even have to run the plates. We ever plucked him together?"

Ljunggren hung his baton back on his belt. "You've got to be kidding me. We've picked him up ten times, at least. You going senile, or what?"

Thomas didn't respond. They approached the car. Weak light inside. Someone moved in the front seat. Thomas leaned over. Knocked on the car window. The light went out.

A voice: "Beat it!"

Thomas cleared his throat. "We're not going anywhere. That you in there, Magnusson? This is the police."

The voice in the car again: "Dammit. I don't got anything tonight. I'm as clean as Absolut."

"Okay, Kent. It's okay. But come out anyway so we can talk."

Indistinct swearing in response.

Thomas knocked again, this time on the roof. A little harder.

The car door opened—the stench from the car: smoke, beer, piss.

Thomas and Ljunggren'd both struck a broad stance. Waited.

Kent Magnusson climbed out. Unshaven, hair a mess, rotting teeth, herpes blisters around his mouth. Faded jeans on half-mast—the guy had to pull them up at least a foot and a half in order not to fall over. A T-shirt with a print ad for the Stockholm Water Festival that must've been ancient. An unbuttoned plaid shirt over the T-shirt.

A complete junkie. Even more worn down than last time Thomas'd seen him.

Thomas shone the flashlight in his eyes.

"Hey there, Kent. How high are you?"

Kent mumbled, "Not at all. I've been cutting back."

His eyes really did look clear. His pupils were a normal size—contracted when the light from the flashlight hit them.

"Yeah, right, you're cutting back. What you got on you?" Ljunggren said.

"Honest, man. I got nothing. I'm trying to quit. It's the truth."

Ljunggren was losing his temper. "Don't give me that crap, Kent. Just give us what you've got and we'll play nice. No fuss, no hassle, and no bullshit. I'm damned tired tonight. Especially of junkie lies. Maybe we can be nice to you. You follow me?"

Thomas thought: Curious thing about Ljunggren—he talked more with the criminals than he did with Thomas during an entire night in the car.

Kent made a face. Seemed to be considering his options.

"Eh, come on. I don't got any."

The junkie wasn't going to make it easy for himself. "Kent, we're going to search your car," Thomas said. "Just so you know."

Kent made another face. "Fuck, man, you can't search my car without a warrant. You ain't seen no drugs. You don't got the right to go through my car, you know that."

"We know that, but we don't give a shit."

Thomas looked at Ljunggren. They nodded at each other. No problem: just write a report afterward claiming that they'd seen Kent fiddling with something in the car when the door opened. Or that they'd seen that he was high. Or whatever the fuck—there was always reasonable doubt. Piece of cake. Cleaning up the streets of Stockholm—that was more important than objections from some whiny junkie.

Ljunggren crawled into the car and began the search. Thomas led the junkie away a bit. Kept the situation under control.

"What the fuck are you doing?" Kent spit. "You can't do this. You know that."

Thomas remained cool. No point in getting worked up. All he said was, "Calm down."

The junkie hissed something. Maybe *pig*.

Thomas had no patience for people like him. "What did you say?"

Kent kept mumbling. If the guy whined and made a fuss, that was one thing. But no way he said *pig*.

"What did you say?"

Kent turned to him. "Pig."

Thomas kicked him hard in the back of the knee. He collapsed like a tower of matches.

Ljunggren popped his head out of the car. "Everything cool?"

Thomas turned Kent over. Belly to ground, arms behind his back. Cuffed him. Put one foot on the guy's back. Called to Ljunggren, "Sure, it's cool."

Then he turned to the junkie.

"You fucking cunt."

Kent lay still.

"Please, can you loosen the cuffs? It fucking hurts, man."

Oh, so now he thought it was time to sulk.

After five minutes, Ljunggren yelled something. Yup, he'd found two bags of hash in the car. No surprise there. Ljunggren handed the baggies to Thomas. He checked—one with ten grams and one with around forty.

Thomas bent Kent's head back.

"Now what you got to say for yourself?"

The junkie's voice jumped up a notch. "Come on now, Officer, someone must've put them there. I didn't know they were in the car. I mean, where'd he find it? Can't you cut me some slack?"

No problem. Fifty grams of hash wasn't much, considering. They'd let it slide, for now. "It's cool," Thomas said. He took the bags. Put them in the inside pocket of his jacket. "But never lie to me again. Got that?"

"No. Never. Thank you so much. Damn, you guys are being nice. Fucking generous. You're cool."

"You don't have to bend over. Just quit lying. Act like a man."

Two minutes later, Kent was crawling back to his feet.

Thomas and Ljunggren walked back to the cruiser.

Ljunggren turned to Thomas. "Did you toss the shit, or what?"

Thomas nodded.

Kent climbed back in the Opel. Started the engine. Turned the volume up high on the stereo. Classic rock. The junkie just got spared a month or so behind bars—despite losing the hash he was as happy as a kid on Christmas.

Back in the cruiser. Thomas pulled his gloves off. Ljunggren wanted to go to some twenty-four-hour café and get a java refill.

From dispatch: "Area two, do we have anyone who can take a call for an unconscious man in Axelsberg? Seriously wounded. Probably intoxicated. He's lying in a basement at Gösta Ekman Road number 10. Over."

A real dirty gig. Silence. They slid on down the road.

No one else took the call. Crap luck.

The radio again: "We're not getting any response for Gösta Ekman Road. Someone's gotta take it. Over."

Dammit, two chill police officers like Thomas and Ljunggren shouldn't have to deal with more small fry tonight. It was enough that Ljunggren'd had to crawl around in the junkie's nasty ride. They kept their mouths shut. Rolled on.

The radio ordered: "Okay. No one's taking Gösta Ekman Road. It'll be car 2930, Andrén and Ljunggren. Copy? Over."

Ljunggren looked at Thomas. "Typical."

Sometimes you just have to eat shit. Thomas pushed the mike button. "Roger that. We'll take it. Any additional info? It was a drunk, right? There gonna be any booze left for us? Over."

The radio voice belonged to one of the boring girls. According to Thomas: a sour pussy. Couldn't kid with her like you could with most of the other chicks on dispatch.

"Quit playing around, Andrén. Just go. I'll get back to you when we know more. Over and out."

The car pulled up to Gösta Ekman Road number 10 a few minutes later. Ljunggren was whining about not getting his coffee yet.

People were lined up outside the entrance to the building as if waiting for some kind of show. A lot of people—the building had eight stories. The sky was beginning to brighten.

They got out.

Thomas took the lead. In through the entrance. Ljunggren dispersed the crowd outside. Thomas heard him say, "Nothing to see here, folks."

Inside, the building felt super sixties. The floor was made of some kind of concrete plates. The elevator door looked like it belonged in a *Star Trek* spaceship. The small entranceway had a door out to a courtyard and a set of stairs leading down. There was a metal railing along the stair leading up to the second floor. He saw some people standing up there on the landing. A woman in a bathrobe and slippers, a man with glasses and a sweat suit, a younger kid who must be their son.

The woman pointed down.

"I'm so glad you're here. He's down there."

"It'd be great if you could go back inside," Thomas said. "We'll take care of this. I'll be up to talk to you in a bit."

She seemed reassured by having done her civic duty. Maybe she was the one who'd called 911 in the first place.

Thomas started to walk down. The stairs were narrow. There was a garbage chute with a sticker on it: *Please—help our sanitation workers— seal the bag!*

He thought about his car again. This weekend he might buy a new motor for the automatic windows.

He checked out the lock on the cellar door. Assa Abloy from the early nineties. He should have a skeleton key that'd work, or else he'd have to ask the family he'd seen on the landing for help.

A few seconds later the electronic skeleton key buzzed. The lock clicked. It was dark in there. He switched on his Maglite. His right hand searched for the light switch.

Blood on the floor, on the bars over the cellar windows, on the stuff in the storage units.

He pulled his gloves on.

Eyed the body. A man. Dirty clothes, now also very bloody clothes. Short-sleeved shirt and corduroy pants. Covered in vomit. Boots with the laces untied. Arm at a weird angle. Thomas thought, Yet another little Kent.

The torso was bent. Facedown.

Thomas said, "Hello, can you hear me?"

No reaction.

He lifted the arm. It felt heavy. Still zero reaction.

Pulled off his glove. Searched for a pulse—stone cold dead.

He lifted the head. The face was totally busted—beat beyond recognition. The nose didn't seem to exist anymore. The eyes were so swollen that you couldn't see them. The lips looked more like spaghetti and meat sauce than like a mouth.

But something was strange. The jaw seemed to be sunk in somehow. He put two fingers inside the mouth, felt around in there. Soft like a baby's palate—the dead man was missing teeth. This was obviously not a junkie who'd lost consciousness by his own doing—this was a murder.

Thomas didn't get worked up.

Considered placing the man in the recovery position, but left him as he was. Skipped CPR. It was pointless, anyway.

He followed the rulebook. Alerted dispatch. Raised the radio mike to his lips, spoke in a low voice so as not to freak out the whole building. "I've got a homicide here. Real grisly. Gösta Ekman Road number 10. Over."

"Roger that. Do you need more cars? Over."

"Yes, send at least five. Over."

He heard the call go out to everyone in the Southern District.

Dispatch got back to him: "Do you need any senior officers? Over."

"Yes, I think so. Who's on tonight? Hansson? Over."

"That's right. We'll send him. Ambulance? Over."

"Yes please. And send a couple rolls of paper towels, too. We've got a lot to mop up. Over and out."

The next step, according to protocol: He talked to Ljunggren on the radio, asked him to make people identify themselves, gather addresses and telephone numbers for potential witness reports. Then have them wait until backup arrived with enough people to ask the usual control questions. Thomas looked around the stairwell. How'd the guy been killed? He didn't see a weapon, but the perp'd probably taken that with him.

What should he do now? He looked at the body again. Lifted the arm. Didn't bother with routine—he should really wait for the technicians and the ambulance.

He looked at the man's hands. They were weird somehow—no missing fingers, not unusually clean or dirty—no, it was something else. He turned a hand over. Then he saw it—the tops of the dead man's fingers were all messed up. On the top of every fingertip: a blood effusion. It looked like they'd been sliced, leveled, erased.

He dropped the arm. The blood on the floor'd dried. How long'd the dead guy been lying down here?

He searched his pockets quickly. No wallet, no cell phone. No money or identification. In one of the back pockets: a slip of paper with a smudged cell-phone number. He memorized the discovery. Put it back.

The man's T-shirt was sticking to his skin. He looked closer. Turned the body over a little, even though he shouldn't. That kind of thing was totally against protocol. Really, they ought to take photographs and search the place before anyone moved the body—but now his interest'd been piqued.

That's when he saw the next weird thing, on the arm. Track marks from an injection needle. Small bruises around every puncture. Completely clear: what he had in front of him on the floor was a murdered junkie.

He heard sounds on the other side of the cellar door.

Backup was coming.

Ljunggren entered the room. Two younger inspectors brought up the rear. Thomas knew them, good guys.

They eyed the body.

"Damn, he sure slipped on all the blood someone spilled everywhere," Ljunggren said.

They grinned. Police humor—blacker than this cellar'd been before Thomas'd switched on the lights.

Orders started sputtering out from their radios—Hansson, the senior officer, had arrived, gave orders to have the area cordoned off. Did what he usually did: ordered, organized, hollered. Still, it was a small operation. If it'd been anything other than a junkie in the stairwell, they would've called in all the squad cars they could get. Cordoned off half the city. Stopped trains, cars, subways. Now there was no real hurry.

The ambulance crew showed up after seven minutes.

Let the body lie there for a while. A technician came down, snapped some photos with a digital camera. Analyzed blood. Secured evidence. Investigated the crime scene.

The ambulance guys brought a stretcher down. Covered the body with blankets. Hauled it up.

Disappeared.

When there's action, it's fun. When it's fun, the night flies by. But they'd combed home zilch. Ljunggren sighed. "Why did we even bother making a whole operation out of this thing? It's just one less drunk who probably would've started a fight 'cause the liquor store opened three minutes late some Saturday morning when we're really not in the mood to deal with bullshit like that." Thomas thought, Sometimes Ljunggren can really talk.

They interrogated some neighbors at random. Photographed the area around the basement. Sent two guys to the subway station. Wrote down the names and phone numbers of people in the building next door, promised to be back the following day. The technicians checked for fingerprints and swabbed for DNA traces in the basement. A couple of cruisers blocked off the street and stopped a sampling of cars down on Hägerstensvägen. Hardly anyone out and about at this hour anyway.

They were quiet on the way back to the station in Skärholmen. Tired. Even though nothing'd happened, it'd been an intense experience. Would feel good to shower.

Thomas couldn't stop thinking about the body in the basement. The busted face and the fingertips. Not that he felt sick or thought it was hard to deal or anything—too much nastiness'd crossed his path already; it didn't affect him. It was something else. The shady aspect of this whole business—the fact that the junkie seemed to have been offed in a way that was just a tad too sophisticated.

But what was strange, really? Someone'd freaked on him for some reason. Maybe a fight over a few milligrams, an unpaid debt, or just a bad trip. It couldn't have been hard to beat the shit out of the guy. He must've been lit like a bonfire. But the missing teeth? Maybe it wasn't so strange. Addicts' bodies tended to give up early—too much of life's good stuff corrodes the fangs. Dentures on forty-year-olds were legion.

Still, the face that'd been beaten beyond recognition, the cut fingertips, the fact that someone'd plucked out the dentures. Getting a positive ID on this guy was going to be a bitch. Someone'd given this some real thought.

It spelled out a job by semipros. Maybe even by total pros.

This wasn't the work of some fellow addict. No way.

Weird.

4

Erika Ewaldsson got on Mahmud's nerves. Annoying, nagging. Wouldn't, like, give up. But, really, he didn't give a fuck about her; she was valueless. Nothing would happen if he broke the probation office's rules just a little bit, anyway. The problem was what they might come up with. What it boiled down to: they thought they could control him, could decide when he went into the city and when he chilled out in the concrete. There was a risk that it looked like he was letting those clowns walk all over him. Make the rules. Control a *blatte* with thick honor—they could go shit themselves.

Still: the red subway line, on his way into the city from the projects. From Alby to the probation office at Hornstull. From his bros—Babak, Robert, Javier, the others—to Erika: parole officer, pussy-marauder, playboy-saboteur. She wouldn't cut him any slack. Refused to understand that he was gonna go straight, or at least really meant it when he told her so. She was riding him worse than the counselor back in school when he was thirteen—the Sven loser who'd decided that Mahmud was troublemaker number one.

Bitch.

The train pounded through the tunnels. Mahmud was nearly alone in the car. He tried to study the pattern on the fabric of the seats across from him. What were those shapes supposed to be, anyway? Okay, he recognized the little ball—the Globen arena. And the tower with the three knobs on top—the city's hall, City Hall, or whatever it was called. But the other stuff. Who drew ugly like that? And who was the train company trying to kid? The subway wasn't some warm and cuddly place and it never would be.

Still: great feeling—chilling in the train car. Being free. Could get off and on wherever he wanted. Flirt freely with the two chicks sitting a few rows down. Life on the inside was like life on the outside except in fast-forward. Time went so much faster, each part seeming more compact—it felt like his latest stint had never even happened. The only thing that disturbed him: the nightmares he'd been having the last two nights. Spinning Russian roulette. Piss stains eating their way down his leg. Gürhan's golden grill gleaming. He had to try to forget. Born to Be Hated.

The train pulled up to the station. He got off. Hungry for something. Walked toward the vending machine. When he was ten yards away he saw that it'd been smashed. What amateurs. If they were gonna rob something, why not go big? What good were a couple bucks from a vending machine? Must be junkies. Tragic losers. Why didn't Erika work on treating them instead? After all, Mahmud didn't bother anyone unless they bothered him. Priorities were all flipped.

He started walking toward the escalators. The station's white brick walls reminded him of the Asptuna pen. A month and a half since he'd gated out of there—six months behind bars. And now he had to go to fucking Hornstull once a week and humiliate himself. Sit and lie to the bitch straight to her face—felt like he was back in middle school again. Didn't work. Some dudes locked themselves into tiny studio apartments that social services lined up for them when they got out. Couldn't handle cribs that were too big, wanted things to be as similar to the pen as possible. Others moved in with their moms. Couldn't really handle life on the outside without someone getting their grub and cleaning up after them. But not Mahmud—he was gonna be a soldier. Get a place of his own, travel, move. Slay mad bitches, make fat stacks. STYLE. But then the image of Gürhan's mug killed all his dreaming like a punch to the face.

He crossed Långholmsgatan. In the background, the traffic thundered. The sky was gray. The street was gray. The buildings were grayest of all.

The parole office shared an entrance with a podiatrist and a pension fund office. He thought, Were only P joints allowed in this pussy place? A janitor was waxing the linoleum floor. Could have been his dad, his *abu*, Beshar. But his *abu* wouldn't have to live that way anymore. Mahmud was gonna provide. Promise.

At the welcome desk, they didn't even slide back the glass partition for him. He had to lean forward to reach the mike.

"Hey, hi. I'm supposed to see Erika Ewaldsson. Ten minutes ago."

"Okay, if you'll have a seat she'll be with you shortly."

He sat down in the waiting room. Why did they always make him wait? They acted like the screws in the slammer. Power-hungry humiliation experts: fags.

He eyed the worthless magazines and papers. *Dagens Nyheter, Café,* and *Gracious Home.* Grinned to himself: What clowns would show up at the parole office and read *Gracious Home*?

Then he heard Erika's voice.

"Hi, Mahmud. Glad you made it. Almost on time, in fact."

Mahmud glanced up. Erika looked the way she usually did. Yellow pants and a brownish poncho thing up top. She wasn't exactly thin—her ass was as wide as Saudi Arabia. She had green eyes and wore a thin gold cross around her neck. Damn, there was that metal taste in his mouth again.

Mahmud followed Erika to her office. Inside, the blinds created a striped light. Posters on the walls. A desk piled with papers, binders, and plastic folders. How many homies did she hassle, anyway?

Two armchairs. A small round table between them. The fabric on the chairs was pilling. He leaned back.

"So, Mahmud, how are you?"

"I'm fine. It's all good."

"Great. How's your dad? Beshar, that's his name, right?"

Mahmud still lived at home. It sucked, but racist landlords were real skeptical toward a prison *blatte.*

"He's good too. It's not exactly perfect, living there. But it'll be fine." Mahmud wanted to tone down the problem. "I'm applying for jobs. Had two interviews this week."

"Wow, that's great! Any offers?"

"No, they said they'd get back to me. That's what they always say."

Mahmud thought about the latest interview. He'd purposely gone wearing only a tank top. The tattoos piled up. The text: *Only trust yourself* on one arm and *Alby Forever* on the other. The ink spoke its own aggressive language: If there's trouble—you'll get in deep. Watch yourself.

When would she understand? He wasn't gonna let a job rob him of his freedom. He wasn't made for a nine-to-five life; he'd known that since he came to Sweden as a kid.

She studied him. For too long.

"What happened to your cheek?"

Wrong question. Gürhan's slap wouldn't ordinarily've busted his cheek—but the dude'd worn a massive signet ring. Had torn up half his face. The cut was covered with surgical tape. What was he gonna say?

"Nothing. Sparred a little with a buddy. You know."

Not the world's best excuse, but maybe she'd fall for it.

Erika seemed to be considering him. Mahmud tried to look out through the blinds. Look unaffected.

"I hope there's no trouble, Mahmud. If there is, you can tell me. I can help you, you know."

Mahmud thought, Yeah, sure you can help me. Irony overload.

Erika dropped the subject. Droned on. Told him about a job-application project that the jobmarketpreparationunemployment-insuranceoffice, or something like that, was running. For guys like him. Mahmud deflected her attention. Had years of training. All the talk with school counselors, meetings with social-service bitches, and inter-rogations with cops'd paid off. Mahmud: expert of experts at shutting his ears when the situation required it—and at managing to still look interested.

Erika kept talking. Blah, blah, blah. Sooooo slow.

"Mahmud, aren't you interested in doing something related to phys-ical fitness? You work out a lot. We've talked about that before. How's that going, by the way?"

"Yeah, it's going good. I like the gym."

"And you never feel tempted to do *that*—you know what I mean?"

Mahmud knew what she meant. Erika brought it up every single time. He just had to smile and take it.

"No, Erika, I've stopped with *that*. We've talked about that hun-dreds of times. Fat-free chicken, tuna, and protein shakes work just as good. I don't need illegal stuff anymore."

Unclear if she was actually listening to what he said. She was writing something down.

"May I ask you a question? Who do you spend time with during the day?"

The meeting was dragging on too long. The point of this shit: short talks so that he could air the problems free life created. But he couldn't let slip about the real problem.

"I hang out with the guys at the gym a lot. They're chill."

"How often are you there?"

"I'm serious about it. Two sessions a day. One before lunch, not too many people there then. And I do another session later at night, around ten."

Erika nodded. Kept talking. Would this never end?

"And how are your sisters doing?"

His sisters were holy, part of his dignity. No matter what punishment Swedish society came up with, nothing could stop him from protecting them. Was Erika questioning something about his sisters?

"What do you mean?"

"Well, do you see her—your older sister? Isn't her man doing time?"

"Erika, we gotta be clear about one thing. My sisters've got nothing to do with the crap I've done. They're white as snow, innocent as lambs. You follow? My older sister's starting a new life. Getting married and stuff."

Silence.

Was Erika gonna get whiny now?

"But Mahmud, I didn't mean anything. You have to understand that. It's just important to me that you see her and your family. When you're released from a penitentiary it often helps to be in touch with stable people in your environment. I've been under the impression that your relationship with your sisters is very good, that's all."

She made a quick pause, eyed him. Was she checking out the mark from Gürhan's slap again? He sought her gaze. After a while, she put her hands in her lap.

"All right, I think we're done for today. Here, take this pamphlet about the Labor Market Board's project I was telling you about before. Their offices are in Hägersten and I really think they might be able to help you. They've got courses in how to succeed at job interviews, stuff like that. It could make you a stronger candidate."

Out on the street. Still hungry. Irritated. Into the 7-Eleven by the entrance to the subway station. Bought an orange soda and two power bars. They crumbled against the roof of his mouth. He thought about Erika's annoying questions.

His phone rang. Unlisted number.

"Yeah."

The voice on the other end: "Is this Mahmud al-Askori?"

Mahmud wondered who it was. Someone who didn't introduce himself. Shadyish.

"Yeah. And what do you want?"

"My name is Stefanovic. I think we may have met at some point. I work out at Fitness Center sometimes. You've collaborated with us before."

Mahmud connected the dots: Stefanovic—the name pretty much said it all. Not exactly a nobody he had on the line. Someone who worked out at the gym, someone who sounded colder than the ice in Gürhan's veins, someone who was Serbian. Mahmud didn't recognize the voice. No face came to mind. But still, it could only mean one thing: One of the heavy hitters wanted to talk to him. Either he was deeper in the shit than he'd thought, or something interesting was in the works.

He hesitated before answering. Wasn't Stefanovic gonna say anything else?

Finally he said, "I recognize your name. Do you work for you-know-who?"

"I guess you could say that. We'd really like to meet you. We think you can help us with something important. You're well connected. And you're good at what you did earlier."

Mahmud interrupted him.

"I've got no plans on rebounding. Just so you know."

"Calm down. We don't want you to do anything that you could get sent back in for. Not at all. This is something completely different."

One thing was certain: this wasn't some normal job. On the other hand: sounded like easy money.

"Okay. Tell me more."

"Not now. Not on the phone. This is what we'll do. We've put a ticket for Sunday in your mailbox. Get there by six and we'll explain then. See you."

The Yugo hung up.

Mahmud walked down the stairs into the subway. Took the escalator to the platform.

He thought, Fuck no, I don't wanna get sent back in. Low odds: the Yugos were gonna trick him into doing something stupid. But it could never hurt a pro *blatte* like Mahmud to meet with them. See what they wanted. How much they'd fork over.

And more importantly: becoming the Yugos' made man could be a way out of the shit he'd ended up in with Gürhan. He felt his mood lift. This could be the beginning of something.

5

Things didn't end up the way Niklas'd planned. One day after he moved into the new apartment, Mom came over. Asked to spend the night.

The whole point of the move was that they wouldn't get on each other's nerves, step too far into each other's territory, disturb each other's routines. But he couldn't say no. She was scared, really scared. Had every right. She had called him on his cell while she was at work.

"Hi Niklas, is that you?"

"Course it's me, Mom, you're calling my number."

"Yes, but I haven't really learned it yet. It's so good that you're home in Sweden now. Something terrible happened."

Niklas could tell by her voice that it was something out of the ordinary.

"What?"

"The police found a murdered person in our building. It's so horrible. A dead person has been lying in our basement all night."

Niklas froze. His thoughts sharpened. At the same time: they turned upside down. This was not good.

"That sounds totally crazy, Mom. What're they saying?"

"Who? The neighbors?"

"No, the police."

"They're not saying anything. I was standing outside half the night, freezing. We all did. Berit Vasquéz was totally broken up."

"Damn, that's terrible. But did you speak more with the police?"

"I'm going in for questioning after work today. But I'm afraid to sleep at home alone tonight. Can I stay with you?"

Not at all what he'd planned. This wasn't good.

"Of course. I'll sleep on a mattress or a bedroll. Why did you go to work today? You should call in sick for a few days."

"No, I can't. And I want to get out of the house, too. It feels good to be at work."

A question in Niklas's head. He had to ask her.

"Do they know who the murdered person was?"

"The police didn't say anything about it. I don't know, anyway. They haven't said anything. Can I come after work?"

He said that was fine. Explained how to get there. Sighed inside.

Niklas put on his shorts and T-shirt: the DynCorp logo in black across the chest. He loved his gear. The runner's socks with no seams to avoid blisters and with a drawstring on the side to hold them up. The shoes: Mizuno Wave Nirvana—nerdy name, but the best shoes the runner's store carried.

The first thing he'd done since he'd come home—and one of the few times he'd traveled any distance from the apartment—was to buy the shoes and the rest of the running stuff. He ran on the treadmill in the store, discussed weight and width, the affect of overpronation on his step and the arch support. A lot of people thought running was a nice sport because it was simple, cheap, no unnecessary gadgets. Not for Niklas: the gadgets made it more fun. The socks, the shorts with the extra slits to avoid chafing on the leg, the heart monitor, and, of course, the shoes. More than fifteen hundred kronor. Worth every cent. He'd already been running more than ten times since he got back. He used to run down there too sometimes, but a limited amount. If you happened to go a few yards down the wrong street, it could end in tragedy. Two British guys from his troop: found with their throats slit. Shoes stolen. Socks still warm on their feet.

He was standing in front of the mirror strapping the heart monitor around his chest. Checked himself out. Fit. Newly sheared crew cut—you could hardly see how blond he really was. But his blue eyes gave him away. Glimpses of another face in the mirror: black streaks smeared under his eyes, greasy hair, steel gaze. Armed for battle.

He put the heart-rate-monitor watch on last. Set it to zero. It gave him the feeling of intensity, the right tempo. And best of all, it gave instant feedback on his training.

He stepped out. Jogged down the stairs. Opened the door. A nice day.

Running: His method of control over loneliness. His medicine. His relaxation in the midst of the confusion over being home again.

He started slow. Felt a mild ache in his thighs from the last run, in

Örnsberg. He ran out toward the Aspudden school. A big, yellow brick building with a flagpole in the schoolyard. A lower wooden building nearby, maybe an after-school center or an elementary-school classroom. He ran past. The trees were sprouting crisp leaves. Nothing was as beautiful as the foliage. He was happy to be home again.

The hill sloped steeper. Down toward what looked like a valley. On the other side: a hill with a wood. At the bottom of the valley was an allotment-garden area—every tenant mommy's big dream: to get her hands on a plot like that. Little cottages, water hoses, and flower beds where things'd really started to grow. The greenery in Sweden was so green.

He couldn't stop himself from analyzing the terrain. Saw it as the FEBA—front edge of battle area. An amphitheater. Perfect for an ambush, an unexpected attack from both sides against an advancing enemy or an enemy convoy at the bottom of the valley. First out: AH-64 Apache helicopters—30-millimeter M230 rotary cannons, a rate of fire of over two thousand rounds a minute. Mow down the trucks and the jeeps. Crush them. Force them to stop. Then bombard them with the helos' Hellfire missiles. After that, the grenade people in the hills would do their bit with 20-millimeter ammunition. Last but not least: the infantry would make sure the jeeps were torched good, spread blankets of fire against any enemy combatants that were still putting up resistance, make sure no militiamen excaped, BBQ the hajis. Deal with the remains. The wreckage. The prisoners.

That's how it was done. The situation was perfect. In the middle of the allotment gardens. He almost longed to be back.

He kept running, toward the hill on the other side. Kept visualizing war scenes. Different images. Bloody people. Burned faces. Blown-up body parts. Men in torn, half-military uniforms screaming in Arabic. Their leaders with guns in their hands and emblems on their shoulder straps, roaring: *"Imshi!"*—charge!

Crawling soldiers. Wounded people. Smoldering bodies.

Everywhere.

In panic.

Distorted faces. Gaping wounds. Empty eyes.

Shit.

He ran. Down toward the water.

The branches arched over the trail like a roof. He continued on toward a residential area.

Felt the fatigue wash over him. Checked his watch. He'd been running for twenty-one minutes. Memorized the time: halfway. Time to turn back. Steady breathing. Could he handle the allotment gardens one more time?

He thought, How am I doing, really? The time at DynCorp marked its men, he knew that. There were plenty of stories about guys who hadn't been able to handle the safe existence in their home countries.

Max 650 feet left to the building's entrance. He slowed down. Walked the last bit. Let his blood sugar settle. His breathing slow. He loved his gadgets. Material that breathed—his shirt was hardly even wet from sweat.

The sky was a clear blue. The leaves in the flower beds lining the street were a clear green.

That's when he saw it. On top of an electrical cabinet.

Dammit.

He didn't know they had those running around outside in Sweden.

Over there, the place was overrun with them. But that was different— there, he was dressed in Kevlar-reinforced camo pants tucked into high, hard military boots. Equipped with weapons—if they came too close, he showed no mercy. Let their little brain substance speckle the gravel. That almost made it okay.

But now.

The rat stared.

Niklas remained still.

No boots—low Mizuno running shoes.

No reinforced pants tucked in—just shorts.

No gun.

It remained still. As big as a cat, he thought.

The panic started creeping up on him.

Someone moved inside the entrance to the building.

The rat reacted. Jumped off the electrical cabinet.

Disappeared along the side of the building.

Niklas opened the door and stepped into the entranceway. Inside, a girl was throwing out trash. Maybe twenty-five years old, long, dark hair, coal-black eyebrows, brown eyes. Pretty. Maybe she was a haji, what the Americans called the civilians down there.

He started walking up the stairs. Sweaty. But it didn't feel like it was from the run. More from the rat shock.

The girl followed. He fumbled with his keys.

She stood outside her door, on the same landing. Checked him out. Opened the door.

Dressed in sweat pants, a big sweatshirt, and flip-flops.

Then he realized—she was his neighbor. He should say hi, even if he didn't know how long he'd be living here.

"Hi, maybe I should introduce myself," he said.

Without really having the time to realize it himself, he heard his own voice say, "*Salaam alaikum. Keif halek?*"

Her face broke into a completely different expression—a broad, surprised smile. At the same time, she looked down at the floor. He recognized the behavior. Over there, a woman never looked a man in the eye, except the whores.

"Do you speak Arabic?" she asked.

"Yeah, a little. I can be neighborly, anyway."

They laughed.

"Nice to meet you. My name is Jamila. I guess I'll see you around. In the laundry room or something."

Niklas introduced himself. Said, "See you later." Then she disappeared into her place.

Niklas kept standing outside his door.

Happy, somehow. Despite the rat he'd seen down there.

In the kitchen, four hours later: him and Mom. Niklas was drinking Coca-Cola. She'd brought a bottle of wine. On the table: a bag with almond cookies that she'd picked up too. She knew Niklas loved those particular cookies. The dry, sweet taste when the cookie got stuck in the roof of your mouth. Nursing-home cookies, Mom called them. He laughed.

The apartment was sparely furnished. There was a worn wooden table in the kitchen. Covered with round stains from warm mugs. Four wooden chairs—extremely uncomfortable. Niklas'd hung a T-shirt over the back of Mom's chair to make it a little softer.

"So, tell me. What really happened?"

It was like pushing a button. Mom leaned over the table as if she wanted him to hear better. It poured out of her. Disjointed and emotional. Hazy and horrified.

She told him how a neighbor'd woken her up. The neighbor said something'd happened in the basement. Then the police showed up.

Told everyone, "No need to worry." They asked strange questions. The neighbors were standing outside, on the street. Talking in low, frightened voices. The police cordoned off the area. Sirens on the street. Armed policemen in motion. They took pictures of the stairwell, the basement, outside. Asked her to produce identification. Wrote down her telephone number. Later, she saw a wrapped human body being rolled out from the basement on a stretcher.

She slurped wine between words. Her head hung over the glass. Her poor posture was apparent even when she sat down.

And then, today, they'd brought her in for questioning. They'd asked all kinds of things. If she had any idea who the dead person could be. Why a murdered man was found in her apartment building. If she'd heard anything, seen anything. If any of the neighbors'd been acting strange lately.

"Was it scary?"

"Very. Just imagine. Being interrogated by the police as if you were involved in a murder, or something. They asked over and over again if I knew who it could be. Why would I know that?"

"So they don't know who it is?"

"I have no idea, but I don't think so. If they did, they wouldn't have asked so many times, right? It's so terrible. How can they not know? The police don't do any good these days."

"Did you see the dead guy?"

"Yes. Or, no, actually. I saw something that could have been a face, but it'd been covered up so much. I don't know. I think it was a man."

"Mom, there's something I need to ask of you. It might sound strange, but I really want you to think about this. You know, considering my background it would be best if—"

He interrupted himself. Poured more Coke. It clucked out from the can.

" . . . I don't want you to tell the police about me. Don't mention that I'm home again. Don't mention that I was living with you. Can you promise me that?" Niklas looked up at Marie.

She was sitting in silence. Staring at him.

6

They stopped for coffee—Thomas and Ljunggren, as usual. Even though it was only four o'clock in the afternoon, Ljunggren was already on his eighth cup of the day. Thomas wondered: Was Ljunggren's stomach made of steel, or what?

The café: a taxi joint by Liljeholmen. A TV in one corner playing an Italian league soccer game on high volume. Uncomfortable metal chairs and tables with checked tablecloths. Spread out on the tables: newspapers and housewares catalogs. Perfect place for cops to chill— they were waiting for an assignment worthy of the name.

Ljunggren's radio handset was on the table. The calls from dispatch could hardly be heard over the soccer announcer's excited commentary. Fiorentina was proving that it wanted to join the top of the Italian league and was mopping the floor with Cagliari. The Dane Martin Jørgensen'd just made the 2–1 goal. Well placed. Beautiful.

They were each reading a newspaper. As always, not much conversation. They nurtured their peaceful rapport.

But Thomas had trouble focusing. The articles in the newspaper just floated on past. He flipped through it, distracted. Couldn't stomach the Fiorentina buzz either. He couldn't drop that basement thing. Normally, he'd forget as soon as he was back at the station. Showered, dried himself off, put on his civilian clothes. Assault, murder, rape—whatever it was—it ran off with the soap. But this was eating away at him. The image of the busted face kept coming back. With every page he turned of the newspaper, he'd see the tatters of flesh; the sunken, broken nose; the swollen eyes. The track marks on the arm. The bloody, peeled fingertips. The empty mouth.

Thomas thought it was a strange routine for real cops—as soon as things got exciting, the crap was turned over to the house mice. Desk cops—the criminal detectives—dudes who'd crawled off the street and into paper shuffling. They were often older officers with bad backs or knee problems—as if sitting still at a desk all day was going to help your back. Or else they came with other baggage, they'd "burned out," as they say. Everyone knew that was just baloney. But sometimes: young jokers fresh out of the Police Academy who were too feeble to do the real job. Thought they could be Kurt Wallander. Thomas knew—90 percent of the investigations they dealt with were shoplifting and bike thefts. Yeah, high drama. Sure.

Dispatch announced, "We've got a drunk driver who thinks he's Ayrton Senna on the E4, southbound. Anyone near Liljeholmen? Over."

There was a break in the soccer game. Thomas heard the radio loud and clear.

Saw on Ljunggren's face that he'd heard it too.

They grinned their usual grins.

Responded, "We can't take it. We're near Älvsjö. Over."

A little white lie to get off scot-free. Dispatch had no idea how close to the place they really were.

Thomas thought, You could call their work ethic shitty. Call it lazy. Call it cheating. But the ones in charge deserved what they got—if you don't invest in the police, don't expect to get anything back. And some drunkard who thought the highway was a racetrack would never get more than a month anyway—so what was the point?

Ljunggren poured his ninth cup. Slurped.

Ljunggren had to drive the last hours of the day's shift alone. Thomas was called to an investigation meeting. Or, as it was formally called, a debriefing. They wanted him to describe his vibes from the early morning of June 3. Give the suits a broader, better, richer story to go on. They needed more than just the technicians' photos, written reports, and interrogation transcripts.

He was going to headquarters, which is to say, Kronoberg. Which is to say: paradise for detective house mice/paper pushers/little girls. He got a ride with a female cop he'd never met before. Didn't have the energy to chat. Greeted her politely—after that, they kept their traps shut for the rest of the ride.

Thomas'd written half a page, his incident report. It was bullshit: standard phrases, abbreviations. *Off. Andrén and Off. Ljunggren were called at 00.10 hours on the night in question. Arrived at 10 Gösta Ekman Road at 0016 hours. Some members of the general public were gathered out-*

side the building as well as ca. 8 people in the stairwell. A list of times, names of officers that'd arrived on the scene, senior officers, info-reporting, and so on. After that, brief descriptions: *Undersigned attempted CPR. CS photographed. Observations: traces of blood and vomit on the walls/floor. VIC, WMA, facedown, severe swelling and wounds. In back pocket: receipts, unidentified slips of paper. BUS on the scene at ca. 0026 hours. SOCO arrived at ca. 0037 hours.*

Thomas hated to write incident reports for two reasons. First of all, he couldn't handle a keyboard. Simple problems tripped him up. He hit the Caps Lock key by accident. Took three minutes to understand what'd happened. He hit the Insert key when he was trying to backspace—every single letter he wrote deleted the text he'd already written. He couldn't handle that shit. Had a fit. Rewrote half the report from scratch because it was deleted in time with the edits he made. His irritation almost boiled over. Who'd invented those keys, anyway?

Second: It didn't matter what actually happened. What mattered was that you showed that you'd followed the rules. In reality, he'd skipped doing CPR. But anyone would've skipped that part. You have to protect yourself—such is the life of a cop. What made it into the report was another thing altogether.

The main entrance on Polhemsgatan was newly renovated. Gleaming marble floors, polished metal, and huge white designer lamps. Thomas couldn't believe how they chose to spend their money. Some dudes in the Southern District'd been using the same service weapons for twenty years, but here, at the home of the fancy cops, they spent millions on redoing an entranceway. How exactly did a luxury foyer give Swedish citizens a better city? No end to the fucked-up priorities.

He flashed his badge at the welcome desk. Asked them to call the inspector he was there to see: the head of the preliminary investigation, Martin Hägerström. Room 547. Fifth floor. Odds were: a great view.

On the ride up the elevator was crammed with desk people, mostly women. He didn't recognize a single face. Did they fill the entire department with girls these days? He fixed his eyes on the elevator buttons—the button with a 5 on it, to be more precise. Adhered to strict Swedish elevator etiquette: get on, sweep your eyes over who's in there, then fix your gaze on a point on the wall, the control panel, or the inspection certificate. Then keep it there. Don't move. Don't turn your head. Don't look around again. Above all: don't, under any circumstances, look any of your fellow passengers in the eyes.

Every single button was lit. Someone was getting off at every floor. It was going to be a long ride.

Fifth floor: he found his way to the room. The door was closed. He knocked. Someone called, "Come in."

Inside: chaos—so messy you could've easily hidden a motorcycle in the room. A bookcase along one wall, filled with books, magazines, and binders. Expanding files bursting with paper in piles on the floor. Incident reports, seizure reports, witness contact information, case documents covered the rest of the floor—some in plastic folders, others not. The desk was cluttered with similar stuff: witness-interrogation transcripts, preliminary-investigation memos, and other junk. Coffee cups, half-empty bottles of mineral water, and orange peels everywhere. Chocolates, tobacco tins, and pens in a pile right in front of the computer screen. Somewhere under all that paper, there must be a keyboard. Somewhere in all that mess, there must be a detective inspector.

A thin guy stepped forward. The dude must've been standing behind the door.

Extended his hand.

"Welcome. Thomas Andrén, right? Martin Hägerström is my name. Detective inspector."

"Newly appointed, or what?" Thomas didn't like his clowny style: the corduroy pants, the green shirt with the top two buttons undone, the chaos in the room, the dude's messy hair. The un-uniformed ease.

"Not really. I was transferred six months ago, from Internal Affairs. They have so much work piled up here. Needed backup, you know. How are things over where you are? Skärholmen, right?"

Hägerström moved some documents piled on a Myra designer chair. Gestured for Thomas to have a seat. Two words were echoing in his head: Internal Affairs—the rat squad. Martin Hägerström was one of Them. The two-timers, the quislings, the traitors. The ones whose job it was to nail other cops, colleagues, brothers. The unit to which they brought people plucked from other districts in the country so that they wouldn't have any buddies in the area where they worked. All cops' number one worry. All normal men's number one enemy. All hierarchies' lowest rung.

Thomas met his gaze with a steely look.

"Okay. You're one of those."

Hägerström stared back, giving him an even harder look.

"That's right. I'm one of those."

Hägerström pulled out a new legal pad and a pen from somewhere.

"This isn't going to take long. I just want you to tell me briefly what you saw, who you spoke to, how you experienced the situation in the stairwell and the basement the day before yesterday. I have your report and all, but we haven't finished investigating the crime scene and I've only brought in about a third of the people in the area for questioning. We really don't know for sure if the basement was the actual scene of the crime. Sometimes you need some fleshing out to get a better picture."

Thomas sat down, too. Looked out through the window.

"What kind of fleshing out do you need? I don't know anything other than what I wrote in the report."

The fastest way to avoid lengthy debriefings was usually to refer to the report. Thomas wanted to get out of there. This was a waste of time.

"Let's start with what happened when you got there. How you discovered the body."

"Doesn't it say in the report?"

"It says here that you, and I'm quoting, 'found the dead person in the basement, outside storage unit number fourteen.' That's all."

"But that's how it was. On the landing, on the first floor, there was a little family dressed in bathrobes wondering what was going on. They told me he was lying down there. I went down. The door was locked so I opened it with a skeleton key. First thing I saw was blood and vomit on the floor of the basement. Then I saw the body. It was lying face-down. But you've got photos of that, don't you?"

The detective wouldn't give up. Kept asking for details. What the family in the stairwell'd looked like. How the basement was built. How the body'd been lying. Thomas realized that he'd applied the wrong tactic—he should've been more detailed to begin with. This was taking all fucking night. After an hour of questioning, Hägerström stood up.

"Want coffee?"

Thomas declined. Remained seated. Hägerström disappeared out of the room.

Thomas's thoughts drifted off. He yearned to be somewhere else. He thought about his shooting club. His Infinity gun, his other guns, the powerful focus he felt when he stood with the ear guards on and fired off ten straight 9-millimeter rounds right in the mug of the paper cutout. He could say it without shame: he was one of the Stockholm police force's best shots.

Hägerström came back into the room again. Seemed to want to make small talk for a while.

"You know, you patrol officers are underrated. I often think your first impressions are important. I mean, we usually nail most of the heavy perps through investigations. All the information we collect lets me sit here in my chamber, tie up the loose ends, and get them prosecuted. You know, from my desk. But we need input from the street, from reality. From you."

Thomas just nodded.

"I've got ideas for new ways of collaboration. The desk people together with the guys who are really out there. Detectives and patrol officers. You'd set up teams with both. There's so much knowledge that's lost today."

"Are we done here? Can I go?"

"No, not yet. I want to discuss one final thing with you."

Thomas sighed.

Hägerström kept going. "We usually talk about different types of violent criminals. I'm sure you remember that from the Police Academy. The professional criminals and the psychologically disturbed. For example, the professional criminals can plan well, are manipulative, and sometimes have psychotic tendencies. Often they are relatively intelligent—at least we'd call them street-smart. The psychologically disturbed, on the other hand, are usually lone wolves. Many have had problems or experienced some sort of trauma growing up. They can live for many years without committing any crime, but then something cracks and they commit some aggravated sexual or violent assault. The thing is that their deeds are different. They move in different fields, commit different kinds of shit. Completely different types of murders. The professional criminals—economically motivated criminals—often kill swiftly and cleanly, leave their victims where they can't be tied to the crime, and don't make any unnecessary bloody business out of the whole thing. The psychologically sick have different motives. It can be sexually related, it can be a real mess, they often go after people in their direct vicinity, or hurt many people at once. They might leave their victims as if they want them to be found, like a message to their surroundings. Or a call for help. Considering the nature of this murder, I'm sure you can already guess what my question is. Spontaneously, what's your view of this murder—professional criminal or psycho?"

The question came as a surprise. For some strange reason, Thomas felt honored—this paper-pushing detective valued his version of things,

his opinion and intuition. He rejected the thought. The dude was sucking up. He answered appropriately—which is to say, rudely.

"I mean, he didn't exactly look happy, so it was probably pretty
painful."

Hägerström didn't get the joke.

"What do you mean?"

"I mean he didn't look happy, he had a strange facial expression.
Bloody, might be the right word."

Their eyes locked again. Neither lowered their gaze.

"Andrén, I don't appreciate your kind of humor. Just answer the
question, please."

"Didn't I just do that? Considering how damn bloody that basement
was, it must've been a real psycho freak who made the hit."

Thirty seconds of silence—a long time between two men who didn't
know each other.

"Don't worry, you'll get to leave soon. I just have one more question. What is your spontaneous, preliminary opinion about the cause
of death?"

No point in making a fuss. If he did, the detective might keep him
there even longer just to fuck with him. He offered his honest view: "I
really don't know. The dead guy had deep track marks on his arm, so it
could've been an overdose that did him in, in addition to the assault."

Hägerström's mouth fell open, looked honestly surprised for a brief
moment. Caught himself. Flipped back to throwing his weight around.
"Didn't I say I didn't like your kind of humor?"

It was Thomas's turn to look surprised. What did the guy mean? It
wasn't a joke.

"Hägerström, I'm gonna be honest now. I don't like people from
Internal Affairs. I think we should stick together and not spend time
ruining the lives of good professionals. But I want to be accommodating and answer your questions, just so I can get out of here. The problem is that, right now, I have no idea what you're talking about."

"No? I mean I want you to answer my question. What is your
spontaneous, preliminary opinion about the cause of death? No fucking track marks, please."

"Like I said, I don't know. It was probably the assault, but it could've
been an overdose, too. Considering the *track marks.*"

Hägerström leaned forward. Articulated, "There were no track marks
or needle wounds. The corpse was completely free of that kind of injury."

Silence again. Both were evaluating the situation. Their faces: less than three feet away from each other.

Finally, Thomas said, "Sounds like you didn't read my report. The corpse's right arm looked like a sieve. If he or someone else pumped drugs into all those holes, he could just as well have caught a chill from an overdose. Do you understand?"

Hägerström rummaged among the papers on his desk. Picked one up; it was Thomas's report. The detective handed it over. Half a page. Terse sentences that he recognized. But there was something wrong about the end. There were words missing. Had he forgotten to save the last lines? Had his problems with the damn keyboard made parts of the text disappear, or had someone else deleted it?

He shook his head. Not a word about the needle wounds in the report.

Thomas looked up from the report.

"This is bullshit."

* * *

AUTOPSY REPORT

The National Board of Forensic Medicine, June 4
The Department of Forensic Medicine
Retzius Road 5
171 65 SOLNA
E 07-073, K 58599-07

A. Introduction
In accordance with an order from the Stockholm County Police Department, an expanded forensic autopsy has been performed on an unknown body, found on June 3 at 10 Gösta Ekman Road in Stockholm, referred to below as "X."

The investigation was carried out by the undersigned at the Department of Forensic Medicine in Stockholm in the presence of the autopsy technician Christian Nilsson.

The body has, according to the Stockholm County Police Department, not yet been positively identified. However, the following can initially be stated:

1. X is a man;
2. X is Caucasian;
3. X is between 45 and 55 years old; and
4. X died between 2100 and 2400 hours on June 2.

B. Additional Circumstances

The additional circumstances of the situation in question are made apparent by a primary report from the Stockholm County Police Department, registration number K 58599-07, signed by Martin Hägerström, Det. Insp.

C. External Examination

1. The dead body is 73 inches long and weighs 174 pounds.

2. General rigor mortis persists.

3. There are extensive and deep surface tissue wounds on the face, on the temples, and on the throat.

4. The hair on the head is ca. 4 inches long and blond, some-what graying around the temples. There is dried blood in the hair.

5. The skin on the right temple has been scraped off within a 4x4-inch area.

6. There is substantial swelling on the left ear. A section of the ear lobe is missing, around 0.4x0.4 inches. Fringe-lined lacerations surround the area. The skin on top of the ear is scraped off within a 0.2x0.1-inch area. Furthermore, the skin is scraped off within a 0.4x0.1-inch area below the right ear.

7. There is substantial swelling, reddish-blue discolor-ations, and deep skin lacerations in a 6x2-inch area across the lower forehead, near the top of the eyebrows. Above the eye-brows, the skin is completely scraped off within a 1.5x0.6-inch area, which is sharply demarcated.

8. Within a 1.6x1.6-inch area 0.4 inches above the right eye-brow, there is a large cut, which also has a blurred, bluish discoloration around it.

9. There is substantial swelling on the eyelids, which also show bluish-red discoloration. There are lacerations with frayed edges on both eyelids.

10. There is a substantial number of cuts, deep skin lacera-tions, swelling, and discolorations on the cheeks, which con-tinue over the edge of the jaw and down on the throat.

11. There is massive, confluent reddish-black bleeding in the eyes' conjunctivae. The conjunctivae have been severed.

12. The nasal bone is broken in three places and the root of the nose is crushed. The skin in a 1.6x0.8-inch area on the upper section of the nose is scraped off. Furthermore, the left nostril is completely missing, replaced by a 0.4-inch-deep cut.

13. There is substantial swelling on the upper and lower lips. There is some confluent reddish-black bleeding in the mucous membrane. Furthermore, there are two 0.4x0.2-inch cuts

that are a few mm deep with fringed edges on the upper lip. There are several large cuts with frayed edges and surrounding bleeding in the tissue and membranes of the lower lip.

14. All the teeth, except for three molars on the upper left side and two molars on the lower left side, are missing. Note: dentures were probably used. There is bloody saliva and vomit in the mouth.

15. All the fingertips on both hands are injured. The bottom side of each fingertip has a 0.3-inch-deep cut that tapers off, measuring 0.08 inches at the lower point.

Stockholm

Bengt Gantz, Head Pathologist, Department of Forensic Medicine

7

Abbou—Mahmud was impressed. According to his own view of things, Mahmud wasn't the guy to get caught off guard by fly whips, boosted bling, or fat stacks. He was the guy who'd rolled in an ill Audi before things went wack. The *blatte* who'd slung juice for a hundred G's a month. Muscle man. Pussy pariah. Million Program myth.

But he felt like a newbie in this situation. They were sitting in the most expensive ringside seats. You had to be someone in fighter Sweden to even be allowed to buy seats like this. And the king who'd made this happen was definitely someone—King of Kings, Radovan.

Things had to be nice when the Yugo boss himself graced the scene. A couple of big fights were being decided tonight. The odds were high: in other words, thick rolls involved. Course the boss wanted to see up close when the boys in the ring had their foreheads smashed in and the dough rose like crazy.

Master's Cup, K-1. K-1 stood for the four K's—karate, kung fu, kickboxing, and knockdown karate—that all went head to head with the same rules. But in reality, most styles were allowed. Ruthless animals who were used to owning the ring at their home gyms had to limp off the mat, beaten to bits. Bare-chested fighters pummeled each other so hard you could feel it all the way up in the nosebleed seats. Eastern European giants tore through Swedish immigrant boys one by one: kneed chins, dislocated arms, elbowed noses. The audience howled. The fighters roared. The judges tried to break up punch sequences that would floor a rhino.

The fighters came from Sweden, Romania, the former Yugoslavia, France, Russia, and Holland. Fought for the titles—and for who would advance to the big K-1 competitions in Tokyo.

Mahmud caught a glimpse of Radovan, eight seats away in the same row. Fired up like everyone else. At the same time, Il Padre maintained his calm, his dignity—a boss never breaks a visible sweat. The Yugo brand equaled dignity, which equaled respect. Period.

Mahmud'd arrived at the arena with time to spare—five-forty. People were lining up outside to buy returned tickets. Security was worse than at the airport. The only advantage: here, they didn't care that he was a Muslim. He had to pass through metal detectors, put his belt, keys, and cell phone through. They ran a manual metal detector over him. Groped his balls like fags.

At six o'clock he sidled up to the seat with the right number. No one was seated around him yet. It was way too early. The Serbs let him wait. Mahmud's thoughts zipped off to an unwanted place. Almost a week since the nightmare in the woods. The wound on his cheek would probably heal fine. But his wounded honor—he wasn't so sure about that. Really, though, he knew—there was only one way. A man who lets someone walk all over him is not a man. But how the fuck would a vendetta go down? Gürhan was VP in Born to Be Hated. If Mahmud so much as breathed cockiness, he'd be as screwed as Luca Brasi.

What's more: Daniel, the Syriac who'd made him eat the gun, had called two days ago. Asked why Mahmud hadn't started paying off his debt yet. The answer was a given: not a chance Mahmud could get anywhere near enough gold in three days. The Daniel dude told him to fuck himself—that wasn't Gürhan's problem. Couldn't Mahmud borrow? Couldn't Mahmud sell his mother? His sisters? They gave him a week. Then he had to make the first payment: one hundred thousand cash. No escaping it. Right now, the knife was at his throat. The Yugos might be his chance.

At the same time: reluctance. He thought about his talk with Dad a few days ago. Beshar'd taken early retirement. Before that, he'd slaved away as a subway engineer and janitor for ten years. Busted his knees and back. Struggled for the Svens, for nothing. Proud. So proud. "I've paid every cent of my taxes and that feels good," he liked to say.

Mahmud's classic answer: "Dad, you're a loser. Don't you get it? The Svens haven't given you shit."

"Don't you call me that. You must understand. It's not about Swedes this or Swedes that. You should get a job. Do right for yourself. You embarrass me. Can't they arrange something through the parole office?"

"Nine-to-fives are no good. Check me, I'm gonna be someone without a job and shit like that."

Beshar just shook his head. He didn't get it.

Mahmud'd known it already when he and Babak'd shoplifted their first candy bars. He could feel it in his whole body when they juxed cell phones from seventh graders in the hallway and when he blazed his first spliff in the schoolyard. He wasn't made for any other life. He'd never get on his knees. Not for the parole people. Not for Gürhan. Not for anyone in Sven Sweden.

Twenty-five minutes later, a ways into the first fight, showtime: Stefanovic slid into the seat next to him. They didn't shake hands, the dude didn't even turn around. Instead he said, "Glad you could make it."

Mahmud kept watching the fight. Didn't know if he should turn to Stefanovic or if they were supposed to take care of the talk on the DL.

"Course. When you guys ask, you come. Right?"

"Usually, yes."

They sat silently in the din.

Now and then Stefanovic turned to a guy sitting on his other side. Mahmud knew who it was: Ratko. He rolled with another huge Yugo, Mrado, who Mahmud used to hang with before he got locked up. It was damn shifty, those guys always said hi to Mahmud when they ran into each other at the gym, but here they didn't move a muscle. Normally, Mahmud didn't tolerate shit like that. But today he needed the Yugos.

Mahmud checked the place out. The Solna sports center: probably four thousand people rubbing elbows in the bleachers. Bodybuilding dudes—he said hi to some of them—young *blattes* with too much juice in their bodies and gel in their hair, combat-sports freaks who loved the smell of blood. Cheaper versions of himself—he loved that he wasn't sitting up there with them. Ringside, another style ruled. More suits, more glamour, more expensive Cartier watches. Older, calmer, more respectable. Stirred into the mix: twenty-five-year-old honeys with tight, low-cut tops and highlighted hair. Somber bodyguards and underlings. Mahmud hoped he'd be spared running into anyone from Gürhan's gang.

The spotlights lit up every fighter that entered the ring. On one short side: the fighters' national flags, size XL, on the wall. On the other: the K-1 logo and the full name of the competition written across a banner: MASTER'S CUP — RUMBLE OF THE BEASTS. Speakers blared out the guys' names, their clubs, and nationalities. 50 Cent on max volume between fights. During breaks, babes with fake tits, hot pants, and tight T-shirts with ads on them held up signs with the number of the next round. Shook their booties as they sashayed around the ring—the crowd howled louder than at a knockout.

The emcee of the night was standing in the ring, his soaring mood cranked up to max: Jon Fagert—full-contact legend, now a suit-clad combat-sports lobbyist.

"Ladies and gentlemen, tonight is the night we've all been waiting for. The night when true sportsmanship, tough training, and, above all, bone-hard spirit decide the fights. Our first real title game tonight is within K-1 Max. As you all probably know, the competitors are not allowed to weigh over one hundred and fifty-four pounds within this subclass of K-1. Let me welcome two fighters into the ring who have solid successes behind them. One is the winner of the Dutch Thai Boxing Society's national tour three years in a row. He's got nasty speed, feared backward kicks, and famous right jabs. The other is a legendary vale tudo fighter with more than twenty knockouts to his name. Ernesto Fuentes from Club Muay One in Amsterdam against Mark Mikhaleusco from NHB Fighter's Gym in Bucharest—please welcome them up!"

In the middle of the applause Stefanovic said something straight out into the air, as if he were talking to himself. "That fairy up there, Jon Fagert. He's a clown. Did you know that?"

Mahmud followed suit—Stefanovic didn't want the whole arena to see that they were talking, of course. He watched how Ernesto Fuentes and Mark Mikhaleusco stretched one final time before the fight. Then he answered, speaking straight out into the air, "Why?"

"He doesn't understand who picks up the tab for this whole spectacle. He thinks it's some kind of charity. But even a player like that's gotta understand that if you put dough in, you want bread back. Right?"

Mahmud wasn't really listening, just nodded along.

Stefanovic continued, "We've built up this business. You with me? The gym where you work out, Pancrase, HBS Haninge Fighting School, and the other joints. We recruit good people from there. Make sure that guy up there and the other enthusiasts can have their fun. Did you put any money down, by the way?"

The discussion was weird. They could've been buzzing about anything. Stefanovic had his poker face on. The entire time: ice cold.

Mahmud responded: "No, who's hottest?"

"The Dutch guy, I put forty G's on the Dutch guy. He's got dynamite in his fists."

The audience was taut, like thousands of rubber bands ready to snap. The fight began.

Mahmud wasn't completely green. He watched fights on Eurosport sometimes. Regular sports didn't interest him; he didn't get anything out of it. But watching the fights on TV gave him an adrenaline rush.

The Romanian had blinding technique, speed, timing, and footwork. Sick round kicks and jump kicks à la Bruce Lee. Punch sequences fast, like Keanu Reeves in *The Matrix*. World-class blocking. No doubt about it—Stefanovic was gonna lose his dough.

The Romanian maintained the upper hand through the end of the first round.

The music switched on: gangsta rap on max. The trainers dabbed the fighters' faces. Rubbed Vaseline on them so the punches would slide off easier. A chick swung her cheeks diagonally across the ring. Held up a sign with the number 2 on it.

The gong sounded. The fighters stepped back into the ring. Sized each other up for a few seconds. Then all hell broke loose. The Romanian continued to impress. Landed a perfect round kick to Fuentes's head. The guy sank to his knees. The judge counted off.

One, two.

The audience roared.

The Dutch man's saliva: like a spider's thread from his mouth down to the floor.

Three, four.

Mahmud'd seen a lot of fights in his life. But this—perfection.

Five, six.

Fuentes stood up. Slowly.

The audience howled.

A few seconds left of the second round. The punches echoed. The Romanian tried to get three punches in. The Dutch guy lowered his chin, raised both gloves in front of his face. Successful block.

Mahmud glanced at Stefanovic. The Yugo's face was rigid like a rock. No sign of panic about the forty G's that were about to be flushed down the toilet.

The third round began.

Something'd happened. It was like the Romanian was kicking in slow motion. Looked tired. But Mahmud was watching from closer up than most—the guy wasn't even out of breath. This had to be rigged. Was that really possible? Massive advantage two minutes ago, and now it looked like he was the one who'd almost been down for the count. Someone ought to react.

Slowly but surely, Fuentes took over the fight. Heavy punches, low kicks, and rapid kicks to the head. The Romanian fought like a girl. Retreated ringside at every advance. Waved his arms in front of his face without even touching the Dutch man on the nose.

It was stupid. Felt like an American WWE fight. Fake.

The rounds passed by one by one. The dudes in the ring grew more tired.

Mahmud almost laughed. Even if it was a rigged fight, Stefanovic was gonna get rich—and his boss, R., would probably get even richer.

The gong sounded. The fight was over. The Romanian was barely standing. The judge grabbed hold of their gloves.

Raised Ernesto Fuentes's arm.

For the first time, Stefanovic turned to Mahmud. A smile barely flickered across his lips—but his eyes glowed like embers.

"Okay, soon we'll talk business. The next fight is going to be huge. I promise, they're giants, he-men. It's what everyone's here to see. The audience is going to be in ecstasy. Deafening support for the Swedish guy. That's when we'll talk. When everyone's attention is directed at the ring and no one can hear us. You follow?"

Mahmud followed. Soon, he'd get his chance. If only the Gürhan fag knew. Mahmud was about to cut a deal with the Yugos.

A half hour later: it was time again. Mahmud was in his seat, waiting. During the intermission, he'd walked around. Said hi to people he knew, buzzed with the guys from the gym. People were happy to see him out. "Welcome back, Twiggy. Now it's time to get cracking and bulk up again." They were right—the slammer was no place to work out. It should be perfect: lots of time, no booze, no unhealthy food. But you couldn't sneak any juice in there, you couldn't even buy dietary supplements in the prison commissary. Plus: the gym at Asptuna sucked. But the biggest difference was that it just wasn't the same thing on the inside. The pen sucked you dry. Mahmud'd lost forty-four pounds.

The Yugos were the right move for him. He wanted up—was *going* up. Six months in the pen couldn't stop him. Not a chance he'd let himself get benched. And anyone who wanted up knew one thing: sooner or later you have to deal with R., so you might as well do it on sweet terms. Play on the same team as the Yugo boss. Mahmud: the Arab they couldn't gyp, the man who went his own way. This was *soooo* right. He just wondered what it was they wanted him to do.

Radovan came walking down a set of stairs. Trailed by a posse. Mahmud recognized a few of them: Stefanovic, of course. Goran: known as the city's booze and smokes smuggling king. The Ratko dude. A couple other beefy guys he recognized from the gym. A trail of skanks.

Stefanovic sat down next to Mahmud again.

Jon Fagert stepped into the ring. Looked out over the sea of people. Silence settled.

"Honored guests. Today is a big day. One of the two men who are soon going to go head to head in the ring will advance. Not just to anything. Not to yet another championship fight in their individual genre. No, on to something much bigger. To the ultimate championship for the sport of sports. What I'm talking about, of course, is the K-1 championship in the Tokyo Dome in December, where more than one hundred thousand people will be in the audience. First prize is over five hundred thousand dollars. One man will advance tonight. One man is strong enough. One man has the best fighting spirit. Soon, we'll know which one."

Smoke billowed out beside two entrances to the ring.

One silhouette appeared at each end.

The music played "Also Sprach Zarathustra" from the movie *2001: A Space Odyssey*.

Fagert raised the volume: "Ladies and gentleman, I have the honor of introducing two giants. From Belarus, straight from Minsk's Chinuks Gym, we have the former Spetsnaz soldier with more than twenty K-1 championships to his name. The man with the iron fists, the beast, the death machine, the legend: Vitali Akhramenko."

The audience roared.

One of the silhouettes moved forward. Took a step out from the smoky fog. The spotlights followed his heavy steps. The feeling: like a god who made an entrance in the valley of death.

He was the biggest human being Mahmud'd ever seen, and Mahmud worked out at Fitness Center. Over seven feet tall. Defined muscles like on a comic-book figure. Chest wide as a sumo wrestler. Biceps broader than Mahmud's thighs.

Jon Fagert continued, making himself heard over the music: "And in the other corner we have a Swedish super fighter, straight from HBS Haninge Fighting School with over ten knockouts to his name. The powerhouse, the tank, the fighting god, our very own Jörgen Ståhl."

The atmosphere felt like a heavy-metal concert. The music pounded. The spotlights played. Jon Fagert's eyes flashed. The little punks in the bleachers were in ecstasy.

Jörgen Ståhl advanced slowly. Allowed the cheering to build gradually. Dressed in a cape with the HBS logo on the back. Black tribal tattoos covered almost his entire upper body. On one forearm in black inked letters: *Ståhl Is King*. Mahmud thought about Gürhan's tattoo.

Stefanovic opened his mouth, kept his eyes on the ring.

"People are crazed. A couple punches and some blood and those kids up in the bleachers think it's a world war. They know nothing. Did you bet, by the way?"

"Didn't bet last time, didn't bet this time. But it seems like you cashed in."

"That's right. This time, I've put in one hundred large. On the Belarusian. He's an animal, I swear. This could be epic. What do you think?"

Mahmud thought, Is Stefanovic trying to make me insecure? He's ending every sentence with a stupid question.

"I don't really think nothing about it. You seem to know what you're doing."

"Listen, the Belarusian is a three-hundred-pound old man, but he's got the technique of a two-hundred-pound kid. And speed isn't the only thing deciding this—timing is even more important. You'll see. He's going to let all hell break loose on that Swede. Course, we've got a hunch about it, too."

Mahmud wondered when Stefanovic was gonna get to the point.

The fight began up in the ring. Akhramenko tried to land a left uppercut on Ståhl. The Swede blocked good. This was like heavy-weight boxing but with low kicks to the legs.

"Mahmud, we trust you. Do you know what that means?"

Yet another question. Might be the beginning of the real talk they were supposed to have.

"You can trust me. Even if I hung out with Mrado, I know he made some trouble for you guys. And even if I'm not a Serb. You use Arabs. Our people don't have anything against each other here."

"That's right. Maybe you already know one of them, Abdulkarim. He's out of the game right now, but you can't find a better man. Are you like him?"

"Like I said, you can trust me."

"That's not enough. We need men who are one hundred and fifty percent loyal. It happens that we bet on the wrong fighters, so to speak."

Mahmud knew what he was talking about—everyone knew. Lately there'd been a lot of shit going down in Stockholm's underworld. That kind of thing happened: someone thought they'd be the new king of the hill, someone wanted to challenge the boys at the top, someone's honor got stepped on. There were plenty of examples. The war between the Albanians and the Original Gangsters, the shoot-out in the Västberga cold-storage facility between different factions within the Yugo mafia, the executions in Vällingby last month.

Up in the ring, Ståhl was landing a series of kicks to Akhramenko's calves and quick alternating punches to his head. Maybe the Sven was gonna take it home after all.

Stefanovic continued, "You could be our man. To see if you make the cut, I'd like to ask you for a little favor. Listen carefully."

Mahmud didn't turn around. Continued to eye the fight. The first round ended. The Swede was bleeding near the eyebrow.

"Have you heard about the hit against Arlanda Airport? It was going smooth but then it went to hell. We'd planned it just as well as we always do. I think you know what I mean. Had the guards in our pockets. Knew the routines, the surveillance cameras, when the delivery of bills would arrive, the emergency exits, the escape routes, the exchangeable cars, caltrops, everything. There were four guys on the team, two of ours and two from your side of town, North Botkyrka. Three went into the grounds at Arlanda, into the storage area where the gear was stashed. One stayed outside. Everything went according to plan. When they'd pushed the bags out on the pallet to the getaway car, they were met by the guy who'd waited outside, dude number four. With gun in hand. Pointed at them. You follow?"

"You got done."

"We got done right up the ass. Hard. There were bills for more than forty-five million. And that dude, he took it all. Had the other three dump the crap in the car. Then he split."

"You're kidding? Who's the guy?"

It took a while for Stefanovic to answer. Ståhl and Akhramenko were dancing around each other slowly. The Belarusian looked tired. Ståhl bounced away as though he knew how Akhramenko was gonna hit. Blocked. Ducked. In the zone, working it. Ståhl almost got a knee in. The ref broke it up. Sent them back to their positions.

"The guy's name is Wisam Jibril. Lebanese. Heavy on CIT gigs. You know, cash in transit. Remember him? Something of a guru in your crowd, I think. He's been missing since the Arlanda hit. Pronounced dead in the tsunami catastrophe a few years ago, just like so many others made sure to be. With forty-five of Radovan's millions."

Suddenly it was obvious why they'd chosen him. Wisam Jibril: one of Mahmud's gods growing up. Three years older. Went to the same school. From the same hood. Same gang. And Mahmud's dad'd known Wisam's mom, too. It was as if they were asking him to rat out family. Fuck.

Still, he heard himself say, "What makes you think I can find him?"

"We think he's back in Sweden. People've seen him around town. But he knows we're not happy. No one seems to know where he lives. He's careful. Never goes out alone. Hasn't even been in touch with his family, at least not as far as we know."

Stefanovic let the words hang in the air for a second. Then he hissed, "Find him."

Up in the ring, the giants were going at it. Ståhl was alternating between feeding uppercuts and jabs. The Belarusian guard was gradually being lowered. His head hung, he seemed unfocused. After two more minutes: bam. The Swede landed a brutal power punch. The Belarusian bounced against the ropes. Ståhl went in close. Grabbed Akhramenko's neck. Pressed the giant down. Kneed him with full force. The sound of something cracking in Akhramenko's jaw. The mouth guard went flying. A brief second: silence in the arena. Then he sank down to the mat.

Mahmud's thoughts were in mad tumult. First and foremost: the offer from the Yugos was in many ways an easy gig. To find a dude like Wisam couldn't be impossible, if he was in Stockholm. At the same time: the guy was a family friend. The guy was from his hood, an Arab. What did that say about Mahmud's honor? At the same time: he needed this more than ever. With the debt to Gürhan. And his own honor to win back.

Stefanovic got up. The man'd just lost a hundred G's. Maybe there were still some clean sports left—the Yugos didn't seem to control everything in this city, after all. Mahmud eyed his face. Completely expressionless.

Stefanovic turned to him.

"Call me when you're done thinking. By Monday."

Then he left.

8

Niklas'd been in the shower for forty minutes. Mom was at work so it didn't matter: he could occupy the bathroom for as long as he liked.

How long was she going to be staying with him? Okay, of course a dead person in the basement was unpleasant. But it was good, too. Maybe it had made her think, change.

Unfortunately, Niklas'd also been dragged into it. Later today he was going in for questioning by the police. Questions were spinning around in the steam under the showerhead. He wondered what they thought they were going to get out of him. How should he deal with questions that got too personal? It was strange—how did they even know that he'd been living with his mom? Maybe some neighbor'd ratted him out, or else it was Mom who'd let it slip.

Damn—this meant trouble. He'd actually thought he'd be spared. It had to be one of Mom's neighbors. Scared, shocked, nervous. Spit out stuff that really should have nothing to do with it. Probably told the cops that a young man'd been living with her, maybe her son. He just couldn't think of who'd even seen him in the building.

The shower was crappy. Rust-brown dirt between the tiles. White residue on the showerhead that looked like old toothpaste. The water barely drained. Didn't seem like the off-the-books broker asshole had the drain cleaned out too often. A thought in Niklas's head: Civilized man couldn't survive long without holes. Holes were the basis of cleanliness. A busted shower drain, and life got difficult. Too much toilet paper in the toilet or hair in the sink—a quick way for a bathroom to quit working. And the kitchen—things ran out through small holes in the drain, disappeared forever from the world of the cushy and comfy. Without them having to think about where it all went. No one cared what really happened with everything that didn't belong in an ordered household: hair, toothpaste spit, food scraps, old milk, excrement. Holes were the most important ingredient in the recipe for comfort.

They maintained Western citizens' embarrassing ignorance about real filth. It was actually pretty remarkable that nothing ever came up out of those holes. Infringed on the pretend spotlessness. Invaded the inner sanctity of the home. But Niklas knew—he didn't trust the holes. Didn't need them. He'd survived without them under circumstances that were significantly worse than anything a Sven could even imagine.

He shuddered at the thought of what could come up through holes. Horror stories from childhood. Real experiences from Basra, Fallujah, the desert, the mountains. Every man who's lived too long in a barracks knew what he was thinking about. As soon as you set your foot outside the zone, the sewage pipes were flooded with floating shit.

Freshly showered and clean, in front of the TV. Newly bought DVD player in gleaming plastic. Fatigue and lethargy, overlapped. He was still sleeping like shit at night. Eight years in tents, barracks, compounds, cramped one-bedrooms with other men—it'd made its mark. Loneliness hit him every night like the recoil from a poorly handled assault rifle. Not that he totally freaked out—just like a pounding in his soul that disturbed the balance.

He abstained from popping some of the pills Mom'd brought yesterday: Nitrazepam. Good for calmer nerves, sweeter thoughts, better sleep. But today he needed to be sharp. The people he was meeting today would be able to tell right away by looking at his pupils if he was on something.

He watched *Taxi Driver*. Really not the right thing for him at the moment. Robert De Niro doing psychotic shooting exercises in front of the mirror. De Niro at a café with the whore—a crazy young Jodie Foster. The shootout with the psycho in the stairwell. Blood everywhere. It didn't look real. Strange red color, too runny somehow.

The loneliness kept ticking away. He thought, Really, a human being is always alone. You can't get closer to your fellow man—no matter how good a friend—than you do to your neighbor in the tent. Physically, it can be so close that his bad breath ruins a whole night's sleep. But in your mind, you never get so close that you can't get up, pull your pants and shirt on, and disappear forever. And your tent neighbor wouldn't give a shit.

Niklas was alone. Just him.

Against everyone else.

He closed his eyes for a moment. Listened to the dialogue in the movie.

Time passed as slowly as on surveillance duty down there. SSDD—Same shit, different day. Same anxious thoughts, but in a living room instead.

It was almost time for him to go. Off to the interrogation.

On the subway into the city. Sweden was a different country than the one he'd left—more anonymous, but at the same time more rushed. Back then, he often felt like he was just visiting. Now he really was just visiting. But all the time.

He thought about his exercises. The knives. Polishing the weapons. Well-known situations. Relaxed tasks. The interrogation didn't really worry him. For the most part, cops were clowns.

Ten minutes later, he walked into the police station. The female guard in the reception area had gray hair parted down the middle. Acted like a stiff soldier. No smile, short, concise questions. Who are you here to see? When? Do you have the extension?

After five minutes, the policeman came and got him.

The interrogation room: empty save for a poster. Pictured a few people around a table toasting one another happily. They might be drinking Aquavit. Maybe it was Midsummer. It was ages since Niklas'd celebrated Midsummer. The cop'd obviously tried to lighten the mood. Two wooden chairs with plush seat cushions, a table that was screwed into the floor, a computer with a small thumb drive attached to it, a cord that was suspended from the ceiling with a wireless mike on the end. The attempt at coziness wasn't too successful.

The police officer introduced himself. "Hi, my name is Martin Hägerström. And you're Niklas Brogren?"

"That's right."

"Okay. Welcome. Please, have a seat. Do you want some coffee?"

"No, I'm fine. Thanks."

Martin Hägerström sat down across from him. Logged in to the computer. Niklas eyed the guy. Corduroy pants, knit sweater. His shirt collar was popped. His hair was too messy, he couldn't be a real cop. Roving gaze. Conclusion: this was a guy who wouldn't survive more than three hours in the desert.

"First, some routine stuff. You're here for informational questioning. That means that you're not suspected of anything. But we're still going to record everything that's said in here. Then I'll transcribe it and you'll get to approve it. That way, there won't be any misunderstandings. If you need to take a break, just let me know. There are coffee machines and bathrooms out in the hall. Anyway, I'm assuming you know why you're here. On June second, a man was murdered at Gösta Ekman Road. Right now, we're gathering as much information as we can about this incident. The man hasn't been identified and he was in pretty bad shape. You've been staying with your mom in the building for a few weeks, so I thought I'd just ask if there's anything in particular you've been thinking about."

The policeman was typing something on the computer while he spoke.

The situation reminded Niklas of his job search the other day. He'd sent his résumé to a couple places. Was called to an interview at Securicor. But, really, he should be able to get a job at significantly more interesting places. The headquarters were in Västberga. Ten-foot-high fence. Three guarded entrances to get through before he met the HR nerd. But with six bullets in a semiautomatic Heckler & Koch Mark 23, he would've made it through their checkpoints, easy as pie.

Sometimes his own thoughts scared him—he could never relinquish his focus on security. But that was also why he was worthy of more than some regular guard job.

The job interview'd almost put him to sleep. The fat interviewer had a crew cut, but probably didn't know what it felt like to have so many lice in the beds in the barracks that it didn't matter how many Tenutex cocktails you took. The only thing that helped was shaving it all off. He droned on about staff and technical surveillance on hire for both the public and private sectors in all of Sweden. Blah, blah, blah. Guard factories, offices, stores, hospitals, and other places in order to create a safe work environment and reduce the risk of unlawful entry. Whatever.

It wasn't Niklas's kind of thing. He didn't ask a single question. Toned himself down. Acted super shy. Didn't get the job.

Back from his thought trip. He looked up. Martin Hägerström's run-through was over. It was Niklas's turn to speak. He took a deep breath, tried to relax.

"I don't really have much to say about what happened in the building. I've worked abroad for a few years and needed somewhere to stay before I got my own place. I mostly stayed at home, at Mom's, went for a run sometimes, and went to a few job interviews. So I basically haven't met anyone else in the building. From what I know, everyone is normal enough."

"How was living with your mom at your age?"

"Pretty hard, actually. But don't tell her that. I don't have anything against my mom, but you know how it is."

"Yeah, I could never handle more than, like, four hours, then I'd pretend I had some important interrogation or something."

They grinned.

The cop continued, "What kind of work did you do abroad?"

"I studied for a few years. And then I was in the security industry, mostly in the States."

Niklas watched the cop's reaction. Some cops could practically sniff out a lie.

"Interesting. Do you know if there was any bad atmosphere in the building? Did anyone have any old beef or something like that?"

"No, I wasn't there long enough and Mom's never said anything about that."

"Can you describe the neighbors in the building?"

"I don't know them. It's been so long since I actually lived there. I was pretty young, back then. Mom's never said anything weird about them. No one criminal, or anything like that. Anymore."

"Anymore?"

"Well, we lived there when I was little, too. Back then it wasn't exactly the calmest building on the block."

"It was rough? How so?"

"Axelsberg in the early eighties, before a lot of young hipsters moved in. Back then, there were real blue-collar people there, if you know what I mean. A lot of alcoholics and stuff."

"Okay, so you weren't thinking of anyone in particular?"

"Well, I guess a few of them still live in the building. Enström, for example. And there were a bunch of characters. Like Lisbet, Lisbet Johansson. She was really fucking weird."

"How so?"

"She screamed in the stairwell and stuff. I remember one time she started fighting with my mom in the laundry room. Tried to hit her with a hamper. They had to call the cops."

Niklas fell silent. Felt like he'd said too much. But that could be a good move, too. He had to give this Hägerström guy something to chew on.

"Well, that doesn't sound like fun. Then what happened?"

"Nothing happened. Mom just tried to avoid her. And I don't remember what I did. I was young back then."

"It sounds like a strange affair. Does she still live in the building?"

"I don't think so. I don't know where she lives."

"We'll have to look into that."

Hägerström typed frenetically on the computer.

"In that case, I only really have one more question for you."

"Okay."

"Where were you between nine o'clock and midnight on June second?"

Niklas was prepared. Figured the question had to come up at some point. He tried to smile.

"I've looked into that. I was having some beers with an old buddy of mine."

"All night?"

"Yeah, I think we watched a movie too." "All right. What's his name?"

"Benjamin. Benjamin Berg."

On the subway platform, on the way back to his illegal rental. The announcer called out, "The trains are running according to schedule." Niklas thought, Sweden is strange. Eight years ago, when he left, it was assumed that the trains would run on time. Now, after the sellouts, the privatization, the alleged professionalism—that shit never seemed to work—it was apparently worth calling attention to the fact that the trains were running on time for once.

He knew better than anyone: private alternatives look shiny, efficient, rational on paper. PMCs—private military companies, also known as security contractors. Private solutions. Cost-efficient. Perfect for low-intensity hotbeds. High-risk international operations. In the Iraqi sand and dirt, it could be catastrophic. Violent beyond all imagination. He tried to fight off the thoughts. How he, Collin, and the others'd been lowered down from the helicopter. Screamed out their warnings and then rushed through the narrow alleys. It'd been raining—the red mud splashed all the way up on his flak jacket. How they'd crushed the wooden door to the house.

The police interrogation'd gone well. They probably wouldn't make any trouble for him or Mom. He hoped Mom would get over the whole thing soon. Move back home. Leave him alone.

Benjamin'd promised him a huge favor: if anyone asked how long Niklas'd stayed there on June 2, he was going to say all night.

The Aspudden stop. He got off.

Long, straight steps along the platform. Not a lot of people around. It was four o'clock in the afternoon.

Then, a movement. Down to the left.

On the tracks.

He looked down. Stopped.

Wrong move.

What he didn't want to see: a large animal behind the electrical cable. Small black button eyes without regard.

Wasn't very visible. Maybe it wasn't visible at all anymore. But he knew it was there. Below. Coming from the tunnel.

Waiting for him.

Five minutes later: he was home. Mom was still at work.

The bedroom in the apartment was hardly furnished. A double bed in one corner. A pillow and a comforter. A poster on the wall from the Moderna Museet in Stockholm—some exhibit fifteen years ago—strangely painted female figures. The word *nonfigurative* was written across the bottom of the poster. Mom brought it when she came over after the incident in her building. White IKEA wardrobes that were needlessly big. On one of them, the door hung crookedly on its hinges.

He lay down on the bed. There were bottles of pills on the floor.

Thought: Rat fuckers in the area. Rat cunts on his running trail. And now rat shits in the subway.

He shook out two 5-milligram tablets. Broke one in half in his hand. Put one whole and one half tablet on his tongue. Went into the kitchen. Drank a gulp of water. Washed them down.

Lay down in the couch in the living room.

Turned on the TV. Tried to relax.

Woke up after only a few minutes.

He heard voices. Sounds from the TV? No.

Loud voices again, close by.

They came from *the other side* of the wall. Someone screaming.

He recognized something. Arabic diphthongs.

He listened. Lowered the volume on the TV.

After a while, he understood. A fight in the apartment next door. It had to be the girl he'd met in the stairwell. Yes, he heard a woman's voice. And someone else. Maybe her guy, dad, lover. They yelled. Screamed. Disturbed.

He tried to hear what they were arguing about. Niklas's Arabic: very basic, but enough to pick up some dirty words.

"*Sharmuta,*" the man's voice yelled in there. That was harsh—whore.

"*Kh'at um'n!*" Harsher—go fuck your mother.

She screamed again. Louder. More aggressive. At the same time, there was panic in her voice.

Niklas sat up on the couch. Pressed his head closer against the wall.

Felt the stress creeping up in him—the unease of taking part, uninvited, in the private lives of other people. And even worse: the unease in the girl's voice over there.

She shrieked. Then there was a sharp sound. The girl grew silent. The man screamed, "I'm gonna kill you."

More thudding sounds. The girl begging. Whimpering. Pleading for him to stop.

Then another tone, without aggression.

Just terror. A tone Niklas'd heard so many times before.

The new sounds felt closer than anything he'd heard in Arabic. More familiar.

More like his own story repeating itself.

The chick in the apartment next door was taking a beating.

9

Dinner: pork tenderloin and a baked potato. Garlicky cream sauce and salad. Thomas didn't touch the salad. Honestly: vegetables were for women and rabbits. Real men don't eat salad, as Ljunggren said.

Åsa, his wife, sat across from him, prattled on as usual. Today, it was about the garden. He picked up a word here and there. Immortelles, planted in May: faintly scented flowers in a blend of colors during the summer.

The only scent he registered: the smell of dirt, violence, and death. The scent that always followed an officer on patrol. No matter how much you tried to think about other things—the city's stench stuck. The only colors he saw: concrete gray, police blue, and blood red from poorly aimed injection needles and assaults. No matter how many flowers Åsa planted, the shades of violence always made up the primary color scales in his mind.

To some people, Stockholm was a charming, cozy, genuine city. Picturesque, with polite and forthcoming people, clean streets, and exciting shopping areas. To cops, it was a city filled with booze, vomit, and piss. To many people, it was egalitarian public-service centers, interesting cultural projects, trendy cafés, and beautiful façades. To others—just façades. Behind them: beer dives, junkie crash pads, brothels. Battered women whose friends ignored their bruised faces, heroin junkies who shoplifted a half hour's worth of bliss in the local grocery store, teen punks from the projects who reigned free—knocked down old people who were on their way to the bank to pay their rent. Stockholm: Mecca of thieves, drug dealers, and gangs. Horndog water hole. Hypocrite playing field. The welfare state'd breathed its last, labored breaths sometime in the eighties, and no one gave a damn. The only place where the two worlds seemed to meet was at the state-run liquor store. One side was looking for upscale, boxed wine for a dinner party, the other was looking for a quart of hard stuff for the night's booze-out. But soon there'd probably be two different liquor stores, too—one where only the dutiful citizenry was welcome and another for the rest. Class warfare in the liquor-store line. Thomas thought about his dad, Gunnar. He'd passed away from prostate cancer three years ago, only sixty-seven years old. In a way, Thomas was glad his old man didn't have to see this shit. He'd been a real working-class hero, a man who'd believed in Sweden.

But someone had to clean up. The question was just if it was his responsibility. He doubted the system too much. Broke the rules too much. Shit, he felt like some bitter detective in a sleepy Swedish crime thriller. Whining about society and solving crime. That wasn't really his thing, was it?

"Maybe we should get a little greenhouse? What do you think, Thomas?"

He nodded. Woke from his reverie. Heard the pain in her voice. How she longed for him to soften. How their problems might be solved through him. He loved her. But the problem involved both of them. They couldn't have kids. Angst squared. No, fuck, cubed.

They'd tried everything. Thomas'd stopped drinking for several months, they tried to have sex as often as they could, Åsa popped hormones. Two years ago, they got close. Huddinge Hospital worked miracles. Åsa got his stuff injected directly through a catheter—artificial insemination. Weeks went by. The pregnancy went according to plan. They passed the twelve-week line, when most people start telling others. When it should be safe. But something went wrong—the baby died in the fifth month. They had to cut Åsa open to get it out. In his fantasies, he saw how they plucked out the dead fetus—his child. Saw arms, legs, a tiny body. He saw a head, a nose, a mouth. Everything.

He wanted it so badly. A must, something that'd seemed given. A condition for the good life. Adoption was always a possibility. They'd get approval. Childless, middle class, stable, orderly—at least on paper. Ready to love a little one above all else. But the idea didn't jibe with him—Thomas didn't like the thought of it. His entire body itched with resistance. Sometimes he was ashamed of the reason. Sometimes he stood by it, straight-backed. It wasn't right. Not at all. But the reason he didn't want to adopt was that he wanted a kid that looked like him and Åsa. No Chinese, African, or Romanian. He wanted a kid who would fit into the kind of family life he wanted to build. Go ahead, call him a racist. A prejudiced ass. A Neanderthal. He couldn't care less, even if he obviously didn't go to work and broadcast his feelings on the issue—he'd never adopt anything but a Nordic child.

Åsa wouldn't forgive him.

Their house was too small to fit a family, anyway. In Tallkrogen. Twelve hundred square feet in white-painted wood. Split level. The hall, the kitchen, a guest bathroom, and the living room were on the first floor. Upstairs: two small bedrooms, a small TV room, and a bathroom. They used the TV room as an office/gym. An exercise bike and a padded bench. A couple of free weights, a barbell in a cabinet along with binders, a sewing machine, and a couple of dress patterns in a pile. An office chair that Thomas'd been allowed to take home when they reorganized the precinct. Otherwise, empty. Thomas didn't like to collect junk.

He called it a dollhouse. That was the feeling he got, anyway. The house didn't even have a mudroom or a real basement. It wouldn't work, especially not if they were able to adopt kids. Where the hell were they going to put a crib, a changing table, a Ping-Pong table?

After dinner, he went in to the computer. Closed the door behind him. Turned it on. The Windows logo jumped around on the screen like a lost soul.

Clicked on the Explorer icon. Was reminded of his greatest fear— that Åsa would get computer savvy enough one day to know how to find his porn searches in Explorer's history. He should ask someone at work if it could be erased.

But that wasn't what he was here to do this time. He rummaged around in his pocket. Pulled out a USB memory stick. Thomas: as far from a computer geek as you could get, but it felt better to carry what he needed in physical form than to e-mail it. At regular intervals, he'd checked nervously that the USB was still there. If he were to drop it, if someone were to find it, check what was on it, and realize it was his—the questions would pile up worse than at a hard-core cross-examination in court.

He inserted the memory stick into the computer. A plopping sound. A window opened on the screen. One file on the memory stick, named Autop.report.

The computer made a spinning sound. Adobe opened up. The autopsy report was less than three pages long. First he scrolled down to the bottom—signed by Bengt Gantz, chief forensic pathologist—as it should be. He started reading from the beginning. It took time. He read it again.

And again.

Something was weird. Nasty weird—in the autopsy report, there was no mention of the track marks in the arm or if they'd tested the body for increased levels of drugs or other junk.

It couldn't be a coincidence. When Thomas'd seen his report at Hägerström's, and realized that the last lines about the potential cause of death were missing, he'd wondered, sure. Thought it was strange, but hadn't thought more about it. But a forensic pathologist didn't miss stuff like that. The track marks were conspicuous. Either the examiner didn't want to write about them for some reason or—the thought hit him and stuck right away—someone else'd edited it out. And this same someone must've edited out the same thing from his report.

He had to calm down. Feel it out. What he should do. How he should act. Never during his years as a cop had he experienced anything like this.

Åsa was tidying in the kitchen. Didn't even look up when he opened the door and stepped into the garage. It was routine. Thomas worked on his Cadillac whenever he had time. Anyway, it was an investment. He could put some of the extra cash he made in the field into it without anyone asking. But even more important: the car was like mediation for him. A place, like the shooting range, where he relaxed. Felt at home. It was his little Nirvana.

There was another thing in the garage too: the big locked gray metal cabinet. Åsa and he called it the tool cabinet, but she was the only one who thought there were tools in it. Sure, he kept some tools and gear for the car in there, but 80 percent of the cabinet was filled with more important stuff: weed confiscated from a bunch of Arabs in Fittja, hash plucked from Turkish druggies in Örnsberg, amphetamines surrendered by Sven junkies in the subway, a couple packs of Russian growth hormone found in a parking garage in Älvsjö, cash from countless hits along stops on the red subway line. And so on. His little gold mine. A kind of retirement fund.

The car gleamed. Cadillac Eldorado Biarritz from 1959. A beauty he'd found online six years ago. It was in Los Angeles, but he didn't hesitate. Every single time he'd confiscated something from the dregs, this car'd been his goal. Without the money he'd made outside of his crappy police salary, it would never have been his. But it was. He'd picked it up with his old man, who was still in good shape back then. Drove it from Los Angeles to Virginia in one stretch. Twenty-seven hundred miles. Fifty-five hours on the road. At the time, Åsa wondered how he'd been able to afford it and it'd been twice as expensive as he'd told her.

It was wonderful. The Cadillac's V8 engine—better known among car lovers as a Q-345—the pistons alone had taken him six months to fix. Now they were like new. It guzzled gas like a truck.

The car that was parked in front of Thomas now was from a different planet than modern junk. He was almost done. Had fixed the chrome, bought new upholstery, installed purple metallic power-seat adjustments, mounted the back fenders, imported a new grille from the States, played around with the new synchromesh gearbox. Gotten the right whitewall tires, fog lights, air-conditioning, tinted windows on the sides. Adjusted the back axle, the carburetor, the brakes. Acid-washed and zinced every single metal part.

Eldorado Biarritz: the car that'd first introduced the back tail fins and the twin back lights. A style icon without compare, a miracle, a legend among cars. The most rock 'n' roll money could buy. Most of these cars were no longer even drivable. But Thomas's car rolled smoothed as hell. It was unique. And it was his.

The only big thing left to do was to fix the hydraulic suspension. Thomas knew what he wanted—to return to the original suspension, it was as simple as that. He'd saved it for last. Otherwise, the car was perfect.

Thomas put on his overalls, strapped on his headlamp. Rolled in under the car. His favorite position. Darkness surrounded him. In the light from the headlamp, the car's undercarriage appeared like a world of its own, with continents and geological formations. A map he knew better than any other place in the world. He didn't pull out the wrench right away. Studied the car's parts. Just lay there for a while.

Someone'd deleted both his and the pathologist's description of the track marks and the possible cause of death. The pathologist himself? Someone within the police? He had to do something. At the same time—it wasn't his problem. Why should he care? If the doctor didn't want anything written about the track marks, maybe he had his reasons. Annoying to have to write a bunch of extra crap about that in the autopsy report. Or else it was one of Thomas's colleagues who didn't want it known that an unidentified dude'd been injected to death. So, let it be that way. He wasn't the type to rat anyone out, to screw things up, to dig up dirt when it concerned other officers. He wasn't like that guy Martin Hägerström.

On the other hand—he could wind up in trouble himself. If the mistake in the autopsy report was investigated, the question could arise as to why he'd left relevant information out of his own report. That was a risk he didn't want to take. And whoever'd deleted his text was unknown. It's not like he was messing things up for some colleague he knew. If you wanted to cover something up, then at least come clean to your co-workers.

It wasn't okay. He should talk to someone. But who? Jörgen Ljunggren was out. The dude was almost dumber than a reality-TV blonde. Hannu Lindberg, one of the men Thomas usually drove with, might understand, but the question was if he'd agree. To Hannu, anything that didn't concern money or police honor was not worth bothering about. The other guys on the beat didn't feel close or reliable enough. They were good men, that wasn't it, but they weren't the kind who wanted to think too much. He thought about Hägerström's comment: "The desk people together with the guys who are really out there. There's so much knowledge that's lost today."

Thomas didn't have the energy to think more about it. He turned the headlamp off. Continued lying where he was for another three minutes before he rolled himself out.

Stood up. Rinsed his hands under a hose in the garage.

Pulled out his cell phone. He'd saved Hägerström's number.

Martin Hägerström picked up. "Hägerström."

"This is Andrén. Are you alone?"

"Absolutely. You're not on patrol?"

"No, I'm off. Calling from home. There's something I want to talk to you about."

"Shoot."

Thomas began in a monotone voice. Didn't want Hägerström to think he'd become friendly toward him.

"I took the autopsy report home. I know it's material that's under investigation and that you're not supposed to take it out of the building, but I don't give a shit about that crap. I didn't want to print and read it at the station. And you're right, it doesn't mention the track marks. You're probably not surprised since you said there wasn't anything written about them in my incident report either, but I know I wrote about them. It's not likely that Gantz, the forensic pathologist, who's used to carving up bodies, would've missed them. To be completely honest, no one, not even you, could've missed them. Did you see the body?"

Silence on the other end of the line.

"Hägerström?"

"Yes, I'm here. I'm thinking. What you're saying sounds very strange. It seems to me there are only two explanations: Maybe you're messing with me. You didn't write shit about any holes or cause of death at all and only want to screw up my investigation. That's the most likely solution to your little mystery. Or something's really wrong. Something that I'm going to get to the bottom of. And I haven't seen the body. But now I intend to do so. Just so you know."

Thomas didn't know what to say. Hägerström belonged to the other side. But, strictly speaking, the guy was handling himself impeccably. Strictly speaking, Thomas should hang up. Never let a rat like Hägerström talk to him that way. Anyway, patrol officers like Thomas shouldn't meddle with detectives' investigations. Still, without knowing why, he heard himself say, "I think it's best if I come with you. So that someone can show you where those track marks were."

10

Early signs of summer: small white flowers in brown lawns, outdoor seating being set up at cafés, defrosted dog shit. Thirteen-year-old girls in too-tiny miniskirts even though it was only fifty-seven degrees out. Soon it would be here: the Swedish summer. Warm. Light. Filled with chicks. Mahmud longed for it. Now he just had to bulk up in time and iron out the shit he'd ended up in.

He was hanging out by a little hole-in-the-wall shop. Hair wet after his workout. Aching muscles. Sweet exhaustion.

Waiting for his homie Babak. It was six o'clock and they should be closing in there by now. Weird that he hadn't come out yet. Mahmud tried to call. No answer. Fired off a text, pulled a standard joke: "Remember when we rode the train and I stuck my head out and you stuck your ass out. Everyone thought we were twins. Call me!"

Irritated. Not really with Babak, the boy was always late, but with the whole situation. Everything was going to hell. Less than five days left. Mahmud hadn't scraped together more than fifteen thousand in cash yet. It didn't even cover a fifth of what Gürhan wanted. What the fuck was he supposed to do? Same thought on repeat like a sampled loop: the Yugos are my only chance.

He eyed the electrical cabinet he was leaning up against. Covered in tags, Ernesto Guerra stickers, the Giant face sprayed on, sticker ads for, like, forty thousand different record stores. He thought, The Svens did so much crap. That was their luxury—they could follow unnecessary, unfathomable, unmanly pursuits: demonstrate in order to trash small shops in Reclaim the Streets riots, organize weird Goth parties in Gamla Stan where everyone looked like corpses, hang out at cafés and study for a whole day. But the Svens didn't know shit about life with a capital L. What it was like when you had to translate at the welfare office so your parents could explain that they couldn't afford winter jackets. What it was like to grow up in the Million Program concrete without a future. To see the dignity in your father's eyes crushed every time some official mistrusted him—a highly respected man where he came from who was dragged through the Swedish dirt like a whore over the square in the home country. They questioned why he didn't get a better job even though he was an educated engineer, why he didn't speak better Swedish—gave him forms to fill out even though they knew he couldn't read the Swedish alphabet. Pork their mothers.

Mahmud loved his dad and his sisters. He had his homies: Babak, Robert, Javier, and the others. The rest could go fuck themselves.

He was gonna beat them all. The Born to Be Hated players. The Sven pussies. The Stockholm brats. The Ernesto Guerra clowns. Make a comeback. Show who was boss. Cash in. The *blatte* from the Million hood was gonna be king. Crush 'em. Pluck 'em. Only the Yugos would help him.

Four hours earlier he'd called and told Stefanovic yes—he was gonna find Wisam Jibril for them. King Mahmud Bernadotte—when he was done with the assignment, Gürhan was gonna taste his fat cock.

Mahmud thought about what he had to do. To count with the Yugos was to count with everyone. If he succeeded with this—plucking the Lebanese, fulfilling Radovan's wishes—his name would spell Mahmud the Man. Not like today: Mahmud the Dude Who Wants Up but Hasn't Gotten Anywhere Yet.

Right after the call to Stefanovic, Mahmud called Tom Lehtimäki—a buddy from way back. Tom was into econ and stuff like that. Worked for some debt-collecting agency. A golden contact who stepped up right away. Two hours after the call, Tom'd already asked a court to fax over all the paperwork from the trial regarding the Arlanda Airport robbery. They refused to fax that much paper. Sent the shit snail mail instead. Apparently the case'd been closed—the prosecutor'd given up the hunt for the perps. But there was still a battle going on between the bank and the transportation company. Mahmud could hardly believe it—the court was giving him good service. Sometimes he loved Svenland.

He woke from his reverie. Checked the time on his cell. Why hadn't Babak shown yet?

They were going out tonight. Gonna do the city. Run their race—the bitches were theirs for the picking. Wham-bam. He hummed in Arabic—*Ana bedi kess*. I love pussy.

He was sick of waiting, climbed the half stair into the store.

Inside: packed.

The store was tiny, like a hot-dog stand. Sweat stench and lots of buzz. Babak was standing behind the glass counter. A shadow of stubble over his cheeks, neatly waxed side part, shirt unbuttoned at the neck. Mahmud would never say it aloud, but Babak had swag. Beside Babak: his dad and a couple other relatives. His dad was dressed in a fake Armani T-shirt. His uncle and cousins in button-downs. They crowded around, peddled and chatted. Babak was busy with a customer. Mahmud loved the place. The atmosphere was mad un-*Suedi*: another world, another country. People haggled like crazy, screamed to make themselves heard. Three young black guys were begging for the best price for a box of stolen cells. Babak's dad threw open his arms, made a face like they'd asked to date his daughter. "You think I made of money? Max hundred each, I give." Mahmud smiled to himself—the guy couldn't get more home country. An island in Sven Sweden.

The shelves were loaded with used cell phones, MP3 players, chargers, wireless phones, calling cards, alarm clocks. There were cell-phone cases in various colors under the counter, along with watches and unlocked iPhones. On the counter: plates with Babak and his dad's dinner. Tomatoes, raw onion, feta cheese, and pita bread. Authentic.

At least fifteen people waited in line. They were selling their old or stolen cell phones, wanted help unlocking SIM locks, were dropping off watches for repair. Most of all they bought calling cards for übercheap international rates. On the walls were ads for different cell-phone manufacturers, everything from old Ericsson legends—black brick phones—*Now with dual band!*—to iPhones. But above all: price lists for the calling cards. Jedda, Jericho, Jordan. You name it.

Babak finished with the customer. Turned to Mahmud. "*Habibi*, give me five minutes. We just gotta close the shop."

A half hour later: they were down on the street together. Walking toward Skärholmen's subway station.

Mahmud laughed. "I love your dad's store, man. Real authentic feel."

Babak threw his arms out, imitated his dad. "Did you see how he was dealin' with his bros? They didn't have a chance, man."

They jumped the turnstiles. Heard the attendant yell something after them. Faggot—let him hide in his booth and scream his throat raw.

They walked toward the platform. Old wads of gum formed a pattern on the ground. Mahmud was in a better mood.

The train rolled into the station. To Babak's place. Time to start poppin'.

Later at Babak's: Mahmud, Babak, and Robert in the apartment in Alby. A one-bedroom, 520 square feet. Pictures of his family and different Egyptian images on the walls. Babak didn't have jack shit to do with Egypt, but for some reason he dug sphinxes, hieroglyphs, and pyramids. Babak used to say, "You know, the Egyptians, they like the baddest empire ever. They invented all that shit you think Europe did. Written language, paper, warfare. All that good shit. You feel me?"

In the living room: two camel-colored leather couches with a glass-top coffee table—covered in empty Coke cans, remote controls for the stereo, TV, DVD, cable box, and projector. Covers to Xbox 360 games: *Halo 3, Infernal, Medal of Honor*. Rizla papers, weapon magazines, porn rags, a dime bag with some weed.

Babak got a Coke from the fridge. Sat down on one end of the couch. Mahmud flipped through a weapons magazine: *Soldier of Fortune*. Eyed sick army knives that the Gurkha warriors used. Couldn't find more hard-boiled killers than that. Robert rolled a fatty. Slowly ran his tongue along the Rizla paper. Stuffed with tobacco and weed. Didn't twist off the end; the weed pouted out like a real zoot. Let the flame lick the outside of the spliff.

He lit up. Took big puffs. In the background, the Latin Kings. Dogge's high-pitched voice speaking right to them.

Rob handed the joint to Mahmud. Between his thumb and index finger. Took a deep hit. Sucking. Sampling. Soaring. Sooo sweet.

He blew smoke out through his nose, slowly.

"Remember back in school? There was a guy named Wisam. Wisam Jibril, I think. He was a couple years older. Word round the way is, he got into some heavy shit."

Rob seemed totally out of it. Nodded like in his sleep.

Mahmud gave him a shove.

"Yo, snap out of it. It wasn't fucking hash you smoked."

He turned to Babak instead.

"Remember him? Wisam Jibril?"

Babak looked up.

"I don't remember no Wisam. What about it?"

"Yo, come on. He was kinda short. Had a couple years on us. Hung with Kulan, Ali Kamal, and those guys. Remember?"

"Sure. That *blatte*. He got fat on cash, I think. You know, his mom and dad went back to Lebanon."

"Why?"

"Don't know."

"But you haven't seen him lately?"

Mahmud thought about what Babak'd said: Wisam's family'd left the country—bad. Might make it harder to find him.

"That was a long time ago. He hung out downtown. Right after I did that grocery store hit, remember? I ran into him at the clubs a couple times."

An opening. "Where'd you run into him?"

"I told you, the clubs."

"But which ones?"

Babak looked like he was thinking hard.

"Thing is, I think it was at Blue Moon Bar every time."

"Oohkaay." Mahmud imitated Tony Montana's pronunciation in *Scarface*. "If you hear anything about him, put the word out I wanna see him."

He shoved Rob.

"Listen up, you too. I wanna see Wisam Jibril."

It felt good. Mahmud'd gotten a lead. Spread the message. Gotten closer. But now it was time to drop the questions for a while.

They lit a new joint an hour later. Deliberated, speculated, syncopated. They could talk for hours. About old homies from the concrete, work-out routines, Babak's dad's store, cool weapons in the magazine, Sven Sweden's pathetic attempt to integrate them. Mahmud told them about the fight gala in the Solna sports center: Vitali Akhramenko's steel jabs, the mouth guard that went flying. But he shut up about the Yugos' assignment—Babak and Rob were soldiers, but you just didn't talk about shit like that.

Most of all: they buzzed about roads to success. Robert told them about four buddies of his from northern Stockholm. Real smart boys who'd cooked up a sick plan. He was getting worked up telling his own story: "You know, the boys made a payment to that cruise company, Silja Line, I think, for thirty-five big ones, cash. Same day, they called Silja and said they'd paid by accident—that Silja wasn't owed any dough. Course the Silja clowns paid it all back with a check. One of the boys' brothers'd worked for a bank or something and knew that it takes a couple days for places like Silja to get their payments registered. If you made a withdrawal on a Thursday or Friday, there's no chance in hell they'll notice anything until Monday. So, they could work for two days, no problem. They copied the check—that's easy, just run it through a color copier—and headed out on tour. They split the banks up between them and marked all the places they were hitting on a map. The point was it'd go faster if they split into two teams. But they fucked it all up."

Mahmud interrupted him.

"How the fuck'd they sink that ship? Those guys sound like mad pros."

"Yeah, I was getting to that. Listen. One of the offices was closed for renovations, but it said you could go to this other office instead. Thing was, the other office was in the part of town the other team was covering. So they went to the same office twice. It coulda worked anyway, but they happened to go to the same teller too. Get it? She started asking questions. Small bank offices like that don't get too many checks for big sums. And both from Silja, too."

Mahmud laughed. "*Habibi*, know what it prove?"

Robert shook his head. Gulped some Coke.

"It prove, no matter how smart you are, it can still fucking go to hell. Violence, that's the only tight way. Right? If they'd had a gun they could've made that bitch shut up."

Robert took a last hit off the doobie. "You're right. Weapons and explosives. So, when we gonna do something big, huh?"

Mahmud winked at him. "Soon." He really wanted to do something big soon.

They ordered a cab. Mahmud was dressed in his usual going-out getup: white button-down with the top buttons undone, jeans that were a little too tight—looked good when his thighs were on display—and black leather shoes.

Mahmud checked for the wad of cash in the inner pocket of his jacket—thirty-five hundred kronor bills that he couldn't burn tonight.

Gürhan's money. But Babak'd promised to treat. Tonight they were gonna blow a big load.

The E4 highway northbound. Mostly taxis and buses. It was eleven-thirty at night. They asked the cabbie to tune the radio to *The Voice*. Mahmud and Robert rocked to the beat in the backseat. Babak sang, "She break it down, she take it low, she fine as hell, she about the dough." Justin, 50 Cent, and plenty of bitches.

Mahmud loved the feeling. Gearing up to go. The camaraderie. Swedish society tried to trample them every day of their lives. Still, there was so much joy left for the weekend.

Twenty minutes later, they arrived at Stureplan. They tipped the cabbie two hundred. Like kings.

The line outside Hell's Kitchen looked more like the fans at the front of the guardrails at a massive concert. People surged forward, waved their arms, gripped their purses tight, jumped to see better, yelled at the bouncers, pressed on. Pressed hard. Pressed in toward the glamour. The head bouncer was standing on an electrical cabinet—pointed at people who were allowed in. The other bouncers patrolled back and forth; the small earpieces they wore made them look like hard-core secret-service agents. The real brats glided easily through the sea of people. Self-tanner chicks with platinum locks trailing. The rest had to hand over crumpled five-hundred-kronor bills, promised to buy drinks for over a thousand kronor, insisted they were famous, rich, people worth betting on. Immigrant guys threatened to beat up the bouncers—they knew they didn't have a chance anyway. The bitches pushed with their boobs out and their lips parted—promised blowjobs, a fuck, a threesome. Anything to get in.

Mahmud saw the same thing in 90 percent of the people in line: desperation. In other words—it was business as usual out here.

Mahmud, Babak, and Robert—they weren't heavy hitters yet. Normally, they didn't have a chance at luxury places like Sturecompagniet and Hell's Kitchen. But Babak was fucking jonesing. Mahmud would rather go to Blue Moon Bar on Kungsgatan, look for Wisam. Ask people in the bar questions. What's more: he didn't understand how Babak thought they were gonna get in.

But Babak wasn't pulling any punches. Eye contact with the head bouncer up on his throne. He spread his fingers. The bouncer raised his eyebrows, didn't get the message. Babak took a step forward, pressed himself against the barricade. Leaned toward the bouncer. "I got the hookup. Ten grams." The bouncer winked. Raised the velvet rope.

They were allowed into the area with the cash registers. Two hundred and fifty kronor each. Shit, it cost to be on top. But who gave a fuck at this point—they were in.

What a fucking miracle. Mahmud and Robert eyed Babak. He grinned. "You didn't know? I'm the snowman."

Inside: the tight boys dominated. Magnum and regular-sized bottles of champagne in ice buckets everywhere. Dudes with silk kerchiefs in their breast pockets, slicked-back hair, and, on the hottest ones: fluffier manes combed back. Unbuttoned striped shirts with cuff links that gleamed, expensive-looking blazers, slim-cut distressed designer jeans, leather belts with monogram-shaped buckles: Fendi, Gucci, Louis Vuitton. Some with ties, but most rocked open necks—that offered the most opportunity to flaunt their chests. What's more: a couple of worn-out rockers with sideburns and trucker hats. Mahmud didn't understand why they'd been let in.

Fine girls were sitting in booths sipping vodka tonics or letting the dudes treat them to bubbly. Silver-spoon bred, young socialites, bumpkins who fronted.

But also a dapple of other types of people: C-list celebs. Reality-TV stars, talk-show hosts, performers. Surrounded by chicks with designer purses over their shoulders and Playboy jewelry around their necks who danced facing out toward the place.

Last but not least: Jet Set Carl, top playboy on all Stureplan bitches' list of dicks to suck. Even Mahmud and his homies knew about the guy. The dude owned three places downtown, his real name was Carl something, Mahmud didn't know what. The only thing he knew: the player was mad jet set. Hence the name.

Not a lot of real *blattes* in there. Maybe a few adopted and well integrated. Like people who did music stuff, media, or other crap. Honestly: Mahmud couldn't feel any less at home—but the honeys were fly. He undid another button on his shirt. Babak ordered a bottle of Dom at the bar.

Mahmud glanced at his reflection in the ice bucket that was brought along with Babak's champagne.

Liked his look. Broad eyebrows, black hair slicked back with so much gel that he could've had the same hairdo for three weeks without a single hair falling out of place. Full lips, solid jaw, perfectly even stubble over his cheeks.

He saw the reflection of Babak and Robert walking toward him behind his back. Turned before they reached him.

Babak, surprised: "How'd you see us?"

Mahmud said, "Ey, buddy, with this many pumas in one place you gotta have eyes in the back of your head. Don't wanna miss one."

A smile played on his lips.

They laughed. Gulped champagne. Did their best to make eye contact with the chicks around them. No success—it was as if they were invisible. Finally, Rob went up to a couple chicks. Said something. Offered bubbly.

They turned him down. Brutal.

Kh'tas—cunts. It was unfair.

"Let's split."

Mahmud wanted out, wanted to go to Blue Moon Bar instead. Ask around for the Lebanese.

Babak laughed. "No, let's *split* a bag o' yay instead." Ha-ha-ha.

An hour later. The C-rush'd settled. But still: Mahmud felt like the city's finest Million Program *blatte*, the world's number one smartest concrete detective—Sherlock fucking Holmes. He was gonna find Wisam. Make him confess where he'd buried Radovan's Arlanda cash. Force him to deliver. Give himself the chance to impress. Get the Yugos' protection.

Robert slid onto the dance floor with a honey that looked like jailbait. Mahmud and Babak stayed put at the bar as usual.

Then he saw something he didn't want to see. The sound died. His head burned. Around him: a little island of panic. A few yards away at the bar—Daniel and two other guys from that night.

Mahmud froze. Stared at the bottles on the other side of the bar. Tried to focus his gaze. Fuck. What was he gonna do? Panic washed in waves against the inside of his skull. The memories returned: the grind of metal in his mouth. The roulette sound from the spinning cylinder. Daniel's grin.

He tried not to glance over at them. Had to keep his cool. Did they see him? If they came up to him he didn't know how he'd react. Babak didn't seem to notice him wigging out. The people around him grew blurry.

Afterward, when Mahmud thought about the situation, he couldn't remember how long he'd been standing that way. Nauseous. Stiff. How many scared thoughts'd zipped through his brain.

But after a good while he looked up. They were gone.

He didn't give a shit about Babak and Robert. Saw that Babak was trying to snare a puma. Coke rings around the girl's nose. Lipstick on Babak's cheeks. Good for him.

Mahmud wanted out. And he had to get to Blue Moon Bar. Now. He slipped out of Sturecompagniet. The line outside was three times as long as when they'd arrived. The desperation in people's eyes—thirty times as thick. The head bouncer was still at his post, deciding in or out, winner or loser, life or death.

Up Kungsgatan. The air was colder. Where'd the summer run off to?

He thought about sinking a burger, but decided not to. Needed to do his thing at Blue Moon. Farther up, he saw the place.

Blue Moon Bar was boasting a good line, too.

Short, wide bouncers in excess. Mahmud thought, You gotta be a midget to get a job here, or what?

Mahmud slid straight up to the VIP entrance. Past the line. Up to a bouncer. Met Mahmud's gaze. That special understanding between big dudes.

He pulled a classic move—this place wasn't as hard to get into as Sturecompagniet—offered a five-hundred-kronor bill, without saying a word.

The bouncer cube asked, "You alone?"

Mahmud nodded.

The bouncer pushed the bill away. "It's cool."

Mahmud went inside. Paid the hundred-kronor entrance fee; the price wasn't as wack as the other place. Surprised by the bouncer's class. Mahmud'd actually been treated good.

He eyed the place. The lower level: surplus of guys—Syriacs with mullets and shirts unbuttoned, showing their shaved chests; Svens with groomed beards; brothas with sideways caps and fake bling in their ears.

A blue glow was blinking in time to the techno: "This is the rhythm of the night."

He moved on. The next level: a more even division of the sexes—

meat market galore. People entwined on the dance floor, dudes squeez-ing tits in couch corners, bitches licking those same dudes' ears and massaging their cocks through their pants. Wunder-Baum—Mahmud would've loved to pick up some little honey.

But not now.

He stepped up to the bar. Ordered a mojito. Usually boozing wasn't his style, other than maybe bubbly for the bitches' sake. He liked smoking up and getting high—but not so loaded you lost control. Only Svens drank away their dignity that way. And if you got in a fight, you didn't have a chance. Plus: too many calories.

He was leaning against the bar. The mojito with a cocktail straw in his hand. Stirred. The ice cubes made his teeth hurt. He counted face-suckers.

He leaned over toward the bartender who'd served him. The guy was in his mid-twenties, Asian appearance.

"You know who Wisam is? Wisam Jibril, chill guy from Botkyrka. Lots of dough. Used to come here. Remember him?"

The bartender shrugged his shoulders. "No idea. Does he come here often?"

"Don't know. But he used to hang here all the time a few years back. Did you work here then?"

The bartender dude wiped a glass. Looked like he was considering. "No, but check with Anton. He's been here every damn weekend for the past five years. Totally crazy." He pointed at another guy in the bar.

Mahmud tried to get the Anton boy's attention for, like, five min-utes. No success. Plenty of time to really check him out. Tight T-shirt that showed off the black tribal tattoos on his biceps, fake-messy hair-style, broad leather bands on both wrists, metal rings on his fingers. The guy wasn't built but in okay shape.

Finally: Mahmud tried another trick. Waved the five-hundred-kronor bill again. Anton reacted. A classic.

He tried to speak over the music. Pointed over toward the first bar-tender. "He said you've worked here awhile. Remember Wisam Jibril? He used to hang here all the time."

Anton smiled. "Course I remember Wisam. A legend in his day."

Mahmud placed the bill on the bar.

"This isn't a good place to talk. Wanna go somewhere quieter for a few? My treat."

Anton didn't seem to get it. Continued pouring a drink for a chick who looked totally stoned. Didn't he understand the most common memory aid of them all?

But after a few seconds, Anton stepped out from behind the bar. Ushered Mahmud in front of him. Toward the men's bathroom.

The dude positioned himself by a urinal. Pulled out his dick.

Mahmud next to him: did the same thing. Bad move—he got stage fright, couldn't squeeze a drop. That'd never happened before. He was usually the fucking pissing king. But he knew why—the memory of the piss stain from the forest returned.

He looked down: the drain was chock full of tobacco and gum.

"Tell me. You seen him here lately?"

Anton zipped his fly.

"Yessiree. Wisam used to hang here all the time. Slayed ladies like a b-ball pro, Dennis Rodman–style. You know, he's had sex with over two and a half thousand chicks. Can you believe that? Two and a half thousand, damn."

"Who? Dennis Rodman or Wisam?"

"Rodman, of course. But Wisam was awesome. He's got that little extra something. When he goes in for the kill, no lady can resist."

Mahmud thought, Yessiree—the dude was an even bigger Sven clown than he looked.

"Okay. But have you seen him lately?"

"Actually, yes. For the first time in three years, I think. There were so many rumors, you know. That he'd made millions on the stock market. That he sold stuff. That he had a manual for how to blow CITs. You know, all kinds of stuff. But people talk so much."

Bingo—Anton'd heard stuff about Jibril.

"All I know is he spent dough with class. I mean, I've seen some stuff."

Ka-ching, right there.

Mahmud had to tread carefully now, wanted to avoid having the bartender think his interest in Wisam Jibril was a little too big.

Mahmud looked around. "Damn," was all he could muster.

Anton looked questioningly at him. What else did he want? Mahmud gripped his arm.

The bartender looked up. Mahmud stared back. Held the guy's forearm hard. Felt the guy's muscles tighten in his grip. Sent a signal, clear as day: If you leave now, there'll be problems.

Mahmud didn't wait. Pulled Anton into a toilet stall.

"Tell me more. What do you know?"

The bartender fidgeted. Eyes wide open. Still, he didn't resist. Mahmud fingered the roll of bills in his pocket. Pulled out a grand.

Anton didn't move a muscle. Looked like he was thinking. Then he spilled.

"He was here for, like, two hours. Picked up two chicks. That was a few weekends ago. I'm pretty sure it was May Day. I don't know that much else. Honestly, I have no idea."

Mahmud picked up on the second to last sentence: "That much else." What did the guy mean? He obviously knew more.

"Anton, out with it. You know something." He flexed the muscles in his forearms. Black letters against olive skin. *Alby Forever*. Had the desired effect.

"Okay, okay. The chicks were here last weekend. They chatted with me for a few minutes and were totally blown away. Wisam'd apparently rained money on them like he was an oil sheik. He took the girls back to his apartment, I don't know where it is. And the girls probably don't know either, 'cause they told me they were shitfaced. He drove them around in his new car. A Bentley."

Mahmud didn't understand.

Anton spelled it out: "B-E-N-T-L-E-Y. Totally insane. That's all I know. I swear."

Someone pounded on the door. "Boys, this isn't a fairy bar. Come outta there."

Mahmud'd gotten enough info for tonight. He had some leads to follow up.

Opened the door. Stepped out of the stall, shoving the jerk who'd bullshitted outside.

Left Anton with the laughs.

* * *

Settergren's Law Offices

To the Sollentuna District Court

COMPLAINT FOR BREACH OF CONTRACT

PLAINTIFF Barclays Bank Plc., 34 George St., London, England
ATTORNEY FOR PLAINTIFF Roger Holmgren, Esq., and Nathalie Rosenskiöld, Esq., Settergren's Law Offices AB, 12 Strandvägen, Stockholm

NEVER SCREW UP

DEFENDANT Airline Cargo Logistics AB
CASE Breach of Contract
APPLICABLE LAW Chapter 9, § 28, The Aviation Act (1957:297)

Barclays Bank Plc ("Barclays") hereby pursues a lawsuit against Airline Cargo Logistics AB ("Cargo Logistics") as follows:

FIRST CAUSE OF ACTION FOR BREACH OF CONTRACT

Barclays claims that Cargo Logistics owes Barclays Capital 5,569,588 U.S. Dollars plus interest according to § 6 of the Interest Law for breach of contract, due within 30 days of the issuance of the District Court's Decision.

Barclays claims the right to compensation for all attorneys' fees incurred, in an amount that will be given at a later time.

GROUNDS

Barclays and Cargo Logistics have entered into an agreement for air transport of a number of courier bags containing different currencies with a total value of 5,569,588 U.S. Dollars. These courier bags have, while they were in the care of Cargo Logistics at Arlanda Aiport, been the subject of armed robbery. Courier bags containing currency equaling the above-mentioned sum have thereby been lost.

According to chapter 9, § 18 of the Aviation Act, the freight carrier is responsible for damages incurred when the checked cargo, in this case the courier bags, is lost, reduced, or damaged while the cargo is in the freight carrier's care at an airport.

Barclays alleges that Cargo Logistics, through severe breach of the requisite care and consideration demanded, is responsible for the incurred damage in full.

THE CIRCUMSTANCES IN DETAIL

Barclays's contract with the Swedish banks and Cargo Logistics

Barclays regularly buys shipments of different currencies from three Swedish banks: SEB, Svenska Handelsbanken, and FöreningsSparbanken (Swedbank).

According to a contract from 2001, Cargo Logistics had, by request of Barclays Bank, on a regular basis agreed to provide pickup and transport of courier bags containing currency from banks in Stockholm and arrange for air transport to London.

The transport relevant to this case followed the procedure

that is routinely applied to Cargo Logistics. Barclays sent a telefax message to Cargo Logistics with the request that Cargo Logistics pick up a number of courier bags containing currency from the three Swedish banks, arrange for air transport from Stockholm to London, as well as fax a copy of the Air Waybill as soon as possible (Attachments 1–5). According to the instructions, the items would be prepared for air transport and the average value of each courier bag would not exceed 500,000 U.S. Dollars. At the time, the dollar was at 7.32 SEK.

Cargo Logistics' pickup of the cargo to bring to Arlanda Airport

On the morning of April 5, 2005, Cargo Logistics picked up a total of 19 courier bags at the three Swedish banks in downtown Stockholm, divided as detailed in Attachment 6. The job was executed by two employees from Cargo Logistics, Göran Olofsson and Roger Boring, using a vehicle adapted to service Cash-in-Transit. Olofsson had worked with Cargo Logistics for 20 years and Boring for 5 years. In accordance with standard procedures, neither Olofsson nor Boring knew anything about the value of the courier bags that were to be picked up.

At 1415 on the same afternoon, Olfsson and Boring arrived at the office of Wilson & Co—the freight agent—at Arlanda Airport, where they picked up the Air Waybill along with documentation marking the cargo. Olofsson and Boring then drove around 165 feet to Cargo Logistics's warehouse on the airport grounds, where they delivered the 19 courier bags.

Cargo Logistics' delivery

At around 1500 on the afternoon of the same day, Cargo Logistics' warehouse acknowledged the receipt of the 19 courier bags by issuing a document entitled "Handling Report—Cargo Logistics—Valuable Cargo" (Attachment 7). Staff from Cargo Logistics placed the courier bags in locked safety boxes that were brought to a room in the warehouse that is called the "strong room" (hereafter referred to as "the vault"), where valuable cargo is locked and stored.

Armed robbery

The flight that the safe boxes would be traveling on was supposed to depart on the evening of April 5, at 1825. At around 1800, Fredrik Öberg, an employee of Cargo Logistics, was working inside the warehouse, moving safe boxes from the vault to the Cargo Logistics truck. The truck, a Nissan King Cab, would transport the courier bags to the airplane. While the work of moving the cargo was being executed, the door to the vault was open, as was the garage entrance to the warehouse, which faced the airport area. The warehouse's emergency-exit door toward the street outside the airport area was also propped open in connection with the recent arrival of a courier from the courier service company Box Delivery. The emergency-exit door is situated directly adjacent to the vault.

At this time, around 1810, three men, two of whom were armed with firearms, entered the warehouse through the open emergency exit. The robbers threatened the courier from Box Delivery and Öberg, who were forced to lie down on the floor while the robbers took nine safe boxes from inside the vault. While Öberg was lying on the floor, he used his cell phone to call Falck Security, the security company at Arlanda Airport, and informed them that a robbery was taking place. Strangely enough, the Falck employee who received the call told Öberg to contact the police instead.

After the robbery, the perpetrators disappeared from the scene using a BMW 528, which has still not been found, and a stolen Jeep Cherokee, which was later found abandoned around 1–2 miles from the scene of the crime, with one safe box remaining inside. The robbery was immediately reported to the Arlanda police.

No camera surveillance

The Cargo Logistics warehouse is equipped with a total of 75 CCTV (video) surveillance cameras that run 24 hours a day. After the robbery, it appeared that the videotape in the camera located in the part of the warehouse where the robbery took place had not been replaced according to standard procedure (the videotape is 27 hours long). The videotape in the camera in question had therefore ceased to record at around 1300 on April 5, and the robbery was consequently not recorded.

Open emergency exit

The vault in the Cargo Logistics warehouse is situated directly adjacent to the emergency-exit door that leads to the street outside the airport area. The emergency-exit door cannot be opened from the outside and, according to Cargo Logistics's standard procedure, is to remain closed. Despite this, the emergency-exit door had been left open at the time of the robbery, which made it possible for the robbers to enter the warehouse from the street outside the airport. The reason the emergency-exit door was not closed after the courier from Box Delivery had entered has not yet been determined.

Open vault

According to Cargo Logistics' standard operating procedure, the door to the vault can only be opened by two persons together, one of whom (of managerial rank) uses an electronic key. In the situation in question, the door to the vault was ajar, whereby the robbers, after they had entered the warehouse through the open emergency-exit door, were granted direct access to the open vault. The reason for the vault door being left open has not yet been determined.

The preliminary investigation has been dropped

No perpetrators have yet been arrested. The prosecutor has decided to drop the preliminary investigation.

Cargo Logistics' responsibility

Barclays alleges that, in the present circumstances, Cargo Logistics either deliberately caused the damage or is guilty of the kind of qualified neglect outlined in chapter 9, § 24 of the Aviation Act and which chiefly corresponds to severe neglect of a commercial contractual relationship. The following circumstances, among others, are of importance:

(i) The robbers were granted access to the warehouse from the street outside the airport area because the emergency-exit door was left open, which is against Cargo Logistics' applicable rules and procedures.

(ii) Against Cargo Logistics' applicable rules and procedures, the door to the vault was open, which granted the robbers immediate access to the open vault once they had entered the warehouse through the open emergency-exit door.

(iii) Cargo Logistics has neglected to follow applicable security rules and procedures by not replacing the videotape in the surveillance camera in the specific part of the warehouse where the robbery took place, whereby the robbery was not recorded.

(iv) This is a matter of a commercial relationship and the demands on Cargo Logistics' organization, security, and professionalism can therefore be high.

(v) Significant damage has been incurred.

Stockholm.

Roger Holmgren, Esq.

11

Niklas worked out in the apartment after his run. He was driven by routine. His philosophy: all training is built on habit, duplication, repetition. Alternating four times fifty push-ups with some leg exercises. Switching up four sets with free weights for his biceps with forty times sixty sit-ups. He sweated like a pig in an army tent. Stretched thoroughly. Wanted to keep the litheness in his muscles. Rested on the couch for fifteen minutes.

Stood back up. Time for the climax—tanto dori katas, knife warfare. Jogging was to measure himself, for conditioning and fat burning. The push-ups and the muscle exercises were necessary to maintain strength and to look decent. He'd admit it any day: vanity was his thing. But tanto dori was something else: relaxation and power. He could do it for hours. Like meditation. Forget everything else. Go into himself. Go into the movements. Go into the knife. The sweeps, the steps. The stabs.

He'd learned the technique six years ago from a couple of elite officers in a company he'd worked with in Afghanistan. Since then, he'd trained as often as he could. You needed space to do the movement sequences, it was like dancing. Couldn't always do it when you were out in the field. But the empty apartment was made for close-combat technique.

First, be still. Heels together. Feet out at a ninety-degree angle. Arms down, in front of your gut. The knife in your right hand with the thumb resting on the flat side of the blade. Left hand in a light grip over the right hand. Head down, chin tucked in. Deep breaths through your nose. Then attack. All the muscles explode. A step forward with your right leg. Weight low. Exhale through your mouth. Air and muscles tighten your stomach. Important: no big movements—or your opponent will see right away what you're planning on doing. Sharp cut with the knife. Twist it on the recoil.

He went through the kata with concentration.

This one took four and a half minutes. Every movement'd been practiced separately at least five hundred times. Stabs to the abdomen. Gutting techniques. Chop-chop methodology.

Originally, it was some Japanese thing. But the soldiers who taught him in Afghanistan mixed and added. The techniques of the different katas covered everything. Cramped spaces like elevators, prison cells, and toilet stalls. Techniques for combat in cars, boats, and airplanes. Unstable environments, combat in heavy vegetation, on slippery surfaces, in silence. Water techniques where the slowness of the motions created new possibilities to predict the opponent's next move, close combat in stairwells—special blocking techniques for punches or stabs coming from diagonally above. As long as Niklas carried a knife, he never needed to be worried up close.

At the same time: worry was a healthy sign down in the sandbox. The men who stopped feeling even so much as a sting of fear in combat often lost their grip. The mercenary industry didn't tolerate any real crazies. They were sent home. Or were eliminated.

He was happy that he'd gotten the chance. Not a lot of Swedes in the world got to fight in real combat. U.N. pussies mostly guarded refugee camps. He knew; he'd tried to be one of them.

After showering, he took two Nitrazepam. Loneliness wore him down. He needed friends. Benjamin, the dude who'd gotten him the dirty real estate hookup, was the only friend he could remember having in high school, before his time in the mountain brigade during his mandatory military service in northern Sweden, up in Arvidsjaur. Maybe Benjamin was the only buddy he'd ever had. Niklas'd seen him last week for the first time in ages. They were meeting up again today.

He popped another downer. Walked out. Toward the subway. Kept his eyes peeled for rats.

The subway car'd been subjected to a graffiti assault. Niklas closed his eyes. Tried to sleep. He thought about the screams he'd heard from the neighbors. The girl in there with the Iraqi accent must've gotten it bad. He hadn't seen the guy who'd done it to her yet. But when he did, Niklas doubted he'd be able to control himself.

He was lost in thought. Human beings lived in Hobbes's world. Niklas knew that better than anyone. You couldn't point out who was good and who was evil. Couldn't paint life over with some sort of morality paint. Pretend like there was right and wrong, good and evil. That was bullshit. Everyone was at war with everyone else. Someone had to go in, take control. Someone had to make sure people didn't beat, shoot, or blow one another up. Someone had to take power. No one had the right to whine about the system without first trying to do something about it, with all their might. That's why the mujahideen deserved to be respected. It was a war. They weren't any worse people than the soldiers in his unit. The only difference was that his men had better weapons. So they took control.

In a way, it was the same deal with the girl in the apartment next door. Her man did his thing. She should do hers—knock him dead. Right way.

He got off the subway. They were meeting up at Mariatorget. Tivoli, a bar. To grab a beer. Niklas sat down at a table.

After a while, he showed up. Benjamin: shaved head with a beard like some old ZZ Top guy. Bull neck. Snub nose that'd probably taken quite a few hits over the years. Still had his sunglasses on. Niklas thought about what the Yanks liked to call those ugly, cheap shades: BCG—birth control glasses—you couldn't get anywhere near a chick with those babies on. Benjamin walked with the same rocking gait he'd always had. Cocky to the max: hands in the pockets of his open jacket, swinging with every step he took.

Niklas's first thought when he'd met Benjamin last time was that he'd seriously changed since they were kids. Back then: he was the guy who wasn't really able to read situations. Who droned on about boring stuff—like that his mom'd accidentally dyed the white load of laundry blue—for a little too long. Who didn't change his T-shirt after gym class. Whom the girls never glanced at, but who still sent little notes to the coolest chick in the class, writing how much he liked her and wondering if she wanted to make out sometime. He was never bullied; there was a reason for that. But he was never part of the group, either. From time to time he'd go berserk. If someone provoked him, taunted him about his hand sweat, teased him about his name, or just made up some crap about his mom. It was scary. He became like a trapped animal. Could whip guys who were two years older than him. Pound their heads into the gravel on the soccer field, pummel them with rocks. And that'd attracted Niklas. It got better in junior high. Benjamin started taking tae kwon do instead. Four years later, he took home bronze in the Junior Nationals. Became someone worth counting on.

They shook hands. Benjamin's handshake: the hypertense grip of a bodybuilder. Was he trying to prove something?

"Hey, Benjamin. Things're good?"

"Absolutely."

"Any questions about me lately?"

"Actually, yeah. Cops called this morning and asked me how long you'd hung out at my place on that night last week."

"And?"

"I said we hung out all night, watched the *Godfather* movies and stuff."

"Thanks. Honestly, I owe you one."

They walked over to the bar and ordered drinks. Benjamin tried to heckle Niklas for speaking such bad Swenglish. Niklas didn't crack a smile.

He ordered a Guinness. Benjamin, a mineral water. Niklas paid for both.

"You don't want anything else?" Niklas asked.

Benjamin shook his head. "No. I'm deffing."

Niklas didn't get it. Eight years in the bush, often without beer, booze, or good grub, had made him yearn for the real stuff.

They sat down.

Chatted. Niklas didn't really understand what Benjamin did these days. Apparently he'd worked as a bouncer. Then a house painter. Then he'd been unemployed. Now something vague.

Niklas thought about his own story. The CV of his life: a few highlights—but mostly his childhood was filled with boredom, alienation, and fear. Boredom while waiting at home in the apartment every Saturday for Mom to come home from work. Alienation at school. How everyone must've known that something wasn't right in Niklas Brogren's household, but never said anything. Terror that the asshole was going to beat Mom to death. Fear of falling asleep at night, of all the nightmares, of the sound of Mom's pleading, screams, tears. Of the rats. And then the highlights. Being drafted. The year with the mountain brigade. The adrenaline kicks before battle. The first time he'd fought under real fire in Afghanistan. Parties with the guys in Iraq after well-executed missions.

Benjamin looked up from his chatter.

"Hello. Earth calling. Are you with me, or what?"

"No worries, I just drifted off a bit." Niklas laughed.

"Oh yeah, where to?"

"You know, thinking about Mom and stuff."

"Oh, okay. I can tell you something that'll put you in a better mood. I joined a shooting club. Did I tell you that already? It's fun as hell. Soon I'll get my license and get to buy a twenty-two. You gotta wait for higher caliber revolvers. But maybe you don't think that's all that special. I bet you've shot up a storm, huh?"

"I guess you could say that. But we mostly practiced with guns for fun down there."

"Cool. You can get tricked by all that stuff, right? You watch a bunch of American movies where they do all those weird grips. Holding the gun sideways in your hand like it doesn't weigh anything."

"Yeah, I know, that doesn't work."

"It doesn't work for shit."

"Yep. That's Hollywood stuff. You get lousy accuracy with a grip like that. Your whole hand shakes with every shot, like on some senile fuck. It's kind of like running. You see them do that all the time in those flicks, too. They run and shoot. But everyone who's been around at all knows that doesn't work."

"You gotta practice. What kind of heat did you guys pack?"

Niklas wasn't really supposed to talk about that stuff. He tried to steer the conversation in a different direction. "I don't really remember. But hey, you got a girl these days?"

"How can you not remember what gun you had? Come on."

It was a matter of honor. Some stuff you just didn't babble about to people on the outside: the arsenal, where you'd done assignments, who the other guys in the company were—and how many people you'd killed. Even if you quit a private army, you had to stick to the rules. The vow of silence was valid until death did you part. Niklas would never leak. He wasn't the type. Why couldn't Benjamin just accept that?

Benjamin eyed him.

Niklas was short: "You just don't talk about that stuff, is all."

Benjamin's eyes narrowed. His brow furrowed. Was he pissed off?

"Okay. I understand. *Nemas problemas.*"

Everything was cool. They chatted for a while longer. The weather was nice. Benjamin told him that he'd bought a game-bred fighting dog. He was proud of the name: Arnold. Had it practice on fenders that he hung up on the carpet rack in the inner courtyard of his building. When its jaws locked, sometimes it kept hanging on for over twenty minutes. Couldn't let go. Helplessly humiliated by its own stubbornness.

In the middle of their chat, Niklas's phone rang. He continued to jive with Yankee taste in music—his signal was that Taylor Hicks song.

"Hi Mom."

"Hi. What are you doing?"

"I'm hanging out with an old friend, Benjamin. Remember him? Can I talk to you later, maybe?"

He didn't try to hide the irritation in his voice.

"No, I have to tell you something."

"Can we talk about it in twenty minutes?"

"Please. Listen. I think I know who they found in my basement."

Niklas's hair stood on end. He felt cold all over. Hoped Benjamin wouldn't hear or understand what they were talking about. Pressed the phone harder against his ear.

"I think Claes tried to be in touch with me that day. We hadn't seen each other for over a year. I didn't think about it then, that's how he is, you know. I know you never liked Classe, but he's meant a lot to me, you know that. Anyway, he hasn't been in touch since. Isn't that strange? I thought of it yesterday and tried to call him. No answer. But he has so many different numbers so I don't really know which one he uses. I tried to call a couple of his old friends. But they weren't worried at all, said Claes is always hard to get ahold of. I even texted him. But he hasn't gotten back to me. This is terrible, Niklas. Awful."

"Mom, it doesn't have to mean anything. He might be out of the country."

"No, wouldn't someone know that, then? And Claes usually calls back. It must've been him. I'm sure of it. He's gone. Murdered. Who could've done something like that?"

"Mom, I'll call you in three minutes."

Niklas hung up. Felt like he was going to hurl. Got up. Benjamin gave him those narrowed eyes again.

"I have to go. Sorry. But this was nice. Let's stay in touch?"

Benjamin looked surprised.

On the way down into the subway. The thoughts were spinning even worse now: insane, bizarre. Niklas called his mom back. Told her to take it easy. That Claes was probably fine. That Claes was an asshole so she shouldn't care either way.

She cried anyway.

He thought, Claes deserved what he got. Justice'd finally been served. God'd answered a prayer.

He said, "Mom, you have to promise me one thing. Don't tell anyone about this. It wouldn't be good. Can you promise me that?"

12

Like a tattoo on Thomas's retina: the basement guy's busted face, torn up like a lottery ticket scratched with a meat cleaver. It was hard core and harrowing. At the same time, genius execution. If he hadn't gotten curious, broken the rules, and checked the guy's arm, everything would be so simple. Now: something was wrong. Okay, to accidentally delete a few lines from his own report—it could happen. But the forensic pathologist's report? That was improbable. He wondered if Hägerström believed him or the reports. Probably the latter.

Usually, it was the opposite. Say someone pounded on a junkie; once everyone saw the track marks on the arms and tests were taken to show the levels of illegal substances in the blood, it was assumed that it was an overdose and the investigation was shut down within a few weeks. Here the assault was the overly obvious part. The track marks were hidden.

He met Hägerström at the entrance to Danderyd Hospital, a large complex just outside the central city. Ljunggren remained in the patrol car. Sulky—he'd been whining about going here the whole way from Skärholmen. "Come on, you really gotta look at that dead drunk again?" Thomas responded that a detective'd asked him to come, that he had to. Ljunggren didn't quit it. "What's he after, that Hägerström? You know where he worked before, right?" Thomas just mumbled in response, "I know, he's a traitor."

Hägerström came walking toward him near the entrance to the hospital. He was shorter than Thomas remembered. Kind of rolled on his feet, rising on his toes at the end of each step. Thomas thought this was a walking style that must've been developed by Hägerström as a teenager in order to gain a few inches in height. Then the walk'd been solidified, made permanent. He wasn't in uniform—dressed in a cotton jacket, jeans, a bag slung over his shoulder. Thomas thought, Typical detective style. They don't understand the importance of wearing a uniform when approaching people—the power it commands. If his type even had uniforms.

Danderyd's morgue was situated a good distance from the regular hospital area. First they walked through the hospital's hallways. Came out the back. Between smaller buildings, special clinics, old housing units for nurses, rehabilitation gyms. A kind of park. An underpass. Onward on a gravel path near the water.

They walked in silence until Thomas said, "You could've told me it was half a day's hike to get to this place. This is wasting taxpayer time, don't you think?"

Hägerström turned to him. Stopped.

"I thought we could use this time to talk."

"Okay."

"You know I'm from Internal Affairs. I know all about people like you. Your kind is everywhere in the Swedish force. People who do everything."

It was an attack. Every policeman knows what it means to be willing to do "everything." Some cops got a little too rough in the field sometimes. Many of them focused on demonstrators—beat animal-rights activists and antifascists bloody. Others made sure heroin addicts, alcoholics, and homeless people got what they deserved. Some cops looked the other way at minor crime in exchange for certain offers—under-the-table rental contracts for apartments, stolen property, free tickets to the racetrack. Others didn't report pimps if they got a lay now and then. Then there were others, not many, who did "everything"—they didn't just rough people up too much sometimes or look the other way at crimes committed by others in exchange for certain favors—they were deep in the shit themselves. Dirty businessmen. Bad seeds. Fallen cops.

Thing was, it really wasn't true. He wasn't like that. "That wasn't a very nice thing to say," Thomas responded coolly.

Hägerström ignored the comment. Just went on, "But you're a smooth player, too. I might call you street-smart. I know your kind, guys like you don't subject themselves to unnecessary risks. And that's why I can't drop the thought that maybe, this time, you're being honest. Your reaction when you were up in my office in Kronoberg seemed unprompted. Your call the other night was unwarranted, unless you really wanted to tell me something. And that's why we're here now, going to the morgue together. I'm not going to rule out that you actually saw something that didn't make it into the report."

Thomas was more impressed than he cared to admit. Hägerström was stretching it, sure—he didn't do *everything*. But still, the guy was right on: he didn't like risks.

"The investigation is ninety-five percent desk work and five percent field research," Hägerström said. "But if something goes wrong with that five percent, like the medical report, for instance, then the whole investigation goes kaput. It's worth double-checking every fact."

Thomas nodded.

"This isn't just any old homicide. Homicides with no known suspects are always tricky. But in this case we don't even know who the deceased is. That's unusual. The face was beaten beyond recognition, so routine methods of identification are out. The fingertips were cut, so that kind of database search is impossible. Which also points to the fact that whoever committed the crime knew that our old print system doesn't read handprints, which they do in a lot of other European countries. We're so damn behind in Sweden."

"Big surprise."

"Lose the sarcasm. It's actually a real problem."

"Yeah, I understand that. And I assume the teeth are busted."

"Unfortunately. The guy hardly had any teeth left in his mouth, so we can't run anything through the dental database either. He probably had dentures, and the murderer pocketed them. We've checked his blood type, but the guy's A positive, the most common type in Sweden. That won't get us anywhere."

Thomas thought about the dead guy's toothless mouth. It sounded totally hopeless; there had to be something to go on. "Can't you run his DNA?" he asked. "We take spit samples on every fucker we pick up these days."

"Yeah, sure. We can check it, but for that to work he needs to be in the database already. Then we can check his liver, scars, birthmarks, whatever. But to search for cirrhosis and scars is difficult. Too general. We need something else. If this dead guy's in the DNA database, great. But the database is pretty new, from 2003. And, like you said, nowadays we swab everyone. But we only started doing that a couple of years ago."

"Right. I'm guessing it's got something to do with a terrorist law."

"That's probably correct. But for him to be in the database from 2003 he must've done some heavy stuff. To be completely honest—and my gut feeling is pretty strong about this—I don't think we're going to find him in the DNA database."

"But since someone went to all the effort to get rid of the dead guy's prints, he should be in the fingerprint database. Right?"

"My thoughts exactly. That seems unnecessary otherwise. And what does that suggest?"

"Lots of stuff, but nothing certain. The person or persons who ended the old guy knew he was in the fingerprint database. But the killer also knew Mr. Dead hadn't been arrested for any serious crimes in recent years, because then he'd be in the DNA database."

"Pretty much, but of course it's not certain that the perps knew him personally. They could've been hired assassins. That doesn't make it any easier."

"So, what do we do?"

"Well, the usual stuff. To start, the technicians've swabbed the whole basement level of the building and half the stairwell. But that kind of thing often doesn't yield as much as you'd think."

"Why not?"

"There are always plenty of clumsy fools messing things up. Someone opens a window, so any potential fiber traces blow off with the wind, people clomp around inside the cordoned-off area so the DNA material gets all mixed up. But we do other stuff, too. Knock on doors in the area, look into missing-persons databases to try to figure out if there's a match. Wait for further answers from SKL—you know, the forensic lab. We've questioned the people who were first on the scene, the neighbor who called in the murder, you, the other officers on patrol. The usual, you know. You have to ask the right questions. Open-ended questions, don't expect specific answers, get people to really remember and not make things up. That's the key."

Thomas'd heard detective talk before. Martin Hägerström sounded like them—tried to make it seem like he was on top of things.

"Right now, the hottest lead we've got is an incomplete phone number. There was a folded piece of paper with a cell-phone number in the victim's back pocket. Unfortunately, it's a bit smeared. The slip must've been sweating in there for quite a while. One digit is illegible. That gives us ten possible numbers that we're checking up on now. Hopefully the person with the number knows who the man is."

Hägerström stopped talking. In front of them: a long, rectangular brick building. White tin roof. Small, square windows and a wide entrance. Above the entrance were big black letters against a gray background: DANDERYD MORGUE — COLD CHAMBERS.

They went in.

A small waiting room. An unmanned reception desk. Hägerström fished out his cell phone. Called someone.

They had to wait. Thomas and Hägerström were standing with their arms crossed. Silent. After ten minutes, a man in a blue county uniform came into the waiting room. He extended his hand.

"Hi, Christian Nilsson, autopsy technician. I'm sorry to have kept you waiting. We're a little understaffed today. You wanted to look at the guy who came in from the Southern District police, right?"

It was cool in the autopsy room. Nilsson explained: it was really cold in the room where they kept the actual cold chambers—freezing. Thomas thought, Is that why the guy looks like he walked through a snowstorm? There was a thick layer of dandruff on his shoulders.

This was Thomas's first time at a morgue. Patent feeling of unease in his gut—something was on the move in there. He looked around. White tiled walls. Two stainless-steel autopsy tables in the middle of the room. Above each: a strong lamp—dentist-style, but bigger. Gigantic floor drains. Thomas thought about what they probably flushed down those drains after a completed autopsy. On the shelves: bowls, instruments, tools, scales. Everything was made out of stainless steel.

Right when they were about to step inside, Nilsson's phone rang. He picked it up. Walked off a few feet. Spoke in a low voice for a minute or so. Thomas and Hägerström remained standing in silence.

Nilsson led them on toward the cold chambers. There was a sticker on the metal door: *At this workplace the atmosphere is good, friendly, and relaxed—but a little stiff.* Thomas thought: Clever—like cop humor.

The room where the bodies were stored was freezing cold. Same white tiles on the walls. They entered through the short end of the room—the two long ends were completely made up of compartments that could be pulled out like drawers: the cold chambers. There were air fresheners strung up. Didn't help. The corpse smell wasn't thick, but it filled the room nonetheless, like a tickling sensation in the nose— Thomas breathed through his mouth.

Nilsson pulled a drawer out. Stainless steel. The corpse was wrapped in a white cloth with the county emblem on it. Two feet stuck out. An identity tag was tied around the big toe in the classic manner. Nilsson looked at it, showed Thomas and Hägerström: *Nr. E 07-073. Identity unknown. Admitted at above given date. Southern Police District, dossier number K 58599-07. Danderyd Morgue's notes: Autopsy completed. Resp. autopsy technician: CNI.*

Hägerström nodded and set his shoulder bag down on the floor.

He lifted the cloth away from the face.

Thomas was cold. Breath rose like steam from everyone's mouth but the corpse's. Just like outdoors on a cold winter's day.

There wasn't much to see. The whole mug: like ground beef. Thomas'd seen a lot of dead people. Examined dead people. Touched and squeezed dead people. Tried to perform mouth to mouth on dead people. He'd seen even more pictures of dead people. Beaten to bits, abused, raped, injured. Flesh wounds, bullet holes, stab wounds. He considered himself a veteran at this. Still—the feel of the morgue disgusted him. The nausea came as a surprise. He turned his face away. Heaved.

His radio crackled. He didn't realize that it was his at first, since he'd set it to only receive calls from his own squad car. "It's yours," Hägerström said.

Thomas responded, "This is Andrén. Over."

"Hey, it's Ljunggren. You gotta come out now. And book it. There's a shoplifter in Mörby Centrum. We're the closest car."

"I'll be there in five. Just gotta wrap up here."

"No, come now. Code red."

"This won't take long. It's just a shoplifter, anyway."

"Get with it. Where are you?"

"I'm still with Martin Hägerström. We're taking a look at the body." Moment of silence.

"Forget Hägerström. Let him look on his own. I'm not waiting. Come out, now."

Hägerström looked at Thomas.

"Ljunggren, we'll talk later. Over and out." Thomas switched the radio off.

Hägerström didn't say anything. The autopsy technician continued to pull away the wrapping, slowly. It was held together with little clips. Took time. Thomas wondered if they'd really be understaffed at this place if this guy just learned to pick up the pace.

Thomas felt the suspense growing in his stomach, pushing the nausea away.

They could now see the entire white body inside the chamber.

The wounds were only visible if you looked closely. The autopsy technicians'd done a good job.

"On which arm did you see the track marks?" Hägerström asked.

Thomas walked over to the right arm. Pointed.

Hägerström picked up the arm. No marks. He ran his hand over the dead man's arm. Thomas wondered what it felt like. Then, in the spot where Hägerström'd run his hand, he saw them: the needle marks.

"Sometimes you have to pull the skin apart a little to see," Hägerström said. "It gets all saggy."

Thomas felt like a badass CSI agent.

Hägerström picked up his bag from the floor. Rummaged around in it. Fished out a digital camera.

"Time to document what the forensic pathologist obviously didn't see."

At that moment, they heard a sound from the autopsy room. The door flew open. A suit-clad man entered. It was Stig Adamsson, unit chief, head of the Patrol Unit in the Southern District. Thomas's boss.

"Hägerström, you have no authority to be here," Adamsson said with a powerful voice. "The same goes for you, Andrén. Put that frozen dead guy back."

Hägerström remained calm. Slowly put the camera back in its case.

"What's going on, Adamsson? I'm in charge of this investigation. I investigate when I want and where I want."

"No, you need a permit from the prosecutor to do this kind of thing. Damn it, Hägerström, you could get charged with official misconduct for this. The dead man's already been autopsied and the forensic pathologist's done his job. You can't just clomp in here and pull out corpses like this."

"I'm sorry, but I disagree."

"In what way, may I ask?"

For the first time, Hägerström raised his voice a notch.

"I don't know what you think you're doing. But I'm the lead investigator on this case. That means I own this investigation. Even if I don't have permission to be here, it's not your place to meddle. Understood?"

Adamsson looked up. He wasn't used to being talked to like this.

The morgue was quieter than death.

Nilsson pushed the corpse back into the chamber. It echoed in the cold room.

Steam rose from Adamsson's nostrils.

"I am your superior, Hägerström. Don't forget that."

Then he walked out. Long, deliberate, angry steps.

They remained silent until they were back out on the gravel path. Thomas assumed that Ljunggren'd left with the car, so he'd have to catch a ride with Hägerström instead.

"Were we just in a movie, or what?" Hägerström asked. Grinned.

Thomas couldn't help himself; he grinned back.

"I don't fucking know."

"If they made a movie about your life, who'd play you?"

"Why would anyone make a movie about me?"

"'Cause of what just happened, for instance. It's like a damn thriller."

Thomas almost laughed out loud. But he held back. To keep his distance.

"He's a real old ballbuster, Adamsson. But I don't get what he was doing here."

"Exactly. Something is way off."

"But what?"

"I have no idea," Hägerström said. "Yet."

13

The gym: beef-marinated, gorilla-infiltrated, muscle-fixated. Fitness Center: the place where Stockholm's meatiest men hung out around the clock. The place where you didn't show unless your biceps were at least sixteen inches in diameter—unpumped. But also—the place where the camaraderie wasn't just based on a shared interest in body-building and Dbols. The gym was open twenty-four/seven, year-round. Maybe that's why it was a watering hole for so many of Radovan's boys. Minions with the right attitude: protein shakes scored high, fat biceps scored higher, the Yugo boss came in first place.

Always techno blaring from the speakers. Tedious, monotonous, and taxing, according to some. According to Mahmud: the only beat that kicked in his will to pump iron. Plastic plants in white pots on the floor. Faded posters of Arnold Schwarzenegger and Christel Hansson on the walls. Old machines with peeling paint. Sweat-soaked handles, fixed up with black electrical tape. Whatever—all serious guys use gloves. Anyway: machines are for pussies. Hard-core players rock free weights.

Mahmud'd started working out there a few years before he got locked up. Now he was back. Loved the place. Loved that it'd given him the chance to work for the Yugos. It was a networking hub. People told stories about R.'s legendary life. The boss who'd started from scratch, who'd arrived with two empty hands at the Scania factory in Södertälje sometime before Mahmud was even born. Two years later, he'd made his first million. The guy was a legend, like a god. But Mahmud knew more: there'd been people at the gym who didn't jibe with Rado. A couple old buddies of his. They weren't exactly living in style these days. If they were even living.

Today: Mahmud did his pecs. Two hundred twenty pounds on the bench press. Slow, controlled lifts. Muscle training was a purely technical sport. Easy to separate the newbies from the vets—the twigs lifted too fast, allowed the arm's angle to change in the wrong way.

He tried to think about the juice he was gonna go on soon; a few shortcuts never hurt anybody.

Impossible to concentrate. Two days left till Gürhan's deadline and Mahmud hadn't scored a single peseta more. His dad couldn't lend him any. Plus, Mahmud didn't want to drag Abu into this. His sis'd already lent him five grand. Maybe her *shabab* could get more, but he wasn't home. He'd tried to buzz with Babak and Robert during their night out the other day. His homies, boys he could trust—but they didn't have any tall stacks to shave off. Babak'd promised to scrounge up thirty grand by Thursday. Robert could loan him ten, but Mahmud couldn't get it till later today. He had other buds too: Javier, Tom Lehtimäki, guys from before that he really dug. But to borrow money? No, a man with honor didn't do that from just anybody.

All in all: he was still short forty big ones. What the fuck was he gonna do? Rob a bodega? Push baking powder on the corner? Beg for more time? Fat chance. He had to find that guy he had to find. Get the Yugos' protection.

Mahmud put the bar back on the bench. The thought remained: WHAT THE FUCK WAS HE GONNA DO? The same feeling of panic hit him as when he'd seen Daniel and the other Born to Be Hated players at Hell's Kitchen. Felt like the room was spinning. His head was pounding.

He stared up at the ceiling. Closed his eyes. Did everything he could not to think about what would happen if Gürhan didn't get his cash at the designated time.

Later, he calmed down. Worked his triceps. One arm at a time over his head. A sixty-five-pound weight in his hand. Lowered it slowly down behind his back. His elbow remained in a straight position. Even slower extension. Smooth movements. An ache in his muscles. Felt good.

He thought more about the assignment. He hadn't understood everything in the lawsuit paperwork Tom'd helped him get. But one thing was certain: someone in the security company responsible for the Arlanda vault was so dirty he must shit bribe dough. Tom'd helped him get the contact info for a couple guards that were known to do some special deals on the side sometimes.

Mahmud'd already called one of the guards, tried to be as polite as he could. Didn't work. The Sven guard went all mall cop on him. Crabby, testy, cocky. Claimed he'd never heard of any Wisam Jibril—or even the Arlanda robbery. No better luck with the other guys whose numbers he'd gotten from Tom—no one wanted to admit they knew Jibril. Maybe they were telling the truth. But that they didn't know about the Arlanda robbery? Real believable. Sure.

Wisam Jibril: ghetto superstar, concrete hero. Was lying low. Trying not to be seen. Discovered. Revealed. But not like a pro—he'd returned to Sweden, to begin with. And: player lived *la dolce vita*, rained bills. Deluxed the luxe. Apparently let the money flow worse than a Kardashian. Mahmud was gonna follow Wisam's cash trail.

Over this past week Mahmud'd asked around for Wisam at as many places as he could think of. The clubs around Stureplan, the pizza places in Tumba, Alby, and Fittja, the gyms in the city. Asked around with old buds of the guy's family, project boys who hadn't rotted all the way through and bitches who used to run around with Wisam when they were kids. He'd even asked around at a couple mosques and prayer centers. Zero success. But he knew about the Bentley.

Babak parked the car at Jungfrugatan. BMW M5: five hundred meaty horsepower under the blue enamel. Sport seats, cherrywood paneling, GPS. Extra everything. Sure, Babak'd borrowed it from his bro, but still—it was a hot whip. The chill part? Babak's bro lived in a rented studio, 345 square feet. Even Babak had to laugh. But everyone knew: we're not like the Svens who dream about some gray house in the shit suburbs. That crap was for squares. We don't care about where we live in the same way. We care about class. And a man without a manly car is a man without dignity.

"*Jalla*, it's time." Mahmud grinned.

They climbed out of the car.

Östermalm in the summer sun. Below them was Strandvägen. On the other side, people were walking out toward the Djurgården park. Lots of boats and seagulls on the water below. What were all these people doing here, anyway? Didn't the Svens work in the middle of the day?

He turned to Babak. "Check this. They whine that we don't work and just look at 'em now."

"Mahmud, no way you can crack *Suedi* thinking. They say we don't work, just live on welfare. But then the same Svens say we take their jobs. How's that make any sense?"

He saw the Bentley dealership a few yards farther up. The sign: BENTLEY SHOWROOM, in black letters on the façade above the display windows that reached all the way down to the pavement. The door was propped open.

It was empty in there. He reached into his pocket: the brass knuckles were in place. Looked at Babak. Nodded. Babak patted his hand over his breast pocket. Mahmud knew what was inside the right side of the jacket: a sawed-off baseball bat.

Mahmud walked into the store. Babak remained standing outside on the street, clearly visible from inside the Bentley place.

White-painted floor and walls. Spotlights in the ceiling. Four big cars on display: two Continental GTs, one Arnage, and one Continental Flying Spur. Normally, Mahmud would've been staring those juicy bits down like crazy. Today, he didn't even check them out.

Still empty in there. Doesn't anyone work here? He yelled, "Hello?" A guy appeared from a door behind a white counter that looked like a bar. Red pleated slacks, light-colored blazer with a kerchief in the breast pocket. Under the jacket: a tailored shirt with broad stripes, the top buttons undone. His cuff links were shaped like the B in the Bentley logo. On his feet: loafers with thin leather soles and gold buckles. Backslick brat times a million. Didn't seem professional. Mahmud thought, Who'd ever consider buying a car from this clown?

"Hi there. How may I help you?"

Raised eyebrows. Was it a diss or a hint of fear? Mahmud didn't look like he belonged in the showroom.

"I just wanna check out your Bentleys. You got more in than these?"

"What you see here is what we have."

The player wanted to play tight-lipped. Signaled: You don't look like a buyer. Mahmud didn't give a fuck, he wasn't here to shop.

"But you got more in storage somewhere, right?"

"Sure, we have a storage facility in Denmark and we build according to demand. It takes two to eight weeks to order a car from there."

"Can you get a Continental GT with nineteen-inch alloy fenders?"

"Absolutely."

"You sold a model like that in the last few months?"

Mahmud glanced outside. Saw Babak out there. Made eye contact. The brat followed Mahmud's gaze. Also saw Babak. Looked back at Mahmud. Was that worry in his eyes?

"I think so," he said.

Mahmud quit playing the interested customer.

"I'm asking 'cause I wanna know if you sold a car like that to a dude named Wisam Jibril."

Silence in the showroom.

"Hey you, I asked you a question."

"Yes, I heard that. But I don't know if we sold a vehicle to anyone by that name. We don't ask our customers what their names are."

"I don't give a shit. You sell a model like that to an Arab lately?"

"May I answer with a question? Why are you asking?"

"Quit it."

"But how am I supposed to know who is an Arab and who isn't? Anyway, there is no reason for me to give a further account of my customers. A lot of people don't want to broadcast this kind of purchase, if you know what I mean."

Mahmud looked out the window again. Babak was in position. Mahmud walked over to the entrance. Closed it. "All right, McBrat. This is how it is." He walked back to the shop boy, or whatever he was. "I need to know if Wisam Jibril bought a car here, either directly or through someone else. That's all. You with me?"

Mahmud was a hard-core guy. His broad jaw formed a square face. Today, he was rocking a tight, short-sleeved V-neck T-shirt and track pants. Freshly pumped arm, shoulder, and pec muscles were clearly visible through the thin fabric. His tattoos accomplished what they usually did. Obvious to anyone: unnecessary to mess with this dude.

Still the guy said, "I can't answer that. I don't know what it is you want, but I am going to have to ask you to leave the store now."

The guy walked over to open the door. Mahmud caught up with him. Three long steps. Grabbed the guy's arm. Hard. The brass knuckles around his fist, hand in his pocket.

"Come with me, buddy."

At first, the brat barely seemed to realize what was happening. Babak came in. "What the hell are you doing?" the brat asked. They couldn't care less about his whining. Mahmud held the hand with the brass knuckles down along the length of his leg. Didn't want it to be visible from the outside.

"Ey, come with us now. We won't do nothing bad."

The brat—not a fighter. They dragged him into the inner room behind the cars. Closed the door. An office: stylin' oak desk, a flashy-looking computer and pens. Bottles with ink, or something. This was probably where they signed the contracts for these million-kronor cars. Mahmud told the shop kid to sit down. The guy looked more scared than a seven-year-old shoplifter caught barehanded.

"It's simple. We're not going to fuck with you anymore. Let's try this one more time. We just wanna know if you've sold a Continental GT to an Arab named Jibril. It's also possible that he was with someone else who bought it, like, on paper. But you know. You're the only place in town that sells these cars and you can't sell too fucking many a month. Am I right?"

"What is it you want, really? You can't do this."

"Shut up. Just answer the question."

Mahmud took a step closer. Stared the kid down. Clear as day how this prejudiced brat saw him: a huge, lethal *blatte* from some war zone somewhere where they killed one another for breakfast. A bloodthirsty demon.

"We sold a car like that two months ago," he finally peeped. "But it wasn't to an Arab."

"Do better."

"No, it wasn't an Arab. It was a company."

Mahmud reacted right away. There was something the kid wasn't saying.

"Stop playing now, bratty, you know more. What, Arabs can't have companies?"

Mahmud opened the door. Peered out. No one in the showroom. He bitch-slapped the shop boy. Gave him his craziest look.

"Racist."

The dude was still sitting on the desk chair. His cheek red like a stoplight. Looking straight up at Mahmud. Babak with the baseball bat in his hand.

Mahmud hit him again. This was awesome—pure American interrogation technique.

The brat's eyes watered. Drops of blood fell from his nose. But at least he held the tears back.

"I don't know. Honestly."

Mahmud exploded. Kicked the guy in the chest. Inspired by Vitali Akhramenko's crazy kicks in the Solna sports center. The desk chair went flying into the wall. The guy fell on the floor. Screamed. His eyes twitched. Maybe a tear.

"Fuck, man, you're crazy."

Mahmud didn't answer. Punched the guy straight in the face. Bull's-eye. Felt like something broke.

The guy shielded his face. Curled up. Mahmud leaned down.

"Tell me, now. 'Cause it'll just get worse for you."

The brat bitch whimpered, "Okay, okay."

Mahmud waited.

The guy whispered, "This is how it was. We sold a Continental two months ago. There were two guys in the store, I think. On paper, the official buyer was a company, but one of the guys was getting the car. Definitely."

In a calm voice Mahmud said, "Can we see that paper?"

*　*　*

The front door slammed shut. It sounded like someone had knocked something onto the floor out in the hall—maybe it was Mom's umbrella, maybe it was the bicycle pump that was always propped up against the dresser.

It must be him.

No one else came over to their house in the middle of the week without ringing the doorbell, and no one else shut doors with such a definitive sound.

It must be Claes.

Niklas raised the volume on the TV. He was watching the same movie for the third time this week: Lethal Weapon. *Mom didn't like it when he watched what she called "scary and violent" movies, but she didn't have the energy to stand up to his protests. He'd learned that a long time ago—Mom always gave in if you asked enough times.*

But Claes, he didn't give in. Niklas knew it was pointless to even ask Mom anything when Claes was there. Not because Mom was less easy to convince, but because Claes got involved and ruined everything. He forbid Niklas to do what he wanted—to watch movies, to go out at night, to get candy from the grocery store. Claes messed everything up. And the old man wasn't even his real old man.

But sometimes he was nice. Niklas knew when—it was when Claes'd gotten money from his job. He didn't keep track of exactly when that happened, but it happened too seldom. On those days, Claes came over with a bag of chips and some Coke, a couple of movies, and raspberry licorice. Always raspberry licorice for some reason, even though there was lots of much better candy. He brought bags for him and Mom that looked heavy. Niklas recognized the white bags with the text RECYCLING AT SYSTEMET, *meaning the state-run liquor store. He knew what the sound of clinking bottles meant. Sometimes they uncorked that very same night. Sometimes they waited until the weekend. The result varied with Claes's mood.*

Claes came into the living room and positioned himself in front of the TV, right when Mel Gibson was about to dislocate his own shoulder. He looked at Niklas where he lay, slouched down in the couch. One of the sofa cushions was about to tip over the edge and fall down on the floor.

"Niklas, turn the movie off," he said.

Niklas sat up on the couch and reached for the remote control. The numbers on the hard buttons'd been worn off. The TV was old and looked like it was sitting in a wooden box. But at least there was a remote control.

He turned the TV off. The video continued to run in silence.

"Turn the video off, too. It's unnecessary to keep it turned on. Don't you care that your mom doesn't like it when you watch shit like that?"

Niklas opened his mouth to say something, but no sound came out.

Mom came in and stood in the doorway.

"Hi Classe. How was your day? Can't he watch the movie a little? You and me can make dinner."

Claes turned to her.

"I'm damn tired, just so you know."

Then he sat down on the couch next to Niklas and turned the TV on again. The news was on.

Niklas got up and went into the kitchen. To Mom.

She was peeling potatoes, but stopped when he came in. She took a beer from the fridge.

"Niklas, can you go bring this to Classe? It'll make him happy."

Niklas looked at the cold beer. There were small drops on the outside of the can, like it was sweating. He thought it looked funny and wondered to himself, The fridge was cold—so why was it sweating? Then he said, "I don't want to. Claes doesn't need a beer, Mom."

"Why can't you call him Classe? I do."

"But his name is Claes."

"Yes, that's true, but Classe is nicer."

Niklas thought Classe was an uglier word than corduroy.

Mom took the beer herself and brought it out to Claes.

Niklas lay down on the bed in his room. It was too short; his toes stuck out. Sometimes it felt a little embarrassing: he was about to turn nine years old and he still slept in a kid's bed. The same bed that he'd had his whole life, Mom said. They couldn't afford a bigger one. But on the other hand, he almost never had any friends over anyway.

He picked up an old issue of Spider-Man *from the floor and started reading. His stomach was growling. He'd learned at school—that meant you were hungry.*

Yes, he was super hungry.

No real food came, even though the hours passed. He ate toast with jam and drank chocolate milk instead. The potatoes that Mom'd peeled were lying unboiled in the pot. Out in the living room were two empty pizza cartons, a bunch of empty beer cans, and Mom and Claes on the couch. They were watching some other movie. His Lethal Weapon, *which a friend's dad had copied for him, was still lying on the floor in front of the VHS player.*

But it wasn't the unfairness of not being allowed to finish the movie that hurt. It was the volume of Claes's voice. Niklas knew what it meant.

Sometimes when he was this drunk, he was nice. But more often, he was scary.

It was only eight o'clock.

He went back into his room. Tried to concentrate on Spider-Man. *There was a huge fight with the Juggernaut. Spider-Man threw his web over the entire street and hoped that it would stop the tank-like man.*

Claes's laughter and Mom's giggles could be heard through his reading.

Juggernaut didn't care about Spider-Man's web. He kept walking with heavy steps that made deep impressions in the New York pavement. The web was stretched more and more.

Suddenly, the door to his room opened.

Niklas didn't look up. Tried to seem unconcerned.

Read a few more panels: Spider-Man's web didn't break. The buildings shook.

It was Claes.

"Niklas, why don't you go down to the basement for a while? You can play that table-hockey game or something. Mom and me, we need some time to ourselves."

It wasn't a question, even though it sounded like one. Niklas knew that.

Still, he kept reading. Juggernaut kept walking. The web held up. But the concrete in the buildings where Spider-Man'd fastened it didn't.

"Did you hear me? Can you go downstairs for a while?"

He hated it when this happened. He wondered what they did when he had to go down to the basement like this. Claes asked now and again. The worst part was that Mom was always on the jerk's side. Since she seemed happy tonight, Niklas did as he was told.

He got up. Rolled the comic book in his hand, grabbed the house keys in his other hand, and left the apartment. The stairwell was dark; he had to turn the lights on.

He pressed the button for the elevator.

It usually didn't last for more than a half hour or so. Then Mom would come down and get him.

14

Last night: Niklas was in a tunnel. Spots of lights in the ceiling. Echoes of heavy breathing. He turned around. He wasn't being chased. He was the one doing the chasing. The tanto knife in one hand. The tunnel brightened. Who was ahead of him? A man. Maybe it was some bearded warrior from down there. Maybe it was the illegal broker. Then he saw: Claes turned his head. Opened his eyes wide. There was spit around his mouth. Niklas took long strides. The Mizuno shoes held up. The old guy stared. White light filled the tunnel. It was impossible to see anything.

Taxi Driver for the second time today. Knife katas for two hours. Niklas, bare-chested. Like Travis. The sweat dried. Concentrating on the katas took its toll. He went into the kitchen and drank a few gulps of water. A luxury: to be able to drink straight from the tap. In Iraq, what came out of the tap was sewer water, if anything came out at all.

He felt nasty tired. The nightmares were really hitting him hard.

He sat down. Looked around. Despondent.

Mom'd moved back home. That heightened his loneliness. Eight years with buddies. Now: six weeks of loneliness. It was about to break him. He needed a job. Needed something to do. A goal in life. Very soon. Then there was the other thing too: Mom's suspicions. She'd told him she was completely certain the dead guy was Claes. Niklas thought of his nightmare again.

It was raining outside. What kind of summer was this, anyway? *Thank God for the rain to wash the trash off the sidewalk.*

He ate from a bag of chips. Saw Claes's face in front of him. Crunched the ruffled, fried potato slices between his front tccth. Claes was gone now. The story'd gotten a happy ending. Niklas felt relieved.

He turned the DVD on again. His favorite scene. Travis tries to apply for a job as a taxi driver. The guy hiring asks, "How's your driving record? Clean?" Travis's pitch-perfect answer: "It's clean, real clean. Like my conscience."

Niklas agreed. Whatever he'd done, his conscience was clean. There was a war out there. Fabricated moral strictures collapsed under extreme circumstances as easily as a concrete Iraqi house under a grenade attack. Just the rebars remained, stuck up out of the ruins like sorrowful arms.

He turned the movie off. Unpacked his real knives, not the weapon he trained with. Spread them out on the coffee table. One MercWorx Equatorian, a heavy knife with a hefty bolster. Amazing to slice with— you didn't even need to put any force into it. Next to it, a CBK, a concealed backup knife. A compact little fucker. The handle was shaped like a half circle at a vertical angle from the blade in order to rest in the palm and make the knife shorter, easier to hide. The sheath was specially designed with a lock mechanism so that you could strap it anywhere: behind your back, under your arm, around your calf. Last but not least, his baby: a Cold Steel Recon Tanto. Crafted according to Japanese tradition with a single blade in layer upon layer of Damascus steel—the Rolls-Royce of knife metal. Freakishly well balanced, the blood groove perfectly positioned on the blade, an ebony handle that fit like it was tailor-made for his hand. He gazed at his reflection in the blade. Beauty defined. So gorgeous. So clean.

It was unusual to use a knife in war. But really, it was the ultimate form of combat. Man to man. No high-tech heat-detecting weapons with night vision. Just you against your opponent. Just you and the cold steel.

Niklas leaned back against the couch. Claes was dead. The world was a little bit better. Mom was a million times freer.

He snapped the movie back on.

"It's clean, real clean. Like my conscience."

Niklas thought about calling her to hear how she was doing. But he was too tired right now.

Something was bothering him. Loud voices. From the neighbors again. He lowered the volume. Got up. Listened. Same Arabic as the last time he'd heard screaming. He turned the TV off completely. Put his ear against the wall. Almost stopped breathing. Heard everything.

A man's voice: "You gotta understand, you're hurting me."

The girl, Niklas's neighbor Jamila: "But I haven't done anything to you."

"You know what you've done. It hurts me. Get that? I can't do this, I can't live my life like this."

They kept on. Screaming. Arguing. Wouldn't give up. Didn't seem like it was going to turn violent this time, at least.

Niklas sat back down on the couch, but didn't switch the TV back on. Heard fragments of sentences from the argument.

Fiddled with one of his knives again. Took out the sheath. Slowly pushed the knife in.

The racket on the other side of the wall continued.

Fifteen minutes went by.

He turned the movie back on. Could barely hear them. Travis got to know Iris, Jodie Foster: they had coffee together.

Half an hour went by.

The fight in the apartment next door grew louder. Niklas raised the volume on the movie.

Iris to her pimp: "I don't like what I'm doing, Sport."

The pimp didn't give a shit. "Ah, baby, I don't want you to like what you're doing. If you like what you're doing, then you won't be my woman."

Niklas stared at the screen. Tried to shut out the sounds from the neighbors. But he could hear them over the movie.

He raised the volume. Iris screamed. The pimp screamed louder. The volume was unbearable. But it shut out the noise from the fight in the apartment next door. Niklas tried to concentrate. His thoughts came crashing down: Claes murdered, his mother unhappy. Niklas's childhood neighbors must've raised the volume on their TV sets, too. Tried to erase the noise from Mom. From him. From Claes.

But somehow, he could still hear it. He knew things weren't right over there on the other side of the wall.

The movie was moving toward its climax. The crescendo. The moment of truth. The victory of justice. Travis takes things into his own hands. He passes by the pimp on the street. "Do I know you? How's Iris? You know Iris?" And the pimp just lies straight to his face. "I don't know nobody named Iris."

This couldn't go on. The volume. The neighbors. Claes. Travis.

He could hear thuds against the wall again. He had to turn the TV off. Couldn't let what was happening over there happen.

The woman on the other side was weeping. Screaming. Niklas knew what was going on. Everyone knew. But no one did anything.

He strapped the Cold Steel knife behind him, under his jeans. Stepped out of the apartment, into the hallway.

Listened. It was still going on in there. The man yelling. The woman whimpering.

He rang the doorbell.

Silence.

He rang it again.

They said something to each other in voices too low for him to hear.

The peephole grew dark; someone was eyeing him from the other side.

The door opened.

A man. Maybe thirty years old. Stubble. Black shirt. Wide jeans.

"Hi, what do you want?" The guy looked completely calm.

Niklas shoved him hard in the chest. Into the apartment. Closed the door behind him. The guy looked shocked. But snapped out of it faster than expected.

"What the hell are you doing? You stupid fuck."

Niklas ignored the provocation. He was a pro. A fighting machine.

In a calm voice, he said, "Never hurt your woman again."

At the same time, he grabbed the back of the guy's head. Shoved it down. Against his knee. Force from two directions. The knee's upward power, and both his arms tearing the head down. Until they met.

The guy tumbled into the wall. Spit blood. Teeth. Howled. Cried.

Niklas let fly three fast jabs with full force into the guy's ribs.

The man collapsed.

Niklas kicked him in the back. The guy shielded his head with his arms. Screamed. Begged for mercy.

Niklas bent down. Pulled his knife out. The tip against the guy's pulsating throat. It gleamed more beautifully than ever.

"Never do that again."

The guy sniffled. Said nothing.

"Where is your woman?"

The guy kept sniffling.

"Where is Jamila?"

He really didn't have to ask.

The neighbor girl stood in the doorway leading to the living room. A fat lip and a bruise over one eye.

In Arabic, Niklas said, "Never let him hurt you again. I'll come back."

15

The reliability of people who claim to have witnessed things was ranked. The National Police had their own internal guidelines: a rating system for eyewitness accounts, evaluation criteria for reliability. Really, it was self-evident stuff that just wasn't formally recognized: what an orderly Swedish small-business owner said held up better in court than what a pot-smoking eighteen-year-old nigger might try to explain. What a regular, working Sven witnessed was always valued higher as evidence than whatever some heroin-rotted disability-check collector claimed. The investigative work had to be focused, which is to say reduced— only prime-minister and foreign-minister assassinations were allocated unlimited resources. The machine-gun method—to shoot at every clue you had in the hopes that you hit something—didn't work. Society couldn't waste endless amounts of cash. So, you knew who to listen to. Whose accounts garnered results. Served as good evidence. For a prosecution and for a conviction.

A policeman's account was always given the highest reliability rating. That's the kind of account you'd put resources toward following, the kind that held up in court.

The situation now: two policemen had seen the track marks on the unidentified man's arm. Two policemen could confirm that the cause of death'd not been properly investigated by the forensic pathologist. That an additional autopsy was required. That Adamsson'd stopped them from photographing the corpse, the arm, the marks. Something was wrong. According to the worldview of the court, two policemen didn't lie.

Still, nothing happened.

Thomas just didn't get it. It was obvious: Stig Adamsson'd wanted to stop them for some reason. But Adamsson wasn't just anybody. Thomas actually liked the guy. Everyone knew him: he belonged to the real old school. A man whom Thomas would ordinarily ally himself with, a man who dared to call a spade a spade, who didn't meddle when something had to get done. In a way, he reminded Thomas of his old man—honest in a tough way—except Adamsson was right wing, politically. Adamsson was a reservist in the army and a shooting fanatic. Warm advocate for tougher caliber, harder methods, fewer weaklings on the force. Well-known opponent of the influx of women and niggers. There were other rumors circulating about Adamsson during the seventies and eighties when he was a part of the Northern District's feared SWAT team. Drunks grabbed by the team and dumped half-dead in abandoned lots outside the city, junkies picked up for nothing and worked over with wet phone books—to avoid visible fractures and wounds—union cops who were bullied, women in the department who were sexually harassed until they transferred out. That kind of stuff often impressed Thomas. A lot of Adamsson's kind'd probably been weeded out over the years, but not him—the old guy was too good.

Hägerström almost seemed to take it lightly. He chuckled when Thomas, with mixed feelings, called him the day after the morgue visit. "That old fart Adamsson is going to feel some heat for this. Promise."

Thomas wanted to know more. To be honest: despite Martin Hägerström's background, what he really wanted was for Hägerström to bring him onto the investigation officially.

They talked about different scenarios for a while. Hägerström had theories. "I think it's probable that the dead guy was an addict. Maybe he was going to break in and rob some stuff or just crash in the basement. Someone followed him down there, or maybe just ran into him by chance, and beat him to death. Afterward, the perpetrator got scared and sliced the guy's fingertips to make things harder for us."

Thomas didn't believe Hägerström's version for a second.

"That can't be it. It can't be a chance encounter. If it was, why all the hush-hush about the track marks? And why would someone go to all that effort for a regular junkie?"

"You might be right."

"And why did someone slice his fingers and pocket the dentures?"

"Okay, okay. You're right. The most likely scenario is that someone probably both shot him full of something—drugs, poison, or whatever—and beat him to death. That seems in line with the rest of the way this was executed. Nothing has been left to chance."

"No, and anyway, the question remains: Why was nothing written about the track marks? Why was my report edited?"

For the first time since Thomas'd gotten to know Martin Hägerström, the man had no ready answer.

There was nothing more to say. But Thomas still wanted to keep talking. He asked, "And the telephone number. That note in his back pocket. Have you gotten anywhere with that?"

Hägerström tried to explain. "We still can't decipher the last digit in the number. We've looked up every possible combination that's linked to a phone plan. That's all of them except for two. We've looked up the people connected to those plans. Of the eight, we've brought five in for informational questioning, and it hasn't led anywhere. You know, they just don't have anything to do with this. They have no idea who the dead man might be, two were under twelve years old, and so on."

Thomas listened tensely. Damn it, not even when he was working on his Cadillac could he drop the thoughts of that murder. He asked the obvious question: "And the two prepaid plans? Have you ordered lists from the phone companies?"

Hägerström laughed. "Maybe you should be a detective, Andrén."

Thomas ignored the comment. Hägerström probably didn't mean to mess with him.

Hägerström went on, "We've ordered and received the lists. We still can't see who took out the prepaid plans; you can't see that with those kinds of plans. But we can see what other numbers the two prepaid cards have called. Based on that, I expect to know who the two plan owners are within a few days. Then we move on and bring them in for questioning. But that's going to take a whole bunch of phone calls."

Thomas thought: that kind of busywork was typical detective crap. Hägerström only had himself to blame, that office rat. Still: Thomas would consider helping him.

Later that night: time for some reality—intervention work. In normal speak: patrolling. Thomas was standing by his locker in the changing room. Preparing himself for a night in the cruiser with Ljunggren. Despite the routine, the uneventfulness of it all, the boredom— patrolling was when things happened. Thomas always looked forward to these rounds. The crackle from the radio, their grins when they ignored a call and chilled in the car instead. And then, sometimes, when shit hit the fan, it really came flying.

Ljunggren hadn't shown up yet. They still hadn't talked about the morgue incident the other day. Thomas looked forward to discussing the case. To hearing Ljunggren's thoughts. He wondered where he was. Ljunggren wasn't usually late.

Thomas got dressed slowly. Like a ritual. The M04 jacket and pants for outerwear: thick, dark blue material made of aramid fibers. Water-repellent, fire-resistant, junkie-hag-with-dirty-fingernails-proof. But Thomas didn't like it—the reflector tape over the chest was nerdy, the absence of a drawstring at the bottom of the jacket made it feel baggy, the crisp noise it made when you walked sounded like ski clothes. The old uniform was better.

His belt rattled like a toolbox: the collapsible baton in a holder, handcuffs, radio, pepper spray, helmet holder, the old baton holder, key chain, a Leatherman, a gun holster. At least twenty-two pounds of gear.

He saw the body in front of him. The track marks. The washed cuts in the face that wasn't a face anymore. The tag around the big toe. The pale, bluish skin that almost looked waxy. He didn't know why he just couldn't just let the issue go.

It was obvious: he ought to do something. With or without Häger-ström. On the other hand—why should he care? Saving the world, that wasn't his calling. It wasn't his style to go out of bounds and be all serious. Not his thing to nail other cops. He should drop it. Stop thinking about it. Keep doing his own little deals. Keep cashing in a few kronor here and a few kronor there.

He got his gun out of the firearms locker. SIG Sauer P229, semiautomatic, 9 millimeter. Eight cartridges. The gun was completely made of matte black metal, with grooves on the grip. Small—but still better than the old gun, the Walther. Everyone in the Southern District knew where Thomas stood on these issues. A few years ago, a petition was made among the patrol officers: all police inspectors with the requisite license should be allowed to carry a personal firearm. Real stuff, like a Colt .45. Thomas's name topped the list. Of course. When you had to fire for effect, the Walther would stop a high-charging lunatic with an ax about as effectively as if you were shooting a spitball through a straw. So, how would that end? With one, two, three shots to the chest. Then the policeman would catch heat 'cause the asshole happened to die. Give the police real weapons so that they could bring down a threatening perp right away, with one shot to the leg. So many fewer would bite the dust. The current SIG Sauer was a step in the right direction. Bullets that expanded on contact with tissue—spread at impact. Perfect.

Where the hell was Ljunggren? Thomas was dressed, charged up. Ready for a ride through reality. He picked up the intercom phone hanging on the wall by the lockers.

Katarina, the coordinator in charge tonight, picked up.

"Hiya, Andrén here. You know where Jörgen Ljunggren is?"

"Ljunggren had to cover for Fransson. So we're having Cecilia Lindqvist drive with you. She's on her way. Should be there in a few."

"Excuse my French, but who the fuck is Cecilia Lindqvist?"

"A new patrol—you haven't met her? She started four months ago."

"You're kidding. You want me to go on the beat with a cadet? I'd rather drive alone."

"Cut it, Andrén. That's against the rules. She'll be there any minute. Stop whining and start loading."

Thomas sighed. Katarina was a hardass. He liked her.

"Hey, you have to double check your scheduling. This is bullshit."

"Yeah, right. You think I'm in charge of this?"

"No, I know. I'll have to talk to management. I gotta go now. See ya."

He started packing. Took out his bag, as big as a hockey trunk. Loaded up the heavier gear first: the leg guards, the helmet, and the gas mask on the bottom. Then the caution tape, flares, an extra radio, a first-aid kit, the old rubber baton, and a reflector vest. In the side pocket: forms, rubber gloves, and the Breathalyzer.

He dragged the bag and the heavy bulletproof vest out to the garage. Straight to their spots in the trunk.

And when exactly was this Cecilia planning on showing up? Did she think she was going out on some little exercise, or something? The rabble couldn't care less that she was green. The rabble didn't wait for late arrivals. He couldn't wait around any longer.

He got into the car. Called Katarina again.

"I'm leaving. Cecilia Lindqvist still hasn't showed. When she deigns to arrive, I can swing by and pick her up."

"Okay, you do what you want. But you know what I think. I'll tell her."

He started the car. It would feel kind of good to be patrolling by himself for a while tonight. He needed time to think.

Right when he started backing out from the parking spot, the door to the garage flew open. A girl came running toward him, her trunk flung over her shoulder. He stopped. Rolled down the window. Looked at her.

She said, "Hi, I think we're patrolling together tonight."

Thomas eyed her: Cecilia looked okay. Medium-dark blond, short hair. Distinct cheekbones. Blue-green eyes. She seemed stressed out. Her forehead: sweaty.

Thomas pointed to the trunk.

"Throw it in back. Did you bring the heavy vest, too?"

"No, I was going to go back in for it. Will you wait?"

Thomas looked at her. He couldn't believe they hired people who couldn't even carry the trunk and the heavy vest at the same time.

An hour of boredom later. Cecilia tried to talk. Thomas thought she almost seemed hysterically scared of silence in the car. She discussed the differences between the Police Academy's current program and the way it'd been back in his day. Thomas wondered why she thought she had a clue. She asked questions about the chiefs in the Southern District. Commented on the attorney general's latest proposal to increase the uniformed presence on the street. Thomas wasn't interested. Didn't she get it? Sometimes it was okay to just listen to the police radio without talking.

After twenty minutes, she seemed to figure it out. Started to calm down, but still asked a bunch of stuff: "Have you heard about the new car thefts they're investigating?" And so on.

Dispatch sent a call for anyone in the vicinity of Skärholmen. Apparently some kind of apartment brawl there.

Thomas didn't even have to lie. They'd just driven past the Shell gas station on Hägerstensvägen, more than a mile away.

"Good thing we're not in Skäris."

Cecilia sat in silence.

They were cruising Thomas's regular route along Hägerstensvägen. Past the center of Aspudden. Past Örnsberg's subway station. It was eight o'clock. Still bright outside. A nice summer night.

The police radio rattled on. A drunk driver was slaloming down the Södertälje road northbound. Attempted robbery in an apartment on Skansbergsvägen in Smista. A teenage brawl down by the water outside the Vårbacka school in Vårby Gård. Maybe they should try to pluck the drunkard on the Södertälje highway. That was in their direction, after all.

Thomas sped up.

The radio crackled again. "The twenty-four-hour bodega in Aspudden. We've got an intoxicated man who is acting very aggressively. Can someone go there immediately? Over."

Cecilia looked at Thomas.

"We have to take that. We're just a minute away."

Thomas sighed. Did a U-turn. Flipped the flashers on. Sped up.

Fifty seconds later, they pulled up next to the bodega. He could see through the window right away that something was wrong: instead of lining up by the cash register to pay for smokes, porn rags, or candy, a bunch of people were standing as if grouped together, but they weren't. All looking at the same thing, but not acting together. Typical Swedish public crime scene. People were there, but still no one was where they were needed.

At the front, by the cash register, a large man with dirty clothes had the shop clerk's arm in a grip, a young guy who looked totally crushed: on the verge of tears, darting gaze, trying to get the support of someone in there. The other clerk was trying to pry the man's grip off. Tore at his huge hands.

The man roared: "You fucking cunts. Every fucking thing is going to hell. You hear me? Every fucking thing."

Thomas took the lead. Rocked his strong, authoritative voice. "Police. It's time to knock it off. Release him, please."

The drunkard looked up. Hissed, "Pigs." Thomas recognized him. The old-timer was big. Completely lethal appearance: ice-blue eyes, boxer's nose, two scars over one eyebrow, bad teeth. But the guy didn't just look lethal. He was a former boxer, used to hang out with the parkbench alcoholics, the so-called A-team, in Axelsberg—a walking barrel of dynamite. Was collecting disability or something, but probably had enough power in his fists to severely hurt the clerk kid. This could really get nasty.

Thomas walked up to the register. Put one hand on the A-teamer's hands. The other clerk let go of his grip. In a calm voice Thomas said, "Let him go. Now."

Cecilia was behind him. Fiddling with the radio. Maybe she was going to call for backup.

Then, something unexpected happened: the old guy released the clerk. Rushed at Cecilia. Thomas didn't have time to react. Turned around.

The guy dealt Cecilia a blow to the chest. She wasn't prepared.

Tumbled into a shelf of penny candy. Yelled, "What the hell are you doing?" Good—finally, some balls.

Thomas tried to lock the guy in a grip. Damn it, he was stronger than you might think. Turned to Thomas. Head butt. Contact almost directly over Thomas's nasal bone. A millimeter down to the middle and his nose would've broken. Hurt like hell. He saw stars. Blacked out for a brief second. He roared.

The drunkard threw himself at Cecilia, who was back on her feet again. The guy was too dangerous. This was chaos. This was not okay. They couldn't wait for backup.

She tried to push him away. The guy tried to get three punches in. Struck her shoulder. Cecilia backed up. Could be immediate blackout if the guy got in a good hit.

Thomas speed-analyzed the situation. It wasn't time to use his service weapon. Too many people in the store and the guy wasn't dangerous enough yet. But Cecilia was weak. They could never take this giant alone. Maybe with their batons.

He made another attempt. His nose was pounding like crazy. He tried to grab hold of the guy's arm, get him in a grip behind his back. A lost cause. The ex-boxer was wild like an animal. High on booze and his little display of power. Knocked Thomas off. Shoved him. He lost his balance. Tripped over a tower of soda bottles. They went flying all over the floor.

"Use the baton, damn it," Thomas yelled, on his knees.

Cecilia tried to shield herself. Pulled out the collapsible baton. Opened it.

The guy threw a punch at her stomach. She hit him over the thighs.

The effect: less than a bitch slap. The old drunk was too crazy to care about the whip of the baton. Pushed her up against the window. Thomas picked up his baton. Hit the guy over the back. Really hard. He reacted. Turned around again. Cecilia was about to collapse. The guy threw a punch in Thomas's direction. He ducked. Struck again with the baton. And again.

Cecilia was on her feet behind the guy. She hit him. He roared. Threw a jab at Thomas again.

Thomas put some real force into it. He had to bring an end to this now. Lashed the old drunk once over the neck. Another time over the thigh. The guy kept on roaring. Thomas hit him again over the legs. The guy sank to the ground. Screamed. Kept kicking Cecilia from where he was, down on the floor. She got more lashes in. The booze-hound shielded his head with his arms. Cecilia gave him hell again. Hit the guy over the head, chest, back.

She was in a panic. Thomas understood her.

This'd spiraled out of control.

16

One of the first things you learn in the slammer: don't pace in your cell. It doesn't lead anywhere. Instead: stay in your head and you can travel far beyond the prison walls. Like Mahmud used to do: fantasize about a BMW Z4 coupe cruising smoothly down Kungsgatan on a sweet spring day, pocket full of bills, headed to a hot party, chill homies, willing honeys. Freedom at its finest.

But now, in his room at Dad's place, he paced back and forth like a monkey in a cage. Nauseated. Dizzy. Head pounding. Only one day left.

He'd managed to scrape together eighty large. Total. He was twenty short. He'd gotten in touch with Daniel the day before—to negotiate with them. But the dude refused to understand: Mahmud was happy to pay interest as long as they were cool with eighty G's in the first installment.

"Forget it. We said one hundred. One hundred is what Gürhan's gonna get. Day after tomorrow."

Click.

Mahmud slept extra crappy that night. His time asleep: shorter than a mosquito's cock. An explosive headache. Anxious thoughts were spinning out of control.

He couldn't even go work out. The only thing he could think about: where Wisam was. When he'd grabbed that gangsta, no one could hurt him. He didn't plan on charging Stefanovic cash. Just asking for a favor in return—that they show Gürhan who's in charge.

He talked to his homeboy Tom Lehtimäki: mad CSI dude—the Finn helped him work with the info he already had. Get facts. Sort possibilities. Analyze leads.

The company that'd bought the car from the Bentley brat down on

Strandvägen was called Dolphin Leasing AB. The paper he'd swiped from the brat didn't say much: Dolphin Leasing AB had a P.O. box in Stockholm. A registration number. The document was signed by a John Ballénius—some fucking name. Tom explained: the registration number was the company's organization number—all companies in Sweden had to have that kind of thing. Mahmud called the Swedish Companies Registration Office. Got information about who was on the board. Two shysters with Swedish names. The first was John Ballénius. The other was Claes Rantzell. Both had P.O. box addresses: classic shadiness. Mahmud paid a visit to the post office. A fatso in a small office in Hallunda. Mahmud rocked the same style as he had toward the boy in the Bentley dealership. Why mess with a winning concept? After ten minutes, he had the home addresses for both of the two men. Tegnérgatan downtown and Elsa Brändströms Street in Fruängen.

Mahmud looked them up with Tom's help. They called the passport authority, went to Kungsholmen—got copies of the old guys' passport photos. They didn't drive any flashy cars, according to the national registry of motor vehicles. But, according to the tax authorities, they were saddled with some heavy tax debt. Mahmud went to John Ballénius's address, Tegnérgatan. Waited outside. After four hours, the guy came staggering up the street laden with two bags from the liquor store. Looked half-marinated in booze. Still good—now he had his eye on the guy. Mahmud went to the other dude's address. Waited all night. Nothing happened. Either Rantzell stayed home twenty-four/seven, or he was abroad, or he didn't actually live there. Craven cunt.

Most likely the guys were front men for the leasing company. Stinky fish like that couldn't buy flashy cars, at least not if they wanted to register and insure them. Wise guys knew the solution was luxury rentals.

The guard lead from the robbery'd unfortunately not panned out. A couple hustlers he'd spoken with'd heard talk that the Lebanese was back in town, maybe they'd even seen him, but no one knew where Wisam Jibril was hiding. Mahmud and Tom's conclusion: the only lead Mahmud could go on was the Bentley.

He had to get one of the golden oldies to talk.

But how? Time was ticking by.

He called Babak and Robert. Even called Javier and Tom. Needed more help than ever. Couldn't face any more attempts at negotiation with Daniel or Gürhan. More humiliation. In twelve hours, he had to have that cash. Twenty grand more. Couldn't be impossible.

They met at Robert's house.

Mahmud served up a blunt—weed rolled in cigar leaves instead of cigarette paper. Tried to seem a thousand times more chill than he really felt. They buzzed quick cash schemes. He needed to get his homies amped. Hoped they didn't see the panic in his eyes.

Robert alternated between hip-hop and Arabic hits. His apartment was so permanently hotboxed that you mellowed out just by walking through the door.

Babak was babbling as usual.

"We should do like the heavy boys, Fucked for Life and those guys. Go to Thailand and just plan."

"*Just* plan?" Robert looked at Babak. "What about the hookers?"

Babak laughed.

"Okay, we'll bukkake some Thai chicks, too. But mostly plan."

Mahmud dug the way they spit.

Babak said, "Who are we, anyway? What should we do? Society already fucked us. We knew that early, right? School, high school, that shit wasn't our beat. College, not on the map. But not slaving away at a McDonald's or working as a cleaner forever either. None of that bullshit. And now there ain't no good jobs for us to get. And honestly, we don't want their normal jobs anyway. Just look at your dad, Mahmud. Sweden isn't for *blattes* like us, not even the straitlaced ones."

Mahmud was listening.

"Imagine a scale, you know what I mean. On one side you put the Sven life, nine-to-five, maybe an okay car, and some bust-your-nuts gig, a house somewhere. On the other side you put excitement, freedom, bitches, and cash. And the feeling. The feeling of being a don. Which side's got the most weight? It's not even a fucking choice, man. Who doesn't want to swag it up, go from ashy to classy? Give society the finger, you feel me? They've pissed on us anyway so why not piss right back on 'em? Just think, the feeling, to be a Yugo boss, Gürhan Ilnaz or one of those real hustlers."

Robert took deep hits off the blunt. "You're right, man. No sane fucker's gonna choose nine-to-five. But, yo, know what the thing is?"

Babak shook his head.

"The thing is, how you get there. Right? You can work corners for years, still someone else's skimming off the top. Or else you can do all that fraud shit, like the guys I was telling you about, who tried to gyp Silja Line. But that's gotta be too much stress."

"True. That's why we gotta go to Thailand. We gotta stop working corners and doing this petty bullshit. Explosives, that's what it's all about, yo, like I always say."

Mahmud and Robert, at the same time: "You mean CIT?"

"Ey, I do. We learn to explode, we can do anything. Know what that's called? The big fish call it technical crime. That's the real shit, the kind of shit that needs planning, that needs technique. Plastic explosives, percussion caps, fuses—I don't got a clue, but the guys who can do explosives can do anything. Imagine, getting ten million on a hit instead of a few grand here and there."

Mahmud thought about the Arlanda hit, and Jibril.

"You can buy recipes for CIT knocks in Södertälje," Robert said. "I know people."

"Yeah, but then they gonna skim off the top again. Fuck, man, we gotta be on our own. Mahmud, don't you know some Yugo who could teach us?"

Mahmud almost got pissed.

"You playin'? Those aren't my people."

"But maybe they know this shit. They're warriors. Seems like most of 'em were down in Yugoslavia ten years ago."

Robert kept sucking on the blunt. "I'll tell you something—never trust the Yugos. They don't got a proper hierarchy, not like the Hells Angels, the OG, or the Brotherhood. No rules. They're not working for the next generation. Every Yugo's just thinking about his own skin and don't build nada for no one else. You know why they done so well in Sweden? 'Cause they were here first and 'cause they get a fuckload of support from their country down there. They've fucking owned this town for twenty years now, kept restocking with Serbian gats from their war, new soldiers who've been primed to come up here for work. But know what I think? They gonna disappear. They a clan, not an organization. They don't got a chance against the HA and the others. The Yugos' time is over. One more thing. They're getting all Sven and shit. You feel me?"

Mahmud was shook—the Yugos' time was over? Had he bet on the wrong fighter? He didn't even want to think about what Rob'd just said. He had to get cash.

They kept buzzing.

After a while, they hatched a tight idea—they should crash a party nearby that Babak knew about. Babak sold E to the guy having the bash, Simon. So it was his time to cash in on some of Simon's debt tonight: sweet Sven with a severe smiley habit. It was the kid's birthday. And Babak wasn't invited. That alone was a reason to show the boy who was boss.

The mood heightened. After a few minutes, it got even better—Robert surprised them with a bonus for the night: Rohypnol.

Three pills and two beers. Unbeatable combination: Benzo-buzz. Aggro-energy.

Mahmud felt it clearly: his blood was pumping better than the others'—he could do whatever he wanted.

They rolled to Simon's birthday party.

It was cold out. They parked Robert's car. Mahmud, Babak, and Robert waited outside the kid's building. Babak'd called. Asked to come up and say happy birthday. Simon'd been reluctant. Worlds colliding—he didn't want his low life to mix with his high life. The whole thing was simple: Babak wasn't invited. Babak wasn't happy. Simon knew that Babak wasn't invited. Ergo: Simon knew that Babak wasn't happy. Simon'd managed to have Babak agree to meet outside. Pleaded, "It's my birthday, can't you cut me some slack today?"

The guy came out of the building. Stood waiting outside by the road. A pale bean pole with hair dyed black. Another guy, maybe Simon's friend, remained standing in the entranceway. Hard to see, the street-light was reflecting in the glass section of the door.

Babak: high as a Dubai skyscraper. Looked at Simon.

"Happy birthday. You got my cash or what?"

Mahmud remained in the background. Eyed Babak's forehead. He was breaking out. His forehead gleamed. Typical side effect of muscle pills.

"Babak, I'm not supposed to pay you until next Sunday. And there's no chance in hell I can get it for today, anyway. Forget about it. You've already pocketed half of what I made last month."

Simon knew the rules. He had to be punished now. But the thing about tonight: he would've been punished either way.

A shove. Simon stumbled back a couple of steps. Babak was steaming. Robert was steaming. Mahmud felt so happy—back on the street, a chance to score. He wanted in. Wanted to feel the kick. Took a step forward.

"You fucking cunt. What are you, slow? Hand over the cash."

The friend stuck his head out through the front door. From a distance, he looked tired, dark circles under his eyes. He yelled, "What the hell are you doing?"

Babak took a solid grip on Simon's arm.

"Tell your nasty little buddy over there to shut up. You say you don't got cash, but someone's gotta pay, right? You bought four bottles from me, but you only paid for two. Who you think's gonna cover the other two, huh? You promised you'd fix it. You want me to spend my own money, huh?"

"But I promised I'd get it."

"Forget that. We're gonna go up to your little fag fest and you're gonna get the dough now."

There were fourteen people in the apartment, a large studio with a spacious kitchen. The boys were playing FIFA on a PS3. Ill graphics.

Babak went straight into the kitchen. Dragged Simon along. Mahmud sat down in front of a computer, scrolled through the MP3s. Fucking pussy music. Didn't they have any black beats?

Robert leaned against the wall. Arms crossed. Both he and Mahmud knew something was gonna pop. Knew they were perceived as gorillas. Waited for Babak's signal.

Obvious: Robert was bugging out. Mahmud could feel the brass knuckles in his pocket. Babak was out in the kitchen with Simon, could feel the vibes, was probably tweaking.

The party seemed more like a dull night in than a birthday bash.

Aside from Babak and Simon, there were some chicks in the kitchen. When Babak walked in, the bitches went into the living room.

One of the chicks put her hands on her hips. Said, "You have to stop playing. It's so boring when you just sit there."

No real response. The soccer playing continued.

Obvious tension in the room.

Babak came into the living room. The number one *blatte*. No sign of Simon. Mahmud dug the situation. Babak nodded. Finally time to rumble. Babak took a step forward. Mahmud positioned himself in front of the couch, broad stance. The gamers looked up.

Babak, with a thicker accent than usual: "Turn off the fucking Play-Station. This is a robbery."

Real R2-aggression, no boundaries. Mahmud slipped on the brass knuckles. "And don't whine, you'll regret it." He slid his hand over his throat. Robert, next to him: backed up with a butterfly.

"Empty your pockets. Cash, phones, subway passes, whatever you got. You know what we want. Put the shit on the table."

The guys looked like they were gonna shit themselves. Mahmud thought the girls' faces grew as white as cocaine, despite the layer of self-tanner. They pulled out their cell phones reluctantly. A couple of them fished out subway passes and wallets.

Mahmud did the collecting. Emptied cash out of wallets. Left the plastic. Gathered the subway passes and cell phones. Hauled stuff over to Babak and Robert. They shoved it all into their jacket pockets.

So easy. The Svens just handed it over.

One of the girls looked totally gone. Like someone'd slipped a Valium in her beer. Mahmud shoved her.

"Ey, yo. Give us your stuff."

She hardly reacted. Handed over her subway pass. Nothing else.

Time to split.

Robert was riled up. Wanted to fight. Started roaring. Waving the knife around. Aimed a kick at one of the guys in front of the TV. Mahmud dragged him out. Babak slammed the door shut.

They ran down the stairs.

The high was still thick. He felt so fucking angry.

Could easily've beaten the shit out of anybody.

Yelled in the stairwell.

Almost forgot all the stress and anxiety over his problems: the Gürhan fucker, Erika at the parole office, Dad's whining.

Down on the street.

Into Robert's car.

Tried to calm down.

One final roar. They rolled the window down, hollered, "Alby for-ever!"

The effect of the Rohypnol was dropping off. Soon back to reality.

They counted the money in the car: 4,800 kronor. Twelve subway passes. Could be flipped for 200 kronor a pass. Sweet phones. Twenty

DVDs from Simon's bookshelf. And, yup: the PS3 game. Nice haul. Mahmud tried to do the math in his head. Hoped the boys would lend him more. Maybe it'd be enough.

Babak and Robert: angel homies—let Mahmud keep the whole enchilada on credit.

Now he had one day to flip the subway passes, the phones, the movies, and the game.

He hoped it would be enough.

17

Niklas and Benjamin ordered a second round of beers. Type: Norr-lands, bottles. The Swedish smoking ban was sweet. But Benjamin was complaining. "Honestly, before all you had to do was treat the ladies to a smoke, get a free reason to start chatting."

His T-shirt today was black with *Outlaws* written in white letters across the front, plus the image of a motorcycle. Niklas thought either his old buddy was acting like a bad boy, or he actually was one.

The bar was situated in Fridhemsplan. According to Benjamin: Fridhemsplan was sweet dank-dive paradise. And this bar, Friden, was apparently the mother of all dank-dives. They laughed.

Niklas liked the place. It wasn't his first time there, but his first in eight years. Exemplary pricing: the beer hardly cost more than when he'd left Sweden. Cute waitresses. Comfy couches, loud volume, cheap grub. Wood paneling along the walls. A number of banners with differ-ent soccer-team emblems were hung up above the paneling. Beer ads and glitter that looked like Christmas decorations. Their beers arrived in warm glasses straight from the dishwasher. The peanuts were served in bowls that resembled ashtrays. Mixed crowd: mostly AIK soccer fans and drunks, but a bunch of younger types, too. He dug the atmosphere.

Benjamin went to the bathroom. Niklas studied his right hand. There was some swelling over the middle knuckle. He remembered: three fast punches. Good technique: 80 percent of the punch'd been absorbed by the knuckles on his pointer and index fingers. Broken at least one of the asshole's ribs. Rightly so.

Benjamin returned. Tried to pinch one of the waitresses in the butt before he sat down in the booth with Niklas. She didn't even react. A relief. Niklas didn't want any trouble.

Benjamin smiled. "It's damn strange. The stench in the bathrooms in this place is exactly the same as the stench in the bathrooms in the ER at Mariapol, remember? That nasty place we got sent when we were smashed as kids?"

"When was the last time you were in the ER there? That's gotta be ten years ago."

"Sure, but I promise you, that stench gets stuck in your nostrils like a fucking piercing."

"Good thing we're near the entrance, then, so you can get some fresh air."

They laughed. Benjamin was okay, after all. Maybe Niklas would get used to living in Sweden.

Two beers later. Niklas was starting to get buzzed. Benjamin claimed that he needed at least eight brewskies for it to even show up in a cop's Breathalyzer. Niklas said he talked more bullshit than a merchant in the souk. They laughed again. It felt good to laugh together.

The entire time, in the back of Niklas's head: he'd made the world a better place the other day. A safer place for innocent women.

They kept talking. Benjamin went on about the shooting club, about some chick he was going on a date with later that night, about some business he had up his sleeve. Sometimes he asked Niklas a lot of questions. About how often he'd been under fire in Iraq, how you reload in the dark, if you could grease a gun with olive oil, when you used dum-dum ammunition. The theater of war, like make-believe. But overall, Benjamin was a know-it-all—thought he knew everything about weapons he couldn't even spell the names of. Niklas told him stories from Iraq. He left out details like names, but he could feel how much he loved to describe life in the sandbox. In actuality, though: no one who didn't have operational experience of combat in war could ever really know what it was about. You couldn't read your way to stuff like that or watch movies or play video games to understand it.

Something was happening by the entrance to the bar. They looked over. A fifty-year-old guy was engaged in a loud discussion with a bouncer in charge of the coat check.

The guy was holding a liquor-store bag in each hand. Apparently wanted to check them and still be allowed to bring a bottle inside. Niklas and Benjamin looked at each other again. Laughed. But it was a fake laugh. The man reminded Niklas of darker times.

Two large men sat down next to them. Ordered a beer each. Benjamin eyed one of them. Leaned over. Spoke to Niklas in a low voice, "Check out his jacket. Looks like he's in the same shooting club as me. Cool." Niklas wasn't as impressed.

Benjamin started to ask him questions again. Niklas thought he was raising his voice. Did he want the men at the table next to them to hear? He couldn't care less. Started telling his story.

"You know, we were lugging around so much equipment that we sounded like a wandering junkyard when we left base camp. Battle rattle, that's what we call it. Call radio, flak jackets, night-vision equipment, at least twenty magazines apiece, grenades, med kits, helmets, sleeping bags and tents in case we weren't coming back that night, food boxes, maps, everything. We thought it'd take three hours there and three hours home, same route. The only good thing about dragging all that junk around was that the beer would be six hours colder when we got back."

Benjamin laughed out loud.

Niklas continued, "In and out, none of our boys were gonna get hurt. That's the rhythm of missions like that. The Red Crescent or Amnesty International can tally the points when we're done. Honestly, we're not the ones turning those villages into targets. They turn themselves into targets. Give food and shelter to suicide bombers and the suicide bombers' brains. They only have themselves to blame. No matter what happens, no way we could kill more people than they did with their car bombs all over Bahgdad."

Even though Niklas was speaking loudly, Benjamin wasn't really listening. His eyes danced. Kept glancing at the man wearing the shooting club's emblem at the table next to them. Finally, Niklas stopped himself.

"If there's something you want to say to that guy, just say it."

Benjamin nodded. Turned to the guy at the table next to them.

"Hey, I just gotta ask. Are you active in the Järfälla Gun Club?"

The man turned his head slowly. Like he was thinking, Are you stupid, or what? Interrupting me in the middle of a conversation? He eyed Benjamin.

But what came out wasn't aggressive.

"Yes, I've been a member for over twelve years. Are you interested in joining?"

"I'm already a member. Joined a few months back. But I gotta say, it's awesome. How often do you shoot?"

Niklas eyed the man. He actually looked interested in the conversation. The guy had short blond hair. Close to forty. A striped shirt unbuttoned at the neck and blue jeans. Maybe it was the focus in his eyes, maybe it was the fact that he looked so put together but still hung out at Friden. The man had to be a cop.

They chatted. The guy told them about the shooting club. About the number of members. About what guns he owned. Benjamin absorbed it all like a sponge. The shooting club guy's colleague joined in. Told them about his firearms. Turned out, they were both cops. Right every time—Niklas's eye for people never failed him.

An hour later. More gun talk than he'd ever experienced among the boys in the barracks down there. The two cops were nice. The bar was nice. The conversation was decent.

Benjamin got up. He had to go meet his date. Was apparently already late. Shook hands with the cops. Niklas and he decided that they'd be in touch later that week. Was Niklas making a friend?

One of the policemen, the one who wasn't a member of the shooting club, also got up. Had to go home to his family. Niklas and the cop who remained seated looked at each other. Really, it was weird to stay with someone you didn't know—but what the hell, why not?

They ordered another round. Kept talking guns. Niklas was getting drunk.

The cop ordered Salisbury steak with pepper sauce. "A classic," as he called it. "This place has really great, classic grub. Might be hard to believe, but."

Niklas ordered more peanuts.

When the gun talk ran dry after fifteen minutes or so, the policeman asked him, "So, what do you do?"

"I'm looking for employment."

Niklas'd learned that that's how you said it. Not "unemployed"—that was not a dynamic state of being. Instead you should be on your way, in motion, on the hunt—for a job. Bullshit. He was unemployed. And he was fine with that for now, but the money would run out at some point.

"Okay. So what kind of job do you want?"

"I could imagine doing some sort of security guard job. Maybe in the subway. But not just sitting still somewhere guarding a building. That's too dull."

"That's good. We need more good security guards. And people who have the guts to roll their sleeves up, if you catch my drift."

Niklas wasn't completely sure he understood. The cop sounded bitter somehow.

"Yeah, sure. I'd roll my sleeves up. I've worked hard in my day."
They looked at each other.

"What kind of work've you done?" the cop asked.

"I've been in the armed forces. I can't really talk about it."

"That's understandable. We need people like you. Do you understand what I mean? Someone's got to clean up the trash. The security guards are often too sissy. Not to mention the police. They've started to recruit such whiny pussies that it makes you wonder if ordinary men are supposed to be in the minority."

"You're right. The police need more authority."

"Addicts, pedophiles, men who beat up their women. People don't care as long as it doesn't affect them. But we're not allowed to get rough, 'cause then everyone gives us a lot of grief. I'm going to tell you something. You really want to listen to a bitter old cop?"

"Absolutely." It was interesting. No one could agree more that the cops should be harder on men who abused women.

The cop really got into it.

"I take my job seriously. I really try to stop the rabble that's taking over this city. So, the other day, they sent me on the beat with a little girl. Fresh out of the Police Academy, no experience at all. Thin, delicate chick. I don't understand how they recruit these days. Anyway, we got sent to a twenty-four-hour bodega where some drunk'd seen red and started picking a fight with the staff. The problem was, I recognized the guy. He's an old boxer, strong as hell. Aggressive like a teenager. But my colleague, she was too green, didn't get what was going on. It got ugly. The boxer-boozer attacked her. She couldn't stand up to him. It got even uglier. He attacked me too. And when we were trying to bring him down, and it wasn't easy, let me tell you, it got uglier still. The old guy was mad as hell, strong as a bull, swinging punches like fucking Muhammad Ali. Look at my nose."

The cop paused. Niklas was into the story.

"What happened?"

"He clocked me. If I'd been out with a male colleague, someone from my usual gang, for example, that never would've happened. But now, now this girl's there and we can't bring the asshole down the normal way. He was just too tough. So we used the batons. A lot. Until we got him down and could cuff him."

Another pause. The cop swallowed. The gravity in his eyes gleamed again.

"And now they're talking excessive force. You understand?"

Niklas was surprised at the turn. This felt private, intimate.

"Sure. It sounds fucked up. You were just doing your job."

"This is society's demise we're talking about. If the police allow a bunch of violent old fuckers to go around and do whatever they want without us being able to fight back, then who's going to stop them? If the police let a bunch of junkies deal drugs, who's going to keep young people from dying prematurely? If the police can't do anything about domestic violence, who's going to make sure innocent women aren't humiliated?"

Niklas nodded in time to the outpouring. The last thing the cop said cut deep. This was bigger than he'd thought—Sweden was in worse shape than he'd expected. If the police didn't do the job, who would do it?

He felt drunk. The cop kept talking about society's decline. Niklas's thoughts galloped off. Again and again: if the cops don't take care of it, then someone else has to.

* * *

AFTONBLADET—EVENING PAPER

Pensioner Assaulted with Batons—and Is Written Up by the Police

Two police officers almost beat a pensioner unconscious with batons. They then wrote him up for assault. A surveillance camera revealed how the police abused the 63-year-old man.

Aftonbladet has acquired the videotape from the store's surveillance camera, which shows the police officers striking the pensioner Torsten Göransson at least ten times with their batons. The tape has also been given to the prosecutor.

The images were captured by a surveillance camera in a twenty-four-hour bodega in Aspudden in southern Stockholm.

"I hope they're prosecuted. The police can't be allowed to do this kind of thing," said Torsten Göransson.

Victim was defending himself

Göransson had driven to the store from his apartment in Axelsberg to buy cigarettes. But the store clerk had refused to sell him cigarettes because the bills he had were too large.

"The ATM machine in Aspudden only had five-hundred-kronor bills," Göransson explained. "Then the police showed up. They started beating me with batons. Over my entire body. I fought back as much as I could in self-defense."

Göransson was arrested and brought to Skärholmen's police station. He was not released until late that night.

Confiscated video footage

The following day, he went to Huddinge Hospital to have his injuries documented. Then he reported the police officers.

Meanwhile, the police officers had written up Göransson for assault.

Judging by the video footage that *Aftonbladet* acquired, Göransson's version of events appears to be the accurate one.

The video footage clearly shows the two police officers using their batons to beat Göransson repeatedly over his entire body.

Bert Cantwell
bert.cantwell@aftonbladet.se

18

Journalists are the rats of humankind; fake-PC-dyke-Communist politicians are the cockroaches of the earth; and Internal Affairs police investigators are the bloodsuckers of the world. They live off of other people's ruin. They thrive on betrayal: spit on loyalty, dignity, and respect. They let Sweden down. Let everyone down who is working for a better country.

Thomas knew that most cops who loved the more confrontational side of police work, those who didn't just waste away behind a desk or pussy out as soon as the heat was turned up, would, at some point during their career, be subjected to internal investigations. That was just par for the course; the police department was forced to stage a little self-scrutiny from time to time to keep the politicians and the public happy. But sometimes it got serious—when the media got involved. When journalists who knew nothing about life on the street started to scrutinize, criticize, theorize. Hunt. The beaters were consequence-neutral—they didn't give a damn what happened to the individual policemen whose heads they wanted on a spit. The media should be outlawed.

That's why he wasn't really too surprised when, three days after the articles appeared in *Aftonbladet, Expressen, Metro, City*, and probably a bunch of other newspapers, he saw the envelope in his mailbox at work. Internal Affairs (IA), Stockholm County. The message was brief.

Ai 1187-07. Chief Prosecutor Carl Holm has decided to commence a preliminary investigation against you and Cecilia Lindqvist in regards to serious professional misconduct, etc., on June 11 of this year on Hägerstensvägen. The Chief Prosecutor has given the undersigned Internal Affairs officer the right to charge you with suspicion of grave professional misconduct or, in the alternative, grave assault. According to the internal database, you are scheduled to work during the day on June 25, therefore, you are called to Internal Affairs

*headquarters on that day at 1300. You are also hereby informed of your right
to have legal representation present at the interrogation.*

His nose was pounding after the head butt from that fucking booze-hound. He felt nauseated.

They were going to commence an investigation against him—and that could lead to suspension and transfer, or, worse, dismissal. It could lead to a charge of professional misconduct being brought against him. He remained standing in front of the mailbox, the letter in hand. Didn't know what to do.

Read the verdict again. Saw the report number again. Ai 1197-07. Thought of all of those who'd been through this before him.

His phone rang.

"Hello, Andrén. This is Stig Adamsson. Are you in?"

After the incident at the morgue, Thomas didn't trust Adamsson one bit. What did he want now? Could it have to do with the murder? More likely, it had to do with the Internal Affairs investigation that he'd just found out about. He responded, "I just got in."

"Great. You think you could come by my office? The sooner the better."

Six colleagues were standing around the coffee machine in the hall. They greeted him. Everyone knew. He could tell. He could see right away which ones were on his side. A discreet nod, a wink, a wave. But two of them stared straight through him—there were quislings among the patrol officers too. Thomas made a point of greeting the four who were his friends.

The door to Adamsson's room was closed. According to police etiquette, that meant you were expected to close it after you when you went inside.

Thomas knocked. Heard a quiet "Come in" from inside.

Adamsson was sitting in front of his computer with his back to the door. A tired, old ballbuster. The unit chief turned around.

"Hey, Andrén. Have a seat."

Thomas pulled out the visitor's chair and sat down. He was still holding the letter from IA in his hand. Stig Adamsson looked at it.

"This is really unfortunate."

Thomas nodded. Could he trust Adamsson?

"So, I'm guessing everyone already knows?"

"Well, you know how it is. Talk spreads faster than wildfire around here. But I heard it by the formal route. They made this a rush job and everything, sent it straight to the prosecutor. They're dragging the girl into it too, Lindqvist."

"So, what do you think? Will the media calm down?"

"They always calm down. But if you're unlucky, some damn politician's going to add his two cents, too. Unfortunately, that usually sets a fire under IA's ass. And then the police commissioner's got to make a decision about where you'll be working, too."

"When will that happen?"

Adamsson put both hands on the table. They were rough hands. Hands that'd taken their fair share of hits in their day: probably been pricked on injection needles, dug through vomit, but also dealt a few more blows than most. He sighed.

"I just spoke to him. He's going to wait for IA's verdict. If they make a case of it, prosecute you and get a conviction, there's a risk that you'll have to quit altogether. If they drop the preliminary investigation, the situation is more hopeful, but even then there's a risk that we'll have to transfer you."

Thomas didn't know what to say.

"Andrén, I just wanted to tell you that I completely understand. I've read your report and the assault report. I mean, I know Torsten Göransson from way back. He was a good boxer, twenty-five or so years ago. Trained at Linnéa. You know that club?"

"Of course."

"A real beast. Then something went wrong. Or else it'd gone wrong already before the boxing. I don't know. Anyway, he's been convicted of assault at least five times before. *Summa summarum:* you were totally right to use the batons. And it's not your fault that the new collapsible batons are too weak. And it's not *your* fault that Cecilia Lindqvist is too weak."

Thomas nodded in time to Adamsson's harangue. He thought, Shouldn't the guy at least mention the incident at the morgue? But he didn't say anything. Instead he said, "Exactly. If we'd been two regular officers we'd have been able to handle him without using the batons so much. I appreciate your support, Adamsson. It feels good. But, can you tell me one thing?"

"I'll do my best."

"Who made the call for me to take the shift with Cecilia Lindqvist? Everyone who knows me knows I don't work too well with little girls."

"I honestly don't know who made that call. But Ljunggren had to cover for Fransson, who was sick. So we had to put someone in. That's just the routine, you know that. But I'll look into it."

Thomas nodded. Adamsson didn't say anything. His facial expression, however, said: This conversation is over.

Thomas wanted to say something about the morgue. Get a sensible explanation.

But no words came. He got up.

"One more thing, Andrén. Take a few weeks off. Go on disability for a month or so. I really think you should. It'll be hard, being here."

It was an order.

On his way home, Thomas drove the roundabout way across Norrmalm. Didn't take the Essingeleden highway. Needed time to think. The lower part of Fleminggatan: Irish pubs and small restaurants. He thought about his and Ljunggren's night at Friden. The places he was driving past now didn't exactly radiate glamour. But Friden still took home the dumpy prize.

Then it hit him: he couldn't exactly put his finger on what it was, but Ljunggren'd been acting weird. First he'd been all about them grabbing a beer after work. And then, when they got to Friden, it was like he had nothing to say. Ljunggren wasn't the world's most talkative person, sure—still, they usually conversed at their own pace, exchanged a few words. Analyzed the day. Complained about their bosses, worthless colleagues. Evaluated the women in the place. But yesterday, Ljunggren'd seemed scattered. Flitted between topics and kept bringing up the same thing over and over: the way Thomas'd dealt with the drunk boxer. And all of that could've been normal, except for his comment after a while, a few minutes before those guys at the next table over started talking to them. As if Ljunggren'd had to force his question out: "Hey Thomas, you're not mad at me, are you? I mean, I got called to something else, that's why they sent that chick." But even that wasn't strange—of course he felt bad about what happened. But the thing he said after that—after Thomas'd shaken his head and said it wasn't his responsibility—was all to hell:

"Andrén, now that they've started this whole internal investigation you'll stop digging around in that Hägerström crap, right?"

At first, Thomas hadn't understood what he meant. Then it became clear what he was implying. His only response was, "I'm still a cop. So I'll keep doing what cops do."

Thomas drove across the Central Bridge toward Slussen. Riddarholmen, with all the courthouses, was on his right. Where they claimed that justice was served in Sweden. Lady Justice was blind, they said. It was true, she was blind.

He added up the facts. Someone'd deleted things from his report. Someone'd deleted things from the forensic pathologist's autopsy report. Adamsson wanted to stop him and Hägerström from taking pictures of the corpse. Then something else hit him: Ljunggren'd called him while he was at the morgue—tried to get him to come on a call, said something about a shoplifter in the Mörby mall. Not only had he asked him to stop the murder investigation, maybe he'd tried to trick him too.

Summation of his analysis: there was only one explanation for all the weirdness piling up in his head. Someone wanted to stop him from continuing his search. That someone might be Ljunggren. But how much power did Jörgen Ljunggren have to make things like that happen? No, it wasn't Ljunggren. And Adamsson? Maybe. Thomas had to find out more.

But right now, he couldn't care less who it was. He had to do something on his own. He made a U-turn at Slussen.

Twenty minutes later he got out of the car in front of Danderyd's morgue. The sky was a clear blue. His nose still hurt like hell. He thought about the smell in the room with the cold chambers. He thought about Hägerström. Suddenly, he changed his mind. Called Hägerström.

He didn't pick up. Thomas left a message. "Hi there, it's Andrén. A lot of shit happened today. You might already know about it, but I'll tell you later. Anyway, I'm going in to see the pathologist right now. Just so you know."

When he'd hung up, he realized that Hägerström was really the enemy. Being disloyal to police colleagues was what Hägerström's past life was all about. Those IA rats.

He rang the bell at the welcome desk. An autopsy technician came out. He looked surprised.

"Hi, may I help you?"

"Yes, I was here a few days ago. Andrén, Southern District."

"Right, now I recognize you."

Not an unusual reaction from people who'd previously only seen him in uniform. As if he were a completely different person in his civilian clothes. But considering the Adamsson incident, maybe this little autopsy technician ought to have a better memory.

"You're Christian Nilsson?"

"Yes, that's me."

Thomas lowered his voice. Unnecessary to speak too loudly. Nilsson might get stressed out by the thought that someone could come into the waiting room and hear.

"You were present at the autopsy of the corpse that me and my colleague were looking at the last time we were here?"

"I don't remember exactly, it's been busy here lately."

"Okay. Then I can tell you that you were present, the autopsy report says so. The dead man's face was basically torn off and the guy had no teeth, so we need more input to make a positive ID. Can you tell me something? Was there anything special about the victim's right arm?"

"As far as I remember, things got a little tumultuous when you were here last. And I can tell you straight away that I don't remember all the details from that autopsy, unfortunately. But if you want, I can get my report so that you can see what it says in it."

Thomas considered his options. The autopsy technician seemed cocky, but it wasn't certain that he was hiding something. Things *had* gotten pretty weird when Adamsson stormed in. Thomas asked him to get the report. There was always a chance that the track marks were mentioned in that version. He came back after three minutes. Without the report.

"Unfortunately, I can't give you the report. You're no longer a part of the investigation, as far as I can tell."

Thomas thought: If the guy says "as far as" one more time, I'll crack his skull. Then he said curtly, "Get your boss, Bengt Gantz. Now, please."

The autopsy technician stared him in the eyes. Turned on his heel and disappeared through the door.

Ten minutes later, a tall, thin man came into the waiting room. The same uniform coat as Nilsson. Thomas wondered why it'd taken so long. The forensic pathologist'd probably been elbow-deep in some corpse, or else he was worried about his major miss in the autopsy report.

Three slow steps. Almost as if he was trying to act dignified.

"Hello. My name is Bengt Gantz." Slow drawl. "I don't want to be unpleasant in any way, but we have been informed that you are not a part of the team involved in this preliminary investigation. Therefore, in the present situation, our privacy rules do not permit us to give you access to journal material, reports, or other things of that nature."

Thomas thought, The doctor dude's language is nerdier than a pompous defense attorney's. He tried to calm down.

"I understand. But I just have a very simple question. You seem to have forgotten certain information in the autopsy report. It concerns findings on the victim's right arm. Do you remember anything in particular about that?"

The forensic pathologist actually looked like he was thinking it over. He closed his eyes. But what came out was all wrong. "As I said, we are unfortunately not able to comment on this case at all. I'm sorry."

Thomas thought Gantz's attempt at a smile to smooth things over was the most disingenuous thing he'd ever seen.

"Okay. Then let me try another tactic. I know that the victim had track marks on his right forearm. At least three of them, on the underside of the arm, about six inches from the wrist. My colleague, Hägerström, can also attest to the injection holes being there. I am now giving you a very simple chance to change your autopsy report so that you won't get slammed with professional misconduct. Grave misconduct, too. What do you say? My suggestion is completely free of charge."

It worked in a way. But not in the intended way.

The doctor breathed heavily. Lost his formal way of talking.

"No. What is it you don't understand? My report was completely correct. There were no track marks. No signs of narcotic influence. Nothing like that. And spare me your insinuations that I'm guilty of some kind of professional misconduct."

Thomas didn't say anything.

"I am going to have to ask you to leave now. This is becoming highly unpleasant."

All the warning bells were ringing. All the vibes were pointing to the same thing. More than ten years on the streets made him good at picking up on the signals when something wasn't right. To read the atmosphere when someone pulled a fast one. The small signs that someone was lying. The movement of the eyes, the sweat on the forehead, the exaggerated emotional outbursts.

Gantz hadn't shown a single physical sign of genuine agitation.

It was crystal clear: the doctor jerk was lying about something.

Thomas went out to his Cadillac as soon as he got home. Rolled into his own world. Tried to shut the thoughts out. There was too much shit.

But maybe that's how it'd always been—full of shit, that is. Just that sometimes the shit all happened in one and the same month.

His thoughts drifted toward the investigation. Hägerström'd asked the National Laboratory of Forensic Science to try to decipher the last digit in the telephone number. Meanwhile, he'd looked up lists he'd gotten from the phone carriers Telenor and Telia for the two prepaid plans. Thomas hadn't been able to resist, even though Hägerström was the enemy—he'd called him. Hägerström'd figured out who the Telenor card belonged to—Hanna Barani, nineteen years old, from Huddinge. The girl said she'd been at a graduation party on June 2, and that agreed with the coordinates. She'd been moving between a cell phone tower in Huddinge and one on Södermalm. Hägerström talked to the girl anyway, even though there was nothing that suggested she had anything to do with it.

But the Telia plan remained. Only three calls made, which was a strangely small number. Hägerström'd looked up the three numbers. They belonged to Frida Olsson, Ricardo's Car Service, and Claes Rantzell.

He called them. Got ahold of Frida Olsson and the car guy. Neither of them had any idea who the prepaid number might belong to. Hägerström couldn't get ahold of Claes Rantzell. They were back to square one.

Thomas tried to focus on the car. Toyed with the suspension. It had to be super comfortable, smoother driving than all the Citroëns in the world. But at the same time it had to exude vitality—couldn't look like some fucking go-cart.

It worked. All the thoughts about the bullshit released their grip on him. He devoted his energy to the car.

Åsa came home two hours later. Went right into the kitchen. Started cooking. Thomas knew: he had to tell her soon. They ate while she talked about their garden and work colleagues who didn't treat each other with respect. Then she went into their big project: adoption. They'd been in touch with an agency. Soon they were going to get a home inspection. Maybe, maybe joy would be theirs within a few months. Thomas couldn't concentrate. He should—the adoption issue was important. Åsa was actually important too, though he often forgot that. But the only thing he was thinking about: why Hägerström didn't call him back.

After dinner, they watched a movie together. *Executive Protection*, a Swedish flick. Åsa saw several movies a week so she had to compromise to lure him to the TV couch. The cop scenes were worthless. But the scenes with weapons were believable enough. For once, they seemed to get that a seasoned cop never shoots with a straight arm. The recoil is all wrong—you'll give yourself a tennis elbow.

They went to bed early. It was only eleven o'clock. She rolled close to him. Åsa: who used to wake such feelings of lust in him. Now they could hardly carry on a conversation, they didn't laugh together the way they used to, they didn't have a normal sex life—he just wasn't turned on anymore.

"I'm tired tonight. Sorry."

Her sigh was deep. She knew that he knew how disappointed she was. It just made it worse.

They turned the lights out.

He couldn't sleep. Thought everything through once more. It was too late to go out to the car; the tinkering was never good when he was too tired.

The room wasn't completely dark. Light seeped through under the curtains. He opened his eyes. Could make out the chair where he always piled his clothes. Åsa's face. He stared up at the ceiling. Tried to calm down.

The phone rang. A quick glance at the clock on the radio. Two-thirty. Who the hell was calling at this time? Thomas fumbled for the phone.

A calm male voice said, "Is this Thomas Andrén?"

Thomas didn't recognize the voice. Åsa moved next to him.

"Yes," he responded quietly.

"Go to the window."

Thomas got up. He was dressed only in his boxers. Peeked through the curtain. The sky was brightening.

"I'm standing by the streetlamp across from your house. I'm here all the time. Even when Åsa is home alone."

"What the hell do you want?"

Thomas saw a man in dark clothes on the other side of the street, about twenty yards away. It had to be him.

"Stop poking around in things that don't concern you."

"What? Who are you?"

"Stop poking around in what you found in Axelsberg."

"Who are you?"

The silence on the line sliced through his ear.

Thomas looked over at the pile of clothes on the chair again. Was his service weapon there?

Then he looked out again. The man by the streetlamp was gone.

He knew there was no point in going out looking for him.

He knew he couldn't leave Åsa alone right now.

19

Afterward, Mahmud felt more naïve than a two-year-old.

They'd met up at the McDonald's in Sergelgången. Mahmud usually dug downtown. Remembered the years in junior high when him and his buds'd hung out there more than at home. The raids between the department stores: Åhléns, Intersport, and PUB. Pit stop at Mickey D's to fuel up before they moved on to Kungsgatan. Down toward Stureplan. Scared the brat kids—stole their Canada Goose jackets, swiped their cell phones, boosted easy money. Carefree moments. They were kings then. When the tight-pants prepsters feared them. Back when the pen felt farther away than, like, Sundsvall up in the north.

But now, on his way to see Gürhan's Born to Be Hated boys, he felt nauseous. Like a nasty punch to his stomach. Maybe an omen.

The cell phones, the video game, the bus passes, and the DVD films'd been sold at majorly discounted prices. *Inshallah*—he thanked the God he didn't believe in for video game markets and Babak's dad's hole in the wall. Even so—the gear didn't get him far. Nine G's total. Fuck. Really couldn't ask Abu about this. If only he'd had something to sell he would've: Dbols, hash, anything—even horse. But he didn't have anything left: had even flipped his gym membership card, with nine months left on it, for one G. Lugged his TV and DVD player to Babak's dad's store. Pulled in another four thousand. Finally, violated his honor: pawned his necklace—it'd belonged to his mother. Made him two G's. If he couldn't buy it back his life wasn't worth piss.

Still, there were four G's missing. Whatever. He couldn't get more paper now and time was running out like water in the desert. They just had to accept it.

He stepped inside. Burger smell. Families with kids. *Blattes* behind the counter—half were probably engineers and the rest doctors. Sven Sweden would rather have them flipping burgers than using their real skills.

Daniel was sitting in the back of the place. Shoving food all over his face like a pig. Next to him: the two other *blattes* Mahmud'd seen at Hell's Kitchen.

Daniel looked at him. "Hey, *habibi*, you don't gotta look like I popped your sister's cherry."

Mahmud sat down.

"Funny."

Daniel was taking big nasty bites out of a Big Mac.

Mahmud's left leg started shaking uncontrollably under the table. He hoped no one saw. Focused—maintained his dignity. Would never let himself be humiliated in front of them again.

Daniel stared.

"Funny? Why aren't you laughing, if you think it's so funny?"

Mahmud didn't have an answer.

They ignored him. Daniel kept buzzing with the other two dudes. In the middle of the chatter, he handed Mahmud an empty McDonald's bag. Nodded. Gestured with his hand: put it under the table.

Mahmud fumbled with his hand in his inside pocket. Quickly shoved the bills in under the table and into the bag.

Daniel accepted the bag with a grin wider than the Joker's in the *Batman* movies. Kept talking to the gorillas. Down with his hand under the table. A quick glance to check the bills' denomination. Then—a classic: don't look down again, count under the table while you keep conversing. Clean.

It took awhile. Daniel looked questioningly at him.

Mahmud leaned over.

"It's only ninety-six. I couldn't get more."

Daniel hissed, "You cunt. Gürhan said one hundred. Take your dirty cash back. Next week, we want two hundred. No joke."

The bag was back on the table again.

Daniel and the other two got up. Walked out.

The dad with his kids at the table next to theirs was staring.

Mahmud was left alone. Stared back.

"What the fuck you looking at, motherfucker?"

That night: slumped down in the leather couch at Babak's place. Tried to tone the whole thing down. Babak was wondering: "Are they *loco*, or what? You give 'em ninety-six in two weeks and they're not happy. What they got on you, man?"

Mahmud acted unperturbed. Almost grinned.

"Eh, you know. I don't wanna get in trouble. You got weed, or what?"

Inside: he knew exactly what they had on him. They were ready to pop him at any time. And they'd seen him piss himself. All he wanted now was to forget the whole thing.

They watched a movie: *Scarface*, probably for the twentieth time. Mahmud's dream: to be as crazy as Tony Montana. "You wanna play rough? Oookey." Bam, bam, bam.

Babak kept talking about how sweet they'd been the other night.

"We juxed those little fags in their own crib. They just sat there. Didja see that bitch who was like in a trance or somethin'? And Simon, he's never gonna mess with me again."

Mahmud wanted to go home.

On the way. Took the train one stop to Fittja. His dad called his cell. Mahmud didn't pick up. Didn't have the energy to talk to him right then. Dad called again. Mahmud hit silent. Let all the signals go through without picking up. He was seeing him in fifteen minutes, anyway.

Across from him: a bleached blonde with long-ass nails. Mahmud liked the look: it was kinky somehow. He thought about his sister. She'd lent him five thousand. They mostly saw each other at Friday dinners at Dad's house and with his little sister, Jivan, once every three months or something. After Beshar'd been to the mosque.

Jamila's dude'd done time, too. At Österåker, for possession. Mahmud'd never liked him. He wasn't good to Jamila. Some girls always seemed attracted to assholes, and Jamila was a girl like that. Something weird'd happened a few days ago: one of Jamila's neighbors'd apparently stormed in during an argument. Beat her guy like he was a snotty schoolkid. And Jamila's guy wasn't the kind who usually took shit. Mahmud tried to understand what'd happened, asked Jamila for details. She just shook her head, didn't want to talk more about it. "He knows Arabic," she said. Maybe there were Svens with honor after all?

Mahmud was standing outside his front door. Dad opened it before he'd even rung the doorbell. Was he looking through the peephole, or what?

Mahmud could see right away: something was wrong. Dad in tears.

Nervous. Scared. When he saw Mahmud he threw his arms around him. Cried. Howled.

"They can never take you away from me."

Mahmud led him into the living room. Sat him down on the couch. Got him a cup of tea with mint leaves. Stroked his cheek. Held him tight. Like Abu'd done for Mahmud so many times before. Calmed him. Hugged him.

Dad told his story. With pauses. Disjointed. Broken.

Finally, Mahmud understood what'd happened.

They'd been there.

Three guys. Dad'd opened the door. They'd handed him a plastic bag. And they'd told him something like, "Your son's in the shit. If he messes with us, we'll crush you."

In the bag: the head of a pig.

For his dad. A religious man.

Impossible to fall asleep. Mahmud was twisting and turning six million times. A single thought in his head: he had to find Wisam Jibril.

He opened his eyes. Stood in front of the window. Looked out at the street through the curtains. Remembered his first showdowns with spitballs when he was seven years old. Him, Babak, and another *blatte* soon figured out that spitballs were for wusses. Moved on to slingshots, blowguns, and throwing stars. Once, Babak accidentally blew a staple that hit a girl in his class in the eye. The chick lost sight in her left eye. The racist teachers put Babak in special ed.

It was two o'clock. The sky would brighten soon.

This wasn't working. He had to do something.

An hour later, he was walking down Tegnérgatan. Hadn't borrowed a car. Had ridden the night bus into the city, jazzed like a speed junkie. Was going to wake up John Ballénius—was gonna whip that fucker until he told him where he could find Jibril.

The entrance to the building was locked. Of course. Even though nothing dangerous happened downtown, all the Svens had to have key codes on their buildings. Why were they so fucking scared of everything?

He walked back and forth on the street for a while. Two people were winding their way home. He let them pass. Picked up a loose cobblestone. Like working out at Fitness Center. Dragged it over to the building's entrance. Threw it through the glass. Damn, the crash was loud. Hoped he only woke up half the building. He reached his hand in, opened the door.

Walked up to Ballénius's door. Rang the doorbell. Nothing happened. The old guy was obviously sleeping.

Rang the doorbell again. Silence. No rattling sound from a door chain. No one shuffling around in there.

Rang the bell for a third time. For a long time.

Totally dead.

Cunt Ballénius didn't seem to be home.

Mahmud considered: pros versus cons. He could try to break in. See if he could find anything that might lead him to Jibril. On the other hand: if the Ballénius fucker was out at a bar and was planning on coming home soon, he'd see that his apartment had been broken in to. Could call the cops, who'd be there in two minutes.

That wouldn't work. The risk of tripping up was too big.

But his next idea was better: the other front man never seemed to be home. Mahmud'd waited outside his house for almost a day and a half. Even paid some kids to ring the guy's doorbell once an hour. Nada.

Sweet. He could do that. Break into Rantzell's house. Pocket some leads.

This was the first time since they'd crashed the party that he'd felt okay. The king was on the move again. The Yugos' new darling would make his grand entrance. He called for a cab—worth spending some of his hard-gathered stash. Had it drive him back to Fittja. Down in the basement. Got his crowbar. Back to Elsa Brändströms Street in the same cab. Wham-bam.

The time: four-thirty. It was light out. Desolate. He tested the door to the building. It was open. What luck. Shouldn't they be more scared about break-ins here in the crap suburbs than downtown on Tegnérgatan?

It said *Rantzell* on a paper slip on a door. Mahmud peeked in through the mail slot. Saw a hall. Should he ring the doorbell? No, others in the building might hear. Might get suspicious. He picked up the crowbar. Ran his hand along the door to find a good place to shove it in. The door moved. It was open. Weirdish.

Was Claes Rantzell at home? Didn't he lock the door? Mahmud slid into the apartment.

Closed the door quickly behind him. Inside: the stench swept over him. Rotten meat. Shit. Junkie crash-pad fumes. He almost threw up. Pulled his sweatshirt up over his nose. Tried to breathe through his mouth. Who lived like this?

Enough light in the apartment so that he didn't have to flip any switches. He called out. Not a sound in response.

In the hall: a couple of worn-out black shoes and two jackets. Flyers and mail on the floor. Mahmud remembered not to touch anything with his fingers. To the right was a kitchen, straight ahead was a living room, to the left a bedroom.

First the kitchen. Unwashed plates and cutlery, the sink brown with dirt. A packet of Jozo salt was standing next to an empty milk carton. The kitchen table was covered in bags, ravioli cans, beer bottles, and glasses. On the floor: old cigarette cartons, paper, a carpet that was so dirty that he couldn't tell what color it really was. What kind of a pigsty was this, anyway? Dig the irony: the guy's company was listed as the owner of a Bentley. Mahmud opened the cupboards. Almost empty, except for a few glasses and two pots.

Then the living room: a leather couch and a leather armchair. Kind of like Babak's place. Two paintings on the wall. One was of a short-haired boy with a tear in his eye. The other looked more like a photo: some army general or something. A couple of shelves filled with old encyclopedias, a dozen paperbacks, and velvet cushions with lots of medals pinned on them. Ugly. A TV, a VHS player, and a dried-up cactus in the window. The living room gave Claes Rantzell away: four or five beer bottles, two wine bottles, half a bottle of whiskey, a handle of vodka. The guy was a boozehound.

Mahmud didn't touch the shit. There wasn't time. He wanted to get out of there quick. Pulled his sweatshirt sleeves down over his hands. Tore the books out of the bookshelf just to take a quick look. Nothing hidden there.

Finally, the bedroom. Double bed. The junkie seemed to live alone—only one pillow. Dirty. Stained comforter. Yellowish sheets. An oriental rug on the floor that had to be fake. A mirror on the ceiling. Porn magazines open on the nightstand: a chick blowing one guy, jerking off another, and getting pissed on by a third. Mahmud approached the closet. There had to be something interesting somewhere. Inside: jeans, shirts, drawers with underwear and socks. A wooden box. He opened it.

Freakshow. Whose house'd he come to, the chairman of the Sodomite Association? Chock-full of sex toys. Dildos—veiny super cocks—Anal Intruder, a strap-on, a leather leash, a riding whip, a couple of thin chains, a leather mask with a zipper over the mouth, a stud choker. Some latex armor, handcuffs, a blindfold, anal beads, lubricant, a couple bottles of poppers, all kinds of oils.

Mahmud: porn watcher, pious Muslim, pornographer. Papa's boy. Thought, This is sick.

Then he grinned. Sven men are losers.

He continued to tear through the closet. Threw out old shoes, T-shirts, bags, LP records. Finally—maybe something of value. Farthest in, attached to the wall: a small locked key cabinet. He applied the crowbar. Pulled. The cabinet cracked open. Inside: small keys that looked like bike keys. And two bigger keys. Looked like they went to padlocks.

He was feeling stressed. Even if he hadn't seen Rantzell for a few days and the guy didn't pick up his phone, he could come home at any moment. He grabbed the larger keys.

Stopped for a second in the hallway. What was he going to do now? Maybe the keys went somewhere. But where? He looked at them again. He recognized them. Assa Abloy. Tri-circle. Like the ones to the padlock on his locker at the gym. Like to the basement storage locker at Dad's house. A little idea worth testing. He left the apartment.

Took the stairs up. There was no attic. Took the stairs down. The basement storage lockers were a mess. Behind the wooden boards and bars: a bunch of *Suedi* gear. Winter jackets, skis, suitcases, books, and boxes. Why didn't they just toss this shit? Did they think they were gonna make big bucks at the Skärholmen flea market, or what?

He tried out the keys in every lock. Thoughts of Wisam Jibril were mixed with thoughts of his father. Images of Gürhan's monster grin mixed with the heads of pigs. He felt manic. The keys just had to fit somewhere.

He tried lock after lock. After at least ten failures: one of the keys fit into a storage locker. It was half-empty in there. A rolled-up carpet, a couple of boxes. Plates in one and porn magazines in the other.

He kept trying the other key in different locks. The other one fit in the lock of the next storage locker over. He thought, Rantzell pulled an old trick—steal someone else's empty storage locker. Mahmud went in. Lots of bags on the floor. Fuck. He looked in one of them: documents. Numbers, names of companies, letters from the tax authorities. He didn't have the energy to keep digging. Could it be valuable? He didn't have the energy to think. Grabbed two bags. Walked up. Out.

The morning sun was glowing beautifully on the street.

Mahmud thought, Maybe I'm back on track.

Sunday. His cell phone clock showed one o'clock. Sweet, he'd slept for six hours. Then he remembered how they'd treated his father. And that Dad hadn't woken him up all morning. An angel, as usual.

He thought about the night; it was hazy in his memory. What'd he achieved? A couple of bags with documents. Congrats, Twiggy. What crap.

Beshar was sitting in the kitchen. Had his usual Middle Eastern coffee with five sugar cubes in it. Murky as a mud puddle. Big, dark eyes. In Arabic, "How did you sleep?"

Mahmud hugged him.

"Abu, how did *you* sleep? It'll be okay. No one's gonna hurt us. I promise. Where's Jivan?"

Beshar rapped the table with his knuckles. "She's at a friend's house. *Inshallah.*"

Mahmud got some juice from the fridge. A cooked chicken breast.

Dad smiled. "I know you work out, but is that really a good breakfast?"

Mahmud grinned back. His dad would never understand what it meant to build for real. Protein-rich food without an ounce of fat didn't even figure in his world.

They sat in silence.

Beams of sun lit up the kitchen table.

Mahmud wondered what kind of person his dad could've been if they'd stayed in Iraq. A great man.

Then: the doorbell rang.

Mahmud saw the panic in Dad's eyes.

His entire body was racked with anxiety. Mahmud went into the bedroom. Got an old baseball bat. Brass knuckles in his pocket.

Looked out through the peephole. A dark guy that he didn't recognize.

The bell rang again.

Dad positioned himself behind Mahmud. Before he opened the door, he said to Beshar. "Abu, would you please go into the kitchen?"

Ready as hell. Just so much as a twitch from the guy outside and he was gonna crack his skull like an egg.

He opened the door.

The guy outside extended his hand. *"Salaam alaikum."*

Mahmud didn't understand.

"Don't you recognize me? We went to school together. Wisam Jibril. I heard you've been looking for me."

Beshar laughed in the background.

"Wisam, it's been ages. Welcome!"

20

Today, Niklas felt safer on his run. He'd bought two pairs of shin guards, the kind made for soccer players. Strapped them to his calves. To reduce the risk of rodent bites.

He thought about his nightmares. Thought about Claes, who was dead. About his mom.

He thought about his visit to the open adult psychiatric clinic in Skärholmen. Mom'd forced him to go.

"You're always complaining about how you can't sleep, that you have nightmares," she said in an accusatory tone. "Shouldn't you get some help?"

She kept nagging, even though Niklas hadn't even told her what the dreams were really about. He didn't need that kind of help, head doctors weren't his thing—but he did need sleeping pills. The nights were crap. Maybe he should follow Mom's advice after all.

He went to the clinic's drop-in hours in the middle of the day. Thought there'd be fewer people at that time, the shortest wait. That was a mistake—the waiting room was full. Another sign that something wasn't right in this country. Niklas felt like turning back at the door. He wasn't a weak person who needed others. He was a war machine. People like him didn't go to shrinks. Still, he stayed. Mostly because he wanted to get a prescription for the pills as soon as possible. But also: to be spared Mom's pestering.

The armchair that the doctor offered Niklas was pretty comfortable. He'd expected some stiff Windsor chair, but this felt nice. The psychologist, the psychiatrist, the doctor—or whatever her formal title was—scooted her armchair closer and took her glasses off.

"So, welcome. My name is Helena Hallström and I'm a psychiatrist here at the clinic. And you are Niklas Brogren. Have you been to see us before?"

"No, never."

He checked her out. Maybe ten years older than he was. Dark hair in a ponytail. A searching gaze. Hands in her lap. He wondered what her family life was like. She was in charge here, that much was clear. But at home?

"So, I'll tell you a little bit about what we do here. I don't know anything about why you're here, but our goal is to work to help you, based on a mutual evaluation of your needs. All to help you achieve an increased quality of life. We have a broad and varied assortment of treatments, and we'll see what is best for you. Maybe pharmacological or psychosocial efforts. Or both. And in a lot of cases, nothing is needed."

Niklas didn't even have the energy to try to listen to what she was saying.

"So, Niklas, why are you here today?"

"I can't sleep. So I thought maybe you could help me with sleeping pills."

Helena put her glasses back on. Gave him that searching gaze.

"In what way can't you sleep?"

"I have a hard time falling aslccp and I wake up several times during the night."

"Okay, and why do you think that is?"

"I don't know. I just think about a lot of stuff and then I have weird dreams, too."

"And what is it you think about?"

Niklas hadn't come here to talk about his thoughts or his nightmares. Maybe he'd been naïve, he realized now. At the same time, he really wanted to get a prescription for those pills.

"I think about all kinds of things."

"Like what, for example?" Helena smiled. Niklas liked her. She seemed to care. Not a soldier like him, but maybe she was still a person who'd understood society's mistakes.

"I think a lot about the war. And about the war here at home that no one is doing anything about."

"I'm not quite following. Could you explain a little more, perhaps?"

"I've been in the military for many years. In active combat, so to speak. And I have a lot of memories from that. They bother me sometimes. I know you have to let that shit go and move on, and that's what I'm doing, so it's fine. But since I got back home, I've come to understand that there's a war going on in Sweden, too."

She wrote something down.

"Did you experience violence in the military?"

"You can say that."

"Maybe those memories are troubling you?"

"Yeah, but the war bothers me more, the war against all of you."

"Against us? How do you mean?"

"Against you women. You're attacked on a daily basis. You're subjected to attacks, offensives. I've seen it. It happens all the time, on the streets, in the workplace, at home in the apartments. And you don't do anything about it. But you're the weaker party so maybe that's not so strange. But society doesn't do shit, either. I often imagine what I could do."

"And what is it you imagine?"

"I think and dream, both. There are a lot of methods and I used a couple of them the other night. I heard noises from the neighbors. Don't forget that I'm an expert at this."

She nodded faintly. "Niklas, there are different terms within psychiatry."

"What are you talking about?"

"There are different names for different types of thoughts. Sometimes we talk about *delusions*. Delusions can be positive symptoms for, for instance, psychoses. There are different types of thoughts like that, but all are more or less incompatible with your immediate surroundings. Your perception of reality becomes skewed. It can cause sleeplessness, but also feelings of anxiety. Sometimes people who have been subjected to trauma or where there are other underlying reasons may experience these kinds of symptoms."

"What?"

"I think it may be a good idea for you to come back here at a regular time, not during our drop-in hours. To talk some more about the thoughts you've been having."

This was starting to go too far. He just wanted the pills. Helena could talk about whatever delusions she wanted. Niklas saw the rats. He saw the women. He'd heard what that cop'd said about society not giving a damn. It wasn't a lie—the police officer'd said so himself. It wasn't some unrealistic perception of reality, not symptomatic of anything but Sweden's slow rot.

"Yes, maybe, but do you think you could give me a prescription for sleeping pills?"

"Unfortunately, I can't do that at this time. But I really recommend that you book a time with us. I'm sure we can help you."

"I don't feel like I've made myself understood. But that's okay. I can take care of myself and I think it's time for me to go. I can work on my sleeping problems on my own."

He got up. Extended his hand.

Helena got up as well. "I think that sounds like a good idea."

They shook hands. She said, "But know that we are always here in case you need to discuss your thoughts again. Would you like to book a time for another appointment?"

"No, that's okay. Thank you for your time."

He left. Was not planning on going back.

Later, he thought about the guy who'd come by to thank him the day before yesterday: Mahmud. Big dude. Wide as a Hummer. Head that somehow continued into a neck that was just as wide—veins like worms along his neck. His face was square, hair so black it almost looked dark blue. Probably too many Dbols and protein shakes. But the guy was genuinely grateful. Apparently the girl who lived next door to Niklas was his sister. The dude rang his doorbell at eleven-thirty at night. Niklas didn't mind that it was so late, but it was still suspicious. He peered out through the peephole. Prepared himself for the worst—that the neighbor's boyfriend'd brought his buddies over for payback. Every muscle tensed as he unlocked the door. The knife in one hand.

But when he opened the door, he was faced with a box of chocolates that was being offered to him. Mahmud's words in Arabic: "I want to thank you. You've given my sister hope back. More people should do as you did."

Niklas accepted the gift.

"Call me if you ever need anything. My name is Mahmud. My sister has my number. I can take care of most things."

That was it. Niklas hardly had time to react. Mahmud walked back down the stairs. The front door slammed shut.

Niklas thought about what he was going to do later that day. Visit a women's shelter—Safe Haven. He'd read an article about it in *Metro* yesterday:

Recently, a Left Party proposal highlighted the great pressure that Stockholm's women's shelters are experiencing, reporting that they are forced to transfer women to their counterparts in neighboring counties for help. But the phenomenon is neither new nor unusual. The guarded shelters frequently become so crowded that they have to send women seeking help to other areas.

It was shocking. Everyone failed women. Shuffled them around like cattle. It couldn't be tolerated.

Maybe this could be his thing: he was planning to get in touch with them to offer his services. Safe Haven ought to be interested, considering the current situation. Protection. Intervention. Security. Just like at the private security company where he'd applied for a job.

On the subway on his way into the city. He was freshly showered. Felt clean.

Mom'd called him earlier today. But it was sick—she was totally crushed because of the Claes thing. Wouldn't stop talking about telling the police. But Niklas knew better. If they ratted to the police, it could all be game over.

She asked him straight out: "Niklas, why is it so important to you that we not tell anyone?"

He tried to explain. At the same time, he didn't want to make her upset. Responded in a calm voice, "Mom, you have to understand. I don't want the police getting suspicious and starting to dig into my past. I've got a whole bunch of money from before that I'm sure the tax authorities would be interested in, too. It's unnecessary. Don't you think?"

He hoped she would understand.

Niklas closed his eyes. Tried to forget the images from his nightmares. The blood on his hands. The way Claes looked when Niklas was young. The world was sick. There was no point in playing along. Someone had to break the silence. Like the cop he'd met at Friden'd said, "This is society's demise we're talking about." Despite that: the logic was disturbed by the fact that his mom was crushed. It was a beautiful thing that Claes was gone. A heroic deed that ought to be celebrated. But she didn't understand this. She, the one for whom the deed was done. She, who gained from it more than anyone else. She should say thank you, like that Mahmud guy.

The train was pounding out a sort of beat in his head. He tried to forget about his mom. Force himself to think about something else. His own problems. The job search that wasn't leading anywhere. His resources that wouldn't last forever. Curse the fact that he'd thought he could double his little fortune on the gambling floor—right before he came home to Sweden he'd done a turn in Macao. Naïve, foolish, risky. But maybe it wasn't so strange, considering all the success stories he'd heard Collin and the others tell. Everyone seemed able to bring it in. Except for Niklas, as it turned out. Half of his assets'd been lost before he could rein himself in.

Niklas opened his eyes. It was almost time to get off. Mariatorget's subway platform was rolling away outside the window. He eyed the Åhléns CD ads on the train car. Thought, Certain things in life never change. The clarity of the starry night sky in the desert, Americans' difficulty learning foreign languages, and Åhléns CD ads on the Stockholm subway. He grinned. It was nice when things remained the same. Except for one thing: some men's attitude toward women. He couldn't drop that shit. Men like that were rats.

He got off at Slussen. Checked the address one more time on the slip of paper he had in his back pocket—5 Svartensgatan. Walked along Götgatan. It had been remade into a pedestrian street. Population: a mix of scenesters in tight jeans, Converse sneakers, sweatshirts, and Palestinian scarves, and trendy families with kids and three-wheeled strollers—the dads sporting thick-rimmed glasses and carefully cropped stubble. Niklas'd been struck by the phenomenon before: in Sweden, young hipsters wore the keffiyeh as if it were something cool, just another piece of clothing. For Niklas, it was just as bizarre as if people ran around in *jellabiya* and a full beard.

Summer was in high gear. Niklas felt at home. Put his sunglasses on. Thought about all the coma-like hours he'd spent on guard duty. In the heat. Always a light sand wind that hit like a gust against your cheeks and forehead.

He took a left. Up a hill. Svartensgatan. Cobblestones. Old-fashioned. Number five: from the outside, it looked like an old church. No windows above the entrance, but higher up—large clerestory windows that must illuminate a huge room inside. A small plaque next to the door: Safe Haven. A heart, the female symbol, a house. Nice. A small camera lens behind a Plexiglas bubble above the buzzer.

He buzzed.

A woman's voice: "Hi, may I help you?"

Niklas cleared his throat.

"Yes, my name is Niklas Brogren and I would like to discuss how I may be of help to Safe Haven."

The woman's voice was quiet for a brief second. Niklas expected to hear a click from the door's lock.

"I'm sorry, but we don't allow any men in here. But we are grateful for all the help we can get in other ways. You can donate money to us. Or call us at zero six forty-four zero nine twenty-five. We're open weekdays from nine to five."

Silence. Had she hung up on him? He gave it a try anyway. As humbly as he could.

"I understand. But I think you need to meet with me in order to understand. I have quite a lot to contribute." Niklas took a deep breath. Could he open up? Yes, he wanted to. "I grew up with a mother who was a victim of domestic abuse."

The woman on the other side of the camera was still there. He could hear her breathing. Finally, she said, "Oh, I understand. Your mother can call us too. At the same number. We have a website, too. But unfortunately I can't let you in. Our rules are pretty strict out of courtesy for the women we help here."

Niklas looked into the camera. This was not what he had expected. All those nights he'd fallen asleep to Mom's whimpers. All he'd been doing lately on behalf of abused women. And now—they refused to let him in. What the fuck was this?

"Wait, come on. Let me in. Please." He grabbed hold of the door handle. Pulled. It was a big door.

"I'm sorry. I'm going to turn the speaker system off soon. The women that we help have often been subjected to such traumatic experiences that they don't even want men in their surroundings. We have to respect that, and that goes for you too. I'm turning this off. Bye-bye."

There was a crackle from the speaker. Niklas pressed the buzzer down again even though he knew it was pointless. Goddammit.

What was he supposed to do now?

He took a few steps out onto Svartensgatan. Looked up at the big windows. Maybe the buzzer woman could see him. Understand that he just meant well. He thought about his conversation with the cop the other night. The cops didn't do jack shit. Safe Haven apparently didn't do jack shit either. No one gave a damn. No one did jack shit. Everyone just capitulated to the power of violence.

21

Thomas was at home all afternoon, doing nothing. Then he tried to work out a little. Boring. Gray feel to the house. Took a cold shower. Not even that gave him a kick, which it usually did. He ran his fingers over his nose. It'd healed okay.

He went down to the grocery store. Bought two car magazines. Boring, too. Gathered his courage. Called Åsa. Told her about the preliminary investigation that'd been initiated against him and the consequences it could have on his job.

She was worried. Very, very worried.

"But Thomas, nothing can happen if you get cleared, right?"

"Unfortunately things can happen anyway; they might decide to transfer me."

"Well, that doesn't sound too bad."

"I might lose my job, too."

"But you've paid unemployment insurance this past year, right?"

Of course he hadn't. Unemployment insurance was for parasites. He tried his best to calm her.

It was all so damned terrible.

At one o'clock, a guy came to install an alarm system in the house. Åsa'd wondered about that too, but he'd explained that break-ins were on the rise in the area.

An hour later: finally—he rolled into the dark under the Cadillac. The beam of light from his headlamp played across the underside of the car. It was cleaner than snow. He waited to pick up his tools. Lay still for a moment. Collected his anxieties like cogs in a row.

The man who'd stood outside his window, Ljunggren's strange behavior, the risk of being fired. The forensic pathologist who insisted that a report that was fucked all to hell was correct. Bullshit, all of it.

He thought about the murder investigation. The few cell-phone numbers that'd been called from the prepaid card didn't lead anywhere. Thomas's conversation with the forensic pathologist yielded nothing. But it'd gotten a reaction—the man outside his house. Hägerström still seemed to think they had something to go on, but Thomas didn't see what. Maybe the lab's further analysis would yield something—fabric fibers, hairs, skin cells—but the odds were low. The prepaid card number ought to lead somewhere. The drunks and junkies always used prepaid cards. Prepaid cards were the street equivalent of pin codes. If you wanted to play safe, you never got a registered phone plan.

Then he thought of something. Crazy that he and Hägerström hadn't thought of it before. Rule on the street: switch out your prepaid card as often as possible and switch out your phone as often as possible. Why would you switch out your phone if you used a prepaid card, anyway? The answer filled his head right away—because everyone knew that a phone's serial number could be tracked even to a prepaid card. In other words: every phone's individual so-called IMEI number showed up in the plan. The IMEI number was always sent to the carrier you used for every phone call that was made. He didn't know what the acronym IMEI stood for, but one thing was certain—the hunt wasn't over yet.

He rolled out from under the car. Stood up in the garage. Took off the headlamp. Stretched. Felt like he'd gotten up after an entire morning lazing around in bed. A new chance. A new day.

The thought was so clear. Life boils down to a few moments and this was one of them. A crossroads. He could choose. Either he had a seat on the bench, let some clowny detectives crush him. Let the rabble win. Or else he and Hägerström solved this thing, even if he risked losing his job doing it, even if Hägerström was a quisling. They wouldn't walk all over him.

He called Åsa again, asked when she was coming home. She would be home in an hour. Didn't dare call Hägerström from the landline or his cell phone. He considered going to police headquarters at Kronoberg to get ahold of him personally. But that wasn't a good idea—the person or persons who were monitoring him didn't need to know what was on his mind right now.

Thomas felt too worked up to roll back under the car again. He sat down in an armchair in the living room and waited. He could hear birdsong outside. It was two-thirty. Summer was in full swing. The neighborhood was silent except for a car or two that was shuttling home grocery bags and kids from soccer practice.

He turned on the stereo. The Boss, rocking.

In Thomas's mind the step was already taken. Maybe he would lose his job. Maybe worse things would happen. But this was one of those moments. When life takes a turn.

22

Mahmud and Wisam Jibril were sitting together with Beshar in the kitchen. Unlikely. Unbelievable. Totally unreal. Dad was serving coffee, wanted to hear what Wisam was up to these days. The *blatte* gave a sketchy answer. "I work with venture capital, invest in different companies. I buy all or part of the stock and try to redesign a little."

Mahmud smiled. His dad probably understood Wisam's so-called business about as much as he understood Swedish stand-up comedians on TV—but he loved it when boys from the block became successful the honest way. Too bad it was a lie.

Dad prattled on. Buzzed about old memories. About excursions to the Alby public pool and the Malmsjön lake near Södertälje, a music festival with the Caravan society, Ramadan nights in the Muslim Cultural Center. Everything used to be better. Before. Before his wife, Mahmud's mom, died. Wisam's parents'd gone back to the home country. "Maybe we should all do that," Beshar said.

Wisam nodded along. Probably to be nice to Dad. Mahmud didn't remember shit. But it was okay—this way he didn't have to come up with what to tell Wisam.

After twenty minutes, Mahmud said, "Abu, is it okay if you let us talk alone for a minute? I have to discuss some business with Wisam."

Dad told him to calm down. Remained seated for another five minutes. Babbling.

When Dad'd settled down in front of the TV in the living room, Mahmud closed the door.

"Your dad is awesome."

"Absolutely. We're a small family, as you know."

"How are your sisters doing?"

"Jamila and Jivan are good. Jamila's dude just caged out from the pen. He's an asshole."

"Why?"

"He beats her."

"Fuck that, man, but you know how some people are. They have to do that shit, or whatever. But you know what happens with people like that on the inside."

"I know. I did time, too."

"I know. How long was your stint? And what was it you didn't do?" Mahmud laughed.

"Six months. And I hadn't sold testosterone ampoules. But it's enough for a *blatte* to have broad shoulders to get nailed for shit like that."

Wisam grinned back. A couple seconds of silence. Mahmud eyed Wisam's watch: a Breitling.

"It's gotta be ten years since we were in school together. What do you live on now?"

"Life is so sweet I can taste it, you feel me? I do business, like I told your dad. Venture capital, sort of. I venture my money, but I can get fat capital back." He laughed at his own joke.

Mahmud laughed along. Acted all nice. Wanted the W-*blatte* to feel trust.

Wisam stopped himself in the middle of his laugh. "But my money is for a good cause. I donate to the Fight."

"The fight?"

"Yeah, twenty-five percent goes to the Fight. We brothers gotta understand what these fucking places, Europe and the U.S., are doing to us. They don't want us here, they don't want us to live like we want to live. They don't want to follow moral codes. Really, if you think about it, they act like the heathen monkeys they are. How did you miss the Fight? What planet've you been living on these last few years?"

"Planet Alby."

"The Zionists, the U.S., Great Britain, all are sworn enemies of us brothers. And you know, they're after me personally, too. The Serbs. You know what they did to people like us in Bosnia? They're worse than Jews."

What was he smoking? Was he kidding? Wisam sounded like fucking Osama bin Laden. Mahmud didn't want to get into that whole discussion.

Wisam kept pouring it on: U.S.A., the great Satan. The humiliation of Muslim brothers. The Western world's contempt for all righteous people.

Mahmud didn't really know what he was supposed to do now. Should he call Stefanovic right away? But he didn't, under any circumstances, want anything to go down in the apartment while Dad was home. Maybe it was better to get as much info as possible out of Wisam about where to find him later. And decide to meet up at some good place, just to be safe.

He brownnosed: "The Fight is important. The crusaders and the Zionists are humiliating our entire world."

Wisam nodded.

Mahmud switched topics. "Another thing, I heard about your business. That's why I wanted to see you. I've got an idea that I'd like to run by you. Maybe you'll dig it. Maybe you'll even want to support it."

"Shit, man. You gotta be eager for some financing. I've heard from, like, five people that you're looking for me. What's your story?"

"It's got to do with hair and tanning salons." Mahmud actually thought the idea was sweet. "You know, there are hair and tanning salons all over the city. My sister works at a tanning salon. It's crazy how people can tan and cut their hair as much as they do, but somehow it runs. The money's almost all under the table. But there's a problem, there're no chains. You follow?"

Wisam looked interested.

"We gotta do a chain, like 7-Eleven or Wayne's Coffee, except for hair and tanning salons."

"You know, chains are hard. There's crazy competition. Hard to get in, like shoving a sofa up Paris Hilton's asshole, you feel me? Not an easy thing to do. It takes investments, slick marketing, all that shit. But it's an interesting idea. I like that you're thinking business. You thought more about it? Like, what places do we buy, for example?"

Mahmud took a deep breath. This was the important part.

"I don't want to talk about it here. Not with Dad sitting in the next room. The idea isn't exactly lily white, you know what I'm sayin', and my dad is the most law-abiding person I know. And, I gotta get to the gym now. But I have a suggestion, can I buy you lunch sometime? What do you think?"

23

Niklas needed alcohol. He went into the Old Beefeater Inn on Göt-gatan. Sat down at a small table. Popped two tablets of Nitrazepam. Ordered a bottle of Staropramen. The waitress arrived with the bottle and a tall glass on a tray. Poured the beer slowly, as if it were a Guinness.

Niklas looked around. Packed with people. The big windows were open toward the street. It was four o'clock. Götgatan went through a costume change—the keffiyeh-wearing hipsters and families with kids were exchanged for a different mix of people. More Benjamin's style: beefy boys with tattoos, tired-looking broads with frizzy hair, young guys in soccer jerseys.

The beer tasted good in the heat. He ordered another one before he'd even drained half the glass. Staropramen, the spring of life.

Niklas's thoughts were spinning. Safe Haven'd given him the cold shoulder. But the battered women out there'd just been given rein-forcement by elite forces number one. The mercenary who gutted more dirty men than a dull Swedish cop could even count. It was time for an offensive strategy, a mission on enemy territory. He'd trained eight years for this.

He fingered his concealed backup knife. It was strapped to his leg, as always. Sipped his beer. Wiped the foam from his upper lip.

Calculated: in Sweden, people always got off work around five o'clock. In an hour, someone ought to come out of Safe Haven.

He ordered another beer.

The air outside was still warm. People were walking slowly back and forth along Götgatan, scouting outdoor spots at the bars and restau-rants. So far, the mood was calm, but in a few hours, loud male roars would explode the night like mortars.

He leaned against the fence across from the entrance to Safe Haven. Waited. The time: quarter to five.

Thought about how he would introduce himself. If he should explain what he wanted right away, or if he should talk about other stuff first. Decided not to refer to the conversation over the intercom system.

Finally, the front door opened. A slight woman dressed in jeans and a jean jacket came out. A shoulder bag slung over one shoulder and a bike helmet in hand. He wondered if she was the one he'd spoken to earlier. He had to act now, or else she would get away on her bike.

Niklas stepped forward.

"Hi, my name is Niklas and I think I can be of help to you."

The woman looked jumpy. Scanned the street. Seemed to be searching for an answer.

"No, I think you're mistaken. I don't think we know each other. Have a nice day."

"Wait. We don't know each other. But I know about you. You're doing good work."

The woman tried to smile. "Are you the person I spoke to on the intercom two hours ago? I'm sorry, I don't think I can help you. But here, take a card and give it to your mother."

This didn't feel right. Perplexing. Confusing. Infuriating. She was turning him down again. What the fuck were they doing at Safe Haven? Here they had a golden opportunity and they didn't even give a damn about it.

He raised his voice: "You've got to believe me. I just want to help you. Why don't we get a beer somewhere so I can tell you more?"

"Sorry, I have to go home now. You'll have to call us instead, during our open hours."

"No, wait. I want to tell you here and now. I used to be a soldier."

The woman started walking toward her bike, which was locked to the fence Niklas'd been leaning against earlier.

Niklas grabbed her arm. "Wait."

She spun around. Eyes wide. "Please, let me go." Her tone was sharp. She was a traitor. If she wasn't going to make more of an effort for the cause, she might as well go fuck herself. If Safe Haven was going to turn down his services, they didn't really want to fight.

He held on to her. "I'm only going to say this one more time. We are going to go talk about this right now."

The woman started screaming. A few yards down the street, two girls in their twenties stopped in their tracks. Niklas wondered where the hell they'd been three seconds ago. But now they were standing there like two idiots, staring. Fumbling for their cell phones.

Niklas made a grab for the woman's shoulder bag. She screamed something about an assault. He tugged at the bag. He was going to get something out of this, goddammit.

Got ahold of it. Pulled. Ran.

The woman shrieked.

He ran down the hill. Heard yelling behind him. Was it the chicks with the cell phones? He headed for the subway. Almost fell down the escalator. It felt like people were hollering. Someone tried to stop him. He ran down the platform.

A train rolled into the station. He jumped on.

The doors closed.

Inside: almost empty. Serene. Stuffy. Still.

He was holding the woman's shoulder bag in his hand.

Opened it.

Paper. A planner. A wallet. A hairbrush. Junk.

Looked again: documents. Information about Safe Haven. Suggested strategies for battered women. Drafts of texts for a website. And a list: women's names and phone numbers. It could only be one thing: battered women. The woman he'd just grabbed the bag from was probably going to call them.

This was huge. An opening. The names of ten women whom Niklas could help. Behind the names: ten men who were going to get what was coming to them.

Two thoughts collided in his head: He was going to find them. He would do his thing to them.

Niklas'd found his calling. His mission. Everything had new meaning. The offensive had begun.

24

The big question: How dangerous could this get for Åsa? Thomas planned to act on his own. Screw the guy outside his window. Screw Adamsson's recommendations—the old-timer was not on his side this time, that much was obvious. Fuck anyone who wanted to stop him. Move ahead with the search for the IMEI number and the prepaid card owner's identity. Find the person who'd murdered a still unidentified man.

Today: Monday. The first day of his foray into the world of detectives. Kurt Wallander, you can hit the showers. Thomas Andrén's in town.

Åsa left home early as usual. She'd wanted to make love again last night. Thomas felt stiffer than he'd felt in ages. Åsa massaged his back, rubbed massage oil on him. Slow motions over his shoulder blades. Hard, softening pinches over the shoulders. She ran the palms of her hands along his lower back. Exactly what he needed. The problem started when she began licking his earlobe. Thomas pulled his head away—it tickled. She wouldn't leave him be. Åsa stroked the inside of his thigh. He settled one leg over the other. She stroked his chest. He lay still. Finally, she gave up. Rolled over to her side of the bed.

Thomas called Hägerström at ten o'clock that morning.

He sounded out of breath when he picked up.

"Hi, it's me."

"Andrén, I think you're bad luck."

"What're you talking about?"

"I just got transferred. Cut off from the investigation."

Thomas looked out the window. Didn't see anyone on the street. What he'd just heard made him feel cold all over.

"What're you talking about? That can't be true. You've got to be kidding me."

"I'm kidding about as little as the boys from Internal Affairs are kidding about you right now. Got called into my boss's office today. Apparently, it was inappropriate that I continue with the investigation on the grounds that you'd been involved and that you're suspended now on suspicion of grave professional misconduct and assault. My boss said it was best that everyone involved was switched out."

"But come on, that's totally insane. It's a conspiracy."

"Yes, it is insane. I don't know what to think. Why the hell did you have to beat up that drunk, anyway?"

"Hey, I don't want to hear that crap. That guy was lethal and they'd paired me up with a hundred-thirty-pound girl. We were forced to use the batons. So you can back off."

Hägerström's shortness of breath seemed to increase on the other end of the line.

"I'm from IA, don't you forget that. The kind of nauseating rationalization you're pulling made my ears rot long ago. There are always excuses, blah, blah, blah. But it's bullshit. You made a fool of yourself, used excessive force against a human being, which I know you've done many times before."

"Hägerström, cut it out. Don't be such a fucking cunt."

"Apparently you think you can talk to me any way you like. It was nice getting to know you too. Good-bye."

Hägerström slammed the phone down.

Thomas continued to stare out the window. Phone still in his hand. Even Hägerström refused to understand how the situation in Aspudden'd ended up the way it did. IA's stained way of thinking apparently didn't wash out too easily. What a fucking asshole. Impossible to understand how that man could've ever seemed even remotely pleasant.

Now he was alone. Alone against an unknown threat. Alone against an internal investigation. Alone in the hunt for a murderer.

He lay down on the bed. Didn't even want to tinker with the car. Didn't want to set his foot in the station. Get stared down, whispered about, gossiped over.

He tried to take a nap. Pointless—it was only ten-thirty. He wasn't tired, but still completely beat.

His brain felt empty.

He remained lying where he was. Didn't have the strength to get up.

He must've fallen asleep after all. His cell phone woke him. He felt groggy. Fumbled for the phone. Didn't recognize the number. Tried to hide how confused and drowsy he was.

"Hello, this is Andrén."

"Hi, my name is Stefan Rudjman. I don't know if you know me?" Slight accent. Thomas didn't recognize the voice. At the same time: the last name rang a bell.

"People also call me Stefanovic."

Thomas was skeptical. Hostile attitude. Could this have something to do with the threat against him and Åsa the other night?

"Okay, what do you want?"

"I understand that you've gotten into some trouble at work. We have an offer for you that we think may be very attractive."

"Know what? Your threats don't bother me."

Stefanovic was silent a second too long—was it genuine surprise or a threatening theatrical pause?

"I am afraid you misunderstand me. This is not a matter of threats at all. We think our offer may provide you with unforeseen possibilities. It's regarding a job. Would you like to meet with us?"

Thomas didn't understand what the guy was talking about. Cockiness mixed with a Slavic accent. Something wasn't right.

"I don't know who you are and I don't understand what this is about. Would you please be so kind as to tell me what job it is you're talking about?"

"With pleasure. But I think it's better if we meet up. Then I can explain in more detail. The conditions may be advantageous for you. Why not give it a chance? Meet us and discuss it. When might you be available?"

Thomas didn't know what to say. Was this some damn telemarketing scheme? Was it a practical joke? On the other hand: he didn't have anything better to do. Everything'd gone to hell anyway. He might as well meet this guy, whoever he was.

"I'm available today."

"That's better than expected. We'll pick you up. Shall we say four o'clock? Is that suitable?"

They took the tunnel under Södermalm, the south side of the city. Rush hour hadn't started yet. Out on Sveavägen. Took a right toward

Roslagstull. And down Valhallavägen. Then Lidingövägen. Turned off toward Fiskartorpsvägen.

Thomas wondered where they were going. The man driving'd introduced himself as Slobodan and asked Thomas to get into the backseat of a Range Rover.

They drove in silence. Thomas wished he had his service weapon, but he'd been forced to turn it in once the internal investigation began.

Along the side of the road he could see the mixed vegetation in the Lill-Jansskogen forest.

They turned onto a narrow gravel road and up a hill.

Finally, the car stopped. Slobodan asked him to get out.

They were on a height. A building in front of him: a sixty-five-foot tower. It must be Lill-Jansskogen's ski-jumping tower. Thomas remembered it from his childhood. He'd been there with his parents. The winters were so much more wintry back then. Someone appeared to have renovated the tower recently. The concrete was almost gleaming in the sunlight.

A burly man walked toward him. He looked to be in his thirties. Dressed in dark-blue pleated slacks and a well-ironed shirt.

The man extended his hand.

"Hi, Thomas. I'm glad you could come so soon. I'm Stefanovic."

Stefanovic showed Thomas into the tower.

The bottom floor looked clean and new. An empty welcome desk with a computer screen mounted on it. There was a poster on the wall: WELCOME TO FISKARTORPET'S CONFERENCE HALL. WE CAN ACCOMMODATE UP TO FIFTY GUESTS. PERFECT FOR YOUR KICK-OFF, COMPANY PARTY, OR CONFERENCE. The floor looked like it'd recently been sanded and finished.

Thomas followed the Yugo up the stairs. Couldn't be much of a conference center yet—it was empty everywhere.

At the top of the tower was a large room. Windows in three directions. Thomas looked out over the Lill-Jansskogen forest. Over Östermalm. Farther off, he could see City Hall, the church spires, and the high rises by Hötorget. The farthest he could see: a glimpse of the Globen arena. Stockholm was spread out before him.

A sofa group, a dining table with six chairs, a minibar against the one windowless wall, filled with bottles and stemware. In the sofa group: a man. He rose. Walked slowly over to Thomas. Shook his hand with a firm grip.

"Hi, Thomas. Thank you for coming on such short notice. It's fantastic. My name is Radovan Kranjic. I don't know if you've heard of me." The man had the same Slavic accent as Stefanovic.

Thomas understood right away. The man in front of him wasn't just anybody. Radovan Kranjic: alias the Yugo Boss, alias R., alias Stockholm's Godfather. A man whom the little guys hardly dared mention by name. Whose reputation was harder than granite. A legend in Stockholm's underworld. It felt bizarre. At the same time, exciting.

"Yes, I've heard of you. You have—how shall I put it?—a certain reputation in my line of work."

Radovan smiled. The dude radiated authority like Marlon Brando.

"People talk a lot. But as far as I've understood it, *you* have a certain reputation as well."

Normally, Thomas would've gotten defensive right away when someone implied something like that. But with this guy—in a way, they were cut from the same cloth; he could feel it instinctively. So instead, he laughed.

They took a seat on the couches. "May I offer you something strong?" Radovan asked.

Thomas said yes. Stefanovic poured two glasses of whiskey. Good stuff: Isle of Jura, aged sixteen years.

Radovan scratched his cheek with the back of his hand. Reminiscent of Don Corleone for real.

The Yugo boss began explaining. Outlined his business. He worked with horses, cars, boats, import/export. A lot from the former Soviet Union. Benzes driven up from Germany. Machine parts from retired Swedish factories to Polish coal plants. It was business development, expansion, and opportunities. Thomas listened. Wondered if Radovan actually believed his own spiel.

Finally: Radovan seemed to be getting to the point. He sipped his drink. "Okay. So, now you know what it is I work with primarily. But I do some other stuff on the side, too. I'm active in what we call the erotica business, if you know what I mean. The subject's gotten so touchy in Sweden these days. We try to provide our customers with the most pleasant environment and staff possible. Erotica doesn't have to be filthy movie theaters where lonely men sneak in at night. Erotica can be professional, businesslike, and well managed. After all, erotica is the world's largest form of entertainment. Our girls are classy and maintain high international standards. Do you understand what I'm getting at?"

Thomas sat in silence. Wound tight. At the same time, elated. What was this all about? Why was Stockholm's most powerful mafia boss sitting here and telling him about the next big thing in pimping? Was it a test? Had they gotten hold of the wrong person? Was this connected to the murder investigation he and Hägerström'd been caught up in?

Then he realized that Radovan'd asked him a question. He met the Yugo boss's gaze. "I think I understand what you're getting at."

Radovan went on, "You can make yourself money when you're young. With money you get boats, fast whips, babes. Whatever you want. But when you get older, like me, you want something more— control over the situation. The ability to feel at ease. And that's where you come in, Thomas. I have, as you noted, a certain reputation. But so do you. We need people like you in our organization. Men who don't back down when the situation calls for some extra effort. Men who don't follow narrow rules out of old habit, but who think about what is right and rational instead. Men who are men, to put it simply."

Radovan made a theatrical pause. Let the flattery sink in.

Thomas dropped his gaze. Looked out over Stockholm again.

"You're a cop, I'm aware of that. That's what makes you so interesting. You've got connections, credibility, insight. At the same time, we know that you, just like me, write your own rules when you need to. It's important to have your own rules, you know. Without your own rules, you won't get far in life. We have information that you do some things on the side now and then. You're a cop who does everything, as people usually say. We need people like you."

Thomas didn't respond.

Radovan went on, "Let me make this brief. You're probably going to lose your job because you defended yourself and your female colleague against an inebriated animal. I can turn that catastrophe into a new beginning for you. I want to hire you for my organization."

25

Mahmud'd talked to his Yugo contact for a helluva long time—the perfect place'd been decided: Saman's Coal Grill in Tumba. It had outdoor seating, there were a lot of people in motion around there, the right kind of joint for a *blatte* like Mahmud to meet up at. Not suspicious. The only downside he could think of was that it was hard to park nearby.

They were gonna meet up at five on Tuesday afternoon. Wisam'd suggested the time himself. Jibril dug Mahmud's chosen meeting spot. "Our kind of grub," he'd said.

Tumba in the summer: almost empty of people except for some teens with too little to do. Mahmud arrived at a quarter to five, grabbed a table near the exit.

Beyond the outdoor seating area, parked more or less on the sidewalk: a pimped Range Rover with tinted windows. Mahmud glimpsed Ratko. Both hands resting on the steering wheel, steel expression. If the 5-0 or some ticket bitch showed up he'd have to move right away. On the other side of the street: a BMW with even darker windows. Mahmud couldn't see who was sitting in it, but his contact, Stefanovic, had instructed him, "If anything derails, you call me. I'll be nearby."

Mahmud waited. Eyed the kids farther down the street. He saw himself in them. Thought about the little marijuana plantation that Robert'd had in that apartment he'd been house-sitting for his aunt.

He wondered why Wisam didn't show. He'd sounded upbeat on the phone the day before. Mahmud was proud of the hair-and-tanning-salon buzz, the made-up business ideas he'd pulled in Dad's kitchen—really, it was Jamila's idea. And all that about the Fight. Mahmud knew the talk—he'd met friends from before who didn't talk about anything else. The U.S.'s hate toward the righteous around the world. The Jewish conspiracy to start a war against the Muslims by plotting 9/11. Great Britain's colonial imperialist capitalism. But Mahmud knew better: cash was king. The secret Jew Americans who sought to repress *blattes* like him didn't have enough power. The British clown-lords who wanted to dominate his brothers—their days were pretty numbered. Lack of cash was the problem. And the answer was simple. His people needed dough. As soon as you got money, everything got solved. Especially for him.

Quarter past five. Wisam still hadn't shown. Stefanovic'd instructed him: we can't wait with the Range Rover for more than twenty minutes. The risk of whiny meter maids and cops was too great.

A couple minutes passed. Mahmud didn't understand what'd happened.

He eyed the clock on his phone. Eighteen minutes past five. Suck a dick.

And then, by the pedestrian crossing—there he was: Wisam. Track pants. Hoodie. Sneakers. Real Million style. Mahmud was surprised by his own thought: Am I doing the right thing? The guy is like me. A project *blatte* with swag. My brother.

No way. He had to let the thought go.

Wisam passed the Range Rover. Saw Mahmud. Nodded. At the same time: two guys jumped out of the car. Dark jeans. Leather jackets. Yugo *classique*. Stepped up behind Wisam. One said something to him. The other was hiding something in his hand. Put it against Wisam's stomach. The *blatte*'s eyes grew wide. Looked down at the thing against his stomach. After that, it was like he grew limp. The beefcakes led him into the Range Rover. It started up.

Mahmud stood up. Slapped a hundred-kronor bill on the table. Left the change.

Saw the Range Rover drive up a side street. Disappear.

* * *

It was always quiet down in the basement. But the silence didn't bother Niklas. He actually liked it, it gave him time to think. But he hated the dark. Or, rather, the risk that the dark would come. Because if you didn't flip the timed switch often enough, the lights would switch off automatically. He had devised his own simple system. He flipped the switch every other minute so as not to risk it. It was lucky that he knew how to tell time.

When he got down there, he pulled out the table-hockey game. It was old. The outer players couldn't move behind the goalie like in the newer games.

But the goalie himself could move behind the goal, which was a big danger—to leave the net unattended. But now it didn't matter—he couldn't trick himself, after all. Instead, he practiced passes. The right wing to the center, who made a goal. The center back to the right wing, who whipped the puck with the back of his stick into the net.

He was really pretty good. Too bad they didn't have a table-hockey game at his after-school program.

Still, time crawled.

He flipped the light switch at even intervals. He had time to do about fifteen strings of passes between times.

Mom should've come down ages ago to tell him to come back up. It was already nine-thirty.

Maybe he should go up on his own. But he wanted to wait. One time he hadn't waited—when he'd tired of the table-hockey game he'd taken the elevator up of his own accord. The living room and kitchen were empty and the door to Mom's bedroom was closed. He called for her without getting an answer. He called again and finally heard her yell from her bedroom, "Stay where you are, Niklas. I'll be out."

Mom came out dressed in a bathrobe—which was strange—and she was really mad. She grabbed his arm, hard, harder than he could ever remember her doing before, and threw him on his bed. Then she yelled at him for a while. Without him really understanding why.

No, he wasn't going to go upstairs of his own accord. She had to come down and get him.

He kept practicing strings of passes at the goal.

A half hour went by. He kept track of the time well since he was flipping the light switch every other minute.

The hockey game was boring, he thought. Tedious: pass from the wing to the defenseman, make shooting motions using his entire arm, usher the puck into the goal, the left defenseman back to the wing, wrist shot, straight in. The monotony made him tired. But what should he do?

He heard a strange sound.

Behind the hockey game.

Something rustling.

He looked carefully. Followed the wall.

An animal.

It stared at him from its perch on the moving box. A rat.

A huge black rat. The eyes were blank, evil, porcelain marbles. The tail like a long worm on the box.

The terror grabbed hold of him at once. Fear that welled up from his gut. He didn't dare move.

The rat sat still. Seemed to be watching him.

Niklas stood even more still. The only thing he could think was, Please don't let it jump at me, please don't let it touch me.

Then the lights went out.

And he screamed. He screamed like he'd never screamed before. Everything came at once: the tears, the horror, the panic. He bawled out his terror, his fear of the dark and the animal that'd been staring at him.

He fumbled for the light switch. At the same time, it felt like his entire brain would explode at the thought of accidentally touching the animal.

Where was the light switch?

He searched with his hands along the wall in quick motions. Hoped that this would scare the rat away.

Finally, he found it.

He turned the lights on. Tumbled toward the door. Opened it. Sprinted up from the basement to the ground floor. Skipped the elevator. Ran up all the seven flights of stairs in one go.

Tore open the front door. Breathless, with a sob still stuck in his throat.

As soon as he came in, he was struck by another kind of panic. The rat was forgotten. The sounds he heard killed off all his other fears. The screams were coming from the living room. He knew them so well. He'd heard them so many times before.

The coffee table was pushed aside toward the TV. All three sofa cushions were scattered on the floor. A beer lay spilled nearby. Beside the sofa was his mother, on her knees.

Above her stood Claes, beating her.

Niklas started screaming.

Mom was crying. She was bleeding from the nose and her blouse was torn over the shoulder.

Claes turned to him. His fist was still held high in the air. "Go back down to the basement, Niklas."

Then he let his fist fall. It hit her across the back.

She looked at Niklas. Their eyes met. He saw terror. He saw sorrow and pain. He saw love. But he also saw something else—he saw hate. And he could feel it clearly, clearer than he'd ever felt anything—he hated Claes. More than anything in the world.

She called to him, "Please Niklas, it's okay. Go to your room. Please."

Claes's fist fell again. He roared. "You fucking cunt, you care more about that little shit than me."

Mom screamed. Collapsed.

Claes kicked her belly.

Niklas ran into his room. Before he closed the door he saw Claes kick her again. This time in the head.

He shut his eyes and covered his ears with his hands.

The sounds pushed their way through.

He tried to think about the rat in the basement.

PART 2

(Two months later)

26

Time flies when you have a calling. A life mission. A mantra: *Si vis pacem, para bellum*. If you wish for peace, prepare for war.

Niklas jogged three times a week. Followed by push-ups, stomach and back exercises. Trained with his knife every day. Practiced the breathing, the control, the feeling. Prepared himself. Exerted himself. One principle was certain: a small war demands as thorough preparation as a big war. The only difference: the number of boots on the ground.

Today, he ran his regular loop. Over the Aspudden school's paved yard. Four stories of yellowish brick, high windows that let in good light. Not like the Afghan mud bunkers where seven kids shared one textbook. The playground was swarming with kids. School must've started again after the summer. Niklas eyed them. Wild, screaming, undisciplined. Still undecided what he thought about kids, anyway. He saw the divide. The guys on one side, the girls on the other. And the subgroups: the nerds, the jocks, the dangerous ones. He saw the violence. A boy, ten years old max, jeans with tears over the knees: pushed a girl who looked to be the same age. She fell. Cried. Lay there by herself. Alone in the world. The boy ran back to his group of friends. Into the camaraderie, the safety of the group. Niklas deliberated: step up, teach the kid a thing or two about pushing people around. Make him feel thirty times more vulnerable than the girl. But now wasn't the time.

It was the end of August. The sun warmed in an unconvincing way: just the hint of a cool breeze and this would turn into a chilly run.

The past few weeks'd been hectic, valuable, illuminating. His strategy was taking shape. The swarm of conflicts was clearing up. The time for attack was drawing closer. *Si vis pacem, para bellum*.

He felt the heat rise in his body. First his gut. Then his legs and head.

He reflected over the past few months.

Two days after he'd gotten hold of the list of women's names from the girl at Safe Haven, he'd gone to a 7-Eleven and bought surf time on the computers. Paper and pen in front of him. Googled the names and telephone numbers. He couldn't find a full name or address for three of them; maybe they were unlisted. He took notes: a total of seven full names with addresses attached to them. Wondered what the woman from Safe Haven was supposed to do with the numbers. Probably work from home or something, make support calls, coddle the poor souls. Even though everyone knew what was really needed—someone to pacify their men.

He sat thinking. How to search further? Brainstormed possible information sources. Only came up with one—Skatteverket, the national tax authority. Called, checked if the women were married and to whom, or if someone else was listed as a resident at the address in question. At the end of the day he'd written down the names of six men plus their addresses. Six abusers—six enemy combatants.

The following day. Niklas made his first investment—a DCU, as he called it: data control unit. In other words, he bought a laptop and ordered high-speed Internet.

That whole week: He worked on ideas on the computer. Took notes. Created folders for different proposals, information on every person on the list. Four days later, his Internet was installed. Now he could start researching for real. He tried to organize. Theorize. Analyze.

First and foremost: he needed a car. But other things too: equipment for private espionage. A reverse door-peephole viewer, waterproof surveillance cameras, extra camera lenses, wall mikes, earpieces, night-vision binoculars, recording devices, fake license plates. A ton of stuff.

He searched for cars on used-car sites online. Niklas hadn't lived a life with a close connection to the Internet, but he'd managed to snoop out info about the men. Still, he was a novice: it took half a day to learn the ropes. Which search engines generated relevant hits, which car sites had the best selection, where you could deal with private people and didn't have to mess with companies, where he could find normally priced future APCs—armored personnel carriers—with four-wheel drive.

He knew next to nothing at this point. He didn't know when/where/how he was going to need the car. If something was going to have to be transported in it, if he might be shot at by the police, on what kind of terrain it would be driven. Only two things were decided: He had to begin watching the men right away. And the car had to have tinted windows.

First, he checked out a Jeep Grand Cherokee from 2006. In the ad, the seller claimed: extremely good condition, only nine thousand miles, diesel engine. Sounded perfect, the car could handle any terrain. The back windows: big, dark, no visibility. The downside: the price—they wanted three hundred G's for it. Niklas went out to Stocksund, a ritzy suburb, just to be on the safe side. The car was nice, would've been perfect. He was sitting on savings, but war cost money. There'd be more expenses than just the car. He had to watch his wallet.

The next alternative: a four-wheel drive Audi Avant from 2002. Seemed awesome: complete service history, GPS, side air bags, winter tires with rims, xenon headlights, tinted windows. The whole shebang. Niklas couldn't care less about the fenders, the wheels, the interior, and stuff like that. But the GPS—it hit him: a navigator was exactly what he needed. He wasn't exactly a pro at finding his way around Stockholm yet. What's more, the ad said the car'd been driven by a chick. The price: two hundred grand, more than okay. *Very good condition, well taken care of! Call to take a look.* He punched the numbers into his phone.

The car was being sold by someone named Nina Glavmo-Svensén in Edsviken, Sollentuna.

Vikingavägen: leafy Sven dreamscape. He tinkered with his waist belt. The money order was in there. One hundred and eighty thousand. Also: twenty thousand cash in case there wasn't any room for haggling. Thanked DynCorp for his financial circumstances. Without their know-how, his money would've been paid in cash down there. But now: their connections with banks all over the world solved that problem. Put the money straight into Chase Manhattan's office, which transferred it directly, via an affiliate in Nassau with better privacy regulations, to safe old Handelsbanken in Stockholm. The remainder of Niklas's savings after the fiasco in Macao: 500,000 kronor. And now he was going to blow almost half the money.

Number twenty-one. A two-story yellow-painted wood house with a garage. In the garden: two fruit trees past blooming. A sprinkler and an inflatable baby pool on the lawn. It was too good to be true. There had to be some dirt hiding behind the perfect façade.

Niklas rang the doorbell.

A woman opened. The seller, Nina Glavmo-Svensén. For about three seconds, Niklas was speechless. He hadn't expected that the seller would be his age. Did people who hadn't even turned thirty yet live in houses like this? He didn't know what to say. Nina Glavmo-Svensén: hot as hell. Dressed in shorts and a tank top. Crooked smile. A baby on her hip. Niklas couldn't judge how old it was or if it was a girl or a boy.

He extended his hand, "Hi, I'm Johannes. I wanted to take a look at your car." A good alias, Johannes.

Nina seemed surprised. Smiled nervously.

Niklas laughed.

Nina looked into his eyes. He returned her gaze. What did he see in there? What was her life like? Who had decided that the car had to be sold? Was it her decision or was there someone else who made the decisions around here? He thought he saw a darkness in her eyes, a hint of sorrow. It wasn't impossible.

"Good thing you didn't drive here, it can be hard to find the way."

They laughed. The mood relaxed.

It was cool in the garage. Three parked cars. The Audi, a Volvo V70, and a black Porsche 911. Niklas pointed to the Porsche. "It was two hundred for that one, right?" Again: laughter.

He checked out the Audi. Good: it wouldn't attract attention. All the windows but the windshield were tinted. Plenty of space if you folded the backseat down. The xenon headlights gave better distribution of light when driving in the dark. Maybe it wasn't quite like the Jeep he'd looked at, but the four-wheel drive should be able to handle most terrains. Nina didn't know exactly how the GPS worked, but Niklas could figure that out on his own. She hadn't driven it many miles and the service history seemed complete. Couldn't be better. It would be his—he just had to bring the price down first.

She showed him where the winter tires were. Niklas rolled one out. Examined it.

"You don't exactly want to think of the winter on a sunny day like today. But these tires are not okay. Much too worn down." He pressed his finger down as far as it would go. "The tread depth here is only a few millimeters."

They discussed the car. The winter tires apparently came from another car. The kid on her hip remained calm. Nina smiled at Niklas, laughed at his attempts at jokes. After ten minutes, he said, "I'm very interested in the car. I'll take it right now for one-eighty. I'm going to need to buy new winter tires, after all."

Nina gazed into his eyes again. "One-eighty should be okay. But then you can't have it now. I have to discuss it with my husband when he comes home tonight."

Again. Niklas's thoughts flashed: under what conditions did this woman really live? What had her baby been forced to witness in this sun-drenched house? His thoughts were spinning, worse and worse. He made an effort. Tried to smile. "What about one-ninety?"

Nina extended her hand. "We've got a deal."

Meanwhile, he'd gotten a job. As a security guard, after all. He sat in a sentry box and controlled vehicles on their way in and out of the pharmaceutical company Biovitrum's complex in Solna. Wasn't even allowed to carry a weapon. Flipped through magazines. The boredom worse than patrolling barbed-wire fences in a sandstorm.

But all the stuff he'd ordered had arrived. It was lined up and waiting on the floor of his apartment.

The base package for eavesdropping through walls: a MW-22 unit. According to the operating instructions, it could handle listening through twelve-inch-thick concrete walls, windows, doors, without a problem. Equipped with an RCA jack: the ability to connect digital functions.

A GPS locating system for vehicles—for cars he needed to track in real time, but couldn't break into. The system was built into a water-proof protective case with powerful magnets and was secured on the underside of the car's body. It ran on twelve batteries—the car could be followed over the course of a week with up to five-second updates without the batteries dying. Heavenly high-tech.

There were two types of cameras. First, three CCD cameras for outdoor use, 480TVL, 25-millimeter lens, black-and-white, 0.05 Lux. They were waterproof and could handle temperatures as low as nega-tive thirteen degrees. Should work for the men who lived in single-family homes. In addition, four small surveillance cameras for concealed application. Could be mounted in junction boxes, in wire covers, under lamps, in fuse boxes. Perfect for the apartment dwellers.

A bunch of regular bugs: small mikes with radio transmitter.

A hard drive. Could hold several days' worth of recordings and transmit remote monitoring through the Internet and other net-works. Could handle four surveillance cameras at once. The heart of his operation.

Finally, the small stuff: the reverse door-peephole viewer, extra lenses for the cameras, two different license plates for the car, binoculars, a ladder, the right clothes, books, tools.

He'd already blown more than seventy-five grand. War was expensive—an eternal truth. With luck, it would total less than three hundred grand. He really needed to keep working his security guard job. DynCorps' money wouldn't last forever. More expenses awaited. More missions to complete. He regretted his naïveté—why'd he try his luck in Macao?

Still: the Internet was magical. In four weeks, he'd built up an FBI-style hub. Now he just had to get the crap mounted.

He called in sick from work. Sat at home in his apartment from eight in the morning until eight at night: practiced with the gear. Hooked up the cameras one by one. Read the manual as thoroughly as if he were building a nuclear reactor. Tested, tested, tested. Poured water on the outdoor cameras, checked their resistance to shock, put them in the freezer. Learned to apply the mini cameras, to conceal them, to pull their cables along edges and borders to locations where the receiver unit could be placed. Played around with the MPEG hard drive, connected it to his TV at home. Repeated the procedure with the cameras without the manual. Assembled them in the dark. With only one hand. By heart. Tried out the wiretap equipment on the girl next door. Her guy'd either split or stayed away. He heard how she talked on the phone or watched miniseries on TV. The equipment was sick: the beeping sound when she punched numbers into her cell phone sounded as though she were standing twenty inches away. He assembled the GPS system. Secured it under the Audi. Drove around Örnsberg. The box stayed in place under the car, made it through the speed bump on Hägerstensvägen. He checked the receiver. Worked better than the worn-out gear he'd operated in the sandbox. He drove around and checked out where the different men lived. Learned the maps, the blind alleys, the stoplights, the one-way streets. Continued to test out the gear at home, learned to use it better than he'd mastered his firearms down there. He analyzed methodology, memorized locations, planned. Hardly talked to Mom, didn't think about the murder in the basement at her place, stopped having nightmares. Responded sparingly to Benjamin's texts. Didn't give a shit about the doctor's note he needed for his disability leave. Time passed. The war would soon be upon them.

———

The following weeks, he went to work as much as he could. They wondered what the hell he was doing, screwing around with the schedule as if it was a grab-a-beer-with-a-bud appointment that you really couldn't care less about. But what could he do: *Si vis pacem, para bellum*. The mission took time.

During the bright summer evenings and nights, he sat in the Audi outside the apartment complexes or houses where they lived. Tried to guage the situation. Which ones he should begin with.

All six of them were normal dudes. From the outside. They didn't have particularly late habits on weeknights. Niklas set the cameras up during three nights in the beginning of August. Worked in silence. It was easy: he'd already zeroed in on the spots where he'd put them. Felt so good not to have to deal with daytime noise pollution: cell phones ringing, the rush of traffic, neighbors pounding on each other. Outside one house: a CCD camera in a tree. Outside the other house: the camera in a bush behind an electrical cabinet. The apartments were harder. How would he be able to see into them? One of the apartments was on the ground floor. He hid the camera in a stairwell on the other side of the street. The distance was a little too great, but it would do for the kinds of photos he needed. The other three apartments wouldn't work. He'd have to guard them personally.

The only thing he wanted to know: Who were the three biggest assholes? Who should he focus on? Him: a pro. Ice water running through his veins. He could wait.

Back in the present. On his way back over Vinterviken's allotment gardens. He didn't see any war scenes today. No blood. No ambush. He thought maybe it was because he was about to begin his own ambush. The weeks'd gone so well. Him: a hunter. A predator. A man who made his mark on history. Who changed circumstances.

The sweat ran down over his eyebrows. His eyes stung. He wiped his forehead with his T-shirt.

The only thing he needed now was a firearm.

It had to come to an end. The rats.

The men.

The enemy combatants.

27

Gloria Palace, Playa de Amadores, Gran Canaria. They could've gone to a flashier place: Aruba, Mauritius, or the Seychelles. But what were they supposed to do there? The only reason Thomas made the trip was to get away. And to calm Åsa.

Still: the hotel, Gloria Palace, had four and a half stars from the charter travel company. You couldn't top that on Gran Canaria. Big rooms with panorama windows looking out over the ocean. A small sofa set and a coffee table with a basket that room service filled with fresh fruit every day. Over thirty channels on the TV, an in-house movie channel, Swedish newspapers, amazing breakfast. One of the pools, the one with seventy-seven-degree water, lay only a few feet away from the Atlantic—you looked out over the waves washing in while calming Muzak played from the hotel speakers. Not to mention the gym: the machines looked like they were bought yesterday. After a workout, his hands smelled of new plastic instead of cop sweat. He worked out every day. It was everything he'd imagined, but better. Åsa loved it. Thomas tried to relax.

His dirty money came in handy. Åsa wondered how they could afford to stay at the closest she'd ever come to a luxury hotel. But it wasn't that expensive, and Thomas explained that they were spending prize money he'd won at the shooting club. He wasn't going to pinch pennies. Åsa could get as many treatments as she liked at the hotel's Thalasso Treatment Center. He rented a Jet Ski and tried scuba diving, tested his swing at the nine-hole golf course, went out for an all-day fishing trip on a boat with some middle-aged Germans. Every night, they ate a three-course meal at one of the à la carte restaurants or took the panorama-view elevator up to the walk on the mountainous strip above the hotel and wandered to Dunas Amadores, the hotel next door.

He grew a beard for the first time, surprised himself every morning in the mirror. It itched, he tried to trim it—but man, it was nice not to have to shave. Åsa claimed that it was prickly. But really: they'd been away for almost two weeks and hadn't had sex once. Okay, maybe they kissed sometimes, but you could count the number of kisses on the fingers of one hand. Both of them knew the beard wasn't to blame.

Sometimes he thought he should go to therapy. He loved Åsa—so why didn't she turn him on? Why did it work better in front of the computer screen than with a real woman? At the same time: therapy wasn't his thing. What if someone found out?

They were each sitting in a beach chair on the sun terrace. Smeared with the right SPF. The pool's clear-blue water lapped peacefully. The hotel towered up behind them like a mountain. Eighty degrees out. Gran Canaria was good in that way: the Atlantic climate didn't turn it into the same kind of oven as, say, Sicily—where they'd been last year.

He tried to read a Dennis Lehane paperback: *Darkness, Take My Hand.* Let it lie on his belly. Restless, couldn't read for too long, even though it was a real page-turner. The dialogue was the best he'd ever read.

Åsa lay with her eyes closed, shiny with lotion and sweat. She was "baking," as she called it. Listening to an audio book. He looked out over the people on the terrace. This wasn't the worst kind of family-friendly hotel. Neither he nor Åsa would've been able to handle seeing happy parents cuddling with their fat little four-year-olds around the edge of the pool every day. The hotel was populated mostly by couples a few years younger than themselves—no kids—and older people in their sixties. As well as a bunch of super chill groups of friends. Four guys who weren't a day over twenty-five were sitting at the pool bar. Downed parasol drinks like it was light beer. Thomas liked their style. Saw himself the way he'd been a few years ago. What was even better: up and down in the pool, a group of chicks the same age as the guys. He thought, There might not be a lot of good in this world, but nothing can take away the pleasure of a string bikini. Any man who denies it just isn't right in the head.

A hand on his thigh. Åsa was looking at him. She'd taken the earbuds out.

"Can you believe we only have two days left? Awful."

Thomas looked at her. Put a hand on her shoulder. He could feel it clearly: she was tenser than usual.

"Yep. Soon it's time to head home to the fall. But we might still get a few warm days at home. Apparently there's some nice Indian summer heat going on right now."

"Thomas, we have to talk. It's not just the fall. You have to tell me what's really going on."

Thomas knew what was on her mind. She couldn't understand why he wasn't freaking out about the internal investigation. But it was more than that: Åsa felt left out. Didn't think he was opening up to her, wasn't saying what he thought would happen next. He couldn't explain, but maybe he should.

"We've already talked about that. I'll get the decision in a few days. Then we know. Either they screw their heads back on and nothing happens, or else they prosecute and then I'll be transferred. But they've got to be pretty damn stupid for that to happen."

"You're not mentioning the last possibility, Thomas."

"Stop it. If I get convicted for this thing, we'll leave the country. It would be a scandal. If that happens, not a single patrol officer should still be working on the force. Everyone would've done what I did. Everyone with a pulse."

"But as far as you can tell, how likely do you think it is that you get convicted and they fire you? Thomas, I need to know. We need to know. We can't live with this uncertainty. I've had a stomachache for two months now. What if it happens? How will we be able to afford the house? How will we be able to take care of a child?"

The final thing sent a burning flare through Thomas. Then he thought, I guess you'll have to start working full-time, then. But he kept his mouth shut. Didn't want to discuss this again. Had already been through it four times on the trip. It always ended with irritation. Åsa wanted him to start looking for other jobs. How could she know— what he'd already been offered was out of the ordinary.

"You're getting all worked up for no reason. They're not going to fire me. I promise."

"*You* stop it. I don't understand how you can be so calm. Don't you understand that this isn't just about you? It's about both of us, we're a team. You're sitting there pretending to be all relaxed when it's going to affect me too—affect us, our family. We've always said that if we adopt a child, it'll get to grow up in a real house with a yard. Living in a house is safe, secure. How will we be able to afford that if you get fired? Do you even understand what a good stroller, car seat, toys, clothes, crib, and all that costs? And I'm *not* going to IKEA."

Her eyes were burning bright against the blue sky.

"To live in a house is not always that safe, I'll have you know." In his head, he saw the man who'd been standing outside their window at home. "But I promise, on my badge. It'll work out. You don't have to worry."

She got up. Jerky movements. Typical fury à la Åsa. Went to the bar, or up to the room. He didn't care either way. Didn't have the energy to argue.

He closed his eyes. The sun warmed. He saw images in his head.

The last few months: some of the worst of his life. On a par with the weeks after Åsa's miscarriage. Sometimes confused, often sleepless. Most of all: exploding with worry. But he still didn't think there was reason to keep going on about it, to talk with Åsa about everything. She hadn't heard his whole side of the story. She couldn't help him. Why should he let his worry rub off on her? That would just be cruel.

The investigation into the so-called assault in the bodega was making crawling progress. After the decision'd been made to start a formal inquiry, he'd had to go in for an interrogation with IA. Tell his side of the story. A small, Hägerstrom-like fucker on the other side of the table: Assistant Detective Rovena. Had probably spent the seven years since cadet school behind a desk. Or even more likely: *under* a desk, 'cause he was so damned scared that something would fall down from the ceiling. Paint, maybe. Or dust? It was insane that a guy like that was even allowed to call himself a cop. He'd probably slid in on some fucking *blatte* quota. It was clear, this guy didn't have the stuff.

Thomas told him the way things were. Rovena was interested in the details. How many times did the man strike Lindqvist? Why hadn't Andrén managed to put handcuffs on the man? When did he decide to use the baton?

"Hey, there's a great movie about this. You should watch it," Thomas said. Rovena didn't laugh at his joke. Didn't want to watch the video from the surveillance camera. Claimed he would rather listen to Thomas's own version of events. Bullshit.

Other than that, the investigation shit was all happening in writing.

After the interrogation, Thomas gathered his strength and got in touch with a lawyer. The old suit wrote two letters. In the first, he demanded to see some of the investigation material that Thomas hadn't been permitted to see. In the second, he attacked the preliminary investigation for allowing an assistant detective to interrogate a police inspector—a subordinate should not be interrogating a superior—and for not noting that Cecila Lindqvist'd actually tried to alert dispatch but had had to abort the attempt due to the fact that Göransson'd acted so aggressively. Thomas wasn't impressed. The only thing the letters led to was that he had to go in for another interrogation—with a detective chief inspector. All he could do was wait for the decision.

He stayed at home, mostly. Gained a certain degree of understanding for the panic that hit the rabble after they'd been in custody for a few days. And he could still watch DVDs and surf unbelievable quantities of porn. Wanted to work on his Cadillac, but it didn't give him any peace of mind. The men sent him a box of chocolate, which made him feel stronger. They'd written him a short letter: "We look forward to having the Sharpshooter back." "The Sharpshooter," that felt good. Thomas was often the best in their practice shoots at work, so the nickname was right on—there were a lot worse things you could be called on the force. Sometimes he lifted weights in the den. But without any real drive. The days passed. The summer rolled by outside his window like an irritating glare on the TV screen.

After four weeks, he'd gotten in touch with Adamsson. The whole thing felt shady. Adamsson ought to understand that it wasn't a problem for Thomas to stay at work while the investigation was going on. But as Thomas'd observed before: Adamsson couldn't be trusted in this case. Thomas knew he should look into things more.

Thomas tried to sound as nice as possible when he called him. "Hey, Adamsson. It's me, Andrén."

"Yeah, I can hear that. How are you doing, anyway?" He tried to sound accommodating. But Thomas hadn't been the one who asked to go on sick leave.

"You know, I don't think I can take this much longer. I'm pacing around at home like a lost soul, waiting for the verdict."

"I understand. But I still think it's best that you stay away. You know, the mood will get weird here if people know you're just waiting. Either they drop it or there'll be a trial—that's just the way it is."

"Stig, may I ask you something?"

Using his first name, Stig, was really too personal, but Thomas couldn't care less at the moment. "I have a great deal of respect for you and I always thought we worked well together. If anyone were to ask who'd been my mentor and role model, I would give your name, without a doubt. You're a straight shooter and don't compromise with the things we all want to preserve. And I've always believed you thought I was one of the good ones. So now I'm wondering, is there anything you can do in this situation? Talk to the police commissioner or someone at IA?"

Stig Adamsson breathed heavily on the other end of the line. "I really don't know. It's dicey."

Thomas could feel it clearly: the irritation was welling up inside him. What was this bullshit? He would've done anything for Adamsson and now the old jerk wouldn't even try for his sake. Adamsson knew something, that much was obvious.

"Come on, Adamsson. I thought we were batting for the same team. Isn't there anything you can do?"

"Do I have to spell it out for you? I. Don't. Know. Is that clear enough?"

Adamsson pulled the carpet out from under his feet. It was a betrayal. Just like when he'd barged into the morgue. Thomas mumbled something in response. Adamsson said good-bye.

They hung up.

He took sleeping pills in order to fall asleep that night.

Another thing'd been eating away at him, too: the unsolved murder. So many questions. The most probable answer was that the dead guy had some sort of connection to someone in the building. Or else he was a simple burglar that one of the neighbors'd caught red-handed. But something told Thomas it wasn't a question of coincidence. There was a connection to someone—but how would they find out who when they didn't even know who the dead man was? The murderer had to have known about the victim's past. On the other hand: the murderer hadn't taken care of the slip of paper with the telephone number on it. Other questions were piling up. Why was there no sign that the victim'd resisted? No traces of blood or torn skin from the murder or murderers. The victim wasn't exactly a small person, there ought to have been a struggle. And the track marks, what was the deal with them? Finally: Whose was the phone number on the slip of paper?

Hägerström'd looked up the registered phone plans—none of the owners appeared to have anything to do with the murder. But could Hägerström be trusted? He didn't want to think about that right now. And no matter what, there were still the prepaid phone plans that hadn't been checked yet. The first'd been used by some young girl without a connection to the murder. But the other one? It was still unclear who owned it. Only three numbers'd been dialed. Two people who claimed not to have a clue and a third who Hägerström hadn't been able to get ahold of.

Just three numbers dialed—something wasn't right. The only people who used prepaid cards that way were troublemakers.

During the first few weeks of his so-called sick leave, he'd had a hard time getting out of bed in the morning. But a few days after his conversation with Adamsson: dammit, he was going to figure this shit out on his own. As an active-duty police inspector or as a cop on sick leave. The idea about the IMEI number'd been in the back of his mind, but had gotten lost when his problems began to pile up.

He'd written down the phone's IMEI number even though bringing home classified investigation material was prohibited. Fifteen numbers. A code. A signal that was sent out every time someone placed a call from the phone. No matter the plan. In other words: if the phone'd belonged to someone else, or had belonged to the same person who, for some reason, switched out the prepaid plans often, it was possible to find other numbers that'd been dialed from it.

The question was how. Thomas was no detective, but he knew that this wasn't exactly rocket science. The detectives did it all the time. He wasn't going to call Hägerström, though. Didn't want to call anyone else in Skärholmen to ask, either. Dammit, he wished he knew this shit. Thomas: alone against the conspiracy.

Theoretically, he should be able to get the information from the major phone companies. Demand a search on all calls that'd been made on plans that they owned from a phone with IMEI number 351549109200565. But what would happen if they asked to call him back at the police's number, just to be certain he was who he said he was? If they asked him to fax his request from a fax machine with the police's official phone number? But what the hell: he was just on sick leave. He was still a cop. It had to work.

Three days later, he called TeliaSonera, Tele2Comviq, Telenor, and a few smaller carriers. Thomas spoke with his most authoritative voice. TeliaSonera and Tele2Comviq promised to check—it would take a few days. They bought his story. Promised to send their findings to a fax number other than the police's usual one—Thomas's private number. No confirmation of who he was, no double-checking from where he was calling. Nothing.

But Telenor.

He introduced himself, but changed certain information. Instead of the Southern District, he said the Western District. If they were to call back to Skärholmen or some other station in his district, everyone would know right off the bat that he was away from work. The Western District was safer. He asked to be connected with someone responsible for technology. He explained the situation. He was calling in regards to a murder investigation with high priority. The police needed to know all the calls that'd been made from the phone with the IMEI number in question. The girl on the other end of the line listened, said yes and mmm—seemed on board. Until he asked her to make it snappy.

"You know, I have to ask you something before you start a bunch of extra work for us here."

"Okay." Thomas hoped it'd be a simple enough hoop to jump through.

"Can I call you back at the police's number? You know, we have our protocol and stuff."

Thomas felt his hands grow cold and sweaty at the same time. What was he supposed to say now?

He put his bet on the authoritative voice again: "This is what we'll do. I'll fax you an official request tomorrow. You'll get our official fax number to your fax. That's what we'll do."

Silence, tension. Thomas thought he could almost hear the seconds ticking inside the cell phone's digital clockwork.

"Okay," the tech chick said. "No problem. We'll do our best. Just send that fax and we'll get started."

Thomas breathed out. Just one problem left now: the fax had to come from the police station. He had to fix this thing with absolutely no suspicion.

The next day he was walking on eggshells. Woke up at 7:00 a.m. without an alarm. Ate breakfast with Åsa. Flipped through travel catalogs with her. It felt good, incredibly good. At the same time: he was thinking of when the best time was to go to the station. When were the least people there? How would he spin it if Ljunggren or Hägertsröm showed up right when he was standing there by the fax machine ready to send the shit? Or worse: Adamsson.

After Åsa left, he sat down in the living room. Remembered how he'd sat there and listened to Springsteen. How he'd made up his mind to keep going. A promise that would be kept.

It felt good. His life needed a boost, to be remodeled from scratch. Like the Cadillac.

Quarter past five: plenty of time before six o'clock. The perfect time of day if you wanted to visit Skärholmen's police station unnoticed. Right after the second shift'd taken over. The first shift'd left. The new guys would be in the locker rooms.

The fax was next to him on the passenger seat. He'd printed it at home in order to speed things up: in, send, out. Just one thing he couldn't forget: to bring the fax receipt.

Weird feeling when Skärholmen's enormous modern-art piece appeared in his line of vision from the highway: a hundred-foot-high rust-colored metal beam with a knot on it. Thomas hadn't been gone this long from Skärholmen over the past ten years. He didn't park in the parking garage—all his colleagues parked their private cars there. The risk of running into someone was too great. He parked by the square behind the mall instead.

The clock struck six. He took a deep breath. Got out.

Walked his usual route. Didn't bump into anyone.

Used the main entrance: most people used the employee entrance when they went home. Swiped his key card. Punched in the code.

The elevator: two detective inspectors in the youth squad stepped out. Greeted him. They weren't close. Either they didn't know that he was under investigation and on so-called sick leave, or else they just didn't give a damn.

Took the elevator up. The hallway looked empty. He walked past his own office, the one he'd shared with Ljunggren and Lindberg. Peeked in. The picture of Åsa was still in its usual place. All the tired old notes from the National Police Association were still pinned to the message board. Ljunggren's Bajen soccer scarf was still hanging on the wall, as usual. Hannu's speedway medals were hanging in their normal spots.

Per Scheele was sitting in a room, typing on a computer. He looked up when Thomas walked past. "Hey there, Andrén. Good to see you. How is everything?"

Scheele, two years in the department. Too green. Probably didn't understand what it was all about or else he was playing dumb. Thomas just nodded, said everything was fine.

The fax was grouped with the other gray plastic monsters: the copy machine, the printer, the scanner.

Preprogrammed phone numbers: Kronoberg, the Western Precinct, the Northern Precinct, the jail, the Southern Prosecutor's Office, and so on. Thomas fed his letter to Telenor into the fax. Double-checked that it was placed with the right side up. The ultimate mistake would be sending it so that Telenor got a blank page.

Dialed the number. Pressed send. The letter was sucked in. A police secretary walked past behind him in the hallway. Elisabeth Gunnarsson. Not someone that Thomas'd talked to much. She greeted him nicely without any small talk.

His calculation'd been correct: this really was the time of day when the place was the most deserted—except maybe for two in the morning when the night shift started.

The letter was fed out the other side.

Thomas heard a voice behind him. Finnish dialect.

"Andrén, it's been ages!" It was Hannu Lindberg. "We were almost starting to think that you'd burned out, as they say these days. Didn't seem like you."

After Adamsson, Ljunggren, and Hägerström: Lindberg was the worst person he could've run into. On the surface: a joking, jovial, happy fart who didn't turn down a drink or shy away from getting a little rough at work. But at the same time: Thomas'd never had any confidence in him, even though he was always entertaining to listen to. He didn't trust Lindberg the way he trusted Ljunggren or any of the other three boys he shared the squad car with. There was something about Lindberg that didn't tally. Maybe it was his smile, which seemed to say: I'll make you laugh as long as I know you've got my back. But if that changes, *I'll* be laughing at *you*.

"Hey there, Lindberg," Thomas said.

Lindberg looked surprised. "What're you doing here, you old boxer?" He laughed.

"I had to come in and deal with something. But you know Adamsson's the one who wants me to be on sick leave, not me."

Lindberg looked down at the fax. The letter lay with the blank back facing up in the tray. No fax receipt yet.

"Yeah, I figured as much. The whole thing is so fucking messed up.

You've got our support, just so you know. A couple of us toasted you when we went out for beers on Friday. Ljunggren, Flodén, and me. You should've been there. Hell, Adamsson can't have anything against that, can he?"

The receipt was fed slowly out of the fax machine. Thomas shook his head. "No idea what Adamsson would think about that. The whole thing makes me sick. But hey, Åsa's waiting down in the car. I just had to fax this one thing. Tell everyone I say hi. *Hasta la vista*, Hannu."

Lindberg grinned. Thomas picked up the letter and the fax receipt. Hannu Lindberg looked at him. Was that a hint of suspicion in his eyes? Thomas tried to see if he was eyeing the letter.

He took the stairs down. His heart was beating in time with his steps.

It was done. Smooth.

Like butter.

Back in the present. There he was, alone in a sun chair on Gloria Palace's terrace. Seventy-seven-degree pool water and a group of smoking-hot Danish twenty-year-olds in front of him. And yet he felt so damned lost.

Still: all cops with balls had to go through tough times sometimes. It was over twelve years since Thomas'd graduated from the Police Academy, always with his sights set on working the streets, to be of some real use. He'd started as a patrol officer in the Southern District right away. Four years later, he was promoted to police inspector. A triumph. A sign that he'd picked the right career. His dad was proud. After that, three calm years. He met Åsa, made sure to end up in the same group as Jörgen Ljunggren and the others. After a while, things went a little too far, he was written up twice for excessive use of force. Some protest in Salem where he'd been called and some fucking wife-beater'd gotten too out of hand. He got off with warnings. And then Åsa had her miscarriage. He'd already realized the world was ankle-deep in shit. Now it just sank a little deeper. He tried to calm down by tinkering with the car. It didn't work. He beat people up ten times worse, several times a month. Pounded on junkies. Split immigrant lips. Smashed shoplifting Sven swillers. But the spirit in the department was good. There was honor, a code. People didn't say anything about Thomas using the harder method. You didn't rat out a colleague who did his job.

Okay, maybe he was a dirty cop. A quasi-racist, overaggressive, degenerate police officer. A rotten human being. But sometimes he missed the good old beat. The part that was about seeking out the truth and nothing else. In the middle of all the shit he'd brought down on himself, in his lust for easy money, there was still a little bit of cop left in him. The one who'd been given a job to do by society: to fight crime. And yet . . . other thoughts elbowed their way to the front. What would he do about Radovan Kranjic's offer? He hadn't made up his mind yet—maybe he'd let the internal investigation's verdict decide.

At home in Sweden, all the reports from the telephone companies would be waiting for him. They'd promised him that.

At home in Sweden, in a few days, he would know if he would stay or not.

At home in Sweden, reality could do what it wanted with him. He felt ready.

Or not.

28

The cunt parole office at Hornstull was lamer than ever. Mahmud's mood: cuntier than ever. He'd been an hour early. The receptionist claimed that Erika Cuntwaldson refused to come out and see him. "I'm sorry, she's in another meeting." Yeah, right—sure she is. Humiliation tactics were their thing. To always let Mahmud wait. He was gonna fucking pork that bitch in her "other meeting."

Mahmud eyed the magazines and newspapers. Thought: *Gracious Home*, *Dagens Nyheter*—so gay. Name a single ordinary *blatte* who read shit like that. But the car magazine was okay. Mahmud flipped through it. An article about the new Ferrari. He drooled for a while. Then he thought: Should he split? Clock on his cell read fifty more minutes to go. He *should* split. But still: Erika was okay, after all. Plus: if things got messy with the parole office the cops would be all up in his shit, and if the cops were up in his shit social services would be all up on him, and so on. If you thought about it, the principle was clear enough: never end up in the system. 'Cause once you're in, they won't let you go. Ever.

Mahmud'd borrowed a cellie from Babak that he'd pocketed at his dad's store. Could hold hundreds of MP3s. Babak'd loaded it with an ill mix. The baddest beat-bangers: P. Diddy, the Latin Kings, Akon. But also: Haifa Wehbe, Ragheb Alama—real Middle Eastern groove. Mahmud leaned his head back. Chilled. He was never gonna let slip that he waited this long to see his parole officer.

He'd dreamed the nightmare again. Back in the woods. Pine trees and fir trees eclipsed the sky. Arms raised to the heavens. The rifle gleamed in a cold light that seemed to be coming from streetlamps. Lamps in the middle of the woods? It seemed weird even in the dreamworld. On the grass in the middle of a ring of men dressed in black—Mahmud was looking diagonally down as if he were floating above the scene—he saw Wisam. Wisam's hands were black from the blood on his face. It ran slowly. Warm. Hot like a stream of lava. He lowered his head. Stefanovic pointed the rifle at his neck: "We're killing you, not because you deserve it but because we need it to show up in our balance sheet." Wisam looked up. Eyes red from crying. A pulsing cut on his cheek. But maybe not. The blood was smearing his cheeks. His chin. Was running like in slow motion. "Help me," he said.

It wasn't the first time. Ever since he'd seen the Yugos pick up the Lebanese bro that afternoon. The dreams were fucking with his head. Patient. Persistent. Sharp like a cocaine rush. The forest clearing. The piss in the grass. Akhramenko's jabs in the ribs of a faceless opponent. Stefanovic's smile. Gürhan's grin. Born to Be Hated. He tried to smoke up before going to bed so that he'd have an easier time falling asleep. Didn't go to the gym or drink Coke too late at night. Only watched boring TV shows. It still didn't work.

The memories were whipping him.

Stefanovic'd asked him to get in the car. He was dressed in a suit, with a cell phone in hand, and he was in a radiant mood. He turned to Mahmud, "Great thanks for your help." Then he kept talking into the phone. In Serbian.

They were driving toward Södermalm. Slavic music on the stereo. A red light on Vasagatan. "Was it hard to get ahold of that asshole?"

Mahmud grinned. "No. Shit, man, I'm a dog-catching king." Now, two months later, that grin almost felt as disgusting as if he'd laughed at his mother's grave.

Erika rapped her knuckles on the table in front of him. He opened one eye. She smiled. What the fuck was she smiling at? Mahmud kept his earbuds on. Couldn't hear what she said.

She knocked him on the knee. Tried to say something that couldn't be heard through the phat beats, 50 Cent.

He took the earbuds off.

Dragged his feet all the way to her room. As messy as usual. Just as much paper, coffee mugs, bottles of mineral water, dead plants, nerdy posters with weird chunky peeps on them. Caption: *Botero*. Fuck, man, Botero, that's what she was—a cow.

"Come on, Mahmud, you don't have to act like a two-year-old just because you showed up early today."

Mahmud rolled up his earbuds. "Who do you think you are?" And, in a softer voice: "Cunt."

Erika stared at him. Mahmud knew: you had to've known her for a while to know how angry she really was. Erika: you could measure that chick's fury by how still she sat. Right now: she was moving less than the naked statue on Hötorget.

Thirty seconds of silence. Then Mahmud said, "Okay, I was too early. It was my fault. Sorry. I just get so pissed at your reception chick. Why couldn't she ask you to see me a little earlier?"

Erika moved her hand—a good sign.

"It wasn't her fault. I was in another meeting. The whole world doesn't revolve around you, Mahmud. You've got to understand that. Anyway. Let's forget that now. It's fly that you're here."

Mahmud grinned at her word choice: *fly*. Man, did she talk like that? In his heart: he couldn't help thinking Erika was okay after all.

"How's the job search going? You've practically got to be CEO somewhere by now."

If it'd been anyone else: Mahmud would've lost his shit. On purpose. Taken it as a diss. A way of making fun of him. The thing with Erika: deep down, he knew that's not what she meant. He usually knew that at other times, too, but here—it's like he couldn't have a beef with her for longer than five minutes.

"Honest, it's not going too good. I haven't been called to interviews lately."

They talked. Erika chatted on as usual. Told him he had to sign up for a course, be in touch with some job-placement agency, his social worker. That he had to stay in touch with his dad, his sisters. A strong family was important. A social context was important. Old friends were important.

He felt a headache come crawling on. Disturbing. Wisam: an old friend.

He switched on the look-like-you're-listening look. But couldn't relax. Tried to soften the headache that was starting to scream: WHAT THE FUCK HAVE YOU DONE?

It felt like he had to hold on to something. Like he was about to collapse. Fall, crawl around like an insect on the linoleum floor. Felt like he wanted to tell everything, spill it all, to Erika. No. *Khara*. That wouldn't work. Never.

He held out. Bit the bullet. Said yes to everything Erika wanted to hear yes to.

Fifteen minutes later, they were done.

Thanks, thanks, see you in two weeks.

Fast. Out.

Two hours later. He was staying with Babak for a few days, couldn't take Dad's whining.

Things were going good for Babak. He'd gotten a new forty-six-inch Sony flat screen. "Not some cheap sale model," as he said. "The real stuff, more pixels than there are *blattes* in Alby. You feel me?" Babak pushed product like never before: blow, weed, even cat. Could talk about it all day: the coke wasn't like before. It wasn't just high-class flyers and the Stureplan clowns that were doing it. The opposite. The Sven Svenssons and the Ali Muhammads next door were ripping lines more often than they downed beers. Everyone was doing it. The prices'd dropped like at an after-Christmas sale. Soon: C would be bigger than weed. Babak transformed every coin into paper. The reward: flat screen, chicks, lackeys. Babak'd gotten two clockers who dealt for him. And that's when the real profits first started pouring in.

Reward of rewards. Two weeks ago, Babak'd bought the number one *blatte* man's wish: a BMW. The ride was an '07, bought as part of a debt settlement with some poor Finn in Norsborg who couldn't deliver.

Mahmud felt it strong: he was so jealous. Of his brother. Hated the feeling. At the same time, he promised himself: one day he'd own even flyer shit.

Babak said, "What're you doing? You're stressing me out. *Habibi*, sit down. Let's watch a flick." Sometimes he sounded so funny: spoke Arabic, but said the word "flick" in Swedish.

Mahmud responded coolly, "Yo, I gotta run some shit by you."

"No problem. The movie can wait. Fire away."

"I did something stupid. Cunt stupid."

Babak did a double take, pretended to look surprised. "Come on, when did you *not* do something cunt stupid?"

"Seriously, Babak. This stays between us. Only. I betrayed someone I didn't wanna betray."

Babak seemed to feel the seriousness. Mahmud paced. Started at the beginning, with the stuff Babak already knew. How he'd been pressed by Gürhan, through Daniel. How his desperation'd grown. How the opportunity'd come like a gift from Allah. The chance to do the Yugos a small favor that they'd pay for royally. To find Wisam Jibril, an old friend from the hood, who'd ripped off Radovan. Babak'd already figured some of it out from before. Been to the Bentley store, heard how Mahmud'd gone door to door in every concrete tower looking for Wisam. But he didn't know the whole story.

Mahmud stopped his pacing in the middle of the room. "You know, when he came to our place that day and I started talking to him, told him my business idea, suggested we meet up, I knew something else right then."

"What did you know?" Babak asked.

"I knew I would regret this for the rest of my life. You feel me?"

Babak just nodded.

Mahmud kept going. He described how he'd tricked Wisam into going to the restaurant in Tumba, how the Yugos'd plucked the Lebanese, how Mahmud'd hopped into a BMW and driven off too. But they hadn't trailed the car that Wisam was in. Instead, they drove in toward the city. Stopped at Slussen. Stefanovic told Mahmud to get out with him. They walked into one of the big buildings behind the Katarina Elevator. Took a cramped elevator up. Stepped out. There was a restaurant up there. White tablecloths, crystal stemware, pro waiters—real deluxe atmosphere. Mahmud'd had no idea there were joints like that on the South Side.

They had a reservation. The waiter seemed to recognize Stefanovic. Like, shit, you know?

Stefanovic ordered a drink. Mahmud didn't plan on drinking, ordered a Diet Coke as usual. "I hope you like this place. I thought we'd celebrate. As thanks for helping us so much."

Mahmud ordered foie gras with some kind of pear vinaigrette that was supposed to come with Serrano ham. He asked to have it without the final ingredient.

Stefanovic chatted. About the money he'd made at the K-1 fights, Jörgen Ståhl's fantastic punches, some new bar by Stureplan. Mahmud liked the way he spit. Stefanovic was drinking wine. The entrées were served. Mahmud'd had a hard time choosing: a lot of fish on the menu and that wasn't his thing. The waiter set his plate down. Grilled rib eye. Real stuff.

During the entire conversation, in the back of his head: he had to ask the Yugo what they could do about Gürhan and Born to Be Hated. Mahmud looked around. Hardwood floors, men in suits, ill view over the city. A couple of old guys at another table were staring at him and Stefanovic in a Sven way.

Stefanovic wiped his mouth with the cloth napkin.

"Okay, let's talk business." He lowered his voice. "First of all, I want to thank you again. It would've been hard to find him without you. The guys are taking care of him now. Do you know what I'm saying?"

Mahmud understood, but not really. For some reason, he shook his head.

"You don't understand? This is how it is. We're not taking him because he deserves it, but because we need it to show up in our balance sheet. You know, he didn't really pocket too much in his little airport heist. We managed to take most of it back. So it's not about the money. It's about the principle. The rules of the game. Our entire business idea is built on one thing." He leaned over, whispered into Mahmud's ear, "Fear."

Stefanovic took a sip of his wine.

"Anyway. You've proven that you're a good guy. You did your job quickly, without making a mess, and in the right way. We appreciate that. Do you know what the most important thing is in this field?"

Mahmud shook his head.

"That we can trust each other. Trust is the only thing that matters. We don't work with written contracts or stuff like that. Just trust. Do you understand?"

Stefanovic took a big bite of his food.

What the Yugo was saying sounded okay to Mahmud's ears. "You can trust me. One hundred percent."

"That's good." Stefanovic finished chewing. "You will get your pay today."

Mahmud almost couldn't keep up. It was all happening too fast. He needed to parry with his proposal. Still play according to the rules. He gathered his courage. Sharpened his talk.

"Hold on a sec, Stefanovic. Thanks for saying all that. It feels damn good to've been able to help you. Honest, it would've been hard for you to find that guy. He hung in my circles, not yours. You gotta be deep in the concrete to pull off a thing like that. And I'd be happy to work more with you. Word on the street is you guys are good. So, I'm yours. But, there's something else I gotta talk about. I don't want cash for the gig. I wanna know if you can help me with something else."

Stefanovic raised his glass as if to make a toast.

"Tell me."

"You know Gürhan Ilnaz, Born to Be Hated, from Södertälje?"

Stefanovic nodded. Everyone in the world he belonged to knew who Gürhan was—just like everybody knew Mr. R.

"He's after me. It's about a debt that I've already paid. But they're piling on more and more, you follow? They're acting like real pigs, threatening my family and stuff."

He paused. "So, I was thinking. I just did you a big favor. Instead of cash, can you talk to Gürhan? You know what I mean, just do your thing."

Mahmud expected another calm nod. Instead: Stefanovic laughed out loud. For at least a minute. Took a gulp of wine. Leaned back in his chair. Kept smiling.

"You can forget about that. Like I said, we're grateful for what you did. But not so grateful that we'll do something stupid. You'll get the money we agreed on. Thirty G's, right? Maybe you can make the Turk happy with that, what do I know."

Mahmud tried, "But I helped you big time, man. It's not a big deal for you to talk to him."

"Didn't you hear what I said? Forget about it. But you can start selling for us. Then maybe you can save up a little."

That's where Mahmud's story ended. He'd gone into the whole thing, quoted every comment, the full transcript. Almost forgotten that Babak was sitting on the couch, listening.

Now, Mahmud looked down at him.

"I'm fucking crushed, man. You feel me?"

Babak was playing with the DVD case.

"You're a fucking idiot."

29

Morning at the pissy guard job. Eyes red. Runny. Ragged underneath. Worse: a headache was pounding on the inside of his skull. Reminded him of his sleep deprivation. Last night again: four hours. Unclear how much longer he could take it. But so far, he was holding it together. The third night in a row that he'd sat outside the different men's apartments from seven until after midnight. Boredom mixed with jittery suspense. In his head: imagined action scenes mixed with feelings of righteousness.

The project'd been named Operation Magnum. Suitable: in the movie, Travis popped the assholes with a .44-caliber Magnum revolver. It was a powerful weapon. This would be a powerful attack.

Niklas was sitting outside an apartment in Sundbyberg. He tried to see as much as he could with the help of his binoculars. The woman, Helene Strömberg, came home around five o'clock. She worked as a dental hygienist at a public dental clinic by Odenplan. The son came home at five-thirty. Ate dinner alone in front of the TV. The only room into which Niklas had good visibility was the living room. The kid was watching some nature show. Niklas, sarcastic: Real exciting, I thought there were video games for kids like him. The man, Mats Strömberg, came home at seven-thirty. He and Helene ate dinner together. Then Mats watched TV with his son. It seemed like Helene was doing laundry. A harmonious home. Had to be fake. Everything was still. Like the calm in the barracks before an attack. But nothing happened.

Later: from twelve-thirty to two-thirty, he collected the tapes from the cameras outside the two single-family homes and across the street from the apartments. Drove home. Downloaded the footage to his hard drive. Fast-forwarded through the video files one by one. For most of the day, the houses were dark. In the afternoon/night, the lights came on. People came home. Moms, dads, kids. They took their dogs for walks. Drove the kids to practice. Made dinner. Ordinary lives.

So far. Or? Maybe the list didn't contain names of battered women after all. Maybe it was a list of potential recruits to the switchboard, the telephone hotline, or the support network at Safe Haven. Maybe everything was to hell. A money pit. Maybe FISHDO—Fuck it, shit happens, drive on. Should he start making other plans?

What's more: he had to watch his finances. The job wasn't earning him much, ten thousand kronor a month, max. He'd poured hundreds of thousands of kronor into equipment, the car, and other stuff. He needed more for living expenses and future expenditures for the Operation. On top of that: the shady broker could reclaim the sublet at any time. What the fuck would he do if that happened?

The dreams returned. He saw Claes in front of him. Bloody hands. Punches to the stomach. Kicks to the face. Images from Iraq. Collin in combat gear. The attack against the mosque. Volumes of the Koran in tattered piles.

August was coming to an end. He waited. Patiently. Something had to happen soon—one of the men would reveal himself for what he was.

Thursday afternoon. End of the workday. One day left till the weekend. Even more time to spend on the Operation.

He called Mom on his way home.

"Hi, it's me."

Niklas could hear water running in the background. She must already be at home, washing dishes or something. Good.

"Hey, honey. It's been too long. Have you stopped picking up my calls?"

He couldn't take that accusatory tone. "No, but I'm working all the time. I can't pick up when I'm at work."

"How is work?"

"Work is shit, Mom. Pure shit."

"Don't say that. Maybe it isn't as exciting as all the stuff you were up to overseas, but it's safer. For all of us."

Niklas was on his way to his car, which was parked in Biovitrum's enormous parking garage. His steps echoed.

"Stop it, Mom. Sometimes you have to do dangerous things to earn your living and sometimes you have to do dangerous things just because you have to."

"What do you mean? Why do you have to do that? What dangerous things are you doing now?"

"No, I didn't mean that." Niklas saw the Audi parked thirty feet away. He unlocked it with the remote-control key. "But maybe you should be more grateful sometimes."

She stopped clattering with the dishes in the background. "What do you mean? What should I be grateful for?"

Niklas opened the car door. Slid into the driver's seat.

"All these years you've been nagging at me to stop with the warring, as you call it. Every time I've been back here you've whined. Then, when I do come home for our sake, what do I get? Even more whining. Mom, you have no idea about all the good stuff I've done for you. There is so much crap in this city. Do you understand that? Dirt that's violating my blood. That's violated you."

He slammed the car door shut.

"Do you know what scares me, Niklas?"

"Other than insects, pigeons, and heights? No."

"You scare me. You're not the way you used to be. Before, you were always hotheaded and full of energy. I know you could get mad then, too, but you were always kind. What's happening? All you do is talk about gratitude, about crap you see around you. About the parks department not doing their job because there are so many rats in Örnsberg. You sound so strange. Did you go to the open clinic like we talked about? How are you really doing, Niklas? Why don't you come over for dinner tonight? I'll order pizza."

First: surprise over her reaction. Quickly replaced by something else: indignation. Disgust. The open clinic was shit. What did she think? He felt his hand begin to shake. He could hardly hold the cell phone steady against his ear.

"Stop it! You'll see. You'll all see. I'm not like you. I'm something much greater; I'll make an impression on people. It's about *impact*, Mom, *changing* the world. And to do that, you have to act. People's lives, the passage of time. Everyone just walks around and accepts this shit, but who's doing anything about it? And you, all you've ever been is spineless."

Niklas hung up. That was enough. If not even Mom understood him, it was pointless trying to explain to anyone.

Operation Magnum had to continue. Niklas drove straight out to Sundbyberg.

The Strömberg family's apartment was on the second floor. Niklas climbed into the backseat of the car. Lay down. Rested the binoculars on his belly. Looked up at the apartment through the windshield. Still dark. It was quarter past five. Good thing he switched out the license plates regularly.

People walked by outside the car. The advantage of getting there so early: easy to find a parking spot. He'd had to give up because of parking a few times. Had to drive to one of the other apartments. It bothered him—he needed the routines.

While waiting for the family to come home he read his newfound genre: Anti-power-imbalance. Anti-porn. Anti-men-who-thought-they-had-the-right-to-do-whatever-the-fuck-they-wanted. Right now: a collection of Judith Butler essays. Scary academic, but it educated him anyway. Made him realize the sickness in Sweden. In the world. The men who abused their strength. The physical imbalance. He saw them as rats who took their chance to suck the blood out of human hearts just because they could. Like filth collecting just because there was room to collect. The shit that soiled every inch of the human body. Invaded the blood, the muscle fibers, the respiratory organs. Dirt. But they didn't know who they were up against—poor devils.

At six o'clock, the son came home. Went through his regular routine. Turned the TV on before he'd even taken his jacket off. Disappeared into the kitchen. Returned with a bowl. Maybe cereal. Sat down in front of the TV.

But Helene didn't come home. Seven o'clock came around. The kid talked on the phone a couple of times.

At seven-thirty, the Mats fucker came home. Disappeared into the kitchen. Time passed. This wasn't going according to the family's routines. Mats came into the living room. Sat down next to his son in front of the TV, beer in hand. The son got up, disappeared out of sight. Maybe he went to bed, but it was early.

The man remained seated. Chugged beer. Watched TV.

It was around ten-thirty when Niklas saw Helene come walking down the street. He already knew the key code to the building—it was easy to make out, just follow people's finger movements over the keypad. He'd tried it out several times just to be sure.

It usually took her forty-five seconds to walk up to the apartment.

Correct: forty-three seconds after she'd walked through the front door, Mats rose from the couch. Swayed slightly. Disappeared out in the direction of the entrance hall.

Damn, Niklas couldn't see what was happening. Considered getting out of the car, positioning himself farther up the street. Getting a better angle, catching a glimpse of the hallway. At the same time: he had to stick to his routines, not rush into anything, not run and wave the binoculars around unnecessarily. He stayed in the car. Waited.

After ten minutes: they came into the living room.

Helene was gesticulating with her arms. Mats was red in the face. Obvious—they were arguing.

Niklas was on tenterhooks. What were they saying in there? How aggressive was the man? He should've rigged a wireless listening device, bugged the whole place.

Then he saw it clearly. The man shoved Helene in the chest. Her face contorted; maybe she cried. He shoved her again. She took a few steps back. Was shoved again. His shoves moved them offscreen. Toward the entrance hall again. It was happening now, now a major assault was coming. Surely, soon.

Niklas threw himself out of the car. Grabbed the reverse peephole viewer and his Cold Steel knife. It was dark out. Streetlamps were hanging on wires between the houses. He punched in the code. A soft click as the lock opened. He tore open the door.

Took the steps four at a time. Advanced—adrenaline-focused, attack-tuned. Stealth position—ready to strike.

Strömberg. On the door: a ceramic plate with a colorful text in relief: WELCOME. The sounds from their argument could be heard faintly. Even though Niklas'd been up here and seen the door before, he now had time to think: The perfect picture is more of a lie than ever. Otherwise quiet in the stairwell. He heard his own panting breaths. Placed the viewer over the peephole in the door. Inside: Mats and Helene in a full-scale war. She was sitting on a stool. He was two feet away from her. Screaming. Niklas could hear it now that his head was only inches from the door.

"You fucking ego-bitch. How do you think this is supposed to work? If you're out on the town all night."

Mats took a step forward. Helene sat with her face in her hands. Sniveling. Sobbing. Weeping.

Mats kept hollering. Yelled about the conditions for their life together. The raising of their son. Cleaning up the kitchen. Lots of shit. Helene ignored him, never looked up.

Mats took another step forward. "Are you even listening to me? You fucking whore." He grabbed her hair. Tore her head up. Swollen, red-rimmed eyes. Niklas could feel it. Her fear. Panic. Maybe she knew what was about to come.

Mats held her hair in a firm grip. Forced her to her feet. She tried to loosen his grip with her hands. He let her go. Pushed her toward the closets. She tumbled, tripped, fell. Tried to get up. He stood with his face inches away from hers. Continued shouting. Scolded, screamed, spit saliva.

She hunched down. Grabbed her shoes.

Niklas hardly had time to react. The door swung open. Helene flicked the light switch in the stairwell. Niklas stood there like an idiot, viewer tight in his fist.

Helene ignored him. Rushed down the stairs, still only in her socks. Shoes in hand.

Niklas walked up to the next landing. Listened.

Heard Mats yell, "Come back, calm down."

His military preparations were worthless—there was nothing Niklas could do.

He waited until Mats closed the door. Walked out to the Audi. Saw Helene farther down the street.

She was walking at a rapid pace, but it looked like she was swaying.

Niklas followed her.

30

On the outside: tan, fit, strong.

On the inside: anxious, expectant, nervous.

The verdict was coming today. Åsa and Thomas'd come home from Gran Canaria the day before. Åsa said that she thought it'd been wonderful. But Thomas knew: the worry was eating away at her too, maybe worse than at him.

The decision would be sent at some point after one o'clock. Åsa was at work.

He went grocery shopping at ten. The sky: hard and gray like concrete, pale like his spirit. The drunks outside the liquor store, the so-called A-team, quieted down when he walked past with his grocery bags—they knew he was a cop. He thought, The A-team must be so damn good at shooting the shit—that's all they do all day, sit together and talk. Hard-core social workout. Maybe he should send Ljunggren there for a while. Thomas smiled to himself—his colleague might be a hopeless case.

Ljunggren: made him miss his job. But also made him think about everything that was strange. The fax machine at home'd been overflowing when he emptied it yesterday, as soon as he and Åsa'd set down their luggage. At least thirty pages from Tele2 Comviq, ten pages from a smaller carrier, and over forty pages from Telenor. Now he just had to dive right in. Organize the information. Work in a structured manner. Åsa wondered if he wasn't tired from the long flight. "It took over nine hours with the layover and everything. I'm beat, anyway." Sure, he was tired, damn tired. But the lists stoked the embers. No, more than that—the lists injected him with pure energy. He wanted Åsa to go to bed right away so that he could start working.

She passed out by nine o'clock. Thomas sat with the lists for four hours. The whole house was dark except for the desk lamp in the office. He crossed off numbers that'd been called from the phone, checked for reoccurring numbers, searched on the Internet. He came up with names—lots of names.

He set down the bags of groceries. Opened the door slowly. Stocked the fridge. He packed in the butter, the pork tenderloin, the cheese, the milk. The last: organic. Åsa was stubborn about that. Thomas didn't have the energy to argue, even though sensible people knew that that was all a crock of shit.

He took a seat by the telephone. Got out the phone lists. Four numbers stood out. Each of them'd been called at least twenty times between May and June. He was going to call the one with the most calls first—thirty-three of them in May alone. The number must be connected to a prepaid phone—he couldn't find a registered contractual plan in any of his searches.

Someone picked up on the other end. "Yes."

Answering the phone "Yes" was weird in and of itself.

"Hi, this is Thomas Andrén. I'm calling from the Stockholm Police Department . . ."

There was a click on the other end of the line.

Thomas called the number again. Got a busy signal like a raised middle finger right in his face.

The next number had been called a total of forty-two times during May and June. Went to a Kristina Swegfors-Ballénius. The third one was yet another unregistered number. The fourth was the most-called number: someone named Claes Rantzell.

He started with Kristina Swegfors-Ballénius.

A relatively young voice: "Yes, hello, this is Kicki."

"Hi, my name is Thomas Andrén and I'm calling from the Stockholm Police Department."

"Okay, and what do you want?" Blatant suspicion on the other end of the line.

"I'm calling in regards to an ongoing investigation into some very serious criminal activity. I need an answer to a simple question. I have a cell phone from which your number was called quite a bit in May and June of this year. The numbers vary, but in May, for instance, you were called eighteen times from this number." Thomas read one of the numbers from a Telenor prepaid phone aloud to her.

"Could you repeat that?"

Thomas read the number again.

"No, I have no idea," the woman said.

What was this bullshit? Kristina Swegfors-Ballénius'd been called over forty times from the phone in question—she must know whom the number belonged to. Thomas tried to gauge the tone in her voice. How much was she lying?

"This is in regards to a murder investigation—I mentioned that, right? Not some regular crime. Someone has called you a total of forty-two times. Someone with the same phone who apparently changes his number as often as regular people change toilet-paper rolls. Please try to remember."

The woman on the other end of the line cleared her throat. "But that's several weeks ago. How am I supposed to remember something like that, huh?"

Something was wrong—the woman didn't even want to remember. Her hostility was too great to be regular old cop skepticism.

"Listen up, Kristina Swegfors-Ballénius. If you don't try to remember fast as hell, I'm going to drive out to Huddinge and go through your cell phone personally."

Thomas hoped she would take the bait—one, that he showed that he knew where she lived; two, the threat to go through her personal life—but, really, that kind of thing was not allowed. Especially not for a police inspector who was on sick leave, potentially soon to be transferred, maybe even fired.

It sounded like the woman on the other end of the line was sucking snot back up her nose. Then, silence. He could almost hear her thinking. This was perfect: she knew something. Finally: "Um, I'll look through my cell phone and stuff. Can I call you back in a few minutes?"

Bingo.

He had a feeling she would call him back.

Ten minutes later, Kicki Swegfors-Ballénius called.

"So, I figured out who those numbers belong to. The calls were from my father, John Ballénius. Don't ask me why, but he changes numbers often. I didn't recognize them right away, because I usually screen his calls." Thomas looked down at the lists in front of him. Correlated with what she said: none of the calls that'd been made to her'd lasted for longer than a second or so. Kicki sounded like she was in a better mood, or else she was just kissing ass. Thomas didn't care either way.

John Ballénius was the name. A shady last name—probably made up; the guy must've changed his name. But it didn't matter. The likelihood that he was about to hit upon his first real breakthrough was greater than ever. The telephone number the dead guy'd had in his back pocket had to belong to this Ballénius guy.

His first day back in Sweden was off to a good start. Thomas was hoping for a lucky day in more ways than one—soon he would be informed about the verdict on his future.

He heated a mini pizza in the microwave and started frying two eggs. Scarfed down the pizza with bizarre speed: less than a minute. A hidden talent: no one ate as fast as he could.

He wasn't going to give up, even if those fuckers did transfer him. He was going to run his own murder investigation on the side. Without that Hägerström clown. Without anyone. Make a triumphant comeback. At the same time, in the back of his mind, a darker thought: What if they didn't drop the preliminary investigation, what if they weren't satisfied with a transfer? What if he was convicted like a criminal, lost his job completely?

He Googled John Ballénius. Zero hits. John Ballénius was apparently not a Web celeb. But on the other hand—who the hell was? Ballénius's address according to the population registry: a post office box. The Internet was useless. He needed access to the police's databases. But that was a problem. Even if he weren't officially on sick leave, every search was registered—not even cops were allowed to snoop around in criminals' lives. You had to swipe your access card to even start up the computer database and every word you punched in was logged.

Despite that, he made an attempt. Called Ljunggren and asked him to run a search through all the central criminal databases at once. Ljunggren was skeptical. "Dammit, Andrén, what is this? You're supposed to be chilling out. We're looking forward to having you back."

At the same time: Ljunggren knew that from one perspective, it was his fault that Thomas was in the shit right now. That had to be exploited. "Come on," Thomas said. "If you'd showed up as usual, I wouldn't even be sitting here. Just do me this one favor."

"Don't tell me this has to do with that dead guy we found at Gösta Ekman Road?"

"Come on, just one search."

Unbelievably enough: Ljunggren agreed. Ran a search while Thomas remained on the line.

Searching all the databases at once meant any relevant hits showed up in the general reconnaissance database, the databases of the tax and the traffic authorities, the National Police's criminal records, the passport database, and the national database of suspected persons. If someone was shady, he'd turn up somewhere.

Ballénius was there: convicted of assault and a drug-related crime in the eighties. There'd been extensive surveillance done on the guy in the mid-nineties. They'd thought he was a front man for a bunch of companies. But he'd only been convicted for a few DUIs and one minor drug offense. Later in the nineties: personal bankruptcy. Debt-rehabilitation measures were decided upon in 2001. A prohibition against owning and running companies was lifted the same year. So-called consumption debt'd apparently been what cracked him. The guy was down in the bankruptcy pit again in 2003. What the fuck was Ballénius doing? He was right back on track by 2006—registered as a board member in seven companies. Thomas could feel it getting warm. Wrong. Warm was an understatement—suddenly this thing was on fire. The dude was shady. Shady as hell.

What's more, there was a street address for Ballénius: Tegnérgatan 46. But there were no listed phone numbers.

It was one o'clock already. Still no call from work about the results from the internal investigation. Should he call? He made up his mind: if he hadn't heard anything by two o'clock, he was going to call.

Åsa called at five past—wanted to hear if the verdict'd come yet. Thomas was irritated. It wasn't her problem. "I'll call you after they've been in touch. Okay?"

She sounded sad.

The clock struck one-thirty. Still nothing. What pigs—making him wait like some humiliated nobody.

At a quarter to two, his home phone rang. Thomas recognized the numbers on the display.

It was Adamsson's extension at the station.

"Good afternoon, Andrén. This is Adamsson."

"Yes, I can see that. Everything okay?"

Adamsson didn't seem steely or stressed, but the stillness in his voice gave him away. No good news was coming.

"All's well with me. And you? How are you doing?"

"Åsa and I were on Gran Canaria for two weeks. Really damn nice. Other than that, it's been a real drag." Thomas made an effort not to sound too bitter. Adamsson would be his boss again if he came back, and Adamsson was the enemy.

"I understand. But it was the right decision. Strong move, Andrén." Dramatic pause. Adamsson made it sound like going on sick leave'd been Thomas's own idea. He continued, "The verdict's in from IA." Thomas was holding the receiver so tightly that his knuckles looked white. "It looks good, actually. They're dropping it. Congrats."

Thomas felt himself sink into the armchair. Exhale. There were still some sane people left in the police department, it seemed.

Adamsson kept going: "But the police commissioner didn't like this whole mess. He's ordering a transfer. And he offered a suggestion, too. Traffic control."

Thomas didn't know what to say. A joke. Ridicule. A fucking spit bomb in his face. Worse than that: this was a matter of police honor.

Adamsson tried to sound sympathetic. "I completely understand that this might be difficult, Andrén. But look on the bright side, you're not being prosecuted. I've always liked you. But you know how it is, the police commissioner doesn't have a choice. It's too bad that things ended up this way, you're a good man. Made of the right stuff. And trustworthy too, as I like to say. But now things are the way they are."

Thomas thought: Thank you, you fucker.

Adamsson continued, "I can just give you one piece of advice. You have to learn self-control. I think you'd do better if you gained a deeper understanding of the situations police work may put you in. Sometimes it's the right time to act forcefully, but sometimes there is no need for that. Believe me, I've been around for enough years to've seen pretty much everything. Hopefully, you'll learn one day."

Åsa came home two hours later. Thomas was under the car with his headlamp switched off. First, he'd tried to concentrate on the chassis. After forty minutes, he'd given up. Everything just went to hell. He kept forgetting tools so that he had to roll out four times, kept dropping stuff, hit his elbow. He just wasn't meant to be working on the car right then.

The door to the garage opened. He saw Åsa's legs and slippers.

"Hi, it's me."

"Hi there, I'm under here."

"I can see that. Did the decision come in?"

Thomas rolled out. Remained lying on the creeper. Looked up at Åsa. He'd made up his mind. It felt overwhelming. Big. But they didn't deserve better, his traitor colleagues.

"They dropped the internal investigation, but I was transferred. To the traffic unit."

Her face was upside down. It was still obvious—a smile, relaxation. She breathed out.

"Oh my God, what a relief. That's wonderful. I thought they'd do something worse."

"Åsa, it's fucking awful. How can you say that this is a good thing? Don't you understand what working in that unit's going to do to me? I'm going to rot. I can't do it, I have to fix this. I don't know how, but please don't say that it's a good thing."

"I'm sorry, but it's still a relief. Imagine if you were convicted. I can't help it."

Thomas got up. "There is one more thing I have to tell you."

"What?" She looked worried.

"I've actually said yes to another job offer. As a head security guard. It's private. Completely outside the force."

Åsa continued to look worried.

"I'm taking it."

"Are you joking with me, Thomas?"

"Not at all. I'm completely serious. It's a part-time job that I think sounds really exciting. So I'm going to call Adamsson tomorrow and tell him that I'm only taking the traffic job part-time and that he can shove his damn sympathy up his ass. The rest of the time, I'll do this other thing."

"Thomas, you can't do that. That doesn't sound stable at all."

Thomas felt tired. Didn't have the energy to argue anymore.

At the same time: maybe this was the beginning of something new.

31

The worst rain all year, even though it was still summer. It pissed on the city. Smattered against the windshield like machine-gun fire. Sick, if you thought about it. Mahmud remembered the sound of machine-gun rounds from when he was a kid. A family wedding in a Baghdad suburb. Back then you shot because you were happy, Dad used to say.

Hopefully, this was his final run to the Shurgard facility for today. Sköndal. The place looked like a cross between a knight's castle and a barn. A tower with a big-ass sign: SHURGARD SELF-STORAGE. OUR SPACE, YOUR PLACE. Pale-pink wood look—in actuality, the place was sheet metal. Surrounded by asphalt: parking lots, ramps to storage areas, unloading docks. Last week it'd been the storage facility in Kungens Kurva, the week before that the one in Bromma. He'd been across half the city, but they looked the same everywhere he went.

Mahmud dug the place. The idea was tight. No need to meet the Yugos' underlings unnecessarily. This operation ran on a strictly need-to-know basis, as Ratko put it. They refilled the stuff as soon as Mahmud informed them he wanted to make a withdrawal. He dropped paper off ahead of time at a Yugo-owned bodega in Bredäng. The Yugos were smart: the rules were tougher than at Guantánamo Bay. Mahmud was a nobody in their world. If he got done, they'd say they'd never seen him, never even heard his name. Again: the setup was thick as cream—from their perspective.

What could he do? His debt to Gürhan was what'd made him do it. Honestly: his promise to Erika Ewaldsson hadn't been 100 percent bullshit. He really didn't want to be rolling like this. Muscle juice, that was his thing. He chowed on the stuff himself, so why not finance his own body by dealing some pills? But this—if he got collared again he'd be benched for the long haul.

He'd borrowed Robert's car. Felt weird. A cute little Golf. Sporty: curved gray leather seats, big Navi Plus, and fresh fenders. Nothing wrong with it, but he'd made his previous rounds in Babak's deluxe ride. That was all over now. Babak'd cut him off. Since Mahmud'd told him about his collaboration with the Yugos. Babak'd asked Mahmud to pack his stuff and move. Shit—Babak was a whiny fucking pussy. A *sharmuta.*

Outdoor storage units were a little more expensive, but much easier to get to with a car. You didn't have to go inside the facility, didn't have to pass by too many surveillance cameras, didn't have to face too many petrified peeps. Ratko'd grinned when he'd told him that the storage unit was even insured.

"Get it? If there's a break-in, at least the insurance company'll pay us back for the store of balsa we supposedly have in there."

Mahmud punched in the pin code. Fiddled with the key. His hands were slippery. The security in these places: pin code, keys, surveillance cameras. Still: he felt weak. Flashes of light in front of his eyes. The Range Rover with Wisam in the backseat. Why did he think about that? A player like him had to keep moving. Ditch the past.

'Cause after he'd sold the shit today, he'd be free. Soon his final payment to Gürhan and the Born to Be Hated *blattes* would be over and done with. Three months of terror drawing to a close. He just had to shovel this last snow. Damn, it was gonna be sweet.

The thirty G's he'd gotten from Stefanovic plus crazy kronor he'd raked in through weed and blow sales over the past few months'd paid off 95 percent of the debt. And tonight at the gym—the deal was basically sealed with Dijma, a big customer. Tight. Then it would be *jalla adios* to Gürhan. But even more tight: good-bye to the Yugo swine too—the ones he'd been dumb enough to help liquidate a homie from the block—who he'd slaved for these two months, who'd reamed him so hard up the dirty when he'd asked them for help. He was gonna quit. Do what Erika Ewaldsson'd recommended: Stop with the criminal activity. Become a free man.

Mahmud locked the bag with the shit into his locker at the gym. The wrapping paper and plastic bulked it up. No risk getting it swiped at Fitness Center—if anyone got caught trying to boost something here, he'd first get his balls squeezed a few turns in the cogs of the ab machine and then get his head smashed under three or four plates on the thigh press. After that, they'd make a protein shake out of the sucker and treat the meatheads to samples.

Mahmud walked into the gym. The Eurotechno was blaring. He

greeted a couple of big guys by the free weights. What was chill about gyms: a *blatte* like Mahmud almost never had to feel alone.

On the schedule today: squats. At other gyms: a ton of hooked-up cardio machines and advanced press-and-pull gear designed to isolate muscles you didn't even know you had. Sci-fi land or whatever. Nothing wrong with that, for some, but according to Mahmud, the key to bulking up was in the basic exercises. Always with free weights. And the squat was king of all free-weight exercises.

There was a lot of talk that squats led to busted backs and other problems. Mahmud knew better: the reason for back pain wasn't the exercise in and of itself, it was bad technique. The solution was simple for anyone with half a brain. Mahmud'd done his research, talked to the others at Fitness Center. Instead of starting the movement at the hip, you should do what the strength guru Charles Poliquin'd always said: start the squat with your knees.

He loved the exercise. And soon he would go on the juice—then things would get even better. He put 180 pounds on each side of the bar. Began the maneuver by bending his knees slowly. As he lowered the bar, he only moved his hips when he needed to in order to maintain balance. He was going to do three sets of ten. He spit, snarled, growled between his teeth. Felt the blood vessels being pressed to the max. His eyes almost popped. *Abbou*—it felt good. He was only thinking about the lift, the move, the bend in his knees. No bad memories, no bad conscience, no bad karma.

When he was on the juice he'd be able to handle much more. And damn, he was gonna bulk up. With good discipline, he could gain twenty-two pounds. Inject Stanol and front-load Deca. The ampoules felt unreal, but Mahmud was happy needles didn't scare him—the injection needles were as big as straws from McDonald's. Then he'd take some Winstrol to dry out—he didn't want to look like a balloon.

There were some minor downsides, too. The word at the gym was that your kidneys could take a hit. But he was only gonna do it for eight weeks.

An hour later: Dijma with a gripper in his hands. Dijma: buyer with a big B who never bought on credit—always cash. Dijma: the Albanian who didn't work out too much, but who sold a crazy bunch of shit. Always applying mad force to the gripper. The muscles in his thumbs big as tennis balls. The nails on the dude's pinky fingers were long like on a porn star.

Mahmud dug him, a straight thug. Dressed in classic gym getup: sweatpants and a long-sleeved shirt, a zippered hoodie. Looked around. No one. A Friday night—the gym was half empty at this time of day.

Mahmud put the weights down. "Hey, Twiggy, stop working your wank muscle and do some free weights instead."

Dijma grinned. Rules of the hierarchy: Mahmud was bigger, Mahmud sat on the goods. Mahmud delivered. So: Dijma laughed at whatever Mahmud said.

In shit Swedish, "The gear, you got it?" Dijma was apparently stressed today.

"Sure. Fifty, in one package."

"Fuck, man, you guys were gonna break it up."

"Chill. You break it up. That's no problem."

"Okay, okay. And the price?"

"Nine hundred pesetas."

"Pesetas?"

"Kronor, man. Fuck, you tired today?"

"Nine hundred kronor? No way. Eight hundred."

"We've said nine hundred every time for months. So don't think you're gonna come changing it now."

"Prices change. And you didn't break it up."

Dijma said it like it was some fucking macroeconomic certainty. Mahmud didn't dig his grouse.

"This is bullshit. Nine hundred, that's the deal."

"Eight fifty, not a kronor more." Dijma was too cocky for his own good.

Mahmud shouldn't put up with this shit. But still: he needed the cash, bad.

His calculation: if he sold fifty times 850 a gram it would be 42,500. Mahmud's cut: twelve G's. Wasn't enough to cover the final payment of fifteen to Gürhan. He needed nine hundred a gram. Or else he was screwed.

Mahmud took a step forward.

"Dijma, the price is nine hundred. We can negotiate next time, then I'll give you eight hundred. But today it's nine hundred. You follow?"

Dijma pumped the grip a few times. Mahmud didn't drop his gaze.

The Albanian nodded. "For today, okay. Next day, eight hundred."

Bull's-eye. Dijma must be stressing about something; he'd folded too easily. Normally, this kind of thing could've made for some tense shit. But not today, and it wasn't Mahmud's problem—he was gonna celebrate.

They walked down to the locker room. Sat next to each other on the bench. Mahmud handed over the bag of gear. Dijma went into a toilet stall to test it. Mahmud, with a raised voice: "Ey, you don't trust me or what?" The Albanian didn't respond. Came out thirty seconds later, thumbs up, pushed over a plastic bucket that said CREATAMAX 300 on the side—normally, bodybuilder milkshake. Today: dough. Mahmud dove his hand in. Fingered the bills.

Totally insane. In a few hours, Mahmud would raise his Stockholm ranking. Lose the Gürhan pigs. Quit the Yugo assholes. Become his own man. Rock for real.

Eleven-thirty, a Friday night in Stockholm: people acted like they were on speed. Had waited all week to go out, plus it'd been pouring all day. But now: the rain'd stopped—summer was back. It might be the last chance for that sweet outdoor buzz, that summer fuck, that weed flight. Muscle cars were driving down Sveavägen to cruise around, around, elbows stuck out through open windows: as *Suedi* as only Svens could be. The kids on their way from the joints in Vasastan that were about to close. Mission: make their way to Stureplan and guzzle some glamour. Mahmud: on his way to freedom.

Carried his gym bag slung over his shoulder. In it: 45,000 cash in a container that'd once held strawberry-flavored creatine powder. Thirty grand had to be repaid to Robert, for the advance for the Yugos. The remaining fifteen were going to Gürhan. No big sums, obviously. But it was Mahmud's key to freedom.

He walked downtown. Played with the contents of his pocket. A Redline baggie, five grams. Ducked into the shadows of a building. Fished out a cigarette. Twisted it between thumb and index finger. The tobacco fell into his hand.

He poured the weed onto the paper, mixed it with the tobacco from the cigarette. Licked. Rolled. Ran the lighter flame along the edge of the paper a few times to dry the shit. Lit the spliff. Three deep hits. Smoke rings in the shadows. Relaxed feeling.

This was going to be an ill night.

Robert was waiting in the Golf outside the kabob place near Hötorget. Phat beats could be heard from a several-yard radius.

Rob smiled. Mahmud smiled broader. Jumped into the passenger seat.

Mahmud asked, "You know Fat Joe's Chinese, right?"

Robert revved the engine. "He's not fucking Chinese. He's an Indian."

"Indian? Haven't you seen the guy? Mix of Zinji and Chinese. *Walla*, I swear, man."

Rob leaned his head back against the seat. Laughed.

Made a U-turn in the middle of Sveavägen. Stepped on the gas. Down to Norrtull. Hardly any traffic. Turned up onto Essingeleden. Southbound toward Södertälje.

Robert changed tracks on the stereo. Sweet Middle Eastern beats. Mahmud liked rap and R & B, but a swinging riff by some Lebanese outclassed most things.

Robert turned the volume down. "Yo, what's Babak's beef with you?"

Mahmud didn't know what to say.

"I don't know. It's between us."

Robert said, "Can't you talk it out?"

Mahmud didn't want to drag Robert into this; there was the risk that he wouldn't understand—react like Babak. Still: the whole thing felt fucked. Babak was his boy.

"It's cool. I just can't handle Babak right now, is all."

Robert didn't ask anything else.

They drove under the train bridge. Södertälje station. Turned right. Toward the city. Over the channel. Mahmud navigated. Had been there many times before. Dug the place: the closest thing to a *blatte*-ruled city you could get without it feeling like a godforsaken slum.

The place: Carwash, City & Södertälje. Detailing. The advertising outside: UNBEATABLE PRICES AND ACCESS TO A REPLACEMENT CAR! Robert parked. Leaned back, looked for something on the floor of the backseat. Fished up a wheel lock. Put it on and clicked it into place.

"You know, this is Södertälje. Every other kid born here is a football pro and the rest boost rides."

A metal door next to the garage. They rang the doorbell. It was dark out.

Mahmud felt for the butterfly knife in his back pocket.

A buzzing sound. A click in the lock. Mahmud opened the door. Concrete floor. Ditec car repair posters on the walls. Ads for maintenance products, car-care packages, equipment, polish, and wax.

Mahmud looked around. Empty.

A voice from the office area. "Look at that, the little Arab. And how are you today?"

Daniel emerged from the shadows. Beside him, a huge dude. Daniel: like a dwarf in comparison. Mahmud'd seen a lot of big guys in his day. At Fitness Center, at K-1, in the concrete, in the pen. Dudes who shat themselves every day under the bench press to get pecs that weren't even half as big as the beef standing next to Daniel right now. The guy was in the same class as the Belarusian at the K-1 gala.

They went into the office area. A desk, a desk chair, two armchairs. Centerfold chicks on the walls.

Gürhan was sitting in the desk chair. Met Mahmud's gaze.

"Welcome." The voice sounded innocent. His eyes were dead.

No chair for Robert and the giant, they had to stand in the background.

Daniel hauled a box with two cords and antennas onto the desk. Mahmud'd heard of that kind of thing in the pen. Some kind of anti-bugging device. Interfered with the 5-0's connection if they'd wired the place. Why all the bells and whistles? Why the giant in the background? Why was Gürhan there at all?

Daniel said, "You got the cash?"

Mahmud set the plastic container on the table. Opened the lid. The smell of candy. Took out the fifteen one-thousand-kronor bills. Turned to Gürhan.

"I know I fucked up. Lost your Winstrol. But now I've paid back every cent plus your interest. One hundred percent. I paid the whole enchilada."

He hid his hands under the desk. Sweating like in a fucking sauna.

Daniel continued to respond instead of Gürhan. "No, we don't agree. You've been messin' this whole time. Been late. Whining like a fucking whore."

Mahmud stared at him. Didn't lower his gaze a millimeter. His heart was beating worse than Fat Joe's base beats. Then: he dissed Daniel.

Turned to Gürhan again. "Bullshit. I paid. And I paid double interest. With these fifteen G's, we're done."

Daniel started barking again. "Shut the fuck up. You don't talk to Gürhan like that. Who do you think you are, you fuckin' fag? Get out. We don't want your filthy Arab money."

Robert looked at Mahmud. Hands in his pockets. Worried. Maybe he had a grip on his knife as hard as Mahmud longed to have on his. The giant took a step forward.

Daniel got up.

"I said leave! And take your nasty candy jar with you."

Robert looked at Mahmud again. His stress was palpable. Mahmud remained seated. Eyes fixed on Gürhan.

"He's not calling me a fag one more time. We're done now. I've paid you what you wanted."

Silence.

Gürhan met Mahmud's gaze.

Mahmud repeated, "We're done."

Daniel lost it. "If you say one more word, I'll kick your skull in."

Then: Gürhan raised his hand. "Sit down."

Daniel turned around. Surprised. Unclear who Gürhan was talking to.

He turned to Daniel. "I said, sit down."

Daniel tried to protest.

Gürhan repeated, "Sit."

Daniel sat down. The giant took a step back toward the wall.

"He's paid what he owed."

Mahmud could hardly believe it was true. Got up. Robert was breathing heavily in the background.

Gürhan said, "Wait."

Mahmud turned around. Gürhan's face was still completely neutral. He said, "Take care, Mahmud."

Cue: string quartet. Hollywood ending. Finally free to flow.

32

Monday. Niklas woke up at eight even though he hadn't gone to bed until 4:00 a.m. He'd been to see a doctor yesterday—talked his way into getting certified sick leave. Run through last night's surveillance videos one more time. One camera'd stopped filming at eleven o'clock. Niklas found it on the ground beneath the tree where it'd been mounted. Someone could've seen it and torn it down, that was possible. As long as it wasn't the guy he was watching. Niklas needed time—he couldn't get found out, couldn't arouse suspicions. The Operation was fragile enough as it was.

Despite that: he'd seen enough. Mats Strömberg would be served his punishment. Operation Magnum's first offensive was in the preliminary stage. Niklas was planning, drawing up an attack strategy. Thought about Collin and the others down in the sandbox. He tried to run through the family's routines over and over again. Realized: he didn't know enough about the swine. Needed to keep close watch over him for a few more days.

The day rolled on. He munched Nitrazepam, ate yogurt. Read a book about the radical feminist Valerie Solanas by some Swedish girl named Sara Stridsberg. She thought the way he did, even if the book was a tough read. But the idea was right on. *SCUM: Society for Cutting Up Men*—a manifesto for action solved problems better than a bunch of pathetic theorizing.

He was supposed to meet Benjamin at six o'clock. Considered canceling. At the same time: Benjamin'd promised to get him a weapons hookup. He needed that.

A few hours left: he read, organized the information he had on the different men, their routines, their patterns, their behavior toward their wives, partners, girlfriends. It was just a matter of domination. The nuclear family was a sealed-off world.

He surfed the Internet. Something new: Niklas'd found websites where people shared his opinions. Feminist chat forums where the comments mirrored his feelings. The hate. The drive. The hunt. For the guilty parties. The men.

It was pouring out. A feeling of purity. Rain'd been a blessing in all the countries where he'd been at war. Often the paramilitary forces, the support units, and the guerrilla men who'd fought on the same side as Niklas would stop for half an hour or so, even in the middle of an attack, to pray to their different gods. Give thanks for the rain, for the ground that would be able to sprout new flowers, bear new crops. Pray for victory on the battlefield. *Inshallah.*

That's why going into Friden felt grodier than usual.

Benjamin was already sitting at a table. His beard was wet. Under the table was his dog, Arnold. It got up when Niklas approached. Wagged its nub of a tail languidly. But the eyes—Niklas met its gaze. Like low, intensely glowing embers.

He ordered a Coke Zero.

"Did you go become one of those health freaks while I wasn't looking?" Benjamin asked.

Niklas didn't want to drink alcohol. In two hours, he had to get back to Sundbyberg, watch over the Strömberg family in general, the so-called patriarch in particular.

"No, but I saw one on my way over. I think there's one of those Hare Krishna places around here."

"Oh man, should I set Arnold loose on 'em?"

Laugh break.

"Did I tell you that I'm gonna start training him for his first fight?"

"Did you dock his tail?"

"Can't you tell?"

"Yeah, but that's illegal."

"Oh, stop. Arnold's imported from Belgium. They don't have those crazy rules over there."

"Okay, and how's the training going?"

"There's a dude who breeds these kinds of dogs in Stockholm. He's taught me a bunch of tricks." Benjamin's eyes gleamed. "You starve the dog and let it eye bitches in heat without letting it touch them. Then you tie its legs together, put a cup over its cock so the dog can't jizz, then spray period blood from the bitches all over the cage, rile it up till it's about to burst. Arnold's gonna be crazier than a *Tyrannosaurus rex*."

Niklas looked at Benjamin like he didn't know him. Thought, You're sick.

He asked if Benjamin'd gotten the hookup. Benjamin smiled, nodded. Looked pleased with himself. Pushed a folded Post-it note across the table. Niklas unfolded it: *Black & White Inn, Södermalm. Lucic. Monday night.* Benjamin'd doodled a gun at the bottom of the note. The guy was so immature.

Niklas shook Benjamin's hand. "I won't forget this."

They kept chatting. Benjamin went on and on about Arnold's potential triumphs, then about chicks and business ideas. He downed one beer after the other. Niklas was stressed out. He had to go in ten minutes.

Benjamin made Arnold sit on the seat next to him. The dog's tongue was dangling from its mouth like a strip of bacon.

Niklas considered his options. Should he stay just to keep Benjamin in a good mood? The guy'd given him a weapons hookup, after all. And the guy'd done him a favor when the cops'd asked about that night this summer. At the same time: he had to go. The Operation was more important right now.

On his way to Sundbyberg. Niklas had too many ideas at once. His goal was clear. To become the kind of person who makes a mark on the world. But he needed resources. The attack demanded cash. The thought ballooned. Maybe he could use Benjamin somehow.

So many people are born who never make a mark. People who might as well not have been born. A hundred years later, who would care if they hadn't ever been born into the world? Who would care if someone made sure they disappeared from the world?

Doing something with Benjamin. Maybe. Could be a possibility. But there were some major problems: Benjamin wasn't made of the right stuff. No matter how many fighting dogs or bad-boy tattoos he got: he was a pussy.

Niklas needed someone else. Someone who would actually be able to go through with what he had in mind. Who did he know? He thought about the websites he'd visited over the past few weeks. The feminist people. Maybe he could find someone there?

33

Formally, he'd been given his service weapon back. But no one packed heat in this unit. Thomas carried his anyway. The gun's weight felt strange in his pocket. His blazer sort of fit crookedly; he kept having to straighten it. Armed, but without a uniform, the way civvies must feel all the time. But for one gigantic difference: that wasn't the service he was in.

His job at the traffic unit was almost duller than the two months he'd spent waiting for the verdict. The people in the unit were like the geeks in school when he'd been a kid. Or rather, these guys were probably the same wimps, but twenty-five years later. Those things never change: geeks are geeks. Laughed at boring word puns, talked about what kind of food they'd cooked their wives the night before, got worked up about how poor the quality of the new plastic binders in the office was. The unit was in Farsta. Thomas tended to go out alone for lunch—grab a burger or a kebob.

But tonight something was going to happen. A new experience in life. From nine o'clock till late at night: his first assignment for the Yugo boss, Mr. Kranjic. Security-guard duty. Bouncer responsibility. Mood-calming utility. If anyone got cocky/violent/inappropriate—it was his job to take care of the situation. Hard manual labor was his specialty.

He thought: the only downside was that the place he was guarding was a strip club. Not that he had anything against strip clubs. You ended up at places like that sometimes. Hannu Lindberg's bachelor party; after a work thing four years ago; together with some buds from the shooting club when they'd been to a competition in Estonia. He liked the whole concept. Sitting with a drink in hand watching the chicks swing their hips, pout, twirl around the pole. Unclasp their bras, slowly release their garter belts, let their panties fall to the floor. Lap dances for the heavy tippers. It was hot, relaxed, a damn good time. Never looked as good as what you got online, but reality is always full of flaws. A visit to a strip joint now and then could spice up the everyday. A little silver lining, in his pants.

So when he arrived at the club, mixed feelings: disgust and horniness. What's more, he felt like he was being unfaithful. Even though things weren't working with Åsa in the sack, he'd promised himself: I don't do that kind of thing. It just wasn't him—the online porn would have to suffice. He told himself the strip club wasn't cheating.

Another thing was his confusion over being on the other side. He'd been a cop for twelve years.

At the same time: the girls were there, so close. Not just frozen images on a screen or dancing goddesses on a stage that, at best, you got to pinch in the butt. But for real. So thin, provocatively dressed, giggly. So simple to get. So easy to take. They ran in and out of the dressing room with their cell phones since there wasn't any service in there. Some were only dressed in their show outfits. Tight thighs, lifted tits, inviting dimples. He was staring like a skeevy old drooler.

It was bizarre. At the same time, awesome. Imagine if Ljunggren or Lindberg could see this. Jealous as horny jackrabbits. Imagine if his bosses got wind of his extra gig. Imagine if Åsa found out what he was doing. Stop—he didn't even want to think that thought.

Thomas was stationed at the cash register out by the entrance. Two other dudes at the joint: a Yugo guy, Ratko, who stayed inside the venue, around the stage. The other guy, Andrzej, a Polack or something, who remained out by the entrance with Thomas.

Andrzej rocked a hard-boiled, testy style. Pushed limits, provoked. When Ratko introduced him to Thomas, he asked, "What are *you* doing here? Aren't you a cop?"

Ratko told him to cool it. Thomas didn't say anything. Just stared straight ahead.

A chick who looked Asian manned the register: Belinda. She tried to make conversation. Thomas, a man of few words. Kept to himself. Didn't bother with her or the Polack. He was just here to do his job tonight. Easy does it.

During the first few hours, the place was dead. Three or four men an hour slid up to the cash register. Some were soft-spoken. Tried not to attract attention. Thomas thought, You're already here, so it's not like anyone's going to think you got lost or something. Others were rowdier. Joked with the chick at the register, asked if she'd do a show later, wondered if she couldn't give him a discount 'cause he was a regular, asked her what she wanted for an hour, just a suck.

Belinda turned to Thomas.

"Has Ratko gone over what the deal is here?"

Thomas shook his head.

"So, most girls just do their show, with fixings. You know, some moves and a lap dance. Maybe they'll allow a slap on the ass and a tongue on their boobs, but no more. But some do other stuff, too. A little hanky-panky, if you know what I mean."

Thomas understood. He'd been a cop longer than this chick'd had tits.

At eleven o'clock, the volume of the music inside the venue was raised. Ratko was switched out. A guy named Bogdan showed up.

Thomas couldn't see inside. A pair of red swinging doors separated the entrance area from the showroom. Did he want to see inside? Yes. No. Yes.

Andrzej and Belinda babbled on with each other. Joked, laughed. Discussed the latest episode of some TV show, real-estate prices in the city, which of the girls in the club had real tits. Andrzej claimed he could always tell.

More guys streamed in. Twenty, thirty of them.

Thomas leaned against the wall. Thought about his own investigation. It'd been more than a week since he called John Ballénius's daughter. Gotten Ljunggren to run a search on the guy in all the government databases. Ordered passport photos. Unfortunately, no phone number seemed to work. But he had an address: 46 Tegnérgatan. Thomas'd gone there both Sunday and Monday nights. Tried on Tuesday and Wednesday morning and night as well. Asked Jonas Nilsson, a former colleague who worked in a squad downtown these days, to swing by and ring Ballénius's doorbell in the middle of the day on Thursday. No one was home. Either the dude was out of the country, or he was a work junkie, or he was dead.

Thomas tried to call the different numbers that Ballénius'd had over the past few months. All of the plans'd been closed out; there was no forwarding information. He tried the most frequently called number again. The person on the other end of the line hung up on him just like last time. It was a prepaid plan. Thomas didn't know who the number belonged to. The next most called number was the daughter he'd talked to earlier. The third most called number turned out to be a pizza place on Södermalm. They had no idea who John Ballénius was. The fourth most called number was a man with a real boozer voice who'd done some business with Ballénius, as he put it. When Thomas started asking questions, he hung up.

So Thomas decided to call her again, the daughter, Kicki. Her answer was loud and clear. "I have no idea where my dad is. We haven't really been in touch in over seven years, but he's been trying to call me a lot over the past few months. I hung up as soon as I realized it was him. But we already talked about that." She sounded sincere. Thomas asked her where she thought her father might be if this'd been seven years ago. Kicki thought the old guy ought to be home at Tegnérgatan. Other than that, she didn't know.

But the fucker wasn't home. Thomas was no detective, but really, how hard could it be to track down a crooked fifty-year-old in Stockholm? That's when it hit him: maybe Ballénius was more famous than he'd realized.

Thomas got in touch with Jonas Nilsson again. Gave him some info on Ballénius that he'd gotten from the comprehensive searches he'd done in the databases. Asked Nilsson to check if he or anyone else in the City District knew anything more. Two hours later, Nilsson called back. When he'd asked around at lunch, a bunch of old-timers'd just laughed. Apparently, John Ballénius was a legend in shady circles. Just as Thomas'd suspected.

Nilsson had more to say. Ballénius was a notorious gambler. Poker, sports betting, horses, everything. Back in the day, the guy'd even hung out at Oxen, the gambling club on Malmskillnadsgatan. Thomas knew the place, infamous underground club in the eighties. Lots of stuff'd been written about Oxen: that it'd been a hangout of Christer Pettersson—the man who the majority of Sweden's population believed murdered Prime Minister Olof Palme.

The best tip the old-timer cops offered was to look for Ballénius at the track at Solvalla or at the casino.

Thomas started at Solvalla. V75. Signs everywhere advertising THE EXTRA SPICE OF THE DAY: THE JUBILEE TROPHY. It was one of the biggest trotting-race events of the year. The informational pamphlets claimed that anyone with a penchant for harness racing should be there. So of course Thomas should be there. Hopefully, Ballénius felt the same way.

The weather was fantastic. People were crowding outside—the worry that the rain would return was as forgotten as the greenhouse effect at a car show. Rowdy atmosphere, excitement in the air. Ads for Agria pet insurance wallpapered the area. Hot dogs, beer, and tote tickets in everyone's hands. The speakers blazoned out the day's races. Soon it would begin.

Thomas didn't think Ballénius would be hanging out in the outdoor grandstands. So, he planned on starting inside the building. It was big, with glass façades, probably 330 feet long. Four stories, but each story was like its own grandstand.

The different floors had different class. At the bottom of the huge building: Ströget, the sports bar. Complete liquor license. Big-screen TVs showing the track better than if you were outside by the standing tables. Cold beer, sausages, burgers made with 100 percent beef. The clientele: mostly younger. Swedish guys in jeans and T-shirts with their wallets slapped down on the tables. A couple of their chicks, girls with their hair pulled into little balls on the top of their heads. A couple of families. Outside: bouncers.

Thomas trusted his gut instinct. If Ballénius was here, he wouldn't hang on this floor.

The speakers were blaring out the special event of the day: "As you all know, Björn and Olle Goop's Conny Nobell was last year's Elite Race champion. But the Goop family never got to make their victory lap in front of our audience. So here at Solvalla we now want to bring your attention to the Elite Race champions. Welcome onto the track, Björn and Olle Goop!"

The next level was called the Bistro—simple tray service with tables on different tiers. View over the track. Still, it cost fifty kronor just to get in. Thomas flashed his badge to the host at the entrance, who asked if something was wrong. Thomas shook his head. Showed the copy of Ballénius's passport photo. "No, but we're looking for this man, John Ballénius, do you know him?" The host's turn to shake his head. The guy was young, couldn't have been working at Solvalla for long. Recommended that Thomas ask the gaming manager in the restaurant today, Jens Rasten. Thomas walked up to the counter, asked a waitress about Rasten. She disappeared into the kitchen. A man with light brown hair and a beer gut came out.

Faint Danish accent: "Hi, you're from the police, I hear. I'm Jens Rasten, responsible for the Bistro. How may we help you?"

"I'm sorry to disturb you on such a busy day. I'm looking for a person named John Ballénius. Do you know him?"

Rasten's eyes turned first to the photocopy of the picture, then angled up to the side. Looked like he was thinking, hard. There was

cheering in the background. Down on the track, the Goops were fin-
ishing their victory lap.

"They're amazing, the Goop family," Rasten said.

Thomas, irritated. What the hell was the Dane talking about?

"Yes, but I was asking you about John Ballénius."

"Sorry. I don't know him. But check with the guy over there, Sami
Kiviniemi. He's been here every race weekend for as long as I can
remember. He knows everybody."

Thomas was tired. What kind of stupid game was this? How many
people would he have to talk to today? Either they knew the Ballénius
dude or he wasn't here. End of story. Still, he approached Kiviniemi.

In Thomas's eyes: the dude looked like a caricature of a Finn. Blond
beard, sunglasses with mirrored lenses, a crooked smile with a front
tooth missing, a baseball cap on his head with the Mercedes-Benz logo
on it, a Solvalla bag in one hand. He was wearing a fleece sweater even
though it was August.

Sami was talking race talk with another guy.

Thomas didn't have the energy to play polite. Knocked the Finn on
the shoulder. Flashed his police badge with one hand and the photo of
John Ballénius with the other. "Do you know who this guy is?"

Sami: shifty eyed. Maybe it was surprise, maybe worry.

He took the passport copy in hand. "Sure, that's Johnny."

Thomas started.

"But you'll never find him here at the Bistro. If he's here today, which
he should be, he'll be in the luxury place, up there, the Congress. He's a
real hustler, that Ballénius. Real slippery. What's he done?"

Thomas: already halfway up the escalator. On his way to the upper-
most story. His heart was beating like after a workout session.

He arrived. Looked down over the Congress Bar and Restaurant: à
la carte restaurant with tables on the grandstand right above the finish
line. White tablecloths, wall-to-wall carpeting, low music playing in the
background, flat screens and forms for V65, V75, and other games on
the tables. The majority: gentlemen in their fifties and sixties. Expectant atmosphere. The first race of the day would start in two minutes.

The host at the entrance referred him to the headwaiter, who looked
through his list of reservations. Yup, John Ballénius'd booked his lucky
table today. Number 118.

Thomas made his way through the tables. Glanced around, checking out the place: people with their own laptops who didn't seem to

give a shit about the view, women in their forties with hoarse laughs, pens, and betting cards, more ads for Agria pet insurance. On a few tables: champagne in ice buckets. Seemed like some people already knew they'd be celebrating.

Table 118: sixteen feet farther off. He saw him, recognized him from the passport photo. It had to be him—Ballénius. He was sitting with three others: two women and a bald man. Ballénius looked tall, pretty thin. According to the printouts he'd pulled from the official register of licensed companies, he should be around fifty-five years old. Worn face, deeply furrowed forehead, the laugh wrinkles cut across his cheeks like cracks. But there was no laughter in that face. Thomas didn't think he'd ever seen anyone with such a gray, hollow, sorrowful appearance before.

On the table were plates with entrées, wineglasses and a half-empty wine bottle, two bottles of beer, cards, pamphlets and folders, calculators, pens, cell phones. The women looked dolled up, more elegant than he would've expected to be with Ballénius. What ruined the picture: one of them had a bag from the discount grocery store Willys by her side instead of a purse.

Thomas stepped up to the table. Flashed his badge.

Saw John Ballénius's panicked look plainly.

"Hi there, John. May I ask you a few questions?"

Ballénius's eyes were unfocused. He was looking off into the distance. Then he nodded.

The women looked like two question marks. One of them wondered if Thomas could wait until after the race. The bald guy didn't seem to give a shit. Ballénius got up. Walked ahead of Thomas.

They made their way through the tables. Out to the gambling booths. It was completely empty up there now. The race was starting in thirty seconds.

"What do you want?" Ballénius asked, still without looking at Thomas.

"I'm glad I got ahold of you. It's regarding something pretty serious. A homicide."

Ballénius faked surprise. "Oh, damn. But what do you want with *me*?"

Thomas explained quickly. That they'd found a phone number in a dead man's back pocket. That the number probably went to a plan that Ballénius'd had earlier, which'd been checked with his daughter. The guy leaned against the wall. Screams and cheers could be heard from down in the Congress. The race'd begun. He was gazing somewhere past Thomas.

The dude: jumpy as hell. This wasn't ideal at all. In a real investigation, they would've brought Ballénius in for informational questioning. But now Thomas was running his own race.

"So, now I want to know if you know who the dead guy is."

John's eyes flitted past his own. "Where did you find him, did you say?"

"Ten Gösta Ekman road. Out in Axelsberg."

"Okay." Ballénius's sad face contorted. To the extent that it was possible, it looked even more crushed than before.

"Do you know who it might be?"

"No idea."

"Do you recognize the address?"

"No, I don't think so."

Thomas was stressed—this was as far from a good interrogation situation as you could get. He had to get something out of him right away. Pulled a fast one.

"Your daughter already told us that you know. I spoke with Kicki yesterday."

John Ballénius looked shocked. Just stared at Thomas and said, "Kicki?"

"Yes, Kristina. We've been speaking quite a bit. I even went out to see her in Huddinge."

It sounded like John was whimpering. "It that true?"

"Yes, as true as the fact that you know who the dead guy is. Isn't that right?"

"It could be an old buddy of mine."

"Are you sure? What's his name?"

"I don't know him anymore. It was a long time ago. I don't know anything."

Loud cheering in the background. A high-odds horse was about to bring home the race..

"Come on, or else we'll have to bring you in for questioning."

"I guess you'll have to do that, then."

"Goddammit. Just tell me his name."

"I told you, I don't know anything. That was many years ago. He was always a little kooky. Was always kind of weird. I felt bad for him. Real bad."

"But what is his name?"

John stood still. Then he said, "Claes."

"Claes what?" Thomas was almost 99 percent sure of the answer. Still: he wanted a confirmation. Come on now, John Ballénius. Come on.

People were coming up from the restaurant. Milling around the gambling booths. The race was over down there. It was time to bet on the next horse. The spaces outside the cash registers were filling up quickly.

Thomas tried to get Ballénius to spill it—it had to be Rantzell who'd been called from Ballénius's phone. Claes Rantzell.

Suddenly, Ballénius made a jerky motion. Threw himself to one side. Thomas tried to grab him. Got hold of his shirtsleeve, held firm for a microsecond. Then the fabric slid through his fingers.

Ballénius rushed toward the lines by the gambling booths. A ten-foot lead plus the element of surprise. Straight into the crowd. The guy hauled ass like a maniac. Thomas ran after him. Chased the tall man for as long as he could. Even more people were pushing their way toward the cash registers. A few were waving tote tickets. Toasting one another, cheering. He tried to push his way through.

Thomas saw John Ballénius's lead grow.

He waved his badge. To no avail. There were too many people.

He yelled. Pressed. Tried to push through.

He had to do something.

34

Mahmud was on his way to see his dad. The Iraqi club in Skärholmen, Dal Al-Salam. Robert gave him a ride. They drove in silence. Listened to Jay-Z's phat beats. Robert drove like a maniac.

It'd been a week since Mahmud'd made his last payment to the Born to Be Hated dudes. He should be happy. He should feel free, independent, unbound. Should.

Everything was fucked up. He was tired. Worn down. Above all, pissed off. They bent him over and did him so hard he wept. Used him like a dumb bitch who just took it. Forced him into the corner of the ring, beat him up mentally like he was a defenseless nobody. A huge betrayal.

Not Gürhan and his boys. But the ones he'd thought would save him: the Yugos—Radovan & Co. Christian fucking crusading Serbs, worse than the Zionists. Fuck them. Easy enough to say, but not so simple to do.

Robert turned to him.

"*Habibi*, what you thinking about? You look crushed, man."

"Nothing. It's cool."

"All right, big-shot hustler. If you say so."

They continued to listen to the music.

Last weekend, Mahmud'd been in touch with Stefanovic. Asked to meet up. They set a time and place: Saturday night, Black & White Inn, a bar in Södermalm, Stockholm's South Side. Stefanovic informed him, "You know, we can't be meeting up all the time. But I'll send someone."

Mahmud was planning on breaking up with the Yugo fuckers. Sell the last round of blow that'd he'd picked up and then: a clean break. Find a normal job. Make Erika E. happy. Above all: make Dad happy.

Tom'd given him a ride that time. The guy liked vintage cars—drove a Chevy from 1981, black with flames painted on the hood. Mahmud didn't get why. Tom assured him, "The engine and the box are from '95, so this baby rolls like a skateboard."

Tom was chill. Had taken a different route than Mahmud, but never looked down on *blattes* like him. Studied real academic stuff in high school. Mahmud grinned at the thought: it took the guy five years to graduate, but look at him now. Tom, twenty-two years old—had learned the debt-collection industry like a crazy college kid. As he put it, "Soon, I'll start my own company and then both Intrum Justitia and the Hells Angels'll have to watch out."

Tom'd asked Mahmud to take the wheel for a sec. Fished out a manila envelope. Poured the powder on a CD case. Almost impossible to make real lines while they were sitting in the car. They had to wing it. Live on the edge. Tom rolled a bill, sucked a noseful. Took back the wheel. Gave Mahmud the bill. He tried to appreciate the amount. Sucked. Shit, that was probably half a gram. The rush was even stronger on days when he'd worked out before. Two seconds later: his gums tickled, grew numb. Then: *schwing*.

The lights on the road floated together like in a photograph. The night was mad beautiful. His emotions were soaring. The road was like a long strip on a racetrack, lined by crazy fireworks.

Black & White Inn: a Yugo-owned place. Everyone needed their laundromats. Mahmud and his buds never really made sums big enough to need washing, but he knew that if you played in the big leagues, you had to do it sooner or later. Gürhan's gang ran their money through dry cleaners, video-rental stores, and other Syriac-run businesses. The Yugos ran restaurants and bars. Maybe even heavier shit: offshore accounts, islands in the West Indies, stocks, and crap like that.

Mahmud had to wait in the car. The rush was too sharp. After fifteen minutes, he felt more normal. They walked in.

Usual pub vibe. Beer ads in old wooden frames and wood paneling along the walls. Wood tables and wood chairs on the wood floor. The people here must have pretty poor imaginations.

The place was half empty. A dude met them. Eyes that looked sunk into his skull. Broad, blanched. Brutal appearance. Led them into some sort of VIP room. Closed the door behind them. Ratko, Stefanovic's gorilla, was in there, leaning back in a chair. The Yugo was dressed in a relaxed way. Chiller style today than anything Mahmud'd seen him or Stefanovic rock before. Ratko today: T-shirt, black jeans, and Sparco racing shoes. Mouth half open, chin up in the air. Don't-fuck-with-me attitude. Fight-picking look par excellence. But the dude was usually cool to Mahmud at the gym.

The Yugo nodded. "Hey Twiggy, you good?"

Real ballbuster comment: "Twiggy." Look in a mirror, Mahmud was twice as beefy as Ratko. But Mahmud was still as high as a skyscraper. Confidence on top. Wanted to take care of this fast. Responded without taking the bait. "I'm a'ight."

Small talk for five minutes. Then Ratko interrupted the chat: "I understand things're going well for you, sales-wise."

Mahmud laughed. Humility wasn't his thing. "You can call me the King Snowman."

Ratko grinned along. "Right?" But then his face changed. The smile vanished.

"There was something you wanted to talk about."

Mahmud rocked, shifted his weight from the right to the left foot.

"I'm gonna start a new life. So I'm gonna quit selling. The gear I picked up a few days ago, that'll be my last gig. But I already paid for that, so."

Ratko didn't say anything.

Mahmud looked at Tom. Tom looked at Mahmud.

Mahmud repeated, "I'm gonna quit selling."

Ratko pretended like he didn't hear what he said.

"Yo, you hear me or what? I quit."

Ratko threw his arms open. "Okay, so you quit. What do you want me to say about that?"

"Nothing."

"Right, and I'm saying nothing. But what'll happen to your sister? And what do you think your dad will think?"

Mahmud didn't understand what he was talking about.

"I mean, if you quit selling, then we're gonna have to sell the tanning salon where your sister works. Oh, you didn't know that? We own the place. And we're gonna have to tell your dad that you've been slinging for us. We've got pictures of you dropping cash off in the store in Bredäng. We've got pictures of you picking the gear up at the storage facilities. We've got pictures of you working corners in the city. Above all, we've got photos of you and Wisam Jibril. It's very possible that he might hear what happened to that Lebanese. Because of you. What'll he think about that?"

Mahmud had trouble producing saliva; his mouth was as dry as sand.

"I think you're starting to understand now, Mahmud.

Tom took a step forward. "Fuck man, let him quit if he wants to."

Ratko still had his gaze glued on Mahmud. "I think Mahmud can speak for himself."

Mahmud just wanted to get out of there. He made an effort. Focused. Had to say something. He said, "Come on. I can quit if I want to."

Ratko's reply was like the bite of whip: "Correct." A short pause, then he added, "But then your sis can forget all about her job and we'll tell your dad. We're honest people. He has to know, that's all."

In Skärholmen. Back to the present. Robert dropped Mahmud off outside Dal Al-Salam. Mahmud opened the door. A small bell jingled.

Inside, the smoke was thicker than in a hammam. The club couldn't care less about any potential no-smoking policies: everyone in there was over fifty anyway—why did they need to be healthy? The room: small, square tables with green tablecloths and ashtrays. Plastic chairs, posters with images of the Spiral Minaret on the Abu Duluf Mosque in Samarra, the martyr monument for the Iran-Iraq war in Baghdad, pictures of the desert in Najaf, herds of sheep, camels. An old-fashioned TV was suspended in one corner: Al Jazeera news was on as usual.

The chatter volume was turned up to max. The old guys were doing their usual things. Eating pita bread, drinking coffee with an extreme amount of sugar in it, smoking strong cigarillos and hookahs, playing *shesh-besh* and patience, flipping through Iraqi newspapers. Mahmud got a kick of nostalgia right away: the bread dipped in baba ghanoush, the hookah smell, the sound of the old men and their frantic discussions, the images of the homeland on the wall.

Mahmud's dad emerged out of the smoky fog. *"Salaam alaikum!"* Kissed Mahmud twice on each cheek. Looked happier than usual: maybe that wasn't so strange—Mahmud hadn't been to the club since he turned fourteen.

"Don't you want to say hello to everyone?" Beshar spoke softly. His Iraqi dialect was stronger than usual—*ch* sounds instead of *k* sounds. But Mahmud knew what his dad's friends thought about people like him, even though he'd only been locked up for a short turn. Iraqis who ruined things for everyone else, who soiled the dignity of the community with their criminal records.

Mahmud said, "No, *jalla* now. I wanna go."

Beshar shook his head. Mahmud thought, No matter what he says, it's a relief for him not to have to drag me around in here.

They walked across Skärholmen's square. The street vendors were hocking their wares as usual. Yelling out their claimed lowest-price guarantees.

They were picking up Jamila at her job, the tanning salon in Axelsberg. Mahmud remembered the Yugos' threat.

Dad said, "Do you know what has come to pass with Jamila's friend? Has he stopped molesting her?"

Mahmud thought he used such old-fashioned Arabic words sometimes. Like, what did *molest* even mean?

"He's not her friend. He was her boyfriend. I think they broke up and that he doesn't bother her anymore. I hope so."

Beshar didn't know too much about the incident a few months ago when Jamila's neighbor'd rushed into the apartment and beaten her guy to a pulp. Neither Jamila nor Mahmud wanted to tell him. The dude'd been hospitalized for eight days after he had surgery on his jaw—sucked breakfast/lunch/dinner through a straw. Still, the guy refused to talk to the cops who showed up and wanted to interrogate him. Despite everything he'd done to Jamila—he was a man of honor.

"Do you know what happened to her neighbor?" Beshar asked.

Mahmud had no idea. The guy seemed lethal.

A man with dark, curly hair, a dirty knit sweater, and a mustache was distributing slips of paper. A picture of a little boy in a fetal position. The text: *My brother is still in Romania. He can't travel. He has a very serious joint disease. He suffers a great deal and needs medical help. My family cannot afford to help him. We ask you for a gift. May God bless you!*

Beshar dropped a ten-kronor coin into the beggar's hand when he passed by collecting the slips of paper again. Mahmud looked at him.

"What are you doing? You can't give money to one of those."

Beshar turned to Mahmud. "An honorable man is always generous. That is the only thing I want to teach you, Mahmud. You need to maintain your dignity through life. Act like a man."

"I do, Dad."

"No, not when you're selling those pills and fighting with the police and prosecutors. Will you ever change?"

"I'm on the right track. Really, I am. I'm not doing that stuff anymore. That was before prison." Mahmud could hardly conceal the disappointment in his voice. When would he be able to start controlling his own life? Be free of all the *sharmutas* who fucked with him. Syriacs, Yugos, the parole office at Hornsfuck.

"You need to act respectfully toward people who deserve it, respect your elders, and always be generous, like toward that poor man we just passed right there. And then you have to take care of your sister. I am too old for that. Just think of all she's been through. Did you thank her neighbor?"

"Absolutely. I thanked him right after that thing happened. I think it made him happy. But he seems a little weird."

"That doesn't matter. Do you know what Allah's messenger—may blessings and peace be upon him—said about that?"

"About what?"

"About woman."

Mahmud remembered certain expressions that his dad'd taught him ages ago. "She is a rose."

"That's right. You must treat her well. The prophet also said that the best among you are those who treat your wives well. He said only an honorable man honors women. Do you understand? Think of your mother."

Mahmud thought about his mom. The memories grew hazier with each passing year. Her eyes, her kisses when he was about to go to sleep. The head scarf that she'd stopped wearing during those last years, but that was always hanging in their house like a reminder. Her stories about bandits and caliphs. He wondered who she'd been, really. What would've happened if she'd come along to Sweden? Then maybe everything wouldn't have gone to hell.

They were almost at Jamila's tanning salon. They passed the indoor subway platform at Mälarhöjden. Beshar moved his prayer beads between thumb and index finger.

Mahmud couldn't drop the irony of the situation. He'd taken a job with the Yugos in order to escape the Born to Be Hated, to get ahead in life. The result: instead of being chased by Gürhan, he was locked in by Stefanovic. Instead of being free but in debt, he was debt-free but a slave. And Abu was involved both times. They'd popped Wisam.

If Dad found out about Mahmud's contribution to that mess—shit, he didn't even want to think about it. Then he might as well just go die in a ditch right away.

Axelsberg, with the usual stores. One ICA grocery store and one video-rental place, an ATM, and a hair salon that looked like it hadn't changed its window display in thirty years. A newly opened Mexican joint in some old building and a beer dive. Finally: Jamila's tanning salon. Well, maybe not Jamila's per se— the Yugos owned the place. But she'd been working there for five years.

They walked in. The tanning booths were hidden behind gray doors. Jamila was mopping the floor. Tanning salons: nasty, sweaty, dirty by default. If you didn't keep it extra clean, not even the worst tanning addicts would show.

Jamila smiled. Beshar smiled. Mahmud watched them. Jamila reminded him of Mom, intense mood swings but always mad nice to Dad. Never talked back, pampered him. But maybe that was good. He got a flashback: the pig head in the paper bag.

Jivan showed fifteen minutes later. She was stressed out, said she had a ton of homework to do. Mahmud remembered his own school years. Babak, Rob, the others—none of them even knew what homework was.

They walked together to the grocery store. Shopped. Then they walked toward Örnsberg, where Jamila lived. Mahmud carried the bags of groceries. Past a playground, a football field, a wooded area. Past the whole Sven suburb with its advantages and privileges. It wasn't the fact that there was a park, a field, or a forest—they had all that in Alby too—it was that it all functioned so calmly and flawlessly. Fag fathers and day-care teachers in the park with the kids, no chaos. School teams on the football field, but no fights. Maybe he exaggerated the image of his own hood.

Beshar asked Jamila lots of questions. She talked about buying the tanning salon. Finally. The storefront and the business couldn't cost more than fifty G's to take over.

Jivan promised, "I'm gonna be a lawyer. Then I can lend you money."
They laughed.

Outside Jamila's house. Some dude was packing stuff into an Audi. At first, Mahmud didn't recognize the guy. Jamila seemed to want to avoid him, turned her face away. After three seconds: Mahmud realized who it was —the neighbor who'd pummeled her boyfriend.

Mahmud stopped. Called out to the neighbor.

The dude looked up. Responded in Arabic, *"Salaam."*

Niklas walked up to Beshar. "Hi, my name is Niklas and I live on the same floor as Jamila. Is she your daughter?"

Beshar looked confused. A Swede who spoke his language?

"May God protect you," Beshar said in a quiet voice.

Mahmud thought, Can't Dad find something better to say?

At the same time: there was something about that neighbor, Niklas. He radiated something. Coolness. Strength. Hardness. Something that Mahmud needed right now.

35

Left-wing types/anarchist feminists/LGBT socialists/gender Communists. Niklas didn't care about labels. Didn't care if they read the same books as he did. Didn't care what they wrote on their message boards, their blogs, their articles. Didn't care who they were, why they thought the way they did. Only one thing was clear: he needed more bodies for the attack—and a few of the people on those websites seemed to think like him. Operation Magnum demanded time. More than he could put in on his own. The thought'd been growing lately: he should recruit. And Benjamin wouldn't do.

Total sleep over the past ten days: less than forty hours. He pursued Mats Strömberg from eight-thirty in the morning until seven-thirty at night, when the guy went home. Most of Niklas's time was spent in the Audi outside the asshole's job, an accounting firm in Södermalm. He rented another car for a few days to avoid drawing attention to himself. Used a fake driver's license that he'd bought online.

He continued to read the right literature—*The Girl and the Guilt*, by Katarina Wennstam, *Under the Pink Comforter*, by Nina Björk—dozed off, drank coffee. The rest of the evenings, he watched over the other apartments. Later at night: changed the tapes in the video cameras, watched the footage, organized his information, practiced with his knife, chatted with the left-wing people. He stopped running, didn't call his mom, Benjamin, or anyone else. But was there anyone else, really? It's not like his social calendar'd been crammed since he'd moved back home.

He was learning more and more about Mats Strömberg. The dude followed strict routines. Took the same route to the train every day. Bought a cinnamon bun and a coffee at the same shop every morning. Threw the coffee cup in the exact same garbage bin on the street. Either he left with his colleagues at eleven-thirty or he went by himself and bought something thirty minutes later. Alternated between three different lunch spots. Niklas could see straight into the pig's office; it was on the bottom floor. Six people worked at the place. He wondered how much they knew about Mats Strömberg's home life.

What's more: things were happening in one of the single-family homes. Roger Jonsson and Patricia Jacobs—the happy little family without kids. Niklas went through the footage. Realized: the guy was coming home later and later at night. Roger and Patricia were arguing. Obvious: things would blow up soon—he could see it in the man's eyes. The way he gesticulated at Patricia. Body language that screamed violence.

Other problems: the dirty real-estate fucker'd been in touch. Niklas couldn't keep living in the apartment. It was just a transitional apartment, as the broker reminded him, and now he'd arranged for a real firsthand rental contract. Ready to go. One hundred and fifty G's and the contract would belong to Niklas. He'd be in the housing system for real, no more subletting. He had a week to make up his mind. No possibility of prolonging his stay in the pad he had now. Dammit. Getting a firsthand rental contract was a good thing, but he just couldn't do it right now. His employer was threatening to fire him—Niklas hadn't gotten a proper doctor's certificate to explain the days he'd missed. What the fuck was he supposed to do? He needed more people. More money. More time. More weapons. More everything.

Solutions. Within a few days: time to make the hit against Mats Strömberg. When that part was over and done with, a certain amount of time would be freed up. Then he had to shore up his finances, maybe rob a bank. Finally: he was going to make a trip out to Biskops-Arnö Community College—a person he'd chatted with studied there, Felicia. She was studying some bogus thing called Ecology and Global Solidarity. A potential recruit, troop reinforcement, another pair of boots on the ground.

On Monday afternoon, he'd gone to the Black & White Inn to get a weapon. Felt stressed out, wanted to miss as little as possible of Mats Strömberg's life.

The place was empty. He ordered a mineral water. Sat down at a table. A lone woman behind the bar was readying things for the night. She was slicing lemons. He eyed the menu: drawn with chalk on a blackboard. Plaice with French fries, pork tenderloin with a green pepper sauce. The woman behind the bar ignored him.

After ten minutes, he asked her if Lukic was there.

The woman shook her head. Then she walked over to the pub's main entrance, turned over the OPEN sign hanging in the little window. Turned to Niklas. "You want stuff?" He nodded. Niklas understood the movement she made with her hand: come with me.

Behind the bar. Through the kitchen. A dude was boiling something in there. A hallway on the other side. Peeling yellow paint on the walls. Flashing fluorescent lights. Past a bathroom, a cleaning closet, a walk-in freezer, a locker room. Like some fucking mafia flick. At the very end of the hall was an office. The woman closed the door behind them. Niklas eyed her. Mouse-colored hair down to her shoulders. Bags under her eyes that makeup couldn't conceal. Still, strength in her gaze. His warrior instinct spoke loud and clear: this is a true fighter.

She unlocked a wooden cabinet. Lifted out a metal suitcase. Hauled it up onto the desk. Turned the coded lock. Opened it. Four fabric-wrapped bundles. She unrolled the contents. Three automatics and one revolver.

He recognized the Beretta immediately. A lot of boys down there used it—the classic 92/96 series, a basic 9-millimeter handgun that came in lots of different models. Chromed steel, camouflage-colored, aluminum frame, even one with real ivory in the grip.

"That is a Beretta."

"I know. A ninety-two ninety-six. Tell me about the others."

"Whatever you want. The other three are Russian. First a revolver, Nosorog, nine millimeter. And this one, this is the same caliber, a Gyurza, special for bulletproof vests. For both righties and lefties. Really good. Finally, a Bagira MR-444, a light handgun, also nine millimeter."

"And the prices?"

"This one and this one, dirty." She pointed to the Beretta and the Gyurza. "You can have the American for five thousand and the Russian for four. But they're good."

"What do you mean, they're dirty?"

"I can't say that they haven't been involved in robberies or other shit."

"Then you can forget about them. I want a new one, in the box. What do you want for this one?" Niklas didn't want a revolver. He picked up the Bagira gun. It was really very light, definitely a plus. But how jam-safe was it? He had no experience with the make.

"Twelve thousand. It's clean." She took it back. Wiped it off with the cloth.

"How much ammo do you have?"

"One pack, twenty rounds."

Problem. He needed at least fifty bullets. Wanted to be able to practice properly with the gun. This wasn't some rush job.

"How many rounds for the Beretta?"

"A lot. Probably a hundred, I can get ammo like that lots of places."

Niklas thought: Dammit, she was really the one running this show. At the same time: he couldn't use a dirty weapon. So far, everything'd been done so meticulously. He'd ordered the spy equipment under a false name and had it delivered to a P.O. box, rotated the license plates on the Audi, used a rental car some days, always hid behind the tinted windows, not spoken with or met anyone who could connect him to his surveillance operation, except for maybe the woman at Safe Haven—but she just had to be on his side. Couldn't risk it with a gun that might be in the police database. He shook his head. This was shit.

"I won't buy dirty guns. I won't buy a revolver that looks like it's made of plastic. I won't buy anything that I can't get at least fifty rounds for. You understand what I'm saying?"

"Calm down. I don't have anything else right now. So, you're interested or not?"

Was she playing hardass or was she really like that? It didn't matter—he needed a weapon. Soon.

"I can't buy any of these weapons. But could I place an order?"

She nodded.

It felt good. The attack would soon take place, his TACSOP—tactical standard operations procedure. Would set a precedent for the rest of the Operation.

In the car on the way out to Biskops-Arnö. Westbound.

He was thinking about the war. Righteous targets.

The day before, outside his building, he'd run into Jamila together with her brother, sister, and father. The dad seemed to be an upstanding man. He'd thanked him. Just like all of Sweden would do when he'd completed the Operation. Applaud him. A beautiful thought.

It was nine o'clock in the morning. Not much traffic at this time of day. The highway out toward Bålsta and Biskops-Arnö: dull. He thought about Mats Strömberg's routines. In two and a half hours, he would, most likely, walk out of the door to his office with two or three colleagues.

Shortly before Sollentuna, Niklas pulled over at a Shell gas station. Reeked of gasoline fumes. He filled his tank. The gas was insanely expensive. He thought about what it'd cost ten years ago, when he'd gotten his license. It was probably 50 percent more expensive now. And the price in Iraq: another story altogether. Kicked his anxiety into full gear again. What would happen if he had to keep working alone? If he was forced to move, pay for a rental contract? If nothing came of the gun he'd ordered?

He went in to pay. Cash. A voice behind him in line.

"Oh, hi there." A smile. He recognized her right away: the woman he'd bought the Audi from, Nina. What the hell was she doing here? Maybe it wasn't so strange after all, she just lived a few miles away.

"I thought it was you. I saw the car outside. Recognized it from twenty yards away."

Niklas, irritated. Not good that someone knew where he was and that he was the one driving the Audi. At the same time: he checked her out. Like an angel. Skin as clear as milk, speckled eyes gleaming in the sunlight that shone in through the big windows in the gas station. She met his gaze. Glittered. Her child looked like a child now. Not like a baby. He felt so bad for her. And for the child. He remembered.

He said, "Yes, hi. It drives well." He felt pathetic. Had to get out of there. Before Nina asked any more questions.

"I see that you got it re-registered. What, you didn't like my license plate? UFO 544. I thought it was pretty cool." Again: the smile, the eyes.

"Yeah, it was cool. But I was worried that someone would report me to the Ministry of Defense and stuff." Good move—a joke, lighten the mood, then leave.

Nina laughed. "You're funny. So, where are you off to?"

"I'm just out for a ride. I'm working."

"Well, I'm still on maternity leave. It's almost getting a little boring. So, what do you do for work?"

Niklas didn't know what to say. *Security guard* was so pathetic. He wanted to sound vague. "I work in the private security industry."

"That sounds exciting. Do you drive the Audi at work?"

"Sometimes."

"I miss it. It's perky, isn't it?"

"Yes, it's nice." He wanted to end the conversation without being rude. "Hey, I've got to get going. But it was nice to see you."

He got into the car. His palms were sweaty. What was happening to him? A normal conversation with a stranger and he felt more nervous than a nineteen-year-old rookie on his virgin tour down in the sandbox.

Farther out. In the countryside. Along the highway: yellow fields about to be harvested. Farms, granaries, tractors.

The exit sign for Biskops-Arnö looked filthy. Reminded him of the signs down there. Always worn down, dirty, buckled. Sometimes riddled with bullet holes.

He drove across a narrow bridge to the island. Parked his car. Looked out over the area. Directly across from the parking lot: large, red-painted wood buildings, old barns. Further off: white stone houses. He kept walking. A grass-covered courtyard. Six flagpoles flying the five Nordic flags and another one, maybe the community college's own emblem. A couple of people were sitting on the lawn in front of the building. Niklas approached them. A guy with a guitar in his lap. His nose, lip, and eyebrow were pierced. He had dreadlocks that were as thick as his forearms and some kind of hooded sweater that looked like it'd been bought at the bazaar in Kabul. The other two were girls. One had red hair, a shirt that was buttoned all the way up, and jeans that were much too wide. The other was dressed in cotton slacks and a black T-shirt. *Ramones* was printed across the chest in white lettering. Her earlobes were stretched out by some kind of earring that expanded the actual hole rather than dangling from it. Niklas could've fit his thumb through the girl's earlobe. He thought, What is this place, anyway?

Felicia'd told him to just ask around. The clowns showed him the way to her cottage.

It was made of brown wood with a black sheet-metal roof, didn't look to be bigger than 320 square feet. He knocked on the door. A girl opened it, wearing just panties and a tank top. Niklas felt awkward. At the same time: there was something incredibly cocky about opening the door for a stranger dressed in so little. The girl knocked on a door. Another girl came out. Shaved head, a ponytail left at the nape of her neck like a Hare Krishna sucker. She was dressed in some kind of kimono and Converse sneakers. Bizarre.

"Hi, are you Johannes?"

Niklas'd kept using his alias in all the conversations he'd had online.

"Yes, hi. It's great to be here, I've looked forward to it. I'm guessing you're Felicia?"

She nodded. Welcomed him. Asked if he'd found the way okay. Seemed nice. Still, there was something about her look, as if she was studying him.

He remained standing in the doorway. Everything felt so strange.

"Come in," she said. He took a step inside. They sat in the little kitchen. The cottage was made up of two small bedrooms and a shared kitchen. "This is how all first-year students live."

She asked him if he'd had a chance to look around the campus at all. Of course he hadn't. She started to talk about the place: courses in photography, film, writing, culture, history, foreign aid, ecology, and solidarity with developing nations. Niklas listened halfheartedly. Wanted to get a feel for her, the people out there, their attitude, strength. His mission today was to recruit.

They'd been chatting every day for almost two weeks. He knew her beliefs through and through. In his world: she could become a warrior. Patriarchy, as she called it, subordinated women. The gender power structure, that's what it was called. A permanent siege of social perceptions. How women should be, who they should be, how they should act—everyone was forced into carefully controlled categories. If you stepped outside the lines of demarcation, you were excommunicated. Were no longer counted as a woman, as suitable, as good, as a docile member of society. Even though everyone should know all this by now, there were so many people who just accepted the shit. Ate the shit. Let the men rule, whip them into submission, and never went out into battle. Like an unbalanced war where one side took the liberty of breaking the rules of the game.

And Felicia—she was impressed by his powerful ideas. He could tell—every time he pulled out some war propaganda she responded by describing missions she'd been a part of or would like to do. Demonstrations—*demos*, as she called them—guard circles outside porn clubs, broken windows, spray-painted façades, trashed interiors, Internet assaults against porn sites, screaming battle cries against government officials, big businesses, and men.

Maybe she was right for him.

Felicia served herbal tea. Her cabinmate, Joanna, chatted about the course she was taking: something about natural medicine. She was going to Brazil next semester to become a shaman, she said. "You can learn so much more in the Amazon than you can in a Western country." Her eyes glittered over the teacup. "So, what do you do?"

He didn't know what to answer. Could feel it instinctively: to mention his soon-to-be former job as a security guard was the wrong move. He let her question float in the air for a bit. Took a swallow of tea.

Finally, he said, "I'm unemployed, unfortunately."

The reaction was not what he'd expected. Felicia almost looked happy. Joanna looked reassured. Felicia said, "Everything's gotten harder since the pigs took power. Damn right-wing government. Don't feel left out. There are a lot of us who support you. Who believe in a different kind of society."

They talked for a while. Felicia was getting riled up talking about how the new government was crushing the old and the weak, women and the low-income bracket. Niklas did his best to keep up, even though Swedish politics wasn't really his thing. He didn't care. The most important thing was that she was angry enough.

After a while, Felicia got up. There was some kind of lecture that was open to the whole student body. She wondered if Niklas wanted to come—bringing visitors wasn't a problem. Of course, okay, that'll be interesting. Inside, he was nervous. He'd never been to a lecture before. Except for the run-throughs at DynCorp before a mission down there.

A large group of people was gathering outside one of the bigger buildings, which looked like a barn. Felica and her roommate greeted a lot of them. Almost half of them looked like the ones Niklas'd seen earlier on the lawn. They didn't exactly look like warriors. Still: Felicia's shaved head gave him hope. A real GI cut, except for the rattail in back.

The barn housed a nice-looking lecture hall. White-painted wood walls, powerful ventilation, lighting, a video projector suspended from the ceiling, chairs with little tables in the armrest that you could fold down and put your notebook on.

The lecturer was dressed in jeans and a red checked shirt. Maybe forty years old. Niklas'd expected something different: a professorial type in a tweed jacket with reading glasses on the tip of her nose. He realized how naïve he was.

Felicia whispered to him, "You're going to like this."

The lecturer got going. Introduced herself, rattled off some introductory story about an ad campaign that was currently being run. According to the lecturer, the campaign privatized female identity and in that way cemented a form of politically created gender identification. After that, it just got denser. Talk about gender roles, the gender power structure, gender hierarchies, and sex changes. Niklas looked around. Mixed ages. Felicia was sitting as though in a trance. Shaman Joanna was drawing flowers in her notebook. She was flaky.

He focused on the younger faces. Soldier material? Were they ready to spend nights curled up in the backseat of a car, to work hard as hell with planning during the day, to kick down doors, take care of crying children, attack the enemy combatants?

Finally: he settled on a guy a little farther down in the same row. Short dark hair. A few rings in his ear, all in a row, as if someone'd riveted the metal spiral on a notebook along the outer edge of his ear. The guy looked young: short-sleeved T-shirt, thin, fit arms. Soldier arms. Niklas'd seen them on so many down there, a toughness in the body that allowed them to handle so much more than the beefcakes did. Above all: the guy had focus. His gaze was steely gray, stone hard, stiffly zeroed in on the lecturer. Resolute. A kind of willpower. Maybe he was right for this.

"It's not as simple as turning the hierarchical world order upside down . . ." The lecturer gazed out over the audience. It felt as though she was looking straight at Niklas. "But to completely free yourself from that kind of a worldview."

Niklas nodded in agreement. Dammit, he was going to turn the hierarchies in the Strömberg and Jonsson families upside down. To begin with.

His concentration drifted. He tried to stop himself from closing his eyes. Still, he saw the same old images in his mind's eye. The ambush at the mosque. The ambushes during his runs in Aspudden. The ambushes from the dream world: Claes Rantzell in bits and pieces. Jamila's dude in a puddle on the floor. Mats Strömberg whimpering. They pleaded for mercy. A mercy that wasn't coming.

Felicia, the shaman, and two dudes from the same course that Felica was taking were sitting around the table in the cottage. They'd eaten in the college dining hall. There was no meat—just veggie grub. Felicia looked at Niklas in bewilderment when he questioned the food.

In the background: noisy music.

"Manu Chao is fantastic," Joanna said. Niklas thought, Maybe for shaman exercises in the woods, but not for war.

Niklas'd bought a couple of bottles of beer and hard cider from Felicia.

Joanna drank out of the bottle without touching the glass to her lips. "It's not good for your energy." Felicia laughed. The shaman broad really wasn't all there in the head.

They discussed their program, the lecture, the general state of the world. Niklas mostly kept his mouth shut. Drank one, two, three, four, five bottles of beer. The dudes were raw—criticizing the U.S.'s invasion of Iraq. Babbled about abuse, illegal weapons, and freedom-fighting bombers. In a couple of days, they were going to partake in a huge demo against the war. Poor nerds—they didn't know what they were talking about.

At nine o'clock, they went down to a bigger cottage across from the dining hall. It looked like an old community center. Twenty or so people were sitting on couches and armchairs, a couple of people were trying to dance, lazily. The same crap music. The same ecological vibe. The same geeky discussions.

He was starting to feel the beer. Felicia was in a quasi-deep discussion with one of the guys from the pre-game. Joanna was dancing around. He thought, What was this shit, anyway? He needed to draft Felicia, but she didn't seem to give a fuck.

Everyone around him was talking. The air was sweet and heavy with marijuana. He chugged more beer. Tried to look relaxed. The dude from the lecture showed up. The earrings in his ears gleamed in the dim light. Niklas approached him. The dude was talking to a girl who actually looked totally normal. He positioned himself beside them. Leaned his head in to listen to their conversation. Something about missions, demonstrations, protest ambitions. The first part sounded okay.

The guy stopped talking. Turned to Niklas. At first: completely indifferent, irritated look. Then he extended his hand. "Hi, my name's Erik. Are you visiting?"

Niklas shook Erik's hand. Introduced himself as Johannes. The guy had a firm grip. That was a good sign.

"Yes, I'm visiting Felicia. Do you know who that is?"

The girl Erik was talking to didn't stop staring at Niklas.

"Sure, we're in the same program, but she's a year above me. How do you know each other?"

Niklas didn't know what to say. The Internet sounded stupid. He mumbled something.

Erik said, "What did you say?"

Niklas spoke louder: "I'm here to discuss women's struggle, the women's movement, stuff like that. What do you think about that?"

Erik laughed. "Define 'the women's movement.'"

The girl was still staring. Just as Niklas was about to respond, she also extended her hand. "Hi, maybe we should be introduced, too. My name is Betty."

"Like sweet Miss Boop?" Niklas thought about the images painted on some of the helicopters down there. Real pinups weren't allowed anymore, but Betty B. always worked.

The chick puckered her lips. An obvious diss.

Niklas didn't get it. Was joking not allowed here, or what? But he didn't want to mess things up with Erik.

"Is your sense of humor part of your investment in the women's movement?" Erik asked.

"It was just a bad joke. That's all. But do you really want me to define the women's movement? I'm passionate about it."

"That sounds good. Because I am too."

Niklas got good vibes. Erik might be the right person.

"I think we men have to help them. Women are vulnerable and defenseless. I've started seeing all the shit around us here in Sweden. On the streets, in the houses, in the apartments. People go too far all the time. Lots of humiliation and violence. The women's movement has to go further."

"Yes, that's probably true."

"We have to fight."

Erik looked lost in thought. "I agree. But what do you mean exactly?"

"I mean what I said, that we have to attack. In some situations, an offensive strategy is the only possible way to defend yourself. And there will never be a war if we just take a defensive stance. Do you understand? We have to use the enemy's tactics. Violence is always the best antidote to violence."

Niklas felt fired up. Finally someone who agreed with him. Someone he could speak openly with. Someone who would understand. After all these evenings and nights. A fellow soldier.

He was spewing military terminology, attack strategies, weapon ideas. He outlined possible missions, targets, torture methods, ways to execute them.

Erik just nodded.

"We have to do this. I'm on my way, actually. I've come far in the planning stage and the operative part, too. It'll go boom in a few weeks. But I need reinforcements. What do you think? Do you want in?"

Silence. That Manu Chao crap in the background.

Niklas repeated his question, "Do you want in?"

"Johannes, that was your name, right? I think Felicia's given you one too many beers."

Niklas shook his head. He was drunk, but thinking clearly. That was bullshit.

"Not at all."

"Maybe not, but your ideas are too aggressive. The stuff you're talking about wouldn't work. But it was nice to meet you." The girl next to Erik smiled a satisfied smile.

Niklas felt cold all over. Shit. The guy was full of shit. The girl could go to hell. Erik could go fuck himself. They had no idea what they were talking about. Knew zilch about the fight. About the Operation. About what had to be done.

"You don't know what you're talking about," Niklas said.

Erik turned to the girl. Shook his head. It was clear what he thought about Niklas.

The girl shook her head, too.

He couldn't believe it. Even here—among the people who claimed to be on his side—they were working against him. They were assholes.

Niklas raised his voice. "You fucking collaborators. You're betraying the fight."

Erik started walking away. Knocked his index finger against his temple. The girl followed him. This was just too much. Now they were mocking him, too.

Niklas threw himself at the girl. Grabbed hold of her cardigan. Threw her down on the floor.

She squirmed. Erik tried to shield her.

Niklas stood over her. Didn't know if he should laugh or cry. Give them a real once-over or get out of there.

36

A week as the Yugos' made man. Not every night—fuck no—but Thursday/Friday/Saturday/Sunday. Åsa didn't ask questions. She said she was happy he'd gotten a side job. During the days, he dozed at his desk at the traffic unit. Gave the other boring cops the cold shoulder. They thought he was arrogant, but he didn't give a damn—respectfully.

Same deal every night. Hung out by the cash register with Andrzej and Belinda or the other stripper/cashier named Jasmine. Easy money— Thomas made two thousand kronor a night. No fuss, no muss, just regular old horndogs who wanted some fun.

Today: a day off. First, he was going to Barkaby Outlet with Åsa. She wanted to buy a fall jacket. She wanted something "durable," as she put it. Thomas knew what she meant. He was the same way. Normally, they didn't give a damn about stupid labels and faggy designer stuff. They cared more about the inside than the outside. But when it came to certain products, Åsa and Thomas wanted the highest quality, which meant the most expensive brands. The clothes had to be able to with-stand rain, cold, and sweat. At the same time, be lightweight and com-fortable. That usually meant supple Gore-Tex material that breathed but also didn't let in damp. That meant a lot of money.

He eyed the people in the outlet. Families with snotty three-year-olds. Younger couples who lived in the inner city but wanted to be well equipped for their trip to the Alps. The ordinary nine-to-five set. Were their lives happier than his? Definitely safer. But he probably made more, he hoped.

He thought about the adoption agency's home visit the other week. Two middle-aged women who seemed totally normal'd came home to their house. Thomas'd expected something different, more wishy-washy types. They'd sat in their kitchen for an hour and discussed child-rearing, parental leave, and the difficulties adopted children face when trying to find their identity. Åsa did the talking, but Thomas made sure to nod in the right places. It actually felt good.

Åsa was overjoyed. "Maybe we'll be parents soon."

Finally, they each bought a jacket. North Face brand. Cost over four thousand kronor a pop. Thomas could pay easily: his new job raked in cold cash.

In the afternoon, Thomas was supposed to meet Ljunggren at the shooting club. For the first time in several weeks. Thomas didn't know if he was getting paranoid, but it felt like Ljunggren was keeping his distance. They'd been close. Hadn't talked much, maybe, but maintained a humorous rapport. Where did it all go? Maybe Ljunggren thought that Thomas'd messed up one too many times. But that wasn't possible. Colleagues like Jörgen Ljunggren never whined about someone getting a little too rough. Ljunggren himself—rough was his middle name. Still, there was something there. A line'd been drawn. Between them. Thomas could feel it clearly.

In the car, he thought about the Solvalla incident. John Ballénius'd freaked out, disappeared into the crowd. According to the phone lists, the guy was nowhere near Axelsberg the night Rantzell was murdered, but something was obviously shady. The most important thing: now, Thomas was certain that Rantzell was the dead guy. That was a big step in the right direction.

Right away on the Monday after the incident, Thomas'd called the house-mouse detective who'd taken over the investigation after Hägerström. Stig H. Ronander, a senior guy, with a name that would've fit right in at Solvalla. For a brief moment, Thomas considered not doing it. But then he changed his mind. After all, this might be his way back. If he solved the mystery of who the dead guy really was, the possibility of solving the larger mystery increased significantly. He was taking a chance; something about this investigation was rotten. But he couldn't see that anything negative could come of him helping it along a bit.

Ronander received Thomas's information skeptically. Questioned how come he'd been asking around about John Ballénius, why the guy'd managed to disappear at Solvalla. Thomas fabricated a little—said that Ballénius'd already been mentioned in the investigation when he'd been helping Hägerström. Tried to refer to the telephone lists without mentioning that he'd ordered them himself. Stig H. Ronander didn't seem grateful. He could go to hell.

The job, the car, the shooting range. Those used to be the three pillars of Thomas's life. Now, he didn't know anymore. The traffic unit was duller than he ever could've imagined. The Cadillac didn't give him any peace. At the same time, he felt right at home at the strip club. Jasmine and Belinda were nice, unaffected.

His transfer and the incident with the man who'd been outside his window that night played tricks on him. Maybe because he lost his ability to defend himself when he rolled into the dark under the car. Maybe it didn't matter when he was alone. But when Åsa was home—no. Even though their marriage wasn't exactly stellar: if anyone hurt her he would never forgive himself.

So the shooting range ought to give him peace. But he didn't like the looks the other guys were giving him after the whole mess at work. He wondered what they thought of him.

The shooting club was located indoors, in a building of its own. Most shooting ranges in Sweden were built inside cabins that'd been opened up along one long end, with shooting booths and targets. You stood and shot, under cover of the roof, but practically outdoors—you froze like a dog. But the Järfälla club was more luxurious: a total of fourteen parallel eighty-foot lanes for precision shooting with the best sound protection Thomas knew of. Everything was located warmly indoors.

Ljunggren was already there. One hand in his jeans pocket, leaning back a little, the other arm extended. A competition gun with an ergonomically correct grip. Baseball cap, protective headgear, broadlegged stance. Ready to shoot. Right before Thomas knocked him on the shoulder, he fired off a shot. A two. Not bad at all.

They shook hands. Ljunggren looked honestly happy to see him. Pounded Thomas on the back. Not like him—usually, the dude avoided physical contact more than he avoided pointless talk. "Didja see the two I just landed?"

Thomas felt happy. "Nice one. You're not used to scoring that high, huh?" Raw, friendly laughter.

They talked for a while. Everything felt like normal.

Thomas positioned himself in his lane. Put on the headgear. The magazine into the 9-millimeter handgun. Closed his eyes for a few seconds. Breathed in. Come on, focus. Even if his job situation hadn't gone the way he'd planned, he always needed to be able to focus at the right moment. Fire a shot in the right way when the situation required it. Hit the target in the right body part.

He raised his right arm slowly. Held the gun as steady as possible. His eye sought out the sight marker. Found it. Still, he was trembling. He relaxed. Clear sight. Carefully now. Focus. Increased the pressure on the trigger slowly and evenly. Avoided any flinching in his arm, hand, gun. Almost closed his eyes. His finger moved of its own accord. Had to lose consciousness of the movement that was about to come. Squeeze slowly. One single movement. One with the sight, the bullet's movement through the air. He felt the recoil, the bullet piercing the target.

The shot came as a shock. The jolt of his hand almost caught him by surprise. Squinted. The hole in the target: a one. Ljunggren said, "It seems like some things don't change, even if you're just nailing traffic sinners all day. I've missed you, just so you know."

Thomas didn't know if he should laugh or cry. It felt so damned good.

After shooting practice Thomas suggested they grab a beer at Friden. Ljunggren had a different suggestion. "Can't we just drive around a little? Like old times."

It felt strange, but good somehow. Ljunggren: COO of integrity. Distance-keeper, no-body-contact specialist, macho dude *numero uno*. His suggestion: a pitying overture. A friend request.

Cops often took their patrol cars to the shooting range. Ljunggren flipped on the police radio, but on low volume. Thomas couldn't read him: maybe he wasn't thinking of what he was doing or else he did it to try to create the right atmosphere. He drove slowly, as if they were out on the beat. They were in a suburban area. The leaves on the trees were dry. Despite the rain, it'd been a warm summer. Real September feel—maybe because it was September.

They drove in circles—really like old times. More than three months ago. Felt like an eternity. An eternity of angst. Angst because everything'd gone to hell so quickly.

"Tell me. How are the traffic geeks?"

Thomas explained. What they talked about, their attitude, their food habits. Ljunggren grinned. Finally someone who understood.

"I've heard rumors about you, Andrén. That you've got a side gig. Is that true?"

Thomas didn't know what to say. How much did Ljunggren know? This wasn't really the time to spill the beans. At least not all of them.

"Yep, that's right. I help a security company. A lot of evenings and nights. So, it's kind of like before. I mean, Åsa's used to it."

Ljunggren nodded. Kept his eyes fixed on the road.

"I bet double my take-home that you make better money."

Thomas laughed. "I'll bet four times my take-home that you've got better retirement and health insurance than I'll ever get there. My new job is outside of all that, so to speak."

"That's what I suspected. Is it worth it?"

Thomas thought about that for a while. The question'd been bothering him for several weeks. And Ljunggren didn't even seem to know what it was he was really involved in.

"Let me be entirely open with you, Ljunggren. I don't know what's worth it and not worth it anymore. The only thing I know is that if someone pisses on you, you don't have to be loyal to them anymore. This whole thing I've been put through—it's bullshit. Do you know what happened? They said you couldn't go on patrol as usual, that you had to cover for someone else. Then they sent me that girl, who could hardly carry the heavy vest to the car. We get called to a crazy boxing champion who goes berserk in a bodega and almost kills her. But, no, we're not allowed to defend ourselves. We're not allowed to restore order. Nope, that'll just lead to whining. Then it's police brutality. Assault. Excessive force. And Adamsson, that old cocksucker, turns his back on me. Makes me go on disability, asks me to more or less go to hell. Thanks for the support, you wrinkly motherfucker! But you and me, we both know Adamsson. He doesn't really mind the kind of thing that happened in the bodega. He should've been behind me, one hundred percent. But no, this time he left me alone in the lion's den. I don't understand why."

Ljunggren didn't say anything. As usual.

Thomas kept going. "Sometimes I think, What if. What if it's all connected? You know that investigation that guy Hägerström was working on? I helped him a little. Okay, I don't like his kind, but something was sketchy about that murder. So I looked a few things up on my own.

And what happens? Just a few days later, all this crap starts coming at me. Like that set it off. Like someone didn't want me helping Häger-ström with that investigation anymore. Like a plot or something."

Ljunggren turned to Thomas again. "Yeah, that stuff was a little weird."

"*A little* weird? It was fucking insane."

Ljunggren ignored Thomas's comment. "I don't know what hap-pened that night. But Adamsson was actually the one who called me and asked me to cover for Fransson. And I just followed orders. But that it's some kind of plot, no, I don't think so. That sounds a little too, what's it called . . . ?"

"Conspiratorial?"

"Yeah, right, conspiratorial." Ljunggren paused. Then, in a lowered voice, as if he was thinking about what the word meant, he said, "Con-spiratorial, yeah."

They kept driving around for another hour. It grew darker. The glowing instrument panel in the patrol car made it feel homey. Thomas couldn't forget what Ljunggren'd just told him. So, Adamsson had been the one who ordered him not to go on patrol. One thought emerged clear as day in Thomas's muddled mind: now it was obvious. Adamsson was involved somehow.

He didn't say anything to Ljunggren.

Ljunggren started driving back toward the shooting club to drop Thomas off at his car.

He turned off the engine, but let the instrument panel continue to glow. His hands remained on the wheel as though he were still driving. His gaze somewhere far off, maybe directed at the clubhouse.

"So, there's something I want to tell you."

Thomas could tell right away by his tone that something was up. "What?"

Ljunggren swallowed several times. Cleared his throat. A minute passed.

"We got a call three days ago. A couple tenants who thought maybe someone was dead in an apartment next door. Through the mail slot they could see that there was tons of mail piled up inside the door and no one'd been seen there for several months. I went there with Lind-berg. An apartment on Elsa Brändströms Street. We rang the doorbell, knocked. The usual routine. Finally, we tried the door. It was open, so we went in. We looked around, a thick film of dust on everything.

Didn't seem like anyone'd been living there for months. But we didn't find any dead guy."

Thomas wondered what his long story had to do with him.

"There was a ton of weird hard-core porn stuff, strap-ons and shit. We found a bunch of booze, a stinking fridge. We didn't find anything else interesting. It didn't seem like anyone'd been there for ages. I thought it was a routine check. But then I found a glass with dentures in the bathroom. Then it hit me that the person who'd lived in the apartment could be the smashed-up corpse we found on Gösta Ekman Road. The one you said you were helping Hägerström with. You told me you saw track marks on his arms and that he was missing teeth and stuff. I thought I should tell you. As a favor. In return."

The silence in the car was complete. Thomas almost thought he could hear Ljunggren's heart beating. What he was doing: breaking the rules, going against investigation confidentiality. Usually, that wasn't the kind of thing that worried Ljunggren. But this—there was something bigger happening.

Thomas tried not to sound too interested. "Okay. Thanks for the info. I'm not doing that anymore, so. But, fuck, course I think it's exciting. So, what was his name? The guy who lived in the apartment?"

Thomas felt goose bumps rise on his arms. Really, he already knew the answer to his question.

"The tenant's name was Rantzell. Claes Rantzell. But that's a new name. You can almost tell just by hearing it."

"What?"

"Rantzell sounds made up, don't you think? The dude's name is actually Cederholm. He changed his name a few years ago. Does that ring any bells? Claes Cederholm?"

Thomas shook his head, but the name did sound familiar.

"Claes Cederholm was the chief witness in the Olof Palme murder trial. Get it? This isn't just some everyday bull. The murder of Olof Palme, Sweden's prime minister."

This was insane.

Thomas was in really deep waters.

Really, really deep.

* * *

NEVER SCREW UP

THE NATIONAL POLICE

THE NATIONAL BUREAU OF INVESTIGATION'S PALME GROUP

Date: September 8 APAL—2431/07

MEMORANDUM

(Confidential according to chapter 9 § 12 of the Secrecy Act)

Regarding Claes Rantzell
(Previous name: Claes Cederholm)
(Database number: 24.555)

Claes Rantzell (previously named Claes Cederholm, database number 24.555 in the suspect and witness database) was most likely murdered on June 2 of this year.

Background

Claes Rantzell was found in a basement at 10 Gösta Ekman Road in Stockholm on the night leading to June 3 of this year (Incident Report, Attachment 1). He was dead at the time of discovery. Rantzell's face was severely wounded due to external force and he showed a variety of other signs of having been gravely assaulted. More notable was the fact that Rantzell's dentures had been removed from the scene and that his fingertips had been cut off (Autopsy Report, Attachment 2).

Due to these circumstances, neither the police in the Southern District nor the National Laboratory of Forensic Science could identify Rantzell until September 7 of this year (Identification Report, Attachment 3).

All of these circumstances point to the fact that Rantzell was murdered.

Claes Rantzell's File in Brief

Rantzell has provided the most testimony in conjunction with the Palme Commission. Between 1986 and 1991, he was interrogated over twenty times (APAL—5970/91). At the time of Palme's murder, Rantzell's name was, as mentioned above, Claes Cederholm.

During the early 1980s, Rantzell was a well-known drug dealer as well as co-owner of the gambling club Oxen on Malmskillnadsgatan. He was convicted of a number of drug-related offenses.

In an interrogation on April 26, 1987 (APAL—151/87), he reported that, among other things, he had been a close friend of Christer Pettersson as well as that, on the night of the murder, Pettersson had been outside of the Grand Cinema—the movie theater Palme and his wife visited shortly before the murder. In an interrogation on February 3, 1988 (APAL–2500/88), Rantzell reported that his memory had changed. He then provided an alibi for Christer Pettersson's whereabouts at the time of the murder. In an interrogation on March 17, 1990 (APAL–3556/90), however, Rantzell said that he had lent a Smith & Wesson Magnum revolver, .357 caliber, to Christer Pettersson. According to Pettersson, the weapon was intended for the shooting of a salute at a friend's birthday. The revolver was never returned to Rantzell.

The most probable murder weapon is precisely such a Smith & Wesson Magnum revolver, .357 caliber. The information about the borrowed revolver was, therefore, one of the central pieces of evidence during the preliminary hearing against Christer Pettersson. The prosecutor aimed to connect Christer Pettersson to the potential murder weapon.

Rantzell has lived the life of a drifter. During the 1980s, he seems primarily to have supported himself by dealing drugs as well as running gambling events. During the 1990s and 2000s, he served as a front man for a number of companies, primarily in the construction industry (Attachment 4).

From the middle of the 1980s to the middle of the 1990s, he cohabitated with Marie Brogren.

Our assessment is that Rantzell's murder does not have a direct connection to the Palme murder. However, it cannot be ruled out that such a connection exists.

Suggested Measures to Be Taken

Considering what has been stated above, we suggest that the following measures be taken:

1. The Palme Group shall be brought into the Rantzell murder investigation. The Palme Group will be informed of all measures taken during the preliminary investigation. The investigator will be informed and will personally report to the Palme Group's representative once a week.

2. The Palme Group will order investigators to go through all documents regarding Rantzell and issue a report no later than October 30.

3. The Palme Group will administer its own investigative team, made up of at least three investigators, to monitor, review, and take their own investigatory measures.

We order that a decision be reached regarding these issues at a meeting to be convened on September 12.

Stockholm

Detective Inspector Lars Stenås

PART 3

(Two months later)

37

Dig the procedure: cut the crystals with the razor blade. To break apart the stones. No face mask like when he'd laced blow with Tetramisole—animal medicine—earlier this week. No latex gloves. No Yugo standing over his shoulder watching his every move. Goading him. Distrusting him. Shitting on him. Just Mahmud, alone at his digs. His crib was a few blocks away from Robert's. Take note: *his own* crib. Stylin'. Even Dad was proud.

On the TV: Brazil against Ghana in some kind of international friendly. He didn't give a shit.

He cut up more than he needed. Like a rhythm. Irritation flowing out of him. Pissed-offness that was about to explode. Everything with the Yugos was fucked. Snorting was sweet. But these last few months, Mahmud'd started going for a heavier rush. Once the cocaine flakes were cut up, all they needed was three drops of water to dissolve. He picked up the disposable needle. The cocaine wasn't like the doping shit—made his veins contract. It was maybe the tenth time in his life that he mainlined blow. Still remembered his virgin crank four weeks ago. White dynamite—the rush like a trip to paradise. Robert and him, together in a mad high-def video-game world. *Grand Theft Auto* number fourteen million. Un-fucking-real.

He pointed the needle toward his arm. Made sure the vein didn't roll away. Pressed. A drop of blood shot up into the barrel. He pressed some more. He let the blood flow up into the barrel again. Then into the vein. Ten second wait. Nine, eight, seven, six, five, four, three, two, one. Blast off! Like a bolt of lightning straight to the brain. Weed paled in comparison, snorting felt weak, boozing was for pussies.

The green color of the football field on the TV screen looked greener than the Amazon. This was life, deluxe.

Where the fuck were Robert and the others? They were supposed to call. Maybe come by and check out his digs. Then they were hitting the town. Mahmud did a line. Regular old feeling. Nice, but once you've tried intravenous, intravenose just doesn't feel the same.

He considered his situation. Other than on nights like this, it sucked fag cock. He worked like a Sven, forty-hour weeks or whatever. Might as well've had a regular nine to five, as Erika'd suggested. He drove around the projects all day. Picked up the shit at Shurgard storage facilities over half of Stockholm. Sold to clockers in Norra Botkyrka, Norsborg, Skärholmen, Tumba, everywhere. At pizzerias after closing, at pubs, clubs, gyms, fighter clubs, in basement storage units, attics, at party pads, in continuing-education hallways, subway stations, the glassed-in meeting spots of the indoor malls, parks, playgrounds. Most of all, he dealt from the driver's seat. 'Cause that's how it was: he rolled in a real sweet ride—a Benz CLS 500. He was paying in installments, sure, but fuck it, you know? And he never would've gotten wheels like that with a regular gig.

Under him he had six, seven dudes, and one chick, as a matter of fact: his regular dealers. Dijma was one of the best. Bought at least seven ounces a month. Mahmud—on his way to becoming the Snow King of southern Stockholm. Flipped at least two kilos a week. At least half a million on the street, cash. He paid the Yugos four hundred and thirty G's for every kilo. Seventy G's left for him. He was riding high, but had to work like a dog for the paper. And the heavy downside: Radovan wouldn't loosen his grip. Mahmud: a well-paid serf. No matter how much he wanted to make his old man, his sisters, Erika, and everyone else happy. He couldn't do it. So, he'd made up his mind: he might as well become the king. It was high time for an Arab at the top. Bigger than the Yugo Godfather.

He got less time over at the gym. His training suffered. He wasn't feeling too hot. The juice he'd been taking'd had side effects. The Winstrol fuckers were lethal, man. Acne'd spread all over his face and back like Ebola or something. His kidneys hurt. Weird, thick hairs'd started sprouting on his back. He hadn't even slept two hours last night. But he had to take the Winstrol. The juice wouldn't work otherwise.

Now he had to take it down a notch. Couldn't crank up both juice and C at the same time. He ordered better protein online instead. Upped his usage. But it could never make up for the fact that he was putting in less time at Fitness Center, or that he wasn't taking steroids.

The thoughts made his head spin: everything he was gonna do with the dough. At the same time: the Yugos could bring him down anytime. They were motherfuckers, all of 'em.

The clock struck eleven. He picked up his cell. Called Robert. Homeboy didn't have proper voice mail, just some blaring Arabic music as his message. No point in recording anything. Rob would see that he'd called, anyway.

The clock kept ticking. Mahmud did another line. Played PlayStation like a video-game god.

His cell phone rang. It was Rob, keyed up like a kid: "Fuck man, come out, we're down the street. We're gonna own this city."

Mahmud put his coat on. A leather jacket with Benz logos on the arms. Tucked a tin-foil ball with two grams in his pocket. Tonight: he was gonna show Stockholm—slay bitches like never before.

First thing, Mahmud and Javier each did a line. Heavy beats on Rob's car stereo. Mood: soaring. The only thing Mahmud was missing: Babak next to him in the backseat.

Obvious: Rob'd tricked himself out for pussy-catching. Major back-slick, short but well-trimmed stubble, gold chain around his neck, tight V-neck silk shirt. His biceps were stretching out the fabric.

"Ey, you hot tonight or what?"

Robert laughed. "Shit, I'm so hot I'm almost coming right now, man."

"Hustler's hustler. Wanna take my CLS instead?"

"If you cool. We'll be big pimpin', man."

Javier just grinned at their buzz. They switched to Mahmud's car. The feeling: so fly.

On the road. Robert turned to Mahmud: wide piranha grin.

"If I don't score a hat trick tonight, I'll give you ten times the cash. You feel me?"

"What, you gonna fuck three chicks, or what?"

"No, *habibi*. Hat trick, you don't know what that is?"

Mahmud could imagine a bunch of things, but he wanted to hear Rob's latest idea.

"Hat trick, okay. That's when you get to spray in all three holes in one night."

Mahmud roared. Javier threw his head back. Rob looked pleased—

laughed at himself. Three fly hustlers on a bitch safari—man, if they didn't score some pussy tonight, they never fucking would.

Mahmud, between the laugh attacks: "Fuck, man, I swear, I'm gonna rock a hat trick tonight too. You watch."

The laughter died down. They were approaching the city.

Mahmud grew solemn. Wanted to run some serious stuff by his buds.

"Something's got me real pissed."

"What, something about Babak? Just drop it, man."

"No, not that. And I swear, I don't wanna fight with Babak. Tell him hey from me, *salaam*."

"So, what's the deal?" Mahmud could see Robert's face in the rear-view mirror. He looked curious for real.

"Man, those Yugos are fucking me so hard. I wanna quit."

"So quit. Tell them to fuck themselves."

"No, I'm not the kinda guy who lights a fire. I burn low and slow like a spliff. But it can boil over. You follow?"

Javier leaned back. "I don't follow. You make mad cheddar. Cruise in an ill car. What's the problem?"

"I'm like their bitch. It's different for you, Rob, you do your own thing. Entrepreneur, or whatever, but they keep me on a leash like a fucking whore. They're like COs, decide what I do, when I do it. Threaten to tell my old man if I don't do what they say, to ruin shit for my sister. They're assholes, man. I gotta do something."

Robert, in a serious tone for the first time all night: "Mahmud, listen to me. I might not believe in the Yugos in ten years, but right now— watch yourself. That's all I'm gonna say. Watch yourself. They're animals, don't play with them. As long as you're bringing it home, keep working and smile while you do it. I swear."

Silence in the car.

The energy in the city: white hot. Mahmud remembered: the Svens were celebrating some kind of All Saints' Day. The November darkness was lit up by platinum-blond pieces of ass rockin' stilettos, legs shivering. Slick brats with Barbour vests that looked more like inner linings than like jackets.

But the night was theirs. Javier'd booked bottle service at White Room. If Mahmud'd tried to make the reservation: he'd have been given the cold shoulder right away. He couldn't gloss over his immigrant Swedish. And there was no way he'd get in the front door without a reservation. Been proven time and time again by some little *blattes* who were college educated or something: the kids'd filmed the apartheid regime ruling the Stockholm nightlife and made a big show of suing the clubs. They ought to be heroes in Sweden—but nothing changed for Mahmud.

But Javier was almost like a Sven. Tight.

Inside at White Room: ice buckets built into the tables, crystal chandeliers hanging from the ceiling, bar lit up in pink with top-shelf vodka and bubbly. Jewelry on the walls—some kind of exhibit. The dance floor was a circle in the middle of the room. Crazy pull. The only shitty thing was that they didn't get into the VIP room. Fuck it: they were gonna throw down. But don't misunderstand: throwing down didn't mean that Mahmud danced. A Million *blatte* like him would never humiliate himself like that. That was reserved for the Svens, the fairies.

Still: the feeling of being on the inside couldn't be beat. He thought of the time he'd seen Daniel and his boys at Hell's Kitchen. The anxiety in his gut. The flashes of panic pulsing through his brain. He wondered what was worse: to owe Born to Be Hated stash or to whore for the Yugos?

Three lines later: Mahmud, Robert, and Javier were sitting at their table. Mahmud went easy on the alcohol, as usual. The booze was for the bitches. The plan: get 'em drunk enough to fuck 'em, but not too trashed—no one wanted to end up with a vomit-stained cock. Mahmud thought the Sven brats were staring at him and his bros threateningly. Weren't digging their game. The *blatte* kings were plucking the honeys.

He felt vibrations in his pocket. His phone was bothering him. And he had to check it. It could be business. The text was an order, straight-up: "D wants 50 tickets tonight." In other words: he had to go to some Shurgard storage place, pick up fifty grams of C, and then deliver the shit to Dijma. Here he was, with his homeboys and three, four willing females, life on top, a hat trick within reach. And right then, Mr. R. had to force him on duty. A bad fucking hand. He ought to refuse, give them the finger. All his hate welled up at once. Knocked around inside him. It was as if his glowing anger was ignited into a roaring fire. Turned into an insane lava stream. He ought to screw the Yugos. Tell them to fuck off. But at the same time—so strong, more powerful than the hate, the rush, the heat: he knew what he had to do. Time to deliver.

He was happy that he'd laid off the booze. Better to drive on a fading

C-rush than with vodka running through his veins. He turned the stereo up to a blare. Snoop killing it. Not the way Mahmud felt right now.

Through the city, over the dreary South Side, the highway a straight
shot south. Past Liljeholmen, Årsta, and so on. Kungens Kurwa—
kurwa, as in whore.

The storage facility was empty of people. Of course: it was twelve-
thirty on a Saturday night. Ice-cold drops of drizzle. He checked in,
rummaged through the boxes in the unit for a while, pocketed all the
grams that were in there—six bags with five G's in each. Back to the car.
Swish-swish through the night. To the next storage unit, Årstaberg. He
knew these places like the back of his hand. In/out like a speed racer.

An hour and a half later: fifty grams in a bag in his pocket. Stupid dangerous: if he got collared by the 5-0 now, he'd get locked up for two
years. At least. The courts made decisions based on a rising scale of
possession, rigid assessments, mad tough sentences for dealers.

Back in the city. Hard to find a parking spot. Mahmud didn't have the
energy to drive around and around. Didn't care if he got a ticket—he
parked the car in front of a building that said Royal Library on it. Fired
off a text to Dijma on the number he thought the Albanian was using
this week. Waited ten minutes. The November night was dark. It was
far between the streetlamps where he was parked. He thought about
Dad. If he found out about this shit he'd cry himself to death.

A silver-colored Saab pulled up next to him. Mahmud almost jumped
in his seat. Had he dozed off in the darkness in the car?

He had time to see Dijma in the front seat. A dude climbed out of
the Saab. Opened the back door of Mahmud's Benz. Slid into the backseat. Mahmud, tense as hell. Didn't recognize the guy. The grams in
his pocket were worth almost three hundred large on the street. Was
Dijma trying to pull a fast one?

The dude looked pasty. Circles under his eyes, mouse-colored hair
with straight-cut bangs that looked Eastern.

"Move," he said in English.

Mahmud started the car. Saw the Saab in front of him.

They rolled out onto Sturegatan. Mahmud was getting bad vibes.
This wasn't the way things usually went down.

The dude in the backseat met his quizzical eyes in the rearview mirror. "Park the car at Stadion." Mahmud got a weird feeling: the guy

pronounced the word *Stadion* a little too good to be a freshly imported Albanian dealer.

He drove up Sturegatan. The Saab took a right at Karlavägen.

"Don't follow him," the pickup man ordered.

Mahmud slowed down. "I don't know you," he said.

"Are you delivering or not?" the Albanian replied.

Mahmud didn't respond. Didn't want to pick a fight. Wanted to get back to the honeys.

They drove across Valhallavägen. Hardly any traffic. Mahmud parked the car next to Stadion's reddish stadium building. The rain continued to fall in fat drops.

Mahmud killed the engine. Played with the grams in his pocket. A dark Volvo pulled up next to the car. Parked, locking the Benz in.

The dude in the backseat leaned forward. Said in Swedish, "You're a good guy, Mahmud." What the fuck was this? Suddenly the Albanian was speaking Swedish. Mahmud had to figure out what was happening. Was Dijma trying to rip him off? Was it the Yugos, playing with him? Or the cops? Tonight, of all fucking nights, his butterfly was at home in his apartment.

"Yo, who the fuck are you, man? Get lost." Mahmud glanced out at the Volvo; two Swedish-looking guys were sitting in the front seats.

"I'll be leaving soon. Don't worry. You can call me Alex."

Mahmud could feel it in his entire body: this was a cop.

"I'm not talking to you."

"Why not? I want you to listen to me, just for a few minutes. I assume you've got something in this car that you're not allowed to have. Am I right?"

"I told you, I'm not talking to you."

"Just tell Dijma that things got hot and I split. I've already messed with him all night, so he won't be surprised."

"I haven't done anything illegal, or whatever you're talking about."

"It's okay, Mahmud. I'm not going to take anything. We're not going to try to write you up for anything tonight. Not this time. Just listen for a minute."

Mahmud didn't get what the cop fucker was babbling about. Everything was messed up. The Volvo outside. His chances of getting away: minimal.

"We know what you're up to. But we need more information. We need someone on the inside. Guys like me can go in and do swift gigs, but we're not let in for real. You're a good guy. Your dad cares about you. You've got sisters you can help. You don't want to get sent back in. Come on, Mahmud, you didn't like the slammer, now did you? Just think about what your old man would say."

Mahmud stared straight ahead, refused to meet the cop fucker's eye. "Pork your mother."

The guy seemed unfazed. Went on, "We're not unreasonable. We can forget what we've got on you so far. I could arrest you now and you'd get two years just for the grams you've got in your pocket. And I've got solid evidence for two more drug-related charges. You'd get eight years at least, you know that. But if you work with us, we'll just strike all that from the record. The only thing we want . . ."

"Are you fucking deaf or what?" This had to end. Mahmud was gonna take the asshole's head, shove it into the gearshift, and then book it. It was worth a try.

"Calm down, Mahmud. Just listen for a second. We need you. We'll drop the stuff we have on you. And the only thing we want is for you to meet us now and then and tell us what's happening."

This: totally loco. They seriously thought he was gonna become a rat. Shit. man, they weren't sane, the popo-pussies.

"You playin' me? You think I'm a snitch? Never."

Alex sounded disappointed. "You should consider it. It's not about snitching. Not at all. We keep everything clean. No one would ever know. But I won't keep you any longer. Think about it. Don't do anything stupid, now. I'm going to get into the car right there."

The cop put one hand on the door handle, held out his other hand. "Here, take my card."

Mahmud ignored him.

The brass named Alex left it on the backseat.

"Call me if you change your mind."

"Forget it."

"Take a few days, think it over. Otherwise, the next time we meet will be when I interrogate you in custody. *Capice?*" Alex didn't wait for an answer. He got out of the car. Turned around before he slammed the door shut. "One more thing. If news of our little chat leaks out for any reason, we'll come get you. Right away."

The cop climbed into the Volvo. Its engine revved.

Mahmud remained sitting for a few minutes in the dark. Picked up the card. It just said ALEXANDER WREN, ENGINEER, and a cell-phone number. Nice cover. He rolled down the window. Tossed out the card.

White Room would be open a little while longer, but he didn't have the energy to go there. What if Dijma was a narc too? Impossible. Dijma felt about as real as only an Albanian could.

He was a loser. Apparently not even the 5-0 thought he was a real G. At the same time: who was he standing up for, really? The ones who'd forced him into this shit by exploiting the fact that he loved his *abu* and sister.

Mahmud texted Dijma. Asked him to come pick up the gear himself. The Albanian met him outside the Royal Library. Dijma was not surprised when Mahmud explained that the asshole who was supposed to do the deal'd started some shit over the price. Mahmud said he'd thrown him out. Mahmud accepted 250 big ones in unfolded thousand-kronor bills. Immediately, everything felt better. Fuck, maybe he should take a turn down to White Room after all. Check if Rob, Javier, and the bitches were still there.

Down among the champagne bottles, it was like the Wild West. Brat players with French-cuff shirts and more wax in their hair than Mahmud used in three months were dousing one another with bubbly. As soon as Mahmud'd had a seat, Rob held out a tin of tobacco. Mahmud peeked below the lid: a nice little pile of C. He went into the bathroom. Did a line. Two hundred and fifty thousand—he was feeling better and better. Okay, it wasn't just his money, but what the hell, he had to relax a little after that turn with the cop.

Back out in the crowd. The dance floor was packed. The spotlights were pumping colors all over the room. The Eurotechno was pounding in time to the girls' arms in the air. This was it. Javier'd picked up some chick. Rob was buttering up a juicy morsel of his own. She gazed into his eyes. Mahmud wondered what kind of sweet lies he was spinning.

Two chicks helped themselves to the final drops of Grey Goose vodka. Mahmud winked at one of them. Yelled over the music, "Hey, sweetie. Let's have some bubbly instead." Unclear if they heard what he said. But three minutes later he was back at the table with the flyest bottle of pink champagne. Then they definitely got it. He poured for them. They toasted him. He didn't drink. But they smiled. The chick he'd winked at was the prettiest he'd seen since Lindsay Lohan. Bleached hair that looked like angel-spun cotton candy. Big doe eyes. A gray top with puffed sleeves. She downed her glass. Mahmud poured more for her. Whispered in her ear: "Do you want to have more fun, real dynamite?"

She laughed. Their hands touched, Mahmud gave her the Redline baggie. When she and her friends pushed past him in the booth, he pinched her butt.

The angel-honey came back five minutes later. Pupils like mechanical pencil lead. Sneezed into her hand. Smiled at him. Mahmud, the king. Tonight, he was gonna score a hat trick. Ha-ha, hat trick!

They were already sucking face in the taxi on their way out to his crib. Her hand inside his pants. Back and forth. He went crazy, wanted to put it in. But unnecessary to pick a fight with the driver.

The rain outside felt clean. The girl's name was Gabrielle. Her jeans hugged her legs and went down over her black heels like drainpipes. She staggered, wasted.

They tumbled into the apartment. He didn't want to turn the lights on—embarrassing how messy and nasty the place was. She took his cock already in the hall. Started sucking. No unnecessary foreplay and cutesy shit. Just the way he liked it.

He was about to come. His breathing grew heavier. Gabrielle noticed. She tried to avoid him jizzing in her mouth.

Mahmud murmured, "Come on, keep it in."

She nodded, his cock moved along with the motions of her head.

They lay down on the bed. He rested for a few minutes. Turned some music on.

Took her jeans off. Kept her top on. Put his cock in.

Gabrielle groaned like in a porno. They went at it for a while. Mahmud slapped her ass.

"Put a condom on, okay?"

"Nah, I'll come on your back."

That seemed fine with her. Mahmud assumed she was on the pill. He kept going, wham-bam. Came after a few minutes, didn't bother pulling out. Unclear if she even noticed. Sweet—second leg out of three done. The guys would hear about this tomorrow.

Gabrielle went to the bathroom. When she came back, he'd served up a line on a CD case. "I'm cool, I don't need any," she said. "Could you call a cab?"

What the fuck was this bullshit? He still had one more thing left to do. Had to complete the hat trick. Spraying in her asshole was the grand finale.

He leaned over her. Began to kiss her neck, up toward her face. Let his lips move over her eyes, cheeks, forehead. He licked her ear, caressed her hair, tits, ass.

"Come on, baby, be nice. Feels good, right?"

They lay down on the bed again. He was gonna fucking enter her, that's all there was to it.

Mahmud took her top off. Her body was hot as hell. He lay down on top of her carefully. He was, like, ten times bigger. Kept kissing her forehead. She closed her eyes. Guided his cock inside her.

Missionary for a few minutes. Then he flipped her over. Pushed his cock toward her asshole.

"No, not there," she whispered.

"It's gonna feel so good. I promise."

He grabbed hold of her ass cheeks. Tried to force his cock in.

"I don't want it there." Her voice was high-pitched now.

"Come on, just a quickie."

Gabrielle wriggled her butt. He grabbed hold of her harder.

"Stop it. I don't want to." Her voice jumped up another notch.

It was insane: him, the muscleman, the pussy king, the bitch-fucker—limp. Ill opportunity, a fine piece of ass on her belly, all he had to do was push it in, do his thing. What the fuck was wrong with him anyway? He let her go. Saw her relax.

"Just stay there, please. You're so beautiful."

He got up. Looked down at Gabrielle. Her legs straight on the bed. He had to do this thing. He rummaged through his clothes, his jacket, his wallet, his jeans. Finally he found what he was looking for: a dime bag with a few milligrams left. He put some cocaine on his finger. Rubbed it against his cock. It had to work. He needed to get it up again.

Now.

38

Niklas held the weapon. Weighed it. Admired the sheen of the metal. Felt like over there, except this weapon'd hardly been used.

Thought back over the past few weeks. The woman at Black & White Inn'd delivered his order. A clean, proper gun: a new Beretta. He test-fired it for the first time in a wooded area in Sätra. Twenty rounds into a couple of beer cans lined up on rocks. Real Baghdad feel in the middle of the Stockholm autumn. He had to learn the weapon. The safety, the slide, the rear sight, the hammer's release, the clamping pin, the sear, the magazine catch, and so on. Him and the Beretta: they would become one. As it should be.

Followed by training at home. The slide motion for this specific piece should be automatic, embedded in his elbow movement. He turned the lights off, practiced in the dark, practiced in baggy clothes, without clothes, walking, lying down, running. Left, right, right, left.

All you fucking wife-beaters—Operation Magnum's offensive begins now. This is your nightmare, and it's coming for you. Go, hide—if you can.

Today was the day. He was going to eliminate the first target. Mats Asshole Strömberg.

The months'd passed by quickly, yielding good results surveillance-wise. The only bad part: Niklas'd been thrown out of his place in Aspudden. The illegal broker fucker'd gotten hold of another apartment and Niklas'd had to pay up. A bigger hit than expected, considering that he'd gotten rid of the Audi and bought a Ford instead. He wouldn't compromise with safety. But the money would run out in a few days. What should he do? The basic principle remained: war has a cost.

His relationship with Mom'd only gotten worse. He couldn't handle being in touch. She'd called, texted, even sent a letter. After their fight a few months ago: it didn't feel right. Mom'd been humiliated for half her life. Still, she didn't seem to want to understand the importance of what he was about to do today. Her way of thinking was so twisted. But therein probably lay the answer. That so many women went along with men beating, repressing, harassing, terrorizing them. That they didn't defend themselves, didn't do something about it, didn't fight back. Niklas was familiar with the hard-core feminists' arguments even though he'd stopped surfing their pathetic websites after the Biskops-Arnö incident. It was about societal structures, gendered power, patriarchy, built-in patterns that every single individual apparently had to ape.

Niklas'd stuck the GPS location device under Mats Strömberg's car on a night in October. Since then, he'd followed the guy's driving route like a fucking map freak. Reminded him of a British sergeant in DynCorp. The guy's greatest pleasure was maps—seriously. When the others listened to their MP3 players, flipped through porn magazines, or played poker, Sergeant Jacobs read maps with incredible intensity. But shit, that dude was sharp in the field. Once he'd studied an area, he knew it better than he knew his own gun.

On the way home, Strömberg often passed by a bodega in Sund-byberg. Parked his car. Got out, hung out in the bodega for fifteen minutes. At first, Niklas didn't understand what the guy was up to. One day, he followed him in. Mats Strömberg wouldn't recognize him, anyway. The deal: gambling. The guy seemed to drop the household kitty on horses and sports, etc. And Niklas began to sense a pattern. It was on the nights that bets were decided that Mats Strömberg found it necessary to take things out on his wife.

When October grew chillier, Strömberg draped himself with a checked scarf, tied it like a fucking fogie—with a simple knot and most of the fabric hanging flat down against his chest. His jean jacket was exchanged for a butt-ugly green nylon jacket. The leather shoes for a pair of boots that looked military-issue. And it was then, in October, that Niklas was able to establish another pattern: the first Monday of every month, Strömberg met a few friends at a pub by Mariatorget. He knew now: same pub, about the same time, same dudes. The pics that Niklas'd snapped were clear. Three months in a row.

And tonight was the first Monday in November. Definitely: time for attack. He knew that Mats Strömberg would be home late without a car. Operation Magnum was entering the next phase.

Niklas'd rented a neutral vehicle, a gray Volvo V50. Didn't want to risk the Mats fucker recognizing the Ford as the one that'd been parked outside his house for so many hours over the past few days. The guy could start wondering. The Volvo was perfect: no one noticed a car that dull.

Waited. Outside the pub where Mats Strömberg was sitting, all happy. It never got boring, strangely enough—letting time lapse with nothing to do but to stare out through the window. Strömberg shouldn't be allowed to be happy. Four days ago, he'd beaten up his wife in front of their son. She just cried. He just hit. The son hid behind the couch.

Niklas wasn't going to take him out here in the city—too many people around. Instead: he would trail the guy out to Sundbyberg. And there, on the street, at a spot he'd identified and analyzed: an end to the tragedy.

His cell phone was on silent. It was in the bag on the passenger seat. Still, he could feel it vibrating as if it'd been in the pocket of his jeans. The display showed: *Benjamin*. This really wasn't the time to talk. On the other hand, Niklas might need Benjamin's help again. His cash problem was too much of a reality to ignore.

"Hey, it's Benjamin."

"I can see that."

"Where've you been these last few months? Fuck, man, this is the first time we're talking in God knows how long. Did you go back to Iraq, or what?"

"Hey, I can't really talk right now. What do you want?"

Benjamin was silent for a few breaths too many. Obviously surprised by Niklas's brashness.

"If you're gonna be like that you might as well go back down to the desert. I don't give a shit. Dammit, man, you've screened my calls at least ten times lately."

That was true. Niklas'd chosen not to pick up the phone, screened the calls, even ignored his voice mail. Focus, that was what mattered, not a bunch of pointless phone calls. Still: his money was running out.

"I know, I'm sorry. I've been swamped. What is it you want?"

"I think you're gonna wanna hear this. If you didn't already check your messages."

Niklas thought, I can't take this.

Benjamin went on. "The police called me a couple weeks ago. Brought me in for questioning and everything. I was there in the middle of October, I think. Take one guess what it was about."

"No idea." Niklas felt a pang of worry.

"It was about that thing this summer. Remember?"

"What?"

"Quit it. Know who they were asking about?"

Niklas's anxiety was rising. He already knew the answer. It could only be one thing—damn it.

"They were asking about you."

"Why?"

"Remember when you asked me to say that you'd been over at my house all night?"

"Yeah, but what did they say this time?"

"You never told me what that shit was about, man. What the fuck did you drag me into? They interrogated me for at least two hours. Pushing me like crazy. Did we really watch a movie? What did we see? When did you get to my house, when did you leave, am I sure about the date? Get it?"

"You didn't say anything, did you?"

"No, I didn't. But I don't know, man. You didn't tell me what the deal was. Murder, man. Niklas, what the fuck is this, anyway? This is insane. Murder."

"I don't know any more than you do. I have no idea. I'm being totally honest. Do they suspect me of something?"

"How the fuck am I supposed to know? Murder, man. Come on, Niklas. What is this about?"

Niklas felt himself grow hot and cold at once. How did this happen? He didn't have an answer for Benjamin.

He was at a crossroads: no way he could take this kind of crap. At the same time: Benjamin's alibi—invaluable. He had to grovel like a fucking brownnoser.

"Yeah, it's about some dead guy that was found in my mom's building. They brought me in for questioning too. And Mom. Some poor sucker who was beaten to bits down in the basement. They really brought out the heavy artillery."

"Okay. But what does that have to do with you? Why'd they drag me in there and interrogate the shit out of me again? And what did you need that gun for?"

"Nothing, that was just for fun. And about the dead guy in my mom's house, I honestly don't know. No idea. But if I'm a suspect I guess they would've picked me up ages ago. But you know, with my background, things can get messy with the police no matter what."

Silence.

More silence.

A drop of sweat along his temple.

In a low voice, Benjamin said, "We're buddies and all, but . . . but this is getting kind of big, I think. What am I getting out of this?"

"What do you mean?"

"I mean, I've got your back like crazy right now, man. And what's in it for me? You don't think I deserve something for making up a story about that movie night?"

"What the fuck are you talking about? You want money?"

"I don't know. But yeah, yeah I do, actually. Don't you think that's fair? I'm putting my neck on the line for you. You've gotta be a little generous."

This was just too much. First the illegal broker, then the vehicle swap and the rental, and now this: a comrade who betrayed. Went the blackmail route. What was he supposed to say? He had to offer the asshole something.

"I didn't expect this from you, Benjamin. But how about this, you did something good for me and that ought to be worth something. I can pay you five grand. I don't have more than that."

Benjamin made a smacking noise with his mouth.

"I'm glad we understand each other. Double that and we'll be completely clear."

At midnight, Mats Strömberg and one of his friends stumbled out of the pub. Flushed face. The fogie scarf sloppily tied.

He jumped into his buddy's car, which, it turned out, was parked three cars in front of Niklas.

Not good if the buddy was planning to give Strömberg a ride all the way home. But Niklas'd seen it before—most often, the Mats asshole was dropped off by the Central Station and took the commuter rail out to Sundbyberg.

Niklas trailed the car without a problem in the light traffic.

Just as he'd expected: Mats Strömberg was dropped off at the Central Station. Walked down to the commuter rail. Niklas'd thought the whole thing through. Had studied the commuter rail timetables for the evening and night. Mats would catch the 12:22 train out toward Bålsta. Might be delays. Niklas checked the traffic info on his smartphone.

Tonight, the 12:22 train was running according to schedule. It would take him nine minutes to drive out to Sundbyberg in the night traffic. The train only took seven minutes, but it didn't leave for another eight minutes. He was safe.

On the highway, one thought running through his head: the shots had to hit the right spots. Take him down quickly. The job had to be done fast and clean. In Operation Magnum, no wounded targets were left behind.

He parked the car about a hundred feet from the exit to the commuter rail station. Rolled down a window. Waited. Cold air streamed in. Checked the train schedule one final time on his phone. The train would arrive in three minutes. He put the Beretta on his lap. A woman with a Labrador walked by on the street. Otherwise, the area was clear of civilians. He double-checked the chamber, the safety, the hammer.

One minute left until the train was supposed to pull into the station below. Niklas bent down, checked again that his shoes were tied properly. Could feel it in his gut, like the hours before an attack. Small, small movements. As if they had a life of their own. At the same time: expectation, excitement in the air. Excitement over doing something for the greater good.

Now he heard the shrieking of the train's brakes. Looked at his watch. Niklas'd test-walked the stairs up from the platform and out through the station. Depending on where on the train the guy got off, it should take between thirty and fifty seconds.

The doors opened automatically. Two people got off. No Mats. Then a family: the mom was pushing a double stroller filled with kids and the dad was carrying a sleeping child. After them: a couple of teens.

Finally: Mats Strömberg.

The flush on his face'd settled. He looked like a model citizen. Walked past the Volvo where Niklas was sitting. Niklas got out of the car. Thirty feet behind the target. The Beretta in his pocket. Strömberg walked at a normal pace. Four hundred yards to the domicile. In about 165 feet, he would cross over a small park. No streetlights there and no houses.

It was almost twelve-thirty at night. Niklas didn't see a single soul out except the target. He'd planned this so well, so long, not just in order to execute this perfectly, but in order to make sure he'd made the correct selection.

One hundred feet left before the park. Niklas sped up. Twenty feet behind Strömberg. The guy didn't seem to notice that he was being followed.

Niklas put his hand in his inner pocket. Felt the warm steel of the revolver.

The trees in the park were clearly visible, dark green.

Niklas knew: aiming for the head is uncertain if you want the target to die. The head can move and is made up of parts that can bust without the victim dying: ears, jaw, skull, parts of the brain, even. The back, on the other hand. If you hit the vertebral column, the shot will be fatal instantly. What's more: enough to shoot at very close range. Large, safe surface to aim at. If you miss the spine there is a great chance that you'll hit the aorta, the inferior vena cava, or the large pulmonary artery. That'll get the job done, too.

Mats was ten feet ahead of him.

To the left was a jungle gym that could hardly be made out in the dark. But Niklas knew that it was there. He'd made up his mind: this was the best spot.

Six feet left.

Mats turned around. Niklas met his gaze. Wondered if the asshole knew what was about to happen.

Three feet. Niklas extended his arm. The black Beretta almost disappeared in the darkness.

A shot.

Immediately followed by another shot.

Perfect hit. The bullets' entry points should be about eight inches below the neck. He couldn't see, exactly. Bent down. Mats lay facedown on the ground. Two small holes. In the correct spot on the back. The bullets' exit points should be significantly larger, but he couldn't check that now.

Niklas turned around. Jogged through the park. Out onto the street: calmer steps. Back to the car.

Three hours later. The Volvo: burned out, cleared. Any possible DNA traces'd gone up in flames. The weapon was washed and buried. Maybe he would use the same gun the next time, he hadn't decided yet.

He was an awesome soldier. A liberator. A hero.

In the Ford on his way home from the charred skeleton of the Volvo, he stopped at a pay phone in Aspudden.

A number of signals went through before anyone picked up. This was going to be a good call.

Groggy or teary, he didn't know how to read her voice.

"Hello, this is Helene."

He'd promised himself to make it short.

"Hi, I'm sorry to be calling in the middle of the night."

"Who is it?"

"I wanted to inform you that I have just set you free."

"Who are you, what do you mean?"

"I've removed him. You don't have to worry anymore. He isn't coming back."

He would've liked to speak longer with Helene Strömberg, she seemed sweet. But he couldn't. Not right now, anyway.

39

Thomas was standing in the kitchen making breakfast. It was eleven o'clock. Last night'd gotten late. He hadn't come home until close to 6:00 a.m. Åsa would be sleeping anyway, so it didn't matter. He could come home at eleven-thirty or six-thirty—she didn't know what he was up to, anyway. Dammit, sometimes the anxiety almost overwhelmed him. He woke up in a cold sweat. Impossible to fall back asleep.

He'd gotten himself a nice deal at the traffic-control unit: worked part-time. Could do late nights at the club on so-called junior Saturdays, a.k.a. Wednesdays, and then sleep in. Flipped the day for half the week. Monday mornings were tougher than he could've ever imagined.

There was an opened envelope on the kitchen table. Beside it, some paperwork. The words: Adoption Center. When he bent down he could feel his heartbeat speed up. It couldn't be true. Please say you've found something for us. Something I can live with.

The papers felt tacky, sticking to one another. He was nervous, his hands were trembling, he tried to read calmly. Lots of filler words. *Information has been verified. A doctor has been consulted. Our ambition is for the family not only to receive word of the child as soon as possible, but that the information received also be as accurate and complete as possible. How much information we have been able to collect about the child, however, varies a great deal between different countries and areas.* He read through it, even though he kept wanting to flip ahead. Maybe to prepare himself in case of bad news. He wondered why Åsa hadn't called.

Then there was a bunch of untranslated official Estonian paperwork, stamps, strange signatures. The pages that followed: descriptions of the orphanage, the boy's age, condition, family situation. Rules for picking him up, demands for further permits, etc. And then, on the final pages: the pictures. Of Sander.

The boy was the most wonderful child he'd ever laid eyes on. A sixteen-month-old angel, chubby, with pale blond curls and brown eyes. He loved the kid immediately: Sander. His heartbeat transformed into rhythmic bells of joy. For the first time in many years, he felt completely warm inside. Happy, he guessed. It was fantastic. He called Åsa.

She picked up on the first ring. Bubbling with joy. Talk interlaced with tears. For once, Thomas didn't get annoyed. He felt the same; they were going to have a son. They began planning right away. When they would pick up the boy, outfitting a nursery. Wallpaper, a lamp, a crib, a car seat, a stroller, a BabyBjörn. All the stuff Åsa'd heard her girlfriends go on about for years.

Åsa said that she hadn't wanted to call and wake him up with the news. She wanted him to see the surprise for himself in the kitchen, the way it'd been for her. Thomas laughed. Maybe he was too hard on her about needing his sleep.

Goddammit—he was going to be a dad. He couldn't decide: Laugh/cry. Cry/laugh. Laugh until he cried.

He worked out up in the TV room. The joy was still there, underneath it all. But the other thoughts'd snuck up on him. It was more than ten weeks since he'd been transferred to the traffic geeks. More than eight weeks since he'd done his first job for his new employer. His side gig as the Yugos' made man was better than he'd expected. The strip club was beginning to feel like home. Life changed so quickly. The way he saw his work. His attitude toward everything. It snuck up on him over the years, a tiny bit at a time. The temptations aren't actually built into the job—they're built into the person. And one fine day you find yourself in a wasteland, where it doesn't matter anymore how you treat the rabble and yourself. When it feels normal. He often thought about his dad. Gunnar'd built Sweden. Believed that everyone deserved to come along for the ride. Back then, Thomas wouldn't have let anyone ruin what his dad'd built. But now he wasn't so sure anymore. How'd he been treated by his own? Ljunggren and Lindberg? Sure, they toasted him at their Friday get-togethers, but what did they do, really? Ljunggren'd agreed to be reassigned that night and not gone on the beat with him. His regret about it came too late, somehow. There was no police spirit when you needed it. In comparison, Ratko, Radovan, and the others he'd met were real men. Honest in their own way. They stood by their word, did what they'd promised. He was paid the salary they'd agreed on without written contracts. But most important of all—nothing leaked out to Åsa or the cops. Thomas trusted the Yugos. More than anyone within the police force. It was strange, but true.

So, no matter how weird it sounded, the job at the club imbued him with a kind of calm. It offered a slow, steady rhythm that he felt at home with. It was more his style: freer rein. Uppity johns at the strip club got a taste of Andrén if they grew too rowdy.

Sometimes he did other things too—more complex, sophisticated. Participated in the security team at more high-class get-togethers. Swedish and foreign businessmen who wanted to have a good time. The strippers were glammed up to look like chicks with class, pro makeup artists were hired, young brats from the fancy Östermalm area organized the parties. Thomas didn't see much of the actual events, but he dealt with the surrounding details. Taught the younger gym guys Ratko introduced him to how to use a baton and a Taser. Explained how to deal with a tanked fifty-year-old: calmly and correctly, but without taking no for an answer. Hard as steel. Made sure the right vests were bought, radio and walkie-talkie systems, belts, handcuffs, and gloves. He knew this stuff like the back of his hand. Ratko loved him. Maybe it was a breakthrough. Maybe he could do this full time.

And then there was the major thing. That kept eating away at him. Like a Post-it note stuck to the inside of his forehead. The Palme thing. Leader of the Social Democrats during Thomas's entire childhood and adolescence, Sweden's prime minister. Murdered. The moment when Sweden lost its virginity. It was insane. Everything pointed to the fact that Rantzell was the murdered man he'd found five months ago. And Rantzell was Cederholm. And Cederholm—that name ought to ring a bell—was the key witness in the entire Palme investigation. The man who claimed that he'd given a Smith & Wesson revolver to Christer Pettersson. The weapon that half the trial'd revolved around. Had Christer Pettersson had such a weapon or not? Was Cederholm credible or not? What was the nature of their relationship? The questions were making his head explode. But worst of all: What'd he stepped into? He thought about the way Rantzell'd been killed. Professionally done. The sliced fingertips, the missing dentures, no other ways to identify the victim. At the same time: so cheap and simple. In a basement, bloody, messy as hell. There had to have been a better way.

And one more thing: it almost felt personal. He thought about his old man again. For his dad, being a Social Democrat was as instinctive as being a man. There were no alternatives. Not because he was actually interested in politics on a theoretical level, but because he voted with his gut. What's good for me is good for Sweden—everyone deserves to come along for the ride. Gunnar'd worked as a housepainter all his life. Hadn't done what everyone did today: worked 80 percent off the books and did a little on the record for the sake of the tax man. Gunnar worked for someone, not for himself. He was an employee, a paycheck slave, his entire life. Union member since he was eighteen. "The Social Democrats," he used to say, "are giving Sweden a chance." People said that Palme was hated because he betrayed his class—the upper class he'd been born into. But Gunnar sang a different tune: "Palme was hated because he could talk so you felt it, all the way into a painter's heavily surface-treated heart."

Thomas remembered his dad in front of the television. Standing with him when Palme spoke at the square at Norra Bantorget. The man's footwork behind the podium. Gunnar's laughter when Palme smiled after delivering a sharp line.

Now someone'd killed Cederholm, the guy who'd ratted out the person who was a hair's breadth from being convicted of the murder of Olof Palme. Thomas didn't know what to do with it all. He'd told the current detective on the case, Ronander, that he'd met Ballénius at Solvalla, and he'd given him all the other info too. But he didn't let slip about his conversation with Ljunggren that night in the car.

He knew it, could feel it in the pit of his stomach stronger than he'd ever felt any other warning—he shouldn't poke around in this mess. And still, he did. To Thomas, it was so obvious. If it'd stopped at Adamsson bursting in on his and Hägerström's visit to the morgue, he wouldn't have given it another thought. But then, when Ljunggren told him that it was Adamsson who'd stopped him from going out on the patrol too, Thomas knew: Adamsson was knee-deep in this shit.

His options were pretty simple: either he forgot about Adamsson or else he proceeded with his own investigation. The conclusion was even simpler: no one would get away with shitting on him—he was going to nail those fuckers. Solve the Rantzell mystery.

It was on that night two months ago, when Ljunggren'd told him who Rantzell really was, that he'd made up his mind.

Right after they parted ways, he'd climbed into his car. Made an effort to keep to the speed limit. The embarrassment if he ended up being investigated by his own traffic unit would be too much. He went into a pizzeria on Sveavägen. Ordered a calzone and a glass of some cheap-brand whiskey. Downed it in two minutes. Everything was spinning. At the time, he'd just found out. Cederholm was Rantzell. Rantzell was Cederholm. Adamsson was involved. How much? In what way? Ljunggren's new information opened up an abyss.

Thomas scarfed down the calzone.

The incidents were being put into a context. If this was connected to something as big as the Palme murder, anyone could be involved. It was sick. The guy outside their window three months ago could be a cop, a South African mercenary soldier, a Mossad agent, a Kurdish PKK terrorist. Anything. Thomas belonged to the camp that thought Christer Pettersson actually was the one who'd popped Palme. But there were some doubts. Sure, he'd heard other theories. Someone didn't want the track marks on Claes Rantzell's arm to come to light. Someone'd swept Thomas out of the picture. Someone with astonishing resources.

So far, Thomas'd acted impeccably, at least according to himself. It couldn't be prohibited for a cop to look around a little on his own— and as soon as he'd found something out he'd called the new detective heading the investigation. But now it was time to go rogue completely. He needed to clear his name.

After the calzone, he walked across the street to a Cuban place. Had a seat at a table. Ordered a glass of Gran Reserva. Felt lonely. The walls were painted black. Big Cuban flags. Should he tell Åsa what he was doing?

He asked to borrow a pen and some paper from the waitress. Started writing down what he knew about the murder in bullet-point form.

Drank the wine in big gulps. The pistol was dangling along one side of his suit jacket. The waitress set down a small plate with grilled scampi. He ordered another glass of wine.

Looked at his list. Names, places, times. Too few bullet points. A big question mark around Rantzell. Who was he?

His cell phone rang. It was Åsa, who wondered where he was. He told her the truth: "I'm sitting at La Habana, alone, drinking red wine." She wondered why. He almost told her the truth: "Seeing Ljunggren put me in a bad mood."

An hour later: when he went to take a piss, he saw himself in the mirror. A reddish-purple grin filled with worry. He thought, Come on now, this'll work itself out.

He walked outside, climbed into the car. Really didn't care about his blood alcohol content. The traffic unit could go fuck itself. He drove toward Fruängen. His buzz felt fine, anyway.

The fall darkness that usually made him depressed felt invigorating. This was his investigation.

He'd realized that something was going on in the building already down by the entrance. Two big notes were posted on the elevator door. *A police investigation is being conducted on the third floor, as well as on certain other floors. Due to this, the county police will be present in your building for a certain period of time. We apologize for any inconvenience. If you have any questions, please call: 08-401 26 00.*

He took long strides. The right floor. The right name on the mail slot. Caution tape. Thomas took a step forward. There was a heavy padlock on the door. He went back down to the car again. Found his skeleton key. Brought his gloves along. Cleared the padlock in under a minute.

Went inside. The hall was dark. He turned the lights on. Jackets on hangers to the right. The floor was bare. His colleagues'd probably cleaned up shoes and other crap. Sent the stuff to the lab. Thomas wondered why they hadn't taken the jackets, too.

The kitchen was small. Dirty dishes and silverware, run-down and nasty—standard protocol in junkie apartments. He knew the drill. Had been inside more crack dens than regular apartments in his life. He tried to analyze what kind of job the cops'd done in there. Felt like the booze was making him sharper. He could follow the sequence of events. How they'd swabbed, searched for fingerprints. Polished surfaces, placed dirty objects in evidence bags. He let his gaze register the details. Rantzell didn't take care of himself. The signs were all there, the filth spoke a clear language.

The living room: a leather couch, a leather chair, flea-market art, shelves empty of books. Thomas took a step forward. Dust in the bookshelf. He remained standing there for a second. Looked, registered. Analyzed. Tried to see things through a detective's eyes. What would Hägerström have seen in here? There was something, his gut told him so. He looked around the room again. The coffee table was cleared, traces in the dust, stains, burn marks. The TV, video: nothing strange.

Hägerström, what would he have been looking for? Things that didn't tally. Anomalies. Departures from the ordinary. Thomas knew all about crack dens. He could visualize the bookshelf before they'd emptied it. A couple of paperbacks maybe, possibly some inherited hardcovers or collected works. Even addicts cared about culture. Probably a few photos, possibly memories from a better time, a time before the present.

Then he saw it: the tracks in the dust on the bookshelf. They weren't straight, regular. As they would've been if the technicians'd pulled the books out one by one and placed them in evidence bags. This was different—the books'd been swept out of the bookshelf. His thoughts came to a halt. Then he repeated the thought: the books'd been swept out. That meant that either Rantzell'd swept them out himself, or else someone'd searched the apartment before the police got there.

He went into the bedroom. The bed was stripped. Ingrained filth and stains covered the mattress. A rug on the floor. A mirror on the ceiling. He searched for traces of the person or persons who'd searched the apartment. Tried again—to think like someone else might. He didn't see anything. Opened the closet. No clothes remained. He saw a box. Opened it. It was empty.

He continued trying to spot something, whatever it might be. On the wall farther down in the closet was a small metal cabinet, eight by eight inches. The door was ajar; it was empty. Looked like a key cabinet with three rows of hooks. He looked closer at the cabinet. It had obvious traces of having been broken into. That decided it: Rantzell wouldn't break open his own cabinet, now would he? And what else did it mean? Maybe there'd never been anything in the cabinet. Or else the technicians'd taken what'd been in there, probably keys. But someone'd broken into the apartment before them. And maybe taken the keys that could've been hanging in the cabinet. What kinds of keys do you keep in a cabinet like that? Could be anything—for your bike, for the attic, the basement, the summer cottage, the car. He thought: no, not the car, it was too impractical to keep keys like that in a cabinet way back in a closet, behind clothes and a bunch of other junk.

He let his eyes scan the room again. Tried to understand what was important. It didn't work. He was tired, his buzz was fading. It felt weird, being there. If he was found out, he could kiss the dull traffic unit good-bye. Pronto.

He left the apartment.

Took the stairs down. It was eleven-thirty at night. Down by the entrance. He stared at the note again. *A police investigation is being conducted on the third floor, as well as on certain other floors.* Other floors? Where could that be? He thought about the key cabinet. Just had to check one more place.

He went down into the basement. One of the storage units in the basement was cordoned off with caution tape. He stepped over the plastic barrier. The unit was open. An old carpet, two moving boxes. In one: dusty porcelain. In the other: old porn magazines. Other than that, the storage unit was empty. Thomas started walking back. The other storage units were more or less crammed with junk. Skis and ski boots, armchairs, bags, furniture, spare beds, crap. The bars felt feeble. The padlocks on the wooden doors were thin. He passed a unit that was almost empty except for a computer that looked like it was twenty years old. Imagine, people saved shit like that. Thomas felt a headache coming on. He just wanted to go home. Coming here was a mistake. He glanced into another storage unit. Froze. It couldn't be a coincidence. Plastic bags. All with the same print on the side: *Willys.* He saw the image in front of him clearly: the woman who'd sat next to Ballénius at Solvalla'd had a bag like that.

His mind cleared. There was a connection. This was his chance. He opened the lock with his skeleton key. Stepped into the storage unit. Bent down. Checked out the dust, looked for footsteps or other signs that his colleagues'd been in here. Didn't seem like it. On the other hand: next to the bags, the layer of dust was a little bit thinner than over the rest of the floor. Obvious: someone'd already taken something from the storage unit.

Thomas went out to his car. Got two big plastic bags from the trunk. Brought them down to the storage unit. Emptied the contents of the plastic bags into the two big bags. Smushed the bags down too. Tomorrow, no one would know he'd been there.

He remembered he had already been completely awake when Åsa woke up. Too many thoughts in his head. He needed to gain control over his ideas. Bring some order to his investigation. Understand what the finds he'd made in Rantzell's basement meant. It was a lot of paperwork. It would take time to go through it and he didn't like paperwork. He had to think things over. Give it time.

The Adamsson trail was the theme of the day. The questions were piling up. At which end would he begin unwinding the knot? When should he begin? In the present or in the past? He tried to analyze.

But how does a traffic cop run an investigation on a superior who is also the boss of all his colleagues in the Southern District? Should he go to the Palme Group, the little that was left of the Palme Commission, and tell them about Adamsson's intrusion at the morgue? Maybe there was some paperwork that would back up the fact that the intervention happened. If not, it all went bust. But even if it was possible to prove that Adamsson was behind the incident at the morgue, it didn't mean anything. Adamsson'd been right about that—they had been at the morgue without the requisite authority.

On the other hand, Thomas was certain that no evidence existed to prove that Adamsson was the one who'd ordered Ljunggren to switch patrols that night. Nothing more than Ljunggren's word, and that wouldn't weigh particularly heavily against Adamsson's.

And Hägerström? Shouldn't he call Hägerström? No, he would never call that IA snake. You had to have some pride.

All his suspicions were founded in the present, but he didn't have much to go on. Maybe it was better if he tried to go back in time, research history. Find out who Adamsson really was and who he'd been. Thomas felt alone. His usual colleagues and friends were not reliable. The people at the shooting club were no support. And Åsa, she was really more of a burden in all of this.

The only person he could think of was Jonas Nilsson. He was simple—didn't think too much. Thomas perceived him as genuinely kind, through and through. After all, Nilsson'd helped him look up Ballénius—without anything leaking about that, at least not that Thomas knew of. The only problem with Nilsson: he was a *former* colleague. In reality, Thomas didn't know him anymore. But it was worth the chance.

He called the guy from Åsa's cell to be on the safe side. They decided to meet up on a night that week. It was dicey: he didn't know if he should tell Nilsson what it was all really about, the murder of a prime minister. He'd have to choose some happy medium.

It all went smoothly. They met up at Friden. Nilsson seemed happy to see him. They ordered beers, started shooting the shit straight off the bat. Compared districts, complained about equipment, bosses, their colleagues. Empathy-whined about Sweden, the National Police, the weather.

Thomas explained his thing: "I'm really damn pissed off about what happened to me."

Nilsson was understanding. To be transferred to the traffic unit was a pure nightmare for a real cop.

Thomas went on. Explained that he thought it was Adamsson's fault, that he wanted to find a way to really stick it to the old fucker. And then he said it. "Nilsson, do you know any old cop who might know what Adamsson was like back in the day? You know, we've all heard a bunch of talk about the guy. What he was up to during the eighties and all that. It would be golden if you knew someone who knew more than we do. Just to have something to hold over Adamsson."

Nilsson promised to think about it. Talk to the old-timers, maybe one of the guys who'd helped him with Ballénius.

Jonas Nilsson delivered a name a few days later: Göran Runeby. Northern District, detective inspector. Not bad. According to Nilsson, Runeby was the kind of man who knew the police force the way a genealogist knows his family tree.

Runeby agreed to meet in an unbiased manner, that's what he told Jonas. Thomas didn't know what to expect and it didn't matter—even if Runeby only knew what anyone could figure out—that Adamsson'd happened to pinch a police secretary in the butt now and then, that he'd had a predilection for excessive force, that he disliked immigrants—then that was good.

Thomas met Runeby at his house in Täby. The old guy lived in an okay house, two stories, more than 2,700 square feet. Thomas wondered if an inspector's salary could really stretch that much further, or if Runeby'd played the game the same way he did.

Runeby's wife was home. Welcomed him at the door.

"Hello, it's so nice to see a fresh face. How do you two know each other?"

Thomas didn't really know what to say. He just smiled and mumbled something about police matters.

"Sure. The usual, in other words." Runeby's wife smiled. Thomas thought she was probably used to the way the men carried on. She reminded him of his own mother.

Runeby came down from upstairs. Led Thomas into the living room. He had white hair and a white mustache. A thin gold watch on his wrist: over thirty years in the service of the state. The guy really was an old hand.

"I'm so glad you were able to come all the way out here. May I offer you something to drink? Cognac, whiskey?"

Thomas had a cognac. Runeby closed the doors to the room.

He was a straight shooter.

"So, Nilsson told me that you've got a particular interest in old Adamsson?"

Thomas liked his style. No small talk. Real police mentality.

"That's right."

"Just so you know—you can trust me," Runeby said. "I've never liked that quasi-fascist."

Thomas reacted inside. A police using the word *fascist* in that way wasn't exactly par for the course.

He looked at Runeby.

"I'm sure you're aware of what happened to me."

Runeby didn't say anything.

"I was transferred after the episode with the boxer. And it's made me bitter as hell. I feel betrayed and poorly treated. Collegiality seems hard to come by in the Southern District. I'll be completely honest with you, Runeby—I blame Adamsson."

Runeby nodded but didn't say anything. Waited for Thomas to go on.

"But that's not what I want to discuss with you. I want to talk history. The past. I've heard quite a lot about Adamsson. But Nilsson said you know even more. That you're well informed about the police in this city. So I would like to ask you, very humbly, if you would tell me about Adamsson, the old quasi-fascist, as you called him. Who is he and who was he?"

"And why do you want to know, if I may ask?"

"I hope you understand that I can't go into that. But he betrayed me. I have no right to demand anything of you. But Nilsson said that you'd probably be willing to share some information with me."

Runeby looked pleased. Even if the old guy hadn't proven himself yet, Thomas couldn't help but like him. There was something calm, dignified, and inviting of respect about the old inspector. Again: genuine cop feel—but with something special, something extra. Thomas couldn't put his finger on what. But he could sense it plainly. Some kind of warmth.

"Okay. I think I understand," Runeby said in a low voice. "I don't really know where to begin. As for Adamsson today, I can tell you right away that I only hear good things. He seems to be well liked by you patrol officers in the Southern District. Isn't that right?"

"If you'd asked me a couple of weeks ago, I would've said yes."

"But now you're less sure? I understand, but that has to do with your transfer, doesn't it?"

"Not only."

"Well, all right. I can't talk about Adamsson as he is today. But I did have a great deal to do with him in the seventies and eighties. Those were strange times for us cops. When did you graduate from the Academy?"

"In ninety-five."

"Ah, you're *that* young. But maybe you've heard stories? Anyway, the political climate was completely different then. We lived in the shadow of the Cold War, as I'm sure you recall. But maybe you were too young to understand the nuances of what that meant."

"I don't know."

Runeby went on at a calm pace. "Maybe it doesn't matter. The first time I met Adamsson was in the military, I guess you could say. I wasn't working in the Northern District at the time, but in the force we had several special units that could be deployed in the event of war. Within the Northern District, the assignment was to, in case of attack, initially—that is, before the military had time to react—defend the royal castle and the government buildings, Riksdagen and Rosenbad. Me and three others from what is now called the Western District were included in that unit because we were in the reserves. So I met Adamsson for the first time during a simulation exercise. He was competent and polite, as I remember. Within the police, he was known as a good shot, with vast knowledge about weaponry. We used to practice together with the National Home Guard, once a year or so. It was amusing, actually. Like a practice drill, except downtown. But there were guys in the unit who were skeptical. Many of them didn't think there was enough invested in defense. They feared that an attack led by, for instance, the Soviet elite forces, Spetsnaz, would be able to occupy Stockholm in a matter of hours. As I remember it, Adamsson was a part of those discussions. And he was one of the ones who agitated the most. A group of us were stationed behind the House of Nobility, on guard. I remember how Adamsson chewed out a younger man. He was really cutting into him. You're letting down the motherland, he barked. I remember that verbatim."

While he listened intently, Thomas looked around Runeby's living room. Dark wood bookcases with photos of the family and volumes of the National Encyclopedia, Jan Guillou's collected works, and photo albums. On another wall were four large framed photographs of a coastline. Thomas assumed that Runeby or his wife'd taken them themselves.

"Maybe I should give you some background information after all. A lot of cops were under the impression that there was a war on. Not just the war we're always fighting, that is to say the war on crime, but something bigger than that. It was the free world against Communism. The Russians could come any day. And a lot of cops saw themselves as part of the line of defense that would resist an attack."

Thomas thought about his dad. No matter how big of a Social Democrat he was, he'd also always gone on about the Russians. "If we don't wise up, we could end up like the Baltic countries," he used to say.

Runeby spoke slowly. "In 1982, I started working in the Northern District. At that time, there were six SWAT teams there. One of them was included in the so-called Troop and was led by a commander who is dead now. His name was Jan Malmström, have you heard of him?"

Thomas vaguely recognized the name, but wanted to know more. He shook his head.

"He was a legend in many ways. But that team kept to themselves, they seldom spoke to the rest of us, only followed Malmström's orders, dealt with appointments behind closed doors. It was generally acknowledged that they acted like real pigs, if you'll excuse the expression, and sympathized with the far right. I remember that one of them, Leif Carlsson, openly called himself a Nazi. The others were bone-hard, too. Anyway, some of the members of the team were also politically active. There was a group that used to meet in Gamla Stan once a month or so. It had connections with a right-wing extremist publication called *Contras*. It was in that context that I met Adamsson a little later on. I myself was, how should I put this, *deeply critical* of the fact that certain elements within the Swedish government showed such weakness in the face of Communism."

Getting warmer. Thomas couldn't help but ask, "Is Leif Carlsson still alive?"

"As far as I know, Carlsson is still alive, but he must be around seventy by now. Where was I? Oh, yeah. The SWAT team and Gamla Stan. I think the Palme Commission looked into the people who ran those meetings. I feel like I've read that somewhere. But the ones who *came* to the meetings were never investigated. Malmström, Carlsson, Adamsson, Winge—no one bothered to ask about them. Since I was an officer in the reserves and connected with the National Home Guard and didn't exactly shy away from being a little rough with the rabble, Malmström considered me reliable. I was invited to one of those meetings in Gamla Stan once."

Runeby paused. The silence echoed in the room.

He took a deep breath, then he went on. "It was a basement venue on Österlånggatan. I think it was used by EAP, the European Workers' Party, a small group made up of crazies that had its roots in the U.S. I remember that the first thing you saw by the entrance was a poster with a cartoon caricature of Olof Palme sitting on a cliff by the ocean. He was covering his eyes with his hands while around him the water was full of periscopes sticking up. It said: *Palme is closing his eyes to the safety of our nation.* I was surprised, almost shocked, to see how many people were there. A colleague of mine who'd been there before told me that there were senior police officers, officers in the navy, secret-service officers, and other high-ranking officials there. I recognized a few cops, but I had no idea who the others were. Lennart Edling, who'd organized the event, was stationed at the entrance to the venue, shaking everyone's hand. When everyone'd arrived, we were served a drink. A police officer who'd been my first commanding officer in the Northern District gave the welcome speech. Maybe it sounds strange, but I remember exactly what it was about. We thought the subject matter was important. Patriotism, the threat against Sweden, Communism's expansionist ideas. We were facing an overhanging threat, the lecturer said. If we didn't do something about the danger, the Russians would come any day now. Then we sat down for dinner and I ended up next to Adamsson. He was my age, but we only knew each other superficially from the simulation exercises with the National Home Guard. This was sometime in 1985, so we must have been around forty—not totally green, in other words. He almost made an insane impression, as I recall. Babbled on about someone needing to do something about the hooknose—Palme, that is. That he, with his influence, was paving the way for the Soviet invasion of Sweden. Later, during the dinner, Adamsson got drunk and almost seemed to want to have a heart-to-heart. Started raving about how he liked me, that the department needed more people like me. Then he moved on to stranger things. He talked about organizing and administering a group that would keep watch over the traitor. That might be forced to do something about that Moscow marionette. I asked him who he wanted in the group. He told me that half the guys in the Troop were already in on it. I didn't want to discuss the matter further because I thought he was embarrassing. After the dinner, there was a lecture. Right after the meeting, I didn't think too much about what Adamsson'd said. There were so many extreme types there. But later, after the assassination, I've often wondered. I was actually the one who called the Palme Group and told them about those meetings."

Runeby fell silent. Thomas was certain that he must have more questions, but he couldn't think of a single one just then. The only thing he knew was that he needed more names, more people to get leads from. Finally, he came up with a question.

"Who gave the lecture after the dinner?"

Runeby leaned forward on the couch and sighed.

"I did."

40

Tonight: a classy party for a guy who'd gated out. Fitness Center was closed. The owners, the dudes who ran the place, half of the beefcakes who trained there—everyone was gonna celebrate. Patrik, a regular, was home from the pen. Mahmud liked him: an ex-skinhead who'd straightened out. The only thing the guy cared about these days was bodybuilding and loyalty to Mr. R.

Fitness people weren't the only ones celebrating: the VIP room at Clara's was crawling with everyone who was anyone in Stockholm's underworld. Like at the gangsta golf that some old OG member started: everyone with a decent swing who'd done more than two years on the inside was welcome. A bunch of old skinheads who'd accepted that White Power music and *heil*ing didn't generate cash and who'd changed gears to bigger bling instead: MC gangs, fighting, professional racketeering. And: Yugo overload. Mahmud saw Ratko. He was sporting a nasty fake tan and bleached hair. Ratko nodded vaguely to Mahmud. But no handshake. Asshole.

Guest list (continued): a couple Albanians, four or five Syriacs, a group of guys from X-Team, the Bandidos' supporter club. Between the Yugos and the Albanians: cheek-kissing and friendly words. You could feel it in the air: this wasn't just to celebrate an insignificant gate-out from the Kumla pen. The purpose: to show generosity, chivalry, to invite future alliances. The Albanians were taking over the city. The Yugos had to watch out, as Robert said.

And, of course, a guest contingent that mustn't be forgotten: the whores. Mahmud'd never seen so many of them at one time. Really, they weren't any different from the bitches at the clubs, except that maybe they didn't look quite as hot. He thought about how close he'd been to pulling a hat trick last weekend. Still, he could sense it clear as day: the hookers were in the room without anyone really giving a damn. If they'd been normal chicks, the guys would've at least stared, flirted, pinched some *bunda*. But now it was like everyone was waiting for something, weren't gonna help themselves to the pussy spread yet. As if the girls were just part of the backdrop in a movie, something that had to be in place before filming could begin. Because everyone was waiting. For Mister Mister. Radovan would show up sooner or later.

Mahmud pushed his way through the crowd to the guy who'd just gated out, Patrik. His jacket felt tight over the shoulders—it was the first time since the tenth anniversary of Mom's funeral that he'd sported threads this dressy. He wasn't used to it, felt fly. Broad grins on both their faces. "Yo, Patrik, good to see you again, man. How many plates didja drop?"

Patrik: scarred, shaved head, pale gray suit and a narrow tie that was tied loosely. The tattoos on his neck were sticking up above his collar. He threw his head back and laughed.

"Mahmud, you little terrorist. I'll be back at target weight in three weeks. Promise." Then, in a more serious voice, "But I was working pretty hard in there. Heard you did a turn, too."

"Just six months. No biggie."

"Then you know how it is. Some guys try to sleep through their time. There's enough downers in there with all the shit they prescribe the ADD clowns. But if you work at it, you can get some good training in."

"Absolutely."

"I heard you're working for us now." Patrik started stretching his arm in the middle of the conversation. Mahmud thought about all of it, this whole situation. They were celebrating Patrik like a fucking king. But really, what'd homeboy done for the Yugos? Run a little coat-check racket, gotten in trouble with some bouncers at a club on Södermalm, lost control, beaten the shit out of a bouncer, been locked up for a few years. Why was he a hero? Why was he celebrated? Patrik'd lost his shit, couldn't do the job professionally. Not like Mahmud—hustler who hustled, made fat stacks. Never fucked up. Anything.

He felt like splitting. Asking Patrik to shut up. Ratko and Stefanovic could go fuck themselves. Radovan, if he ever showed up, could pork his own mother.

"But you were sitting in a sweet place, right?" Patrick asked. Mahmud'd almost drifted off, forgot that he was standing in the middle of some buzz.

"Yeah, Asptuna. Basically my hood, you know, Botkyrka. Not close security at all, really."

"You should be happy you were in a place like that. Times are tough for us on the inside these days."

"What're you talking about?"

"Didn't you hear? They tried to cut a guy at Kumla this weekend. One of ours. Seven guys went into the shower, six came out. They stabbed him nine times with a sharpened toothbrush. He's in the ICU but he's gonna live, he's a tough devil. Warred down in the Balkans and shit. Guys like that don't go down too easy, even if those fuckers tried."

Mahmud was somewhere else. His concentration was directed at the other side of the room. All the voices'd died down a little. Everyone's eyes were directed at the entrance—Radovan and his entourage'd walked in. Two chicks behind him. The crowd divided itself—created an aisle as though he was some big star at an MTV gala. Mahmud'd seen Radovan once before, about six months ago at the K-1 gala. But that was at a distance. Now: the first time he saw the boss close up. Or, rather, the first time he felt him. The guy reeked of authority. Even the Albanians froze. Stepped up, took the Yugo boss's hand, kissed, smiled, fake-laughed.

Radovan was definitely not the biggest man, didn't have the hardest stare, the most spring in his step—even if it was obvious that the boss would've been one of the toughest guys twenty years ago. It was something else: he spread a feeling around him, moved with a kind of ease that could only mean one thing: power. And his exterior: not that Mahmud knew much about suits, but the one R was rocking looked mad exclusive.

The girls behind him: completely different. One: had to be a whore, or some kind of mistress. High boots, plunging neckline, clown makeup. And the other one: young, very young, and strangely properly dressed. She reminded him of Jivan. He wondered who she was.

Stefanovic took a step forward, kissed Radovan's hand. Mahmud's gaze locked on the finger that the ass-licking fags were kissing: Radovan was wearing a large signet ring. Obvious: this was the man, the myth, the master of masters—the massive legend—Stockholm's Godfather of ten years.

Patrik walked up to the boss. Did as everyone else did—kissed Radovan's finger. You could tell he was a vet; Svens didn't normally do that kind of thing. Radovan said some words of welcome. Introduced his women. With one, he just introduced her by name. But the other one surprised Mahmud—she was his daughter. Then he made a small gesture toward Patrik: fixed the Sven's tie knot. An open signal: nice that you're out, but you're a nobody. Hammered it home: this party isn't for Patrik. Maybe it was just about the Albanians.

Mahmud was less than two feet away from R. Could feel his presence deep in his gut. Then, a surprise—the boss turned to Mahmud. Raised his eyebrows.

"And who are you?"

Mahmud didn't know what to say. Managed to spit out, "Mahmud al-Askori. I work for you."

Radovan looked even more surprised. "No, I don't think so. I know who's employed in my businesses."

Stefanovic, right behind Radovan, leaned forward. Whispered something in Radovan's ear.

Mahmud'd understood enough. Understood that he'd made a fool of himself. At the same time: understood that he couldn't roll with this.

Radovan moved on. Mahmud wouldn't be able to have a good time tonight. He might as well go home. But he didn't. Didn't mesh with his self-image. He went to the bathroom. Did a line instead. Tried to perk up.

The next day, Ratko called. Mahmud felt groggy. He'd partied hard the night before. It just ended up that way. A couple of noses of blow and some sweet talk with a chick'd gotten him going. Not good for his training. He downed a glass of water. Two tablets of Diazepam Desitin—for his anxiety.

Ratko'd been hounding him last night. Buzzed about Mahmud doing a good job. Flattered. Buttered. Uttered, "I want you to help us with some stuff."

Mahmud was doubtful. He wanted to get away from them. Get ahold of his life. Sure, he was raking it in, but he couldn't take the humiliation. The Yugos were fucking with him. Still, he didn't say anything.

Ratko explained. They needed help during the day. Keep an eye on some girls, as he put it. Mahmud assumed he was talking about whores. The girls lived in trailers at a campground. Ratko wanted Mahmud to make sure the girls had what they needed during the day. "And that they don't head out on their own. If they do, they might get lost." Smile. Wink-wink, you-know-what-I-mean.

"Don't know if I got time."

"You've got time for this," Ratko said and patted him on the shoulder. It was an order.

41

Iraq. With his company. Mike as sweaty as usual. Collin with black-painted streaks under his eyes. Joking that maybe they'd run into Harry, the prince of England, somewhere in the bush. The British accent. The mannerisms. The body language. The strap of the machine gun heavy over his back. Farther up, they glimpsed black smoke. Bubble-gum taste in his mouth. Collin always carried a couple packs of Stimorol with him. Pleasure in the heat. A Jeep was coming toward them. But he couldn't see the driver. The landscape around him was changing. The stones and cliffs disappeared, were exchanged for burning oil drums. Fires everywhere. The world ignited by heat. The Jeep drew closer. Collin, Mike, and the others'd disappeared. Niklas approached the car. There was a man lying on the backseat. Blood was running from one of his ears. The face was turned down toward the seat. Niklas flipped him over. He could see him now—it was Mats Strömberg. "Why?" he said. The flames around them were licking the sky.

Niklas woke up. Tried to calm down. His heart was beating like crazy. Thought about the dream he'd just had.

He couldn't fall back asleep. In today's world, moral standards were served as a smorgasbord. You chose your ethical rules depending on your worldview. The bearded warriors down there chose their ethics based on their hate for the United States. Found support for their beliefs in the Koran and sunna. The Americans chose their rules based on their terror of no longer being the kings of the hill. But Niklas knew the important rules of the game. There was no right or wrong; there were no rules at all, really. Morality grew in the human mind. But there was still one rule: if you don't act, you can't change anything. You reach your goals through action. Morality was a human construct, it had no value. His mission was to create peace for women. No nightmares would stop him. Nothing in the real world would stop him.

He stared straight into the wall. Dreary grayish color. The structure of the fibers in the wall were clearly visible.

He thought about the two entry points in Strömberg's back. Considered whom he should take next. Roger Jonsson or Patric Ngono? Niklas'd trailed both guys even more intensively over the past week, since taking care of Strömberg. Ngono was worse to his woman. But there was something about Roger Jonsson, too. Something that didn't tally. Niklas'd seen him several times over the past few weeks. The guy checked out of his work. Took the car to Fruängen. Picked up a woman outside a mall. They drove home. Came out again after about an hour. Roger drove her back. Obvious: he was playing two hands. Classic infidelity. But who was the woman? A prostitute, of course. The guy visited prostitutes. Double trouble.

But something else determined Niklas's decision. He'd ordered as much public information as was available on the two assholes. Not much. Patric Ngono appeared in some old Immigration Services case, but the guy was on the safe side now. Had gotten permanent residency, lived here for more than eight years. Collected welfare at some point, but now he was working. Probably under the table, but still.

There was nothing like that on Roger Jonsson. But there was something much worse. A conviction. Gross Violation of a Woman's Integrity, between 1998 and 2002. And Aggravated Rape. Jonsson'd served three years. The sentence was public. Niklas ordered all the documents.

The reading almost crushed him. No, never—nothing crushed an elite soldier, one who'd seen the real shit down in the sandbox. On the contrary: it made him stronger. More sure of Operation Magnum. *Si vis pacem, para bellum.*

* * *

STOCKHOLM SOUTHERN DISTRICT

PUBLIC PROSECUTOR'S OFFICE

LAWSUIT Nr: C-98-25587

Defendant, full name: *Roger Karl Jonsson*
Personal Identification Number: 671001-8573
Telephone Number: 08-881 968
Address: *Gamla Södertäljevägen*
Public Defender: *Tobias Åkermark, Esq.*
In custody: *Arrested on March 3, 2002, placed in custody on March 5, 2002*

NEVER SCREW UP

DEMAND FOR CONVICTION

GROSS VIOLATION OF A WOMAN'S INTEGRITY

Plaintiff
Carin Engsäter, through the Plaintiff's Counsel, Lina Eriksson

Charges
Roger Jonsson has, between March 1998 and January 2002, threatened and abused Carin Engsäter on numerous occasions. The actions, each of which formed part of a repeated violation of the Plaintiff's integrity, have been aimed at severely harming her self-esteem. Thus, Roger Jonsson has:

1. in April 2008, delivered several slaps to her face. Later the same day, in Tumba, he beat her several times with clenched fists over her upper arms. Finally, on the same day, he held her throat in a choke grip. The abuse caused the Plaintiff pain and a swollen eye as well as bruises on the throat;

2. on one occasion at some point on October 14–15, 1998, in her residence in Stockholm, with the consequence of pain, he abused her by gripping her neck with his arm and pressing her down on her back. After she tried to break free, he beat her several times with clenched fists on her upper arms;

3. on one occasion at the end of December 1998, in their residence, with the consequence of pain, he dealt her several blows with clenched fists on her thighs and back;

4. on one occasion in June 1999, in their residence, he kicked her right knee, making her fall to the floor, after which he delivered another kick that struck her right thigh. The abuse led to pain and bruising;

5. on one occasion in the middle of September 2000, in their residence, he dealt her several punches with clenched fists that struck her on the back. On the same occasion, he dealt her punches with clenched fists that struck her on her upper arms as well as slapped her head with an open palm. The abuse led to pain and bruising;

6. on one occasion in October 2000, in their residence, he dealt several slaps with an open palm on the face and head with the consequence of pain and a bloody nose;

7. on August 14, 2001, in their residence, he grabbed her face in his hand and squeezed, then threw her to the ground. He also pulled her hair. The abuse, which led to pain and bruising, took place in front of their four-year-old child;

8. on one occasion in September, 2001, he called the Plaintiff at their residence and—in a way that was intended to make her seriously fear for her life—made remarks claiming that she would be hurt or killed.

Finally, Roger Jonsson has, on multiple occasions, called the Plaintiff at her place of work and—in a way that was intended to make her seriously fear for her life—threatened her by saying that she would not get away from him alive, that he would dance on her grave, and that if he saw her with another man he would cut her head off.

AGGRAVATED RAPE

Plaintiff
Carin Engsäter, through the Plaintiff's Counsel, Lina Eriksson

Charges
Roger Jonsson has, on over fifty occasions between 1999 and 2001, forced Carin Engsäter to have intercourse with him, orally, vaginally, as well as anally, by forcing her, through the use of violence, down on the floor or bed, holding her wrists and pushing her face into a pillow or against the floor. He has also, on at least twenty occasions, forced objects—among other things, a dildo and pliers—into her vagina, with the consequence of pain and injuries.

Section of the Penal Code
Chapter 4, 4a § 2, Chapter 3 § 5, Chapter 4 § 5, and Chapter 6 § 1 of the Penal Code.

42

He'd driven out to the nursing home on a clear day in the middle of September. The surroundings were beautiful. Thomas could glimpse a lake behind the main brick building. The trees were still green, but you could sense that fall was on its way; there was a kind of damp in the air that snuck up on him when he climbed out of the car.

Tallbygården: a private nursing home on the shore of Lake Mälaren. High standard of living and good care, that's what it said on the place's website. The home for your idyllic final years. The home where quality care was valued highest. The home where Leif Carlsson– former police inspector, SWAT team member, neo-Nazi—lived.

Stig Adamsson'd claimed that he was going to start a right-wing group whose mission would be to keep an eye on Olof Palme. But what did that mean, really?

Thomas'd tried to read up on the story. A couple of borrowed books and the Internet—it was almost too much for him. The murder of Olof Palme was Sweden's equivalent of the Kennedy assassination twenty-three years earlier. A web of conspiracy theories that never seemed to end. He made a list of a couple of theories before he lost interest—they flourished like weeds. One basically amounted to: members of Augusto Pinochet's feared death squads were in Stockholm the week of the murder, but since the intelligence chief, Holmér, thought the two professional Chilean assassins, Michael Canes and Robert Tartino, were one and the same person, the lead was never followed. Another theory claimed that Christer Pettersson'd made a mistake; he'd actually intended to shoot Rantzell—then known as Cederholm—but due to the clumsy work of the police, they were forced to cover up parts of the investigation. Bullets were missing, phone-tapping transcripts were forged, the police authorities refused to explain what the two patrol cars that'd been parked outside the Grand Cinema on the night of the murder'd been doing, exactly. It was endless.

Thomas needed real information. From people. Not from a bunch of circumstantial evidence, detail obsession, and conspiracy craziness. Above all: he needed to understand the connection to the present day—to Rantzell's mangled body in the basement at Gösta Ekman Road.

Runeby'd mentioned the SWAT team that Adamsson'd been a part of. That's where Thomas had to begin. Among the people who knew Adamsson—who shared his views—during the time of the murder with a capital M. There'd been eight cops in total, of which Adamsson was one. Their boss, Malmström, was dead. Six people remained. It wasn't too difficult to find information on them. Jonas Nilsson knew all of them well, most of them were still on the police force, but no longer in positions that were as conflict-ridden. The classic fate of a patrol officer: sit out your final fifteen years in a basement, registering bike thefts.

He made up his mind easily: his first visit would be paid to Leif Carlsson. He was the oldest. He'd been an outspoken Nazi. Above all: the guy had Alzheimer's—he was the perfect interrogation victim.

Tallbygården appeared peaceful. He saw old people on a few of the balconies facing the greenery. Narrow walking paths wound their way through the trees. He walked into the entrance hall. Ficus trees, couches with Josef Frank fabric, and a message board with notices and information materials pinned up on it: *Singing with Lave Lindér on Thursday. Trosa's librarian will be here to speak about new books at the library on the 17th, at 8 a.m. Gentlemen's Aerobics on Tuesday morning is canceled.*

Thomas waited awhile. There was no welcome desk. He thought about Runeby. The final thing the inspector'd told him was that he'd been the one to hold the lecture that time in Gamla Stan. Really, it wasn't as strange as it sounded—the guy'd served two years in some kind of private army in South Africa in the late seventies. "For the battle's sake," as he'd said. "Not because I was a racist." Thomas didn't really care what his reasons were—but he had to watch out. How mixed up was Runeby really in that Gamla Stan organization?

After a few minutes, a nurse came walking out through a glass door. "Is Leif Carlsson here?" Thomas asked.

The nurse led him up one flight of stairs. Flowers in the windows, framed prints with Swedish art classics: Zorn, Carl Larsson, Jirlow. A TV room, a cafeteria, plenty of staff. The nurse knocked on a door. Never even asked who Thomas was.

Leif Carlsson didn't look as frail as Thomas'd imagined. Neatly combed side part. Blond hair that was going gray at the temples. A crooked smile, a glimmer of challenge in his blue eyes. Did he really have Alzheimer's? Leif Carlsson was tall. Thomas could picture what he'd looked like thirty years ago, probably significantly bigger: a terrifying vision to the rabble on the street.

The TV in the room was switched on. Carlsson seemed to have been sitting in a chair in front of it. He'd stood up when Thomas came in. The nurse left them alone. Closed the door.

"Good morning. My name is Thomas Andersson, inspector, the Palme Group."

Carlsson dropped his hand. "So, you're coming now?"

Thomas couldn't judge if it was an accusation or a fateful declaration.

The old man sat down. It looked as though he was constantly tasting something in his mouth with his tongue. Probably a tic.

Thomas sat down on a chair by a small desk. The assisted-living apartment was small: a bedroom with the door ajar and a living room, where they were sitting now. Carlsson'd furnished it like a real home. A Persian carpet on the floor, a couple of paintings on the walls, an armchair and a desk in rococo style.

"I just want to ask you some questions. I hope that's all right."

Apparently, Carlsson'd been seriously ill for five years. His resistance to an interrogation ought to be weaker than a kid's.

Carlsson nodded. "I have nothing to hide."

Thomas pressed record on an audio recorder he had in his pocket.

"Tell me about the Troop."

"You mean the A-route?"

"Yes, that's the only group that's ever been called the Troop, isn't it?"

"That's right, I think that's what we called it."

"Who were 'we'?"

"Who are you, anyway?"

Thomas responded calmly, "Thomas Andersson, the Palme Commission." Well, the geezer sure had Alzheimer's.

Carlsson moved his tongue around in his mouth again. Repeated, "So, you're coming now."

Thomas went on, "Tell me about the Troop, the A-route. Who was in it with you?"

"In the Troop? It was Malmström, of course. Then it was Jägerström, Adamsson, Nilsson, Wallén. A couple more. I don't remember."

"And Malmström, he was the boss?"

"Oh yeah. Malmström. He was a real officer. The kind we need in the police force. But he quit. He lives out by Nykvarn nowadays."

"Malmström is dead."

"Really? That's too bad. I haven't seen him since I retired."

Thomas started thinking about ending the interrogation. Carlsson was obviously too confused. But the question was if his memory from the eighties was better than his memory from the present.

"Who used to go to those meetings in Gamla Stan, in the EAP offices?"

Leif Carlsson looked disoriented. "I was never there."

Thomas felt his surprise grow. The old guy wouldn't lie, would he? "Is that true?"

"Yes, it's true. The guys who organized it, Ålander and Sjöqvist, didn't invite me. Not because I had anything against them, or that they had anything against me. That wasn't it. I shared their patriotism and worry in the face of the Red infiltration. But I was never invited. Maybe it wasn't so strange, though. My father worked at one of the companies that Bolinder owned. So he was afraid to get me mixed up in it."

"What did you say?"

"They were afraid to get me mixed up in it."

"But why?"

"Dad worked at Bolinder's company."

"And who was this Bolinder?"

"The financier."

"The financier of what?"

Suddenly Carlsson got that gleam in his eye again, tasted the roof of his mouth with his tongue. Then he said, "Bolinder. He was the one who funded those meetings, the organization, the project. All of it. But I think I was the only one who knew that."

"Why were you the only one who knew that?"

Leif Carlsson started giggling. "Just because I'm sitting here talking a load of crap doesn't mean I didn't do my part for Sweden."

"I understand. But tell me more about Bolinder."

"I don't remember Bolinder. But Bohman, he was too weak."

"Bohman who?"

"Gösta Bohman, I mean. The head of the right-wing party. Are you too young to remember him?"

Carlsson looked pleased.

Gösta Bohman was the Moderate Party leader in the seventies. Leif

Carlsson was confused. The Alzheimer's made it difficult to know what was relevant and what wasn't. Thomas tried to ask a few more questions, but was just given confused answers in response.

He needed someone else.

On his way home. Thomas's thoughts were spinning. Bolinder—where'd he heard that name before? It didn't fit. He wasn't a cop. He wasn't one of the security-service people that Runeby'd mentioned. Who was Bolinder?

Then it clicked: he'd heard Ratko talking about planning "higher-class events" at some Bolinder's place. Thomas'd even instructed a couple of gorillas how a set of walkie-talkies worked because they might be needed at one of those events—was it the same person?

43

He stayed in bed. His thoughts were churning around, around. In the same old tracks. He thought about the narc who'd approached him about a week ago. Maybe they tried that on others, too. Who could be trusted? Robert felt safe. Tom and Javier, too. But Babak? Fuck, man—he missed Babak.

At around two o'clock, he got up. Made coffee. Dumped sugar into it. Perked up a little. Popped a Diazepam. Later, he'd need an upper to make it to the gym. Pressed play on a porno. Tried to jack off. He thought about the honey from last weekend. Gabrielle. The porno felt lame in comparison.

Ratko called at three o'clock. Mahmud'd almost managed to forget his order. He got dressed. Jeans, a hoodie. Baseball jacket. Fall—the worst season. The weather needed to make up its mind. Not shilly-shally like some tranny.

Ratko'd given him directions: "Go to Bigge's Hot Dog Palace and wait." Shit, they were really pushing him around. He was their bitch.

A half hour later. Mahmud knew these projects like the back of his hand. Maybe he should check into the university. Honestly. Lecture on Shurgard storage facilities and housing project sociology. He knew why they built areas like this. They created a world where no one would get it into their minds to try to get ahead. Just stay down there in the shit, without getting too worked up about it. Society'd made him into what he was.

The business signs didn't even try to be sexy around here. State Dentistry, the library, the Coop Konsum grocery store, Swedbank, the accounting firm Håkansson & Hult, a barber, the Pasta House: Extra Much Extra Cheap, Svedin's Shoes, a pizzeria, a pharmacy. And, finally: Bigge's Hot Dog Palace. He sat down. Ordered a Diet Sprite.

Tried to call some peeps. First Rob, then Tom, then Javier, then his sis. No one picked up. Time crawled slower than an old lady with a walker. He waited.

After twenty minutes, Dejan walked in. The guy was a sly mother-fucker. Rimmed Radovan for pennies. Talked smack about Arabs as soon as he got the chance. They shook hands.

Mahmud climbed into his Benz. Followed Dejan's car. First the high-rises. Then a couple of single-family homes. Then industrial buildings. A bunch of nature. The road was winding. Away from the concrete. After ten minutes: a sign. THE VIEW, CAMPGROUND — TRAILER AND RV.

Set up in the November rain: twenty-odd trailers. Five run-down cars. A sea of mud. Sparse trees all around. Electrical wires led to the trailers from poles.

Dejan parked his car. Mahmud pulled in behind him. What a nasty fucking trailer park.

Dejan walked up to one of the campers. The white paint was gray. A faded sticker on one of the windows said: *Go Gästrikland!*

They walked in. The smell of smoke hit Mahmud in the face like an uppercut. Low radio music. First, he didn't see the girls. It was like they were a part of the furnishings. Gray, beige, brown. Boxes of food, pizza cartons, Coke bottles on the kitchen counter. They were sitting at the doll-sized table. Dark brown hair. Chopstick skinny. One was very pale. Thin lips. Sorrowful eyes. The other: rosier cheeks, but even darker eyes. In front of them on the table: packs of counterfeit Marlboros. The feeling: grody. Dejan said something in Russian or a similar language. The girls seemed disinterested. Didn't even look up.

Dejan explained in his crap Swedish: "This, Natascha and Juliana. Maybe not juiciest meat we got, but okay." He grinned. "Here, we got real tasty ones. Promise."

Mahmud didn't know what to say.

"Now you know who they are. That's enough," Dejan said.

They stepped out. Dejan brought him to seven more campers. Two whores in each. The same bored attitude. The same smoke-saturated rooms. The same empty stares.

On the way back to the car, Mahmud asked, "So, what do you want me to do?"

Dejan stopped. Threw his arms open.

"This our stockpile, yes? You keep track a little of stockpile. Make sure nothing get lost, transport sometime. If client here—not allowed to hurt stockpile. Days, only. When you not do your other business."

Mahmud got it: they saw him as some kind of fucking poon-nanny. Man, if his dad found out.

That night, he took care of his usual business. Slung more than sixty grams to a contact who represented an Iraqi family that owned restaurants.

Jamila called around ten o'clock. Wanted help installing a new DVD player. Shit, she was living it up on the bills he slipped her when his business boomed. Just these past few weeks, she'd bought a Gucci bag with a bamboo handle for eight thousand, high-heeled shoes for three G's, and a silver necklace with fat letters on it: *Dior*. Crazy, but Mahmud couldn't help but love the glitter in her eyes when she came home with the stuff. He was gonna keep outfitting her and his little sis. The real deal.

He fiddled with the DVD player. Was planning on hitting the town later. Had arranged to meet up with Robert. Piranhasize Stockholm. Maybe that Gabrielle chick would be out tonight. If not, he was gonna find someone else.

Jamila told him about the latest Louis Vuitton bag, the latest Britney gossip, and her plans for the future: start her own tanning salon. Mahmud thought, Don't let the Yugos fuck it up for her. She told him about nasty texts she'd gotten from her ex.

"He doesn't dare do shit," Mahmud said. "That loser."

Jamila sighed. "I don't know, Mahmud. He's crazy. And that Niklas guy moved away, too. He was so sweet."

"Yeah, he was tight. Where'd he move?"

"Not far." He'd given her the address.

"Okay, he like you, or what? You know what Dad would say about him."

"He doesn't feel like that kind of guy. I think he just wants to help me. Honestly, you know?"

"Maybe."

Mahmud had a thought. Niklas seemed like a good Sven. What's more: like a real commando, special-ops style. Maybe he should get to know him better. And another thing: the soldier guy could keep an eye on Jamila now and then.

Jamila dug the idea. And she was the one who usually screamed and sulked as soon as Dad said she needed to be controlled more. Mahmud grinned at her. "Come on, sis, you're a little sweet for that Sven. Admit it."

They decided to pay him a visit. Niklas didn't live far away.

They rang the doorbell.

Niklas opened the door. In his face: both surprise and joy. He began to speak with Jamila in his half-assed Arabic. Mahmud eyed the guy properly for the first time. Dressed in a T-shirt with *DynCorp* written on it; it was tight over his pecs and biceps. The guy looked built. Not like Mahmud—built like a safe—but tougher, more sinewy, endurance muscles. He wondered what DynCorp was. The guy looked sweaty. Maybe he was working out at home. Mahmud tried to catch a glimpse of the apartment. Saw a computer, a bed, lots of paperwork, tools, junk. Saw something else too, on the table: a long, shiny knife. Shit, Niklas seemed a little psycho.

They left a short while later. It'd been nice, anyway. Jamila was glowing. Mahmud laughed again.

"Cut that out. You know what Dad would think."

Jamila turned to him. Her eyes: serious.

"Don't talk about what Abu would say to me. If he even knew a tenth of all you do, he'd die."

Mahmud stopped. "What're you talking about?"

"You know what I mean. He'd die of shame."

It hurt. Like a knife being twisting into his gut.

Die.

Of shame.

He knew how right she was.

His entire body was screaming at him. Get away from them. Step off before it's too late.

Break up with the Yugos.

44

Niklas got out of bed. More tired than usual. Four hours of sleep. His cameras kept rolling at night. The footage he'd speed-scrolled through didn't show anything interesting. But it would come. He wanted proof. Righteousness was his thing. Strömberg, Jonsson, Ngono—he already knew enough about them. Niklas was a man of honor: if one of them didn't show himself to be that kind of man, he wouldn't attack. It wasn't about morals, it was about action.

After breakfast, he strapped the heart-rate monitor on. Got dressed: underwear, workout clothes.

The air was colder now. The asphalt was wet. He jogged at a calm pace. The air was cool to breathe. It felt so good.

Home again: He practiced katas with the knife. Felt in better shape than in a long time. The sweeps through the air. The knife's arch-shaped movements staked out a blocking area in the room. Smooth stabs. Nimble jabs. The knife had to follow the will of the hand's muscles as if it were a sixth finger.

He showered longer than usual. Yesterday, he'd seen Jamila's brother, Mahmud, again. Not the kind of person he would've gotten to know ten years ago. Even less the kind of person he would've met down there. The question at hand: Was he a person he ought to know now? Maybe Mahmud could help him with the fight? Niklas knew the dude didn't share his beliefs, but the guy had drive. Something in his eyes. Not the vermin's sparking spitefulness. Something else.

Above all, the Arab seemed as hot for cash as Niklas was. Niklas couldn't care less what Mahmud wanted to do with his money. Money was a means to an end. But maybe, maybe the Arab could be something else for him? Benjamin was a traitor. The anarchist-feminist activists weren't willing to participate in the Operation. Mom was out of the match. The Arab might prove to be a puzzle piece in the war.

After the shower, he ate again. His financial situation was starting to reach crisis level. He didn't have the energy to think about that right now. He didn't know what to do.

He climbed into the Ford. Missed the Audi, somehow. He needed to think.

He drove slowly. Tried to figure out where he wanted to go.

Thought about his money situation again.

He drove out of the city via Nortull. Kept thinking about Mahmud. How could he use the Arab? The Biskops-Arnö people'd just talked and talked. The only people they influenced were one another—the rest of society didn't give a damn about them. Then he thought about Mom again. Why couldn't they talk anymore? Why couldn't she just accept? Everything he did, he did for her.

Niklas looked around. It was strange. He was in Edsviken, Sollentuna. Where Nina Glavmo-Svensén lived. The woman who'd sold him the Audi. He drove toward her street. Pictured her green eyes. The baby on her arm. Her crooked smile.

He reached the area. Vikingavägen ran like an artery through adjoining plots of land. The small streets were like detours leading into the inner realms of an idyllic world.

There, a hundred feet farther up, was the house where she lived. Number twenty-one. The yellow wood siding didn't look as shiny in the drizzle as it had during the summer, when he'd been there last. The trees were barren. He thought about what things must be like for her. A man who denied her the right to a life. She needed Niklas. That much was clear. Crystal clear.

The car rolled slowly down the street. He leaned his head back. Tried to look in through the windows, see if there was a light on in there. Fifty feet from the house. He saw that the garage doors were closed. The autumn sky was the color of chromed steel. Nina lived somewhere in there, in the warmth.

He could feel it: she was home. He drove past the house. Slowly. Peered. Stretched to try to see in. Saw a movement further in, inside a room. She was there.

Niklas turned right. Up a hill. His palms were sweaty. The wheel was sticky. Right again. Down. Back on the street. His heart was pounding. Number eleven. *Da-dum*. Number fifteen. *Da-dum.* Soon, number twenty-one again.

He wanted to ring her doorbell so badly. See her. Touch her. And she probably wanted to see him.

He stopped the car outside the house. Too bad it wasn't the Audi anymore. That would've made Nina happy.

So happy.

45

Jasmine showed up late to the club. Thomas saw it right away. Thought: There's something different about her tonight. She was wearing a baseball cap pulled down low over her eyes, a baggy hoodie, a knee-length skirt over tight jeans. Tanning-salon bronzed like a mulatto after two weeks on *la playa*. What was it that didn't tally? He looked again. She wanted to hide something. Her choice of dress was speaking loud and clear: the hoodie, the skirt. The tan, the baseball cap.

Then he saw: the lips. They were pouting like on someone goofing off. Then he saw more: the breasts. Also pouting a stupid amount—either she'd stuffed two handballs under her sweater or, more likely, she'd filled up with at least two pounds of implants in each tit.

Thomas grinned. "You look—how should I put this? Thriving."

At first, Jasmine was dead serious. Acted like she didn't understand. After three seconds: she grinned back at him. "Whaddya think?"

Thomas gave a thumbs-up. "Sure. But the lips? Are they gonna settle a little, or what?"

Jasmine laughed. "I think so. I'm switching fields, so I need this."

"Chapstick model, or what?"

"Ha-ha, real funny. I'm gonna make a career."

"Oh yeah? Are you gonna tell me what you're gonna do, or do I have to guess?"

"Erotica."

Thomas was silent for a second too long. Jasmine noticed his reaction.

"What? You got a problem with that?"

He didn't want to argue. To bare your body in front of people and run the register now and then at a well-guarded strip joint maybe wasn't the best gig in the world, but still—it paid good money. And he was there to keep track of the rabble-rousers. But porn felt dirtier somehow. He couldn't explain why. He liked porn. But he also liked Jasmine—they laughed a lot. Not just *at* the same jokes, but *together* at the same jokes. As if they understood each other. He didn't want her ending up in trouble.

"The producer paid for the implants and everything. It's totally free. Can you believe it? You know what this kind of thing costs?"

"I have no idea. But is it really the right thing for you?"

"Of course." Jasmine went on to describe how good the erotica business was going to be for her. Told him about her plans, different career paths, routes to fame.

"Erotica is, like, much better than stripping. There's no money in stripping in Sweden. And, you know, the strippers are bitches with a nasty attitude. But everyone says it's the opposite in the film industry. That it's like one big, happy family, you know?"

Thomas shut her out. It hurt to listen. He'd watched too much porn to care to imagine Jasmine in the scenes he usually jerked off to.

Later that night, Ratko showed up. Laughed at Jasmine too. "I think things're gonna go well for you, honey," he said, like he was her dad or something. What bullshit.

Ratko sat down next to Thomas. Put his arm around his shoulders. Jasmine was inside, doing a show. One of her last.

"What do you think about Jasmine's plans?"

Thomas looked around the room. Wondered what Ratko was trying to get at. Was it a provocation? He didn't care either way—he always spoke his mind.

"I think it sounds like shit. That's a dirty business."

"So, you think this is a lot better, then?"

"We keep order here."

At first, Ratko didn't answer. Thomas turned to him. "Was there something you wanted?"

A crooked smile on Ratko's lips. "You do a good job, Thomas. We think you're performing. Just so you know."

Ratko got up. Walked into the show area.

Thomas didn't bother trying to interpret what the Yugo'd just said.

When the right moment came along, he was going to ask about Sven Bolinder, the so-called financier, the one Leif Carlsson'd babbled about.

He woke up around eleven o'clock. Åsa'd gone to work without waking him up, as usual.

In the bathroom. He let the shaving cream soak in for an extra long time. Shaved meticulously: short strokes with a fresh razor. He looked at himself in the mirror. Tried to really see himself, not just his reflection. Who was he? What did he want?

He knew what he wanted: to track down Rantzell's killer and bring home his adopted child. It felt like a good balance. One project to solve outside the home. One to solve at home. But who was he? During the day, he was an upright citizen. At night, he belonged to the underworld. Just like the enemy. Maybe he was the enemy?

He thought about Leif Carlsson's muddled answers. Then he thought about Christer Pettersson, who'd almost been convicted for the Palme murder. It wasn't a question of *if* there were any connections. It was a question of *how strong* the connections were. Too bad he couldn't ask Pettersson himself. The guy'd bit the dust a couple of years ago in what seemed like a natural enough cerebral hemorrhage.

Thomas'd mixed what everyone in Sweden who was over thirty years old knew about the murder with his more specialized knowledge from the police force. And then he'd done some research too, lately.

A picture was emerging. Of one of Sweden's most wanted men: Christer P. The biggest murder investigation ever, a national trauma: the unsolved murder of a prime minister. An unhealed wound in the Swedish consciousness. An unpleasant, stinging mystery for anyone who came from the same background as Thomas—regular Swedish middle-class people who still knew where they had their roots. Whom they had to thank for being where they were today.

Olof Palme'd been shot in the open, on a public street, more than twenty years ago. Thomas wasn't as politically interested as his dad'd been, but according to him: Palme—Sweden's biggest ever politician internationally. A man of honor, a friend to regular Swedes. Executed with a clean shot to the back. It was a good shot, he had to admit.

Three years later, the District Court convicted Christer Pettersson of the murder and sentenced him to life in prison. The guy was identified by Olof Palme's wife, Lisbet Palme, during a lineup arranged by the investigators. What's more, there were apparently witnesses who placed him at the scene of the crime and who said he had the same limp the perpetrator apparently had. Pettersson: an aggressive deadbeat alcoholic. Maybe the perfect scapegoat. But this was the murder of a prime minister. You couldn't just make a conviction based on cir-cumstantial evidence and shady claims—the Court of Appeals freed Pettersson. There was not proof beyond a reasonable doubt, that was the claim.

Claes Rantzell, previously Claes Cederholm, showed up as one of the key witnesses in the federal prosecutor's appeal to the Supreme Court a few years later. The state really wanted to get Pettersson convicted.

Claes Rantzell: drug dealer, front man, finally run down on booze and pills himself. In the fall of 1985, a few months before the murder, he said he'd lent Pettersson a Magnum revolver, make: Smith & Wes-son, .357 caliber. Rantzell said he never got the revolver back. What's more, Pettersson'd been over at Rantzell's house on the night of the murder. Rantzell was the witness who'd been interrogated the most during the entire preliminary investigation, but his memories seemed to vary—Magnum delivery boy, ammunition Santa, canary. A perfect witness to identify Pettersson.

But the Supreme Court didn't hear the case. The appeal collapsed. There was no new trial for Pettersson. No conviction for the legend from Sollentuna that time either. But in most people's eyes, he was still guilty. Lisbet Palme's poorly handled ID, along with Claes Rantzell's claims about the Magnum revolver, sank him. The logic of the Swedish people was simple: Lisbeth somehow recognized Pettersson, he'd been near the scene of the crime, and he'd had access to a revolver of the same make as the murder weapon. On top of that: he was an aggressive, down-and-out drunk—that made it all easier, somehow.

And now Rantzell'd been killed. It might not to be so strange—men like Claes Rantzell died of cirrhosis or other diseases that took out people with crappy lifestyles. Or through violence.

But in this case: someone was trying to cover up the tracks in a much too sophisticated way.

This thing was ten times bigger than he'd thought before he knew who Rantzell was.

So much bigger that it gave him vertigo.

The two leads emerged slowly. Adamsson in the past. Rantzell in the present.

After the sloppy interrogation with Leif Carlsson, the Alzheimer's patient, he needed to speak with someone else. He'd been thinking about calling Hägerström again. But no, not now.

Who of the other members of the Troop, the SWAT team that Adamsson'd been a part of, could he get something out of? Malmström was dead. Adamsson was the enemy. He'd already talked to Carlsson. Remaining: Torbjörn Jägerström, Roger Wallén, and Jan Nilsson, who were all still active-duty cops, and Carl Johansson and Alf Winge, one of whom was retired while the other ran a private security company. And he should do some more research about this Sven Bolinder guy, too.

Thomas decided to begin with Alf Winge: the guy seemed to live a calm life without needing to break too much of a sweat. What decided it: Winge wasn't a cop anymore and Runeby'd mentioned him as one of the guys at the meetings in Gamla Stan. He'd been an insider.

Alf Winge walked out of 32 Sturegatan at five-thirty. The trees in the Humlegården park were almost bare of leaves. The offices of Alf Winge's private security company, WIP—Winge International Protection AB—were situated on the third floor of the building. Thomas'd checked out the website. WIP detailed their services openly: they did specialized surveillance and protection assignments, as a complement to other actors on the surveillance and security market. The field'd grown like an avalanche since 9/11.

Alf Winge was around fifty years old. Still had a spring to his step that seemed powerful. Cop style: integrity, good posture, gaze fixed on something farther down the street. He had a shaved head, stern furrows along his cheeks, light-blue eyes that looked gray. He was dressed in a dark-blue coat, sturdy black shoes, a Bluetooth headset still in his ear even though he wasn't using it right then.

Thomas saw him get into his car, an Aston Martin, real sports-car feel. WIP was apparently doing well. Thomas started the engine of his own car. Winge's killer ride rolled down Sturegatan. Thomas followed. He knew where Winge lived. He knew the road Winge usually took home. He knew where on that road he was going to stop the old riot-squad cop.

Forty minutes later: Bromma, a luxury suburb where, probably, not too many cops could afford to live—except for the ones who abandoned the force and put their cards on something private instead. Kiselgränd: a day-care center surrounded by sparsely growing trees. It was deserted now, after its six o'clock closing. The only movements were the cars that drove past, on their way home.

It didn't look like Winge was reacting to being followed. Or else he saw, but didn't give a shit. Maybe he was a real hardass.

Thomas stepped on the gas. Drove up alongside Winge's super ride. He'd borrowed a blue light from the traffic unit. Put it on the dashboard. Flashed the lights. Saw Alf Winge turn his head to the side. Register that an undercover cop car was trying to get him to pull over.

Winge hit the brakes. Pulled over to the side of the road. Thomas turned in slowly. Parked diagonally in front of the Aston Martin. Was almost surprised that Winge'd stopped so easily.

Thomas flashed his police badge in front of Winge's face. The guy didn't move a muscle.

"What do you want?"

"License and registration, please."

Winge extended his arm, showed his license. He looked young in the picture. Alf Rutger Winge.

"This is just a routine check. Would you mind stepping out of the car for a moment?"

Winge remained seated. "What is it you claim I've done?"

"Nothing. It's just a routine check. We're on the lookout for certain things in this area." He added something that he thought Winge would like: "You know, there's got to be limits for the rabble. We don't want them here in Bromma."

For a brief moment, Winge looked like he was thinking it over. Then he opened the car door. "Okay." A car drove past on the road. Thomas waited, the baton in one hand. Then he went into action. Hit Winge in the kneecaps as hard as he could. The guy crumpled, sank slowly down to his knees. He didn't even scream. Thomas was over him immediately. Slapped the cuffs around one wrist. Winge turned around, tried to hit back. Thomas was faster: sprayed him with pepper spray. At least he was screaming now. Thomas was acting as if in a trance—the other wrist in the handcuffs behind his back, dropped the spray, pulled out his gun, pressed it up against Winge's side, and spoke in a clear voice, "Get up."

Winge got up. Must think Thomas was some kind of road pirate who'd gotten his hands on a police badge. Thomas pushed him into his own car. Tears from Winge's red eyes: blinked, blinked, blinked.

He started the car, secured Winge's cuffed hands to the car door with another pair of handcuffs. Pulled up in the empty yard of the day-care center. Away from the road. Away from where people could see them. Free to begin the interrogation.

Winge'd collected himself a little. "Who the fuck do you think you are?"

Thomas steeled himself. "Shut up."

"Do you know who I am?"

"I don't give a shit who you are."

"I don't have any money on me and they'll track the car down in five minutes; it's got a built-in GPS. What do you want?"

"I said, shut up. I'm the one asking the questions."

Winge stopped. Did he recognize the most hackneyed of cop inter-rogation phrases?—"I'm the one asking the questions."

"Are you a cop?"

"Did you hear what I said? I'm asking the questions."

Tears were still running from the old guy's eyes.

"Alf Rutger Winge, this is not about your money or your car. This is about the Troop, the meetings in Gamla Stan, and Bolinder. We already know most of it, so I just need you to answer a few questions."

"I don't know what you're talking about. The Troop, that was ages ago."

"Yes, you know what I'm talking about. Just answer the questions. Were you a part of Adamsson's group?"

"Like I said, I have no idea what you're talking about."

"I will repeat what I said: Were you a part of Adamsson's group?"

Winge didn't drop his gaze. But he didn't say anything.

"I will only repeat the question one more time: Were you a part of Adamsson's group?"

Nothing.

Thomas knew what he was about to do now was the riskiest game he'd played so far. It was one thing to slap around drunks, junkies, and immigrant gangbangers. Another thing entirely to run that race with an ex-cop who knew his rights better than a fucking defense lawyer. Still, it was all or nothing.

He put his gloves on. Hit Winge right over the nose. It broke. Blood sprayed the inside of the windshield. Dammit—Thomas would have a whole bunch of cleaning up to do. He struck Winge over the ear. Then on the forehead, jaw, ear again. Alf Winge's face in pieces.

"Were you a part of Adamsson's group?"

"Forget it." Slurring mixed with bubbles of bloody spit.

Thomas hit him one more time on the nose.

"Where you a part of Adamsson's group?"

Silence.

Winge's head hung. Saliva, blood, snot, drool dripped down in his lap.

Thomas: felt like on the beat. Excitement. Adrenaline, the smell of blood, sweat. The combination was better than alcohol and Rohypnol. He wouldn't let Alf Winge mess this up for him. He had to answer.

"For the last time, were you a part of Adamsson's group?"

No response.

Thomas hit him a third time on the nose. It would never heal properly.

Winge whimpered. Slowly raised his head. Stared straight into Thomas's eyes. Thomas tried to read his gaze. It was completely blank, empty. Maybe there'd never been anything in it.

He said, "You don't know what you're doing."

After the incident with Alf Winge, Thomas'd taken it easy for a few days. Waited to see what would happen.

He'd released Winge. He couldn't take it any further. If he beat him more there was a real risk of sustaining injuries, and that was a risk he couldn't take. Dammit.

But there were other threads to tug at in order to try to unravel the knot. Right after he found them, Thomas'd started going through the bags he'd plucked from Rantzell's storage unit. That was about eight weeks ago. Reading documents wasn't his thing, but he tried. It felt insurmountable: contracts, records, registration documents, tax documents, certifications, receipts, bank notices, account details, paper. So much information that he didn't understand. And so difficult to know what might be relevant.

Giving his nights to the Yugos and his days to the traffic unit took time. He felt like he was constantly jet-lagged. One night he worked until five in the morning. The next day he drank coffee and talked hybrid cars with the traffic cops in the afternoon. He didn't have time to go through the documents. Still: after a few weeks, he began to get some sense of what was going on. It was obvious that Rantzell'd been busy lately: as a front man, or what they called a goalie, in eighteen companies over the past seven years. Thomas thought about the old cops' jokes about John Ballénius: "There's just one goalie who can compete with him, and that's Thomas Ravelli." In about half of the companies where Rantzell was a board member, Ballénius was an alternate, and the other way around. A couple other old deadbeats showed up in some of the companies. Thomas made a note to look them up.

He couldn't see any particular pattern for the companies where the fogies'd been active, except that a bunch of them were in the construction business, but that was pretty much always the case. Täby's Chimney & Sheet Metal, Frenell's VVS AB, Yellow Bend Building AB, Roaming GI AB, Skogsbacken AB, Stockholm's Speedy Delivery AB, Dolphin Leasing AB, and so on. Eleven of the companies appeared to have gone bankrupt. Three were involved in disputes with the tax authorities. Seven of the companies'd spit out invoices like a fucking assault rifle—probably invoice fraud. Two had real boards with people who seemed to be a part of other legitimate companies as well. Five of the companies used the same auditor. One company sold porn films.

He didn't know enough about this kind of stuff. Where should he begin looking?

Finally, he arranged the crap in chronological order. Thought, I'll start with the most recent stuff. Maybe there's someone there who's met Rantzell alive, and the closer I can get to the deed itself, the closer I ought to get to the murderer.

The most recent document was a contract of sale between the company Dolphin Leasing AB and a car retailer. For a Bentley. It looked like it was signed by Rantzell, on the day before he was rubbed out.

The Bentley store was on Strandvägen. Stockholm's sunny side, the classic address for the upper crust. Thomas thought about his dad's exaggerated class contempt.

Thomas went to the store in the middle of November. The city was warmer than usual. As a rule Thomas didn't give a shit about all the climate-change chatter, but today he actually thought about the weather. Warm summers with an excessive amount of rain, dams breaking in the Jönköping area, weird winters with too much snow and icicles that formed in the slushy weather and fell down on poor law-abiding souls walking on the sidewalk. Sometimes, it was like it was all going under, the whole shebang. The political clowns who tried to clean up the city, the climate, his life.

He walked in.

Spotlights gleamed on the six cars that were lined up on display. This wasn't some ordinary Sven car dealership. Hell no. Instead: small, exclusive, disgustingly expensive.

A young brat was standing behind a counter, trying to look busy. Longish hair casually combed back, a suit jacket, the top buttons of his shirt undone like a fucking fag. Thomas wondered, Shouldn't they have real men working with cars this powerful?

There were two other customers in the store. He waited till they left. Flashed his police badge for the shop kid.

"Hi, I'm from the police. May I ask you a few questions?"

Thomas purposely didn't give his name.

Richie Rich looked surprised. He probably didn't see too many cops in his store—an honest police salary even times ten wouldn't be enough for the kinds of cars they were flipping here.

They stepped into a small office behind the counter. An oak desk, a computer, and a fountain pen in a marble holder. Elegant.

Thomas laid the contract of sale for the Bentley on the desk.

"Are you the one who signed this? Are you Niklas Creutz?"

The guy nodded. "But I don't remember this contract."

Thomas eyed him. How many cars could they sell a month in this store? Five, six? Maybe fewer. Every car sold ought to be a pretty big deal. Every car sold ought to equal a decent commission for this little brat. He ought to remember.

"Are you sure? How many cars of this model have you sold this year?"

The guy closed his eyes. Tried to look like he was giving it some thought. But why did he have to give it some thought? He ought to be able to check some list or something.

"Four, I think," he said after a while.

Thomas asked again, "Are you completely sure you don't remember? It's pretty important."

"May one ask what this is in regards to?"

"One may certainly ask. But one won't get an answer."

"Okay."

"I'll ask you one last time, just so you feel that I've given you some time to think it over. Do you remember the person who bought this car?"

The guy shook his head.

Thomas thought, The brat's a bad liar.

* * *

Hello boys,
My name is Juliana. I'm a sexy, fun, and sociable young woman.
I'm 21 years old, 5'3" and 114 lbs. I look even younger.
I'm visiting Stockholm for a few weeks and look for generous men here for
pleasure. My tight body want to make you happy.

Half hour with me: 1,000 SEK plus taxi.
One hour with me: 1,500 SEK plus taxi.

I do normal sex in any position you like. I give pleasure with my body,
mouth, and tight pussy. You may cum as many times as you can ;)
Everything with condom for your and my safety. I do not do anal.
If you want to cum on my breast it cost +500 SEK.

You contact me easiest by phone. I don't reply to hidden numbers or texts. I
have male friend who look after me.

46

Mahmud: whore handler, hooker guard, hussy driver. For two weeks, he'd spent more than half his time at the campground. He sat in one of the trailers for most of the days. With a window facing out toward the rest of the grounds. A total of twenty-two dirty-white trailers. Nine belonged to Dejan and his people. A bunch of half-baked white trash lived in four of the others, like in a fucking Eminem song. The rest of the trailers: empty, waiting for the summer.

Damn, it was dull. He listened to his iPod: Akon, Snoop, and music from the home country: Majida El Roumi, Elissa, Nancy Ajram. Flipped through porn and auto magazines. Texted Rob, Tom, Javier, and his sis. Whined, moped. Tried to make the time pass. Almost hoped that one of the chicks would come running over the field. Flying the coop. So there'd be a little hunt. A little action.

But, nope. They stayed put. Now and then, a car rolled into the area. Dejan usually called to give forewarning. Sometimes the man went right into the trailer. Sometimes the girl came out. Climbed into the car. Mahmud could see her expression, even from a distance—the slave trade was written on her face. They came back a few hours later. Or else they called and let the phone ring only once—a sign that everything was fine. Same, same, but different somehow.

Mahmud had to drive them. Natascha, Juliana, and the others. Skinny girls. Pale, worn-down, worn-out. They went to addresses all over the city—mostly the crappy boroughs, but sometimes to the fancy areas downtown. A few times, he drove four girls at once. Dropped them off at the same address. When they came back they were made up better, their hair done. Mahmud drew his own conclusions: someone'd tried to give them a little class and style.

Mahmud never hung with the whores. He didn't know why, really. Just felt it strongly: I couldn't handle what they'd tell me. But maybe it didn't matter, really. Their Swedish was even worse than Dad's.

Dejan came out to the trailer park sometimes. Dealt with practicalities: booked hotel rooms and transport for the girls. Administered the Internet ads. All the girls were online. Called the customers: informed them of prices and services. The dude stank. Mahmud'd smelled most things in the slammer. You got a little too close to your neighbors sometimes, a lot of guys didn't wash properly. The worst ones skipped the showers but still rolled deodorant on top of the sweat every day. Dejan: like one of them. Nasty-sweet perfume stench ruined by sweat and dirt.

At sixish, sevenish every day, Mahmud was rotated out. He drove into the city. Took care of his real business. Why did the Yugos do this to him? He knew the answer. They wanted to show him that there were no shortcuts in their organization. You start at the bottom and if you're good, you can work your way up. But he didn't even want to run their race.

Fuck the whole fucking shit.

A guy who looked like a mouse came to switch off with Mahmud today. Small, yellow lower row of teeth and a little-girl walk. Mahmud didn't bother asking what his name was. Felt better that way. He'd just done a fat line, 90 percent pure. Just wanted to get out of there. The guy eyed Mahmud's porn magazine, which was lying open on the table. Close-up of a monster cock stuffing a chick's ass. Mahmud closed it. Was ashamed. The dude said, in crap Swedish, "Why you read that?"

Mahmud didn't feel like having a discussion. Just wanted to sit in his car and enjoy the C-rush. He flexed his neck muscles. "You got a problem with that?"

"In trailers, is real stuff."

Mahmud put his jacket on. Opened the door. "Know what? I like willing bitches. Ever met one of those?"

The guy stared back. Mahmud slammed the door.

It was snowing out. Wasn't it too early for that? It'd been okay warm the other day. November 21. White against a black background: TV blizzard. Crackling, flickering. Like in his head.

His mood improved a little once he'd climbed into the Benz. When he was leaving the shit behind. He thought about the cop that'd been in touch with him a few weeks ago. He had to be more careful. The pigs could have eyes out right now, for instance. He stopped the car by the side of the road. No one behind him. A car passed in the opposite lane. Should be cool.

Still: he pulled out his cell phone. Took the batteries out. Picked out the SIM card. Rolled down the window. Flicked it out. Like one of the snowflakes.

On his drive into the city, he thought about Babak. Okay, Mahmud'd tripped up. Never imagined that the Yugos would do Wisam like that. But Babak'd overreacted. Despite that: Mahmud wanted to call him. Talk a little. Straighten it all out. Get back to normal. Be homies. Blood brothers.

He passed Axelsberg on the highway. Thought about his sister. Thought about her crazy ex-neighbor. The Niklas guy. What was his deal? A week after he and his sis'd visited, Mahmud's phone'd rung. Unknown number. Could be any buyer, dealer, Yugo fucker—but it was Niklas. Weird. Mahmud wigged out. Thought something'd happened to Jamila. But that wasn't it, the Niklas guy just wanted to talk. Maybe get together. During the conversation, like, all the time, the dude got onto the subject of battered women, johns that should be shot, and what he called "the rot in Sweden." Mahmud didn't dig his lingo. He was grateful that Niklas'd tenderized his sister's ex. But what was all this about johns, society's decline, and a rat invasion in the boroughs?

The next day: in the trailer again. The weather was better. Ragheb Alama on low volume in his earbuds. Dejan'd called before lunch. Talked about a massive delivery. Ratko'd called, too. Worked up. Amped. "Mahmud. Make sure to keep an extra good eye. You follow? We've got a massive delivery going." Mahmud thought they were beating a dead horse. Were all repeating the same words: *massive delivery.* MASSIVE DELIVERY.

In the afternoon, a van pulled up. A woman with Dejan. Mink coat. Looked so Russian it was almost funny. She didn't speak a word of Swedish. Dejan tried to interpret, introduced her as the makeup artist. "Tonight, we're doing a massive fucking delivery. They're all going to the same address."

Mahmud couldn't care less. They could have as big whore parties as they wanted, he didn't give. As long as he got out of there in time.

A few hours later, a Hummer showed up. Two guys climbed out. Mahmud saw right away through the trailer's filthy windows—those weren't some regular Yugos or clients. They were ultra players. He even recognized one of them: Jet Set Carl. The guy who owned a bunch of clubs, ran the slickest parties, cashed in the illest cash. The guy who, according to rumor, had slayed more bitches on Stureplan than Mahmud'd seen in his whole life. A legend. A king among brats. A force of power even among Svens. Mahmud wondered what the guy was doing here.

Mahmud turned off the music. Got closer to the window. Saw how the whores were ordered into one of the trailers where Dejan and the Russian were holding court. He waited. The girls came out, one by one. Finally: all sixteen'd been taken care of. Made up, styled, fixed for fucking. They went to their campers. The Jet Set guy was smoking with his buddy. A camel-colored coat to the knees, dark blue jeans, and a colorful scarf. Thin suede desert boots. His hair: more carefully slicked back than the coat of a cat. The two Sven slicks were eyeing the procedure.

After forty minutes, all the chicks were ready. Time stood still. Mahmud stared. Scouted. Spied.

Dejan walked around and knocked on all the trailer doors. The chicks came out. Miniskirts, tight tops, garter belts, high boots, heels, silk scarves nonchalantly wrapped around their necks. More dolled up than usual. Classier than Mahmud'd ever seen them.

They lined up in the cold. Sixteen in a row. Like a fucking horse show. The Jet Set guy and his buddy walked down the line. Checked the girls out one by one. Measured them with their eyes. Sucked them in with their gazes. Deliberated, negotiated, evaluated.

After ten minutes. Her, her, and her, and so on. Jet Set Carl pointed to twelve of the girls. The chosen ones.

Dejan and the Russian herded them into the van and another car. Jet Set Carl had another cigarette. The smoke was clearly visible.

Mahmud thought: a massive delivery. He didn't even know where they were going.

He couldn't drop what'd just happened. Two hours left before he was being switched out. He didn't put the music back on. Didn't bother Tom about their evening plans. Mahmud: not a guy who had anything against hookers. It was the world's oldest profession, and all that. In his home country, dads often took their sons for a little test drive in Bahgdad's seedier neighborhoods for their eighteenth birthday. It was good practice, good education. Young studs had to let off some steam. But still: he couldn't handle this. The girls in the trailers were treated like objects. Were advertised on the Internet just like any other items for sale. Honestly, how could people be into chicks who didn't want to spread 'em on their own? It was sick, somehow.

He looked out at the parking lot. Everything was calm. He wondered if the girls who hadn't been picked felt safe or desperate.

His cell phone rang. Unknown number. At first, he wasn't gonna bother picking up. Then he thought: I have to get out of my own depressed head right now. Might as well see who it is.

As he picked up the phone, he was struck by a weird feeling. A feeling that something big was about to happen. The signal sent a message through the depth of his gut: This call will change my life.

"Yo, this is Mahmud."

"Hey, Mahmud, I roll with your boy Javier."

Mahmud didn't recognize the voice. But he knew all about accents. Latino. Sounded pretty much like Javier, actually. After his years in the Million concrete, Mahmud could read accents like a fucking speech expert. The height of his knowledge: he could even hear the difference between some Kurdish languages—Sorani and Kurmanji, you name it. The dude on the line now: the *s* sounds were softer than on other Latinos. Crystal-clear Chilean accent.

Mahmud responded, "Okay, Javier's my boy. And what do you want?" Really, he didn't want to talk to some coke-tweaking junior meal ticket right now. He wanted to chill with Robert and the boys tonight.

"I want to meet you. My name is Jorge. I don't know if you've heard of me. I did time at Österåker with your sister's man. They still together?"

"No."

"Good. Can I be real with you?"

"Yes."

"Your sister's dude was a real *cabrón*."

Mahmud couldn't help himself, he laughed. Who was this *chico*?

"Anyway. Javier's told me about your little hang-up. And it interests me."

"Whaddya mean 'hang-up'? What're you talking about?" The name Jorge reminded Mahmud of something. He knew he'd heard people talk about this guy a couple years ago. Plenty.

"You've been running your mouth. I think half the city knows how you feel about Mr. R."

"What do you want?"

"I want to see you, live. Talk this through. I think we've got an enemy in common. And you know what we say in my hood: my enemy's enemy is my friend."

Then it hit Mahmud who Jorge was. A couple of years ago: a lotta talk about a newbie who'd revolutionized the coke business in Stockholm. Helped the Yugos take the blow to the boroughs, the projects. Spread the shit among the Svens, the middle-class yuppies, the immigrant kids. Made doing a line as normal as grabbing a beer at the bar. But then things'd derailed somehow. Rumor was that the Yugos massexecuted the guys who'd helped them build the empire, that those same guys'd tried to jack a massive shipment from R., that it'd all been about internal fights within the Yugo mafia. Jorge, the name was familiar. Sure, Mahmud'd heard Javier talk about that guy—he'd been the Yugos' own little dealer consultant. He wondered what the Latino wanted from him.

Jorge kept talking. "You're not a big talker, but I think you're curious and want to meet up. Do you know who I am? Does Västberga Cold Storage facility ring any bells? Abdulkarim? Mrado Slovovic? Do you know who those guys were?"

Mahmud remembered. He knew. And he admitted to himself: he really wanted to meet this Latino.

Jorge suggested a place. A day. A time. They hung up.

After the call a thought in his mind, crystal clear: This might be an opening.

47

Niklas sat up within a microsecond. A crackling sound'd woken him. Was there someone in the room? He reached for the knife on the floor next to the bed. Listened again.

Silence.

Stillness.

Darkness.

He held the knife in front of him, combat grip. Crawled out of bed. Crouched. He could make out vague outlines in the room. There was some light coming from the kitchen. There were no shades in there.

The crackling again. No big movement in the room that he could see. He made his way along the length of one wall. Every muscle tense. Every step a practice in stealthfight.

The apartment only consisted of one room and a kitchen. So the room was a quick check. It appeared empty. Of people, at least. But there was always the risk that *they*'d gotten in. Like they always succeeded in doing, in the end.

He went into the kitchen. Significantly brighter in there. The light from the streetlamps farther down the street were shining in through the window. The kitchen wasn't bigger than fifty square feet. He could see right away that there were no humans in there. But what about the others? He had to search more carefully: his empty cupboard, under the sink, the shelves where he kept granola and bread. Under the pizza cartons, the yogurt packages, the plastic bags. He didn't find them. The apartment was secured.

It must've been his dream that woke him. It'd been stronger than before. First, the mosque over there. Glass shards from the windows and torn prayer mats. The typical Iraq smell from fermenting trash and sewers. Then: scene change. Back in Sweden, except twenty years ago. Claes shoving Mom into the wall. A painting came tumbling down. She fell. Headfirst. Remained. Niklas bent down, grabbed her arm. Pulled, tugged. He screamed. Yelled. But not a single word came out.

Niklas dressed. He peeked through the blinds. The darkness outside was complete. It was seven-thirty in the morning. Today would be a hectic day.

He ate yogurt. Boiled two eggs. Four minutes, exactly. Soft-boiled, but not too soft-boiled.

He sat down in the room. Inspected the Beretta. Tonight he was going to use the silencer. Picked up the black metal cylinder that he'd also bought at the Black & White Inn. Screwed it on, screwed it off. Test-aimed at the window. Weighed the weapon in his hand. Put his jacket on. Slipped the gun into his inner pocket. Tore it out and went through a rapid reloading sequence. Repeated. Fast. Faster. Fastest. He would need to shoot at close range, using hollow-point ammunition, to counteract the limiting effect of the silencer.

He thought about Nina. There was something special between them, that much was obvious. She needed his help. She'd suddenly emerged while he'd been sitting outside her door. Completely alone. Niklas's first thought'd been, Where is the child? He got out of the car. Looked at her. Fifty feet away. She didn't seem to see him.

Nina: dressed in a white coat with a black belt. Collar popped like some badass agent. Tight blue pants and black leather boots with a low heel. On her head: a red knit hat that wasn't pulled down properly. He couldn't tear his eyes from her. Whatever it was she radiated, it hit him like a sandstorm down there.

She walked toward him, but didn't seem to recognize him. Then it struck him: she didn't want anything to do with him. Of course. She knew that he'd seen through her. Looked into her sorrowful eyes and unveiled the truth of how she was feeling. How she was treated. Humiliated.

Niklas remained motionless. Nina's gaze was fixed straight ahead. Purposeful steps. A faint smile on her lips.

Ten feet. Her purse swung in time with her steps.

Six feet. He remained motionless. His breath billowed out in small clouds.

Three feet. He had to say something, grab her. She passed him. A whiff of her perfume. They almost touched. Almost.

He called out, "Nina!" At the same time he thought, What am I going to say now?

Nina turned around. Three feet away. Surprised, quizzical. She clearly didn't recognize him. But she still smiled sweetly.

"Don't you recognize me? I'm the one who bought your Audi."

Nina's smile broadened. "Right, of course. And we saw each other at the gas station, too." She glanced at his car. "You don't have it anymore?"

Niklas didn't know what to say. He didn't want to disappoint her.

"I do, but I have several cars." He tried to laugh, but it felt like the chuckle got caught somewhere in his throat.

Nina didn't seem to notice anything.

"Oh. Do you live in the area?"

Yet another question he couldn't answer.

"No, I was just passing through." What an answer. It sounded dumb as hell. "Passing through," what did that even mean?

"Oh, okay. Well, nice to see you again. We seem to bump into each other now and then, so I bet we'll be seeing each other again." She turned to resume walking. But Niklas glimpsed it again. Her look. The sorrow that came over her. The feelings of powerlessness. Repression. Torturous humiliation. He had to help her. She was so beautiful.

"Nina, wait a minute."

She turned around again. This time: her smile was more uncertain. "Yes?"

"Where are you going?"

"Why do you ask?"

"I was just wondering."

"I'm going to the stables with a friend. You have to make the most of having a babysitter. But I have to hurry. She's waiting for me."

"Can't we get together sometime? And talk through it all."

Nina's smile was even more uncertain. But her eyes: he saw that she was asking him for help. Wanted him close.

"What do you mean?"

"Talk about how you're doing and stuff."

"I don't know what you mean. We don't know each other that way, you just bought a car from me. That's all. But it was nice bumping into you. See you." Her steps were faster. Away from him.

Niklas remained standing, watching her. Her butt swayed rhythmically. And he'd seen it clearly when she said, "See you"—she wanted to see him again. To tell him. Make him understand. She needed him. How could she know that he already understood, all too well.

The run felt extra good today. His thoughts were clear. Nina's perfect face. Tonight's mission was planned in such detail that even Collin would've been jealous. Ready for Operation Magnum's second offensive. What bothered him: that Benjamin fucker. But Niklas knew what he would do about it.

After the push-ups and sit-ups, he did practice exercises with the knife. In order to relax, mostly. He needed peace of mind. He took a shower. Ate lunch. Went through the tapes from the surveillance cameras. He knew the routines of his targets better than they did.

At two o'clock, he made the call that he'd been planning to make for a few days now. To Mahmud, Jamila's brother. He hoped it would lead to results.

Niklas went down to the car. Drove to Alby. Mahmud'd said he'd be home now.

Back home. An hour since his meeting with Mahmud. Niklas was pleased. The conversation'd gone well. Mahmud wasn't a warrior of his caliber, but the Arab was okay. And the best part: he owed Niklas a favor. What Mahmud'd promised to do for him solved some of his problems. Sure, it stretched his finances even more, but that was inevitable. Too many risks hanging over you wouldn't do.

He packed his bag with the usual stuff. The binoculars, concealable transmitters, tapes and memory cards for the surveillance cameras, the computer, the knife, the gloves. And: the Beretta and the silencer.

Took two tablets of Nitrazepam. Sat down on the couch. Turned the TV and DVD on. The taxi drivers talking over coffee at night. Travis was bare-chested. Tested his Magnum. Later: the child whore, Jodie Foster, met Travis.

Niklas remembered who he'd met a few days ago. He'd shadowed Roger Jonsson one night. Seen him drive to downtown Fruängen. Park the car outside the bus station. Niklas saw the guy walk past the subway station. He got out of the car, too. Remained sixty feet or so behind him. Roger: walked leaning forward as if he were constantly about to grab something.

Niklas'd weighed his options. It wasn't time for the offensive yet, but if things got messy, he had no problem doing what was going to happen to Roger Jonsson anyway. It was late at night, hardly any people out except for a group of half-trashed teens who were hanging out inside the glass doors of the subway station. Probably trying to find warmth while they waited for something to happen.

Roger, that asshole, kept walking for a while. Went into Fruängen's Pizzeria. Niklas stopped. Didn't, under any circumstances, want to raise suspicion. Inside the pizzeria: dimly lit. Something was weird.

He got an idea. Ran back to the car. Rummaged through the bag. Got out the equipment. Ran back. Approached the pizzeria carefully. He snuck along one wall. When he was right outside the window of the place, he bent down. Pretended to tie his shoes. Actually, taped a bug outside the window, right at the edge of the concrete.

He didn't know if it'd work. The bug he'd stuck there was meant to be used in the same room as the object under surveillance. The question was how much he would be able to hear now. But maybe, with luck.

Ten minutes later: two other men walked into the pizzeria. Niklas at a proper distance. Sitting on a bench. A bottle in hand. Pretended to be drinking.

The earpiece was in place. The rest of the equipment fit in his jacket pocket. It was cold out. He was already shivering.

So far, he hadn't heard anything from inside the place, but now things started happening. First, two men who spoke some other language. Sounded like Serbian. Then they switched to Swedish. More men. A low crackle, almost like he was listening through a pillow. Some words were muffled, sometimes entire sentences. But he got the gist: they were waiting. Yearning. Lusting. Soon there'd be a display. Of women.

A few minutes passed. The conversation seemed to dry up. The men in the pizzeria sat in silence. Sometimes the Serbian-speaking dudes exchanged a few remarks.

For a short while, Niklas considered storming the place. Make it quick, put those assholes out of their misery. But alone against five men—could get difficult.

Yeah, not now.

Then he heard a gravelly new voice. First Serbian. Then Swedish with a heavy accent. He was able to pick out enough words to understand what was going on.

The gravelly voice said, "Six fine things. Very fine."

"Is one styled the way I like it?"

"Absolutely. I always keep my word."

Then a brief exchange followed that he couldn't hear properly. But he picked up how it was concluded: "They are your very own white slaves."

The man with the accented Swedish went on, "They're back here. As usual. Gentlemen. Have your pick."

The voices disappeared.

Niklas remained sitting for a few minutes. His mind was exploding with thoughts. Maybe the chance of slaughtering the pigs'd increased now that their attention was so obviously directed elsewhere. Maybe it'd be enough if he took down two or three of them and then split? But no, now wasn't the time. He needed to plan.

They must've brought the women in through a back door or else they'd been there long before Roger arrived. He looked around. Deserted. The streetlights were illuminating small islands of asphalt. He walked up to the pizzeria again. It was empty in there. He peeled off the bug. Walked around the building. It was connected to the indoor mall. Seemed like there were offices on the second story. The street level contained restaurants, hair salons, a shoe shop, a bank. He walked in the other direction. The building ended after two hundred feet. In the back, he saw metal doors, loading docks, garage doors. Now he just had to figure out which door belonged to the pizzeria.

He waited. A man and a woman came out from the door Niklas'd been betting on. It wasn't Roger. Darker appearance, maybe Indian or Pakistani. The man was dressed in a brown leather jacket and baggy jeans. Almost looked like a bum. Worn down, unkempt hair, stubble. The girl looked young. Much too thinly dressed, she hugged herself as soon as they stepped outside.

The man was holding an arm around her back. Niklas thought: As if they were a real couple. What a lie.

They walked toward some parked cars. Niklas made up his mind: it wasn't worth waiting for Roger. He was going to find out more about this guy. Now.

He ran back to his car again. Panted so hard his lungs hurt. He couldn't lose them. His pants were tight over the knees, his shoes felt heavy compared with his running gear. He didn't give a shit about anything. Increased his pace. Jumped into the Ford. Stepped on the gas, drove to where he'd seen them. He just had time to spot a yellow Volvo driving off. He glimpsed the john's curly hair in the driver's seat.

He followed the car. Southbound. Out on the highway.

It stopped in Masmo. The man led the girl again. In through the entrance of a building. In the same calm, overly confident way. Like he owned her. Like he thought his behavior would go unpunished.

Two hours later, the girl came out alone. She made a call on her cell phone. Leaned against the building's façade. Lit a cigarette. Niklas thought he could smell the smoke, even though he was sitting in his car.

She sat down on a low fence. Leaned her torso forward. Clasped her arms around her knees. Hung her head. She must be freezing. In both body and soul.

Niklas got out of the car. Planned on offering her a ride away from there. Offering her a safe haven. To take her away from the war. The shit. The filth.

THE FILTH.

He walked up to her. The girl didn't seem to hear him. He scraped his feet on the asphalt intentionally. No reaction. He was standing in front of her, tapped her on the shoulder.

She looked up. She had a thin face, dark hair pulled back in a ponytail and light-brown eyes that glittered in the light from the streetlamp. Her gaze: full of shame. At the same time, she looked indifferent.

Niklas extended his hand.

"My name is Niklas."

She shook her head. In poor Swedish, "I not understand Swedish so good."

Niklas repeated himself, in English. The girl continued to look surprised.

"What do you want?"

He hadn't used his English in a long time, but it was still good.

"I came to take you away from here."

The girl stood up. He saw her entire body up close for the first time. A short skirt and thick, nude-colored tights. Long legs. A leather jacket that didn't appear to close. Under it, he glimpsed her pouting breasts. She stood in silence. Seemed to be reading him as much as he was checking her out. Niklas was ashamed: he'd just looked at her like she was a piece of meat. Just like it said in all those feminist books he'd read.

Finally, she asked, "What do you mean?"

"I'm taking you away from here. You shouldn't have to do what you do. And I'm going to punish them."

"You can take me away from here. But it cost. One thousand five hundred for one hour."

"No, no. You misunderstood. I don't want to buy you. The opposite, I want you to stop with this. You'll be free. And I'll punish the ones who think you can be sold. I promise."

A dark blue Opel stopped on the street. The girl looked over at it. Then back at Niklas.

"Now, I have to go."

"Don't go. Come with me."

"No, I go."

Niklas glanced at the Opel. A man in the driver's seat. Looking at them.

Niklas said, "I'll punish him too."

The girl started walking toward the car. Right before she climbed in the car, she turned around.

"You can never punish them all."

Finally, it was time. Crouched as if in battle. Approaching the back of Roger Jonsson's house. Because he knew that today the pig's partner, Patricia Jacobs, was away at a conference. And he knew more: the asshole followed Swedish hockey finals like a well-trained dog follows its owner. Tonight at seven, Färjestad versus Linköping. Huge game between two fan favorites.

He thought about the last thing the prostitute'd said. Tonight, he'd show her. Roger Jonsson—whore buyer, wife cheater, woman torturer. He was going to be punished so hard he'd wish he'd never been born.

Niklas was dressed in dark, lightweight clothes that were made for winter runners: thick, tight leggings and a thin Gore-Tex windbreaker. On his head: a homemade balaclava, a hat that he'd cut eye and mouth holes out of. He was going to roll it down when it was time. A small backpack was strapped tightly to his back. The Beretta, in a holster.

In front of him: a small lawn, a deck with a set of stairs, a balcony door onto the deck. He reached the house in five steps. The TV was in a room with a window overlooking the street, so there was no risk that Roger would discover anything. What's more: it was the middle of the second period right now. The risk that the guy'd so much as leave to take a piss: less than zero.

He picked the deck door. He'd already tried it out twice before while the couple was at work.

He could hear the sounds from the game faintly. The applause from the audience, the worked up clichés from the commentators, the rapid sounds from the skate blades captured in a close-up.

Niklas knew the layout of the house. Had sat outside and stared in for so many days. Had created a picture of how the rooms were laid out. If there was an alarm, where the wireless phone was usually kept, if they locked the front door, which way the hinges opened. And, again: he'd broken in twice before for a visit. Just to get a quick look around. To feel at home.

He stopped. His heart was beating louder than the feet stomping in the bleachers from the cheering section on TV. A short second: he brought his hands into starting position for tanto dori. Took a deep breath. Let the air out through his mouth. Felt the calm wash over him.

A few more steps. The sounds from the hockey battle were clearer now. He pulled out his gun. He was one with his weapon.

Niklas could've gotten a sniper rifle. Camped out on some rooftop across the street. A single shot to the face—easy. Sprayed wife-beater brain matter on the wall of the house. He could've attached a bomb to the TV, blown up 430 square feet of the idyllic suburbs with the tap of a finger. Or why not simply poison Roger Jonsson? There were many easier ways than the one he'd chosen. But that wasn't what it was about. Operation Magnum was a school. A pedagogical signal to all perpetrators. You will be punished. You will suffer.

It was time. Niklas walked into the TV room. Striped wallpaper. A couch and two armchairs. Nasty wall-to-wall carpeting and a stereo console. On the couch: Roger Jonsson. Pudgy, pale, pathetic.

Niklas pointed the Beretta at the guy's head. Picked up the remote control, switched channels.

"I don't like hockey."

Roger Jonsson looked like he was going to shit his pants. If he'd been pale before, he was more green now. He tried to say something.

Niklas shushed him.

"Don't say anything. Then I'll have to shoot you."

There was a risk that someone would see them from the outside. The house across the street didn't have a direct view into this room. But if someone drove past in a high car, like an SUV, for instance, they would be able to see in. Niklas brought out his backpack. Taped Roger's mouth. Taped his hands, feet. Threw him on the floor.

"I know you like eating carpet, you fucking pig."

Niklas was pleased with his comment. He'd thought it out way ahead of time.

He sat down on the couch. Put the Beretta in his lap. Now no one could see them from the outside. Time for some action.

He explained. Held a planned lecture. For at least ten minutes. The gender power structure was over. Everyone who beat, humiliated, exploited their physical strength would soon find out. Everyone who bought women, raped people, played with lives.

He dealt Roger kicks with even intervals.

The beads of sweat on the guy's forehead must be stinging his eyes.

Niklas unfolded a piece of paper. It was Roger Jonsson's conviction. Gross Violation of a Woman's Integrity and Aggravated Rape.

Niklas dug around in his backpack. Fished out a small blowtorch. Roger's eyes widened.

Go time.

Niklas read sections of the conviction aloud.

A long night for a wife beater and whore buyer.

Four hours later. Niklas left the same way he'd come. Through the garden. Out on the other side of the house. The rental car was parked around seven hundred feet farther away. Maybe someone would see him walk through the area. But they wouldn't see his hair color or facial features. It was pitch-black outside and he'd broken the streetlights the night before.

He fished out his cell phone. He'd prepared a prepaid card.

He'd memorized the number of Patricia Jacobs.

Loud music in the background. Disco at the company party? He hoped Patricia got to dance.

"Hello?"

"Hi, can you hear me?"

"Wait a sec, let me go somewhere quieter."

Seven seconds. The noise in the background diminished.

"I think I can hear you better now. Who is this?"

"You can call me Travis."

"What did you say?"

"You can call me Travis."

"I don't think I know you."

"You don't need to. I just wanted to let you know that I've removed him. You don't have to worry anymore. He's not coming back."

"What do you mean? Who are you?"

"Ask the police what it feels like to get your private parts treated with a blowtorch. I know what he's done to you. I know what he did to his last woman."

48

He thought about his private investigation over the past few weeks. Alf Winge hadn't leaked shit. But the Bentley dealer was hiding something. Thomas wasn't a seasoned detective. But his gut was speaking loud and clear. Shouldn't he call one of his old colleagues after all? The answer to that question still hadn't changed. The rest of the guys in the Southern District were too close to Adamsson. Should he be in touch with Hägerström? Nah, he didn't need that piece of shit. Still: there was so much to dig deeper into. Runeby's info about Adamsson's project in the eighties. The impenetrable material he'd gotten from Rantzell's basement. The Bentley kid's insecurity.

Thomas found out as much as he could about the guy in the store. Niklas Creutz. Didn't show up in the criminal registry, no tax debt or late-payment notices. Came from an old banking family. Daddy probably still paid for the brat's rent and the car he drove. Still: he got the feeling that something wasn't quite right. Could see Niklas Creutz's face in front of him. Went over the sequence of events. The guy's almost panicked expression.

Thomas ran a search through the multiple databases on his own this time. Really didn't give a shit if someone wondered why he'd done a search on Creutz. No hits on suspects or people with claims filed on them—but on people who'd filed claims, bingo: Niklas Creutz'd been subjected to some unpleasantness this summer. Thomas ordered the criminal report from the City District: aggravated assault in the dealership on Strandvägen. Perps unknown. The only thing the brat'd said in the report was that he remembered that the perps were dark, with a foreign appearance, one pretty short but hefty—very hefty. They'd forced their way into the small office. Given Creutz a real going over. The doctor's certificate pointed to a broken rib, swelling and bruises on the face, as well as two lost teeth in the upper row. In the report taken at the scene of the crime, he'd explained why: *They wanted to know if I'd sold a Continental GT to someone named Wisam. Then they wanted to see all the paperwork on the car. Then they called me a racist. Wisam Jibril, I think. I don't understand why. Then they beat me up. I thought I was going to die.*

It couldn't be a coincidence. The last document that Rantzell'd signed: a contract of sale, Bentley Continental GT, 1.4 million kronor. And then this: someone'd beaten that poor sucker bloody. For the sake of the very same car. Why?

He had to find Wisam Jibril. Ran the same searches on him as he'd done on the Bentley dealer. Got a hit right away. The guy had a solid criminal record: unlawful threats, assault, armed robbery, drug-related crimes, etc. A gangster, a robber, a guy who'd been around the block. Thomas ordered copies of court records, preliminary-investigation paperwork, surveillance notes, printouts from the general reconnaissance register. Worked like a maniac. The guy was a suspect in at least three big robberies, emphasis on big. A CIT robbery in Tumba in the spring of 2002 and one in the Norrtälje area in the fall of the same year. Total value: 1.5 million kronor. But even bigger: a robbery at Arlanda. Thomas remembered the newspaper articles vaguely. An airplane load of bills. Many, many million kronor. Wisam Jibril was definitely not some nobody.

Horrendous sums. A legendary coup. Exquisitely elegant execution. But no one saw, heard, or knew shit. Still: the talk around town was buzzing according to the report that Thomas'd read: Wisam Jibril'd supposedly died in the tsunami catastrophe in Thailand. But, in reality, he'd been back in Sweden for a year or so. Jibril: king of robberies. Jibril: consumed his capitalist gains like crazy. Pimped apartment, flat-screen machines, a Bentley, a Porsche, a BMW. According to another report: the cars the suspect drove were actually leased from one and the same company—Dolphin Leasing AB.

Jibril: a dude who wanted to hide that he was sitting on a pot of gold. A guy like that had every imaginable reason to get rid of a poor, run-down front man who might be a burden if he started letting his mouth run.

Summa summarum: Thomas might've found a perp. There was a connection to Rantzell and, most important, there was a motive. The only puzzle piece that didn't fit: how did Rantzell's Palme connection come into the picture if Jibril was the one who snuffed him out? He couldn't let it go. Something still wasn't right.

Despite that: Thomas had to get ahold of Wisam Jibril.

Thomas got in touch with Jonas Nilsson again. Nilsson was a man of honor. His latest good deed: introducing Thomas to old Runeby

The days passed. Thomas kept working like crazy. Days at the traffic unit. Nights at the club. Him and Jasmine, Belinda, Ratko, a new guy named Kevin. His side gig felt normal. More than that, he actually dug the place. The camaraderie, the freedom.

He needed to check off all the old-timers from the Troop. He ran through the list in his head again. Malmström, Adamsson, Carlsson, and Winge: nothing more he could do there. Left: Torbjörn Jägerström, Roger Wallén, Jan Nilsson, and Carl Johansson. Four former riot policemen. Someone ought to know more about Adamsson's hatred of Palme. But Thomas'd rethought things—these guys appeared tougher than he'd initially anticipated. Winge'd proved as much. He needed to turn to other tactics.

In one way, he was surprised the man hadn't returned—the one who'd threatened him and Åsa from outside their house that time. He understood that his interrogation with Leif Carlsson might not've gone public—the guy was so far gone he probably didn't even remember what he'd had for breakfast. But Winge—shouldn't something happen soon? On the other hand: maybe Winge didn't want to make a thing of it until he knew who Thomas was, and he couldn't know that at this point. Thomas patted himself on the back: he hadn't been driving his own car when he'd followed Winge.

Thomas got the number of Kent Magnusson, the old junkie he and Ljunggren'd collared in the schoolyard in Skärholmen during the summer. Thomas knew a lot of deadbeats like him, but Kent was the one he'd done a favor for most recently.

Thomas called him. The junkie didn't understand whom he was talking to at first. Thomas asked what he'd called to ask. Kent didn't sound like he was doing too well, but finally Thomas got a promise out of him: The junkie was going to check with his contacts. Ask if they could get Morfin-Scopolamin, for injection.

Early morning: Thomas out on his private beat again. This time, outside Torbjörn Jägerström's house in Huddinge. He thought about his failure with Winge. The risk he'd taken. Again: What if Winge'd figured out who he was? He ought to make sure Åsa armed herself. Or even better, moved somewhere for a few months until this was all over and done with. Dammit, they were supposed to pick up Sander soon.

Torbjörn Jägerström lived in a house that was the same size as Thomas's own. Not in an upper-class neighborhood like Bromma, where Winge held court. Not a huge mansion like Runeby's. Just normal. Jägerström was the youngest of the guys in the Troop, forty-seven. He couldn't have been more than twenty-five when he took up with those other old guys. Nowadays he was in charge of the task force in Norrmalm, the northern part of the inner city. Senior officer. He'd made something of himself.

Thomas'd already spent three or four mornings sitting outside his house like this. Checked Jägerström and his wife's morning routine. He knew it by now: the wife left a half hour before Jägerström went to work. The same morning routine should apply today.

He checked the thermometer in the car. The cold'd come creeping. November was the worst month of the year. A whole winter stretched out ahead, no pleasure to await.

Jägerström's wife emerged from the front door of the house at exactly the same hour, down to the minute, as the last time he'd been out scouting. Stressed steps. A purse over her arm. Proper, business casual. He wondered what she did for a living.

He waited a little while longer.

Checked the contents of the small leather bag on the seat beside him one more time. An injection needle. An ampoule with Scopolamin. He opened the car door. Walked up to the house. Rang the doorbell.

A long time passed before Torbjörn Jägerström opened the door. Burly guy. Shirt unbuttoned. Chinos. Thick gold chain with the hammer of Thor around his neck. His facial expression was stiffer than on a corpse.

"Good morning," Thomas said.

"Good morning? And what do you want, if I may ask?"

"I'm from Länsförsäkringar, the insurance company. We're conducting a study in the area about what home insurance people have."

Jägerström stared. "I recognize you."

Fuck. Thomas'd actually thought the same thing when the door opened. He must've met Torbjörn Jägerström in some work context. But there was no time to lose. He shoved the Taser into Jägerström's chest. Felt the vibrations all the way up his own arm, the muscles contracted involuntarily. Jägerström collapsed. Thomas closed the door behind them. Bent down, dug through his bag. Pulled out the rubber hand, tightened it over one of Jägerström's biceps. Ran his fingers over his forearm. Searched for a vein. Picked up the injection needle. Drove it in. Injected two full doses of Scopolamin.

Waited. Thought about the drug. Morfin-Scopolamin: muscle relaxant with a calming effect. The drug was normally used as a painkiller before surgery. But also: the active substance in truth serum.

Jägerström revived after half an hour. Thomas'd put him in an armchair in the living room. Taped his hands, just to be on the safe side. He was such a genius.

The room reminded him of Runeby's living room. The same darkwood bookshelves with framed photos of family, an encyclopedia, Jan Guillou's collected Hamilton books and a couple by John Grisham and Tom Clancy. The only thing that differed from Runeby's living room was the absence of photographs on the walls. Instead, there was a large lithograph: two drummer boys marching beside each other on a snowcovered field. Thomas recognized the theme: Björneborgarna's March. The two drummer boys dressed in old army uniforms were meant to represent Finland's two peoples, Swedes and Finns, fighting together for their country's independence. But this motif had another significance too: "Björneborgarna's March" was a piece of music. The salute and parade march for the Finnish Defense Forces. But it was also the march the Troop used to sing when they did their so-called special operations on the street. Common knowledge in the police department: Björneborgarna's March'd been hummed countless times while drunks, *blattes*, and bums were beaten to bits in the eighties. A war march. A call to arms.

Thomas thought, Fuck you people.

Jägerström was still groggy. Drooling like a baby. He was mumbling something.

Showtime.

Thomas had a seat in the armchair across from him.

"I'm going to ask you some questions. Do you understand what I'm saying?"

Jägerström nodded, blinked. A strand of saliva hung from his chin. Thomas wiped it off with Jägerström's shirt.

"You're going to tell me everything exactly the way it was. I thought I would begin by asking your name."

"Torbjörn Elias Jägerström."

"Good. What is your wife's name?"

"Eva Elisabeth Jägerström, maiden name Silverberg."

"Good. How is your sex life?" A control question.

"It's gotten better since our son moved out."

"Okay. And how was it before?"

"Probably better than yours, anyway." The guy's great sense of humor didn't seem to be suffering. Thomas couldn't let the joke get to him. He had to concentrate on his interrogation.

"Now I'm going to ask you some other questions about the old Troop. Were you a part of it?"

"Absolutely. That was my best time on the force."

"Were you a part of the meetings that were organized by Lennart Edling in the eighties?"

The left corner of Jägerström's mouth made a jerking motion. Thomas put his hand on his shoulder. "Take it easy. It's okay, you can tell me."

Jägerström leaned back in the armchair. He actually looked like he was relaxing further, if that was even possible.

"Lennart Edling, that crazy old guy. He was a little extreme, but a man of honor."

"What do you mean by 'a man of honor?'"

"You know what I mean. There aren't too damn many left in this country, but Edling is one of them. If he's alive, that is."

"Yes, but what do you mean by that?"

"I told you, you know what I mean. Men who care about Sweden's future. Who stand up for who they are, who don't let Arabs, Communist cunts, and Jew swine take over this country. Do you understand what I'm saying? Now when we've finally gotten a center-right-wing government, they make a fucking nigger minister. It's a joke. I haven't voted for those parties since ninety-four."

"Are you a man of honor?"

"I do my best. Duty above all."

"Tell me about those meetings in Gamla Stan."

Jägerström explained slowly. He hadn't been to every meeting—he was young, had just met his current wife, there wasn't time for everything. But Malmström was a good boss and there was a lot to learn. For Jägerström, the meetings were mostly pleasant get-togethers, a way to network. But also: a way to safeguard the police department and Sweden. The Scopolamin was working better than expected—Jägerström kept on talking without pause.

Thomas asked about Adamsson.

"Adamsson? You can't find a better guy. He's done well, I think. Runs the Southern District like his own little platoon. A real patriot. An upright citizen."

"Were you a part of Adamsson's Palme group?"

Jägerström stopped. The corner of his mouth started jumping again. He brought his taped hands up to shield his face. Mumbled something again.

"What did you say?" Thomas asked.

"I can't talk about that."

Thomas tried to cajole, to speak calmingly to him, to try to make him relax.

His only answer: "I can't. You have to understand that. I can't."

This wouldn't do. There was only one option left: Thomas brought out the injection needle again. Shot another ampoule of truth serum into Jägerström's body. Waited fifteen minutes. Jägerström almost looked like he was sleeping.

Thomas tried again. "Were you a part of Adamsson's Palme group?"

Torbjörn Jägerström's power of resistance was gone with the wind. It was almost funny. Jägerström: iron fist, macho man, super cop—babbled like a three-year-old. Still, his answer was razor sharp.

"I was a part of it. It was necessary. Protecting Sweden, that's the job assigned to the police and the secret service by the parliament, and that job had to be done no matter who was in power in the government. Since Palme was a threat to Sweden, we had to watch him the way we would any other potential national threat. Palme was too close with the Russians."

"So, what did you do, practically speaking?"

"I was only twenty-five years old. I wasn't a commanding officer or in a leadership position. So I don't know too much, but we were divided into cells. The ones in my group didn't know who was in the other groups. At least I didn't. My area of responsibility was weapons. I made sure the group had access to a big enough arsenal and combat equipment. There was a coup in the air."

It was insane. Thomas could hardly believe what he was hearing. He felt like taking a break. Calling the evening newspapers or Hägerström. Doing something. But he had to keep asking questions, learn something tangible.

"Tell me more."

Jägerström explained how often they'd met up. Who'd been a part of his group. What they'd discussed, how they'd organized themselves, planned. How they'd feared the Russians, Communist conspiracies, tried to recruit trusty senior police officers, naval officers, secret-service people. Still: Thomas couldn't get anything out of him that pointed to Adamsson or anyone else being directly involved in the murder of Olof Palme. He had to make the pieces fit. There had to be a connection. What Adamsson's men'd been doing then: attempted treason. What Adamsson was doing now: muddling the murder investigation of a key witness.

"Are you at all in touch with Adamsson today?" he asked.

"No, not with him."

"Why not?"

"We just grew apart. Nothing more."

"And what about anyone else from that group?"

"Yes, a few of us get together now and then, maybe twice a year. Me, Roger Wallén, a couple others. Sven Bolinder has even joined us a few times. When he does, things get a little fancier, some company picks up the bill."

Thomas tried to get Jägerström to say more. The clock was ticking. Jägerström's cell phone was ringing nonstop. People were probably wondering where he was. Why he hadn't showed up to work, called back, picked up. Thomas switched off the phone. But it was still dangerous. He couldn't stay here much longer. Jägerström babbled on. About the meetings, about honorable men, about patriots. The Scopolamin made him too talkative. It was mostly nonsense. Rubbish that was difficult to understand. Disjointed slurring.

Thomas had to bring this to an end. The question was if he'd even gotten any information of interest. Not really, but he had to leave. Someone might come by the house.

He'd have to do his thinking at home.

Jonas Nilsson called one night a few weeks later.

"Hey, it's me."

Thomas sensed that he was calling for a reason.

"Hey there, Nilsson. What's up?"

"Things're swell, let me tell you. I just bought a new car."

"Nice, what kind is it?" Actually, Thomas just wanted him to get to the point. Did Nilsson know something about Jibril?

"A Saab 9-5 Aero." Right kind of car for a cop, Thomas thought. Cops didn't drive super fly models, but they didn't ride around in junk buckets either, no Japanese duds or Škodas.

"Damn, that's awesome. And have you heard anything about what we talked about?"

"Yes, that's why I'm calling. I met one of our informants today. A real hard-boiled guy who decided to straighten out. The guy got married and has a couple of kids, but sometimes he gives us a few leads to show his goodwill."

"Okay. And?"

"Jibril is dead. Word on the street is the Yugos got him."

Dammit.

Thomas tried to find out more. But Nilsson didn't know anything. They ended the conversation. Thomas remained standing where he was. Suddenly, he grew worried. How dumb was it to have that conversation over the phone? For the thousandth time, he thought about the man outside his window. Winge. Jägerström. Bolinder. They were prepared to go far to stop him. Maybe they didn't know who he was yet. But then, the man outside his window'd known.

They'd gotten him kicked out of his job. Had threatened him and Åsa. Messed with his report. Murdered his father's hero. Sweden's morale was on the line. If even middle-aged Swedish police officers were rotten to the core—there was no hope. Fuck no, he wouldn't let them succeed. This was his way back.

Thomas picked up the phone again.

When he punched in the numbers he felt an almost childish excitement. Nervousness paired with suspense.

He didn't like Hägerström. At the same time, he knew he should've made this call a long time ago.

When the signal went through, he heard a short click on the other end of the line.

"Hi, you've reached Martin Hägerström. Please leave a message after the beep."

Fucking voice mail. Major letdown.

Thomas kept the message short: "This is Andrén, call me."

49

Mahmud was on his way home from the gym. In one hand, the wheel. In the other, a plastic container with the Lionhart mix: creatine and other dietary supplements. Sipping strawberry-flavored gunk with a straw, like a milkshake. The side effects of the last juice he'd been cranking were still making themselves known. He had to wait before he started up again. It was lame. But true.

Right now, he was on his way to meet the Latino who'd called him. Jorge.

The car stereo was blaring. Ragheb Alama was crooning like a god.

He thought about Niklas, the commando guy, who'd come over to Mahmud's house the other day. Asked for a favor. A very, very big favor. The guy wanted Mahmud to fuck up a friend of his. Mahmud didn't give a shit about the details.

Niklas really did seem crazy somehow. His eyes were always darting around. Above all, the guy was probably lethal—at least if you judged by what he'd done to Jamila's ex. Why couldn't he spook that Benjamin guy himself?

"*Habibi*," Niklas said in Arabic. "You really have to help me. I'm in a tight spot and I might get locked up. So this Benjamin has to understand that if he rats me out, there are others on the outside who'll punish him. Do you understand?"

Mahmud thought, Really, I shouldn't bother with this. But honor was honor. Niklas'd helped his sister. And nothing in the world was more important than a sister. He owed Niklas.

Mahmud nodded. "I'll do it, buddy. Where does this pussy live?"

Niklas seemed ecstatic.

The rest was simple. Yesterday, before he went on whore guard duty, he drove out to the guy's address. Niklas'd tipped him off that Benjamin was home. It didn't take long for Mahmud to figure out where in the building the guy lived. Did a quick line in the entranceway. Took the elevator up. Hummed to himself, "Coke gives you wings."

Rang the doorbell. Felt angry as hell. Life was sour on him so now he'd get sour on this Benjamin chump.

A bearded guy of average height opened the door. Looked surprised. Mahmud delivered a straight right cross. His brass knuckles were in place. The guy tumbled backward into the apartment. Bleeding from the nose. Tried to raise his guard, swung at Mahmud. But it wasn't an even fight—Mahmud had brass knuckles, after all. He landed another punch. The guy fell over. Was lying down. Trying to shield his head while he yelled, "Who the fuck are you? Stop. My nose, man."

Mahmud pulled out a roll of electrical tape. Taped the guy's hands and feet. Stared into panicked eyes. Felt powerful. It was like he was Gürhan now. Ey, whatcha say now? Not so cocky, huh? Snitching bitch.

Benjamin was lying completely still. Whimpering. Mahmud sat down on a stool.

"Hey, Brillo-face."

Benjamin didn't say a word.

"If you rat my friend Niklas out, I'll come get you for real. You feel me?"

Benjamin closed his eyes.

Mahmud didn't wait for an answer. Opened the door, walked out. Thought, Shit, maybe I should become a bruiser after all. He had to work a full week to make thirty grand on blow. This had taken fifteen minutes, including the drive.

Malmvägen. A black guy came toward him. Flow in his step. His walk was reminiscent of Robert's. But more exaggerated. One of his legs jerked with every other step. Was he walking to the beat of some song in invisible earbuds? Dressed in a hoodie pulled up over his head and tucked behind his ears, which stood straight out like on Mickey Mouse. A down vest over the sweatshirt. Baggy camo pants. Around his neck: Africa's silhouette in Rasta colors: green, yellow, and red. The grass, the sun, the blood.

Walking toward Mahmud, without a doubt.

He crossed his arms. This was definitely not Jorge.

The Rasta guy tilted his head. Crap teeth—looked like they were gonna fall out of his mouth at any moment. Spoke English with a thick accent—sounded like Sean Paul, almost incomprehensible. "Hey you, Arab man. My friend wants to meet you."

Mahmud dropped his arms. Relaxed. The nigger was apparently

Jorge's messenger. Introduced himself as Elliot. Mahmud followed him. The jerk in his step. The flow in his walk.

Malmvägen was big, spread out. Satellite dishes hung like ears off the high-rises. This was northern Stockholm's Million district.

Elliot didn't look back.

They walked into a building. Up the stairs.

Elliot rang a doorbell. Music could be heard through the door: reggae rhythms.

A broad dude opened the door. At first, Mahmud couldn't see if he was black or Latino. Thick dreads. Fat ganja grin when he saw Elliot. The door slammed shut in front of Mahmud's face. He remained standing outside alone.

He thought: What the fuck is he doing?

Mahmud didn't know what to do. Ring the doorbell? Bang on the door? Split? The last was probably the best alternative. He started walking back down the stairs.

Then the door opened halfway. Elliot peered out again. Called, "Hey, Arab brother, you welcome."

Mahmud turned. Walked in.

In the hall: music was blaring even louder from the other rooms. Back beat. Sweet weed smell. A hallway. A blue throw rug. White-painted walls. There was a large animal skin pinned up on one wall. The lion of Judah with a crown and one paw raised in greeting. The *blatte* with the dreads sat down in a chair and started rolling a joint.

Elliot nodded.

Led Mahmud down the hallway.

The living room: Marijuana paradise. Couches, pillows, and cushions spread out. Blankets covered other areas of the floor. Ten or so people were sitting and lying down. Above all: they were smoking. There was a hookah between two couches. Two hollowed-out wood hash pipes on the coffee table. Piles of Rizla papers. Bags of weed. Pictures of Bob Marley, Haile Selassie, and the silhouette of Africa. A stereo stood next to one of the other couches. A vinyl record with a green, red, and yellow label was turning.

The people in there: stoned out of their minds.

Elliot showed him to a spot. Mahmud ended up on a cushion next to a pretty girl who seemed to be sleeping. Blond dreadlocks tied back with a hair band. This place was mad wack.

One of the guys on the couch got up. Approached Mahmud. The

guy's voice was barely audible over the music. He extended his hand. Someone lowered the volume.

"Welcome to Sunny Sunday. I'm Jorge, Jorgelito. And you're Javier's friend, right?"

Mahmud nodded.

"May I offer you a smoke?"

Mahmud accepted the bag of weed. Picked up a pipe. But didn't do anything. Gaze glued on Jorge.

Jorge smiled. "They come here every Sunday. Worship Jah. Relax with some weed. Do what the black man should do. Chill, dig the music, feel the power."

Mahmud didn't know if he should laugh or split. He maintained an interested look.

Jorge went on. "You're not African. Me neither. But we're still niggers. Do you understand what I'm saying?"

Mahmud didn't get what the Latino was talking about. He put the pipe back on the table. Got up.

Jorge put his hand on Mahmud's shoulder. "Chill, man. I just wanted you to relax a little. We'll go into the kitchen."

They had a seat in the kitchen. Jorge closed the door. Poured two glasses of water.

Mahmud eyed him. The dude was thin but still built, somehow. Short hair and a small, ugly mustache. Dark eyes with something in them besides weed haze.

"Okay, I'm sorry if you don't like this place. I love it."

Mahmud grinned. "I've got nothing against it. But I always get a little jumpy when there are too many Zinjis around."

"Not a problem with me, man, but don't say anything to them out there. And, like I said, we're all niggers. Do you understand what I mean?"

"Nope."

"Let me put it this way. Segregation is like apartheid. The Million Program has the same effect on us as slavery. You understand now?"

Mahmud had a vague notion. Jorge was trying to be serious. Comparing immigrant guys like Mahmud with how black people'd lived in South Africa. He didn't have the energy to have a discussion. Just nodded.

Jorge starting telling his story. The Latino'd only been in Sweden for a month. Really, he lived in Thailand. It was easier because he was wanted in Sweden since the drug incident by the Västberga Cold Storage facility.

It'd all begun when the Yugos'd wrapped him in a trial many years ago. Slaughtered him like a dog. But Jorge busted out of the pen by climbing over a wall, like fucking Spider-Man. Mahmud recognized the story, but honestly—he'd thought it was a tall tale. Jorge explained: he'd known all along that things wouldn't end well with the Yugos. They should've helped him, taken responsibility for him since he'd worked for them, but instead they'd gone south on him. So Jorge'd started fucking with them. Shit hit the fan—they beat him real bad and from that day forward he hated Radovan more than anything else in the world. Jorge wasn't the kind of guy to let a beating slide.

Mahmud saw himself in the story. Jorge'd had an energy he couldn't feel right now, but still. They were driven by the same obsessions.

Jorge kept telling his story. How he'd tried to come up with ideas to sink the Yugo empire. Shadowed Radovan, found out a bunch of things about the organization: smuggle routes, dealing technology, drug methodology. He looked at Mahmud. "Do you still use those Shurgard storage units out by the parking lots?"

Mahmud grinned. The Latino knew what he was talking about.

But it all went to hell. Jorge got played. Had to bust the border. Now he was sitting on a good pile of dough and a Yugo hate that was hotter than lava. But, as Jorge said, "If that'd been all, I would've dealt with it. Swallowed the sperm with a smile." But there was something else, too. Something worse. Darker. Harder. He didn't want to go into details. "It was about dirty human trafficking" was all he said. He focused in on Mahmud. "I think you understand what I mean."

Mahmud wondered if the Latino knew what he did besides sell blow. The *blatte* seemed to know about everything.

Maybe Jorge knew what he was thinking. He said, "I know what you do, man. It's not pretty, but I don't blame you. You're in their clutches now. I know you're cool. Javier's told me. And I trust him. He's *un hermano*."

Jorge swallowed a gulp of water.

"You feel what I feel. You hate them. You want to get out. Let me tell you, man."

Jorge began explaining stuff about Radovan's other businesses. Blackmail, financial fraud, brothels. Mentioned the organized luxury whore parties. Mahmud felt like the pieces were falling into place.

It agreed with what he'd seen the other day: the way the hookers'd been collected, made up, fixed up, the slick players who'd run the operation.

It took Jorge ten minutes to finish. He stared out into space. Seemed like his thoughts were still stuck in the story.

"It's messed up," Mahmud said. "But what can I do about it?"

Jorge's reply was slow in coming. "You and me, we're not the only ones who feel like this. I've got contacts who want the Yugos to get what's coming to them even more than we do. If you want, I've got a job for you."

Mahmud didn't really understand what Jorge was talking about.

"You earn dough by taking a hit at Radovan's whore business. A contract. With good pay. And everything you find, you can keep."

Mahmud still didn't really follow, asked him to explain further.

Jorge explained. Someone was willing to cough up 300,000 if Mahmud took a hit at the Yugos and the luxury-whore johns.

Three hundred thousand. Shit. Even though business was booming now, that was a lotta cash.

Still: he asked to think about it. Needed to digest everything. Jorge understood that he couldn't give an answer right away. "Get in touch with me within a week. Or we'll have to find someone else."

When they'd walked back into the living room, Mahmud asked, "I still don't get it. Why do you want *me* to do it?"

Jorge's response wasn't very helpful: "Because you're perfect." Then he laughed. "Forget it for now. You can think about it, remember?"

They sat down on the couch.

"Stay awhile," Jorge said. "Listen to some Marley. Take a hit and feel the power. Haile Selassie Jah, as they say around here."

Mahmud relinquished control for a while. Leaned back. Took four hits on the joint that Jorge'd rolled. A man with a knit Rasta-colored hat was half-lying on a cushion next to them. Accepted the joint from him. Took deep hits.

The smoke, the music. He inhaled the atmosphere.

Mahmud: relaxed for the first time in a long time.

No woman, no cry.

With flow. Rhythm.

One of life's tranquil moments.

His irritation over everything was released in the fog. Three hundred thousand glimpsed on the horizon.

He floated away.
Praise the Rastafari, Jah.
Sunny Sunday shines.

* * *

AFTONBLADET—EVENING PAPER

November 25

SUSPECTED SERIAL KILLER IN STOCKHOLM

A man was found dead this morning in a single-family home in northern Stockholm. The police suspect that he was murdered and that there are connections to a previous murder in the Stockholm area.

According to the police's press secretary, Jan Stanneman, the dead man is in his forties. No arrest has been made and there are no suspects in the case so far.

The police believe that the murder is connected to another murder that was committed in Sollentuna, where a man of the same age was shot outdoors.

"What makes us see a connection between the murders is that both the men's wives received a phone call from a person who may have been the perpetrator," says an inside source.

The murders appear to have been professionally carried out and very few witnesses have been able to report observations to the police. It has also come to light that one of the murdered men was convicted of abusing his wife and that the other man's wife has reported that she had been abused over a number of years.

"We're not ruling out that it could be a question of some kind of vendetta by a madman, but it is too early to speculate," *Aftonbladet*'s source says.

The man who was found this morning had reportedly been tortured.

Karl Sorlinder
karl.sorlinder@aftonbladet.se

50

It was still dark out when Niklas was woken by a text from Mahmud: *I heard they found a corpse with dirty feet, saggy balls & a hairy ass—call me so I know you're still alive.* Niklas assumed the Arab was trying to joke.

Still, he waited to call. Needed to process the information he'd received during the night. The Operation'd advanced to the third phase: Patric Ngono. Niklas was well trained by now: he knew the mission and the SOP. The planning of the actual attack was already under way.

It wasn't just about Ngono: there were three others in line after him.

Part of the victory was that the media'd started to understand what he was doing. Soon, they would get more material.

He thought about Nina Glavmo-Svensén. He thought about what he should do with Benjamin. Hoped that Mahmud's treatment'd sent a clear message. So many human beings in so many different roles. And he was the only one who cleaned up—made sure that Sweden became a little more fair, a little more logical.

Niklas sat down at his computer. Opened the folder that he'd labeled "Johns." Roger Jonsson wasn't the only one who bought women.

In the afternoon, after training exercises, he called Mahmud.

"Hey, it's me. The corpse."

Mahmud laughed. "So you're alive, *habibi*. You got time to meet up today?"

Niklas wondered what he wanted. Mahmud didn't want to tell him over the phone—they decided to meet up later that night.

"You want in on something I'm doing?" That was the first thing Mahmud asked when they met up at his house.

Niklas thought his apartment was nasty. He could handle his own filth. But Mahmud's dirt disgusted him: crusty dishes, bottles of protein shakes, bowls with dried powder mixes. And the Arab's way of dressing: sweat pants and a T-shirt that said *Beach Wrestling* across the front. Was that really a way to dress when you had company? But Niklas owed him one. He didn't say anything.

What Mahmud told him was the best thing he'd heard since he'd arrived back in Sweden. He almost felt religious. How could something fit so well into Operation Magnum? Mahmud's question was simple: he'd been asked to do a job—on contract. It wasn't just anything—it was about striking against some big-time pimps in Stockholm. Plus hurting the people and the organization that ran the human trafficking as much as possible.

Mahmud didn't want to go into details. Maybe he didn't know much more. He just said that someone who had some unfinished business with Radovan and the whore business wanted to get things done. The Arab didn't know it, but no one was more suited for this job than Niklas.

They discussed some ideas briefly. Mahmud wanted to establish certain principles: no conversations on cell phones or landlines, no talking to anyone on the outside, when they needed to talk they'd fire off a text first—he outlined a bunch of different codes they would use.

They discussed if they needed to get anyone else on board. Benjamin is out, Niklas thought to himself. Would someone from Biskops-Arnö work, maybe? Felicia? Erik? No, they were too weak. Couldn't handle the fight when the storm really blew in. They'd already proven as much.

Mahmud had a stringency and a warrior instinct that Niklas hadn't expected. Niklas really got going. Started discussing types of weapons, attack methods, strategic planning. Mahmud smiled.

"Buddy, everything in its own time. We'll get to that."

"But you've got to give me something to get started on now."

Mahmud thought it over. "Okay, I have the address of the place where we're going to make the hit. We have to know the area. So it'd be perfect if you checked it out."

Mahmud: like a badass general. Niklas loved it. Above all: he loved having a partner. To be a part of a TF again—a task force.

The next day, Niklas drove the Ford out to Smådalarö, in the Stockholm archipelago. The address Mahmud'd given him wasn't a street, it was just the name of a place, maybe a house: Näsudden, and a zip code. Mahmud'd been talking about their employer's warning: be careful—these guys have security. They've made a mistake before and don't want to do it again. It was unclear if Mahmud knew whom it was they were going to be dealing with. Niklas had no clue, but he was an expert, after all.

A good day: clear weather. Fall was turning into winter. He looked forward to the snow. When it'd been at its worst down there, he used to think about clean, white, glittering snow. Icicles dripping as spring approached. The crunching sound when you walked over hard-crusted snow. It was his childhood. Not a happy childhood, but at least it'd been clean. Not filled with dust, gun oil, sweat, and sand.

Still, he missed the real war. Everything felt so natural when he was among the other men. He knew the shape of each day. What was expected of him. How he would make his bed, care for his equipment, joke with Collin and the others, run through the day's guard-duty schedule, bodyguard mission, or whatever it was. And sometimes their extra missions, the stuff that was too dangerous or too dirty for the official forces. The raids in the suburbs, the villages, the small communities where the enemy gathered, prayed to their god, and hoped for luck in war. Niklas knew why he'd become a soldier. It was a meaningful life. A life with dignity.

He drove over the bridge to Dalarö. Took a left by the sign: Smådalarö. A twisting road along the water. There were boats pulled up and protected by wood structures and tarps. It was one o'clock. Darkness would fall in less than two and a half hours. Sweden is a strange country, he thought. During the winter, you live in the dark for more than half the time.

He continued on. Golf courses, pine forest, private drives that branched out from the road and probably led to flashy summer homes. Niklas'd memorized the map and the aerial photos that he'd downloaded from Google Earth.

Six hundred and fifty feet left.

The small turnoff was blocked by a black metal gate. He stopped the car. There was a camera and a big sign on one side of the gate: PRIVATE PROPERTY. GUARDED BY G4S. They could guard as much as they liked.

He parked by a small forest road. Walked back through the woods. His boots clucked through the wet underbrush.

After a few minutes: a metal fence. Nearly seven feet high—like an industrial fence except without any barbed wire along the top—but not impossible to climb over. Still: there could be surveillance cameras. He walked along the fence, arrived at the gate after a few yards. Now he knew. Walked back along the fence, up into the woods. Lucky that the leaves'd fallen off the trees. After 330 feet or so, he glimpsed buildings beyond the trees.

He pulled out his binoculars. The main building was easy to see. Three floors. Pillars around the entrance. Crazy castle style. Gravel in front, a parked car. Next to the big house: a building that looked like a garage and a smaller outbuilding, maybe a stable, maybe a barn. He pointed the binoculars at the big house. Could see an entrance. He counted the windows, estimated the number of rooms, the height of each level.

Continued along the fence, his eyes locked on the trees behind it. He didn't see any cameras. Looked closer at the fence posts and ground mounts. Concluded: no electricity. No motion sensors. It would be easy to get through.

After another few yards, the fence began to curve. Now he could see the house clearly, just 130 feet off on the other side. Hardly any trees. He picked up the binoculars again. The back of the house. There was another entrance there. He eyed the lock, what material the door was made of, tried to calculate where it led to. He could see straight in through a couple of rooms. A kitchen, a dining room, some kind of living room. He could clearly see motion sensors in the corners, in the ceilings, in the rooms.

He continued around the back. Estimated the distance, the possibility of climbing in through the windows. He needed answers to two big questions. First of all: Where would the target be located on the night of the attack? Second of all: Would the security staff be heavily armed?

They should be able to calculate the answer to the first question. Figure out the floor plan. The party would be in the largest room. Phallic compensation on this scale must've demanded more building permits and authorization than the entire Söderleden highway. The application documents for all those building permits must be in the county archives. And those kinds of documents were public information.

He was a fucking genius.

Question number two might prove more difficult. But maybe Mahmud could get some information.

On his way home, he saw images in his mind. Instead of scenes from Iraq: the attack against the house. The familiar rat-tat-tat from assault rifles mixed with the sound of glass shards crashing down on the ground. The panic in the eyes of those horndogs. Himself in full gear, battle rattle.

It would become a killing zone.

With pleasure.

51

There was too much information. Where should he begin? How would he possibly understand it all? He tried to grasp what was relevant, and what was just false leads. How did one carry out this kind of investigation? Dammit, the Palme Group'd probably had fifteen people working on it full time for over twenty years, without getting anywhere. How would Thomas Andrén, by himself, alone, hunted—above all, a patrol officer—do this?

Still: Thomas'd gotten certain information. Adamsson's surveillance group'd met in Skogsbacken AB's office space in the eighties. The company was owned by Sven Bolinder. The deal: in the bugs from Rantzell's basement, Thomas'd found documents that had to do with none other than Skogsbacken AB—one annual report, a few payment orders and verifications. The conclusion was clear as day: there was a connection—past, present.

Sven Bolinder: well-known multimillionaire, finance shark, player on the black market. Maker of spare parts for the car industry, supplier of retail services. But apparently also a whore hound, a john shepherd, an arranger of so-called finer events. Bolinder was suspected of being the chief owner of a business empire that included over twenty-five companies in seven countries. And the white-collar-crime cops Thomas'd spoken to probably didn't even know the half of it.

Thomas worked like a maniac. Continued to go to the traffic unit for show and for access to the databases. Continued to work nights at the club: with a new fire inside—there were connections to the investigation here as well. Thomas inquired, inspected, investigated Ratko without the Yugo understanding what he was doing. Apparently, Bolinder usually invited his friends to a party twice a year. Always when his wife was abroad. And it was the Yugos, along with some finer party boys, who arranged the revelry.

Thomas continued to try to work through the material from Rantzell's basement. Over and over again. With increased effort, concentration, organization. More focus on Skogsbacken AB. How long'd the company existed, what exactly did the business comprise, who was on the board, what did the ownership structure look like, where were the bank accounts? There was a lot that wasn't in the bags, but he learned as he went along. The Swedish Companies Registration Office, the National Tax Authority, annual reports, details about the companies' operations. He worked as methodically as he could. But really, he probably needed help. At the same time: something just had to surface soon.

He'd read a book about the Palme murder by a journalist, Lars Borgnäs. There was a connection, in theory. The investigators' tunnel vision'd steered their view of the murderer and the murder of the prime minister. It'd also steered their vision of another important detail: the weapon.

Borgnäs described the theory in detail. In the same way that they'd gotten stuck on the idea that it'd been Christer Pettersson or possibly some other lone lunatic who snuffed out Palme, they'd zeroed in on a single hypothesis when it came to what kind of gun was used and, therefore, what kind of gun'd been sought. Things locked into place pretty much right after the murder. The national chief of police, Hans Holmér, appeared at a press conference where he held up a couple of guns. They were all the same caliber: .357 Magnums. "What we know now," Holmér apparently said, "is that the murder weapon with all certainty was a Smith &Wesson revolver, .357 caliber." There were a few other, less common makes that were also under consideration, the chief of police explained. But most likely, it was a Smith & Wesson. And it was completely clear that a Magnum revolver, .357 caliber, was what'd been used. After that, all investigative work regarding the weapon was carried out with the assumption that it had to be a .357 caliber Magnum. The Palme weapon became synonymous with a Magnum revolver. Thomas tried to remember. He and everyone he knew'd always assumed that the murder weapon was a Magnum.

But, according to Borgnäs, the truth was different. And it wasn't only him—most weapons experts agreed with him. The murder weapon *could* have been of that caliber, but it *could also* have been of a completely different caliber. But no other type of weapon had been searched for, even though they were more common than the Magnum revolver.

The connection was in the murder weapon. Rantzell was the one who'd tied Christer Pettersson to a revolver that probably didn't even have anything to do with the Palme murder. Rantzell'd planted it all nicely. The revolver, the time, the opportunity. Framed Pettersson as the murderer. And now someone'd murdered Rantzell. Maybe someone who didn't want the fake connection to come to light.

Åsa wondered what was going on. They saw less and less of each other. Thomas was always tired—the bags under his eyes looked like black bruises. The people from the adoption agency were coming for another home visit. The final one before Sander.

"We have to make things even cozier here so they can see that we care. That we're nesting."

Thomas sighed. "What does 'nesting' even mean?"

"You know, to prepare the nest for a child."

"But we can't set up the baby room before we actually get Sander, can we?"

"Yes, we have to take care of that now. So that they see that we know how and that we want a child here. We should buy a stroller and enroll in that parenting class, too."

Thomas shook his head. Åsa turned her face away. Pulled her hair back in that way she always did when she was sad. They tried to talk it through. From Thomas's perspective: he wanted nothing more than to bring the boy home, that was his dream. But right now he didn't have time to really get involved.

The feeling lingered: this wasn't good, this wasn't good at all.

He went out to the garage. Glanced at the Cadillac. It'd been weeks since he'd even touched it. Same thing with the shooting club—he hadn't been there since he'd seen Ljunggren. It was strange: as if his entire life'd been turned upside down. He'd dived into the investigation in a way that he'd never done before. It was scary. He climbed into his regular car. The garage door opened automatically.

He drove to the station. Listened to Springsteen. Tried to collect his thoughts.

He arrived. The garage in the police station. The only advantage of the traffic unit: your own garage.

Thomas climbed out of the car. Breathed in the smell of exhaust that never really aired out properly. The fluorescent lights gave off a pale glow. The concrete looked grainy, almost like wood. He heard his own footsteps. Eyed the parked cars: tried to calculate which of his colleagues'd already arrived at work.

He heard footsteps behind him. The door to the stairwell was sixty-five feet farther off. Thomas began to search for the key card in his pocket.

The steps behind him sped up. Thomas slowed down, didn't see a reason not to wait for a colleague who was clearly in a rush.

But something was wrong. The footsteps were too fast. Thomas turned around. Saw too late: a man with a ski mask over his face. He was wearing dark clothes. Thomas didn't have time to react. The man came charging at him, holding something in his right hand. A gun. Thomas flash evaluated: maybe a Colt, maybe a Beretta.

"Stay where you are," the man said in a clear voice.

Thomas tried to read the situation. There was nothing he could do. The muzzle of the gun, in a steady grip. This was a pro.

The man pointed him toward a darker corner of the garage. Where the overhead lights weren't working.

"What the fuck do you want?"

"You know what I want. Stop snooping around." The man's low voice—he was almost whispering.

"Forget it. I'm not afraid of you. I've recorded the interrogations I've done with multiple people, just so you know."

"Don't talk so fucking much. If you're not afraid now, you will be soon. Stop snooping. This is the last time you'll be getting this message."

"Fuck you."

Thomas felt something hard hit him over the head. As he fell toward the concrete floor he had time to think: You shouldn't hit someone with a weapon that nice. Weapons like that are made for shooting.

Then he hit the hardness below.

Thomas opened one eye. The other eye. Breathed in the smell of exhaust. The man was gone. He brought a hand to his forehead. The blood was sticky.

A vibration in his jacket pocket. Then the ringer on his cell phone. He just didn't want to answer right now. But still: he had to get his phone out either way, in order to call for help.

A familiar voice on the other end of the line. It was Hägerström.

"Hiya Andrén, sorry for not calling you back."

Thomas was completely taken aback. For a moment, he forgot his current situation.

"Hägerström. I'm glad you're calling. Sorry for being such a dick last time."

"No worries. How is everything?" Hägerström sounded happy.

Thomas considered. Should he tell him that he was lying beat up like an idiot in the police station garage? No. Yes. The answer: Yes—now was the time. He couldn't continue working alone any longer.

"Not so good, actually," he said. "I was just threatened and assaulted by a masked man."

"You're joking? Are you all right?"

"Yes, it's true, and no, I'm not completely okay. But it's nothing alarming, either."

"Are you sure?"

"I'm sure."

"But why?"

"I'll tell you later. We have to meet up. As soon as possible. When are you available?"

"Let's say the day after tomorrow. But are you sure that you're all right?"

Thomas tried to truly evaluate. His forehead was pounding, but it didn't seem to be bleeding anymore. "I'll be fine," he said. "Nothing too serious. So, I'll see you the day after tomorrow?"

"Absolutely. There's just one more thing I want to tell you."

"What?"

"Adamsson is dead."

52

It'd been easy to rope Niklas into the job. Yeah, the dude was strange somehow, but Mahmud couldn't think of a better partner for this gig.

A few days after Mahmud'd told him the address, Niklas'd already been out at the house on Smådalarö and done some reconnaissance. A real pro: he'd brought binoculars, a range finder, a camera with a serious lens. Taken photos of the house from all angles, zoomed in through the windows, snapped close-ups of the fence, the locks, the alarm systems, the gate, the distance from the windows to the ground.

According to Mahmud: the house was the perfect place to rob. It was just like when he, Babak, and Rob'd stormed that Ecstasy junkie's apartment. Once they were inside, no one would bother them. No one would discover them from the outside. But this would be an even better home invasion: they'd be walking into a fucking prostitute party—no risk that anyone'd be calling the 5-0. It was genius.

The Yugos were gonna taste his fat cock. The nasty old johns were gonna get hit hard. Mahmud was gonna get the easiest money in town. Rastafari Jah! That little Sunny Sunday'd changed his life. Jorge was the king, man.

After this, all the running around to Shurgard storage units would be over, he wouldn't have to poon-nanny anymore, wouldn't have to sling any more shit. He was so fed up with Dejan, Ratko, Stefanovic, and the other cunts that just hearing their names made him feel sick. The hit against Smådalarö would be the last thing he did. Honest, he was gonna listen to Erika Ewaldsson, his dad, and his big sis. Use Jorge's money to start something clean. Something honest. Something that fit into *Suedi* society.

He and Niklas'd met twice. Studied maps and floor plans that Niklas'd gotten ahold of. Dude had mad Tom Lehtimäki–style skillz. Actually, more than that: hard-core Special Forces shit. Mahmud felt like fucking SEAL Team Six.

They studied the house from above. Checked out the roads, height differences in the terrain, the way the forest grew in the area. It was winter now: no dense trees would hide them. They analyzed where they could put out caltrops, if they'd need a distraction—maybe torch the garage or some other side building.

The architectural drawings of the house were even cooler. Niklas'd gotten them from the county offices. Sweden was weird—you could basically get anything out of a public institution. Magical transparency. The house was big, more than five thousand square feet. Massive kitchen, dining room, spa area in the basement, gym, living rooms, bedrooms, guest bedrooms, walk-in closets. Questions: What was the best way to get into the house? Where might there be surveillance or guards on duty? Which doors would be locked and which would be open? The biggest question of all: Which room would the pussy party be in? They compared the blueprints with the photos that Niklas'd snapped. Identified the rooms, saw the interiors through Niklas's camera lens. Could cross some rooms off the list. The johns were not likely to be in the kitchen, not in the dining room. More likely: the big living room, the spa area, maybe the guest rooms. It depended on what kind of event this was really gonna be. Mahmud had to try to do some snooping on his end.

They discussed how many bodies they needed. Niklas wouldn't budge: he and Mahmud would never pull it off alone. It messed with Mahmud's line of thinking, but he didn't protest. They evaluated alternatives for weapons. Niklas had sick know-how. It was almost scary— what'd this player done in his previous life? Assault weapons, laser sights, night vision. Maybe they would need a grenade, flak jackets, proper dark clothes that they could burn when it was all over. This was gonna be done right. Beautiful.

They planned, chatted, fantasized. Strategized, made lists, memorized the photos, the terrain, the maps. Tried to visualize the different stages of the attack, understand the dangers. Still: they knew too little. Mahmud also had to go out to the house and look around. Niklas wanted to go out there again too. At night.

Again: he was weird. Used military terminology like a crazy commando or something. Rattled off a bunch of abbreviations, tactical terminology, weapon vocab that totally blindsided Mahmud. At the same time: he was perfect.

They ended their last meeting with homework. Mahmud was gonna get weapons and bolt cutters and talk to some guys he trusted, see if they wanted in. Niklas was responsible for clothes, bulletproof vests, night-vision goggles, grenades, and caltrops.

As Niklas said: It was gonna be a killing zone.

Mad *Call of Duty* shit.

53

It was as though Niklas was in a trance. His thoughts wouldn't stop spinning. His sleep was reduced to brief moments of rest between planning sessions on the computer, time spent in the woods around the house on Smådalarö or in front of the tapes from the surveillance cameras he'd mounted in the trees around the house. His mantra rhymed: don't loiter, reconnoiter.

Patric Ngono was on hold—the whore parties were so much bigger. Abusive men in action at a high level. Society's absolute deterioration in relief. The filth that invaded society would be dealt with, cleaned up, driven out.

Benjamin'd stopped calling. That was a relief. When Niklas was done with this, he would teach that traitor a lesson. Mahmud'd done him a big favor by talking to the guy. Benjamin must understand that Niklas wasn't alone.

He couldn't bring himself to answer Mom's calls or texts. She wouldn't understand, anyway. The same thought kept coming back: He was doing all of this for her.

He didn't go running. Didn't even train with the knife.

This was the last stretch, the finish, the final sprint.

The surveillance cameras did provide some interesting information. The security company visited the house a few times every week. Neither Sven Bolinder—the guy who lived in the house—or his wife seemed to be home too often. But Niklas had a feeling that there'd be a whole lot more security on D-Day. The question was how it would be handled.

Mahmud'd also gotten hold of certain information. The Yugos usually ran the security operation with their own men. But it was unclear what that meant. He didn't know if they were armed. If they wore bulletproof vests. If they were trained for war.

And: Mahmud'd started to understand how this so-called luxury event went down. There was going to be a big party; a couple of party planners took care of the food, bartenders, a dance floor. Spruced up the women. Niklas studied the blueprints of the house. Came to some conclusions. Guessed: party ground zero ought to be the big living room along one of the house's short ends, on the ground floor.

Everything was going according to plan. But it would take time for the Arab to get weapons. As long as he didn't mess that stuff up. Maybe Niklas should take care of that himself? At the same time: Mahmud'd assured him that his contacts were legit. And Niklas didn't like dealing with the chick at the Black & White Inn.

He took care of his own homework right away. Ordered equipment online. Now all he had to do was wait—like an Advent calendar: count down, day by day. Four weeks, then it was time. Bolinder's event was being held on New Year's Eve. Operation Magnum would reach a crescendo.

A few snowflakes'd fallen during the night, but they soon melted. Niklas thought about tears on a bone-hard cheek. A face that'd been forced into resilience. Like the black tarmac when it gleamed in the winter darkness.

Niklas was on his way home from the mansion. Eighth time he'd been out there. He knew the area now. The terrain felt like the patches of grass in Axelsberg where he'd grown up. He'd identified the ultimate way in. There needed to be four to six people for the attack, depending on the number of security personnel. The question was if Mahmud would be able to scrounge up that many boots.

He thought back on his time in Sweden since his return. The whole world was at war. The trick was to see where the front lines were drawn. People abroad thought that Sweden was so peaceful, happy, perfect. It was actually worse than that—even people in Sweden thought harmony reigned. That was bullshit. If you scratched the surface, it was rat shit through and through.

He got on the highway at Handen. Not a lot of cars out. Maybe he should call Mom after all? Images flashed through his mind. Claes Rantzell. Mats Strömberg. Roger Jonsson. Sometimes the opposition was victorious after all.

Nynäsvägen. Down to Södra Länken, the highway. Toward Årsta. There was some kind of artwork around the entrance to the tunnel.

It almost felt magical. Like a blue light that lit up the entire upper part of the tunnel. Between the two entrances to the tunnel: lots of small lights, like stars with a large orb in the center. Maybe a celestial body. He thought, Yet another hole in life. He fell into his usual line of thought. The basic pillar of civilization was its cavities, the holes. It was strange. Society was dependent on its tunnels, pipes, garbage chutes, cables, holes. But all that just underscored the reality. No matter how good something looked on the surface, the truth was to be found in the holes.

Niklas drove through Årsta. Turned on Hägerstensvägen. Almost home. He felt tired. But still not. His thoughts kept him awake. Like constant adrenaline kicks.

He couldn't find a parking spot near his building, had to park four blocks away. Left the duffel with the equipment in the car; he could leave it there until the next time he went out to Smådalarö. It would be soon.

He slammed the car door shut. Walked toward his building.

The glow from the streetlights made the tarmac glitter again. His breath was billowing like smoke.

He pushed in the key code. Opened the door.

Stepped inside. Flipped the light switch.

He stared into the barrels of four MP5s.

Someone yelled, "Hands up, Brogren! You're under arrest!"

Four cops from the SWAT team. Suited up like they were on the front line: black clothes, vests, helmets, visors—the whole shebang. Smaller-model police assault rifles, pointed at him. Behind him, more cops were pouring in. Snapped handcuffs on him. Pushed him to the ground. It was too late. Too late to think. He was arrested.

He wondered what for.

* * *

K0202-2008-30493

INTERROGATION OF NIKLAS BROGREN, NR 2

December 7, 10:05-11:00
Present: The suspect, Niklas Brogren (NB), Interrogator Stig H. Ronander (INT), Public Defender Jörn Burtig (JB)

INT: Hi, Niklas. First, I want to inform you that we are recording this as usual. Just so you know.

NB: Okay.

INT: Good. Let's get going, then. I will begin by informing you of the charges against you. You are suspected of murder, or, in the alternative, accessory to murder, on June 2 of this year.

NB: I don't know anything about that. I'm innocent.

INT: Okay. Well then, maybe you can tell us a little bit about what you did that day?

JB: Wait a minute. The suspected crime must be specified in order for my client to discuss the accusations against him.

INT: What do you want specified?

JB: It's not enough for you just to name a type of crime. What is it exactly that you believe Niklas has done? And where?

INT: Was that not clear by what I just said?

JB: No. How is he expected to know what it is you think he did?

INT: I think it's pretty clear. But I'll give it another try. Niklas Brogren, you are suspected of murdering or aiding in the murder of Claes Rantzell on the night of June 2 of this year, in a basement at 10 Gösta Ekman Road in Axelsberg. Is Mr. Burtig happy now?

JB: Hm . . . (inaudible)

INT: So, Niklas, what do you have to say?

NB: I know who Claes Rantzell is. But I did not murder him. I wasn't even at Gösta Ekman Road that night.

INT: So, you are denying it?

NB: I'm denying it.

INT: Can you tell us what you were doing on June 2?

NB: Yes, hm . . . (inaudible)

INT: Perhaps you remember something, even though it was a long time ago. You said you weren't at that address. That much you remember.

NB: But I've already told you. I think I was at a job interview during the day. I had just arrived back in Sweden after a few years abroad. Then I met up with an old friend in the evening. His name is Benjamin Berg. I have his number in my phone. And I told you that too, the last time I was called in for questioning. Haven't you talked to him?

INT: That's right, we have.

NB: Okay. So, what else do you want to know?

INT: Why don't you keep telling us about what you did that night? In a little more detail.

NB: It's a while ago, so I probably can't remember all the details. But we watched a movie. I think it was *The Godfather*. It's pretty long, so we ate too. I got there at around seven o'clock, and that's when we went and rented the movie. We started watching it pretty much right when we got back, I think. Watched the first two hours, or something. Then we ordered pizza that I went to pick up. We ate and finished watching the movie. That's how it was.

INT: Well, what did you do after watching the movie?

NB: I stayed at Benjamin's place for a few hours. We drank some beer and talked about old times. We're friends from school. But you can check all that with him. Didn't you already do that? He can confirm everything. Why exactly am I here?

JB: Yes, that is a legitimate question. Niklas apparently has an alibi for the night in question.

INT: We've brought Benjamin in for questioning before. But I don't intend to recount that interrogation now. It is classified under pretrial confidentiality, as Mr. Burtig surely can explain to you.

JB: Yes, but my client must have the opportunity to defend himself against your allegations. This is a question of very serious charges. If he is not permitted to know the information that Benjamin Berg has given, he doesn't have a chance. He has an alibi.

INT: I think he has had the opportunity to tell us about the night in question today. So that's not what this is about. On the other hand, I wanted to tell you that we have interrogated your mother. Niklas, do you have anything to say about that?

NB: No. She knows who Claes Rantzell is, too. He was her old boyfriend.

INT: That's right, she told us that. Do you think there is something else she might have told us—about that night this summer, so to speak?

NB: No, not about this. What would that be?

INT: I will make this brief. What she said does not correspond with what you have told me today.

NB: Why not? In what way?

INT: I am not going to go into that now. But the prosecutor will order you detained, just so you know. We believe we have enough information on you.

NB: Then I have nothing more to say.

INT: Nothing?

NB: Absolutely nothing. I'm not going to say anything.

PART 4

(Three weeks later)

54

Three weeks'd passed since the attack in the parking garage—still, the thoughts revisited him at least once an hour. Not just because the attack itself'd been so scary—he'd experienced worse violence before—but because of how big this snowball he'd started'd grown. This wasn't just about a threat against him, it wasn't even just about Sweden's most famous murder—it was about a goddamned conspiracy in the middle of his own home: the National Police. And he had no idea how to stop it.

Months ago, when someone'd been standing outside his house that night, he'd been able to push his fear away into some corner of himself. Reacted like he always reacted: let the worry dissolve into cynicism and denial. His goals were more important. He was driven by anger. He was driven by the thought that reflection equaled capitulation. And when he'd begun to understand the connections to the Palme murder, he was also driven by a strange feeling—some kind of duty to his old man and to Sweden. But now, after the assault, and after Hägerström's phone call about Adamsson, he no longer knew if he should allow himself to be driven at all.

Adamsson'd died in a car accident on the E18 highway, by the Stäket rest stop. According to Hägerström, the investigation showed that the guy'd driven into the middle divider and bounced back out into the lane. That's when a forty-ton trailer truck made mush of Adamsson's Land Rover. Maybe it was a coincidence, maybe it was part of something bigger.

Something would happen to him, with all certainty. He could live with that thought. But the second thought was harder: it could happen to Åsa. The third thought almost crushed him: it could happen to the child that they still hadn't been given, Sander.

Still: let whatever was going to happen, happen. Thomas couldn't think of any alternatives. He had to keep searching.

He talked to his brother, Jan. They didn't really have too great of a relationship. Worn down after too many years of silence. The only thing that still made it feel like they were brothers was the irritation: it was different from what you felt toward a stranger. But they still cared for each other, sent postcards from their vacations, Christmas greetings, and birthday cards. Thomas'd made sure that he and Åsa were invited over to Jan's house for Christmas Eve.

The next night, Christmas Day, he went up to speak with Åsa. The TV was on: some documentary about right-wing extremists in Russia. They looked fat and stupid, the lot of them. He wondered why they were showing such tragic shit today of all days.

She was sitting with her legs pulled up on the couch. On the coffee table was the folder that was so often in front of her these days, the one with the pictures of Sander.

The adoption agency's final home visit a week ago'd gone well. It felt like the women who'd come by thought that Åsa and Thomas were well prepared to receive a small child. Åsa'd decorated the house more than usual for Christmas this year. Maybe to show off for the adoption agency women, maybe in preparation for the family life they would soon have.

She looked up. The Russians on the TV show babbled on in the background about how the motherland's property was being sold off to foreigners.

"It was really very nice yesterday, at Jan's," Åsa said.

Thomas took a deep breath. "Åsa, we have a difficult decision ahead of us."

She was breathing with her mouth open; it looked pretty dumb.

Thomas went on, "Sander will be here soon. It's going to be the best moment of our lives."

She smiled. Nodded. Continued to flip through the folder—uninterested in Thomas again. Almost as though she was trying to say, I agree with you, now leave.

"I don't want to ruin that moment," Thomas said. "And I don't want to jeopardize it either. So we have to make certain changes. Together."

Åsa's smile faded.

"I am in the middle of a bad situation right now. A dangerous situation. It's an investigation I'm involved with. Do you remember that Internal Affairs guy I was complaining about before?"

Åsa looked uncomprehending.

Thomas felt himself twist uncomfortably. "He and I are mixed up in something that I can't handle, and the National Police can't either. There are people who are out to get me on a personal level. Who have threatened to hurt me and who have already attacked me."

"Why haven't you said anything?"

"I didn't want to worry you. Not now when Sander is coming and everything. But it's gone too far now. And I can't stop. I have to keep going, get to the bottom of this thing. There is no one else who can take over."

"Can't we get some sort of protection?"

"We can't get enough protection. This is the price you have to pay as a police officer. I am so damn sorry. If it'd just been about me it would've been okay, but now it involves you, too. It might involve Sander too, when he gets here."

"But there's got to be some protection we can get. There's got to be help for police officers involved in dangerous investigations. Right?"

"I'm sure that exists, but it won't help now."

"But it's Christmastime!"

"That's never mattered less."

"What do you mean?"

"What I said. The police can't help us now. Christmas won't stop anyone. No one can stop what I'm involved in."

She sat in silence. Thomas waited for her to say something. Instead, she flipped through the folder.

"You can stay with Jan for a few weeks, until this is all over," he said. "And if it isn't over in two months, then we can't bring Sander here. That would be too dangerous."

She didn't say anything.

"Åsa, I'm just as upset about this as you are. But there is no other solution."

The industrial area by Liljeholmen. Hägerström's car was parked facing the water. Thomas's car was parked next to him, but facing in the opposite direction. It was already dark out. Hägerström rolled down his window first.

"So, how was Christmas Eve?"

"We were at my brother's place. They have a huge family. Tons of kids everywhere, dogs, cats, even a hamster. It was the first time I celebrated Christmas with him in more than fifteen years. How about you?"

"I was at my parents' place, then I went to Half Way Inn. You been there?"

"Once or twice. It's near the police station in Södermalm, right? The one that's next door to that gay place?"

"That's right. My haunt. Not the gay place, that is."

"Maybe I should've come?"

"You're welcome next year."

"Next year I'll have my own family. Hopefully no hamster, though." Hägerström looked unhappy.

"How long do we have to meet up like this?" he said. "We'd work better if we had some proper place to be."

Thomas nodded. "I've sent Åsa away now. So I feel better, safer."

"Damn, how'd it go?"

"Felt like shit. But I think she understood. We can meet up at my house later."

"Good."

Thomas turned up the heat even more. There was half an inch of snow on the hood of the car.

"So, what do we have to discuss today?"

Hägerström leaned out through the open window. "I actually have a whole lot to tell you. I was at work today and heard some talk in the hallway. They've arrested someone for the murder of Rantzell."

Thomas felt himself stop breathing for a few seconds.

"His name is Niklas Brogren, the one I brought in for informational questioning a few months ago. The guy had a good alibi then. But it's starting to fall apart. He said he'd been at a friend's house the entire night of the murder, until late. The friend's been in for questioning and confirms that Brogren was there, but the investigator is skeptical about his testimony. Apparently, the guy seems disjointed and stressed out. But the most important part is that the mother has started talking. She says that Niklas Brogren came home pretty early that night and that he was drunk and in a bad mood. You know how it is with alibis, either you have one or else you're really deep in the shit 'cause you tried to lie."

"Hm."

"You sound skeptical."

"That Niklas guy doesn't have anything to do with what we're looking at."

"No, but his mom had a long-term relationship with Rantzell at the end of the eighties and the beginning of the nineties. So there are some connections and possible motives."

"So, what's the motive?"

"Rantzell apparently beat the mother."

"How do they know that?"

"I guess the investigators ordered old medical records and stuff like that, I know I would've. They say she had to go to the hospital several times, sometimes with fractures."

"Damn."

"You can say that again."

Thomas sighed. "Maybe I'm too set on our lead, but I don't know. It just sounds too easy, that the son of an old battered woman is out for revenge. Like some pathetic crime thriller. The past visits the present, all that crap. But that's never the way things are in reality."

"I've got the same gut feeling. But what the hell. There's a lot pointing at this Niklas Brogren. Except the forensic lab hasn't found any matches."

Thomas took a deep breath. "I don't think we should end our project."

"Absolutely not. But what does it give us? Adamsson died, but there's nothing pointing to anything shady about it. Wisam Jibril died and we can't get any further there. We haven't gotten hold of Ballénius. What do we have, exactly? You've got a bunch of documents at home that we haven't been able to get anything substantial from. You've tricked and forced answers out of a few old cops that suggest they're right-wing extremists. So? It doesn't lead anywhere."

"Stop it, Martin. We have a lot. But so far, nothing that points to the actual murderer. But soon we'll have gone through all the documents from Rantzell's basement—I never would've been able to do it without you—and there are lots of weird things there. Lots of names of people to interrogate, companies to take a closer look at, payment streams to follow."

It was true. Thomas and Hägerström'd divided the document piles between them. Thomas'd already gone through a bunch of it, but there was still too much he didn't understand. They had to do it together. Hägerström knew numbers and finance stuff—explained as well as he could, but it wasn't enough. The sheer amount of information almost felt overwhelming. All the numbers, addresses, names. They worked methodically. Thomas sorted and structured the material, Hägerström analyzed it. They were using a point system of their own divising. Graded the level of suspicion for the information they were investigating. Made lists of people, telephone numbers, company names. Created an order of priority: everything that pointed to a connection between Rantzell and Bolinder's company, everything that pointed to a connection between Skogsbacken AB and something illegal.

So far, no traces led to Adamsson. But there was still so much they hadn't gone through.

"It's going to take us several months. Maybe years," Hägerström said. "You can't have Åsa living somewhere else for that long, and if they find out that I'm involved, I'll have to look around for another job pretty quick. That won't work. We need a breakthrough soon or else we'll have to drop it and let the prosecutor nail that Brogren guy. Anyway, if you ask me, it doesn't seem improbable that he did it."

Thomas was breathing through his nostrils. The winter cold pushed down into his lungs. Filled him even though it was still warm in the car. He wasn't going to bother commenting on whether Brogren was the murderer or not.

"I'm going to keep at it, in any case. I believe in our lead, even if it seems fuzzy right now. And there's a particular lead we have to follow up on. We have to find Ballénius. He knows something, I can feel it. An old fox like that wouldn't have acted the way he did at Solvalla if not for something special. He knows something."

The Stockholmers were running around, harried as they made exchanges, returned Christmas gifts, and did post-Christmas shopping while, at the same time, everyone was trying to rest up and be on vacation. Thomas talked to Åsa a million times a day. She was sitting at home at Jan's house with all the animals, bored. She was maybe going to spend New Year's Eve with some friends and wanted him to come. He couldn't say no to everything. Thankfully: what Åsa was most worried about was how she would hide the fact that she was staying with her brother-in-law from her friends at the New Year's party. That felt like the biggest triviality ever.

Thomas'd scaled back work at the club while still doing his utmost to find facts on Bolinder. He spoke with cop acquaintances. Searched on the Internet. Asked Jonas Nilsson for help again—he was going to ask his older colleagues. Went to a library and asked to look through the newspaper archive. He asked around at the club. "Bolinder," Ratko said. "Why are you so interested in him all the time?" After that, Thomas lay low at the club for a few days.

It was Sunday. High, clear blue sky, for once. The air was crisp. Thomas and Hägerström were standing outside the entrance to Solvalla. The day's race was called the Silver Horse. It was a high-class V75 championship with a trophy statuette shaped like a royal silver horse as icing on the cake. The place would be packed with people. Ballénius ought to be there. This time, they wouldn't lose him.

Agria pet insurance was still dominating the ad space. The excitement in the air was almost as thick as the mashed potatoes on the old guys' steak platters. But there were fewer people outside than the last time Thomas'd been there—the colder weather was sending people indoors.

They worked their way through the outdoor crowd. Even though Thomas was certain that Ballénius wouldn't be there, he wanted to be sure.

Ballénius wasn't there.

They went into Ströget, the sports bar. Pretty much the same crowd with their jackets still on, just like last time. Definitely the same bacon chips in the bar. Mostly younger dudes here, downing burgers and beer. They wouldn't find Ballénius here, he was certain.

Thomas eyed Hägerström; he looked nervous. Or else he was just tense, on alert. Double emotions: Thomas was grateful that the ex-IA guy was with him. At the same time, he was ashamed—hoped no old colleagues would see them together.

They moved on, up to the Bistro. The entrance was crammed with Finnish gypsies. Thomas pushed his way through. Walked up to the bar. He recognized the Danish restaurant boss with the beer gut whom he'd talked to last time. It looked like the beer gut'd swelled somewhat. He got the Dane's attention. Asked his questions. The Dane shook his head—sorry, he didn't know anything. Thomas asked for Sami Kiviniemi, the man who'd pointed Thomas to the right floor last time. But the Finn wasn't there. So far, their Solvalla lead was worthless.

Thomas and Hägerström took the escalator up toward the Congress. The names of the horses that'd won the big championship were printed on the wall, year by year. Gum Ball, Remington Crown, Gidde Palema.

Before they walked into the Congress, Hägerström looked at Thomas.

"Are you armed, Andrén?"

He patted the front of his jacket. Felt the SIG Sauer through the fabric.

"Even though I'm just a traffic cop these days, I'm still the best shot in the Southern District."

Hägerström smiled a little. Then he said, "It's probably best if I stay by the entrance, right? You go in, because you'll recognize him. If the old guy tries the same thing as last time, I'll be a brick wall up here."

Thomas nodded.

Hägerström continued, "And you call my cell as soon as you go in. It'll be our own little radio that no one will look twice at."

Hägerström seemed competent. Thomas tried to relax, walked into the Congress Bar and Restaurant. He held the phone in his left hand. Positioned himself at the top of the room. Tried to see down into the bleachers. Looked around. All the tables looked completely booked. He reported to Hägerström, "I don't see him. But it's big in here. Probably four hundred people at the tables."

He began walking along the top row. His head constantly turned toward the tables farther down. People were loving the race, their attention was directed fiercely on the track. The voice over the loudspeaker in the venue sounded worked up: a high-odds horse was apparently about to win. Eighty feet farther off, he saw Table 118. Ballénius's favorite spot. The place where Thomas'd found the old guy last.

Four people were sitting at the table. He could only see two of them head-on: a woman with massive lips that had to be fake, and a man in his thirties who was almost standing up in excitement over the action on the track. Thomas only saw the backs of the two others at the table. One of them could be Ballénius. Tall, thin.

He took a step closer. It would make things easier if the man didn't turn around.

Closer. Thirty feet left. Thin, gray hair—it could definitely be him. Closer.

He spoke to Hägerström, "I'm twenty feet away from a man who could be him."

Thomas approached the table. Saw the guy head on.

Reminded him of Mr. Bean, except with gray hair.

It was definitely not Ballénius.

55

There were three reasons Mahmud took the job seriously: Jorge was a cool cat—Mahmud could feel it in his entire body. He and the Latino shared the same attitude, the same agenda. On top of that: Mahmud really wanted to fuck those Yugo cunts, show them that they couldn't just play an Arab with honor any which way. There were rules, even for those who stood outside the law. Finally: it was mad exciting—an ill special-ops gig that could lead to some sick cheddar.

He'd been to see Erika Ewaldsson for the last time today. She'd led him into her office as usual. The mess, the blinds, the coffee cups—everything was the same as always. Except for one thing: she was speaking more slowly than she normally did. And she almost looked a little angry. Not like her—a pissy Erika sat still and didn't peep. Not like today: babbled on, but still looked unhappy.

Then he had a different thought. Maybe she wasn't pissed off. Maybe she was sad. Motherfucker, it sounded shadyish, but maybe she was gonna miss him. The longer he sat there and listened to her drone, the more obvious it became. She didn't like that this was their last meeting. But it was even stranger: Mahmud felt funny too, like sad or something. Shit, Erika was kinda okay after all. He beat the thought away. Tried to picture Erika in front of him naked instead, coax his inner chuckle. She always wore baggy clothes. She wasn't thin, but was she really that chunky? Her tits might still be nice. Her ass was wide, but maybe it gave her sick curves. No laughs—the opposite. Didn't suit a G like him. But finally, he grinned to himself. Between her legs: she just had to rock a crazy Queen of Spades, major bush. Sooo *Suedi*.

The meeting was over.

"Okay then, Mahmud, we won't be seeing each other again. How do you feel about that? Strange?"

What? She was the one who thought it was sad. He didn't care.

"It's cool. You'll probably see me on TV when I'm a millionaire."

Erika smiled. "I thought you already were a millionaire, that's what you usually say."

"Yeah, sure I'm a Millionaire, a child of the Million Program. Did you people really think that was gonna work? Pile all of us into a bunch of towers out in the concrete?"

You could see it in Erika's eyes again: she wasn't happy. "I don't know, Mahmud. But I really hope things go well for you. But how are you going to be become a millionaire? You haven't actually gotten a job yet."

Maybe she was grinning a little bit, after all.

"Okay," Mahmud said. "Then maybe I'll see you at the employment agency, or whatever it's called."

"That would be nice."

"Yes."

"There's just one place I don't want to see you again, Mahmud."

"Where is that?"

"Here."

They laughed together. Mahmud got up. Extended his hand.

She extended her hand, too. They looked at each other. Stood still. Then they hugged.

"Take care, now," Erika said.

Mahmud didn't say anything. Tried to keep himself from hugging her again.

Mahmud'd been to the gym. It was snowing out. Stockholm was still decked out for the holidays. The Swedes'd sat at home with their families and celebrated a few days ago. Mahmud'd gone over to his dad and Jivan's house. Jamila came over that night. She'd brought gingersnaps and baklava. They ate dinner, watched a movie that Mahmud'd been allowed to pick: *I Am Legend*. Dad didn't like the flick.

In a way, they celebrated Christmas too, except Beshar refused to say the word *Christmas* in front of Mahmud. "That's the Swedes' thing. Not ours."

Mahmud'd taken care of his homework. The first thing he had to do was the weapons. He got contacts through Tom. A couple of real heavy hitters from Södertälje. Tight networks—Syriacs. Cash-in-transit pros. Dynamite vets. Weapons fetishists. Tom didn't know them well, but well enough to be able to buy three pieces. Two AK4s that'd probably been stolen from some army stockpile and a Glock 17. Felt epic: to hide three badass pieces at home in the apartment. Mahmud removed the bolts, wrapped them in a bedsheet. He put the rest of the weapons under the bed, behind a couple of bags of documents that he'd picked up at that apartment many months ago. Then he put the bed sheet with the bolts up on a beam in the attic. Couldn't be too careful: if the 5-0 got him, at least he'd be able to say that the weapons had important parts missing. That they weren't fit to use.

Another piece of homework'd been even easier: to get bolt cutters. First he thought of boosting one, but changed his mind. Unnecessary to take risks. Instead, he bought it at Järnia in Skärholmen's mall—the phattest model they had. He paid cash.

The final piece of homework was the most difficult: to get manpower. Not that he didn't know a lot of people. But who did he trust? Who would never snitch, kept shit synced, could handle the job? He already knew who he would ask: Robert, Javier, and Tom. But the questions still remained: Could he trust his homies?

Tom was traveling over New Year's—fuck. Niklas wanted a total of ten boots on the ground, as he put it. Mahmud had to have a planning meeting with the other guys anyway. Robert and Javier came over to his house that night. Javier was wearing a shirt so tight his nipples were popping out like that fucking British bimbo Jordan. Robert was rocking his usual baggy ghetto style, like Fat Joe himself: track pants and an oversized hoodie. Mahmud couldn't help but think, Will these *blattes* really be able to handle the attack? They saw themselves as real G's and maybe they were hard core. But this—this was different. He just couldn't blow this thing. Could never fuck up.

They split a doobie. Watched *Bourne Ultimatum*. Mahmud tried to get himself pumped up. Soon he was gonna lay it all out. Couldn't sound lame. Had to do it right.

He ejected the DVD. Turned to the guys. "Boys, I've got a thing cooking. A big thing."

Rob took a hit on the joint. "What? You got a connect?"

"No, this is personal. And there'll be easy money."

"Sounds good."

"It's like that home invasion we rocked, Rob, in that crib. Remember?"

Rob smiled. "Sure. Damn, we were fucking saints, giving you all the gear we lifted."

"This is my turn to give back, promise. This is like that invasion times a hundred. We're gonna hit a huge fucking house on Smådalarö."

"Smådalarö. Where the fuck is that? Way up north or something?"

They laughed.

Mahmud began explaining. How he'd met Jorge in the reggae apartment. How the Latino'd been set on revenge on the Yugos, 110 percent. Old wrongs and shit, mafia style. He told them about Niklas, who'd floored Jamila's ex and who hated the whore business more than a broad-backed feminist dyke. He explained about the upper-class horndogs who thought they were gonna fuck young pussy but would get slammed with a high-stylin' *blatte* attack instead. They could trust Niklas. The commando dude knew his shit: the planning, the surveillance, the maps, the photos, everything.

Mahmud could feel that they were listening. They nodded. Asked semismart follow-up questions. Dug it. What sealed the deal: the weapons. When they heard what Mahmud'd gotten ahold of, they wanted in right away.

Mahmud: the meanest attack *blatte* on the Stockholm battlefield. The only downside was that he should've talked to Niklas ages ago, but the guy was impossible to reach. Mahmud didn't want to call, since they'd decided to send coded texts. He fired off about ten texts a day instead. No answer. Maybe he'd misunderstood the code. So he stopped by Niklas's crib, rang the doorbell, even put a note in the mail slot: *Hey corpse, call me!*

But nothing happened. One day, two days, three days passed. New Year's Eve was approaching. Where the fuck was that guy?

What's more: he had to find another soldier. Niklas wanted five people for the attack. If it even happened.

Mahmud thought about his buddies. Dejan, Ali, lots of other players. They wouldn't be able to pull this off. He didn't even know if Robert and Javier would man up, seal the deal. The same thought came sneaking back—Babak would be perfect.

But how? Babak'd totally turned his back on him. Regarded him as a massive traitor. With every right, as he'd realized too late—the Yugos were the enemy. His conscience boiling like heartburn.

He got out a pen and paper. Did something he'd never done before: wrote down what he was gonna say. After ten minutes, he was done. Read through it. Made some changes. He remembered from school: bullet points, that's what it was called.

He hoped they would help.

He picked up his phone. Called Babak.

56

The air in the jail was heavy with smoke and bad karma. Even though the smoking ban that applied in the rest of Sweden'd reached this place, too. The linoleum in the hallways and the thick, blue-painted doors to the cells were so marinated in smoke that you could probably scrape a Marlboro from them.

Niklas took note of everything. The uniforms the correctional staff wore: baggy, green, worn down until they were pajama soft. The white-painted metal borders on the windows, the four-inch-thick flameproof mattress on the bed, the wooden chair, the mini desk, the fourteen-inch TV. The three PlayStation games that you could check out in the unit were worth their weight in gold. There was nothing wrong with the COs, they were just doing their job. But the detained men shuffled around in state-issued slippers—unshaven, languid, depressed. There was no need to rush in here. Life was measured out in the windows of time between hearings or, for the ones with privileges, conversations with loved ones.

He felt lost, and at the same time, superior. Most of the people in here were duds. According to Niklas, the logic was simple: that's why people ended up in here.

He felt like the robot in the *Terminator* movies. Registered his surroundings, the rooms, the people, like a computer. Scanned the placement of the cells, the guards' equipment, tones of voices, attitude. Possibilities. He was classified as restricted, so he wasn't permitted to speak with anyone, to make or receive phone calls, or to send or receive mail. They thought he might tamper with evidence if he gained access to the outside world. It was insane.

He thought about the interrogations he'd been through. A few'd only been fifteen minutes long. Others several hours. The investigators went over the same things over and over again. When he'd arrived at Benjamin's place on the night in question, where they'd rented the

DVD, who'd paid for the movie, if he knew what Benjamin'd been doing earlier during the night, if he'd like to comment on his mother's testimony, when he'd left Benjamin's place for home, what his mother'd been doing when he got home. And, yesterday: they started asking questions about Mats Strömberg and Roger Jonsson. They were on to him.

They sat in a small interrogation room in the same hall as his cell. There was a sticker on the eternal linoleum floor that pointed out the direction of the Kaaba in Mecca—someone was apparently permitted to pray in there. There was an intercom phone on the table, but outbound calls were blocked. There was a note on the wall: *Important! Contact unit personnel before the client is released into the hallway.* He couldn't complain about security. His overall conclusion: breaking out of the jail at Kronoberg wouldn't be easy.

Today: another interrogation, even though there was nothing to say. He didn't have anything to do with Claes's murder, that's all there was to it.

His lawyer sat with him for a few minutes before the interrogation.

"Have you thought of anything since the last time we saw each other? Anything you want to bring up with the interrogator?"

Niklas said what he was thinking. "I don't want to talk about the way Claes treated Mom and me. That's none of the police's business."

"Then I suggest that you breathe through your nose and keep your mouth shut," Burtig said. "Do you understand? Legally, you don't have to answer any questions about that."

Niklas understood. Burtig was good, but would that be enough?

The chief interrogator, Stig Ronander, came in. Gray hair and a spider's web of wrinkles around his eyes. The old guy exuded experience and calm: a relaxed style, composed movements. Above all: a gleam in his eye and a sense of humor that allowed the interrogations to be punctuated by a laugh now and then. It was smart, nasty smart.

The other cop was named Ingrid Johansson. She was the same age as Ronander, but more quiet, watchful, on her guard. She brought a tray with coffee and cinnamon buns.

Niklas'd spent a few hours in his cell trying to analyze their interrogation technique. It was significantly more subtle than his and Collin's methods in the heat, down in the sand. An interpreter, the butt of a gun, a boot: that was usually enough to get the information you needed. Ronander/Johansson rocked the opposite style: pleasantness attack. Self-controlled and thoughtful, tried to create a connection, trust. Force more details out of him by asking the same things over and over again. Good cop/bad cop—seemed to belong to the old school. Both oozed trust, consideration. But Niklas was on to them. They were slippery.

The first real question came after ten minutes of coffee sipping and small talk. "You wouldn't mind telling us about your childhood, would you? Your mom already has."

"No comment."

"Why no comment? Come on."

"No comment."

"But Niklas, be nice. We're just talking here. Do you remember a lot from your childhood?"

Silence.

"Did you like sports?"

Silence.

"Did you used to play outdoors?"

Silence.

"Did you read books?"

Even more silence.

"Niklas, I understand if this is difficult to talk about. But it could be worth it, for your own sake."

"I said, no comment."

"Your mom worked as a cashier, right?"

Niklas drew a line through the crumbs on the table.

"That's private."

"But why is it private? She told us so herself. So it can't be private." Silence.

"Is it true that she worked as a cashier?" Ronander's eyes darted quickly to the right, toward Ingrid Johansson. Niklas didn't respond.

And that's how it went. Repetition, gentle questioning, repetition. The lawyer couldn't do much, they had every right to ask questions. Two hours went by. More repetition. Wasted time. His childhood was an important subject, he'd give them that. But they didn't know *how* important. They didn't understand what ought to be done to stop people like Claes Rantzell.

He wasn't guilty of this.

Only two days left till New Year's Eve. Niklas thought about Mahmud and their preparations. Wondered if a haji like him would've gotten his shit done: the weapons, the foot soldiers, the bolt cutters. Niklas himself'd done everything before he was arrested. But now: time was running out. He hoped the Arab would sit tight on the gear for a later occasion.

He tried to work out in his cell. Push-ups, sit-ups, triceps exercises, back, legs, shoulders. He brainstormed, planned, organized. There had to be a solution. A way out. At night, other, darker thoughts visited him. The face of the prostitute. Images of how they would assault, beat, and rape her. Glimpses of her vulnerability: the girl crying in a bed, pleading for help. Where was help? Where was freedom? And other images: Nina Glavmo-Svensén in the idyllic suburb. The child on her arm. The locked doors of the house. He didn't know if he was dreaming or imagining things.

It was almost time for another hearing. They'd already had two, without success. His lawyer, Burtig, explained, "First, they weren't allowed to hold you for more than four days without the court making a decision about the charges brought against you. After that, they have to hold a hearing every other week in order to continue to coop you up like this. But I think we have a pretty good case. You have an alibi. There are no witnesses. No technical evidence so far; they haven't found anything on you through the forensic lab database. The question is just what your mom is actually saying. And what they've found on your computer about those other guys."

Niklas already knew what to answer: "I want a hearing. As soon as possible."

The lawyer took notes.

Niklas had a plan.

* * *

JENS LAPIDUS

THE NATIONAL POLICE
The National Bureau of Investigation's Palme Group
Date: December 29 APAL–2478/07

MEMORANDUM
(Confidential according to Chapter 9 § 12 of the Secrecy Act)
Regarding the murder of Claes Rantzell
(previous name: Claes Cederholm,
Reg. nr 24.555)

The investigation of the murder of Claes Rantzell
The preliminary investigation of the murder of Claes Rantzell (previously named Claes Cederholm) is led by Detective Inspector Stig H. Ronander of the Southern District in Stockholm. Ronander is reporting personally to the Palme Group.

Fredrik Särholm, the Palme Group's specially appointed investigator, as designated on September 12, has compiled a report regarding Rantzell (Attachment 1).

In a previous memo from October 28 (APAL–2459/07), the Palme Group described the advances in the investigation regarding the murder of Rantzell.

In this memo, certain recent developments are detailed. In summary, the following:

1. A man named Niklas Brogren has been arrested for the murder of Rantzell (further details in the Detention Hearing Memo, Attachment 2). Niklas Brogren is the son of Marie Brogren, who, during the end of the eighties and the beginning of the 1990s, periodically lived with Rantzell. She has informed the investigators that, during this time period, she was assaulted by Rantzell on a number of occasions. Several people connected with Marie Brogren have confirmed that Rantzell abused her during this time (Interrogation Notes, Attachments 3-6). Therefore, there appears to be a motive to kill Rantzell.

2. During a search of Niklas Brogren's residence, a computer, notebooks, certain surveillance equipment, and a number of knives were found. The computer's hard drive has been searched by the police's IT unit. It contains information that suggests that Niklas Brogren may be involved in the murder of two men in Stockholm on the 4th and the 25th of November of this year. A preliminary investigation has been commenced. (Further details: crime reports etc., Attachment 7).

3. Within the framework of the investigation, information has been gathered from a man named John Ballénius, 521203-0135, who

was supposedly a close friend of Rantzell's. John Ballénius is well known to the police as a front man in a number of companies suspected of white-collar crime. During the 1980s and 1990s, he frequently socialized with Claes Rantzell. According to the information that has been gathered, he apparently did not want to be interrogated in connection with the investigation. A certain level of suspicion can therefore be directed at Ballénius, either for involvement in the murder or for harboring knowledge of relevant information (Interrogation, Attachment 8).

4. Rantzell's apartment has been searched by the police's technicians (Lokus), and tests have been sent to SKL (the National Laboratory of Forensic Science). The following conclusions can be drawn from SKL's DNA analysis: the apartment has been visited by persons who are not Rantzell or close relatives of Rantzell. There are traces of DNA from at least three such people. It cannot be ruled out that the persons have been present in the apartment during the time *after* the murder of Rantzell (SKL's statement, Attachment 9).

5. The police's technicians further suspect that an unknown person, who is not Rantzell, has seized objects from a basement storage unit that was very probably used by Rantzell. The seized objects probably consisted of plastic bags with unknown contents.

Suggested measures to be taken
Based on the above, the following measures are suggested:

1. The Palme Group is to be given permission to attend interrogations with Niklas Brogren.

2. The Palme Group orders Fredrik Särholm to investigate all the suspicions directed at Niklas Brogren parallel with the police's regular investigation.

3. The Palme Group is to be given permission to allocate resources toward the search for John Ballénius.

We request that decisions regarding these questions be reached at a meeting on December 30 of this year.

Stockholm

Detective Inspector Lars Stenås

57

They were sitting at Thomas's house, on the ground floor. If Åsa'd been there, she would've been watching TV upstairs. Thomas felt as though deep inside, she'd understood him. That made him feel warm. But his fear of the people he was searching for made him colder.

There was an illuminated Christmas star hanging in one of the windows. Even if Åsa'd decorated more than usual this year, they hadn't gotten a Christmas tree or an Advent candelabra. But when Sander came they were going to decorate so damn much for the holidays that even the window displays at the NK department store would seem un-Christmassy in comparison.

Hägerström was sitting in an armchair that Thomas'd inherited from his dad. The frame was in cherrywood. Worn red seat cushion and backrest. Maybe it wasn't the most stylish chair in the world, but it meant a lot. If you smelled closely: the old man's cigarillo smell still clung to it. Thomas thought, I ought to reupholster it. Someday.

On the coffee table and on the floor: papers, documents, files spread out. They'd eliminated a certain amount through their point system. For an outside observer, it would've looked like chaos. For the cop duo, it was chronology, order, structure.

The mission: to sift through the material and find information that could lead them to Ballénius. They'd been naïve; thought if only they went to Solvalla, Ballénius would be sitting there, waiting, just like the last time. But the old fox wasn't dumb: he understood that something was going on. He knew that Rantzell was dead.

The Wisam Jibril trail obviously pointed toward some form of crime. But they weren't able to complete the puzzle, didn't see how that part fit in. Jibril'd been some kind of robber king, a professional criminal, but nothing seemed to indicate that he'd had any kind of personal contact with Rantzell. When it came to Adamsson's death, it probably meant something, but it could be a coincidence, too. Hägerström'd asked around. Thomas'd made the rounds. No one believed the man'd lost his life through foul play. Everything pointed to the car accident being as normal as a car accident can be. What was left were a few members of the Troop, all the documents, the companies, the front men, the transactions, the more or less shady businesses. What was left was Ballénius, who knew something. And what was left was Bolinder's party that the Yugos were arranging on New Year's Eve. Thomas hadn't told Hägerström about that yet.

Through Jasmine, Thomas'd found out some more information about the party at Bolinder's. They didn't try to hide what they were up to from Thomas—but this, the fact that they were going to do an event at Bolinder's right now, wasn't just crazy. It was insane. He had to tell Hägerström, he might make something of it. Still, he was reluctant. He didn't want to advertise his side job. Even if Hägerström was smart—he'd already understood that Thomas was involved with something sort of shady—he didn't know how deep it was. Telling him could wait.

Hägerström'd brought a large bar of chocolate that he'd put on the table. He broke pieces through the foil. "Dark chocolate is still damn good. And healthy, they say." He grinned. The chocolate was like a brown film over his teeth.

Thomas laughed. "I'm not going to say what it looks like you're eating." He got up. Went to the kitchen. Got two beers. Handed one to Hägerström. "Here, have something manly instead."

They continued to go through the piles of paper. Company by company. Year by year. It all went so much better when Hägerström was there. They'd looked up the addresses where Ballénius'd been registered. Fourteen different street addresses and P.O. boxes over the years. Other people in the companies: he mostly served on boards alone. Sometimes he was an alternate. Often with Claes Rantzell. Sometimes with someone named Lars Ove Nilsson. Sometimes with someone named Eva-Lena Holmstrand. In older documents, he was often on the board with some other guys whom Thomas'd looked up—they'd all passed away. He ordered printouts from the national criminal records: a few convictions for white-collar crime and many for drunk driving. Typical alcoholic front men.

Lars Ove Nilsson and Eva-Lena Holmstrand weren't impossible to get ahold of. Hägerström'd talked to the man. Thomas'd interrogated the woman. They didn't know anything. One'd taken early retirement and the other was living on welfare. Both'd applied for debt relief orders. They said they recognized the names—both Claes Rantzell and John Ballénius—but claimed that they'd never met them. That they'd agreed to have their names on the paperwork in exchange for a few grand. Maybe they were lying, maybe it was the truth. Thomas'd still applied quite a bit of pressure. The woman'd cried like a child. Hägerström'd rocked the same tactic—if they knew anything, it would've come out.

Furthermore: they'd looked up the auditors in a couple of the companies. Hägerström'd talked to them. In some cases, he'd done regular interrogations, according to the rules. Or as close to the rules as you could get in an investigation that was being carried out completely outside the rules. The most important part: he got them sufficiently scared. They didn't want to be involved in any illegalities, blamed everything on the bookkeepers. And the bookkeepers—the companies all used the same accounting firm—had gone bankrupt. The two owners, who were also the only employees, lived in Spain. Maybe Thomas and Hägerström would be able to find them—further down the line.

More: the apartment on Tegnérgatan was empty. Ballénius was really lying low. Thomas dug up two acquaintances of Ballénius and Rantzell's, from recent years. They said they didn't have a clue. They were probably lying too—but no one really seemed to know too much about Rantzell's last months alive.

The day after the fiasco at Solvalla, Thomas and Hägerström went to see Ballénius's daughter, Kristina Swegfors-Ballénius, in Huddinge. She was younger than Thomas'd imagined when they'd spoken on the phone. Kicki knew right away that they were cops. Thomas thought, How come people always know?

"Are you the one who called me this summer?" she asked before they'd even introduced themselves.

They pressured her like crazy—ran over her whole story with a fine-toothed comb. She worked off the books as a waitress at a restaurant in the city. Still, she reacted just like the two old front men. Thomas told her how it was. "We're going to make sure you lose your job and are reported to the tax authorities if you don't tell us how we can get ahold of your father." But she held firm to the same story the whole time: "I don't know where he is; it's been a long time since I heard from him."

They gave her a day to get back to them with instructions on how to find him.

They could look up places where the companies'd had their business. Check if there were people there who knew Ballénius. They ought to talk to the banks, check if there was a specific bank office that usually made payments to him. Maybe look up the customers—see if anyone'd ever met the people who supposedly ran the company they were doing business with. There was a lot left to do and it would take time. Thomas couldn't drop the thought: on New Year's Eve, that Bolinder character was going to have a party that Ratko and the other Yugos were helping to organize. He must be able to make use of that somehow. There must be some way.

Hägerström was chugging beer and chewing chocolate. Dropping lame jokes that Thomas grinned at. Even if the guy was a quisling, he was pretty fun, after all. Sharp, a good investigator. He was sitting bent over a pile of paperwork when he suddenly looked up.

"I don't think Kicki will get back to us."

"Why?" Thomas asked.

"I could just see it in her face. My unfailing instinct."

"What do you mean, unfailing instinct? I didn't think cops had anything like that."

"Maybe you're right. But I let a colleague get ears on Kicki Swegfors-Ballénius's cell phone. We've been tapping it since our little visit yesterday. She called him."

"You're kidding? So we've got a number."

"We've got a number, but he killed it right after that call. It doesn't exist anymore. And she told him that someone was looking for him and that he shouldn't call her for a while. She's protecting him."

Thomas felt angry, at the same time, mystified—why hadn't Hägerström told him earlier? "That's fucked up," he said. "What a cunt."

"You can put it that way. Basically, I don't think the Kicki trail is going to lead anywhere. That's why I didn't say anything at first. But I have another idea."

Thomas leaned forward from the couch.

"I've looked up the addresses that Ballénius has had over the years. There's a pattern with those P.O. boxes. For all the companies that are still alive, he still uses or recently used a P.O. box in Hallunda."

"And?"

"And that means that address is probably still in use. Which is to say, that he still uses it to pick up mail."

"Let's go there right now."

They reached Hallunda an hour later. Thomas'd driven carefully. He was thinking about all the chaos in the city. A huge snowstorm was blowing in over Stockholm like a premonition: the citizens needed to be protected in the face of a catastrophe. Soon a new year would begin—with plenty of white snow, for once. Without there being time for it to be soiled and turn the usual color of snow in Stockholm: grayish-brown, full of gravel, dirt, and the inhabitants' melted expectations.

Welcome to the Hallunda Mall. They'd created a logo for the mall that appeared on every sign: a red H followed by a period. Thomas thought about the way it'd been when he was growing up—early eighties, before the age of the malls—he and his buddies used to travel in to Södermalm and wander all the way downtown, to Sergels Torg, by cruising between shops. Records, clothes, stereo equipment, comics, and porn magazines. Maybe he saw a connection: that was the time before the malls and before the scum from the projects took over the city.

The P.O. box company didn't have any windows facing out toward the actual mall. Instead, you entered through an anonymous glass door. They looked up the company's name on a board, took an elevator up, above all the stores. It said, P.O. BOX CENTER in the same colors as the letters of the Hallunda Mall signs. The tagline was: *Do you need a P.O. box? Are you new in town and haven't been able to secure a permanent residence?* What bullshit—everyone knew what type of people used P.O. boxes like this.

A door. A doorbell. A surveillance camera.

Thomas rang the doorbell.

"P.O. Box Center, how may I help you?"

"Hi, this is the police. May we come in?"

The voice on the other end fell silent. The speaker crackled like it was trying to speak on its own. A few too many seconds passed. Then the lock clicked. Thomas and Hägerström stepped inside.

The space: max 320 square feet. The walls: lined with two different sizes of metal-colored mailboxes with Assa Abloy keyholes. Along one short end: a small built-in booth covered with a sheet of Plexiglas. In the booth was an overweight man with a downy mustache.

Thomas walked up to him, flashed his badge. The guy looked scared out of his mind. He was probably trying frenetically to remember the instructions he'd been given in case a cop stopped by for a visit.

"Would you mind stepping out from behind there?"

The guy spoke in broken Swedish: "Do I have to?"

"You don't have to, but I guess then we'll have to drag you out."

Thomas tried to smile—but he could sense that it wasn't a very pleasant smile.

The guy disappeared for a few seconds. A door opened next to the booth.

"What do you want?"

"We want you to get in touch with one of your customers and tell him that he has to come here."

The guy thought it over. "Is this a search?"

"You'd better fucking believe it, buddy. We have every right to get information about your customers. You know that. And if you don't know that, I'll make sure that every single box in here is broken into at your expense, and you'll have to take full responsibility for the damage. Just so you know."

The P.O. box guy started going through a binder with customer contracts. After a few minutes, he seemed to find Ballénius's contract.

"Okay, so what are you going to do now?"

Thomas was growing impatient. "Call him and tell him a package arrived for him that is too big for you to take care of and that he has to pick it up today, or else you'll send it back."

"What did you say?"

"Quit it. Either you do what I just told you to do, or else we'll make life really fucking sour for you." Thomas walked into the booth. Pulled binders out. Started flipping through them. He found Ballénius's contract. Actually: there was a number listed that he didn't recognize.

Hägerström watched the situation unfold. The P.O. box guy seemed bewildered.

Thomas looked at him. "What, you want something?"

The P.O. box guy didn't respond.

Thomas stepped back out from booth. "Maybe you didn't understand what I just told you." He walked over to a P.O. box. Rummaged around in his pocket. Fished out the electrical skeleton key. Started working on the lock.

The guy looked terrified. "Shit, man, you can't do that."

"Call John Ballénius right now and tell him that there's a huge package here for him," Thomas said. "Big as a bike or something like that. Just call."

The postbox guy shook his head. Still picked up the phone. Dialed the number. Sandwiched the receiver between his chin and shoulder.

Thomas could hear his own breathing.

After fifteen seconds.

"Hi, this is Lahko Karavesan at P.O. Box Center in Hallunda."

Thomas tried to hear the voice on the other end of the guy's phone. He couldn't.

"We've got a package for you that's way too big for us to keep here."

Something was said on the other end of the line.

"It's big like a bike or something, but I don't know what it is. Unfortunately, if you don't pick it up today we're gonna have to send the package back."

Silence.

Thomas looked at the P.O. box guy. The guy looked at Hägerström. Hägerström looked at Thomas.

The guy hung up the phone. "He's on his way, soon."

Damn, that was some luck.

The buzzer in the office went off. Four customers'd passed through the P.O. Box Center while they'd been waiting. Said hi discreetly to the poor guy who worked there, exchanged a few words, emptied their boxes. Continued running their anonymous companies, their frontman operations, their porn stashes hidden from their wives.

The P.O. box guy signaled to Thomas and Hägerström. A man walked in. The same sad, gray face. Same thin hair. Same thin, rickety body. Ballénius.

The guy didn't have time to react. Hägerström was positioned by the door and stepped up behind him. Thomas, in front, leaned in close. Ballénius didn't even seem surprised; he looked despondent.

Hägerström cuffed him.

Ballénius didn't resist. Didn't say anything. Just stared at Thomas with tired eyes. They led him out. The P.O. box guy exhaled, as though he'd been holding his breath for the entire time that Thomas and Hägerström'd been in there.

Hägerström climbed into the front seat. Thomas in the back, next to John Ballénius. It was snowing so much outside that Thomas couldn't even see the Hallunda Mall sign anymore. Warm air was pouring out of the car's air vents.

Ballénius was sitting with his hands in his lap; the handcuffs weren't pulled too tightly. Waiting for them to drive him to the interrogation.

Hägerström turned around. "We're going to conduct the interrogation right here, just so you know."

"Why?" Ballénius asked. The guy'd been around the block—knew: regulation interrogations were never conducted in a car.

"Because we don't have time to mess around, John," Thomas responded.

Ballénius groaned. His exhalation created a cloud of steam—it still wasn't all that warm in the car.

"You know the drill. You're an old hand at this, John. We can goof around and play nice. Laugh at your jokes to pretend to be pleasant. Coddle you, cajole you into talking."

Theatrical pause.

"Or else we can just be straight with you. This is not an ordinary investigation. You know that, too. This is the fucking Palme murder."

Ballénius nodded.

"You've laid low. You know something and you know that someone wants to know what you know. Me and Hägerström here, we also want to know. But there are others, too. Understood?"

Ballénius kept nodding.

"I understand that you don't want to talk. You might get in trouble. But let me put it this way: you've probably read in the papers that they've arrested a man for the murder of Rantzell. Do you know who it is? The media isn't printing his name. He's Marie Brogren's son."

Thomas tried to see if Ballénius reacted to the news. The guy lowered his gaze. Maybe, maybe a reaction.

Thomas briefly went over the suspicions against Niklas Brogren. Hägerström sat with his gaze fixed on Ballénius. Five minutes passed.

"You know what this means. Niklas Brogren is probably going to be convicted of the murder of Claes. But he isn't the one who did it, is he? Niklas Brogren is innocent. And the ones who are really behind all this, and who were behind Palme, will go free. But you can change that, John. This is your chance. The chance of a lifetime. And that's because Hägerström and I are not part of an official investigation. We're doing this privately, on the side. So everything you tell us will stay between us, it'll never go public. Never."

Ballénius looked down again. Near silence in the car. It was warm now. Too warm. Thomas was still sitting with his jacket on. Saw his own reflection in the window across from him. He felt tired. This had to end now.

Hägerström broke the silence.

"John, we're as deep in the shit as you are. Ask any cop. Andrén's been transferred because of his investigation and I've been cut off. We're not desirable anymore, we're outside the system. And we've gone rogue on this. If that comes out, we're done as cops. Do you understand what I'm saying? If you want, you can call one of your police contacts and ask."

"That's not necessary," Ballénius said. "I've already heard about you." A vein was pulsing in Ballénius's neck. "I'll talk, on two conditions."

"What?"

"That you release me right afterward and that you don't tell anyone how you got ahold of me or what you know about me."

Thomas stared at Hägerström. Then he said, "That's fine, granted you give us useful information."

"That's not enough. If it is as you say, you really don't have any right to sit here and interrogate me. I want something to hold over you as security. I want to take a picture of us together on my cell phone. If things get bad, I'll give it to some appropriate inspector who can draw his own conclusions about you."

Dangerous horse trading. They'd be taking a huge chance. A massive risk. Thomas could feel Hägerström glancing at him again. The decision was his. He was the one most personally affected by this whole thing. He was burning the most. Was pushing the hardest.

Thomas said, "Okay, we'll buy that. You talk, you take a picture, then you can go."

Hägerström turned off the heat. The silence sounded like a scream in the car.

The old guy opened his mouth as if to say something. Then he closed it again.

Thomas stared.

Ballénius leaned back. "Okay. I'll tell you what I know."

Thomas could feel himself tense up.

"Claes and I weren't close for long. We spent a lot of time together in the eighties and nineties. Especially in the middle and end of the eighties—you know, there was quite the time being had at Oxen, the bar, and then there were all the companies we were on the boards of. Between us, we made some hefty dough. But neither me nor Classe have ever been any good at holding on to money. Ask my daughter, you know about her, I gather. Claes's money mostly went to booze and you can guess where mine went. I've always loved horses."

John Ballénius continued to describe his and Claes Rantzell's lives twenty years earlier. Hash parties, gambling winnings, goalie jobs, alcohol problems, fights, all that crap. Early business structuring in the beginning of the nineties, before the police'd understood how big the front-business bubble was. Names went flying by. Thomas recognized a bunch of them from the tales the old cops'd told from earlier days. Places were mentioned, apartment brothels, underground clubs, drug hideouts. It was a rundown of the rabble of the past.

"I didn't see Claes more than once or twice a year over the past few years. He was worn down, I was worn down. We didn't have the energy, you know? But this spring, I heard rumors about him. Apparently he was living it up like he'd won big-time at the track. And then he started calling me. We spoke a few times, then we got together at a bar in Södermalm."

Thomas couldn't hold back. "What did he say?"

"I don't always remember things too good, but I remember that night clearly. He looked like a real suave player. Newly pressed suit, gold watch on his arm, new cell phone. And damn, was he ever in a good mood; ordered bottle after bottle for us to split. I wondered what was up, and when I asked he wanted to go somewhere private. We sat down in a booth. I remember that Classe acted as if every guest was a civvy on the lookout. It was obvious that he'd made a little too much cash for it all to be clean. But that's how we'd lived all our lives, so. Then he told me how he'd thought it over, turned it over every which way, been racked with angst, shilly-shallied, but finally—*they'd* paid him. After all these years he'd finally dared make demands and that's when they folded. He was fucking ecstatic."

"Who were *they*?"

Ballénius looked at Thomas.

"Don't you know that already?"

58

Niklas still hadn't been in touch and it was the day before New Year's Eve—the attack wouldn't happen. Fuck, this was some gay shit. Mahmud didn't want to let Jorge down, lose the promised cash, let the Yugos win. But without the commando guy, nothing would work.

Where was he, anyway? Mahmud'd continued, today even, to send texts like a maniac. His note under Niklas's door hadn't had any effect. But he was gonna wait another few hours.

They'd been over at his place again this morning. Prepped the weapons. Tried not to snort or smoke. They weren't exactly experts— even if they were always talking about gats and Glocks. They needed to concentrate. They inserted and removed the cartridges from the magazines. Secured them on the weapons. Flipped the safeties, changed between semiautomatic and single-shot settings.

Above all: he'd seen Babak yesterday. First a short phone call. His former homeboy kept his style clipped.

"What do you want?"

"Ey, man. Come on, can't we start hangin' again?"

"Why?"

"Can't we meet up? I promise to explain. *Jalla, si.*"

Babak agreed. They met up in the afternoon, in the Alby mall. Mahmud drove his Benz even though it was just half a mile. Wanted to show Babak: things're going good now.

It was snowing like the North Pole outside. Big, fluffy flakes that whirled around. Mahmud remembered the first time he'd seen snow: he'd been six years old, at the refugee camp in Västerås. He'd run outside. First stepped carefully on the thin layer of snow. Then dragged his hand over the picnic tables, gathered enough to make a snowball. And finally, while giggling—attacked Jamila. Beshar didn't get mad that time. The opposite—he laughed. Made a snowball too that he threw at Mahmud. It missed him. Mahmud knew already then, as a six-year-old, that it was on purpose.

Inside McDonald's, in Alby: Babak was sitting way in the back, as usual. Hadn't even bought any food—according to Babak, this meeting wasn't going to be long. His boy was munching on something from a green bag.

Mahmud greeted him.

Babak remained seated at the table. Didn't get up. No handshake, no hug.

"Shit, Babak, it's been a long time, man."

Babak nodded. "Yeah, long time." He fished out some green balls from the bag.

Mahmud sat down. "What're you eating?"

"Wasabi peas." Babak leaned his head back. Opened his mouth wide. Dropped the wasabi peas in one by one.

"Wasabi? Like in sushi? You gay now?"

Babak popped a few more peas. Didn't say anything.

Mahmud tried to grin. His joke'd bombed. Said, "I'm really sorry, man."

Babak continued to eat his peas.

"I made a mistake. You were right, *habibi*. But if you listen to me, you'll understand. Big things're happening. Real big. *Ahtaj musaa'ada lau simacht.*"

Mahmud pushed the bag of wasabi peas to the side. Leaned forward. Mahmud spoke in a low voice. About how he'd been working more and more as a whore guard, then gotten in touch with Jorge, that he'd talked to his sister's ex-neighbor, who was a crazy fucking raider or something. He told him about the planning, the photos, the maps, the bolt cutters. And above all, he told him about the weapons: two assault rifles and one Glock. The illest arsenal since the CIT heist in Hallunda. All the talking probably took twenty minutes. Mahmud didn't usually talk that much in one go. The last time was probably when he'd told Babak how the Yugo cunts'd picked up Wisam Jibril. That time, he felt angst. This time, he felt pride.

"You follow? We're gonna storm that Sven party. We're gonna lay out the Yugos. We're gonna jizz in their skulls."

Finally. After that last thing he'd said: a smile on Babak's lips.

While Mahmud was driving home from Alby, he thought about the dream he'd had the other night. He was back with Mom. Back in Baghdad. They were sitting together under a tree. The sky was blue.

Mom was telling him how you knew when the spring'd come because that's when the almond tree bloomed. She stood up, picked a small pink flower. Showed Mahmud. Said something in her soft Arabic that Mahmud didn't completely understand: "When the soul is happy, it has the same color as the almond tree." Then it looked like the flowers were falling off the tree. Mahmud looked up. Saw the sky. Saw the tree. It wasn't flowers falling, he realized. It was snow.

He was in a good mood. Homies again—he and Babak. His boy dug what he'd heard. Had held Mahmud by the shoulders—looked him in the eyes. They'd embraced. Like two brothers reuniting after many years. That's how it was: Babak was his brother, his *akh*. A pact that couldn't be broken.

After he'd explained everything, Mahmud finally asked the question: Did Babak want in?

Babak thought it over for a while. Then he said, "I'm in. But not for the cash. I'm in for the honor."

Now there was just one thing that seemed like it would kill everything. Niklas was a no-show.

59

The cell was situated fifty feet above the ground, not a chance. If Niklas managed to break into a hallway, the doors had armored Plexiglas that he could probably smash in a minute or so, but that wouldn't be enough. Even if he made his way through them, he'd need to take the elevator to get down, and it didn't go further than to the sixth floor. After that, you had to pass through several more doors equipped with surveillance cameras before switching to a new elevator. The hallway route was a no-go too. Other alternatives: getting ahold of a weapon—taking a hostage. The crux: the jail staff only carried batons. The cops that came to conduct interrogations checked their weapons somewhere downstairs. If only he hadn't had these vile restrictions—someone, maybe Mahmud or Benjamin, could possibly've smuggled in a firearm. But probably not: the metal detectors sniffed every fucking thing that moved. Another possibility was taking apart the ventilation duct in the ceiling—somehow crawling and slithering his way out. But he wasn't thin enough for that. He could try to start a fire—split during the fake-fire chaos. Start an uprising—escape while the jail was in riot mode. Niklas crossed out the alternatives quickly from his inner list. You couldn't escape from the Kronoberg jail—not without massive aid from the outside.

There was a better way. The other day his lawyer, Burtig, had explained that they weren't allowed to detain him for more than two weeks at a time without a court ruling. Today it was time for his hearing in the District Court.

Niklas ate breakfast early. He did push-ups and sit-ups. When he stood up, it felt like all the blood rushed from his head. At around ten o'clock, there was a knock at the door: Markko, a big detention officer. Niklas asked to change his shirt—he was soaked in sweat and wanted to feel fresh in court.

Markko put handcuffs on him. He and two other detention officers led him down the hall. There was nothing wrong with them, they were just doing their job. Niklas eyed the information panels on the cell doors. *Allergies: Nuts. No pork. Allergies: Fish. No pork.* Reminded him of the Americans and their weird prisons down in the sandbox.

They walked into a small room with a metal detector. Markko undid the handcuffs. Niklas walked through the metal detector: it remained silent. The cuffs went back on. They took an elevator down. This was a part of the building that he hadn't known existed.

"We're going to the tunnel under the Kronoberg Park," Markko explained. "They call it the Path of Sighs."

The guards unlocked two metal double doors. The road to the District Court, underground. Like a bomb shelter dug out by al-Sadr's mujahideen. Their steps echoed. The fluorescent lights gave off a cold glow, the concrete looked like the sand down there after rain: full of small holes. Markko tried to make conversation, be as nice as possible. Niklas couldn't concentrate.

They reached another set of metal doors. He was led into the bottom level of the District Court. Granite hallways and reinforced wooden doors. A small detention room. A wooden table. Two chairs. On the other side of the table: his lawyer, Burtig, was sitting, waiting.

"Hey there, Niklas, how are you?"

"I'm fine. At least they let me make a snowball yesterday."

"Was there snow in the rec yard?"

"Tons."

"Yeah, it's some climate thing, all this. It's snowing like never before. Do you feel prepared for what's going to happen today?"

"I'm assuming it's pretty much the same deal as last time."

"In principle. Some new things have come to light. They've gone through your computer."

"What've they found?"

"Take a look at this." Burtig handed him a pile of papers. Niklas flipped through them. Realized already by the fourth page—the seizure report—that they'd gotten ahold of his surveillance videos.

He didn't really have the energy to read more. If it was all over, fine. There were more important things to think about right now. He couldn't wait around for a conviction.

"Are we meeting in the same room as last time?" Maybe his question seemed strange.

Burtig held his poker face. "No, we're meeting in room number six."

"And where is that?"

"How do you mean?"

"I was just wondering. I'm feeling a little nervous. Is it on the same floor as last time?"

"I think we were in room four last time. So yes, it's on the same floor."

Niklas nodded. Continued to flip through the arrest memo. The cops hadn't only found the files with the videos he'd saved. They had the info he'd written down, too: lists of routines, photos of the wife-beaters, bugging equipment. They had nearly everything.

He asked Burtig a few more questions. At the same time: laser focus on a different target.

The case was called a little while later. Burtig rose. The detention officers came back into the room. Put the handcuffs on. Led him through a hallway.

They stepped into the courtroom.

It was large: high windows with long curtains, the prosecutor's desk, Niklas and his lawyer's desk, the witness stand, a raised platform, the railing. The judge was sitting up there, along with a thin, dark-haired guy who was going to take down the transcript: the court reporter. The judge: the same old man as at the last hearing. He was in his sixties. Concentrated gaze. Tweed jacket, pale-blue shirt, green tie with ducks on it. It might actually be the same tie as last time. There was a computer on the table and a law book in front of the judge.

Niklas turned around. Stared for a brief moment. The room was filled with spectators. Burtig'd already warned him—journalists, law students, the curious public. They'd be crowding outside trying to get a seat. In the last row, he spotted his mom.

The detention officers spread out. Markko and one of the other two sat down behind Niklas. The third sat down by the entrance. Kept watch.

Markko unlocked the handcuffs and told Niklas to sit down.

On the other side: the two prosecutors. In front of them: piles of paper, notebooks, pens, and a laptop. They were also the same team as last time—one man and one woman. The man was apparently the chief prosecutor. Burtig'd explained, "You have to understand, Niklas, that this isn't just any old case. The key witness in the Palme trial has been killed—and everyone thinks you're the murderer." Niklas agreed. It really was not just any old case.

The judge cleared his throat.

"The Stockholm District Court will conduct a hearing on detention in case B 14568-08. The suspect, Niklas Brogren, is present."

Burtig nodded. The judge went on.

"And his public defender, Jörn Burtig, is present. On the side of the prosecution, we have Chief Prosecutor Christer Patriksson and County Prosecutor Ingela Borlander."

The prosecutors responded affirmatively. Niklas thought it seemed like they were making an effort to sound authoritative.

The judge leaned forward. "Mr. Prosecutor, please present your charges."

"We move for the continued detention of Niklas Brogren based on reasonable suspicion for the murder of Claes Rantzell on June second at Gösta Ekman Road in Stockholm. He is also reasonably suspected of the murder of Mats Strömberg on the fourth of November of this year as well as the murder of Roger Jonsson. The sentence prescribed for these crimes constitutes imprisonment for not less than two years. The special reasons for detention are due to the risk that, if Niklas Brogren is able to move freely, he may impede the investigation by tampering with evidence, that he may continue his illegal activities, and that he may evade punishment. Furthermore, we move for a private hearing for the remainder of the hearing."

The clerk was taking notes like a maniac.

The judge turned to Burtig.

"And how does Brogren view the matter?"

Burtig was flipping his pen back and forth between his thumb and index finger.

"Niklas Brogren objects to the request for continued detention and seeks his immediate release from pretrial detention. He denies that reasonable suspicion exists for the alleged murder in June and for the alleged murder on November fourth. He also objects to the special reasons for prolonged pretrial detention. However, there is no objection to a private hearing."

"Okay," the judge said. "In that case, the District Court rules that the hearing will proceed as a private hearing. All spectators must leave the courtroom."

Niklas didn't turn around. The sound of rustling, whispering people could be heard behind him. Two minutes later, the room was empty of spectators. Go time.

Christer Patriksson, the chief prosecutor, began to read details about the Rantzell murder. How he was found, what the cause of death was, who he'd been. Then he went on. He described Niklas's relationship to Rantzell. What'd emerged regarding Rantzell's treatment of Marie. Finally, the information from her interrogation—in which she claimed that Niklas's alibi didn't hold up. Why the hell did she say that? Niklas didn't get it. The cops must've pulled a fast one on her.

He waited. Thought about Claes. Those nights down in the basement. With the table-hockey game, with Mom's old clothes and suitcases. Those nights when Rantzell'd beaten. Repressed. Humiliated.

His lawyer began to speak. Went on and on about what Niklas'd been doing that night, the movie he'd watched at Benjamin Berg's house, the pizzas they'd bought at the local pizzeria. Burtig argued, attacked the prosecutor's purported evidence. Burtig kept flipping his ballpoint pen back and forth the entire time. Soon they would turn to Niklas and ask him questions. He wasn't listening.

Niklas was breathing in through his nose. Out through his mouth. Slowly. Was filling his lungs with oxygen. Focusing on Burtig's pen.

Tanto dori feel. The pen. As if he were holding it in his own hand.

Weighed it.

Breathed in.

Relaxed.

Breathed out.

He stood up. Tore the pen from Burtig's hand.

Ran toward the railing. The judge stood up. Yelled something. A guard reached for Niklas. Missed. Rushed after him.

Niklas leaped up onto the raised platform. The clerk looked scared out of his mind. The judge backed up. The detention officer grabbed hold of Niklas. That was to be expected.

He breathed quickly. Pen in hand. The detention officers weren't evil, but Niklas's mission was more important.

He made a perfect straight-motion jab. Out and back.

The pen stuck out of the guard's gut like an arrow. The man realized what'd happened. Started howling. Staggered backward.

Niklas lifted the judge's chair. Threw it at the window. The sound of the window breaking reminded him of Claes's bottles, which he used to throw straight down the garbage chute on Gösta Ekman Road.

Niklas picked up the law book. Used it to break off the sharp edges of jagged glass that were still sticking up. They shattered. Would give him fewer wounds. He stepped up onto the windowsill. Markko ran toward him, yelling something. Niklas actually didn't want to hurt him. But this was war. He kicked. Saw Markko fall backward.

It was over now.

He jumped out the window. Not more than ten feet. Easy fall in the soft snow.

Pulsed forward.

His breath steamed.

Up on the sidewalk. He was panting. Could feel the cold against his feet. He was wearing only socks. The jail slippers were left behind in the snow.

He concentrated. Knew where he was going.

Toward the subway station.

The cold filling his lungs.

Focus on his mission objective.

On his steps.

He saw the entrance to the subway station. No cops'd showed up yet.

Tomorrow was New Year's Eve.

60

The snow continued to fall. The precipitation lay like a four-inch layer of cotton on the windowpanes. The greenhouse effect could go to hell, all the fuss about the end of winter was seriously exaggerated.

They were sitting at Thomas's house again. Documents in piles everywhere. Searching. Looking for signs, leads, information about what Ballénius'd told them—payments to Rantzell. They worked feverishly. Like during a preliminary investigation. No mistakes allowed. Time was running out—they'd gotten hold of Ballénius, but the guy might sing, whoever'd attacked Thomas in the parking garage might understand that they were onto something, the Palme Group might get wind of their private little parallel investigation. And tonight was the night of Bolinder's party. Thomas still hadn't said anything about it to Hägerström. Really: if there was no reason to go to the party, there was no reason to tell him about it, either. And so far, Thomas couldn't see that there was anything to gain from going.

The hours passed. At six at the latest, Thomas was going with Åsa to the New Year's Eve party their friends were having. What he really wanted to do was work through the night with Hägerström, but a man has to have his limits.

On the floor, they lined up all the documents that they'd designated with the highest priority according to their point system, as well as those that had to do with finances. The total amount'd shrunk, but it was still more than five hundred documents. They crawled around like two toddlers. The crux: How would they know what was shady and what wasn't? There were verifications for payments made to suppliers and payments made by customers, bank statements that listed transfers, price quotas, tax returns, balance sheets, ledgers. They were looking for large sums. Preferably during the spring. Hägerström decided on a minimum figure: anything over 100,000 was of interest. They checked cash withdrawals and amounts that were moved to strange accounts.

Four o'clock rolled around. They scrutinized thirty or so documents more carefully. A few concerned the more than three million kronor that'd been paid by a company named Revdraget in Upplands Väsby AB to a private account at the Nordea Bank. But the private account number didn't correspond with Rantzell's information. Still—the sum'd been transferred straight from the company to a private person. It could be a salary, but there was nothing noted in the accounts to suggest that this was so.

Several sums were only recorded as withdrawals in four different companies' account statements—for example, Roaming GI AB: one million kronor. No receipts, verifications, or other documents indicated what the sum was intended for. Suspicious. But there was nothing that pointed directly to the payments having been made to Rantzell. And nothing connected the payments to any other person, either. But it was Rantzell, together with a few other front men, who'd formally run the companies.

Even more information: sums that were paid into company accounts without any indication of the identity of the recipient, sums that were paid out as loan repayment without any documents supporting the existence of a loan, dividends made out to unidentified stockholders without records of such a decision in the minutes from the shareholders' meeting. The document piles contained a lot of oddities. Hägerström saw things that Thomas didn't understand, even after Hägerström'd tried to explain.

Time was running out. Should he say something about Bolinder's party? Maybe Hägerström would think of a reason to go there that he hadn't thought of. But no, that was just too much. They'd have to continue tomorrow instead. Åsa wouldn't be happy, but that's just how it had to be.

Thomas went to the kitchen to put on some coffee. When he came back out, Hägerström was sitting down on the couch again. Was staring into space with an empty gaze.

"How's it going, H.? You getting tired? I made coffee."

"Aren't you leaving in half an hour?"

"Yup. And what about you? You going to Half Way Inn again tonight?"

"Not impossible."

Thomas looked at him. Weird, if you thought about it—it was five-thirty on New Year's Eve and they hadn't even talked about how Hägerström would be spending the evening until now.

Hägerström smiled. Slowly—the corners of his mouth slid up like on a cartoon character. He remained sitting like that for a few seconds.

"What is it?"

"I just found a very strange payment."

Thomas looked at the piece of paper Hägerström was holding in his hand. "What? Where?"

Hägerström remained sitting calmly. "It's a payment from a foreign account to Dolphin Leasing AB for over two million kronor, made in April of this year. And that wouldn't be strange in and of itself, but I checked the IBAN number on the account from which the payment was made."

Thomas interrupted him, "What's i-ban?"

Hägerström spoke slowly, almost as if he wanted to keep the suspense going. "It's the international bank account number, abbreviated to IBAN. It's used to identify a bank account for a transaction between different countries." Hägerström played with the piece of paper he was holding. "And the first thing I noticed was that the IBAN number for this payment denoted an account on the Isle of Man. What do you know about the Isle of Man?"

"Not much. I think it's outside England. Isn't it one of those tax havens?"

"Yes, and more than that, it's a secrecy haven too. Companies with accounts on the Isle of Man usually want to hide something. It's difficult to find out who they belong to because there is complete bank secrecy."

"Very suspicious."

Hägerström kept on smiling. "You can say that again. But so far it's not any shadier than a lot of the other stuff we've seen. But, later, Dolphin Leasing paid an invoice to a company registered in Sweden called Intelligal AB for the exact same sum of money as the payment from the Isle of Man. The account number on that invoice is an account with the Skandia Bank. I recognize those kinds of accounts. It's a private account."

He let his last word hang in the air.

Thomas got worked up. Analyzed, connected the dots in his head: a large sum is paid from a secret offshore account to a company in

Sweden that then pays an invoice to another company whose account is actually held by a private person.

Thomas's big question: "Whose Skandia Bank account is it?"

"Guess."

Two hours later. Thomas called Åsa and apologized—he was going to be super late. He tried to explain. Something'd come up at work that was just too important. She said she understood, but still, she didn't. You could tell by her voice.

He and Hägerström'd gone through as many documents as they'd had time for. Tried to find information about who or what company the account on the Isle of Man belonged to. They couldn't find anything. They just had to accept it—the shit wasn't here. They saw the payment, the connection to Rantzell. But the essential part was missing—who'd paid.

"What we should really do is search Bolinder's house," Hägerström said.

Thomas looked at him quizzically. "But we don't have probable cause to believe that any crime was committed by him yet, do we?"

"No, but one of the auditors who I scared a little told me that Bolinder is a control freak. Apparently, he saves copies of everything at his house. And he meant *everything*: every single document that has been issued is, according to the auditor, filed in Bolinder's private archive. That old fox doesn't leave anything to chance."

Thomas felt a lurch in his gut. He knew what he had to do.

Tonight.

* * *

EXPRESSEN–EVENING NEWSPAPER

December 30

MAN SUSPECTED OF MURDERING PALME WITNESS ESCAPED FROM DISTRICT COURT. The hearing in Stockholm's District Court had to be cancelled. The 29-year-old man made an extraordinary escape from the District Court today by leaping through a window. The police are now issuing a warning to the public.

The man was detained with probable cause for the murder of Claes Rantzell, previously Cederholm, one of the key witnesses against Christer Pettersson in the Olof Palme trial. It was today, December 30, that the man was supposed to go to a hearing in the Stockholm District Court. He had been detained for about four weeks and the District Court was supposed to decide whether or not he would remain in custody.

No handcuffs

For some reason, the man was not forced to wear handcuffs in the courtroom. The hearing took place on the ground floor of the building.

When the spectators had left the room, the man rushed to his feet and broke a window in the courtroom. When the detention officers tried to stop the man, he stabbed one of the officers with a steel pen. He then disappeared in the direction of the Rådhuset subway station.

The detention staff is defending itself with the claim that suspects' handcuffs are always taken off during hearings and that there did not appear to be a reason to make a different assessment for this man.

Expressen has tried to reach the District Court for comment as to why the hearing was held on the ground floor.

The police issue a warning

The county police are now issuing a warning to the public. The man is also suspected of two other murders. According to the police, he is armed and may be very dangerous.

Ulf Moberg
ulf.moberg@expressen.se

61

The apartment felt overstuffed with people. But really, only Mahmud, Rob, Javier, Babak, and two of Javier's buds were there. On the stereo: some monster hit by Akon. On the TV: MTV on mute. On the table: a bottle of bubbly in an ice bucket, a transparent baggie filled with weed, and Rizla papers.

Mahmud should have felt overjoyed—his boys, the music, the smokes, the champagne. The mood. New Year's Eve was gonna be top of the line. They were hitting the town later, were gonna snort the snort, party the party, nail bitches—rock the piranha race straight up. Hump in the New Year so hard the chicks wouldn't be able to walk till Saint Knut's Day, or whatever that Sven shit was called.

Still: he'd wanted to do the hit against the Yugos and the old pervs. Jorge's story'd got him going. Niklas's planning'd felt legit, like a real war. There was gonna be an attack, a massive guerrilla ambush. A hardcore invasion—on Million Program terms.

But Niklas'd disappeared. Mahmud was angry as hell. The elite soldier guy could go fuck himself—he wasn't so elite after all.

He went into the kitchen. Brought out the champagne glasses.

Babak smiled. "Ey, brother, you're doing good. Not just an ice bucket, I see you got yourself real glasses now too."

Mahmud popped a bottle. It was only seven o'clock, but he didn't plan on waiting with the bubbly.

Rob laughed. "You stacking them bills, or what?"

Mahmud nodded. Poured for the guys.

"I'm working double. But fuck, man, not for much longer."

"Why, man? You deal, you watch the whores. I think it sounds like a perfect combo, like Big Mac & Co."

"Cut it, Twiggy. I'm gonna quit the whores. That shit's wack. Skank wack, that's all it is."

Babak set his glass down. Looked at him.

"*Habibi*, I don't get you. You get to work with easy pussy all day.

446

You can do whatever you want to them. Double team, triple team, hat trick."

"Man, I don't wanna hear it. Hookers, that's some loser shit."

Babak shook his head. Turned to Rob instead. Mahmud pretended like he didn't hear—thought about Gabrielle instead, the chick he'd banged this fall when things'd gotten embarrassing. He was gonna forget that now. Party. Hopefully get between the sheets. With someone who wanted it.

The night rolled on. The clock struck eight. Babak was holding court. Bullshitting about new blow schemes, ideas for CIT robberies, bouncers he knew downtown, the new Audi R8 super car that he'd test-driven before Christmas.

Robert laughed louder and louder. The bubbles were starting to work their magic. Javier and his buddies were talking amongst themselves, half the time in Spanish.

Mahmud heard a sound that stood out from the general din. Not from the music. Not from anyone's cell phone. Not from outside the window. He understood what it was: someone was ringing his doorbell. He got up.

The speakers were blasting top-shelf Timbaland.

Babak yelled over the music, "Who's coming?"

Mahmud shrugged. "No idea. Maybe one of all those bitches you're talkin' about."

He peered through the peephole. The hallway outside was dark. He couldn't see shit.

It was eight o'clock on New Year's Eve—who wouldn't turn the lights on in the stairwell? He remembered how Wisam Jibril'd shown up at his dad's apartment on that summer morning.

He opened the door.

A dude. It was still dark. Mahmud tried to see who it was. The person was pretty tall, shaved head.

He said, "I'm back. *Jalla*, Mahmud, let's do this."

Mahmud recognized the voice.

"Yo man. Where the fuck've you been?"

Niklas stepped into the apartment. He looked different. Shaved head. Thin beard. Darker eyebrows than the last time they'd seen each other.

Mahmud repeated the question.

"Where've you been? We were supposed to do the thing tonight. You fucked it, man."

"Don't use that tone with me." Niklas sounded pissed. Then he grinned. "Didn't you hear what I said? I'm back. Let's do this thing. Now. *Jalla*."

A half hour later. The mood was completely different from when the bubbly'd been on the table and the stereo'd been jacking up the atmosphere. Serious, calm, focused. At the same time: ready to roll, pumped, sharp. At first, Mahmud hadn't understood what Niklas was talking about. But when he understood, it felt good. Damn good. They were gonna go through with the attack. As long as his homeboys were into it—it would be the phattest shit ever. They kicked out Javier's friends. Their swagger sagged, but Mahmud offered them the bag of weed to take with them. They still looked sulky, but accepted. There were lots of other parties in town tonight.

Babak, Javier, and Robert were sitting on the couch. Niklas and Mahmud, each on a chair. Mahmud was still a little buzzed. But in a few hours, he would be on point. The Rizla papers, the cell phones, the champagne, and the glasses'd been put away. Instead: maps, aerial photos taken off the Internet, blueprints, photos of the house. And weapons: the AK-47s, the Glock, and Niklas's own gun, a Beretta. A goddamned arsenal.

Niklas went over the plan with the boys. Mahmud tried to fill in here and there, mostly for show. Niklas was in charge.

Babak raised his hand, like the good schoolboy he'd never been. "The Yugos that're running this party, they armed?"

Niklas looked at Mahmud. "Mahmud, you work with these assholes."

Mahmud cleared his throat. Weird feeling: to sit here with his homies planning the big gig together with a half-crazed mercenary soldier who didn't seem to give a fuck about the money, who just cared about punishing people. Like in a movie somehow—Mahmud just couldn't think of which flick.

He tried to answer Babak's question. "I don't know for sure. But I've never seen them pack heat. I think some of them have gear like that, maybe Ratko. But why, really? The whores just need a good slap to be put in their place. The johns usually don't pull any shit. And it's not exactly like they're expecting the SWAT *blattes* from Alby to make an entrance, right?"

The guys laughed. Babak smiled, said, "Shit, man. The SWAT *blattes*, that's us." The mood lightened.

Robert said, "The Yugos are on the decline, I've always said so, right?" The boys relaxed. Even Niklas cracked a smile.

At around ten o'clock, they got up. Packed a bag and put it in Mahmud's car: the weapons and the bolt cutters. They divided up in different cars. Niklas directed them to Gösta Ekman Road in Axelsberg. Parked outside. It was deserted. Everyone who wanted to be somewhere at ten o'clock on New Year's Eve'd already made sure to get there.

Niklas turned to Mahmud. "The bulletproof vests, the clothes, and the other gear's inside. But I can't go in there. Can you and one of your buddies get the stuff?"

"Isn't this your mom's place? Why can't you go in? What's your mom doing tonight? Is she home?"

"I have no idea. And we're not going upstairs to ask. Haven't you read the papers? Haven't you understood my situation?"

Mahmud didn't read the papers. He looked at Niklas. The guy really did look different from the last time he'd seen him. Thinner, harder. His eyes were darting around more than ever. Then there was the thing with the shaved head and beard, too. "No," he said. "What's the deal?"

"What you don't know won't hurt you," Niklas responded. "Forget about it, I'll tell you some other time. But I can't go in. You have to do it."

Mahmud let a few seconds pass. Thought: The guy really is quasi crazy. But still okay, somehow. He's got guts, he fights back. Just like I should've done, a long time ago.

Mahmud climbed out. Keys in hand. Babak got out of his car. He was wearing a ski hat pulled down low. Walked leaning slightly backward, trying to look chill.

It was cold.

They walked in through the entrance. Down to the basement. There was a sticker on the garbage chute: *Please—help our sanitation workers—seal the bag!* They walked down a staircase. A steel door. A lock from Assa Abloy. Mahmud opened it. Turned the overhead light on. Inside: a row of storage units. He looked for number twelve. One minute.

Found the unit. He opened it. Two black garbage bags filled with soft things. He looked. Inside: the bulletproof vests, the clothes, and the rest of the gear.

Back to the car. Mahmud started the engine. Javier in the passenger seat. Robert in the back. Niklas'd climbed in with Babak in his car.

He started. Followed Babak's car.

Robert leaned forward from the backseat.

"Honest, man, are we gonna pull this off?"

Mahmud didn't know how to respond. He just said, "Check out that commando guy. The dude's as cold as a glacier. I trust him."

Robert reached out his hand. A matchbox. A thin Redline baggie. Mahmud turned to Robert.

"Is that some white dynamite?"

Robert gave him a crooked smile.

"I think we need a little extra strength tonight."

Mahmud fished out a snort straw from his inside pocket. Put it in the bag. Sucked.

Outside, it was snowing like crazy.

Like the ice age was back.

62

Niklas repeated to himself: *Si vis pacem, para bellum*—If you wish for peace, prepare for war. His mantra, his life's mission. He'd armed himself, planned his attacks, guarded the perpetrators, hit the right people, at the right time, in the right way. Then came the latest incidents: the arrest, the escape, and now: a bunch of clowns. BOG, boots on the ground: five people—but really, they ought to count as three. Sure, Mahmud was okay enough, might hopefully equal one soldier, but he counted the other players as one. These were circumstances he hadn't been able to prepare for.

And somehow, it was all Mom's fault. She was the one who'd cracked his alibi—the video night at Benjamin's place was all to hell. He wouldn't have had a chance if there'd been a trial, even if the lawyer seemed sharp.

His escape from the hearing'd almost gone smoother than expected. As soon as Niklas'd made it down into the subway, he zeroed in on a man. It was almost New Year's Eve, so there were a lot of people out. Still, on the platform: mostly retirees and moms on maternity leave. The man was one of the former. Niklas forced him down on the ground, didn't even have to strike him. Took his shoes and coat. People around him hardly missed a beat—no one tried to stop him. Symptomatic: the losers just stood there and watched. That was part of the problem. Society was made up of bystanders. A train rolled in. So far, he didn't see any cops. Everything'd gone so fast, just a few seconds since he'd leaped out of the window in the District Court. His thoughts in battle position. Strategic considerations in fast-forward. He didn't get on the train. When it rolled out of the station, he jumped down behind it on the tracks and walked into the tunnel in the opposite direction. Hopefully, the people who'd seen him would think he'd gotten on the train, disappeared in the direction of the next subway stop.

A thousand feet or so in darkness. The light from the next station glowed like a white dot farther off. There were blue signal lights and thick cables on the walls. He ran. The old man's shoes fit okay. He'd only need them until he got to his own gear. So far, no trains, and that wouldn't stop him anyway—the margin between the track and the wall was several feet wide. What could stop him: the rats that ran in the gravel down there.

Rats.

A few seconds of silence. The darkness closed in around him. Sounds from the animals' jaws.

Niklas stopped. He had to get out.

The rats were moving down there on the tracks.

He repeated to himself: I have to get out.

Images came flashing back. The basement storage unit when he was a child. All the rats down in the sandbox.

The thought was as clear as the light farther off down the tunnel: If I don't get out now and complete the mission, my right to live ceases to exist. I will die. I WILL DIE.

He refused.

Refused to remain a passive observer of his own fate. So far, he'd let the circumstances control him. Yes, he made decisions—but always based on the situation at hand, on what others did, how he felt, what Mom thought. External facts, circumstantial occurrences that didn't originate in the depth of his soul. He didn't transcend himself. He didn't steer his own path. Today, he would change course. He was a living force to be reckoned with. A counterweight to everyone else.

He saw other lights farther up.

The tracks vibrated. A train approached through the tunnel.

He pressed himself against the wall. Tried to see if the rats were still there.

A minor blast wave in the tunnel. As if the air was being pressed in front of the train.

The train rushed by. He stood still. Close, close.

Then he ran. Toward the light.

He didn't hear the animals. He just moved.

Scrambled up onto the platform.

It was eleven o'clock. A mother with a stroller eyed him.

Niklas ran up the escalator.

He made it.

Back in the present. The car, the snow. The Arab he was sharing the car with was named Babak.

Niklas told him about the mansion. Gave directions. Explained the plan of attack over and over again. Babak just nodded. Held the steering wheel tight, as if he was afraid of losing it.

They took Nynäsvägen out toward the archipelago. Hardly any cars. Gray snow drifts along the roadside. Deep tracks in the snow.

Niklas thought about Mahmud and his men. They had energy. They were cocky. But that wasn't enough. Guys like that: they didn't know what structure, order, and teamwork were. They were individualists who ricocheted their way through life. Didn't understand the importance of organization. Hopefully they knew how to handle weapons— they'd practiced, according to Mahmud. Maybe they could handle the deep snow—panting their way through one and a half feet. They might possibly pull off the attack, the storming, the invasion. But would they be able to handle the situation that followed? Niklas hadn't had enough time. He felt unsure of himself.

He called Mahmud and ordered him to tell everyone to kill their phones.

Babak turned up toward Smådalarö. The darkness outside was compact against the windows. It'd stopped snowing.

He had to stop worrying. Get into the mood. Think about battle rattle.

The cars stopped seven minutes later. They were actually supposed to have stolen or rented cars for tonight, but there'd been no time to do that now when everything'd happened so quickly. They parked outside a large white house. Niklas knew what it was: the clubhouse that belonged to the golf course.

Niklas stepped out. Opened the trunk. Hoisted out one of the black plastic bags. Good that Mahmud'd been able to pick them up in Mom's basement. The cops were most definitely keeping the house under surveillance, waiting to pick him up again. The media'd heated up the debate around the whole escape.

He walked over to Mahmud's car with the bag. The sky was dark and it'd stopped snowing. The Arab opened the door. "Here, change in the car," Niklas said. "It's better than standing out here. If someone comes by, we don't want to call attention to ourselves." Mahmud accepted the bag. Niklas walked back to Babak's car. Hoisted out the other bag. Brought it into the car.

They began dressing.

Long underwear that Niklas'd bought at the Stadium sports store. There'd be a lot of time spent out in the cold. Over that: the bullet-proof vest—with the protective panels tightly packed, molded to the body. It was made to be worn directly against the body: the harness was attached to the protective panels so that the weight was distributed evenly. Maybe this stuff wasn't the best gear on the market, but it would do. The vests would still feel lighter than they actually were. Would protect heart, lungs, liver, kidneys, spleen, and spine.

He put on the black wind pants. It was tight, getting dressed in the car. He laced up his boots. High, fourteen holes, leather, over four-hundred-gram Thinsulate lining. Waterproof, ventilated membranes for winter cold, guard duty, and armed attack. He pulled on his gloves: lined, black leather. And then the thin puffy over the vest. The heat in the car almost felt damp.

Finally: the ski mask—rolled up, ready to be pulled down over his face.

Babak in the front seat: trying to wriggle into his pants.

"I'm sorry I didn't get any shoes for you," Niklas said. "I didn't have time."

Babak chuckled.

"My regular winter shoes'll have to work, I guess."

Niklas looked down. Babak was wearing a pair of white sneakers. Those were going to get cold and wet. He hoped the guy would be able to hack it.

They climbed out. The road was dark. The air felt clean. Farther up, beyond the golf course, he saw the trees. Niklas brought a backpack out from the trunk of the car. Opened it. Thanked himself for his careful preparations. Pulled out the Beretta. Tucked it into one of the front pockets of his jacket, put the ammunition in the other.

He walked over to Mahmud's car. The Arab rolled down the window. They looked like they were all dressed in there.

"Okay, boys, it's almost game time," Niklas said. "From now on, we're operating according to military rules. Is that clear?"

Mahmud nodded.

Niklas continued, "I'm going to be completely honest with you. We haven't had the planning time we needed. But this has to happen tonight. So we're going to have to improvise a little. There are a few things you have to think about."

The wind was picking up. Niklas had to raise his voice to be heard. "We're going to speak English with each other. Is that clear?"

The guys in the car and Babak nodded.

"And we will never use each other's names. Only use numbers. I am number one, Mahmud is number two, Babak is three, Robert is four, and Javier is five. Can you repeat that? Who are you, Mahmud?"

They repeated their assigned numbers a few times, until Niklas was satisfied.

"Never touch anything without wearing gloves. And finally—don't, under any circumstances, remove your ski masks. Not even if you've taken a hit to the face. Never. Is that clear?"

The boys nodded.

"Now I want you, Javier, to repeat what I just said," Niklas said.

Javier opened the car door. Recounted briefly about the names, the language, the ski masks.

"You forgot the gloves," Niklas said. "Never, under any circumstances, take off your gloves. Is that clear?"

The boys nodded again. Niklas asked Robert to repeat. Then Babak.

After each time, they nodded. Niklas hoped that it meant something.

They'd walked through the woods, in the snow, up to the fence. Waded through the snow. None of the boys were whining, yet. Niklas stopped. Took his backpack off. Dug around inside. Fished out four handsets.

"I have four walkie-talkies here. They are much better than cell phones. No one can track that we've used these. Mahmud and I will have two of them, for those of us going inside the house. Robert, you'll have the third handset and Javier will have the fourth. For the men remaining outside the house."

He pointed down, toward the road. "Now we're going to go check out the entrance gate."

One hundred and sixty-five feet farther off they saw the lights from the road. A car drove by, slowly. They walked closer. Saw the silhouette of the fence against the headlights. The car stopped: a Range Rover, model XL. Niklas watched the gates. Two men walked up to the car. The windows were rolled down. One of the men poked his head in. Said something. Then he waved: all clear.

The gates slid open. The car rolled in.

It was eleven-forty.

The moon was cold and large. Niklas led his men up along the fence again. The snow was reflecting the little light that was filtering through the trees from the house and the moon. It was enough, he didn't need to get out the night-vision goggles.

He knew this area. Knew the house's façade, angles, distance from the fence. He knew the course of the fence, where there were larger stones and gaps in the trees.

They walked another hundred feet. Silent. Calm. Focused.

Niklas stopped. "Here, Robert, this is your position. You know what your job is. Sit on this rock and wait. I'll inform you over the radio when it's time to get going. It'll be around midnight."

Robert looked like he understood the gravity of the situation. Nodded grimly. Gripped the AK4 with both hands. Mahmud shook his hand.

"See you later, *habibi*. This is gonna be big."

They pushed through the snow.

Three hundred feet. They glimpsed the back of the house through the trees. A warm light glowed from the windows.

He ran through the same procedure with Javier. Javier got in position with the AK4 held high. Ready. Prepared for his mission.

It actually felt good. So far.

Fifty more feet. Just Niklas, Mahmud, and Babak. Dressed in black, dark as the desert night. Niklas felt for the Beretta in his jacket pocket. Picked it up one final time. Popped out the magazine. Inspected it in the moonlight. He knew this piece by heart. He thought about Mats Strömberg and Roger Jonsson. Pigs who'd faced their butcher. Soon, justice would be served. The New Year would be off to a good start.

They stopped by the designated spot in the fence, where the distance to the back entrance of the house was the shortest. Niklas took off his backpack. Fished out the bolt cutters. Crouched by the fence. Began from the bottom. Cut into the thin steel: easy as paper.

After five minutes: a hole nearly three feet high and twenty inches wide.

They crouched down. Crawled through. Behind enemy lines.

Eighty feet. Slowly. Niklas in the lead. Staying low to the ground, military posture.

Sixteen more feet. They approached the house.

Another sixteen feet. Niklas stopped. Looked ahead. No people outside the house as far as he could see. He fished around in the bag again. Brought out the night-vision goggles after all. Mahmud and Babak sat down behind him. He scanned the façade. Window by window. The light from the inside was intensified by the effect of the goggles, hurt his eyes. He eyed the door: no people outside. All appeared quiet.

He took the goggles off. Turned to Mahmud. The Arab still had his ski mask rolled up. Niklas whispered, "We move in ten minutes."

Mahmud smiled widely. Made thumbs up.

Something was fishy. Mahmud looked strange. Niklas didn't drop his gaze. Took a step closer to Mahmud.

"Can you show me your mouth again?"

Mahmud smiled again.

His teeth were dark, almost looked bluish. Maybe it was the moonlight.

"What the fuck did you eat?"

Mahmud grinned. Responded in a low voice, "Rohypnol, of course. It makes your mouth a little blue. You didn't know that, buddy? You want some?"

Niklas didn't know what to do. For a brief second, he considered shooting Mahmud in the face. Bolinder could happily find a defrosted Arab corpse in the spring. Then another thought passed through his mind: he should abort the mission. Get up and sneak back out the same way they'd come. Leave these two clowns to do whatever they wanted. Still, he remained where he was in the snow. Crouching. Shivering. Completely paralyzed. It couldn't end like this. He'd promised himself. I'm in charge. I make the decisions. I don't give up. I make a difference.

"How long ago did you take that shit?"

"Right before we saw the Range Rover. I want to be ready. It's not a big deal, Niklas. I promise. I always take roofies when there's gonna be action."

"You've made a mistake. But we'll have to let it slide for now. You won't take any more of that stuff. Is that clear?"

Mahmud's smile died. He looked down. Maybe he understood his slip. Maybe he just didn't want to argue.

Fifteen minutes passed. They were lying down. The snow was touching their chins. The house: fifty feet off. The kitchen entrance was clearly visible. A wood door—90 percent certain it was locked. Niklas could hear music from inside. Could see people moving around behind the curtains. Music, laughter. Whore sounds.

He fished around in his backpack. His very own IED: improvised explosive device. His homemade grenade. It looked like a black beer can.

Mahmud and Babak were lying diagonally behind him.

Niklas held the grenade in his right hand. Looked at his watch. It was five minutes to midnight.

Soon time to catapult the whore hounds into the New Year.

63

There was music coming from the floor above. Thuds in the ceiling. A bass. Laughter. Thomas thought about his dad's old favorite poet, Nils Ferlin, and his poem about a ceiling being someone else's floor. Then he thought, There is no room for poets in today's Sweden. Way too few who even know Swedish well enough to read stuff like that. What's more: the ones who speak Swedish don't care about poetry anyway. He was pining. Not just for his old man. He was pining for a Sweden that no longer existed.

In front of him: high metal storage shelves. Probably a total of thirty yards of shelving. Classic black binders with felt spines. Binders that locked around the paperwork. Around the bookkeeping material, the verifications, the documents. Hopefully the same stuff that Hägerström and Thomas'd just gone through. Hopefully something else too. Proof.

New Year's Eve's night was running on. Finally, right before he got here and made his way inside, the weather'd calmed down—Åsa would get a perfect view of the fireworks. Thomas was inside, alone—alone against the power. Alone against the ones fucking with him. Now it was his turn to show some people who's boss.

Hägerström'd looked shocked at first. "You work a side job at a strip club?" But his surprise settled quickly—the case was more important. Still, he advised against going to the party. Went on and on about how they should wait till tomorrow, try to talk to some superior, give an account of all the information they had. Rantzell's connection to the Palme murder and Bolinder's organization. Get a formal search warrant.

Thomas grew irritated, mostly. "You know as well as I do that what we have won't get us anywhere. Really, what proof do we have? That

459

Rantzell guy'd been given shady payments. It has to do with the murder weapon, that much I'm certain of. But in what way does our information really point to someone having something to do with the murder? And it certainly doesn't point to the murder of Olof Palme. But when we add up what Ballénius told us about Rantzell and the payments that you found, we know that we're on the right track."

Hägerström squeezed his eyes shut. Looked pained. He probably knew that Thomas was right. Still he said, "But come on, Andrén. We've been doing this on the side long enough. We have to get back on the formal route now. Do the right things in the right way. Or else it could all go to shit. Right?"

Thomas looked at him for a moment. "I'm going to be honest with you. I don't think too highly of cops who work against other cops. People like that aren't real cops in my eyes."

Hägerström stared back at him.

Thomas went on, "What's more, you're a little know-it-all who thinks a bit too highly of yourself. You bitch about irrelevant stuff, you don't have any sense of comradeship, and I'm not sure you could even handle a SIG Sauer."

Hägerström continued to stare back at him.

"But, on the other hand," Thomas made a dramatic pause, "you're the best, sharpest, quickest cop I've ever met. You've been loyal to this private investigation we're running. You've been loyal to me despite everything that's happened. You're funny, I laugh at every joke you make. You're thoughtful and brave. I can't help it—I like you a lot."

Continued silence.

"I understand where you're coming from," Thomas said. "You have significantly more to lose than I do. I've already put myself outside the system. I just have myself to blame while you might lose your job. And practically speaking, there's one other thing. You'd never be let in there, at that party. But I might be. I'm going to finish this thing. Tonight. With or without you."

Hägerström rose. Didn't say anything. Thomas tried to read his facial expression. Hägerström walked toward the hallway. Turned around. "Well, this is what I was thinking. My night is going to consist of me going home and changing, then going to the Half Way Inn and hanging out there for the rest of the night. Drinking lots of beer and maybe a few glasses of champagne. At around two o'clock, I'll probably be so drunk that I'll already have forgotten about midnight, ringing in the New Year, all that. What do I have to lose? That's not a New Year's Eve worth remembering. I'll come with you. You're not doing anything without me."

They were driving on the road out to Dalarö, each in his own car. Hardly any traffic. Almost felt cozy. The warm air and the heating in the seat. The sound of the car's engine was like a blanket of security in the background. The light from the headlights was reflected in the snowdrifts that edged the road like high banks. Hägerström was in front; he'd entered the address into his GPS. Thomas didn't think they had the same things on their minds.

He'd called Åsa again and told her he had to work all night. She became sadder this time, started crying, questioned how it was all going to work when Sander came. Would Thomas take his role as a parent seriously? Did he understand what it meant to have a family? What did he value in life? He didn't have any answers. He couldn't tell her anything about what was happening right now.

Who was he, really? A mix of police mentality and self-righteousness was deeply rooted in him. At the same time, he'd changed over the last few months. Seen, close up, the people he usually worked to nail. Felt a kind of kinship with them. There was a life, a moral code, on the shady side of society, too. They were people he could become close to. They made choices based on what was the right thing to do in their situations. Thomas'd crossed the line. The step he'd taken—a cardinal sin. But there, in the valley of death, among the people he used to call the dregs, the rabble, he'd found people who felt like friends. And if they could be his friends and if their choices were the right choices—then who was he, as a police officer?

He tried to dismiss the thoughts. Concluded to himself: Tonight, it was different.

Forty minutes later, Hägerström's car stopped by a dark forest road out on Smådalarö. Thomas parked behind him. Remained sitting in the car and called Hägerström. They decided that Hägerström would park his car on the forest road. Thomas would try to make his way in. They put all their chips on this one hand.

He drove slowly along the road until he saw the driveway. There was a full moon. A black metal gate. He stopped the car ten yards from the sign. Waited. Next to the gate was a camera and a large sign: PRIVATE PROPERTY. PROTECTED BY G4S.

Fifteen minutes later, a car pulled up. Not just any car: a limousine. Felt weird: a stretch limo à la Las Vegas on a winter road in the countryside. The car pulled up to the gate. Thomas couldn't see exactly what was happening. After thirty seconds, the gates slid open. The car rolled through.

Thomas thought about the man outside his house and the guy who'd attacked him in the garage. Maybe it was the same person. He thought about Cederholm alias Rantzell, Ballénius, and Ballénius's daughter. The cops who used to feel like his friends: Ljunggren and Hannu Lindberg. In his mind's eye he saw Adamsson, the forensic pathologist Bengt Gantz, Jonas Nilsson. It'd been a long journey leading up to the situation he was facing now. Still, it almost felt like everything'd been going according to some predetermined plan.

He put the car in first gear. Drove slowly up to the gate. The car's exhaust billowed out behind him like a minor heating plant. He stopped. Rolled down the window. Looked into the surveillance camera. A voice from the speakers: "Good evening. How may we help you?"

"My name is Thomas Andrén, let me in please."

A faint buzz on the other end of the line.

"Tell Ratko, Bogdan, or whoever else you've got in there right now that I'm supposed to work tonight."

A rustling sound in the microphone, then a different voice. "Hey there, Thomas. I didn't know you were working. No one informed me." It was Bogdan, a guy who usually helped out at the club.

The gates opened.

He drove through.

Outdoor lights were hidden in the bushes along the road and illuminated the snow on the branches of the trees. A hundred or so yards, maybe, then the forest opened up. An enormous three-story house, big windows, pillars by the entrance. Probably twenty cars parked outside. The limousine was turning around. A few of the rooms were lit up. He could hear faint sounds. Thomas parked next to a black Audi Q7. Walked up to the house. Thought, What is this insane thing I've gotten myself into?

He didn't have time to ring the doorbell. The door slid open. A guy he recognized but didn't know the name of opened it. Huge Yugo. Had been down at the club with Ratko once or twice. Smiled. "Hey there, copper. I didn't know you were working tonight. Ratko and Bogdan are around here somewhere. Do you need to talk to them?"

Thomas responded politely that he was there to work. He didn't need to see Ratko or Bogdan. He knew the drill.

He walked in. A hallway. There was a real Persian carpet on the floor. Yards and yards of sconces, paintings, and tapestries along the walls. The room was bigger than the entire downstairs of his and Åsa's house in Tallkrogen. At the other end of the entrance hall: a number of men—they must've come in limousines. They were all dressed in tuxes. Loud, hungry for a ho-down. In front of them—it looked like a cloakroom. Coats were hanging in rows. A girl was in the process of taking them. Thomas should've been able to guess what this would all be like, but he was still surprised. Mini-mini-miniskirt, the lower part of her ass cheeks visible. Thigh-high stockings that ended in an edge of lace a ways up on her leg, a provocative show of skin, taut corset, black high-heeled shoes. Her top didn't look cheap, but it was low cut enough for her breasts to be a perfect target for the men's eyes. Like the strippers at the club, but even more spruced up somehow.

He needed to act quickly. He picked up his cell phone, fired off a text to Hägerström: *Inside.* Then he looked around again. There were three doors in front of him. The men who'd checked their coats disappeared through one. Thomas heard noise coming from in there. Not the right choice for him. He turned back around to the guard. "Hey, actually, where did you say Ratko was?"

The beefcake laughed, nodded toward one of the doors. "Where he always is during these events, in the kitchen of course." Thomas was a fucking genius. Process of elimination must be as old as the job these chicks were working. He walked over to the last door. Opened it. Didn't worry about whether or not the beefy Yugo wondered what he was doing.

It was almost completely dark in there. A table: probably thirty feet long. Rococo chairs in pale wood, a crystal chandelier, candelabras on the table, parquet floor. A dining room. Two doors. Both were half open. From one, he saw lights and heard the sound of men talking. That must be the kitchen. He walked through the other door.

Another type of room. Sparsely furnished: a narrow sofa against one wall. On the walls: paintings, paintings, and more paintings. Spotlights placed everywhere, like little islands of light. He didn't know anything about art—what he saw looked mostly like pastel-colored lines on fuzzy backgrounds. On the other hand: difficult apparently equaled expensive.

He walked into the next room. The sound of music and laughter increased. If what he was looking for was in there or in the kitchen, he could forget about it. He looked around. The room was small. Again, paintings on the walls. Garish wallpaper. And one more thing: a railing wrapped in leather, a staircase. Leading down. It was too good to be true. Where do you store archive material? Not where you entertain. Not in your private quarters. In the basement. He hoped.

Walked down.

The staircase ended in a door. He tried the handle—locked. Bolinder wasn't that stupid after all. But neither was Thomas Andrén. He fished out the electronic skeleton key. For a real cop like him, it was the most important tool, after his baton. He inserted it into the lock. Thought about the basement door at Gösta Ekman Road. How he'd found Rantzell in pieces. He was nearing the end of the story.

Down on the basement level: a spa section, a sauna, a swimming pool. A laundry room, a room filled with paintings that apparently weren't suitable enough to hang on the walls upstairs, a smaller room with a stationary bike, a treadmill, and a weight machine. Narrow windows high up near the ceiling. Farthest in: the archive. Metal storage shelves. What looked like a hundred binders of material. Bingo.

He checked the time on his phone: eleven o'clock. He didn't have any service down here. It was time to start searching.

Almost midnight: he hadn't found jack shit. Still, he was familiar with the material. Recognized the company names, the names of the board members, the banks that provided accounts, the businesses. He only looked through the binders that had to do with Dolphin Leasing AB, Intelligal AB, and Roaming GI AB.

He couldn't stay here forever. Sooner or later the guard or one of the others would wonder where he'd gone. If he was supposed to work tonight—then why wasn't he working? He looked at his cell phone again. Three minutes to midnight. He had the feeling he was going to find something soon. He stopped briefly. Considered: Had he done the right thing? Ditched Åsa, gotten himself into this situation. He refused to think the thought: Maybe he wouldn't come out of here alive tonight.

The sounds from upstairs seemed to be dying down.

And then: the explosions. The men cheered. Thomas climbed up on a stool and looked out through a small window. The sky was illuminated by the crackle of fireworks. The moon was like a pale disk beside the play of colors in the sky. It was beautiful.

The partygoers were making even more noise. Thomas didn't see anyone outside. Maybe they'd walked outside but were standing somewhere where he couldn't see them. Maybe they were still inside.

Then he heard another explosion. It was definitely closer. Harder. Sounded like something crashing. He was certain: that wasn't the sound of fireworks.

64

It was the biggest bang Mahmud'd ever heard. Niklas'd pulled the ski mask down over his face—reminded Mahmud of the images of militiamen in his dad's Iraqi newspapers. He'd moved forward crouching in the dark. Planted the grenade by the back door. Crawled back ten yards. It exploded. Incredible sound. The blast wave was like a kick to the chest. A screaming inside him. A beeping in his ears. Niklas hollered, "Game time!" The night was lit up by fireworks. Crackling sounds across the sky. It felt like a dream. Maybe it was just the effect of the roofies.

Niklas rushed forward. Like in slow motion.

Mahmud gasped for air. Ran after him, toward the house. The Glock in his right hand. Shit, it was cold. He could hardly feel his feet: cold, wet, stiff.

A hole gaped where the back door'd been. Gunpowder was splashed along the wall. Wood, bricks, plaster—in pieces. The light from the kitchen glowed out into the backyard. The night in color—painted green, red, and blue.

Niklas was approaching the hole. Then him. Last, Babak.

Agitated voices. Rapid gunfire in the background. It had to be Rob and Javier letting the Swedish Army's AK4s loose on the house. Ha-ha-ha—the *blattes* were fighting back. Jorge the Latino's plan was gonna kick some fat ass.

They stepped in through the hole.

The kitchen was gigantic. Felt old-fashioned. Fancy cabinets, marble countertops, clinker floor. Spotlights in the ceiling. Two sinks, two ovens, two tables, two microwaves. Two of fucking everything. Even two shocked-looking dudes. They rose. Tall. Broad. Steaming Yugos.

One of them was Ratko. Who'd humiliated Mahmud. What's more: one of the guys Jorge'd talked about as being Radovan's man. Who was part of the mission. Whom he needed to pop.

Mahmud stopped. Looked at Niklas. The soldier dude knew where he was going, was already about to disappear through a door. Yelled, in English, "Take that motherfucker out!"

Mahmud was tripped up by the English for a second. Double emotions: confused, at the same time, riled up. The dudes in front of him started screaming in Serbian. That's when he reacted. He was holding the Glock out in front of him. Now he aimed it at Ratko. The Yugo was wearing jeans, a white shirt with the sleeves rolled up. Testosterone-squared jaw, his thin blond hair parted to the side, surprise in his eyes. Mahmud saw Wisam Jibril in front of him. Images in his head: how they'd picked up the Lebanese outside the grill joint in Tumba. How Stefanovic'd taken him to dinner at Gondolen and explained the situation: we snuff out anyone who messes with us. How Ratko'd laughed in his the face when he'd wanted to quit dealing. He felt the effects of the roofies pumping through his blood. The Yugos were gonna eat shit tonight.

Mahmud raised the gat toward Ratko's head. Ratko stopped. Fell silent. Babak behind him. "Come on." He didn't see Niklas. The Yugo dude's face: contorted. Panicked. Mortal terror.

Mahmud walked closer. Slowly squeezed the trigger with his finger. Ratko saw what was about to happen.

Images in his head. Like the din of the fireworks outside. In the forest clearing with Gürhan's piece in his mouth. In the Bentley store with the scared sales kid before him. Finally: Beshar. Dad. His voice in serene Arabic: "Do you know what the prophet—peace be upon him— says about killing the innocent?"

The handle of the Glock felt sweaty. The white of the kitchen was hurting his eyes. Fucking pigs.

Ratko was not an innocent.

He fired.

Bam-bam-bam.

For Dad.

65

First POC—point of contact—with the enemy. They were inside the house. Niklas scanned the room: white, white, white. Two whore guards. Ordered Mahmud to SBF—support by fire. Pop that fucker. Woman user, abuser, enemy combatant.

Niklas felt at home with the situation at hand. The adrenaline was pumping like in the good old days. He took a deep breath in through the nose, breathed out through the mouth. He was mentally prepared. At war again. Not just man to man—but with soldiers, a battalion, a battle.

Continued through the door toward where the men must be. FEBA—forward edge of battle area. A dining room. Wrong. He walked up to another door. Opened, looked in. A hallway. Turned around. Saw Babak taping up the remaining guard in the kitchen. Nice. Ordered him and Mahmud to follow him.

Outside: Javier and Robert'd stopped shooting at the house. But everyone inside must've gotten the message: area controlled. If anyone were to walk outside the house, they'd have to start firing again like madmen. Pepper everything that moved.

Through the hall. The Beretta safe in his hand. A large man who seemed to understand that something was happening. Probably the guy who let people in the front door.

"What the fuck are you doing? Who are you?"

Niklas landed a bullet in the guy's knee. He crumpled like a dead man but he howled like a wild dog.

Niklas gave Mahmud an order: "Put some tape on that asshole."

They taped the bouncer's wrists and mouth. Niklas kept advancing. Alone.

Got in touch with Robert over the radio. A few rapid comments: "We've neutralized three combatants in here, and that's most of the ones we believe may be dangerous. But maintain eyes on the big room that I pointed out. I'm making contact now."

A gigantic room. Red wallpaper. Crystal chandeliers and spotlights in the ceiling. Large windows along one long end of the room. A fifteen-foot bar in the other end. Probably fifty people in there: half girls, half old guys. But they weren't just any old guys. The ones Niklas'd spied on at the pizzeria'd been middle-class Svens, Eastern Bloc pimps, and dudes from the kind of countries where he'd been at war. These johns: thriving Swedish men in black tie. They were here to party and to get something more. Mahmud'd told him earlier what he'd been told by their employer: these weren't your everyday horndogs—these were the leaders of the Swedish business world. Industry men, finance moguls, majority shareholders. Sweden's head honchos. Here to taste fresh young pussy.

The old guys and the girls were gathered at the windows. Impressed by the New Year's Eve fireworks. Champagne glasses in hand. The last fanfare of gunpowder and color blasted across the sky. They still hadn't realized that they were under attack. Hadn't heard the explosion from the IED, or at least not distinguished it from the noise of the fireworks. Everything'd gone according to plan: they would never be able to close or lock the hole out back. Always an open retreat route: assault tactics.

Two seconds was enough. He read the mood in the room: as if they were at a regular New Year's Eve party where some younger single girls just happened to be. As if there was nothing wrong. Nothing dirty. Nothing humiliating about the whole situation. But Niklas knew: buying women equaled abuse. And his calling was to exterminate abusers.

Most of them were still turned away from him. Looking out at the sky or at one another. Except for two younger guys who were manning the bar. One of them reacted to Niklas in the doorway: a man with a ski mask pulled down over his face attracts attention. Niklas walked farther into the room. Mahmud followed behind him. Niklas'd ordered Babak to wait outside, guard the entrance, cover their backs.

The bar guy starting yelling something. Niklas raised the Beretta in both hands. A firm grip. He knew: this is the decisive moment—everything could go to hell. A turning point. A bottleneck in the exercise. Ready. Get set. Run.

The gun in one hand. One step. Two steps. Flew. Reminded him of his escape from the District Court.

He breathed in once. Twice. Twenty feet. Reached the guy. Raised the gun. Heard him say, "What the hell?"

Bam. Rapped the guy's forehead with the Beretta, hard. The kid collapsed. Niklas turned around. Met the faces of the men and the girls—they'd turned around as well.

It was like time stood.

Still.

Everyone'd seen the attack.

Niklas and Mahmud: in control. Niklas'd informed Robert, "We've made contact, we're gonna get this show on the road. Shoot everything that moves outside the house."

The guys were lined up against the wall. The girls were standing next to them. Mahmud with his Glock pointed at the cluster of people the whole time. The bar guy and his friend were taped up on the floor. There could be more pimps, whore guards, in the house. Or, rather, there *should* be more: someone must've been responsible for the outdoor fireworks display. The advantage that Niklas and his troops had: because of what the men were up to, they weren't exactly overly inclined to call the cops. The men knew it too. Still, he had to be smooth. He wanted to get ahold of those in charge.

Niklas took a step forward. In English: "I want Bolinder!"

No movement among the men.

"Who is Bolinder?"

A voice in the crowd, in English with a heavy Swedish accent: "There is no Bolinder here."

Niklas responded in his own way. Fired off a shot at one of the chandeliers. Heard the bullet bounce around up there. Pulled the ski mask up halfway, bared his mouth.

"Don't fuck with me 'cause then I'll take you out, one by one. For the last time, who is Bolinder?"

The silence in the room was louder than the shot itself.

A man stepped forward. Said in a thin voice, "I am Bolinder. What do you want?"

He was slightly overweight, had carefully combed gray hair, and wore his tuxedo shirt unbuttoned to reveal a tuft of gray chest hair. He met Niklas's gaze. The man's eyes were gray.

Niklas stared back. Didn't bother saying anything. This was the guy who arranged everything.

Bolinder was made to stand in the middle of the parquet floor. The light from a couple of spotlights in the ceiling hit him in the face. Niklas could see it clearly: the old john was scared as hell.

Mahmud pulled out the tape. Had Bolinder put his hands behind his back. The Arab wrapped them carefully. Laid the old guy down on the floor. The duct tape gleamed serenely.

Mahmud went closer. Gun pointed at the herd of men. He waved the Glock slowly from right to left and back again. If anyone tried anything, he'd hopefully be able to take down five or six people before he was overpowered. Instinctively, the men knew it too. No one wanted to take the chance.

Niklas yelled in English, "Down on the ground, every fucking one of you. Now. Put your hands on your head. Anyone who moves . . ." He made two shooting motions with the gun. They understood.

Niklas rummaged around in his backpack. The moment he'd been waiting for. He pulled out the plastic bag he'd prepared months ago. His own little project, parallel to surveillance of the wife beaters. It was pretty heavy, probably thirteen pounds. From the outside, it looked innocent enough: a gray bag with black electrical tape wound around it and a compact mass within. On the inside, it was highly lethal.

Everything'd gone so fast. Just a little while ago, he'd been sitting in a courtroom, about to be detained. And now: the final battle. He thought about his mom. She didn't understand anything. Thought repression was intrinsic to life, built in. He remembered. He was maybe eight years old, but he still understood more than they thought. The bags that Claes brought home, the mood when he and Marie'd started gulping from their glasses, which they refilled quickly with whatever was in the bottles. They told him to go down to the basement for an hour or so. He had his own life down there. He didn't remember exactly, but something scared him. Maybe it was a sound, or maybe he saw something. He was a child then. Thought the fear down there was the worst thing in the world. When he came upstairs, he saw Mom being beaten more than he'd ever seen before. She had to go to the hospital. Stayed there for two weeks.

Afterward, he'd asked Mom if it was right. Should Claes really be allowed to come over to their house? Should it really be like this? Her answer was simple but firm: "I've forgiven him. He's my man, and he can't help that he gets angry sometimes."

It was Niklas's duty to restore balance.

He placed the bomb on Bolinder's chest. The old guy was fluttering like a flag in the evening breeze outside Falluja. In contrast: Niklas's hands were steady.

66

Thomas came up the stairs. Something was wrong. First the explosion at the same time as the fireworks. He could've misheard. But not what followed: the peppering that sounded parallel to the rest of the New Year's spectacle—even a simple cop like him, who was used to his little 9-millimeter SIG Sauer, knew what that was: assault weapons. He was a gun freak, after all. Completely clear: something was really fucking wrong.

As soon as his phone had service again, he called Hägerström. It rang once. More rings went through. Was he not going to pick up? Thomas looked around. The room with the hypercolorful wallpaper was empty. He peeked through the opening in the doorway to the room with the paintings. Empty. He tried to call Hägerström again. Five rings. Then there was Hägerström's panting breath on the other end of the line: "Good, you're alive."

Thomas whispered into the receiver, "What the fuck is happening?"

"I don't know, but I've called for backup. There was insane shooting going on somewhere inside the building where you are. And an explosion that sounded like they were blowing something up."

"When is backup getting here?"

"You know, it's New Year's Eve, on Smådalarö, out in the archipelago. They won't be here for another twenty minutes, at best."

"Fuck. But what should I do? Something's definitely going on in here."

"Just wait for the squad cars. I can't get past the gate by myself."

"No, Hägerström, that won't cut it. This is our chance to get some hard evidence. I've got to see what's happening. It might be connected to our case."

Hägerström was silent. Thomas felt a drop of sweat on his forehead. He waited for Hägerström's response. Would he support him in this or not?

Hägerström cleared his throat. "Okay, take a quick look. But for fuck's sake, don't do anything stupid. You said it yourself—this could be the solution to our case. So don't blow it."

Thomas put his cell phone back in his inner pocket. Groped for his gun. Looked at it for a second. Fully loaded. Recently cleaned. Safety on. Felt good.

Thomas went back into the salon where all the paintings were hung. Then into the entrance hall.

His first discovery surprised him: the huge Yugo—the bouncer—in a heap on the floor. Around his feet, his forearms, and his mouth: looked like miles' worth of duct tape. A puddle of blood on the floor—the guy's knee: ground meat mixed with pants fabric. The guard was staring sluggishly into space. Thomas bent down. Ripped the tape from his mouth in one tear.

"What happened?" he whispered.

The guard seemed groggy. Maybe the loss of blood, maybe the shock, maybe he was on his way out. Thomas loosened the tape on his forearms. The guard: completely silent. Thomas listened to his breathing. It was there. Thin but still clear. He used the tape he'd torn off to wrap the wound on his knee. Tightened—tried to stop the flow of blood. Better than nothing. Checked the guy's back, stomach, head—he didn't seem to be injured anywhere else. Thomas placed him in the recovery position. The guard would survive.

Thomas texted Hägerström: *Call amb. Pers shot in knee.*

Moved on. Silence in the house. The beat, the music, the laughter couldn't be heard anymore. The house felt like a grave, like the basement where he'd found Claes Rantzell. Thomas thought about the guard's breathing: so thin. Like the air in this house. Like this entire investigation. It might all go to hell now—Bolinder's bizarre party, the Yugos' involvement, the payments to Rantzell, the key witness in Sweden's most important trial.

Everything was thin.

Thomas stopped.

Took a deep breath. Was there something wrong with the air in here?

Felt like he was getting less oxygen. As if he was forced to breathe deeper. As if his lungs needed more.

He raised his gun. Closed his eyes. Saw an image in front of him. A boy. A face.

Sander.

Then he opened his eyes.

It was time to keep going.

Made his way through a couple of rooms. Empty of people. Colorful wallpaper, paintings, a sculpture or two, the right lighting, the right color choices, the right designer furniture. Couches, armchairs, Persian carpets, harmonious feel. Thomas thought, These types of men hide their real selves behind fancy art that no ordinary people understand. Criminal classic—the bigger the crook, the bigger the artists on the walls. It felt good to relax into a normal, bitter line of thought.

He walked through a hallway. The lighting was built into the floorboards.

He grabbed hold of the door handle. Carefully. Slowly. Pushed down. The door opened outward. A crack. He raised his gun. Sank down to his knees to be safe. Looked in.

A large room. The crystal chandeliers in the ceiling were the first things he saw. The room felt too bright. It sparkled. Immediately thereafter he saw the people. At least fifty of them. Men and women. On their stomachs, hands over their heads. Facedown on the floor. Thomas couldn't see who they were. Could only guess.

He looked closer. Three people were lying in front of them. Taped up, folded up. One of them looked like he was unconscious. The second one was just staring, wide-eyed. The third: wrapped in something. A heavy-looking plastic bag on his stomach. A wire led from the plastic bag to a small gray box.

There were two more people in the room. Two men with concealed faces. Ski masks rolled down, dark clothes; they looked like they were wearing bulletproof vests underneath. Maybe they were pros. One was thinner, with a Beretta in one hand and maybe something else in the other. Standing a little way off from the people. Steady, calm, focused on safety. The other was incredibly beefy. He approached the group on the floor. Said, in crap English, "Everyone hands over their watches and wallets. Now." Thomas could distinguish a thick Swedish immigrant accent in the English. Clear: this was a Swedish *blatte*.

He looked again. These weren't real pros—the beefy guy was wearing light-colored sneakers.

Thomas read the situation. Weighed possibilities. Judged alternative courses of action. What he should really do is get out. Report to Hägerström where the hostage holders and the people were. Wait for backup. Let things take their course.

Or else he could wait and see what happened. He had a personal interest in this investigation. It was completely outside the rule book, after all. If it came to light, he'd be screwed as a cop forever. Häger-ström too. He was also lured by the thought of solving the situation going on in the room by himself. Become a hero—make a triumphant return to the Southern District. The lone cop who went in on his own instead of waiting for backup. Dumb as hell. Stubborn as a four-year-old. Idiot risk taker—but still a hero.

That's exactly how he felt. But he didn't do it. He remained where he was. Backup was on its way, after all.

The guys in there pocketed the stuff that the men'd laid out on the floor in front of them.

The guy with the Beretta was clearly taking it easier than the one with the gym shoes. Moved with ease above the men's heads. Held the gun in a relaxed grip, but still with full control. Looked like he'd done this before.

He opened his mouth. His English was significantly better than the beefcake's. "I want all the whores to stand up."

No one seemed to understand. He repeated, "I want all the girls to stand up."

He pointed the gun at one of the men. Then he screamed, "Now!"

67

Mahmud didn't understand what Niklas was doing. The commando guy'd suddenly started asked the hookers to stand up.

In his smooth English: "Everyone point to the man who last bought you."

They didn't seem to understand what he meant. Mahmud didn't either.

This wasn't part of the plan.

His bag was full of wallets and watches. Nice stuff—he immediately saw a solid gold Rolex Submariner. Mahmud calculated. The gold watch alone: probably 200,000. The total value: at least 500,000 in just Rolex, Cartier, IWC, Baume & Mercier, and the rest of the watches. Plus: the plastic. Even if they would cancel a bunch, Tom Lehtimäki would be able to trick enough systems to get another 500,000 or 600,000 kronor. What's more: Jorge's promised payment—he'd popped Ratko, one of Radovan's men. Avenged his humiliation. Completed the Latino's mission: hurt the Yugo mafia. It tasted so good.

Time to retreat.

Then again, he hadn't taken pictures of the men with the hookers yet. That'd been Jorge's idea. When he'd explained, the Latino's grin'd been wider than a fucking smiley face. "Bring a good camera, man. You're gonna be able to use the photos for years. They'll pay. I promise. I know." Mahmud got the point. Blackmail was a wonderful thing.

He turned to Niklas—screw the whole speak Yankee thing.

"What the fuck are you doing?"

Niklas didn't respond. Kept raving.

"All the whores stand up. Or else I'll blow this old fuck into so many pieces you'll have to wipe up brain matter all night."

A few of the girls started to get up. One by one. Most of them looked Eastern, around ten mulattos or Asians, a few Swedes. Dressed like the sluts they were, but more deluxe. Short skirts, tight jeans, fishnets, boots, stilettos, low-cut tops in thin materials. Mahmud recognizcd Natascha and Juliana and several others from the trailers. They'd clearly been dolled up tonight. Girls he'd driven around over the entire city.

Niklas yelled at them. The soldier boy seemed to've lost his grip. The girls didn't want to follow his orders. But he kept on making commands.

"I don't care if you don't recognize these men. Just stand next to one who's ever humiliated you. Stand there, goddammit!"

Mahmud tried again.

"Cut this shit, man. I'm done collecting. We did what we came here to do."

Niklas turned to him. Continued in English, "I told you, no Swedish! What are you? Fucking retarded?"

68

Niklas was close to the finish line. The women would point out the guilty parties. He would serve the justice that society was waiting for. That his mom'd waited for all her life. He was a one-man judge and jury.

He was holding the remote detonator in one hand. The Beretta in the other. The attack was in its final stage. Judgment within reach. In a few minutes, it would be time to pull back the forces.

But first he had to make the Arab, who'd started interfering, shut his trap. Didn't Mahmud understand that WILCO—will comply—was in force? Shut up and follow orders.

Niklas never dropped his eyes from the whore hounds.

The Arab kept pestering him: "Let's split. Now. We're done here."

He tried to calm Mahmud down. Might need him to finish things here.

This couldn't become a SNAFU—situation normal, all fucked up. He tried a WO—warning order: "Shut up. Now. Just follow orders or you'll wish you had."

Mahmud, in a raised register: "Fuck man, chill out, Niklas. We're splitting. Or else Babak and me'll split without you."

Niklas couldn't wait. He raised the Beretta toward one of the men. One by one, the order determined by the gravity of their crime. The man looked up. Three prostitutes were standing over him.

69

Did he hear that right? The situation in the room'd definitely started to derail. This would end badly. Very badly.

The men in the ski masks were arguing with each other. The immigrant guy'd started speaking Swedish. Apparently wanted to leave. The pro wanted to stay. Finish something that had to do with lining the whores up. Thomas could only imagine.

But did he hear that right? The immigrant guy'd said the name of the dude who wanted to stay—Niklas. He'd called him Niklas.

It was scary. A man named Niklas was attacking Bolinder.

Only one Niklas came to mind. The guy who'd escaped from the hearing in the District Court yesterday. The guy he and Hägerström'd discussed so many times. Maybe they were on the wrong track. Thomas'd dismissed all that—too much pointed to Adamsson, Bolinder, and the others. But now: what did the altercation and the hostage taking he'd just witnessed mean?

It couldn't be a coincidence. It must be Niklas Brogren who was standing in the room right now. Prepared to kill all the johns. Above all: prepared to blow Bolinder into a million pieces.

There was a connection between Bolinder and the man who was suspected of murdering Rantzell. Again: it couldn't be a coincidence. Niklas Brogren wanted something from Bolinder.

It meant two things. One: Thomas and Hägerström'd been right—the guy wasn't innocent, he was involved in the murder somehow. Two: Bolinder wasn't innocent either. Why else was someone who was involved in the murder here at his house, of all places?

There wasn't time to think. The immigrant guy remained where he was reluctantly. Brogren'd forced all the girls to stand over different men. Unclear if they'd actually had sex with them or if they just went somewhere out of fear and confusion over Brogren's order.

What should he do? Backup obviously wasn't here yet. Not his fault—what was happening in the room would've happened even if he hadn't come up from the basement. Now he was the only policeman on the scene. His duty: to stop what was happening in there. Or? No one knew that he and Hägerström were here. Maybe he should just sneak out of this cursed house. Let the hostage taker deal with the hostages. Let a murderer murder an instigator. Let Bolinder meet the fate he deserved.

But no. He'd promised himself to get to the bottom of this. Despite his thoughts in the car coming out here—that some of the people he'd gotten to know were his friends—he was a police officer. A regular cop—as he'd thought so many times before: far from the most honest one in the world. But, despite that, about as honest as you can expect a cop like him to be. It still boiled down to the same principle: he liked to see the law win. He didn't care when it was a matter of petty shit, an ounce here and an ounce there. But he wanted the law to pluck the real rabble. And deep inside he thought he knew who they were. Suit-clad, wealthy, extremist men like Sven Bolinder should rot in the same cells as the drunk drivers, the dealers, and the wife beaters. That's what he wanted. Even if it rarely, or never, turned out that way. Actually, he didn't know of a single instance when it'd happened. But he didn't give a shit, that was still his goal. This was his opportunity to change things—to see the law win. They'd taken Palme. The workingman's hero. This was his way out. To change Sweden. At least just this once.

He speed-analyzed different alternatives. Rush in, try to arrest the intruders. Wait for the *blatte* to possibly leave and overtake him on the way out. Shoot the guys from a distance.

To rush in was dangerous. At least seven to nine yards. Niklas would have time to detonate the bomb and shoot a fuckload of people before he reached them. To wait for the *blatte* to leave—might never happen. That wouldn't work.

Try to play sniper? Yes, maybe—that was Thomas's thing. He was one of the best shots in the police force, after all.

If he'd had his Strayer Voigt Infinity, it would've been easy. But now—the police gun wasn't exactly suited for sniper duty. At the same time: he should be able to handle nine yards. First Brogren, then the *blatte*.

He positioned himself with one knee on the floor. Straightened his back. Stretched his arms out. As long as they didn't see him through the crack in the door. Remembered his bull's-eye at the Järfälla club's shooting range on the same night that Ljunggren'd told him that they'd found Rantzell's apartment. He held the gun as still as he could. Sought out the sight. It was slow on the SIG Sauer. Fixed the notch. Subtle tremble. Relaxed. Didn't bother with the poor lighting. Focused on one of Niklas's legs. No point in aiming at his chest—the guy was wearing a bulletproof vest. Thomas squeezed the trigger, slowly. The founding principle was clear: squeeze, massage, stroke it. He squinted. Lost consciousness of everything else. Even slower. One single movement. The only thing he saw was Niklas's thigh. It was the only thing in the world right now.

The shot rang out. Reality came crashing in. The sound hurt his ears.

Niklas stumbled. But didn't fall.

The opposite. He roared. Took a step forward toward the man he was about to pop.

This wouldn't do. He had to do something else.

Thomas regained his position.

Aimed for Niklas again.

The right side of his chest this time. Wouldn't injure the lunatic too much. The guy was wearing a bulletproof vest, after all.

70

Fuck. Fuck. Fuck. Some fucker was still around. Some cunt that Babak hadn't spotted.

Niklas stumbled. But didn't fall.

"I've been hit!"

Mahmud didn't know what he should do. This was not part of the plan. What a fucking idiot he'd been. It could be the 5-0. A blue storm rolling in.

FUCK.

Babak yelled from the room next door, "*Habibi*, what's happening?"

Mahmud responded, "We gotta go."

Babak ran in to Mahmud and the others.

Niklas roared, "Wait, I want to complete the mission."

Babak approached him. Mahmud wondered why he'd come in. They were gonna split now.

Babak grabbed hold of Niklas. Tried to drag him away.

Tugged at his arm. Tore. Screamed, "Fuck, man, we gotta go."

Another shot rang out in the room.

Mahmud saw Niklas. Like in slow motion. He collapsed like a rag.

On the left side of his head: the skull was busted.

Someone'd shot him again.

Khara. KHARA.

Niklas on the floor. They had to get out.

"Come on, man. Can you get up?"

Niklas tried to say something.

Gurgled.

Babak howled in the background.

Mahmud ran.

71

The second shot was bad.

Niklas dropped the Beretta.

But he was still holding the detonator in his hand.

Tight grip.

He felt the blood over his cheek and chin. Didn't feel the blood. Didn't feel anything.

He saw images. So many people, stories, faces.

Mom on the couch at home. The men in the mosque they'd torched down there. Collin.

The faces drifted past as if he were seeing them in a mirror.

Jamila. Benjamin. The cop who'd interrogated him.

He didn't see anything anymore.

No johns, no old guys.

He saw a crystal chandelier swing above him.

Swing.

All the men who'd beaten and abused.

Mats Strömberg, Roger Jonsson, Patric Ngono.

Claes. Remembered him. All the punches.

Remembered Bolinder.

Niklas gripped.

Squeezed.

So still.

The detonator.

Everything was so still.

EPILOGUE

Thomas was sitting in the squad car with Ljunggren. They were both staring at the new radio system. Rantzell, that's what it was called. Now dispatch could keep track of where all cars were situated at all times. Serious drawbacks: they couldn't pull their usual excuses and evasive maneuvers. They would be forced to take the crap calls that the cadets should really be dealing with. But there was an advantage. Thomas and Ljunggren'd been given a new topic of conversation that would last for several days—whining about management that didn't trust them. And there was maybe an even greater advantage: no downtime on the job. Less time to think. To bury yourself in guesswork. To brood. Have regrets.

Two months'd passed.

At first, Thomas'd been given a complete leave of absence from the force. To rest up, as they put it. What they were actually doing was investigating him again. Fuck, he couldn't handle more investigations. But it was perfect timing. Sander'd arrived. He was the most fantastic little person Thomas'd ever met. He already loved the boy more than anything. It was beautiful and felt so good.

Niklas Brogren'd detonated the bomb that he'd strapped on Bolinder. The walls, the crystal chandeliers, the johns, the whores: smeared in old-man matter. Thomas'd rushed into the room, tried to do CPR on the man. But it was too late. What was left of Bolinder couldn't be saved.

Thomas went over to Niklas. The guy looked up, but there was no life in his eyes. He was wheezing. Gurgling. He'd taken Bolinder with him to the other side.

The *blatte* boys'd disappeared.

The men and the hookers were in shock. People were whimpering, weeping, screaming. He was used to that kind of thing.

He hadn't meant to shoot Niklas in the head. He'd aimed at his chest. But when that other *blatte* surprised him by coming into the room and pulling on Niklas, it'd messed up his aim. Niklas's body was pulled down. Enough for a disastrous miss. A bad hit.

Maybe he never should've stepped into that room to save Bolinder. Maybe he should've split just like the immigrant guys. After a minute or so, he walked out of the room. Into the hall. Saw the blue lights. Heard the sounds of police in the house.

Hägerström stormed in, followed by ten or so men.

Their entire case seemed to go up in smoke, just like a New Year's firecracker.

Two weeks after the incident, Stig H. Ronander, the detective inspector who'd taken over the Rantzell case after Hägerström, called.

The guy had a nasal voice.

"Good morning. This is Inspector Stig H. Ronander."

Thomas's first thought: What a douche to say his own rank like that. I know very well who he is.

"I want to talk to you about the incident on Smådalarö."

That someone would call was expected, but Thomas didn't know what to expect from Ronander, of all people. He was actually in charge of the other investigation.

"Yeah, you call that an incident?"

Ronander didn't bother responding.

"We have to meet up."

Two hours later, Thomas was sitting across from Ronander in the inspector's office. He noted: framed photos of Ronander's wife and some young children in overly cutesy clothes. They had to be grandchildren. Thomas thought about Sander. Longed to go home.

"Okay, Andrén, I'll be brief."

Thomas was tense as hell, ready for anything.

"What happened out there was a tad too much for little old Sweden."

Thomas maintained his calm.

"Above all, it was a tad too much for you."

One of the grandchildren in the photos looked like Sander.

"If it ever comes out that you were there in connection with some rogue investigation, or that you were the one who killed that crazy hostage-taker Brogren, you won't be allowed to keep your job, not even part-time. And you'll be charged with gross professional misconduct or something else bad."

Thomas continued to sit in silence.

"You'll be kicked out. Hägerström will be kicked out. A lot of other fucking good police officers will risk getting kicked out. You understand that, of course."

Thomas leaned forward in his chair. "You don't have to tell me things I already know. And there's nothing that can be done about it, right?"

Ronander smiled. "There might be. I have a little suggestion. Why don't we forget about the fact that you fired the shots? Most of the men who were out there are going to be very tight-lipped about what was going on, it was tumultuous, and no one actually saw you shoot, if I've understood things correctly. What's more, two unknown perps were able to get away. So it can be arranged. We've arranged things like this before. And you'll be the one gaining from it. You'll get to keep your job. Not just that, we'll make sure you get back to the Southern District, to your regular position. Hägerström will be happy too—he'll stay at his job."

Thomas understood that there was something more. "What's the catch?"

Ronander's smile broadened. "The catch? I don't want to call it that. It's more of an agreement. The preliminary investigation into the murder of Rantzell has really already been completed. Niklas Brogren's alibi for the night of the murder was a bluff. What's more, now his mother's given us some new information, that Brogren came home drunk and was babbling about Claes Rantzell on the night of the murder. And we've analyzed the films, the photos, and the other documentation that we found at his house. It's completely clear that Brogren was the one who murdered those other men this fall—Mats Strömberg and Roger Jonsson. They were regular, honest family men. Innocent. And this maniac killed them. And do you know what he did in his previous life?"

Thomas shook his head.

"He was a mercenary soldier. Contracted by one of those American private military companies. But that might not be of much interest. Anyway, everything points to the fact that Niklas Brogren killed Claes Rantzell. On top of that, add Mats Strömberg, Roger Jonsson, and Sven Bolinder. Four ordinary Swedish men. So, to put it simply, the preliminary investigation would've led to a prosecution, which would've led to a guilty verdict—another Swedish serial killer. So there really isn't a catch. You don't need to dig any deeper, you don't need to continue your own little investigation. The case is closed. You get your job back and don't have to face any consequences. Hägerström gets to keep his job. You stop poking around, because there's nothing more to poke around in."

There it was—the catch.

Back in the squad car. He tried to wrap his head around it all. Rantzell must've threatened to reveal the truth. That his testimony about the Palme murder weapon'd been a lie. That someone was behind it, someone who'd made sure he dreamed up that story about the weapon. Someone who now, many years later, had paid him hush money. But maybe Rantzell'd wanted more, or meddled in some other way. They were forced to get rid of him. The link was in the payment—and that was the one document he didn't have. Possibly it'd been at Bolinder's house. But Thomas was certain—it wasn't there anymore. So, he'd accepted. Not right away, but after a few days. Not so much for his own sake as for Åsa's and Hägerström's. He needed his job in order to be happy, but he could've let it go all the same. He wasn't going to say anything to Hägerström—he never had to know. What's more, there was something to what Ronander'd said: everything did point to the fact that Niklas Brogren killed Rantzell. The thought settled after a few weeks—maybe there wasn't a group behind it all, maybe there wasn't any conspiracy.

That's how it must be.

That was the logical answer. It was a relief.

Thomas looked at Ljunggren. Everything almost felt like normal.

He opened the door to his house. Heard Sander's cooing from the living room. Felt joy. There was a letter on the doormat. He picked it up. Broke the seal with his finger. It was a picture of Sander. It looked like it'd been taken through one of the windows of their house. The boy was lying on a blanket on the floor. A huge smile on his face. Thomas turned the photo over. A short message on the back: *Stop poking around.*

* * *

Beshar was in Mahmud's apartment for the first time. Rays of sun danced on the table in the kitchen. Beshar was preparing coffee. He'd brought the pot himself. With the coffee powder and lots of sugar. Stirred while it boiled. Always clockwise. Beshar always wanted to explain how he made coffee. Probably saw it as some sort of child-rearing principle.

He poured the coffee into the tiny cups.

"Wait, Mahmud. Always wait for the grounds to settle."

There was a picture of Mom hanging on the wall.

Mahmud thought about the attack. Niklas'd gone berserk. Totally flipped out, started lining up the whores next to the johns. Then the first shot was fired. He didn't have time to grasp what was happening. Babak started to pull Niklas down to the floor. Another shot rang out. Niklas crumpled. Mahmud and Babak ran. Through the house. Weird rooms. Paintings and carpets like in a fucking museum. He held the Glock tight. Hauled ass outta there. Heard the explosion. Hoped it wasn't the man that Niklas'd strapped his bomb to.

Room after room. Paintings of fat ladies. Paintings of cities. Paintings that looked like nothing more than a few black streaks.

They reached the kitchen. The hole in the wall was black like the night outside. They could feel the cold wafting in. They stepped out. Niklas was still in there. It was his own fault.

Mahmud was panting like an idiot. His shoes felt like they were about to fall off.

The bulletproof vest weighed hundreds of tons.

He saw Babak four yards in front of him. Out in the snow. Back through his own tracks.

The hole in the fence. They crawled through. Mahmud was careful not to leave any evidence on the jagged wire.

Through the snow on the other side of the fence.

Down to the road.

Mahmud groped for the walkie-talkie in his pocket.

Got ahold of it.

Kept running.

He almost screamed to Robert and Javier. "It's time to go. We've got the gear, but shit got crazy."

Dad looked at him. "What are you thinking about?"

"I was thinking about how I could help Jamila buy the tanning salon. I've made some money lately."

"I hope you did so legally."

"No innocent people have suffered, Dad. I promise."

Beshar said nothing. Just shook his head.

They were having a *fika*, as the Svens liked to say. Drinking coffee together. Mahmud thought the coffee was too sweet, but he didn't say anything, Dad would take it personally. Beshar said that he'd been thinking about going to Iraq for a few weeks to visit family. Maybe Mahmud could come along. Just for a few weeks.

Mahmud got up. "I have something for you, Dad. Wait here."

He went into the bedroom.

Crouched down. Peered in under the bed. Reached in.

Pushed some plastic bags to the side. Looked at them again. Recognized them. They were the bags that he'd taken from that basement when he'd been looking for traces of Wisam Jibril. There was just a bunch of documents in them. Looked like financial stuff. He didn't even know why he'd saved them. Whatever—he'd clean up someday when he had the time. Throw out all the crap.

He reached farther in under the bed. Found what he was looking for—the small green box he'd bought on an auction site online. In silvery lettering: SANTOS, CARTIER.

It was a present for Dad.

The watch would look like new when it came in an original box.

He held it in his hand for a few seconds.

Dad's idea wasn't bad at all—disappearing to the home country for a while. Could be just what he needed.

* * *

The forest-lined cemetery felt enormous. Marie Brogren'd arrived too early, before the chapel'd even opened, so she went for a walk.

So many graves. Names of people and families who'd lived their lives. Maybe some in chaos, but most of them in relative peace. They didn't harbor terrible secrets. Not like Niklas. Not like her.

The sky was gray, but she could glimpse the sun behind the trees—like a bright spot on a dull piece of fabric. She didn't know if anyone would come. Maybe Viveca and Eva from work. Maybe the cousins: Johan and Carl-Fredrik and their wives. Maybe some other relative. Maybe Niklas's old classmate Benjamin. But she hadn't arranged anything after. There wasn't enough money for that.

She thought about the time they'd had together since he'd come back. Even if things'd gotten weird a few months ago, she was still happy that he hadn't died down there, in the sandbox, as he used to say.

Why was death what people feared most in life? Those who'd been in her situation knew that was all backward. To live—to survive—was worse. Especially when it felt like it was your own fault that things ended up the way they did.

It was still unclear how it'd all happened. A policeman—Stig H. Ronander was his name—had come over to her house. Tried to tell her that Niklas'd committed some sort of robbery and that he'd been shot there, probably by his cronies. The policeman also explained that Niklas with all certainty would've been convicted of the murder of Claes Rantzell. He expressed his regrets for her loss, both of them.

Deep inside, she'd always known it would end in violence.

Marie approached the chapel. She could see Viveca and Eva from far away. It felt good that they'd come after all. She straightened her coat. It was cold out and it would be nice to go inside.

Three other women were standing a few yards from her colleagues. Marie didn't recognize them. She came closer. Were they some distant relatives? No, she really didn't recognize them. Maybe they were friends of Niklas's.

They looked strange. Certainly not Swedish. Didn't walk toward her like Viveca and Eva'd started doing. They must be in the wrong place. Because they couldn't be people Niklas had known, could they?

Things went pretty much as she'd expected, with the exception of the three unknown women and without Benjamin. Her, Viveca, Eva, the cousins, and their wives. And then the priest, of course.

The priest talked about human vulnerability. How every person adds something to the world, no matter what. Marie thought about the last thing he'd said. To add something to the world. To contribute. She didn't know what Niklas'd contributed, but she was sure it was something.

She knew what she herself had done. What was strange is that it'd taken the police several months to figure out that Claes was the one who'd been murdered down there. She'd never understood why. He couldn't be unknown in their registries. The policeman, Ronander, had said something else strange: "We apologize that everything took so long. But Claes Rantzell was very difficult to identify—he didn't have teeth or fingerprints, actually."

The images haunted her thoughts. How she'd gone downstairs that night on her way to the laundry room. How he'd appeared, in the entryway, outside the elevator. Terribly high on something. Much worse than alcohol. More like he was sick. He'd asked her for help, told her that someone'd poisoned him. Someone who didn't want it all to come out. Doing laundry wasn't actually allowed this late, but she didn't care. The building was quiet, except for his whining. They hadn't seen each other in several years. What the hell was he doing here? Why was he coming to her? After everything he'd done. This was the only place he could flee to, he said. The only place where they wouldn't find him. They'd managed to inject him with something. He needed her help. It was too much for her. She steered him out toward the entrance to the building. He staggered. Vomited. Fell toward the set of stairs leading to the basement. She opened the door. Tried to push him in front of her. He didn't seem to understand what was happening. The door slammed shut behind them. The basement—where Niklas used to spend time as a child. Everything welled up in her. The memories, the pain, the humiliation. She was almost shocked by what she felt. She pushed him again.

Why hadn't he had teeth or fingerprints? Now in retrospect, she thought that maybe "they," the ones he'd been talking about, had found him in the end.

He'd swayed.

She'd kicked his shins. Punched him in the stomach.

He'd doubled over.

She'd kicked him again.

Punched, kicked.

The sequence was played over and over again in her head.

His face.

Her rage.

THANKS TO:

Hedda for being wonderful and for all your invaluable help.

Mamma for always telling me about the people you meet who like my writing.

Pappa and my bro, Jacob, for all the tips and support—without you this wouldn't work. We support one another.

All my buds and family who read this book and made comments. Lasse M. for great information about the police. The boys in the jail-house for facts. Mr. Eriksson for good details.

Annika, Pontus, and Anna-Karin at Wahlström & Widstrand for your phat support. Sorry if I'm stressed out sometimes—a lawyer's duty calls.

Månpocket for doing fantastic work. Salomonsson Agency for doing a magical job—now we take the world.

Sören Bondesson for kicking me back into action once again.

All of you who read the last book and encouraged me to write another one.

Jack for being alive. The joy you bring to our lives defies description.

A Note About the Author

Jens Lapidus is a criminal defense lawyer who represents some of Sweden's most notorious underworld criminals. He lives in Stockholm with his wife.

A Note About the Translator

Astri von Arbin Ahlander is a writer and translator from Stockholm, Sweden. She is a cofounder and editor in chief of the interview project the Days of Yore (www.thedaysofyore.com), which features interviews with successful artists about the time before their breakthroughs. She translated the first book in the Stockholm Noir Trilogy, *Easy Money*.